DICK FRANCIS

FOUR COMPLETE NOVELS

DICK FRANCIS

FOUR COMPLETE NOVELS

ODDS AGAINST

FLYING FINISH

BLOOD SPORT

RAT RACE

AVENEL BOOKS
NEW YORK

This volume contains the complete and unabridged texts
of the original editions. They have been completely reset for this volume.

This Omnibus edition was previously published in separate volumes under the titles:

This 1984 edition is published by Avenel Books,
distributed by Crown Publishers, Inc.,
225 Park Avenue South, New York, New York 10003
by arrangement with Harper & Row, Publishers, Inc.

Manufactured in the United States of America

Library of Congress Cataloging in Publication Data
Francis, Dick.
Four complete novels.
Contents: Odds against—Flying finish—
Blood sport—[etc.]
1. Detective and mystery stories, English. I. Title.
PR6056.R27A6 1984 823′.914 83-22466
ISBN: 0-517-38806-5

m l k j i h g

CONTENTS

ODDS AGAINST

1

I WAS never particularly keen on my job before the day I got shot and nearly lost it, along with my life. But the .38 slug of lead which made a pepper shaker out of my intestines left me with fire in my belly in more ways than one. Otherwise I should never have met Zanna Martin, and would still be held fast in the spider threads of departed joys, of no use to anyone, least of all myself.

It was the first step to liberation, that bullet, though I wouldn't have said so at the time. I stopped it because I was careless. Careless because bored.

I woke up gradually in the hospital, in a private room for which I got a whacking great bill a few days later. Even before I opened my eyes I began to regret I had not left the world completely. Someone had lit a bonfire under my navel.

A fierce conversation was being conducted in unhushed voices over my head. With woolly wits, the anesthetic still drifting inside my skull like puffball clouds in a summer sky, I tried unenthusiastically to make sense of what was being said.

"Can't you give him something to wake him more quickly?"

"No."

"We can't do much until we have his story, you must see that. It's nearly seven hours since you finished operating. Surely—"

"And he was all of four hours on the table before that. Do you want to finish off what the shooting started?"

"Doctor—"

"I am sorry, but you'll have to wait."

There's my pal, I thought. They'll have to wait. Who wants to hurry back into the dreary world? Why not go to sleep for a month and take things up again after they've put the bonfire out? I opened my eyes reluctantly.

It was night. A globe of electric light shone in the center of the ceiling. That figured. It had been morning when Jones-boy found me still seeping gently onto the office linoleum and went to telephone, and it appeared that about twelve hours had passed since they stuck the first blessed needle into my arm. Would a twenty-four-hour start, I wondered, be enough for a panic-stricken ineffectual little crook to get himself undetectably out of the country?

There were two policemen on my left, one in uniform, one not. They were both sweating, because the room was hot. The doctor stood on the right, fiddling with a tube which ran from a bottle into my elbow. Various other tubes sprouted disgustingly from my abdomen, partly covered by a light sheet. Drip and drainage, I thought sardonically. How absolutely charming.

Radnor was watching me from the foot of the bed, taking no part in the argument still in progress between medicine and the law. I wouldn't have thought I rated the boss himself attendant at the bedside, but then I suppose it wasn't every day that one of his employees got himself into such a spectacular mess.

He said, "He's conscious again, and his eyes aren't so hazy. We might get some sense out of him this time." He looked at his watch.

The doctor bent over me, felt my pulse, and nodded. "Five minutes, then. Not a second more."

The plainclothes policeman beat Radnor to it by a fraction of a second. "Can you tell us who shot you?"

I still found it surprisingly difficult to speak, but not as impossible as it had been when they asked me the same question that morning. Then, I had been too far gone. Now, I was apparently on the way back. Even so, the policeman had plenty of time to repeat his question, and to wait some more, before I managed to answer.

"Andrews."

It meant nothing to the policeman, but Radnor looked astonished and also disappointed.

"Thomas Andrews?" he asked.

"Yes."

Radnor explained to the police. "I told you that Halley here and another of my operatives set some sort of a trap intending to clear up an intimidation case we are investigating. I understand they were hoping for a big fish, but it seems now they caught a tiddler. Andrews is small stuff, a weak sort of youth used for running errands. I would never have thought he would carry a gun, much less that he would use it."

Me neither. He had dragged the revolver clumsily out of his jacket pocket, pointed it shakily in my direction, and used both hands to pull the trigger. If I hadn't seen that it was only Andrews who had come to nibble at the bait I wouldn't have ambled unwarily out of the darkness of the washroom to tax him with breaking into the Cromwell Road premises of Hunt Radnor Associates at one o'clock in the morning. It simply hadn't occurred to me that he would attack me in any way.

By the time I realized that he really meant to use the gun and was not waving it about for effect, it was far too late. I had barely begun to turn to flip off the light switch when the bullet hit, in and out diagonally through my body. The force of it spun me onto my knees and then forward onto the floor.

As I went down he ran for the door, stiff-legged, crying out, with circles of white showing wild round his eyes. He was almost as horrified as I was at what he had done.

"At what time did the shooting take place?" asked the policeman formally.

After another pause I said, "One o'clock, about."

The doctor drew in a breath. He didn't need to say it: I knew I was lucky to be alive. In a progressively feeble state I'd lain on the floor through a chilly September night looking disgustedly at a telephone on which I couldn't summon help. The office telephones all worked through a switchboard. This might have been on the moon as far as I was concerned, instead of along the passage, down the curving stairs and through the door to the reception desk, with the girl who worked the switches fast asleep in bed.

The policeman wrote in his notebook. "Now, sir, I can get a description of Thomas Andrews from someone else so as not to trouble you too much now, but I'd be glad if you can tell me what he was wearing."

"Black jeans, very tight. Olive-green jersey. Loose black jacket." I paused. "Black fur collar, black and white checked lining. All shabby . . . dirty." I tried again. "He had gun in jacket pocket right side . . . took it with him . . . no gloves . . . can't have a record."

"Shoes?"

"Didn't see. Silent, though."

"Anything else?"

I thought. "He had some badges . . . place names, skull and crossbones, things like that . . . sewn on his jacket, left sleeve."

"I see. Right. We'll get on with it then." He snapped shut his notebook, smiled briefly, turned, and walked to the door, followed by his uniformed ally, and by Radnor, presumably for Andrews' description.

The doctor took my pulse again, and slowly checked all the tubes. His face showed satisfaction.

He said cheerfully, "You must have the constitution of a horse."

"No," said Radnor, coming in again and hearing him. "Horses are really quite delicate creatures. Halley has the constitution of a jockey. A steeplechase jockey. He used to be one. He's got a body like a shock absorber . . . had to have to deal with all the fractures and injuries he got racing."

"Is that what happened to his hand? A fall in a steeple-chase?"

Radnor's glance flicked to my face and away again, uncomfortably. They never mentioned my hand to me in the office if they could help it. None of them, that is, except my fellow trap-setter Chico Barnes, who didn't care what he said to anyone.

"Yes," Radnor said tersely. "That's right." He changed the subject. "Well, Sid, come and see me when you are better. Take your time." He nodded uncertainly to me, and he and the doctor, with a joint backward glance, ushered each other out of the door.

So Radnor was in no hurry to have me back. I would have smiled if I'd had the energy. When he first offered me the job I guessed that somewhere in the background my father-in-law was pulling strings; but I had been in a why-not mood at the time. Nothing mattered very much.

"Why not?" I said to Radnor, and he put me on his payroll as an investigator, racing section, ignoring my complete lack of experience, and explained to the rest of the staff that I was there in an advisory capacity, owing to my intimate knowledge of the game. They had taken it very well, on the whole. Perhaps they realized, as I did, that my employment was an act of pity. Perhaps they thought, I should be too proud to accept that sort of pity. I wasn't, I didn't care one way or the other.

Radnor's agency ran Missing Persons, Guard, and Divorce departments, and also a section called Bona Fides, which was nearly as big as the others put together. Most of the work was routine painstaking inquiry stuff, sometimes leading to civil or divorce action, but oftener merely to a discreet report sent to the client. Criminal cases, though accepted, were rare. The Andrews business was the first for three months.

The Racing section was Radnor's special baby. It hadn't existed, I'd been told, when he bought the agency with an army gratuity after the war and developed it from a dingy three-roomed affair into something like a national institution. Radnor printed "Speed, Results, and Secrecy" across the top of his stationery; promised them, and delivered them. A life-long addiction to racing, allied to six youthful rides in point-to-points, had led him not so much to ply for hire from the Jockey Club and the National Hunt Committee as to indicate that his agency was at their disposal. The Jockey Club and the National Hunt Committee tentatively wet their feet, found the water beneficial, and plunged right in. The Racing section blossomed. Eventually private business outstripped the official, especially when Radnor began supplying prerace guards for fancied horses.

By the time I joined the firm, "Bona Fides: Racing" had proved so successful that it had spread from its own big office into the room next door. For a reasonable fee a trainer could check on the character and background of a prospective owner, a bookmaker on a client, a client on a bookmaker, anybody on anybody. The phrase "O.K.'d by Radnor" had pressed into racing slang. Genuine, it meant. Trustworthy. I had even heard it applied to a horse.

They had never given me a Bona Fide assignment. This work was done by a bunch of inconspicuous middle-aged retired policemen who took minimum time to get results. I'd never been sent to sit all night outside the box of a hot favorite, though I would have done it willingly. I had never been put on a racecourse security patrol. If the stewards asked for operators to keep taps on undesirables at race meetings, I didn't go. If anyone had to watch for the pickpockets in Tatterstalls, it wasn't me. Radnor's two unvarying excuses for giving me nothing to do were first that I was too well known to the whole racing world to be inconspicuous, and second, that even if I didn't seem to care, he was not going to be the one to give an ex-champion jockey tasks which meant a great loss of face.

As a result I spent most of my time kicking around the office reading other people's reports. When anyone asked me for the informed advice I was supposedly there to give, I gave it; if anyone asked what I would do in a certain set of circumstances, I told them. I got to know all the operators and gossiped with them when they came into the office. I always had the time. If I took a day off and went to the races nobody complained. I sometimes wondered whether they even noticed.

At intervals I remarked to Radnor that he didn't have to keep me, as I so obviously did nothing to earn my salary. He replied each time that he was satisfied with the arrangement, if I was. I had the impression that he was waiting for something, but if it wasn't for me to leave, I didn't know what. On the day I walked into Andrews' bullet I had been with the agency in this fashion for exactly two years.

A nurse came in to check the tubes and take my blood pressure. She was starched and efficient. She smiled, but didn't speak. I waited for her to say that my wife was outside asking about me anxiously. She didn't say it. My wife hadn't come. Wouldn't come. If I couldn't hold her when I was properly alive, why should my near-death bring her running? Jenny. My wife. Still my wife in spite of three years' separation. Regret, I think, held us both back from the final step of divorce: we had been through passion, delight, dissension, anger and explosion. Only regret was left, and it wouldn't be strong enough to bring her to the hospital. She'd seen me in too many hospitals before. There was no more drama, no more impact, in my form recumbent, even with tubes. She wouldn't come. Wouldn't telephone. Wouldn't write. It was stupid of me to want her.

Time passed slowly and I didn't enjoy it, but eventually all the tubes except the one in my arm were removed and I began to heal. The police didn't find Andrews, Jenny didn't come, Radnor's typist sent me a get-well card, and the hospital sent the bill.

Chico slouched in one evening, his hands in his pockets and the usual derisive grin on his face. He looked me over without haste and the grin, if anything, widened.

"Rather you than me, mate," he said.

"Go to bloody hell."

He laughed. And well he might. I had been doing his job for him because he had a date with a girl, and Andrews' bullet should have been his bellyache, not mine.

"Andrews," he said musingly. "Who'd have thought it? Sodding little weasel. All the same, if you'd done what I said and stayed in the wash-room, and taken his photo quiet-like on the old infrared, we'd have picked him up later nice and easy and you'd have been lolling on your arse around the office as usual instead of sweating away in here."

"You needn't rub it in," I said. "What would you have done?"

He grinned. "The same as you, I expect. I'd have reckoned it would only take the old one-two for that little worm to come across with who sent him."

"And now we don't know."

"No." He sighed. "And the old man ain't too sweet about the whole thing. He did know I was using the office as a trap, but he didn't think it would work, and now this has happened he doesn't like it. He's leaning over backwards, hushing the whole thing up. They might have sent a bomb, not a sneak thief, he said. And of course Andrews bust a window getting in, which I've probably got to pay for. Trust the little sod not to know how to pick a lock."

"I'll pay for the window," I said.

"Yeah," he grinned. "I reckoned you would if I told you."

He wandered round the room, looking at things. There wasn't much to see.

"What's in that bottle dripping into your arm?"

"Food of some sort, as far as I can gather. They never give me anything to eat."

"Afraid you might bust out again, I expect."

"I guess so," I agreed.

He wandered on. "Haven't you got a telly then? Cheer you up a bit, wouldn't it, to see some other silly buggers getting shot?'' He looked at the chart on the bottom of the bed. ''Your temperature was one hundred and two this morning, did they tell you? Do you reckon you're going to kick it?

''No.''

''Near thing, from what I've heard. Jones-boy said there was enough of your life's blood dirtying up the office floor to make a tidy few black puddings.''

I didn't appreciate Jones-boy's sense of humor.

Chico said, ''Are you coming back?''

''Perhaps.''

He began tying knots in the cord of the window blind. I watched him, a thin figure imbued with so much energy that it was difficult for him to keep still. He had spent two fruitless nights watching in the washroom before I took his place, and I knew that if he hadn't been dedicated to his job he couldn't have borne such inactivity. He was the youngest of Radnor's team. About twenty-four, he believed, though as he had been abandoned as a child on the steps of a police station in a pushchair, no one knew for certain.

If the police hadn't been so kind to him, Chico sometimes said, he would have taken advantage of his later opportunities and turned delinquent. He never grew tall enough to be a copper. Radnor's was the best he could do. And he did very well by Radnor. He put two and two together quickly and no one on the staff had faster physical reactions. Judo and wrestling were his hobbies, and along with the regular throws and holds he had been taught some strikingly dirty tricks. His smallness bore no relation whatever to his effectiveness in his job.

''How are you getting on with the case?'' I asked.

''What case? Oh . . . that. Well, since you got shot the heat's off, it seems. Brinton's had no threatening calls or letters since the other night. Whoever was leaning on him must have got the wind up. Anyway, he's feeling a bit safer all of a sudden and he's carping a lot to the old man about fees. Another day or two, I give it, and there won't be no one holding his hand at night. Anyway, I've been pulled off it. I'm flying from Newmarket to Ireland tomorrow, sharing a stall with a hundred thousand pounds' worth of stallion.''

Escort duty was another little job I never did. Chico liked it, and went often. As he had once thrown a fifteen-stone would-be nobbler over a seven-foot wall, he was always much in demand.

''You ought to come back,'' he said suddenly.

''Why?'' I was surprised.

''I don't know. . . .'' He grinned. ''Silly, really, when you do sweet off all, but everybody seems to have got used to you being around. You're missed, kiddo, you'd be surprised.''

''You're joking, of course.''

''Yeah. . . .'' He undid the knots in the window cord, shrugged, and thrust his hands into his trouser pockets. ''God, this place gives you the willies. It reeks of warm disinfectant. Creepy. How much longer are you going to lie here rotting?''

''Days,'' I said mildly. ''Have a good trip.''

"See you." He nodded, drifting in relief to the door. "Do you want anything? I mean books or anything?"

"Nothing, thanks."

"Nothing . . . that's just your form, Sid, mate. You don't want nothing." He grinned and went.

I wanted nothing. My form. My trouble. I'd had what I'd wanted most in the world and lost it irrevocably. I'd found nothing else to want. I stared at the ceiling, waiting for time to pass. All I wanted was to get back onto my feet and stop feeling as though I had eaten a hundredweight of green apples.

Three weeks after the shooting I had a visit from my father-in-law. He came in the late afternoon, bringing with him a small parcel which he put without comment on the table beside the bed.

"Well, Sid, how are you?" He settled himself into an easy chair, crossed his legs and lit a cigar.

"Cured, more or less. I'll be out of here soon."

"Good. Good. And your plans are . . . ?"

"I haven't any."

"You can't go back to the agency without some . . . er, convalescence," he remarked.

"I suppose not."

"You might prefer somewhere in the sun," he said, studying the cigar. "But I would like it if you could spend some time with me at Aynsford."

I didn't answer immediately.

"Will . . . ?" I began and stopped, wavering.

"No," he said. "She won't be there. She's gone out to Athens to stay with Jill and Tony. I saw her off yesterday. She sent you her regards."

"Thanks," I said dryly. As usual I did not know whether to be glad or sorry that I was not going to meet my wife. Nor was I sure that this trip to see her sister Jill was not as diplomatic as Tony's job in the Corps.

"You'll come, then? Mrs. Cross will look after you splendidly."

"Yes, Charles, thank you. I'd like to come for a little while."

He gripped the cigar in his teeth, squinted through the smoke, and took out his diary.

"Let's see, suppose you leave here in, say, another week. . . . No point in hurrying out before you're fit to go. That brings us to the twenty-sixth . . . hm . . . now, suppose you come down a week on Sunday, I'll be at home all that day. Will that suit you?"

"Yes, fine, if the doctors agree."

"Right, then." He wrote in the diary, put it away and took the cigar carefully out of his mouth, smiling at me with the usual inscrutable blankness in his eyes. He sat easily in his dark city suit, Rear Admiral Charles Roland, R.N., retired, a man carrying his sixty-six years lightly. War photographs showed him tall, straight, bony almost, with a high forehead and thick dark hair. Time had grayed the hair, which in receding left his forehead higher than ever, and had added weight where it did no harm. His manner was ordinarily extremely charming and occasionally patronizingly offensive. I had been on the receiving end of both.

He relaxed in the armchair, talking unhurriedly about steeplechasing.

"What do you think of that new race at Sandown? I don't know about you, but I think it's framed rather awkwardly. They're bound to get a tiny field with those conditions, and if Devil's Dyke doesn't run after all the whole thing will be a non-crowd puller par excellence."

His interest in this game only dated back a few years, but recently to his pleasure he had been invited by one or two courses to act as a Steward. Listening to his easy familiarity with racing problems and racing jargon, I was in a quiet inward way amused. It was impossible to forget his reaction long ago to Jenny's engagement to a jockey, his unfriendly rejection of me as a future son-in-law, his absence from our wedding, the months afterward of frigid disapproval, the way he had seldom spoken to or even looked at me.

I believed at this time that it was sheer snobbery, but it wasn't as simple as that. Certainly he didn't think me good enough, but not only, or even mainly, on a class distinction level; and probably we would never have understood each other, or come eventually to like each other, had it not been for a wet afternoon and a game of chess.

Jenny and I went to Aynsford for one of our rare, painful Sunday visits. We ate our roast beef in near silence, Jenny's father staring rudely out of the window and drumming his fingers on the table. I made up my mind that we wouldn't go again. I'd had enough. Jenny could visit him alone.

After lunch she said she wanted to sort out some of her books now that we had a new bookcase, and disappeared upstairs. Charles Roland and I looked at each other in dislike, the afternoon stretching drearily ahead and the downpour outside barring retreat into the garden and park beyond.

"Do you play chess?" he asked in a bored, expecting-the-answer-no voice.

"I know the moves," I said.

He shrugged (it was more like a squirm), but clearly thinking that it would be less trouble than making conversation, he brought a chess set out and gestured to me to sit opposite him. He was normally a good player, but that afternoon he was bored and irritated and inattentive, and I beat him quite early in the game. He couldn't believe it. He sat staring at the board, fingering the bishop with which I'd got him in a classic discovered check.

"Where did you learn?" he said eventually, still looking down.

"Out of a book."

"Have you played a great deal?"

"No, not much. Here and there." But I'd played with some good players.

"Hm." He paused. "Will you play again?"

"Yes, if you like."

We played. It was a long game and ended in a draw, with practically every piece off the board. A fortnight later he rang up and asked us, next time we came, to stay overnight. It was the first twig of the olive branch. We went more often and more willingly to Aynsford after that. Charles and I played chess occasionally and won a roughly equal number of games, and he began rather tentatively to go to the races. Ironically from then on our mutual respect grew strong enough to survive even the crash of Jenny's and my marriage, and Charles's interest in racing expanded and deepened with every passing year.

"I went to Ascot yesterday," he was saying, tapping off his cigar. "It wasn't a bad crowd, considering the weather. I had a drink with that handicap fellow, John Pagan. Nice chap. He was very pleased with himself because he got six abreast over the last in the handicap hurdle. There was an objection after the three-mile chase—flagrant bit of crossing on the run-in. Carter swore blind he was leaning and couldn't help it, but you can never believe a word he says. Anyway, the Stewards took it away from him. The only thing they could do. Wally Gibbons rode a brilliant finish in the handicap hurdle and then made an almighty hash of the novice chase."

"He's heavy-handed with novices," I agreed.

"Wonderful course, that."

"The tops." A wave of weakness flowed outward from my stomach. My legs trembled under the bedclothes. It was always happening. Infuriating.

"Good job it belongs to the Queen and is safe from the land-grabbers." He smiled.

"Yes, I suppose so. . . ."

"You're tired," he said abruptly. "I've stayed too long."

"No," I protested. "Really, I'm fine."

He put out the cigar, however, and stood up. "I know you too well, Sid. Your idea of fine is not the same as anyone else's. If you're not well enough to come to Aynsford a week on Sunday you'll let me know. Otherwise I'll see you then."

"Yes, O.K."

He went away, leaving me to reflect that I did still tire infernally easily. Must be old age, I grinned to myself, old age at thirty-one. Old tired battered Sid Halley, poor old chap. I grimaced at the ceiling.

A nurse came in for the evening jobs.

"You've got a parcel," she said brightly, as if speaking to a retarded child. "Aren't you going to open it?"

I had forgotten about Charles's parcel.

"Would you like me to open it for you? I mean, you can't find things like opening parcels very easy with a hand like yours."

She was only being kind. "Yes," I said. "Thank you."

She snipped through the wrappings with scissors from her pocket and looked dubiously at the slim dark book she found inside.

"I suppose it is meant for you? I mean somehow it doesn't seem like things people usually give patients."

She put the book into my right hand and I read the title embossed in gold on the cover. *Outline of Company Law.*

"My father-in-law left it on purpose. He meant it for me."

"Oh well, I suppose it's difficult to think of things for people who can't eat grapes and such." She bustled around, efficient and slightly bullying, and finally left me alone again.

Outline of Company Law. I riffled through the pages. It was certainly a book about company law. Solidly legal. Not light entertainment for an invalid. I put the book on the table.

Charles Roland was a man of subtle mind, and subtlety gave him pleasure. It hadn't been my parentage that he had objected to so much as what he took to be Jenny's rejection of his mental standards in choosing a jockey for a husband. He'd never met a jockey before, disliked the idea of racing, and took it for granted that everyone engaged in it was either a rogue or a moron. He'd wanted both his daughters to marry clever men, clever more than handsome or wellborn or rich, so that he could enjoy their company. Jill had obliged him with Tony, Jenny disappointed him with me: that was how he saw it, until he found that at least I could play chess with him now and then.

Knowing his subtle habits, I took it for granted that he had not idly brought such a book and hadn't chosen it or left it by mistake. He meant me to read it for a purpose. Intended it to be useful to me—or to him—later on. Did he think he could maneuver me into business, now that I hadn't distinguished myself at the agency? A nudge, that book was. A nudge in some specific direction.

I thought back over what he had said, looking for a clue. He'd been insistent that I should go to Aynsford. He'd sent Jenny to Athens. He'd talked about racing, about the new racing at Sandown, about Ascot, John Pagan, Carter. Wally Gibbons . . . nothing there that I could see had the remotest connection with company law.

I sighed, shutting my eyes. I didn't feel too well. I didn't have to read the book, or go wherever Charles pointed. And yet . . . why not? There was nothing I urgently wanted to do instead. I decided to do my stodgy homework. Tomorrow.

Perhaps.

2

FOUR DAYS after my arrival at Aynsford I came downstairs from an afternoon's rest to find Charles delving into a large packing case in the center of the hall. Strewn round on the half-acre of parquet was a vast amount of wood shavings, white and curly, and arranged carefully on a low table beside him were the first trophies out of the lucky dip, appearing to me to be dull chunks of rock.

I picked one of them up. One side had been ground into a smooth face and across the bottom of this was stuck a neat label. "Porphyry" it said, and beneath, "Carver Mineralogy Foundation."

"I didn't know you had an obsessive interest in quartz."

He gave me one of his blank stares which I knew didn't mean he hadn't heard or understood what I'd said, but that he didn't intend to explain.

"I'm going fishing," he said, plunging his arms back into the box.

So the quartz was bait. I put down the porphyry and picked up another piece. It was small, the size of a squared-off egg, and beautiful, as clear and translucent as glass. The label said simply, "Rock Crystal."

"If you want something useful to do," said Charles, "you can write out what sort they all are on the plain labels you will find on my desk, and then soak the Foundation's labels off and put the new ones on. Keep the old ones, though. We'll have to replace them when all this stuff goes back."

"All right," I agreed.

The next chunk I picked up was heavy with gold. "Are these valuable?" I asked.

"Some are. There's a booklet somewhere. But I told the Foundation they'd be safe enough. I said I'd have a private detective in the house all the time guarding them."

I laughed and began writing new labels, working from the inventory. The lumps of quartz overflowed from the table onto the floor before the box was empty.

"There's another box outside," Charles observed.

"Oh no!"

"I collect quartz," said Charles with dignity, "and don't you forget it. I've collected it for years. Years. Haven't I?"

"Years," I agreed. "You're an authority. Who wouldn't be an authority on rocks, after a life at sea?"

"I've got exactly one day to learn them in," said Charles, smiling. "They've come later than I asked. I'll have to be word perfect by tomorrow night."

He fetched the second lot, which was much smaller and was fastened with important-looking seals. Inside were uncut gem quartz crystals, mounted on small individual black plinths. Their collective value was staggering. The Carver Foundation must have taken the private detective bit seriously. They'd have held tight to their rocks if they'd seen my state of health.

We worked for some time changing the labels while Charles muttered their names like incantations under his breath. "Chrysoprase, aventurine, agate, onyx, chalcedony, tiger's-eye, carnelian, citrine, rose, plasma, basanite, blood-stone, chert. Why the hell did I start this?"

"Well, why?"

I got the blank stare again. He wasn't telling. "You can test me on them," he said.

We carried them piece by piece into the dining room, where I found the glass-doored bookshelves on each side of the fire had been cleared of their yards of leather-bound classics.

"They can go up there later," said Charles, covering the huge dining-room table with a thick felt. "Put them on the table for now."

When they were all arranged he walked slowly round learning them. There were about fifty altogether. I tested him for a while, at his request, and he muddled up and forgot about half of them. They were difficult, because so many looked alike.

He sighed. "It's time we had a noggin and you went back to bed." He led the way into the little sitting room he occasionally referred to as the wardroom, and poured a couple of stiffish brandies. He raised his glass to me and appreciatively took a mouthful. There was a suppressed excitement in his expression, a glint in the unfathomable eyes. I sipped the brandy, wondering with more interest what he was up to.

"I have a few people coming for the weekend," he said casually, squinting at his glass. "A Mr. and Mrs. Rex van Dysart, a Mr. and Mrs.

Howard Kraye, and my cousin Viola, who will act as hostess."

"Old friends?" I murmured, having ever heard only of Viola.

"Not very," he said smoothly. "They'll be here in time for dinner tomorrow night. You'll meet them then."

"But I'll make it an odd number. . . . I'll go up before they come and stay out of your way for most of the weekend."

"No," he said sharply. Much too vehemently. I was surprised. Then it came to me suddenly that all he had been doing with his rocks and his offer of a place for my convalescence was to engineer a meeting between me and the weekend guests. He offered me rest. He offered Mr. van Dysart, or perhaps Mr. Kraye, rocks. Both of us had swallowed the hook. I decided to give the line a tug, to see just how determined was the fisherman.

"I'd be better upstairs. You know I can't eat normal meals." My diet at the time consisted of brandy, beef juice, and some vacuum-packed pots of stuff which had been developed for feeding astronauts. Apparently none of these things affected the worst-shot-up bits of my digestive tract.

"People loosen up over the dinner table . . . they talk more, and you get to know them better." He was always carefully unpersuasive.

"They'll talk to you just as well if I'm not there—better in fact. And I couldn't stand watching you all tuck into steaks."

He said musingly, "You can stand anything, Sid. But I think you'd be interested. Not bored, I promise you. More brandy?"

I shook my head and relented. "All right, I'll be there at dinner, if you want it."

He relaxed only a fraction. A controlled and subtle man. I smiled at him, and he guessed that I'd been playing him along.

"You're a bastard," he said.

From him, it was a compliment.

The transistor beside my bed was busy with the morning news as I slowly ate my breakfast pot of astronaut paste.

"The race meeting scheduled for today and tomorrow at Seabury," the announcer said, "has had to be abandoned. A tanker carrying liquid chemical crashed and overturned at dusk yesterday afternoon on a road crossing the racecourse. There was considerable damage to the turf, and after an examination this morning, the Stewards regretfully decided that it was not fit to be raced on. It is hoped to replace the affected turf in time for the next meeting in a fortnight's time, but an announcement will be made about this at a later date. And here is the weather forecast. . . ."

Poor Seabury, I thought, always in the wars. It was only a year since their stable block had been burned down on the eve of a meeting. They had had to cancel then too, because temporary stables could not be erected overnight and the National Hunt Committee in consultation with Radnor had decided that indiscriminate stabling in the surrounding district was too much of a security risk.

It was a nice track to ride on, a long circuit with no sharp bends, but there had been some trouble with the surface in the spring, a drain of some sort had collapsed during a hurdle race: the forefeet of one unfortunate horse had gone right through into it to a depth of about eighteen inches and he had broken a leg. In the resulting pile-up two more horses had been injured and one jockey badly concussed. Maps of the course didn't even warn that the drain existed, and I'd heard trainers wondering whether there were any more antique waterways ready to collapse with as little notice. The executive, on their side, naturally swore there weren't.

For some time I lay daydreaming, racing round Seabury again in my mind, and wishing uselessly, hopelessly, achingly, that I could do it again in fact.

Mrs. Cross tapped on the door and came in. She was a quiet, unobtrusive mouse of a woman with soft brown hair and a slight outward cast in her gray-green eyes. Although she seemed to have no spirit whatever and seldom spoke, she ran the place like oiled machinery, helped by a largely invisible squad of "dailies." She had the great virtue to me of being fairly new in the job and impartial on the subject of Jenny and me. I wouldn't have trusted her predecessor, who had been fanatically fond of Jenny, not to have added cascara to my beef juice.

"The Admiral would like to know if you are feeling well today, Mr. Halley," said Mrs. Cross primly, picking up my breakfast tray.

"Yes, I am, thank you." More or less.

"He said, then, when you're ready would you join him in the dining room?"

"The rocks?"

She gave me a small smile. "He was up before me this morning, and had his breakfast on a tray in there. Shall I tell him you'll come down?"

"Please."

When she had gone, and while I was slowly dressing, the telephone bell rang. Not long afterward, Charles himself came upstairs.

"That was the police," he said abruptly with a frown. "Apparently they've found a body and they want you to go and identify it."

"Whose body, for heaven's sake?"

"They didn't say. They said they would send a car for you immediately though. I gathered they really rang here to locate you."

"I haven't any relatives. It must be a mistake."

He shrugged. "We'll know soon, anyway. Come down now and test me on the quartz. I think I've got it taped at last."

We went down to the dining room, where I found he was right. He went round the whole lot without a mistake. I changed the order in which they stood, but it didn't throw him. He smiled, very pleased with himself.

"Word-perfect," he said. "Let's put them up on the shelves now. At least, we'll put all the least valuable ones up there, and the gem stones in the bookcase in the drawing room—that one with the curtains inside the glass doors."

"They ought to be in a safe." I had said it yesterday evening as well.

"They were quite all right on the dining-room table last night, in spite of your fears."

"As the consultant private detective in the case I still advise a safe."

* * *

He laughed. "You know bloody well I haven't got a safe. But as consultant private detective you can guard the things properly tonight. You can put them under your pillow. How's that?"

"O.K." I nodded.

"You're not serious?"

"Well, no . . . they'd be too hard under the pillow."

"Damn it. . . ."

"But upstairs, either with you or me, yes. Some of those stones really are valuable. You must have had to pay a big insurance premium on them."

"Er . . . no," admitted Charles. "I guaranteed to replace anything which was damaged or lost."

I goggled. "I know you're rich, but . . . you're an absolute nut. Get them insured at once. Have you any idea what each specimen is worth?"

"No, as a matter of fact . . . no. I didn't ask."

"Well, if you've got a collector coming to stay, he'll expect you to remember how much you paid for each."

"I thought of that," he interrupted. "I inherited them all from a distant cousin. That covers a lot of ignorance, not only costs and values but about crystallography and distribution and rarity, and everything specialized. I found I couldn't possibly learn enough in one day. Just to be able to show some familiarity with the collection should be enough."

"That's fair enough. But you ring the Carver Foundation at once and find out what the stones are worth just the same, and then get straight onto your broker. The trouble with you, Charles, is that you are too honest. Other people aren't. This is the bad, rough world you're in now, not the navy."

"Very well," he said amicably. "I'll do as you say. Hand me that inventory."

He went to telephone and I began putting the chunks of quartz on the empty bookshelves, but before I had done much the front doorbell rang. Mrs. Cross went to answer it and presently came to tell me that a policeman was asking for me.

I put my useless, deformed left hand into my pocket, as I always did with strangers, and went into the hall. A tall, heavy young man in uniform stood there, giving the impression of trying not to be overawed by his rather grand surroundings. I remembered how it felt.

"Is it about this body?" I asked.

"Yes, sir, I believe you are expecting us."

"Whose body is it?"

"I don't know, sir. I was just asked to take you."

"Well . . . where to?"

"Epping Forest, sir."

"But that's miles away." I protested.

"Yes, sir," he agreed, with a touch of gloom.

"Are you sure it's me that's wanted?"

"Oh, positive, sir."

"Well, all right. Sit down a minute while I get my coat and say where I am going."

The policeman drove on his gears, which I found tiring. It took two hours to go from Aynsford, west of Oxford, to Epping Forest, and it was much too long. Finally, however, we were met at a crossroads by another policeman on a motorcycle, and followed him down a twisting secondary road. The forest stretched away all round, bare-branched and mournful in the gray, damp day.

Round the bend we came on a row of two cars and a van, parked. The motorcyclist stopped and dismounted, and the policeman and I got out.

"ETA 12.15," said the motorcyclist, looking at his watch. "You're late. The brass has been waiting here twenty minutes."

"Traffic like caterpillars on the A.40," said my driver defensively.

"You should have used your bell," the motorcyclist grinned. "Come on. It's over this way."

He led us down a barely perceptible track into the wood. We walked on dead brown leaves, rustling. After about half a mile we came to a group of men standing round a screen made of hessian. They were stamping their feet to keep warm and talking in quiet voices.

"Mr. Halley?" One of them shook hands, a pleasant, capable-looking man in middle age who introduced himself as Chief Inspector Cornish. "We're sorry to bring you here all this way, but we want you to see the er . . . remains . . . before we move them. I'd better warn you, it's a perfectly horrible sight." He gave a very human shudder.

"Who is it?" I asked.

"We're hoping you can tell us that, for sure. We think . . . but we'd like you to tell us without us putting it into your head. All right? Now?"

I nodded. He showed me round the screen.

It was Andrews. What was left of him. He had been dead a long time, and the Epping Forest scavengers seemed to have found him tasty. I could see why the police had wanted me to see him *in situ*. He was going to fall to pieces as soon as they moved him.

"Well?"

"Thomas Andrews," I said.

They relaxed. "Are you sure? Positive?"

"Yes."

"It's not just the clothes?"

"No. The shape of the hairline. Protruding ears. Exceptionally rounded helix, vestigial lobes. Very short eyebrows, thick near the nose. Spatulate thumbs, white marks across nails. Hair growing on backs of phalanges."

"Good," said Cornish. "That's conclusive, I'd say. We made a preliminary identification fairly early because of the clothes—they were detailed on the wanted-for-questioning list, of course. But our first inquiries were negative. He seems to have no family, and no one could remember that he had any distinguishing marks—no tattoos, no scars, no operations, and as far as we could find out he hadn't been to a dentist all his life."

"It was intelligent of you to check all that before you gave him to the pathologist," I remarked.

"It was the pathologist's idea, actually." He smiled.

"Who found him?" I asked.

"Some boys. It's usually boys who find bodies."

"When?"

"Three days ago. But obviously he's been here weeks, probably from very soon after he took a pot at you."

"Yes. Is the gun still in his pocket?"

Cornish shook his head. "No sign of it."

"You don't know yet how he died?" I asked.

"No, not yet. But now you've identified him we can get on with it."

We went out from behind the screen and some of the other men went in with a stretcher. I didn't envy them.

Cornish turned to walk back to the road with me, the driver following at a short distance. We went fairly slowly, talking about Andrews, but it seemed more like eight miles than eight hundred yards. I wasn't quite ready for jolly country rambles.

As we reached the cars he asked me to lunch with him. I shook my head, explained about the diet, and suggested a drink instead.

"Fine," he said. "We could both do with one after that." He jerked his head in the direction of Andrews. "There's a good pub down the road this way. Your driver can follow us."

He climbed into his car and we drove after him.

In the bar, equipped with a large brandy and water for me and a whisky and sandwiches for him, we sat at a black oak table, on chintzy chairs, surrounded by horse brasses, hunting horns, warming pans and pewter pots.

"It's funny, meeting you like this," said Cornish, in between bites. "I've watched you so often racing. You've won a tidy bit for me in your time. I hardly missed a meeting on the old Dunstable course, before they sold it for building. I don't get so much racing now, it's so far to a course. Nowhere now to slip along to for a couple of hours in an afternoon." He grinned cheerfully and went on, "You gave us some rare treats at Dunstable. Remember the day you rode that dingdong finish on Brushwood?"

"I remember," I said.

"You literally picked that horse up and carried him home." He took another bite. "I never heard such cheering. There's no mistake about it, you were something special. Pity you had to give it up."

"Yes. . . ."

"Still, I suppose that's a risk you run steeplechasing. There is always one crash too many."

"That's right."

"Where was it you finally bought it?"

"At Stratford-on-Avon, two years ago last May."

He shook his head sympathetically. "Rotten bad luck."

I smiled. "I'd had a pretty good run, though, before that."

"I'll say you did." He smacked his palm on the table. "I took the Missus down to Kempton on Boxing Day, three or four years ago. . . ." He went on talking with enjoyment about races he had watched, revealing himself as a true enthusiast, one of the people without whose interest all racing would collapse. Finally, regretfully, he finished his whisky and looked at his watch. "I'll have to get back. I've enjoyed meeting you. It's odd how things turn out, isn't it? I don't suppose you ever thought when you were riding that you would be good at this sort of work."

"What do you mean, good?" I asked, surprised.

"Hm? Oh, Andrews of course. That description of his clothes you gave after he had shot you. And identifying him today. Most professional. Very efficient." He grinned.

"Getting shot wasn't very efficient," I pointed out.

He shrugged. "That could happen to anyone, believe me. I shouldn't worry about that."

I smiled, as the driver drove me back to Aynsford, at the thought that anyone could believe me good at detective work. There was a simple explanation of my being able to describe and identify—I had read so many of the Missing Persons and Divorce files. The band of ex-policemen who compiled them knew what to base identification on, the unchanging things like ears and hands, not hair color or the wearing of spectacles or a mustache. One of them had told me without pride that wigs, beards, face-padding, and the wearing of or omission of cosmetics made no impression on him, because they were not what he looked at. "Ears and fingers," he said, "they can't disguise those. They never think of trying. Stick to ears and fingers, and you don't go far wrong."

Ears and fingers were just about all there was left of Andrews to identify. The unappetizing gristly bits.

The driver decanted me at Charles's back door and I walked along the passage to the hall. When I had one foot on the bottom tread of the staircase Charles himself appeared at the drawing-room door.

"Oh, hullo, I thought it might be you. Come in here and look at these."

Reluctantly leaving the support of the bannisters I followed him into the drawing room.

"There," he said, pointing. He had fixed up a strip of light inside his bookcase and it shone down onto the quartz gems, bringing them to sparkling life. The open doors with their red silk curtains made a softly glowing frame. It was an eye-catching and effective arrangement, and I told him so.

"Good. The light goes on automatically when the doors are open. Nifty, don't you think?" He laughed. "And you can set your mind at rest. They are now insured."

"That's good."

He shut the doors of the bookcase and the light inside went out. The red curtains discreetly hid their treasure. Turning to me, more seriously he said, "Whose body?"

"Andrews'."

"The man who shot you? How extraordinary. Suicide?"

"No, I don't think so. The gun wasn't there, anyway."

He made a quick gesture toward the chair. "My dear Sid, sit down, sit down. You look like d . . . er . . . a bit worn out. You shouldn't have gone all that way. Put your feet up, I'll get you a drink." He fussed over me like a mother hen, fetching me first water, then brandy, and finally a cup of warm beef juice from Mrs. Cross, and sat opposite me watching while I dispatched it.

"Do you like that stuff?" he asked.

"Yes, luckily." I grinned.

"We used to have it when we were children. A ritual once a week. My father used to drain it out of the Sunday joint, propping the dish on the carving fork. We all loved it, but I haven't had any for years."

"Try some?" I offered him the cup.

He took it and tasted it. "Yes, it's good. Takes me back sixty years. . . ." He smiled companionably, relaxing in his chair, and I told him about Andrews and the long-dead state he was in.

"It sounds," he said slowly, "as if he might have been murdered."

"I wouldn't be surprised. He was young and healthy. He wouldn't just lie down and die of exposure in Hertfordshire."

Charles laughed.

"What time are your guests expected?" I asked, glancing at the clock. It was just after five.

"About six."

"I think I'll go up and lie on my bed for a while, then."

"You are all right, Sid, aren't you? I mean, really all right?"

"Oh yes. Just tired."

"Will you come down to dinner?" There was the faintest undercurrent of disappointment in his casual voice. I thought of all his hard work with the rocks and the amount of maneuvering he had done. Besides, I was getting definitely curious myself about his intentions.

"Yes," I nodded, getting up. "Lay me a teaspoon."

I made it upstairs and lay on my bed, sweating. And cursing. Although the bullet had missed everything vital in tearing holes through my gut, it had singed and upset a couple of nerves. They had warned me in the hospital that it would be some time before I felt well. It didn't please me that so far they were right.

I heard the visitors arrive, heard their loud cheerful voices as they were shown up to their rooms, the doors shutting, the bath waters running, the various bumps and murmurs from the adjoining rooms; and eventually the diminishing chatter as they finished changing and went downstairs past my door. I heaved myself off the bed, took off the loose-waisted slacks and jersey shirt I felt most comfortable in, and put on a white cotton shirt and dark gray suit.

My face looked back at me, pale, gaunt and dark-eyed, as I brushed my hair. A bit of a death's-head at the feast. I grinned nastily at my reflection. It was only a slight improvement.

3

By the time I got to the foot of the stairs, Charles and his guests were coming across the hall from the drawing room to the dining room. The men all wore dinner jackets and the women, long dresses. Charles deliberately hadn't warned me, I reflected. He knew my convalescent kit didn't include a black tie.

He didn't stop and introduce me to his guests, but nodded slightly and went straight on into the dining room, talking with charm to the rounded, fluffy little woman who walked beside him. Behind came Viola and a tall dark girl of striking good looks. Viola, Charles's elderly widowed cousin, gave me a passing half-smile, embarrassed and worried. I wondered what was the matter: normally she greeted me with affection, and it was only a short time since she had written warm wishes for my recovery. The girl beside her barely glanced in my direction, and the two men bringing up the rear didn't look at me at all.

Shrugging, I followed them into the dining room. There was no mistaking the place laid for me: it consisted, in actual fact, of a spoon, a mat, a glass, and a fork, and it was situated in the center of one of the sides. Opposite me was an empty gap. Charles seated his guests, himself in his usual place at the end of the table with fluffy Mrs. van Dysart on his right, and the striking Mrs. Kraye on his left. I sat between Mrs. Kraye and Rex van Dysart. It was only gradually that I sorted everyone out. Charles made no introductions whatever.

The groups at each end of the table fell into animated chat and paid me as much attention as a speed limit. I began to think I would go back to bed.

The manservant whom Charles engaged on these occasions served small individual tureens of turtle soup. My tureen, I found, contained more beef juice. Bread was passed, spoons clinked, salt and pepper were shaken and the meal began. Still no one spoke to me, though the visitors were growing slightly curious. Mrs. van Dysart flicked her sharp china-blue eyes from Charles to me and back again, inviting an introduction. None came. He went on talking to the two women with almost overpowering charm, apparently oblivious.

Rex van Dysart on my left offered me bread, with lifted eyebrows and a faint noncommittal smile. He was a large man with a flat white face, heavy black rimmed spectacles and a domineering manner. When I refused the bread he put the basket down on the table, gave me the briefest of nods, and turned back to Viola.

Even before he brought quartz into his conversation I guessed it was for Howard Kraye that the show was being put on; and I disliked him on sight with a hackle-raising antipathy that disconcerted me. If Charles was planning that I should ever work for, or with, or near Mr. Kraye, I thought, he could think again.

He was a substantial man of about forty-eight to fifty, with shoulders, waist and hips all knocking forty-four. The dinner jacket sat on him with the ease of a second skin, and when he shot his cuffs occasionally he did so without affectation, showing off noticeably well-manicured hands.

He had tidy gray-brown hair, straight eyebrows, narrow nose, small firm mouth, rounded freshly shaven chin, and very high unwrinkled lower eyelids, which gave him a secret, shuttered look.

A neat enclosed face like a mask, with perhaps something rotten underneath. You could almost smell it across the dinner table. I guessed, rather fancifully, that he knew too much about too many vices. But on top he was smooth. Much too smooth. In my book, a nasty type of phony. I listened to him talking to Viola.

". . . So when Doria and I got to New York I looked up those fellows in that fancy crystal palace on First Avenue and got them moving. You have to give the clotheshorse diplomats a lead, you know, they've absolutely no initiative of their own. Look, I told them, unilateral action is not only inadvisable, but impracticable. But they are so steeped in their own brand of pragmatism that informed opinion has as much chance of osmosing as mercury through rhyolite. . . ."

Viola was nodding wisely while not understanding a word. The pretentious rigmarole floated comfortably over her sensible head and left her unmoved. But its flashiness seemed to me part of a gigantic confidence trick: one was meant to be enormously impressed. I couldn't believe that Charles had fallen under his spell; it was impossible. Not my subtle, clever, coolheaded father-in-law. Mr. van Dysart, however, hung on every word.

By the end of the soup his wife at the other end of the table could contain her curiosity no longer. She put down her spoon and with her eyes on me, said to Charles in a low but clearly audible voice, "Who is that?"

All heads turned toward him, as if they had been waiting for the question. Charles lifted his chin and spoke distinctly, so that they should all hear the answer.

"That," he said, "is my son-in-law." His tone was light, amused, and infinitely contemptuous; and it jabbed raw on a nerve I had thought long-dead. I looked at him sharply, and his eyes met mine, blank and expressionless.

My gaze slid up over and passed his head to the wall behind him. There, for some years, and certainly that morning, had hung an oil painting of me on a horse going over a fence at Cheltenham. In its place there was now an old-fashioned seascape, brown with Victorian varnish.

Charles was watching me. I looked back at him briefly and said nothing. I suppose he knew I wouldn't. My only defense against his insults long ago had been silence, and he was counting on my instant reaction being the same again.

Mrs. van Dysart leaned forward a little, and with waking malice murmured, "Do go on, Admiral."

Without hesitation Charles obeyed her, in the same flaying voice. "He was fathered, as far as he knows, by a window cleaner on a nineteen-year-old unmarried girl from the Liverpool slums. She later worked, I believe, as a packer in a biscuit factory."

"Admiral, no!" exclaimed Mrs. van Dysart breathlessly.

"Indeed yes," nodded Charles. "As you might guess, I did my best to stop my daughter making such an unsuitable match. He is small, as you see, and he has a crippled hand. Working class and undersized . . . but my daughter was determined. You know what girls are." He sighed.

"Perhaps she was sorry for him," suggested Mrs. van Dysart.

"Maybe," said Charles. He hadn't finished, and wasn't to be deflected. "If she had met him as a student of some sort, one might have understood it . . . but he isn't even educated. He finished school at fifteen to be apprenticed to a trade. He has been unemployed now for some time. My daughter, I might say, has left him."

I sat like a stone, looking down at the congealed puddle at the bottom of my soup dish, trying to loosen the clamped muscles in my jaw, and to think straight. Not four hours ago he'd shown concern for me and had drunk from my cup. As far as I could ever be certain of anything, his affection for me was genuine and unchanged. So he must have a good reason for what he was doing to me now. At least I hoped so.

I glanced at Viola. She hadn't protested. She was looking unhappily down at her place. I remembered her embarrassment out in the hall, and I guessed that Charles had warned her what to expect. He might have warned me too, I thought grimly.

Not unexpectedly, they were all looking at me. The dark and beautiful Doria Kraye raised her lovely eyebrows and in a flat, slightly nasal voice, remarked, "You don't take offense, then." It was halfway to a sneer. Clearly she thought I ought to take offense, if I had any guts.

"He is not offended," said Charles easily. "Why should the truth offend?"

"Is it true then," asked Doria down her flawless nose, "that you are illegitimate and all the rest?"

I took a deep breath and eased my muscles.

"Yes."

There was an uncomfortable short silence. Doria said, "Oh," blankly, and began to crumble her bread.

On cue, and no doubt summoned by Charles's foot on the bell, the manservant came in to remove the plates, and conversation trickled back to the party like cigarette smoke after a cancer scare.

I sat thinking of the details Charles had left out: the fact that my twenty-year-old father, working overtime for extra cash, had fallen from a high ladder and been killed three days before his wedding day, and that I had been born eight months later. The fact that my young mother, finding that she was dying from some obscure kidney ailment, had taken me from grammer school at fifteen, and because I was small for my age had apprenticed me to a racehorse trainer in Newmarket, so that I should have a home and someone to turn to when she had gone. They had been good enough people, both of them, and Charles knew that I thought so.

The next course was some sort of fish smothered in mushroom-colored sauce. My astronauts' delight, coming at the same time, didn't look noticably different, as it was not in its pot, but out on a plate. Dear Mrs. Cross, I thought fervently, I could kiss you. I could eat it this way with a fork, singlehanded. The pots needed to be held—in my case inelegantly hugged between forearm and chest—and at that moment I would have starved rather than taken my left hand out of my pocket.

Fluffy Mrs. van Dysart was having a ball. Clearly she relished the idea of me sitting there practically isolated, dressed in the wrong clothes, and an object of open derision to her host. With her fair frizzy hair, her baby-blue eyes and her rose-pink silk dress embroidered with silver, she looked as sweet as sugar icing. What she said showed that she thoroughly understood the pleasures of keeping a whipping boy.

"Poor relations are such a problem, aren't they?" she said to Charles sympathetically, and intentionally loud enough for me to hear. "You can't neglect them in our position, in case the Sunday papers get hold of them and pay them to make a smear. And it's especially difficult if one has to keep them in one's own house. One can't, I suppose, put them to eat in the kitchen, but there are so many occasions when one could do without them. Perhaps a tray upstairs is the best thing."

"Ah, yes," nodded Charles smoothly, "but they won't always agree to that."

I half choked on a mouthful, remembering the pressure he had exerted to get me downstairs. And immediately I felt not only reassured but deeply interested. This, then, was what he had been so industriously planning, the destruction of me as a man in the eyes of his guests. He would no doubt explain why in his own good time. Meanwhile I felt slightly less inclined to go back to bed.

I glanced at Kraye, and found his greenish-amber eyes steady on my face. It wasn't as overt as in Mrs. van Dysart's case, but it was there: pleasure. My toes curled inside my shoes. Interested or not, it was hard to sit tight before that loathsome, taunting half-smile. I looked down, away, blotting him out.

He gave a sound halfway between a cough and a laugh, turned his head, and began talking down the table to Charles about the collection of quartz.

"So sensible of you, my dear chap, to keep them all behind glass, though most tantalizing to me from here. Is that a geode, on the middle shelf? The reflection, you know . . . I can't quite see."

"Er . . . " said Charles, not knowing any more than I did what a geode was. "I'm looking forward to showing them to you. After dinner, perhaps? Or tomorrow?"

"Oh, tonight, I'd hate to postpone such a treat. Did you say that you had any felspar in your collection?"

"No," said Charles uncertainly.

'No, well, I can see it is a small specialized collection. Perhaps you are wise in sticking to silicon dioxide."

Charles glibly launched into the cousinly-bequest alibi for ignorance, which Kraye accepted with courtesy and disappointment.

"A fascinating subject, though, my dear Roland. It repays study. The earth beneath our feet, the fundamental sediment from the Triassic and Jurassic epochs, is our priceless inheritance, the source of all our life and power. . . . There is nothing which interests me so much as land."

Doria on my right gave me the tiniest of snorts, which her husband didn't hear. He was busy constructing another long, polysyllabic and largely unintelligible chat on the nature of the universe.

I sat unoccupied through the steaks, the meringue pudding, the cheese and the fruit. Conversations went on on either side of me and occasionally past me, but a deaf-mute could have taken as much part as I did. Mrs. van Dysart commented on the difficulties of feeding poor relations with delicate stomachs and choosy appetites. Charles neglected to tell her that I had been shot and wasn't poor, but agreed that a weak digestion in dependents was a moral fault. Mrs. van Dysart loved it. Doria occasionally looked at me as if I were an interesting specimen of low life. Rex van Dysart again offered me the bread; and that was that. Finally Viola shepherded Doria and Mrs. van Dysart out to have coffee in the drawing room and Charles offered his guests port and brandy. He passed me the brandy bottle with an air of irritation and compressed his lips in disapproval when I took some. It wasn't lost on his guests.

After a while he rose, opened the glass bookcase doors, and showed the quartzes to Kraye. Piece by piece the two discussed their way along the rows, with van Dysart standing beside them exhibiting polite interest and hiding his yawns of boredom. I stayed sitting down. I also helped myself to some more brandy.

Charles kept his end up very well and went through the whole lot without a mistake. He then transferred to the drawing room, where his gem cabinet proved a great success. I tagged along, sat in an unobtrusive chair and listened to them all talking, but I came to no conclusions except that if I didn't soon go upstairs I wouldn't get there under my own steam. It was eleven o'clock and I had had a long day. Charles didn't look round when I left the room.

Half an hour later, when his guests had come murmuring up to their rooms, he came quietly through my door and over to the bed. I was still lying on top of it in my shirt and trousers, trying to summon some energy to finish undressing.

He looked down at me, smiling.

"Well?" he said.

"It is you," I said, "who is the dyed-in-the-wool, twenty-four-carat, unmitigated bastard."

He laughed. "I thought you were going to spoil the whole thing when you saw your picture had gone." He began taking off my shoes and socks. "You looked as bleak as the Bering Strait in December. Pajamas?"

"Under the pillow."

He helped me undress in his quick neat naval fashion.

"Why did you do it?" I said.

He waited until I was lying down between the sheets, then he perched on the edge of the bed.

"Did you mind?"

"Hell, Charles . . . of course. At first anyway."

"I'm afraid it came out beastlier than I expected, but I'll tell you why I did it. Do you remember that first game of chess we had? When you beat me out of sight? You know why you won so easily?"

"You weren't paying enough attention."

"Exactly. I wasn't paying enough attention, because I didn't think you were an opponent worth bothering about. A bad tactical error." He grinned. "An admiral should know better. If you underrate a strong opponent you are at a disadvantage. If you grossly underrate him, if you are convinced he is of absolutely no account, you prepare no defense and are certain to be defeated." He paused for a moment, and went on. "It is therefore good strategy to delude the enemy into believing you are too weak to be considered. And that is what I was doing tonight on your behalf."

He looked at me gravely. After some seconds I said, "At what game, exactly, do you expect me to play Howard Kraye?"

He sighed contentedly, and smiled. "Do you remember what he said interested him most?"

I thought back. "Land."

Charles nodded. "Land. That's right. He collects it. Chunks of it, yards of it, acres of it. . . ." He hesitated.

"Well?"

"You can play him," he said slowly, "for Seabury Racecourse."

The enormity of it took my breath away.

"What?" I said incredulously. "Don't be silly. I'm only—"

"Shut up," he interrupted. "I don't want to hear what you think you are only. You're intelligent, aren't you? You work for a detective agency? You wouldn't want Seabury to close down? Why shouldn't you do something about it?"

"But I imagine he's after some sort of take-over bid, from what you say. You want some powerful city chap or other to oppose him, not . . . me."

"He is very much on his guard against powerful chaps in the city, but wide open to you."

I stopped arguing because the implications were pushing into the background my inadequacy for such a task.

"Are you sure he is after Seabury?" I asked.

"Someone is," said Charles. "There has been a lot of buying and selling of the shares lately, and the price per share is up although they haven't paid a dividend this year. The clerk of the course told me about it. He said that the directors are very worried. On paper, there is no great concentration of shares in any one name, but there wasn't at Dunstable either. There, when it came to a vote on selling out to a land developer, they found that about twenty various nominees were in fact all agents for Kraye. He carried enough of the other shareholders with him, and the racecourse was lost to housing."

"It was all legal, though?"

"A wangle; but legal, yes. And it looks like it's happening again."

"But what's to stop him, if it's legal?"

"You might try."

I stared at him in silence. He stood up and straightened the bedcover neatly. "It would be a pity if Seabury went the way of Dunstable." He went toward the door.

"Where does van Dysart fit in?" I asked.

"Oh," he said, turning, "nowhere. It was Mrs. van Dysart I wanted. She has a tongue like a rattlesnake. I knew she would help me tear you to pieces." He grinned. "She'll give you a terrible weekend, I'm glad to say."

"Thanks very much," I said sarcastically. "Why didn't you tell me all this before? When you so carefully left me that book on company law for instance? Or at least this evening when I came back from seeing Andrews, so that I could have been prepared, at dinner?"

He opened the door and smiled across the room, his eyes blank again.

"Sleep well," he said. "Good night, Sid."

Charles took the two men out shooting the following morning and Viola drove their wives into Oxford to do some shopping and visit an exhibition of Venetian glass. I took the opportunity of having a good look round the Krayes' bedroom.

It wasn't until I'd been there for more than ten minutes that it struck me that two years earlier I wouldn't have dreamed of doing such a thing. Now I had done it as a matter of course, without thinking twice. I grinned sardonically. Evidently even in just sitting around in a detective agency one caught an attitude of mind. I realized, moreover, that I had instinctively gone about my search methodically and with a careful touch. In an odd way it was extremely disconcerting.

I wasn't of course looking for anything special: just digging a little into the Krayes' characters. I wouldn't even concede in my own mind that I was interested in the challenge Charles had so elaborately thrown down. But all the same I searched, and thoroughly.

Howard Kraye slept in crimson pajamas with his initials embroidered in white on the pocket. His dressing gown was of crimson brocade with a black quilted collar and black tassels on the belt. His washing things, neatly arranged in a large fitted toilet case in the adjoining bathroom, were numerous and ornate. He used pine-scented aftershave lotion, cologne friction rub, lemon hand cream, and an oily hair dressing, all from gold-topped cut-glass bottles. There were also medicated soap tablets, special formula toothpaste, talcum powder in a gilt container, deodorant, and a supersonic-looking electric razor. He wore false teeth and had a spare set. He had brought a half-full tin of laxatives, some fruit salts, a bottle of mouthwash, some antiseptic foot powder, penicillin throat lozenges, a spot-sealing stick, digestive tablets, and an eye bath. The body beautiful, in and out.

All his clothes, down to his vests and pants, had been made to measure, and he had brought enough to cover every possibility of a country week-end. I went through the pockets of his dinner jacket and the three suits hanging beside it, but he was a tidy man and they were all empty, except for a nail file in each breast pocket. His six various pairs of shoes were handmade and nearly new. I looked into each shoe separately, but except for trees they were all empty.

In a drawer I found neatly arranged his stock of ties, handkerchiefs, and socks: all expensive. A heavy chased silver box contained cuff links, studs, and tiepins; mostly of gold. He had avoided jewels, but one attractive pair of cuff links was made from pieces of what I now knew enough to identify as tiger's-eye. The backs of his hairbrushes were beautiful slabs of the gem stone, smoky quartz. A few brown and gray hairs were lodged in between the bristles.

There remained only his luggage, four lavish suitcases standing in a neat row beside the wardrobe. I opened each one. They were all empty except for the smallest, which contained a brown calf attaché case. I looked at it carefully before I touched it, but as Kraye didn't seem to have left any telltales like hairs or pieces of cotton attached, I lifted it out and put it on one of the beds. It was locked, but I had learned how to deal with such drawbacks. A lugubrious ex-police sergeant on Radnor's payroll gave me progressively harder lessons in lock-picking every time he came into the office between jobs, moaning all the while about the damage London soot did to his chrysanthemums. My one-handedness he had seen only as a challenge, and had invented a couple of new techniques and instruments entirely for my benefit. Recently he had presented me with a collection of fine delicate keys which he had once removed from a burglar, and had bullied me until I carried them with me everywhere. They were in my room. I went and fetched them and without much trouble opened the case.

It was as meticulously tidy as everything else, and I was particularly careful not to alter the position or order of any of the papers. There were several letters from a stockbroker, a bunch of share transfer certificates, various oddments, and a series of typed sheets, headed with the previous day's date, which were apparently an up-to-the-minute analysis of his investments. He seemed to be a rich man and to do a good deal of buying and selling. He had money in oils, mines, property, and industrial stocks. There was also a sheet headed simply S.R., on which every transaction was a purchase. Against each entry was a name and the address of a bank. Some names occurred three or four times, some only once.

Underneath the papers lay a large thick brown envelope inside which were two packets of new ten-pound notes. I didn't count, but there couldn't have been fewer than a hundred of them. The envelope was at the bottom of the case except for a writing board with slightly used white blotting paper held by crocodile and gold corners. I pulled up the board and found underneath it two more sheets of paper, both covered with dates, initials, and sums of money.

I let the whole lot fall back into place, made sure that everything looked exactly as I had found it, relocked the case, and put it back into its covering suitcase.

The divine Doria, I found, was far from being as tidy as her husband. All her things were in a glorious jumble, which made leaving them undisturbed a difficult job, but also meant that she would be less likely than her husband to notice if anything were slightly out of place.

Her clothes, though they looked and felt expensive, were bought ready-made and casually treated. Her washing things consisted of a plastic zippered case, a flannel, a toothbrush, bath essence, and a puffing bottle of talc. Almost stark beside Howard's collection. No medicine. She appeared to wear nothing in bed, but a pretty white quilted dressing gown hung half off a hanger behind the bathroom door.

She had not completely unpacked. Suitcases propped on chairs and stools still held stirred-up underclothes and various ultra-feminine equipment which I hadn't seen since Jenny left.

The top of the dressing table, though the daily seemed to have done her best to dust it, was an expensive chaos. Pots of cosmetics, bottles of scent and hair spray stood on one side, a box of tissues, a scarf, and the cluttered tray out of the top of a dressing case filled the other. The dressing case itself, of crocodile with gold clips, stood on the floor. I picked it up and put it on the bed. It was locked. I unlocked it, and looked inside.

Doria was quite a girl. She possessed two sets of false eyelashes, spare fingernails, and a hairpiece on a tortoiseshell headband. Her big jewel case, the one tidy thing in her whole luggage, contained on the top layer the sapphire and diamond earrings she had worn the previous evening, along with a diamond sunburst brooch and a sapphire ring; and on the lower layer a second necklace, bracelet, earrings, brooch, and ring all of gold, platinum, and citrine. The yellow jewels were uncommon, barbaric in design, and had no doubt been made especially for her.

Under the jewel case were four paperback novels so pornographic in content as to raise doubts about Kraye's ability as a lover. Jenny had held that a truly satisfied woman didn't need to read dirty sex. Doria clearly did.

Alongside the books was a thick leather-covered diary to which the beautiful Mrs. Kraye had confided the oddest thoughts. Her life seemed to be as untidy as her clothes, a mixture of ordinary social behavior, dream fantasy and a perverted marriage relationship. If the diary were to be believed, she and Howard obtained deeper pleasure, both of them, from his beating her than from the normal act of love. Well, I reflected, at least they were well matched. Some of the divorces which Hunt Radnor Associates dealt with arose because one partner alone was pain-fixated, the other being revolted.

At the bottom of the case were two other objects of interest. First, coiled in a brown velvet bag, the sort of leather strap used by schoolmasters, at whose purpose, in view of the diary, it was easy to guess; and second, in a chocolate box, a gun.

4

TELEPHONING FOR the local taxi to come and fetch me, I went to Oxford and bought a camera. Although the shop was starting a busy Saturday afternoon, the boy who served me tackled the problem of a one-handed photographer with enthusiasm and as if he had all the time in the world. Between us we sorted out a miniature German 16 mm. camera, three inches long by one and a half wide, which I could hold, set, snap and wind with one hand with the greatest ease.

He gave me a thorough lesson in how to work it, added an inch to its length in the shape of a screwed-on photoelectric light meter, loaded it with film, and slid it into a black case so small that it made no bulge in my trouser pocket. He also offered to change the film later if I couldn't manage it. We parted on the best of terms.

When I got back everyone was sitting round a cozy fire in the sitting room, eating crumpets. Very tantalizing. I loved crumpets.

No one took much notice when I went in and sat down on the fringe of the circle except Mrs. van Dysart, who began sharpening her claws. She got in a couple of quick digs about spongers marrying girls for their money, and Charles didn't say that I hadn't. Viola looked at me searchingly, worry opening her mouth. I winked, and she shut it again in relief.

I gathered that the morning's bag had been the usual mixture (two brace of pheasant, five wild duck and a hare), because Charles preferred a rough shoot over his own land to organized affairs with beaters. The women had collected a poor opinion of Oxford shop assistants and a booklet on the manufacture of fifteenth-century Italian glass. All very normal for a country weekend. It was my snooping that seemed unreal. That, and the false position Charles had steered me into.

Kraye's gaze, and finally his hands, strayed back to the gem bookshelves. Again the door was opened, Charles's trick lighting working effectively, and one by one the gems were brought out, passed round and closely admired. Mrs. van Dysart seemed much attached to a spectacular piece of rose quartz, playing with it to make light strike sparks from it, and smoothing her fingers over the glossy surface.

"Rex, you must collect some of this for me!" she ordered, her will showing like iron inside the fluff; and masterful-looking Rex nodded his meek agreement.

Kraye was saying, "You know, Roland, these are really remarkably fine specimens. Among the best I've ever seen. Your cousin must have been extremely fortunate and influential to acquire so many fine crystals."

"Oh, indeed he was," agreed Charles equably.

"I should be interested if you ever think of realizing on them . . . a first option, perhaps?"

"You can have a first option by all means," smiled Charles. "But I shan't be selling them, I assure you."

"Ah well, so you say now. But I don't give up easily. . . . I shall try you later. But don't forget, my first option?"

"Certainly," said Charles. "My word on it."

Kraye smiled at the stone he held in his hands, a magnificent raw amethyst like a cluster of petrified violets.

"Don't let this fall into the fire," he said. "It would turn yellow." He then treated everyone to a lecture on amethysts which would have been interesting had he made any attempt at simplicity: but blinding by words was with him either a habit or a policy. I wasn't certain which.

". . . Manganese, of course occurring in geodes or agate nodules in South America or Russia, but with such a world-wide distribution it was only to be expected that elementary societies should ascribe to it supra rational inherencies and attributes. . . ."

I suddenly found him looking straight at me, and I knew my expression had not been one of impressed admiration. More like quizzical sarcasm. He didn't like it. There was a quick flash in his eyes.

"It is symptomatic of the slum mentality," he remarked, "to scoff at what it can't comprehend."

"Sid," said Charles sharply. "I'm sure you must have something else to do. We can let you go until dinner."

I stood up. The natural anger rose quickly, but only as far as my teeth. I swallowed. "Very well," I muttered.

"Before you go, Sid," said Mrs. van Dysart from the depths of a sofa, ". . . Sid, what a deliciously plebeian name, so suitable. . . . Put these down on the table for me."

She held out both hands, one stone in each and another balanced between them. I couldn't manage them all and dropped them.

"Oh dear," said Mrs. van Dysart, acidly sweet, as I knelt and picked them up, putting them one by one on the table, "I forgot you were disabled, so silly of me." She hadn't forgotten. "Are you sure you can't get treatment for whatever is wrong with you? You ought to try some exercises, they'd do you the world of good. All you need is a little perserverance. You owe it to the Admiral, don't you think, to *try*?"

I didn't answer, and Charles at least had the grace to keep quiet.

"I know a very good man," went on Mrs. van Dysart. "He used to work for the army . . . excellent at getting malingerers back into service. Now he's the sort of man who'd do you good. What do you think, Admiral, shall I fix it up for your son-in-law to see him?"

"Er . . . ," said Charles, "I don't think it would work."

"Nonsense." She was brisk and full of smiles. "You can't let him lounge about doing nothing for the rest of his life. A good bracing course of treatment, that's what he needs. Now," she said turning to me, "so that I know exactly what I'm talking about when I make an appointment, let's see this precious crippled hand of yours."

There was a tiny pause. I could feel their probing eyes, their unfriendly curiosity.

"No," I said calmly. "Excuse me, but no."

As I walked across the room and out of the door her voice floated after me. "There you are, Admiral, he doesn't *want* to get better. They're all the same. . . ."

I lay on my bed for a couple of hours rereading the book on company law, especially, now, the section on take-overs. It was no easier going than it had been in the hospital, and now that I knew why I was reading it, it seemed more involved, not less. If the directors of Seabury were worried, they would surely have called in their own investigator. Someone who knew his way round the stock markets like I knew my way round the track. An expert. I wasn't at all the right person to stop Kraye, even if indeed anyone could stop him. And yet . . . I stared at the ceiling, taking my lower lip between my teeth. And yet . . . I did have a wild idea. . . .

Viola came in, knocking as she opened the door.

"Sid, dear, are you all right? Can I do anything for you?" She shut the door, gentle, generous, and worried.

I sat up and swung my legs over the side of the bed. "No, thanks, I'm fine."

She perched on the arm of an easy chair, looked at me with her kind, slightly mournful brown eyes, and said a little breathlessly, "Sid, why are you letting Charles say such terrible things about you? It isn't only when you are there in the room; they've been, oh, almost sniggering about you behind your back. Charles and that frightful Mrs. van Dysart. . . . What has happened between you and him? When you nearly died he couldn't have been more worried if you'd been his own son . . . but now he is so cruel, and terribly unfair."

"Dear Viola, don't worry. It's only some game that Charles is playing, and I go along with him."

"Yes," she said, nodding. "He warned me. He said that you were both going to lay a smoke screen and that I was on no account to say a single word in your defense the whole weekend. But it wasn't true, was it? When I saw your face, when Charles said that about your poor mother, I knew you didn't know what he was going to do."

"Was it so obvious?" I said ruefully. "Well, I promise you I haven't quarreled with him. Will you just be a dear and do exactly as he asked? Don't say a single word to any of them about . . . um . . . the more successful bits of my life history, or about my job at the agency, or about the shooting. You didn't today, did you, on the trip to Oxford?" I finished with some anxiety.

She shook her head. "I thought I'd talk to you first."

"Good." I grinned.

"Oh dear," she cried, partly in relief, partly in puzzlement. "Well, in that case, Charles asked me to pop in and make sure you would come down to dinner."

"Oh he did, did he? Afraid I'd throw a boot at him, I should think, after sending me out of the room like that. Well, you just pop back to Charles and say that I'll come down to dinner on condition that he organizes some chemmy afterwards, and includes me out."

Dinner was a bit of a trial: with their smoked salmon and pheasant the guests enjoyed another round of Sid-baiting. Both the Krayes, egged on by Charles and the fluffy harpy beside him, had developed a pricking skill for this novel weekend parlor game, and I heartily wished Charles had never thought of it. However, he kept his side of the bargain by digging out the chemin-de-fer shoe, and after the coffee, the brandy, and another inspection of the dining-room quartzes, he settled his guests firmly round the table in the drawing room.

Upstairs, once the shoe was clicking regularly and the players were well involved, I went and collected Kraye's attaché case and took it along to my room.

Because I was never going to get another chance and did not want to miss something I might regret later, I photographed every single paper in the case. All the stockbroker's letters and all the investment reports. All the share certificates, and also the two separate sheets under the writing board.

Although I had an ultra-bright light bulb and the exposure meter to help me get the right setting, I took several pictures at different light values of the papers I considered the most important in order to be sure of getting the sharpest possible result. The little camera handled beautifully, and I found I could change the films in their tiny casettes without much difficulty. By the time I had finished I had used three whole films of twenty exposures on each. It took me a long time, as I had put the camera down between each shot to move the next paper into my pool of light, and also had to be very careful not to alter the order in which the papers had lain in the case.

The envelope of ten-pound notes kept me hoping like crazy that Howard Kraye would not lose heavily and come upstairs for replacements. It seemed to me at the time a ridiculous thing to do, but I took two flat blocks of tenners out of the envelope, and photographed them as well. Putting them back I flipped through them: the notes were new, consecutive, fifty to a packet. One thousand pounds to a penny.

When everything was back in the case I sat looking at the contents for a minute, checking their position against my visual memory of how they looked when I first saw them. At last satisfied, I shut the case, locked it, rubbed it over to remove any finger marks I might have left, and put it back where I had found it.

After that I went downstairs to the dining room for the brandy I had refused at dinner. I needed it. Carrying the glass, I listened briefly outside the drawing-room door to the murmurs and clicks from within and went upstairs again, to bed.

Lying in the dark I reviewed the situation. Howard Kraye, drawn by the bait of a quartz collection, had accepted an invitation to a quiet weekend in the country with a retired admiral. With him he had brought a selection of private papers. As he had no possible reason to imagine that anyone in such innocent surroundings would spy on him, the papers might be very private indeed. So private that he felt safest when they were with him? Too private to leave at home? It would be nice to think so.

At that point, imperceptibly, I fell sleep.

The nerves in my abdomen wouldn't give up. After about five hours of fighting them unsuccessfully I decided that staying in bed all morning thinking about it was doing no good, and got up and dressed.

Drawn partly against my will, I walked along the passage to Jenny's room, and went in. It was the small sunny room she had had as a child. She had gone back to it when she left me and it was all hers alone. I had never slept there. The single bed, the relics of childhood, girlish muslin frills on curtains and dressing table, everything shut me out. The photographs round the room were of her father, her dead mother, her sister, brother-in-law, dogs and horses, but not of me. As far as she could, she blotted out her marriage.

I walked slowly round touching her things, remembering how much I had loved her. Knowing, too, that there was no going back, and that if she walked through the door at that instant we would not fall into each other's arms in tearful reconciliation.

Removing a one-eyed teddy bear I sat down for a while on her pink armchair. It's difficult to say just where a marriage goes wrong, because the accepted reason often isn't the real one. The rows Jenny and I had had were all ostensibly caused by the same thing: my ambition. Grown finally too heavy for flat racing, I had switched entirely to steeplechasing the season before we were married, and I wanted to be champion jumping jockey. To this end I was prepared to eat little, drink less, go to bed early, and not make love if I were racing the next day. It was unfortunate that she liked late-night parties and dancing more than anything else. At first she gave them up willingly, then less willingly, and finally in fury. After that, she started going on her own.

In the end she told me to choose between her and racing. But by then I was indeed champion jockey, and had been for some time, and I couldn't give it up. So Jenny left. It was just life's little irony that six months later I lost the racing as well. Gradually since then I had come to realize that a marriage didn't break up just because one half liked parties and the other didn't. I thought now that Jenny's insistence on a gay time was the result of my having failed her in some basic, deeply necessary way. Which did nothing whatsoever for my self-respect or my self-confidence.

I sighed, stood up, replaced the teddy bear, and went downstairs to the drawing room. Eleven o'clock on a windy autumn morning.

Doria was alone in the big comfortable room, sitting on the window seat and reading the Sunday papers, which lay around her on the floor in a haphazard mess.

"Hello," she said, looking up. "What hole did you crawl out of?"

I walked over to the fire and didn't answer.

"Poor little man, are his feelings hurt then?"

"I do have feelings, the same as anyone else."

"So you actually can talk?" she said mockingly. "I'd begun to wonder."

"Yes, I can talk."

"Well, now, tell me your troubles, little man."

"Life is just a bowl of cherries."

She uncurled herself from the window seat and came across to the fire, looking remarkably out of place in skin-tight leopard-printed pants and a black silk shirt.

She was the same height as Jenny, the same height as me, just touching five foot six. As my smallness had always been an asset for racing, I never looked on it as a handicap for life in general, either physical or social. Neither had I ever really understood why so many people thought that height for its own sake was important. But it would have been naïve not to take note of the widespread extraordinary assumption that the mind and heart could be measured by tallness. The little man with the big emotion was a stock comic figure. It was utterly irrational. What difference did three or four inches of leg bone make to a man's essential nature? Perhaps I had been fortunate in coming to terms early with the effect of poor nutrition in a difficult childhood; but it did not stop me understanding why other short men struck back in defensive aggression. They were the pinpricks, for instance, of girls like Doria calling one "little" and intending it as an insult.

"You've dug yourself into a cushy berth here, haven't you?" she said, taking a cigarette from the silver box on the mantelpiece.

"I suppose so."

"If I were the Admiral I'd kick you out."

"Thank you," I said, neglecting to offer her a light. With a mean look she found a box of matches and struck one for herself.

"Are you ill, or something?"

"No. Why?"

"You eat those faddy health foods, and you look such a sickly little creature. . . . I just wondered." She blew the smoke down her nose. "The Admiral's daughter must have been pretty desperate for a wedding ring."

"Give her her due," I said mildly. "At least she didn't pick a rich father figure twice her age."

I thought for a moment she meant to go into the corny routine of smacking my face, but as it happened she was holding the cigarette in the hand she needed.

"You little shit," she said instead. A charming girl, altogether.

"I get along."

"Not with me, you don't." Her face was tight. I had struck very deep, it seemed.

"Where is everyone else?" I asked, gesturing around the empty room.

"Out with the Admiral somewhere. And you can take yourself off again too. You're not wanted in here."

"I'm not going. I live here, remember?"

"You went quick enough last night," she sneered. "When the Admiral says jump, you jump. But fast, little man. And that I like to see."

"The Admiral," I pointed out, "is the hand that feeds. I don't bite it."

"Bootlicking little creep."

I grinned at her nastily and sat down in an armchair. I still didn't feel too good. Pea green and clammy, to be exact. Nothing to be done though, but wait for it to clear off.

Doria tapped ash off her cigarette and looked at me down her nose, thinking up her next attack. Before she could launch it, however, the door opened and her husband came in.

"Doria," he said happily, not immediately seeing me in the armchair, "where have you hidden my cigarette case? I shall punish you for it."

She made a quick movement toward me with her hand and Howard saw me and stopped dead.

"What are you doing here?" he said brusquely, the fun-and-games dying abruptly out of his face and voice.

"Passing the time."

"Clear out, then. I want to talk to my wife."

I shook my head and stayed put.

"Short of picking him up and throwing him out bodily," said Doria, "you won't get rid of him. I've tried."

Kraye shrugged. "Roland puts up with him. I suppose we can too." He picked up one of the newspapers and sat down in an armchair facing me. Doria wandered back to the window seat, pouting. Kraye straightened up the paper and began to read the front page. Across the back page, the racing page, facing me across the fireplace, the black, bold headlines jumped out.

"ANOTHER HALLEY?"

Underneath, side by side, were two photographs: one of me, and the other of a boy who had won a big race the day before.

It was by then essential that Kraye should not discover how Charles had misrepresented me; it had gone much too far to be explained away as a joke. The photograph was clearly printed for once. I knew it well. It was an old one which the papers had used several times before, chiefly because it was a good likeness. Even if none of the guests read the racing column, as Doria obviously hadn't, it might catch their eye in passing, through being in such a conspicuous place.

Kraye finished reading the front page and began to turn the paper over.

"Mr. Kraye," I said. "Do you have a very big quartz collection yourself?"

He lowered the paper a little and gave me an unenthusiastic glance.

"Yes, I have," he said briefly.

"Then could you please tell me what would be a good thing to give the Admiral to add to his collection? And where would I get it, and how much would it cost?"

The paper folded over, hiding my picture. He cleared his throat and with strained politeness started to tell me about some obscure form of crystal which the Admiral didn't have. Press the right button, I thought . . . Doria spoiled it. She walked jerkily over to Kraye and said crossly, "Howard, for God's sake. The little creep is buttering you up. I bet he wants something. You're a sucker for anyone who will talk about rocks."

"People don't make a fool of me," said Kraye flatly, his eyes narrowing in irritation.

"No. I only want to please the Admiral," I explained.

"He's a sly little beast," said Doria. "I don't like him."

Kraye shrugged, looked down at the newspaper and began to unfold it again.

"It's mutual," I said casually. "You daddy's doll."

Kraye stood up slowly and the paper slid to the floor, front page up.

"What did you say?"

"I said I didn't think much of your wife."

He was outraged, as well he might be. He took a single step across the rug, and there was suddenly something more in the room than three guests sparring round a Sunday-morning fire.

Even though I was as far as he knew an insignificant fly to swat, a clear quality of menace flowed out of him like a radio signal. The calm social mask had disappeared along with the wordy, phony, surface personality. The vague suspicion I had gained from reading his papers, together with the antipathy I had felt for him all along, clarified into belated recognition: this was not just a smooth speculator operating near the legal border line, but a full-blown, powerful, dangerous big-time crook.

Trust me, I thought, to prod an anthill and find a hornets' nest. Twist the tail of a grass snake and find a boa constrictor. What on earth would he be like, I wondered, if one did more to cross him than disparage his choice of wife?

"He's sweating," said Doria, pleased. "He's afraid of you."

"Get up," he said.

As I was sure that if I stood up he would simply knock me down again, I stayed where I was.

"I'll apologize," I said.

"Oh, no," said Doria, "that's much too easy."

"Something subtle," suggested Kraye, staring down.

"I know!" Doria was delighted with her idea. "Let's get that hand out of his pocket."

They both saw from my face that I would hate that more than anything. They both smiled. I thought of bolting, but it meant leaving the paper behind.

"That will do very nicely," said Kraye. He leaned down, twined one hand into the front of my jersey shirt and the other into my hair, and pulled me to my feet. The top of my head reached about to his chin. I wasn't in much physical shape for resisting, but I took a half-hearted swipe at him as I came up. Doria caught my swinging arm and twisted it up behind my back, using both of hers and an uncomfortable amount of pressure. She was a strong, healthy girl with no inhibitions about hurting people.

"That'll teach you to be rude to me," she said with satisfaction.

I thought of kicking her shins, but it would only have brought more retaliation. I also wished Charles would come back at once from wherever he was.

He didn't.

Kraye transferred his grip from my hair to my left forearm and began to pull. That arm was no longer much good, but I did my best. I tucked my elbow tight against my side, and my hand stayed in my pocket.

"Hold him harder," he said to Doria. "He's stronger than he looks." She levered my arm up another inch and I started to roll round to get out of it. But Kraye still had his grasp on the front of my jersey, with his forearm leaning across under my throat, and between the two of them I was properly stuck. All the same, I found I couldn't just stand still and let them do what I so much didn't want them to.

"He squirms, doesn't he?" said Doria cheerfully.

I squirmed and struggled a good deal more—until they began getting savage with frustration, and I was panting. It was my wretched stomach which finished it. I began to feel too ill to go on. With a terrific jerk Kraye dragged my hand out.

"Now," he said triumphantly.

He gripped my elbow fiercely and pulled the jersey sleeve up from my wrist. Doria let go of my right arm and came to look at their prize. I was shaking with rage, pain, humiliation . . . heaven knows what.

"Oh," said Doria blankly. "Oh."

She was no longer smiling, nor was her husband. They looked steadily at the wasted, flabby, twisted hand, and at the scars on my forearm, wrist and palm, not only the terrible jagged marks of the original injury but the several tidier ones of the operations I had had since. It was a mess, a right and proper mess.

"So that's why the Admiral lets him stay, the nasty little beast," said Doria, screwing up her face in distaste.

"It doesn't excuse his behavior," said Kraye. "I'll make sure he keeps that tongue of his still, in future."

He stiffened his free hand and chopped the edge of it down across the worst part, the inside of my wrist. I jerked in his grasp.

"Ah . . . ," I said. "Don't."

"He'll tell tales to the Admiral," said Doria warningly, "if you hurt him too much. It's a pity, but I should think that's about enough."

"I don't agree, but—"

There was a scrunch on the gravel outside, and Charles's car swept past the window, coming back.

Kraye let go of my elbow with a shake. I went weakly down on my knees on the rug, and it wasn't all pretense.

"If you tell the Admiral about this, I'll deny it," said Kraye, "and we know who he'll believe."

I did know who he'd believe, but I didn't say so. The newspaper which had caused the rumpus lay close beside me on the rug. The car doors slammed distantly. The Krayes turned away from me toward the window, listening. I picked up the paper, got to my feet, and set off for the door. They didn't try to stop me in any way. They didn't mention the newspaper either. I opened the door, went through, shut it, and steered a slightly crooked course across the hall to the wardroom. Upstairs was too far. I shut the wardroom door behind me, hid the newspaper, slid into Charles's favorite armchair, and waited for my various miseries, mental and physical, to subside.

Some time later Charles came in to fetch some fresh packages of cigarettes.

"Hullo," he said over his shoulder, opening the cupboard. "I thought you were still in bed. Mrs. Cross said you weren't very well this morning. It isn't at all warm in here. Why don't you come into the drawing room?"

"The Krayes . . ." I stopped.

"They won't bite you." He turned round, cigarette in hand. He looked at my face. "What's so funny?" and then more sharply, looking closer. "What's the matter?"

"Oh, nothing. Have you seen today's Sunday *Hemisphere?*"

"No, not yet. Do you want it? I thought it was in the drawing room with the other papers."

"No, it's in the top drawer of your desk. Take a look."

Puzzled, he opened the drawer, took out the paper, and unfolded it. He went to the racing section unerringly.

"My God!" he said, aghast. "Today of all days." His eyes skimmed down the page and he smiled. "You've read this, of course?"

I shook my head. "I just took it to hide it."

He handed me the paper. "Read it then. It'll be good for your ego. They won't let you die! 'Young Finch,' " he quoted, " 'showed much of the judgment and miraculous precision of the great Sid.' How about that? And that's just the start."

"Yeah, how about it?" I grinned. "Count me out for lunch, if you don't mind, Charles. You don't need me there any more."

"All right, if you don't feel like it. They'll be gone by six at the latest, you'll be glad to hear." He smiled and went back to his guests.

I read the newspaper before putting it away again. As Charles had said, it was good for the ego. I thought the columnist, whom I'd known for years, had somewhat exaggerated my erstwhile powers. A case of the myth growing bigger than the reality. But still, it was nice. Particularly in view of the galling, ignominious end to the roughhouse in which the great Sid had so recently landed himself.

On the following morning Charles and I changed back the labels on the chunks of quartz and packed them up ready to return to the Carver Foundation. When we had finished we had one label left over.

"Are you sure we haven't put one stone in the box without changing the label?" said Charles.

"Positive."

"I suppose we'd better check. I'm afraid that's what we've done."

We took all the chunks out of the big box again. The gem collection, which Charles under protest had taken to bed with him each night, was complete; but we looked through them again too to make sure the missing rock had not got among them by mistake. It was nowhere to be found.

"St. Luke's stone," I read from the label. "I remember where that was, up on the top shelf on the right-hand side."

"Yes," agreed Charles, "a dull-looking lump about the size of a fist. I do hope we haven't lost it."

"We have lost it," I remarked. "Kraye's pinched it."

"Oh no," Charles exclaimed. "You can't be right."

"Go and ring up the Foundation, and ask them what the stone is worth."

He shook his head doubtfully, but went to the telephone and came back frowning.

"They say it hasn't any intrinsic value, but it's an extremely rare form of meteorite. It never turns up in mines or quarrying of course. You have to wait for it to fall from the heavens, and then find it. Very tricky."

"A quartz which friend Kraye didn't have."

"But he surely must know I'd suspect him?" Charles protested.

"You'd never have missed it, if it had really been part of your cousin's passed-on collection. There wasn't any gap on the shelf just now. He'd moved the others along. He couldn't know you would check carefully almost as soon as he had gone."

Charles sighed. "There isn't a chance of getting it back."

"No," I agreed.

"Well, it's a good thing you insisted on the insurance," he said. "Carver's valued that boring-looking lump more than all the rest put together. Only one other meteorite like it has ever been found: the St. Mark's stone." He smiled suddenly. "We seem to have mislaid the equivalent of the penny black."

5

TWO DAYS later I went back through the porticoed, columned doorway of Hunt Radnor Associates a lot more alive than when I last came out.

I got a big hullo from the girl on the switchboard, went up the curving staircase very nearly whistling, and was greeted by a barrage of ribald remarks from the Racing Section. What most surprised me was the feeling I had of coming home: I had never thought of myself as really belonging to the agency before, even though down at Aynsford I had realized that I very much didn't want to leave it. A bit late, that discovery. The skids were probably under me already.

Chico grinned widely. "So you made it."

"Well . . . yes."

"I mean, back here to the grindstone."

"Yeah."

"But," he cast a rolling eye at the clock, "late as usual."

"Go stuff yourself," I said.

Chico threw out an arm to the smiling department. "Our Sid is back, his normal charming bloody self. Work in the agency can now begin."

"I see I still haven't got a desk," I observed, looking round. No desk. No roots. No real job. As ever.

"Sit on Dolly's, she's kept it dusted for you."

Dolly looked at Chico, smiling, the mother-hunger showing too vividly in her great blue eyes. She might be the second-best head of department the agency possessed, with a cross-referencing filing-index mind like a computer, she might be a powerful, large, self-assured woman of forty-odd with a couple of marriages behind her and an ever hopeful old bachelor at her heels, but she still counted her life a wasteland because her body couldn't produce children. Dolly was a terrific worker, overflowing with intensely female vitality, excellent drinking company, and very, very sad.

Chico didn't want to be mothered. He was prickly about mothers. All of them in general, not just those who abandoned their tots in push-chairs at police stations near Barnes Bridge. He jollied Dolly along and deftly avoided her tentative maternal invitations.

I hitched a hip onto a long-accustomed spot on the edge of Dolly's desk, and swung my leg.

"Well, Dolly, my love, how's the sleuthing trade?" I said.

"What we need," she said with mock tartness, "is a bit more work from you and a lot less lip."

"Give me a job, then."

"Ah, now." She pondered. "You could . . . ," she began, then stopped. "Well, no . . . perhaps not. And it had better be Chico who goes to Lambourn; some trainer there wants a doubtful lad checked on. . . . "

"So there's nothing for me?"

"Er . . . well . . . ," said Dolly. "No." She had said no a hundred times before. She had never once said yes.

I made a face at her, picked up her telephone, pressed the right button, and got through to Radnor's secretary.

"Joanie? This is Sid Halley. Yes . . . back from Beyond, that's right. Is the old man busy? I'd like a word with him."

"Big deal," said Chico.

Joanie's prim voice said, "He's got a client with him just now. When she's gone I'll ask him, and ring you back."

"O.K." I put down the receiver.

Dolly raised her eyebrows. As head of the department she was my immediate boss, and in asking direct for a session with Radnor I was blowing agency protocol a raspberry. But I was certain that her constant refusal to give me anything useful to do was a direct order from Radnor. If I wanted the drain unblocked I would have to go and pull out the plug. Or go on my knees to stay at all.

"Dolly, love, I'm tired of kicking my heels. Even against your well-worn desk, though the view from here is ravishing." She was wearing, as she often did, a crossover cream silk shirt; it crossed over at a point which on a young girl would have caused a riot. On Dolly it still looked pretty potent, owing to the generosity of nature and the disposal of her arrangements.

"Are you chucking it in?" said Chico, coming to the point.

"It depends on the old man," I said. "He may be chucking me out."

There was a brief, thoughtful silence in the department. They all knew very well how little I did. How little I had been content to do. Dolly looked blank, which wasn't helpful.

Jones-boy clattered in with a tray of impeccable unchipped tea mugs. He was sixteen; noisy, rude, anarchistic, callous, and probably the most efficient office boy in London. His hair grew robustly heavy down to his shoulders, wavy and fanatically clean, dipping slightly in an expensive styling at the back. From behind he looked like a girl, which never disconcerted him. From in front his bony, acned face proclaimed him unprepossessing male. He spent half his pay packet and his Sundays in Carnaby

Street and the other half on week nights chasing girls. According to him, he caught them. No girls had so far appeared in the office to corroborate his story.

Under the pink shirt beat a stony heart; inside the sprouting head hung a big "So what?" Yet it was because this amusing, ambitious, unsocial creature invariably arrived well before his due hour to get his office arrangements ready for the day that he had found me before I died. There was a moral there, somewhere.

He gave me a look. "The corpse has returned, I see."

"Thanks to you," I said idly, but he knew I meant it. He didn't care, though.

He said, "Your blood and stuff ran through a crack in the linoleum and soaked the wood underneath. The old man was wondering if it would start dry rot or something."

"Jones-boy," protested Dolly, looking sick. "Get the hell out of here, and shut up."

The telephone rang on her desk. She picked it up and listened, said "All right," and disconnected.

"The old man wants to see you. Right away."

"Thanks." I stood up.

"The flipping boot?" asked Jones-boy interestedly.

"Keep your snotty nose out," said Chico.

"And balls to you. . . ."

I went out smiling, hearing Dolly start to deal once again with the running dogfight Chico and Jones-boy never tired of. Downstairs, across the hall, into Joanie's little office and through into Radnor's.

He was standing by the window, watching the traffic doing its nut in Cromwell Road. This room, where the clients poured out their troubles, was restfully painted a quiet gray, carpeted and curtained in crimson and furnished with comfortable armchairs, handy little tables with ash trays, pictures on the walls, ornaments, and vases of flowers. Apart from Radnor's small desk in the corner, it looked like an ordinary sitting room, and indeed everyone believed that he had bought the room intact with the lease, so much was it what one would expect to find in a graceful, six-storied, late Victorian town house. Radnor had a theory that people exaggerated and distorted facts less in such peaceful surroundings than in the formality of a more orthodox office.

"Come in, Sid," he said. He didn't move from the window, so I joined him there. He shook hands.

"Are you sure you're fit enough to be here? You haven't been as long as I expected. Even knowing you . . ." He smiled slightly, with watching eyes.

I said I was all right. He remarked on the weather, the rush hour and the political situation, and finally worked round to the point we both knew was at issue.

"So, Sid, I suppose you'll be looking around a bit now?"

Laid on the line, I thought.

"If I wanted to stay here . . ."

"If? Hm, I don't know." He shook his head very slightly.

"Not on the same terms, I agree."

"I'm sorry it hasn't worked out." He sounded genuinely regretful, but he wasn't making it easy.

I said with careful calm, "You've paid me for nothing for two years. Well, give me a chance now to earn what I've had. I don't really want to leave."

He lifted his head slightly like a pointer to a scent, but he said nothing. I ploughed on.

"I'll work for you for nothing, to make up for it. But only if it's real, decent work. No more sitting around. It would drive me mad."

He gave me a hard stare and let out a long breath like a sigh.

"Good God. At last," he said. "And it took a bullet to do it."

"What do you mean?"

"Sid, have you ever seen a zombie wake up?"

"No," I said ruefully, understanding him. "It hasn't been as bad as that?"

He shrugged one shoulder. "I saw you racing, don't forget. You notice when a fire goes out. We've had the pleasant, flippant ashes drifting round this office, that's all." He smiled deprecatingly at his flight of fancy: he enjoyed making pictures of words. It wasted a lot of office time, on the whole.

"Consider me alight again, then." I grinned. "And I've brought a puzzle back with me. I want very much to sort it out."

"A long story?"

"Fairly, yes."

"We'd better sit down, then."

He waved me to an armchair, sank into one himself, and prepared to listen with the stillness and concentration which sent him time and time again to the core of a problem.

I told him about Kraye's dealing in racecourses. Both what I knew and what I guessed. When at length I finished he said calmly, "Where did you get hold of this?"

"My father-in-law, Charles Roland, tossed it at me while I was staying with him last weekend. He had Kraye as a house guest." The subtle old fox, I thought, throwing me in at the deep end: making me wake up and swim.

"And Roland got it from where?"

"The clerk of the course at Seabury told him that the directors were worried about too much share movement, that it was Kraye who got control of Dunstable, and they were afraid he was at it again."

"But the rest, what you've just told me, is your own supposition?"

"Yes."

"Based on your appraisal of Kraye over one weekend?"

"Partly on what he showed me of his character, yes. Partly on what I read of his papers. . . ." With some hesitation I told him about my snooping and the photography. ". . . The rest, I suppose, a hunch."

"Hmm. It needs checking. . . . Have you brought the films with you?"

I nodded, took them out of my pocket, and put them on the little table beside me.

"I'll get them developed." He drummed his fingers lightly on the arm of the chair, thinking. Then, as if having made a decision, said more briskly, "Well, the first thing we need is a client."

"A client?" I echoed absent-mindedly.

"Of course. What else? We are not the police. We work strictly for profit. Ratepayers don't pay the overheads and salaries in this agency. The clients do."

"Oh . . . , yes, of course."

"The most likely client in this case is either Seabury Racecourse executive, or perhaps the National Hunt Committee. I think I should sound out the Senior Steward first, in either case. No harm in starting at the top."

"He might prefer to try the police," I said, "free."

"My dear Sid, one thing people want when they employ private investigators is privacy. They pay for privacy. When the police investigate something, everyone knows about it. When we do, they don't. That's why we sometimes get criminal cases when it would undoubtedly be cheaper to go to the police."

"I see. So you'll try the Senior Steward—"

"No," he interrupted. "You will."

"I?"

"Naturally. It's your case."

"But it's your agency—he is used to negotiating with you."

"You know him too," he pointed out.

"I used to ride for him, and that puts me on a bad footing for this sort of thing. I'm a jockey to him, an ex-jockey. He won't take me seriously."

Radnor shrugged a shoulder. "If you want to take on Kraye, you need a client. Go and get one."

I knew very well that he never sent even senior operatives, let alone inexperienced ones, to arrange or angle for an assignment, so that for several moments I couldn't really believe that he intended me to go. But he said nothing else, and eventually I stood up and went toward the door.

"Sandown races are on today," I said tentatively. "He's sure to be there."

"A good opportunity." He looked straight ahead, not at me.

"I'll try it, then."

"Right."

He wasn't letting me off. But then he hadn't kicked me out either. I went through the door and shut it behind me, and while I was still hesitating in disbelief I heard him inside the room give a sudden guffaw, a short, sharp, loud, triumphant snort of laughter.

I walked back to my flat, collected the car, and drove down to Sandown. It was a pleasant day, dry, sunny, and warm for November, just right for drawing a good crowd for steeplechasing.

I turned in through the racecourse gates, spirits lifting, parked the car (a Mercedes 230 SL with automatic gears, power-assisted steering, and a strip on the back saying NO HAND SIGNALS), and walked round to join the crowd outside the weighing-room door. I could no longer go through it. It had been one of the hardest things to get used to, the fact that all the changing rooms and weighing rooms which had been my second homes for fourteen years were completely barred to me from the day I rode my last race. You didn't lose just a job when you handed in your jockey's license, you lost a way of life.

There were a lot of people to talk to at Sandown, and as I hadn't been racing for six weeks I had a good deal of gossip to catch up on. No one seemed to know about the shooting, which was fine by me, and I didn't tell them. I immersed myself very happily in the racecourse atmosphere and for an hour Kraye retreated slightly into the background.

Not that I didn't keep an eye on my purpose, but until the third race the Senior Steward, Viscount Hagbourne, was never out of a conversation long enough for me to catch him.

Although I had ridden for him for years and had found him undemanding and fair, he was in most respects still a stranger. An aloof, distant man, he seemed to find it difficult to make ordinary human contacts, and unfortunately he had not proved a great success as Senior Steward. He gave the impression, not of power in himself, but of looking over his shoulder at power behind: I'd have said he was afraid of incurring the disapproval of the little knot of rigidly determined men who in fact ruled racing themselves, regardless of who might be in office at the time. Lord Hagbourne postponed making decisions until it was almost too late to make them, and there was still a danger after that that he would change his mind. But all the same he was the front man until his year of office ended, and with him I had to deal.

At length I fielded him neatly as he turned away from the clerk of the course and forestalled a trainer who was advancing upon him with a grievance. Lord Hagbourne, with one of his rare moments of humor, deliberately turned his back on the grievance and consequently greeted me with more warmth than usual.

"Sid, nice to see you. Where have you been lately?"

"Holidays," I explained succinctly. "Look sir, can I have a talk with you after the races? There's something I want to discuss urgently."

"No time like the present," he said, one eye on the grievance. "Fire away."

"No, sir. It needs time and all your attention."

"Hm?"

The grievance was turning away. "Not today, Sid, I have to get home. What is it? Tell me now."

"I want to talk to you about the take-over bid for Seabury racecourse."

He looked at me, startled. "You want . . . ?"

"That's right. It can't be said out here where you will be needed at any moment by someone else. If you could just manage twenty minutes at the end of the afternoon . . . ?"

"Er . . . what is your connection with Seabury?"

"None in particular, sir. I don't know if you remember, but I've been connected" (a precise way of putting it) "with Hunt Radnor Associates for the last two years. Various . . . er . . . facts about Seabury have come our way and Mr. Radnor thought you might be interested. I am here as his representative."

"Oh, I see. Very well, Sid, come up to the Stewards' tearoom after the last. If I'm not there, wait for me. Right?"

"Yes. Thank you."

I walked down the slope and then up the iron staircase to the jockeys' box in the stand, smiling at myself. Representative. A nice big important word. It covered anything from an ambassador down. Commercial travelers had rechristened themselves with its rolling syllables years ago; they had done it because of jokes, of course. It didn't sound the same, somehow, starting off with "Did you hear the one about the representative who stopped at a lonely farmhouse? . . ." Rodent officers, garbage disposal and sanitary staff; pretty new names for rat catchers, dustmen, and road sweepers. So why not for me?

"Only idiots laugh at nothing," said a voice in my ear. "What the hell are you looking so pleased about all of a sudden? And where the blazes have you been this last month?"

"Don't tell me you've missed me?" I grinned, not needing to look round. We went together through the door of the high-up jockeys' box, two of a kind, and stood looking out over the splendid racecourse.

"Best view in Europe." He sighed. Mark Witney, thirty-eight years old, racehorse trainer. He had a face battered like a boxer's from too many racing falls, and in the two years since he hung up his boots and stopped wasting he had put on all of forty pounds. A fat, ugly man. We had a host of memories in common, a host of hard-ridden races. I like him a lot.

"How's things?" I said.

"Oh, fair, fair. They'll be a damn sight better if that animal of mine wins the fifth."

"He must have a good chance."

"He's a damn certainty, boy. A certainty. If he doesn't fall over his goddamned legs. Clumsiest sod this side of Hades." He lifted his race glasses and looked at the number board. "I see poor old Charlie can't do the weight again on that thing of Bob's. . . . That boy of Plumtree's is getting a lot of riding just now. What do you think of him?"

"He takes too many risks," I said. "He'll break his neck."

"Look who's talking. No, seriously, I'm considering taking him on. What do you think?" He lowered his glasses. "I need someone available regularly from now on and all the ones I'd choose are already tied up."

"Well, you could do better, you could do worse, I suppose. He's a bit flashy for me, but he can ride, obviously. Will he do as he's told?"

He made a face. "You've hit the bull's-eye. That's the snag. He always knows best."

"Pity."

"Can you think of anyone else?"

"Um . . . what about that boy Cotton? He's too young really. But he's got the makings. . . ." We drifted out in amiable chat, discussing his problem, while the box filled up around us and the horses went down to the start.

It was a three-mile chase, and one of my ex-mounts was favorite. I watched the man who had my old job ride a very pretty race, and with half my mind thought about housing estates. Sandown itself had survived, some years ago, a bid to cover its green tempting acres with little boxes. Sandown had powerful friends. But Hurst Park, Manchester and Binningham racecourses had all gone under the rolling tide of bricks and mortar, lost to the double-barreled persuasive arguments that shareholders liked capital gains and people needed houses. To defend itself from such a fate Cheltenham Racecourse had transformed itself from a private, dividend-paying company into a non-profit-making holdings trust, and other racecourses had followed their lead.

But not Seabury. And Seabury was deep in a nasty situation. Not Dunstable, and Dunstable Racecourse was now a tidy dormitory for the Vauxhall workers of Luton.

Most British racecourses were, or had been, private companies, in which it was virtually impossible for an outsider to acquire shares against the will of the members. But four—Dunstable, Seabury, Sandown and Chepstow—were public companies, and their shares could be bought in open market, through the stock exchange.

Sandown had been played for in a straightforward and perfectly honorable way, and plans to turn it into suburban housing had been turned down by the local and county councils. Sandown flourished, made a good profit, paid a 10 per cent dividend, and was probably now impregnable. Chepstow was surrounded by so much other open land that it was in little danger from developers. But little Dunstable had been an oasis inside a growing industrial area.

Seabury was on the flat part of the south coast, flanked on every side by miles of warm little bungalows representing the dreams and savings of people in retirement. At twelve bungalows to the acre—elderly people liked tiny gardens—there must be room on the spacious racecourse for over three thousand more. Add six or seven hundred pounds to the building price of each bungalow for the plot it stood on, and you scooped something in the region of two million.

The favorite won and was duly cheered, I clattered down the iron staircase with Mark, and we went and had a drink together.

"Are you sending anything to Seabury next week?" I asked. Seabury was one of his nearest meetings.

"Perhaps. I don't know. It depends if they can hold it at all, of course. But I've got mine entered at Lingfield as well, and I think I'll send them there instead. It's a much more prosperous-looking place, and the owners like it better. Good lunch and all that. Seabury's so dingy these days. I had a hard job getting old Carmichael to agree to me running his horse there at the last meeting—and look what happened. The meeting was off and we'd missed the other engagement at Worcester too. It wasn't my fault, but I'd persuaded him that he stood more chance at Seabury, and he blamed me because in the end the horse stayed at home eating his head off for nothing. He says there's a jinx on Seabury, and I've a couple more owners who don't like me entering their horses there. I've told them that it's a super track from the horses' point of view, but it doesn't make much difference, they don't know it like we do."

We finished our drinks and walked back toward the weighing room. His horse scrambled home in the fifth by a whisker and I saw him afterward in the unsaddling enclosure beaming like a Halloween pumpkin.

After the last race I went to the Stewards' tearoom. There were several Stewards with their wives and friends having tea, but no Lord Hagbourne. The Stewards pulled out a chair, gave me a welcome, and talked, as ever, about the racing. Most of them had ridden as amateurs in their day, one against me in the not too distant past, and I knew them all well.

"Sid, what do you think of the new-type hurdles?"

"Oh, much better. Far easier for a young horse to see."

"Do you know of a good young chaser I could buy?"

"Didn't you think Hayward rode a splendid race?"

"I watched the third down at the Pond, and believe me that chestnut took off outside the wings. . . ."

". . . do you think we ought to have had him in, George?"

". . . heard that Green bust his ribs again yesterday . . ."

"Don't like that breed, never did, not genuine. . ."

"Miffy can't seem to go wrong, he'd win with a cart horse. . . ."

"Can you come and give a talk to our local pony club, Sid? I'll write you the details. What date would suit you?"

Gradually they finished their tea, said good-bye, and left for home. I waited. Eventually he came, hurrying, apologizing, explaining what had kept him.

"Now," he said, biting into a sandwich. "What's it all about, eh?"

"Seabury."

"Ah yes, Seabury. Very worrying. Very worrying indeed."

"A Mr. Howard Kraye has acquired a large number of shares—"

"Now hold on a minute, Sid. That's only a guess, because of Dunstable. We've been trying to trace the buyer of Seabury shares through the stock exchange, and we can find no definite lead to Kraye."

"Hunt Radnor Associates do have that lead."

He stared. "Proof?"

"Yes."

"What sort?"

"Photographs of share transfer certificates." And heaven help me, I thought, if I've messed them up.

"Oh," he said somberly. "While we weren't sure, there was some hope we were wrong. Where did you get these photographs?"

"I'm not at liberty to say, sir. But Hunt Radnor Associates would be prepared to make an attempt to forestall the takeover of Seabury."

"For a fat fee, I suppose," he said dubiously.

"I'm afraid so, sir, yes."

"I don't connect you with this sort of thing, Sid." He moved restlessly and looked at his watch.

"If you would forget about me being a jockey, and think of me as having come from Mr. Radnor, it would make things a lot easier. How much is Seabury worth to National Hunt racing?"

He looked at me in surprise, but he answered the question, though not in the way I meant.

"Er . . . well, you know it's an excellent course, good for horses and so on."

"It didn't show a profit this year, though."

"There was a great deal of bad luck."

"Yes. Too much to be true, don't you think?"

"What do you mean?"

"Has it ever occurred to the National Hunt Committee that bad luck can be . . . well, arranged?"

"You aren't seriously suggesting that Kraye . . . I mean that anyone would damage Seabury on purpose? In order to make it show a loss?"

"I am suggesting that it is a possibility. Yes."

"Good God." He sat down rather abruptly.

"Malicious damage," I said. "Sabotage, if you like. There's a great deal of industrial precedent. Hunt Radnor Associates investigated a case of it only last year in a small provincial brewery where the fermentation process kept going wrong. A prosecution resulted, and the brewery was able to remain in business."

He shook his head. "It is quite ridiculous to think that Kraye would be implicated in anything like that. He belongs to one of my clubs. He's a wealthy, respected man."

"I know, I've met him," I said.

"Well then, you must be aware of what sort of person he is."

"Yes." Only too well.

"You can't seriously suggest—" he began.

"There would be no harm in finding out," I interrupted. "You'll have studied the figures. Seabury's quite a prize."

"How do you see the figures, then?" It seemed he genuinely wanted to know, so I told him.

"Seabury Racecourse has an issued share capital of eighty thousand pounds in fully paid-up one-pound shares. The land was bought when that part of the coast was more or less uninhabited, so that this sum bears absolutely no relation to the present value of the place. Any company in that position is just asking for a takeover.

"A buyer would in theory need fifty-one per cent of the shares to be certain of gaining control, but in practice, as was found at Dunstable, forty would be plenty. It could probably be swung on a good deal less, but from the point of view of the buyer, the more he got his hands on before declaring his intentions, the bigger would be his profit.

"The main difficulty in taking over a racecourse company—its only natural safeguard, in fact—is that the shares seldom come on the market. I understand that it isn't always by any means possible to buy even a few on the stock exchange, as people who own them tend to be fond of them, and as long as the shares pay any dividend, however small, they won't sell. But it's obvious that not everyone can afford to have bits of capital lying around unproductively, and once the racecourse starts showing a loss, the temptation grows to transfer to something else.

"Today's price of Seabury shares is thirty shillings, which is about four shillings higher than it was two years ago. If Kraye can manage to get hold of a forty per cent holding at an average price of thirty shillings, it will cost him only about forty-eight thousand pounds.

"With a holding that size, aided by other shareholders tempted by a very large capital gain, he can outvote any opposition, and sell the whole company to a land developer. Planning permission would almost certainly be granted, as the land is not beautiful, and is surrounded already by houses. I estimate that a developer would pay roughly a million for it, as he could double that by selling off all those acres in tiny plots. There's the capital gains tax, of course, but Seabury shareholders stand to make eight hundred per cent on their original investment, if the scheme goes through.

Four hundred thousand gross for Mr. Kraye, perhaps. Did you ever find out how much he cleared at Dunstable?''

He didn't answer.

I went on, ''Seabury used to be a busy, lively, successful place, and now it isn't. It's a suspicious coincidence that as soon as a big buyer comes along the place goes downhill fast. They paid a dividend of only sixpence per share last year, a gross yield of under one and three-quarters per cent at today's price, and this year they showed a loss of three thousand, seven hundred and fourteen pounds. Unless something is done soon, there won't be a next year.''

He didn't reply at once. He stared at the floor for a long time with the half-eaten sandwich immobile in his hand.

Finally he said, ''Who did the arithmetic? Radnor?''

''No . . . I did. It's very simple. I went to Company House in the city yesterday and looked up the Seabury balance sheets for the last few years, and I rang for a quotation of today's share price from a stockbroker this morning. You can easily check it.''

''Oh, I don't doubt you. I remember now, there was a rumor that you made a fortune on the stock exchange by the time you were twenty.''

''People exaggerate so.'' I smiled. ''My old governor, where I was apprenticed, started me off investing, and I was a bit lucky.''

''Hm.''

There was another pause while he hesitated over his decision. I didn't interrupt him, but I was much relieved when finally he said, ''You have Radnor's authority for seeing me, and he knows what you have told me?''

''Yes.''

''Very well.'' He got up stiffly and put down the unfinished sandwich. ''You can tell Radnor that I agree to an investigation being made, and I think I can vouch for my colleagues agreeing. You'll want to start at once, I suppose.''

I nodded.

''The usual terms?''

''I don't know,'' I said. ''Perhaps you would get onto Mr. Radnor about that.''

As I didn't know what the usual terms were, I didn't want to discuss them.

''Yes, all right. And Sid . . . it's understood that there is to be no leak about this? We can't afford to have Kraye slapping a libel or slander action on us.''

''The agency is always discreet,'' I said, with an outward and an inward smile. Radnor was right. People paid for privacy. And why not?

6

THE RACING section was quiet when I went in next morning, mostly because Chico was out on an escort job. All the other heads, including Dolly's, were bent studiously over their desks.

She looked up and said with a sigh, "You're late again." It was ten to ten. "The old man wants to see you."

I made a face at her and retraced my way down the staircase. Joanie looked pointedly at her watch.

"He's been asking for you for half an hour."

I knocked and went in. Radnor was sitting behind his desk, reading some papers, pencil in hand. He looked at me and frowned.

"Why are you so late?"

"I had a pain in me tum," I said flippantly.

"Don't be funny," he said sharply, and then, more reasonably, "Oh . . . I suppose you're not being funny."

"No. But I'm sorry about being late." I wasn't a bit sorry, however, that it had been noticed; before, no one would have said a thing if I hadn't turned up all day.

"How did you get on with Lord Hagbourne?" Radnor asked. "Was he interested?"

"Yes. He agreed to an investigation. I said he should discuss terms with you."

"I see." He flicked a switch on the small box on his desk. "Joanie, see if you can get hold of Lord Hagbourne. Try the London flat number first."

"Yes, sir," her voice came tinnily out of the speaker.

"Here," said Radnor, picking up a shallow brown cardboard box. "Look at these."

The box contained a thick wad of large glossy photographs. I looked at them one by one and heaved a sigh of relief. They had all come out sharp and clear, except some of the ones I had duplicated at varying exposures.

The telephone on Radnor's desk rang once, quietly. He lifted the receiver.

"Oh, good morning, Lord Hagbourne. Radnor here. Yes, that's right. . . ." He gestured to me to sit down, and I stayed there listening while he negotiated terms in a smooth, civilized, deceptively casual voice.

"And of course in a case like this, Lord Hagbourne, there's one other thing: we make a small surcharge if our operatives have to take out-of-the-ordinary risks. . . . Yes, as in the Canlas case, exactly. Right then, you shall have a preliminary report from us in a few days. Yes . . . good-bye."

He put down the receiver, bit his thumbnail thoughtfully for a few seconds, and said finally, "Right, then, Sid. Get on with it."

"But—" I began.

"But nothing," he said. "It's your case. Get on with it."

I stood up, holding the packet of photographs. "Can I . . . can I use Bona Fides and so on?"

He waved his hand permissively. "Sid, use every resource in the agency you need. Keep an eye on expenses though, we don't want to price ourselves out of business. And if you want legwork done, arrange it through Dolly or the other department heads. Right?"

"Won't they think it odd? I mean . . . I don't amount to much round here."

"And whose fault is that? If they won't do what you ask, refer them to me." He looked at me expressionlessly.

"All right." I walked to the door. "Er . . . who . . . " I said, turning the knob, "gets the danger money? The operative or the agency?"

"You said you would work for nothing," he observed dryly.

I laughed. "Just so. Do I get expenses?"

"That car of yours drinks petrol."

"It does twenty," I protested.

"The agency rate is based on thirty. You can have that. And other expenses, yes. Put in a chit to accounts."

"Thanks."

He smiled suddenly, the rare sweet smile so incongruous to his military bearing, and launched into another elaborate metaphor.

"The tapes are up," he said. "What you do with the race depends on your skill and timing, just as it always used to. I've backed you with the agency's reputation for getting results, and I can't afford to lose my stake. Remember that."

"Yes," I said soberly. "I will."

I thought, as I took my stupidly aching stomach up two stories to Bona Fides, that it was time Radnor had a lift installed; and was glad I wasn't bound for Missing Persons away in the rarefied air of the fifth floor. There was a lot more character, I supposed, in the splendidly proportioned, solidly built town house that Radnor had chosen on a corner site on Cromwell Road, but a flat half acre of modern office block would have been easier on his staff. And about ten times as expensive, no doubt.

The basement, to start at the bottom, was—except for the kitchen—given over entirely to files and records. On the ground floor, besides Radnor himself and Joanie, there were two interview-cum-waiting rooms, and also the Divorce Section. On the first floor, the Racing Section, Accounts, another interview room and the general secretarial department. Up one was Bona Fides, and above that, on the two smaller top floors, Guard and Missing Persons. Missing Persons alone had room to spare. Bona Fides, splitting at the seams, was encroaching on Guard. Guard was sticking in its toes.

Jones-boy, who acted as general messenger, must have had legs like iron from pounding up and down the stairs, though thanks to a tiny service lift used long ago to take nursery food to top-floor children, he could haul his ten trays up from landing to landing instead of carrying them.

In Bona Fides there was the usual chatter of six people talking on the telephone all at once. The department head, receiver glued to one ear and finger stuck in the other, was a large bald-headed man with half-moon spectacles sitting halfway down a prominent nose. As always, he was in his shirt sleeves, teamed with a frayed pullover and baggy gray flannels. No tie. He seemed to have an inexhaustible supply of old clothes but never any new ones, and Jones-boy had a theory that his wife dressed him from jumble sales.

I waited until he had finished a long conversation with a managing director about the character of the proposed production manager of a glass factory. The invaluable thing about Jack Copeland was his quick and comprehensive grasp of what dozens of jobs entailed. He was speaking to the glass manufacturer as if he had grown up in the industry; and in five minutes, I knew, he might be advising just as knowledgeably on the suitability of a town clerk. His summing up of a man went far beyond the basic list of honesty, conscientiousness, normality and prudence, which was all that many employers wanted. He liked to discover his subject's reaction under stress, to find out what he disliked doing, and what he often forgot. The resulting footnotes to his reports were usually the most valuable part of them, and the faith large numbers of industrial firms had in him bore witness to his accuracy.

He wielded enormous power but did not seem conscious of it, which made him much liked. After Radnor, he was the most important person in the agency.

"Jack," I said, as he put down the receiver. "Can you check a man for me, please?"

"What's wrong with the Racing Section, pal?" he said, jerking his thumb toward the floor.

"He isn't a racing person."

"Oh? Who is it?"

"A Howard Kraye. I don't know if he has a profession. He speculates on the stock market. He is a rabid collector of quartz." I added Kraye's London address.

He scribbled it all down fast.

"O.K., Sid. I'll put one of the boys on to it and let you have a prelim. Is it urgent?"

"Fairly."

"Right." He tore the sheet off the pad. "George? You still doing that knitting-wool client's report? When you've finished, here's your next one."

"George," I said. "Be careful."

They both looked at me, suddenly still.

"An unexploded bomb," I observed. "Don't set him off."

George said cheerfully, "Makes a nice change from knitting wool. Don't worry, Sid. I'll walk on eggs."

Jack Copeland peered at me closely through the half specs.

"You've cleared it with the old man, I suppose?"

"Yes." I nodded. "It's a fraud query. He said to check with him if you wanted to."

He smiled briefly. "No need, I guess. Is that all then?"

"For the moment, yes, thanks."

"Just for the record, is this your own show, or Dolly's, or whose?"

"I suppose . . . mine."

"Uh-huh," he said accenting the second syllable. "The winds of change, if I read it right?"

I laughed. "You never know."

Down in the Racing Section I found Dolly supervising the reshuffling of the furniture. I asked what was going on, and she gave me a flashing smile.

"It seems you're in, not out. The old man just rang to say you needed somewhere to work, and I've sent Jones-boy upstairs to pinch a table from Missing Persons. That'll do for now, won't it? There isn't a spare desk in the place."

A series of bangs from outside heralded the return of Jones-boy, complete with a spindly plywood affair in a sickly lemon color. "How that lot ever find a missing person I'll never know. I bet they don't even find their missing junk."

He disappeared and came back shortly with a chair.

"The things I do for you!" he said, setting it down in front of me. "A dim little bird in the typing pool is now squatting on a stool. I chatted her up a bit."

"What this place needs is some more equipment," I murmured.

"Don't be funny," said Dolly. "Every time the old man buys one desk he takes on two assistants. When I first came here fifteen years ago we had a whole room each, believe it or not."

The rearranged office settled down again, with my table wedged into a corner next to Dolly's desk. I sat behind it and spread out the photographs to sort them. The people who developed and printed all the agency's work had come up with their usual excellent job, and it amazed me that they had been able to enlarge the tiny negatives up to nine-by-seven-inch prints and get a clearly readable result.

I picked out all the fuzzy ones, the duplicates at the wrong exposures, tore them up, and put the pieces in Dolly's wastepaper basket. That left me with fifty-one pictures of the contents of Kraye's attaché case. Innocent enough to the casual eye, but they turned out to be dynamite.

The two largest piles, when I had sorted them out, were Seabury share transfer certificates, and letters from Kraye's stockbroker. The paper headed S.R. revealed itself to be a summary in simple form of the share certificates, so I added it to that pile. I was left with the photographs of the bank notes, of share dealings which had nothing to do with Seabury, and the two sheets of figures I had found under the writing board at the bottom of the case.

I read through all the letters from the stockbroker, a man called Ellis Bolt, who belonged to a firm known as Charing, Street and King. Bolt and Kraye were on friendly terms; the letters referred sometimes to social occasions on which they had met; but for the most part the typewritten sheets dealt with the availability and prospects of various shares (including Seabury), purchases made or proposed, and references to tax, stamp duty, and commission.

Two letters had been written in Bolt's own hand. The first, dated ten days ago, said briefly:

> Dear H.
>
> Shall wait with interest for the news on Friday.
>
> E.

The second, which Kraye must have received on the morning he went to Aynsford, read:

> Dear H.
>
> I have put the final draft in the hands of the printers, and the leaflets should be out by the end of next week, or the

Tuesday following at the latest. Two or three days before the next meeting, anyway. That should do it, I think. There would be a lot of unrest should there be another hitch, but surely you will see to that.

E.

"Dolly," I said. "May I borrow your phone?"

"Help yourself."

I rang upstairs to Bona Fides. "Jack? Can I have a rundown on another man as well? Ellis Bolt, stockbroker, works for a firm called Charing, Street and King." I gave him the address. "He's a friend of Kraye's. Same care needed, I'm afraid."

"Right. I'll let you know."

I sat staring down at the two harmless-looking letters.

"Shall wait with interest for the news on Friday." It could mean any news, anything at all. It also could mean the News; and on the radio on Friday I had heard that Seabury Races were off because a lorry carrying chemicals had overturned and burned the turf.

The second letter was just as tricky. It could easily refer to a shareholder's meeting at which a hitch should be avoided at all costs. Or it could refer to a race meeting—at Seabury—where another hitch could affect the sale of shares yet again.

It was like looking at a conjuring trick: from one side you saw a normal object, but from the other, a sham.

If it were a sham, Mr. Ellis Bolt was in a criminal career up to his eyebrows. If it was just my suspicious mind jumping to hasty conclusions I was doing an old-established respectable stockbroker a shocking injustice.

I picked up Dolly's telephone again and got an outside line.

"Charing, Street and King, good morning," said a quiet female voice.

"Oh, good morning. I would like to make an appointment to see Mr. Bolt and discuss some investments. Would that be possible?"

"Certainly, yes. This is Mr. Bolt's secretary speaking. Could I have your name?"

"Halley. John Halley."

"You would be a new client, Mr. Halley?"

"That's right."

"I see. Well, now, Mr. Bolt will be in the office tomorrow afternoon, and I could fit you in at three thirty. Would that suit you?"

"Thank you. That's fine. I'll be there."

I put down the receiver and looked tentatively at Dolly.

"Would it be all right with you if I go out for the rest of the day?"

She smiled. "Sid, dear, you're very sweet, but you don't have to ask my permission. The old man made it very clear that you're on your own now. You're not accountable to me or anyone else in the agency, except the old man himself. I'll grant you I've never known him give anyone quite such a free hand before, but there you are, my love, you can do what you like. I'm your boss no longer."

"You don't mind?" I asked.

"No," she said thoughtfully. "Come to think of it, I don't. I've a notion that what the old man has always wanted of you in this agency is a partner."

"Dolly!" I was astounded. "Don't be ridiculous."

"He's not getting any younger," she pointed out.

I laughed. "So he picked on a broken-down jockey to help him out."

"He picks on someone with enough capital to buy a partnership, someone who's been to the top of one profession and has the time in years to get to the top of another."

"You're raving, Dolly, dear. He nearly chucked me out yesterday morning."

"But you're still here, aren't you? More here than ever before. And Joanie said he was in a fantastically good mood all day yesterday, after you'd been in to see him."

I shook my head, laughing. "You're too romantic. Jockeys don't turn into investigators any more than they turn into . . ."

"Well, what?" she prompted.

"Into auctioneers, then . . . or accountants."

She shook her head. "You've already turned into an investigator, whether you know it or not. I've been watching you these two years, remember? You look as if you're doing nothing, but you've soaked up everything the bloodhounds have taught you like a hungry sponge. I'd say, Sid love, if you don't watch out, you'll be part of the fixtures and fittings for the rest of your life."

But I didn't believe her, and I paid no attention to what she had said.

I grinned. "I'm going down to take a look at Seabury Racecourse this afternoon. Like to come?"

"Are you kidding?" she sighed. Her in-tray was six inches deep. "I could have just done with a ride in that rocket car of yours, and a breath of sea air."

I stacked the photographs together and returned them to the box, along with the negatives. There was a drawer in the table, and I pulled it open to put the photographs away. It wasn't empty. Inside lay a packet of sandwiches, some cigarettes, and a flat half bottle of whisky.

I began to laugh. "Someone," I said, "will shortly come rampaging down from Missing Persons looking for his missing lunch."

Seabury Racecourse lay about half a mile inland, just off a trunk road to the sea. Looking backward from the top of the stands one could see the wide silver sweep of the English Channel. Between and on both sides the crowded rows of little houses seemed to be rushing toward the coast like Gadarene swine. In each little unit a retired schoolmaster or civil servant or clergyman—or their widows—thought about the roots they had pulled up from wherever it had been too cold or too dingy for their old age, and sniffed the warm south salt-laden air.

They had made it. Done what they'd always wanted. Retired to a bungalow by the sea.

I drove straight in through the open racecourse gate and stopped outside the weighing room. Climbing out, I stretched, and walked over to knock on the door of the racecourse manager's office.

There was no reply. I tried the handle. It was locked. So was the weighing-room door, and everything else.

Hands in pockets, I strolled round the end of the stands to look at the course. Seabury was officially classified in Group Three: that is to say, lower than Doncaster and higher than Windsor when it came to receiving aid from the Betting Levy Board.

It had less than Grade Three stands: wooden steps with corrugated tin roofs for the most part, and drafts from all parts of the compass. But the track itself was a joy to ride on, and it had always seemed a pity to me that the rest of the amenities didn't match it.

There was no one about near the stands. Down at one end of the course, however, I could see some men and a tractor, and I set off toward them, walking down inside the rails, on the grass. The going was just about perfect for November racing, soft but springy underfoot, exactly right for tempting trainers to send their horses to the course in droves. In ordinary circumstances, that was. But as things stood at present, more trainers than Mark Witney were sending their horses elsewhere. A course which didn't attract runners didn't attract crowds to watch them. Seabury's gate receipts had been falling off for some time, but its expenses had risen; and therein lay its loss.

Thinking about the sad tale I had read in the balance sheets, I reached the men working on the course. They were digging up a great section of it and loading it onto a trailer behind the tractor. There was a pervasive unpleasant smell in the air.

An irregular patch about thirty yards deep, stretching nearly the whole width of the course, had been burned brown and killed. Less than half of the affected turf had already been removed, showing the grayish chalky mud underneath, and there was still an enormous amount to be shifted. I didn't think there were enough men working on it for there to be a hope of its being returfed and ready to race on in only eight days' time.

"Good afternoon," I said to the men in general. "What a horrible mess."

One of them thrust his spade into the earth and came over, rubbing his hands on the sides of his trousers.

"Anything you want?" he said, with fair politeness.

"The racecourse manager. Captain Oxon."

His manner shifted perceptibly toward the civil. "He's not here today, sir. Hey! Aren't you Sid Halley?"

"That's right."

He grinned, doing another quick change, this time toward brotherhood. "I'm the foreman. Ted Wilkins." I shook his outstretched hand. "Captain Oxon's gone up to London. He said he wouldn't be back until tomorrow."

"Never mind," I said. "I was just down in this part of the world and I thought I'd drop in and have a look at the poor old course."

He turned with me to look at the devastation. "Shame, isn't it?"

"What happened, exactly?"

"The tanker overturned on the road over there." He pointed, and we began to walk toward the spot, edging round the dug-up area. The road, a narrow secondary one, ran across near the end of the racecourse, with a wide semi-circle of track on the far side of it. During the races the hard road surface was covered thickly with tan or peat, or with thick green matting, which the horses galloped over without any trouble. Although not ideal, it was an arrangement to be found on many courses throughout the country, most famously with the Melling Road at Aintree, and reaching a maximum with five road crossings at Ludlow.

"Just here," said Ted Wilkins, pointing. "Worst place it could possibly have happened, right in the middle of the track. The stuff just poured out of the tanker. It turned right over, see, and the hatch thing was torn open in the crash."

"How did it happen?" I asked. "The crash, I mean?"

"No one knows, really."

"But the driver? He wasn't killed, was he?"

"No, he wasn't even hurt much. Just shook up a bit. But he couldn't remember what happened. Some people in a car came driving along after dark and nearly ran into the tanker. They found the driver sitting at the side of the road, holding his head and moaning. Concussion, it was, they say. They reckon he hit his head somehow when lorry went over. Staggers me how he got out of it so lightly, the cab was fair crushed, and there was glass everywhere."

"Do tankers often drive across here? Lucky it's never happened before, if they do."

"They used not to," he said, scratching his head. "But they've been over here quite regularly now for a year or two. The traffic on the London road's getting chronic, see?"

"Oh . . . did it come from a local firm, then?"

"Down the coast a bit. Intersouth Chemicals, that's the firm it belonged to."

"How soon do you think we'll be racing here again?" I asked, turning back to look at the track. "Will you make it by next week?"

He frowned. "Strictly between you and me, I don't think there's a bleeding hope. What we needed, as I said to the Captain, was a couple of bulldozers, not six men with spades."

"I would have thought so too."

He sighed. "He just told me we couldn't afford them and to shut up and get on with it. And that's what we've done. We'll just about have cut out all the dead turf by next Wednesday, at this rate of going on."

"That doesn't leave any time for new turf to settle," I remarked.

"It'll be a miracle if it's laid, let alone settled," he agreed gloomily.

I bent down and ran my hand over a patch of brown grass. It was decomposing and felt slimy. I made a face, and the foreman laughed.

"Horrible, isn't it? It stinks, too."

I put my fingers to my nose and wished I hadn't. "Was it slippery like this right from the beginning?"

"Yes, that's right. Hopeless."

"Well, I won't take up any more of your time," I said, smiling.

"I'll tell Captain Oxon you came. Pity you missed him."

"Don't bother him. He must have a lot to worry about just now."

"One bloody crisis after another." He nodded. "So long, then." He went back to his spade and his heartbreaking task, and I retraced the quarter mile up the straight to the deserted stands.

I hesitated for a while outside the weighing room, wondering whether to pick the lock and go in, and knowing it was mainly nostalgia that urged me to do it, not any conviction that it would be a useful piece of investigation. There would always be the temptation, I supposed, to use dubious professional skills for one's own pleasure. Like doctors sniffing ether. I contended myself with looking through the windows.

The deserted weighing room looked the same as ever: a large bare expanse of wooden board floor, with a table and some upright chairs in one corner, and the weighing machine itself on the left. Racecourse weighing machines were not all of one universal design. There weren't any left of the old type where the jockeys stood on a platform while weights were added to the balancing arm. That whole process was much too slow. Now there were either seats slung from above, in which one felt much like a bag of sugar, or chairs bolted to a base plate on springs: in both these cases the weight was quickly indicated by a pointer which swung round a gigantic clock face. In essence, modern kitchen scales vastly magnified.

The scales at Seabury were the chair-on-base-plate type, which I'd always found simplest to use. I recalled a few of the before-and-after occasions when I had sat on that particular spot. Some good, some bad, as always with racing.

Shrugging, I turned away. I wouldn't, I thought, ever be sitting there again. And no one walked over my grave.

Climbing into the car, I drove to the nearest town, looked up the whereabouts of Intersouth Chemicals, and an hour later was speaking to the personnel manager. I explained that on behalf of the National Hunt Committee I had just called in passing to find out if the driver of the tanker had fully recovered, or had remembered anything else about the accident.

The manager, fat and fiftyish, was affable but unhelpful. "Smith's left," he said briefly. "We gave him a few days off to get over the accident, and then he came back yesterday and said his wife didn't fancy him driving chemicals any more, and he was packing it in." His voice held a grievance.

"Had he been with you long?" I asked sympathetically.

"About a year."

"A good driver, I suppose?"

"Yes, about average for the job. They have to be good drivers, or we don't use them, you see. Smith was all right, but nothing special."

"And you still don't really know what happened?"

"No," he sighed. "It takes a lot to tip one of our tankers over. There was nothing to learn from the road. It was covered with oil and petrol and chemical. If there had ever been any marks, skid marks I mean, they weren't there after the breakdown cranes had lifted the tanker up again, and the road was cleared."

"Do your tankers use that road often?"

"They have done recently, but not any more after this. As a matter of fact, I seem to remember it was Smith himself who found that way round. Going over the racecourse missed out some bottleneck at a junction, I believe. I know some of the drivers thought it a good idea."

"They go through Seabury regularly, then?"

"Sure, often. Straight line to Southampton and round to the oil refinery at Fawley."

"Oh? What exactly was Smith's tanker carrying?"

"Sulfuric acid. It's used in refining petrol, among other things."

Sulfuric acid. Dense, oily, corrosive to the point of charring. Nothing more instantly lethal could have poured out over Seabury's turf. They could have raced had it been a milder chemical, put sand or tan on the dying grass and raced over the top. But no one would risk a horse on ground soaked with sulfuric acid.

I said, "Could you give me Smith's address? I'll call round and see if his memory has come back."

"Sure." He searched in a file and found it for me. "Tell him he can have his job back if he's interested. Another of the men gave notice this morning."

I said I would, thanked him, and went to Smith's address, which proved to be two rooms upstairs in a suburban house. But Smith and his wife no longer lived there. Packed up and gone yesterday, I was told by a young woman in curlers. No, he didn't leave a forwarding address, and if I was her I wouldn't worry about his health as he'd been laughing and drinking and playing records till all hours the day after the crash, his concussion having cured itself pretty quick. Reaction, he'd said when she complained of the noise, against not being killed.

It was dark by then, and I drove slowly back to London against the stream of headlights pouring out. Back to my flat in a modern block a short walk from the office, down the ramp into the basement garage, and up in the lift to the fifth floor, home.

There were two rooms facing south, bedroom and sitting room, and two behind them, bathroom and kitchen, with windows into an inner well. A pleasant sunny place, furnished in blond wood and cool colors, centrally heated, cleaning included in the rent. A regular order of groceries arrived week by week directly into the kitchen through a hatch, and rubbish disappeared down a chute. Instant living. No fuss, no mess, no strings. And damnably lonely, after Jenny.

Not that she had ever been in the place; she hadn't. The house in the Berkshire village where we mostly lived had been too much of a battleground, and when she walked out I sold it, with relief. I'd moved into the new flat shortly after going to the agency, because it was close. It was also expensive, but I had no fares to pay.

I mixed myself a brandy with ice and water, sat down in an armchair, put my feet up, and thought about Seabury. Seabury, Captain Oxon, Ted Wilkins, Intersouth Chemicals, and a driver called Smith.

After that I thought about Kraye. Nothing pleasant about him, nothing at all. A smooth, phony crust of sophistication hiding ruthless greed; a seething passion for crystals, ditto for land; an obsession with the cleanliness of his body to compensate for the murk in his mind; unconventional sexual pleasures; and the abnormal quality of being able to look carefully at a crippled hand and *then hit it*.

No, I didn't care for Howard Kraye one little bit.

7

"CHICO," I said. "How would you overturn a lorry on a predetermined spot?"

"Huh? That's easy. All you'd need would be some heavy lifting gear. A big hydraulic jack. A crane. Anything like that."

"How long would it take?"

"You mean, supposing the lorry and the crane were both in position?"

"Yes."

"Only a minute or two. What sort of lorry?"

"A tanker."

"A petrol job?"

"A bit smaller than the petrol tankers. More the size of milk ones."

"Easy as kiss your hand. They've got a low center of gravity, mind. It'd need a good strong lift. But dead easy, all the same."

I turned to Dolly. "Is Chico busy today, or could you spare him?"

Dolly leaned forward, chewing the end of a pencil and looking at her day's chart. The crossover blouse did its stuff.

"I could send someone else to Kempton. . . ." She caught the direction of my eyes and laughed, and retreated a whole half inch. "Yes, you can have him." She gave him a fond glance.

"Chico," I said. "Go down to Seabury and see if you can find any trace of heavy lifting gear having been seen near the racecourse last Friday . . . those little bungalows are full of people with nothing to do but watch the world go by. You might check whether anything was hired locally, but I suppose that's a bit much to hope for. The road would have to have been closed for a few minutes before the tanker went over, I should think. See if you can find anyone who noticed anything like that . . . detour signs, for instance. And after that, go to the council offices and see what you can dig up among their old maps on the matter of drains." I told him the rough position on the subsiding trench which had made a slaughterhouse of the hurdle race, so that he should know what to look for on the maps. "And be discreet."

"Teach your grandmother to suck eggs." He grinned.

"Our quarry is rough."

"And you don't want him to hear us creep up behind him?"

"Quite right."

"Little Chico," he said truthfully, "can take care of himself."

After he had gone I telephoned Lord Hagbourne and described to him in no uncertain terms the state of Seabury's turf.

"What they need is some proper earth-moving equipment, fast, and apparently there's nothing in the kitty to pay for it. Couldn't the Levy Board . . . ?"

"The Levy Board is no fairy godmother," he interrupted. "But I'll see what can be done. Less than half cleared, you say? Hmm. However, I understand that Captain Oxon assured Weatherbys that the course would be ready for the next meeting. Has he changed his mind?"

"I didn't see him, sir. He was away for the day."

"Oh," Lord Hagbourne's voice grew a shade cooler. "Then he didn't ask you to enlist my help?"

"No."

"I don't see that I can interfere then. As racecourse manager it is his responsibility to decide what can be done and what can't, and I think it must be left like that. Mm, yes. And of course he will consult the clerk of the course if he needs advice."

"The clerk of the course is Mr. Fotherton, who lives in Bristol. He is clerk of the course there, too, and he's busy with the meetings there tomorrow and Monday."

"Er, yes, so he is."

"You could ring Captain Oxon up in an informal way and just ask how the work is getting on," I suggested.

"I don't know—"

"Well, sir, you can take my word for it that if things dawdle on at the same rate down there, there won't be any racing at Seabury next weekend. I don't think Captain Oxon can realize just how slowly those men are digging."

"He must," he protested. "He assured Weatherbys—"

"Another last minute cancellation will kill Seabury off," I said with some force.

There was a moment's pause. Then he said reluctantly. "Yes, I suppose it might. All right then. I'll ask Captain Oxon and Mr. Fotherton if they are both satisfied with the way things are going."

And I couldn't pin him down to any more direct action than that, which was certainly not going to be enough. Protocol would be the death of Seabury, I thought.

Monopolizing Dolly's telephone, I next rang up the Epping police and spoke to Chief Inspector Cornish.

"Any more news about Andrews?" I asked.

"I suppose you have a reasonable personal interest." His chuckle came down the wire. "We found he did have a sister after all. We called her at the inquest yesterday for identification purposes as she is a relative, but if you ask me she didn't really know. She took one look at the bits in the mortuary and was sick on the floor."

"Poor girl, you couldn't blame her."

"No. She didn't look long enough to identify anyone. But we had your identification for sure, so we hadn't the heart to make her go in again."

"How did he die? Did you find out?"

"Indeed we did. He was shot in the back. The bullet ricocheted off a rib and lodged in the sternum. We got the experts to compare it with the one they dug out of the wall of your office. Your bullet was a bit squashed by the hard plaster, but there's no doubt that they are the same. He was killed with the gun he used on you."

"And was it there, underneath him?"

"Not a sign of it. They brought in 'murder by persons unknown.' And between you and me, that's how it's likely to stay. We haven't a lead to speak of."

"What lead do you have?" I asked.

His voice had a smile in it. "Only something his sister told us. She has a bed-sitter in Islington, and he spent the evening there before breaking into your place. He showed her the gun. She says he was proud of having it; apparently he was a bit simple. All he told her was that a big chap had lent it to him to go out and fetch something, and he was to shoot anyone who got in his way. She didn't believe him. She said he was always making things up, always had, all his life. So she didn't ask him anything about the big chap, or about where he was going, or anything at all."

"A bit casual," I said. "With a loaded gun under her nose."

"According to the neighbors she was more interested in a stream of men friends than in anything her brother did."

"Sweet people, neighbors."

"You bet. Anyway we checked with anyone we could find who had seen Andrews that week he shot you, and he hadn't said a word to any of them about a gun or a 'big chap,' or an errand in Cromwell Road."

"He didn't go back to his sister afterwards?"

"No, she'd told him she had a guest coming."

"At one in the morning? The neighbors must be right. You tried racecourses, of course? Andrews is quite well known there, as a sort of spivvy odd-job messenger boy."

"Yes, we mainly tried the racecourses. No results. Everyone seemed surprised that such a harmless person should have been murdered."

"Harmless!"

He laughed. "If you hadn't thought him harmless you'd have kept out of his way."

"You're so right," I said with feeling. "But now I see a villain in every respectable citizen. It's very disturbing."

"Most of them are villains, in one way or another," he said cheerfully. "Keeps us busy. By the way, what do you think of Sparkle's chances this year in the Henessy? . . . "

When eventually I put the telephone down Dolly grabbed it with a sarcastic "Do you mind?" and asked the switchboard girl to get her three numbers in a row, "without interruptions from Halley." I grinned, got the packet of photographs out of the plywood table drawer, and looked through them again. They didn't tell me any more than before. Ellis Bolt's letters to Kraye. Now you see it, now you don't. A villain in every respectable citizen. Play it secretly, I thought, close to the chest, in case the eyes looking over your shoulder give you away. I wondered why I was so oppressed by a vague feeling of apprehension, and decided in irritation that a bullet in the stomach had made me nervous.

When Dolly finished her calls I took the receiver out of her hand and got through to my bank manager.

"Mr. Harper? This is Sid Halley . . . yes, fine thanks, and you? Good. Now, would you tell me just how much I have in both my accounts, deposit and current?"

"They're quite healthy, actually," he said in his gravelly base voice. "You've had several dividends in lately. Hang on a minute, and I'll send for the exact figures." He spoke to someone in the background and then came back. "It's time you reinvested some of it."

"I do have some investments in mind," I agreed. "That's what I want to discuss with you. I'm planning to buy some shares this time from another stockbroker, not through the bank. Er . . . please don't think that I'm dissatisfied; how could I be, when you've done so well for me. It's something to do with my work at the agency."

"Say no more. What exactly do you want?"

"Well, to give you as a reference," I said. "He's sure to want one, but I would be very grateful if you would make it as impersonal and as strictly financial as possible. Don't mention either my past occupation or my present one. That's very important."

"I won't, then. Anything else?"

"Nothing . . . oh, yes. I've introduced myself to him as John Halley. Would you refer to me like that if he gets in touch with you?"

"Right. I'll look forward to hearing from you one day what it's all about. Why don't you come in and see me? I've some very good cigars." The deep voice was amused. "Ah, here are the figures. . . ." He told me the total, which for once was bigger than I expected. That happy state of affairs wouldn't last very long, I reflected, if I had to live for two years without any salary from Radnor. And no one's fault but my own.

Giving Dolly back her telephone with an ironic bow, I went upstairs to Bona Fides. Jack Copeland's mud-colored jersey had a dark blue darn on the chest and a fraying stretch of ribbing on the hip. He was picking at a loose thread and making it worse.

"Anything on Kraye yet?" I asked. "Or is it too early?"

"George has got something on the prelim, I think," he answered. "Anybody got any scissors?" A large area of jersey disintegrated into ladders. "Blast."

Laughing, I went over to George's desk. The prelim was a sheet of handwritten notes in George's concertinaed style. "Leg mat, 2 yrs. 2 prev, 1 div, 1 sui dec.," it began, followed by a list of names and dates.

"Oh, yeah?" I said.

"Yeah." He grinned. Kraye was legally married to Doria Dawn, nee Easterman, two years ago. Before that he had two other wives. One killed herself; the other divorced him for cruelty." He pointed to the names and dates.

"So clear," I agreed. "When you know how."

"If you weren't so impatient you'd have had a legible typed report. But as you're here . . . " He went on down the page pointing. "Geologists think him a bit eccentric . . . quartz has no intrinsic value, most of it's much too common, except for the gem stones, but Kraye goes round trying to buy chunks of it if they take his fancy. They know him quite well along the road at the Geology Museum. But not a breath of any dirty work. Clubs: he belongs to these three, not over-liked, but most members think he's a brilliant fellow, talks very well. He gambles at Crockfords, ends up about all square over the months. He travels, always first class, usually by boat, not air. No job or profession, can't trace him on any professional or university lists. Thought to live on investments, playing the stock market, etc. Not much liked, but considered by most a clever, cultured man, by one or two a hypocritical gasbag."

"No talk of him being crooked in any way?"

"Not a word. You want him dug deeper?"

"If you can do it without him finding out."

George nodded. "Do you want him tailed?"

"No, I don't think so. Not at present." A twenty-four-hour tail was heavy on man-power, and expensive to the client, quite apart from the risk of the quarry noticing and being warned of the hunt. "Anything on his early life?" I asked.

George shook his head. "Nothing. Nobody who knows him now has known him longer than about ten years. He either wasn't born in Britain, or his name at birth wasn't Kraye. No known relatives."

"You've done marvels, George. All this in one day."

"Contacts, chum, contacts. A lot of phoning, a bit of pubbing, a touch of gossip with the local tradesmen—nothing to it."

Jack, moodily poking his fingers through the cobweb remains of his jersey, looked at me over the half-moon specs and said that there wasn't a prelim on Bolt yet because ex-sergeant Lamar, who was working on it, hadn't phoned in.

"If he does," I said, "let me know? I've an appointment with Bolt at three thirty. It would be handy to know the setup before I go."

"O.K."

After that I went down and looked out of the windows of the Racing Section for half an hour, idly watching life go by in Cromwell Road and wondering just what sort of mess I was making of the Kraye investigation. A novice chaser in the Grand National, I thought wryly; that was me. Though, come to think of it, I had once ridden a novice in the National, and got round, too. Slightly cheered, I took Dolly out to a drink and a sandwich in the snack bar at the Air Terminal, where we sat and envied the people starting off on their travels. So much expectation in the faces, as if they could fly away and leave their troubles on the ground. An illusion, I thought sourly. Your troubles flew with you; a drag in the mind . . . a deformity in the pocket.

I laughed and joked with Dolly, as usual. What else can you do?

The firm of Charing, Street and King occupied two rooms in a large block of offices belonging to a bigger firm, and consisted entirely of Bolt, his clerk and a secretary.

I was shown the door of the secretary's office, and went into a dull, tidy, fog-colored box of a room with cold fluorescent lighting and a close-up view of the fire escape through the grimy window. A woman sat at a desk by the right-hand wall, facing the window, with her back toward me. A yard behind her chair was a door with ELLIS BOLT painted on a frosted glass panel. It occurred to me that she was most awkwardly placed in the room, but that perhaps she liked sitting in a potential draft and having to turn around every time someone came in.

She didn't turn round, however. She merely moved her head round a fraction toward me and said, "Yes?"

"I have an appointment with Mr. Bolt," I said. "At three thirty."

"Oh, yes, you must be Mr. Halley. Do sit down. I'll see if Mr. Bolt is free now."

She pointed to an easy chair a step ahead of me, and flipped a switch on her desk. While I listened to her telling Mr. Bolt I was there, in the quiet voice I had heard on the telephone, I had time to see she was in her late thirties, slender, upright in her chair, with a smooth wing of straight, dark hair falling down beside her cheek. If anything, it was too young a hair style for her. There were no rings on her fingers, and no nail varnish either. Her clothes were dark and uninteresting. It seemed as though she were making a deliberate attempt to be unattractive, yet her profile, when she half turned and told me Mr. Bolt would see me, was pleasant enough. I had a glimpse of one brown eye quickly cast down, the beginning of a smile on pale lips, and she presented me again squarely with the back of her head.

Puzzled, I opened Ellis Bolt's door and walked in. The inner office wasn't much more inspiring than the outer; it was larger and there was a new green square of carpet on the linoleum, but the grayish walls prevailed, along with the tidy dullness. Through the two windows was a more distant view of the fire escape of the building across the alley. If a drab conventional setting equaled respectability, Bolt was an honest stockbroker; and Lamar, who had phoned in just before I left, had found nothing to suggest otherwise.

Bolt was on his feet behind his desk, hand outstretched. I shook it, he gestured me to a chair with arms, and offered me a cigarette.

"No, thank you, I don't smoke."

"Lucky man," he said benignly, tapping ash off one he was half through and settling his pin-striped bulk back into his chair.

His face was rounded at every point, large round nose, round cheeks, round heavy chin; no planes, no impression of bone structure underneath. He had exceptionally heavy eyebrows, a full, mobile mouth, and a smug, self-satisfied expression.

"Now, Mr. Halley, I believe in coming straight to the point. What can I do for you?"

He had a mellifluous voice, and he spoke as if he enjoyed the sound of it.

I said, "An aunt has given me some money now rather than leave it to me in her will, and I want to invest it."

"I see. And what made you come to me? Did someone recommend . . . ?" He tailed off, watching me with eyes that told me he was no fool.

"I'm afraid . . . " I hesitated, smiling apologetically to take the offense out of the words, "that I literally picked you with a pin. I don't know any stockbrokers. I didn't know how to get to know one, so I picked up a classified directory and stuck a pin into the list of names, and it was yours."

"Ah," he said paternally, observing the bad fit of Chico's second-best suit, which I had borrowed for the occasion, and listening to me reverting to the accent of my childhood.

"Can you help me?" I asked.

"I expect so, I expect so. How much is this, er, gift?" His voice was minutely patronizing, his manner infinitesimally bored. His time, he suspected, was being wasted.

"Fifteen hundred pounds."

He brightened a very little. "Oh, yes, definitely, we can do something with that. Now, do you want growth stock or a high rate of yield?"

I looked vague. He told me quite fairly the difference between the two and offered no advice.

"Growth, then," I said, tentatively. "Turn it into a fortune in time for my old age."

He smiled without much mirth, and drew a sheet of paper toward him.

"Could I have your full name?"

"John Halley . . . John Sidney Halley," I said truthfully. He wrote it down.

"Address?" I gave it.

"And your bank?" I told him that too.

"And I'll need a reference, I'm afraid."

"Would the bank manager do?" I asked. "I've had an account there for two years. He knows me quite well."

"Excellent." He screwed up his pen. "Now, do you have any idea what companies you'd like shares in, or will you leave it to me?"

"Oh, I'll leave it to you. If you don't mind, that is. I don't know anything about it, you see, not really. Only it seems silly to leave all that money around doing nothing."

"Quite, quite." He was bored with me. I thought with amusement that Charles would appreciate my continuing his strategy of the weak front. "Tell me, Mr. Halley, what do you do for a living?"

"Oh . . . um . . . I work in a shop," I said. "In the men's wear. Very interesting, it is."

"I'm sure it is." There was a yawn stuck in his throat.

"I'm hoping to be made an assistant buyer next year," I said eagerly.

"Splendid. Well done." He'd had enough. He got cumbrously to his feet and ushered me to the door. "All right, Mr. Halley, I'll invest your money safely for you in good long-term growth stock, and send you the papers to sign in due course. You'll hear from me in a week or ten days. All right?"

"Yes, Mr. Bolt, thank you very much indeed," I said. He shut the door gently behind me.

There were now two people in the outer office. The woman with her back still turned, and a spare, middle-aged man with a primly folded mouth, and tough stringy tendons pushing his collar away from his neck. He was quite at home, and with an incurious, unhurried glance at me he went past into Bolt's office. The clerk, I presumed.

The woman was typing addresses on envelopes. The twenty or so that she had done lay in a slithery stack on her left; on her right an open file provided a list of names. I looked over her shoulder casually, and then with quickened interest. She was working down the first page of a list of Seabury shareholders.

"Do you want something, Mr. Halley?" she asked politely, pulling one envelope from the typewriter and inserting another with a minimum of flourish.

"Well, er, yes," I said diffidently. I walked round to the side of her desk and found that one couldn't go on round to the front of it: a large old-fashioned table with bulbous legs filled all the space between the desk and the end of the room. I looked at this arrangement with some sort of understanding and with compassion.

"I wondered," I said, "if you could be very kind and tell me something about investing money, and so on. I didn't like to ask Mr. Bolt too much, he's a busy man. And I'd like to know a bit about it."

"I'm sorry, Mr. Halley." Her head was turned away from me, bent over the Seabury investors. "I've a job to do, as you see. Why don't you read the financial columns in the papers, or get a book on the subject?"

I had a book all right. *Outline of Company Law.* One thing I had learned from it was that only stockbrokers—apart from the company involved—could send circulars to shareholders. It was illegal if private citizens did it. Illegal for Kraye to send letters to Seabury shareholders offering to buy them out: legal for Bolt.

"Books aren't as good as people at explaining things," I said. "If you are busy now, could I come back when you've finished work and take you out for a meal? I'd be so grateful if you would, if you possibly could."

A sort of shudder shook her. "I'm sorry, Mr. Halley, but I'm afraid I can't."

"If you will look at me, so that I can see all of your face," I said, "I will ask you again."

Her head went up with a jerk at that, but finally she turned round and looked at me.

I smiled. "That's better. Now, how about coming out with me this evening?"

"You guessed?"

I nodded. "The way you've got your furniture organized. Will you come?"

"You still want to?"

"Well, of course. What time do you finish?"

"About six, tonight."

"I'll come back. I'll meet you at the door, down in the street."

"All right," she said. "If you really mean it, thank you. I'm not doing anything else tonight. . . ."

Years of hopeless loneliness showed raw in the simple words. Not doing anything else, tonight or most nights. Yet her face wasn't horrific; not anything as bad as I had been prepared for. She had lost an eye, and wore a false one. There had been some extensive burns and undoubtedly some severe fracture of the facial bones, but plastic surgery had repaired the damage to a great extent, and it had all been a long time ago. The scars were old. It was the inner wound which hadn't healed. Well . . . I knew a bit about that myself, on a smaller scale.

8

SHE CAME out of the door at ten past six wearing a neat well-cut dark overcoat and with a plain silk scarf covering her hair, tied under her chin.

It hid only a small part of the disaster to her face, and seeing her like that, defenseless, away from the shelter she had made in her office, I had an uncomfortably vivid vision of the purgatory she suffered day in and day out on the journeys to work.

She hadn't expected me to be there. She didn't look round for me when she came out, but turned directly up the road toward the tube station. I walked after her and touched her arm. Even in low heels she was taller than I.

"Mr. Halley!" she said. "I didn't think—"

"How about a drink first?" I said. "The pubs are open."

"Oh no—"

"Oh yes. Why not?" I took her arm and steered her firmly across the road into the nearest bar. Dark oak, gentle lighting, brass pump handles, and the lingering smell of lunchtime cigars: a warm beckoning stop for city gents on their way home. There were already half a dozen of them, prosperous and dark-suited, adding fizz to their spirits.

"Not here," she protested.

"Here." I held a chair for her to sit on at a small table in a corner, and asked her what she would like to drink.

"Sherry, then . . . dry."

I took the two glasses over one at a time, sherry for her, brandy for me. She was sitting on the edge of the chair, uncomfortably, and it was not the one I had put her in. She had moved round so that she had her back to everyone except me.

"Good luck, Miss . . . ?" I said, lifting my glass.

"Martin. Zanna Martin."

"Good luck, Miss Martin." I smiled.

Tentatively she smiled back. It made her face much worse: half the muscles on the disfigured right side didn't work and could do nothing about lifting the corner of her mouth or crinkling the skin round the socket of her eye. Had life been even ordinarily kind she would have been a pleasant-looking, assured woman in her late thirties with a loving husband and a growing family: years of heartbreak had left her a shy, lonely spinster who dressed and moved as though she would like to be invisible. Yet, looking at the sad travesty of her face, one could neither blame the young men who hadn't married her nor condemn her own efforts at effacement.

"Have you worked for Mr. Bolt long?" I asked peaceably, settling back lazily into my chair and watching her gradually relax into her own.

"Only a few months. . . ." She talked for some time about her job in answer to my interested questions, but unless she was supremely artful, she was not aware of anything shady going on in Charing, Street and King. I mentioned the envelopes she had been addressing, and asked what was going into them.

"I don't know yet," she said. "The leaflets haven't come from the printers."

"But I expect you typed the leaflet anyway," I said idly.

"No, actually I think Mr. Bolt did that one himself. He's quite helpful in that way, you know. If I'm busy he'll often do letters himself."

Will he, I thought. Will he, indeed. Miss Martin, as far as I was concerned, was in the clear. I bought her another drink and extracted her opinion about Bolt as a stockbroker. Sound, she said, but not busy. She had worked for other stockbrokers, it appeared, and knew enough to judge.

"There aren't many stockbrokers working on their own any more," she explained, "and . . . well, I don't like working in a big office, you see . . . and it's getting more difficult to find a job which suits me. So many stockbrokers have joined up into partnerships of three or more; it reduces overheads terrifically, of course, and it means that they can spend more time in the House. . . ."

"Where are Mr. Charing, Mr. Street, and Mr. King?" I asked.

Charing and Street were dead, she understood, and King had retired some years ago. The firm now consisted simply and solely of Ellis Bolt. She didn't really like Mr. Bolt's offices being contained inside of those of another firm. It wasn't private enough, but it was the usual arrangement nowadays. It reduced overhead so much. . . .

When the city gents had mostly departed to the bosoms of their families, Miss Martin and I left the pub and walked through the empty city streets toward the Tower. We found a quiet little restaurant where she agreed to have dinner. As before, she made a straight line for a corner table and sat with her back to the room.

"I'm paying my share," she announced firmly when she had seen the prices on the menu. "I had no idea this place was so expensive or I wouldn't have let you choose it. Mr. Bolt mentioned that you worked in a shop."

"There's Aunty's legacy," I pointed out. "The dinner's on Aunty."

She laughed. It was a happy sound if you didn't look at her, but I found I was already able to talk to her without continually, consciously thinking about her face. One got used to it after a very short while. Sometime, I thought, I would tell her so.

I was still on a restricted diet, which made social eating difficult enough without one-handedness thrown in, but did very well on clear soup and Dover sole, expertly removed from the bone by a waiter. Miss Martin, shedding inhibitions visibly, ordered lobster cocktail, fillet steak, and peaches in kirsch. We drank wine, coffee and brandy, and took our time.

"Oh!" she said ecstatically at one point. "It is so long since I had anything like this. My father used to take me out now and then, but since he died . . . well, I can't go to places like this by myself. I sometimes eat in a café round the corner from my rooms, they know me there . . . it's very good food really, chops, eggs and chips . . . you know . . . things like that." I could picture her there, sitting alone with her ravaged head turned to the wall. Lonely unhappy Miss Martin. I wished I could do something—anything—to help her.

Eventually, when she was stirring her coffee, she said simply, "It was a rocket, this." She touched her face. "A firework. The bottle it was standing in tipped over just as it went off, and it came straight at me. It hit me on the cheek bone and exploded. It wasn't anybody's fault. I was sixteen."

"They made a good job of it," I said.

She shook her head, smiling the crooked tragic smile. "A good job from what it was, I suppose, but . . . they said if the rocket had struck an inch higher it would have gone through my eye into my brain and killed me. I often wish it had."

She meant it. Her voice was calm. She was stating a fact.

"Yes," I said.

"It's strange, but I've almost forgotten about it this evening, and that doesn't often happen when I'm with anyone."

"I'm honored."

She drank her coffee, put down her cup, and looked at me thoughtfully. She said, "Why do you keep your hand in your pocket all the time?"

I owed it to her, after all. I put my hand palm upward on the table, wishing I didn't have to.

She said "Oh!" in surprise, and then, looking back at my face, "So you do know. That's why I feel so . . . so easy with you. You do understand."

I shook my head. "Only a little. I have a pocket; you haven't. I can hide." I rolled my hand over (the back of it was less off-putting) and finally retreated it onto my lap.

"But you can't do the simplest things," she exclaimed. Her voice was full of pity. "You can't tie your shoelaces, for instance. You can't even eat steak in a restaurant without asking someone else to cut it up for you—"

"Shut up," I said abruptly. "Shut up, Miss Martin. Don't you dare to do to me what you can't bear yourself."

"Pity . . . ," she said, biting her lip and staring at me unhappily. "Yes, it's so easy to give—"

"And embarrassing to receive." I grinned at her. "And my shoes don't have shoelaces. They're out of date, for a start."

"You can know as well as I do what it feels like, and yet do it to someone else . . . " She was very upset.

"Stop being miserable. It was kindness. Sympathy."

"Do you think," she said hesitantly, "that pity and sympathy are the same thing?"

"Very often, yes. But sympathy is discreet and pity is tactless. Oh . . . I'm so sorry." I laughed. "Well, it was sympathetic of you to feel sorry I can't cut up my own food, and tactless to say so. The perfect example."

"It wouldn't be so hard to forgive people for just being tactless," she said thoughtfully.

"No," I agreed, surprised. "I suppose it wouldn't."

"It might not hurt so much . . . just tactlessness?"

"It mightn't."

"And curiosity—that might be easier, too, if I just thought of it as bad manners, don't you think? I mean tactlessness and bad manners wouldn't be so hard to stand. In fact *I* could be sorry for *them,* for not knowing better how to behave. Oh why, why didn't I think of that years ago, when it seems so simple now. So sensible."

"Miss Martin," I said with gratitude. "Have some more brandy. You're a liberator."

"How do you mean?"

"Pity is bad manners and can be taken in one's stride, as you said."

"You said it," she protested.

"Indeed I didn't, not like that."

"All right," she said with gaiety, "we'll drink to a new era. A bold front to the world. I will put my desk back to where it was before I joined the office, facing the door. I'll let every caller see me. I'll—" Her brave voice nearly cracked. "I'll just think poorly of their manners if they pity me too openly. That's settled."

We had some more brandy. I wondered inwardly whether she would have the same resolve in the morning, and doubted it. There had been so many years of hiding. She too, it seemed, was thinking along the same lines.

"I don't know that I can do it alone. But if you will promise me something, then I can."

"Very well," I said incautiously. "What?"

"Don't put your hand in your pocket tomorrow. Let everyone see it."

I couldn't. Tomorrow I would be going to the races. I looked at her, appalled, and really understood only then what she had to bear, and what it would cost her to move her desk. She saw the refusal in my face, and some sort of light died in her own. The gaiety collapsed, the defeated, defenseless look came back, the liberation was over.

"Miss Martin . . . " I swallowed.

"It doesn't matter," she said tiredly. "It doesn't matter. And anyway, it's Saturday tomorrow. I only go in for a short while to see to the mail and anything urgent from today's transactions. There wouldn't be any point in changing the desk."

"And on Monday?"

"Perhaps." It meant no.

"If you'll change it tomorrow and do it all next week, I'll do what you ask," I said, quaking at the thought of it.

"You can't," she said sadly. "I can see that you can't."

"If you can, I must."

"But I shouldn't have asked you . . . you work in a shop."

"Oh." That I had forgotten. "It won't matter."

An echo of her former excitement crept back.

"Do you really mean it?"

I nodded. I had wanted to do something—anything—to help her. Anything. My God.

"Promise?" she said doubtfully.

"Yes. And you?"

"All right," she said, with returning resolution. "But I can only do it if I know you are in the same boat. I couldn't let you down then, you see."

I paid the bill, and although she said there was no need, I took her home. We went on the underground to Finchley. She made straight for the least conspicuous seat and sat presenting the good side of her face to the carriage. Then, laughing at herself, she apologized for doing it.

"Never mind," I said, "the new era doesn't start until tomorrow," and hid my hand like a proper coward.

Her room was close to the station (a deliberately short walk, I guessed) in a large, prosperous-looking suburban house. At the gate she stopped.

"Will . . . er . . . I mean, would you like to come in? It's not very late . . . but perhaps you are tired."

She wasn't eager, but when I accepted she seemed pleased.

"This way, then."

We went through a bare tidy garden to a black-painted front door adorned with horrible stained-glass panels. Miss Martin fumbled endlessly in her bag for her key and I reflected idly that I could have picked that particular lock as quickly as she opened it legally. Inside there was a warm hall smelling healthily of air freshener, and at the end of a passage off it, a door with a card saying "Martin."

Miss Martin's room was a surprise. Comfortable, large, close carpeted, newly decorated, and alive with color. She switched on a standard lamp and a rosy table lamp, and drew burnt orange curtains over the black expanse of French windows. With satisfaction she showed me the recently built tiny bathroom leading out of her room, and the suitcase-sized kitchen beside it, both of which additions she had paid for herself. The people who owned the house were very understanding, she said. Very kind. She had lived there for eleven years. It was home.

Miss Martin had no mirrors in her home. Not one.

She bustled in her little kitchen, making more coffee: for something to do, I thought. I sat relaxed on her long comfortable modern sofa and watched how, from long habit, she leaned forward most of the time so that the heavy shoulder-length dark hair swung down to hide her face. She brought the tray and set it down, and sat on the sofa carefully on my right. One couldn't blame her.

"Do you ever cry?" she said suddenly.

"No."

"Not . . . from frustration?"

"No." I smiled. "Swear."

She sighed. "I used to cry often. I don't any more, though. Getting older, of course. I'm nearly forty. I've got resigned now to not getting married. I knew I was resigned to it when I had the bathroom and kitchen built. Up to then, you see, I'd always pretended to myself that one day . . . one day, perhaps . . . but I don't expect it any more, not any more."

"Men are fools," I said inadequately.

"I hope you don't mind me talking like this? It's so seldom that I have anyone in here, and practically never anyone I can really talk to. . . ."

I stayed for an hour, listening to her memories, her experiences, her whole shadowed life. What, I chided myself, had ever happened to me that was one tenth as bad? I had had far more ups than downs.

At length she said, "How did it happen with you? Your hand. . . ."

"Oh, an accident. A sharp bit of metal." A razor-sharp racing horseshoe attached to the foot of a horse galloping at thirty miles an hour, to be exact. A hard kicking slash as I rolled on the ground from an easy fall. One of those things.

Horses race in thin light shoes called plates, not the heavy ones they normally wear; blacksmiths change them before and after, every time a horse runs. Some trainers save a few shillings by using the same racing plates over and over again, so that the leading edge gradually wears down to the thickness of a knife. But jagged knives, not smooth. They can cut you open like a hatchet.

I'd really known at once when I saw my stripped wrist, with the blood spurting out in a jet and the broken bones showing white, that I was finished as a jockey. But I wouldn't give up hope, and insisted on the surgeons' sewing it all up, even though they wanted to take my hand off there and then. It would never be any good, they said; and they were right. Too many of the tendons and nerves were severed. I persuaded them to try twice later on to rejoin and graft some of them and both times it had been a useless agony. They had refused to consider it again.

Miss Martin hesitated on the brink of asking for details, and fortunately didn't. Instead she said, "Are you married? Do you know, I've talked so much about myself that I don't know a thing about you."

"My wife's in Athens, visiting her sister."

"How lovely," Miss Martin sighed. "I wish . . . "

"You'll go one day," I said firmly. "Save up, and go in a year or two. On a bus tour or something. With people anyway. Not alone."

I looked at my watch, and stood up. "I've enjoyed this evening a great deal. Thank you so much for coming out with me."

She stood and formally shook hands, not suggesting another meeting. So much humility, I thought, so little expectation. Poor, poor Miss Martin.

"Tomorrow morning . . . " she said tentatively, at the door.

"Tomorrow," I nodded. "Move that desk. And I . . . I promise I won't forget."

I went home cursing that fate had sent me someone like Miss Martin. I had expected Charing, Street and King's secretary to be young, perhaps pretty, a girl I could take to a café and the pictures and flirt with, with no great involvement on either side. Instead it looked as if I should have to pay more than I'd meant to for my inside information on Ellis Bolt.

9

"Now look," said Lord Hagbourne, amid the bustle of Kempton races, "I've had a word with Captain Oxon and he's satisfied with the way things are going. I really can't interfere any more. Surely you understand that?"

"No, sir, I don't. I don't think Captain Oxon's feelings are more important than Seabury Racecourse. The course should be put right quickly, even if it means overruling him."

"Captain Oxon," he said with a touch of sarcasm, "knows more about his job than you do. I give more weight to his assurance than to your quick look at the track."

"Then couldn't you go and see for yourself? While there is still time."

He didn't like being pushed. His expression said so, plainly. There was no more I could say, either, without risking his ringing up Radnor to cancel the whole investigation.

"I may . . . er . . . I may find time on Monday," he said at last, grudgingly. "I'll see. Have you found anything concrete to support your idea that Seabury's troubles were caused maliciously?"

"Not yet, sir."

"A bit farfetched, if you ask me," he said crossly. "I said so to begin with, as you remember. If you don't turn something up pretty soon . . . it's all expense, you know."

He was intercepted by a passing Steward who took him off to another problem, leaving me grimly to reflect that so far there was a horrid lack of evidence of any sort. What there was was negative.

George had still found no chink in Kraye's respectability, ex-sergeant Lamar had given Bolt clearance and Chico had come back from Seabury with no results all along the line.

We'd met in the office that morning before I went to Kempton.

"Nothing," said Chico. "I wagged my tongue off, knocking at every front door along that road. Not a soggy flicker. The bit that crosses the racecourse wasn't closed by diversion notices, that's for sure. There isn't much traffic along there, of course. I counted it. Only forty to the hour, average. Still, that's too much for at least some of the neighbors not to notice if there'd been anything out of the ordinary."

"Did anyone see the tanker before it overturned?"

"They're always seeing tankers nowadays. Several complaints about it, I got. No one noticed that one, especially."

"It can't be coincidence. Just at that spot at that time where it would do most harm. And the driver packing up and moving a day or two afterwards with no forwarding address."

"Well . . . " Chico scratched his ear reflectively. "I got no dice with the hiring of lifting gear either. There isn't much to be had, and what there was was accounted for. None of the little bungalows saw anything in that line, except the breakdown cranes coming to lift the tanker up again."

"How about the drains?"

"No drains," he said. "A blank back to doomsday."

"Good."

"Come again?"

"If you'd found them on a map the hurdle race accident would have been a genuine accident. This way, they reek of tiger traps."

"A spot of spadework after dark? Dodgy stuff."

I frowned. "Yes. And it had to be done long enough before the race meeting for the ground to settle, so that the line of the trench didn't show."

"And strong enough for a tractor to roll over it."

"Tractor?"

"There was one on the course yesterday, pulling a trailer of dug-up turf."

"Oh yes, of course. Yes, strong enough to hold a tractor . . . but wheels wouldn't pierce the ground like a horse's legs. The weight is more spread."

"True enough."

"How fast was the turf-digging going?" I asked.

"Fast? You're joking."

It was depressing. So was Lord Hagbourne's shillyshallying. So, acutely, was the whole day, because I kept my promise to Miss Martin. Pity, curiosity, surprise, embarrassment and revulsion. I encountered the lot. I tried hard to look on some of the things that were said as tactlessness or bad manners, but it didn't really work. Telling myself it was idiotic to be so sensitive didn't help either. If Miss Martin hadn't kept her side of the bargain, I thought miserably, I would throttle her.

Halfway through the afternoon I had a drink in the big upstairs bar with Mark Witney.

"So that's what you've been hiding all this time in pockets and gloves," he said.

"Yes."

"Bit of a mess," he commented.

"I'm afraid so."

"Does it hurt still?"

"No, only if I knock it. And it aches sometimes."

"Mm," he said sympathetically. "My ankle still aches too. Joints are always like that; they mend, but they never forgive you." He grinned. "The other half? There's time; I haven't a runner until the fifth."

We had another drink, talking about horses and I reflected that it would be easy if they were all like him.

"Mark," I said as we walked back to the weighing room, "do you remember whether Dunstable ran into any sort of trouble before it packed up?"

"That's going back a bit." He pondered. "Well, it certainly wasn't doing so well during the last year or two, was it? The attendances had fallen off, and they weren't spending any money on paint."

"But no specific disasters?"

"The clerk of the course took an overdose, if you call that a disaster. Yes, I remember now, the collapse of the place's prosperity was put down to the clerk's mental illness. Brinton, I think his name was. He'd been quietly going loco and making hopeless decisions all over the place."

"I'd forgotten," I said glumly. Mark went into the weighing room and I leaned against the rails outside. A suicidal clerk of the course could hardly have been the work of Kraye, I thought. It might have given him the idea of accelerating the demise of Seabury, though. He'd had plenty of time over Dunstable, but owing to a recent political threat of nationalization of building land, he might well be in a hurry to clinch Seabury. I sighed, disregarded as best I could a stare of fascinated horror from the teen-age daughter of a man I used to ride for, and drifted over to look at the horses in the parade ring.

At the end of the too-long afternoon I drove back to my flat, mixed a bigger drink than usual, and spent the evening thinking, without any world-shattering results. Late the next morning, when I was similarly engaged, the doorbell rang, and I found Charles outside.

"Come in," I said with surprise: he rarely visited the flat and was seldom in London at weekends. "Like some lunch? The restaurant downstairs is quite good."

"Perhaps. In a minute." He took off his overcoat and gloves and accepted some whisky. There was something unsettled in his manner, a ruffling of the smooth, urbane exterior, a suggestion of a troubled frown on the high domed forehead.

"O.K.," I said. "What's the matter?"

"Er . . . I've just driven up from Aynsford. No traffic at all, for once. Such a lovely morning, I thought the drive would be . . . oh damn it," he finished explosively, putting down his glass with a bang. "To get it over quickly, Jenny telephoned from Athens last night. She's met some man there. She asked me to tell you she wants a divorce."

"Oh," I said. How like her, I thought, to get Charles to wield the ax. Practical Jenny, eager for a new fire, hacking away the deadwood. And if some of the wood was still alive, too bad.

"I must say," said Charles, relaxing, "you make a thorough job of it."

"Of what?"

"Of not caring what happens to you."

"I do care."

"No one would suspect it," he sighed. "When I tell you your wife wants to divorce you, you just say, 'Oh.' When that happened"—he nodded to my arm—"the first thing you said to me afterwards when I arrived full of sorrow and sympathy was, if I remember correctly, and I do, 'Cheer up, Charles. I had a good run for my money.' "

"Well, so I did." Always, from my earliest childhood, I had instinctively shied away from too much sympathy. I didn't want it. I distrusted it. It made you soft inside, and an illegitimate child couldn't afford to be soft. One might weep at school, and one's spirit would never recover from so dire a disgrace. So the poverty and the snickers, and later the lost wife and the smashed career, had to be passed off with a shrug, and what one really felt about it had to be locked up tightly inside, out of view. Silly, really, but there it was.

We lunched companionably together downstairs, discussing in civilized tones the mechanics of divorce. Jenny, it appeared, did not want me to use the justified grounds of desertion. I, she said, should "arrange things" instead. I must know how to do it, working for the agency. Charles was apologetic: Jenny's prospective husband was in the diplomatic service like Tony, and would prefer her not to be the guilty party.

Had I, Charles inquired delicately, already been . . . er . . . unfaithful to Jenny? No, I replied, watching him light his cigar, I was afraid I hadn't. For much of the time, owing to one thing and another, I hadn't felt well enough. That, he agreed with amusement, was a reasonable excuse.

I indicated that I would fix things as Jenny wanted, because it didn't affect my future as it did hers. She would be grateful, Charles said. I thought, knowing her, she would very likely take it for granted.

When there was little else to say on that subject, we switched to Kraye. I asked Charles if he had seen him again during the week.

"Yes, I was going to tell you. I had lunch with him in the Club on Thursday. Quite accidentally. We both just happened to be there alone."

"That's where you met him first, in your club?"

"That's right. Of course he thanked me for the weekend and so on. Talked about the quartz. Very interesting collection, he said. But not a murmur about the St. Luke's stone. I would have liked to have asked him straight out, just to see his reaction." He tapped off the ash, smiling. "I did mention you, though, in passing, and he switched on all the charm and said you had been extremely insulting to him and his wife, but that of course you hadn't spoiled his enjoyment. Very nasty, I thought it. He was causing bad trouble for you. Or at least, he intended to."

"Yes," I said cheerfully. "But I did insult him, and I also spied on him. Anything he says of me is fully merited." I told Charles how I had taken the photographs, and all that I had discovered or guessed during the past week. His cigar went out. He looked stunned.

"Well, you wanted me to, didn't you?" I said. "You started it. What did you expect?"

"It's only that I had almost forgotten . . . this is what you used to be like, always. Determined. Ruthless, even." He smiled. "My game for convalescence has turned out better than I expected."

"God help your other patients," I said, "if Kraye is standard medicine."

We walked along the road toward where Charles had left his car. He was going straight home again.

I said, "I hope that in spite of the divorce I shall see something of you? I should be sorry not to. As your ex-son-in-law, I can hardly come to Aynsford any more."

He looked startled. "I'll be annoyed if you don't, Sid. Jenny will be living all round the world, like Jill. Come to Aynsford whenever you want."

"Thank you," I said. I meant it, and it sounded like it.

He stood beside his car, looking down at me from his straight six feet.

"Jenny," he said casually, "is a fool."

I shook my head. Jenny was no fool. Jenny knew what she wanted, and it wasn't me.

When I went into the office (on time) the following morning, the girl on the switchboard caught me and said Radnor wanted me straight away.

"Good morning," he said. "I've just had Lord Hagbourne on the telephone telling me it's time we got results and that he can't go to Seabury today because his car is being serviced. Before you explode, Sid . . . I told him that you would take him down there now, at once, in your own car. So get a move on."

I grinned. "I bet he didn't like that."

"He couldn't think of an excuse fast enough. Get round and collect him before he comes up with one."

"Right."

I made a quick detour up to the Racing Section where Dolly was adjusting her lipstick. No crossover blouse today. A disappointment.

I told her where I was going and asked if I could use Chico.

"Help yourself," she said resignedly. "If you can get a word in edgeways. He's along in Accounts arguing with Jones-boy."

Chico, however, listened attentively and repeated what I had asked him.

"I'm to find out exactly what mistakes the clerk of the course at Dunstable made, and make sure that they and nothing else were the cause of the course losing money."

"That's right. And dig out the file on Andrews and the case you were working on when I got shot."

"But that's all dead," he protested, "the file's down in records in the basement."

"Send Jones-boy down for it," I suggested, grinning. "It's probably only a coincidence, but there is something I want to check. I'll do it tomorrow morning. O.K.?"

"If you say so, chum."

Back at my flat, I filled up with Extra and made all speed round to Beauchamp Place. Lord Hagbourne, with a civil but cool good morning, lowered himself into the passenger seat, and we set off for Seabury. It took him about a quarter of an hour to get over having been maneuvered into something he didn't want to do, but at the end of that time he sighed and moved in his seat and offered me a cigarette.

"No, thank you, sir. I don't smoke."

"You don't mind if I do?" He took one out.

"Of course not."

"This is a nice car," he remarked, looking round.

"It's nearly three years old now. I bought it the last season I was riding. It's the best I've ever had, I think."

"I must say," he said inoffensively, "that you manage extremely well. I wouldn't have thought that you could drive a car like this with only one effective hand."

"Its power makes it easier, actually. I took it across Europe last spring . . . good roads, there."

We talked on about cars and holidays, then about theaters and books, and he seemed for once quite human. The subject of Seabury we carefully bypassed. I wanted to get him down there in a good mood—the arguments, if any, could take place on the way back—and it seemed as if he was of the same mind.

The state of Seabury's track reduced him to silent gloom. We walked down to the burnt piece with Captain Oxon, who was bearing himself stiffly and being pointedly polite. I thought he was a fool: he should have fallen on the Senior Steward and begged for instant help.

Captain Oxon, whom I had not met before, though he said he knew me by sight, was a slender, pleasant-looking man of about fifty, with a long pointed chin and a slight tendency to watery eyes. The present offended obstinacy of his expression looked more like childishness than real strength. A colonel *manqué,* I thought uncharitably, and no wonder.

"I know it's not really my business," I said, "but surely a bulldozer would shift what's left of the burnt bit in a couple of hours? There isn't time to settle new turf, but you could cover the whole area with some tons of tan and race over it quite easily, like that. You must be getting tan anyway, to cover the road surface. Surely you could just increase the order?"

Oxon looked at me with irritation. "We can't afford it."

"You can't afford another cancellation at the last minute," I corrected.

"We are insured against cancellations."

"I doubt whether an insurance company would stand this one," I said. "They'd say you could have raced if you'd tried hard enough."

"It's Monday now," remarked Lord Hagbourne thoughtfully. "Racing's due on Friday. Suppose we call in a bulldozer tomorrow; the tan can be unloaded and spread on Wednesday and Thursday. Yes, that seems sound enough."

"But the cost—" began Oxon.

"I think the money must be found," said Lord Hagbourne. "Tell Mr. Fotherton when he comes over that I have authorized the expenditure. The bills will be met, in one way or another. But I do think there is no case for not making an effort."

It was on the tip of my tongue to point out that if Oxon had arranged for the bulldozer on the first day he could have saved the price of casual labor from six hand-diggers for a week, but as the battle was already won, I nobly refrained. I continued to think, however, that Oxon was a fool. Usually the odd custom of giving the managerships of racecourses to ex-army officers worked out well, but conspicuously not in this case.

The three of us walked back up to the stands Lord Hagbourne pausing and pursing his lips at their dingy appearance. I reflected that it was a pity Seabury had a clerk of the course whose heart and home were far away on the thriving course at Bristol. If I'd been arranging things, I'd have seen to it a year ago, when the profits turned to loss, that Seabury had a new clerk entirely devoted to its own interests, someone moreover whose livelihood depended on its staying open. The bungle, delay, muddle, too much politeness and failure to take action showed by the Seabury executive had been of inestimable value to the quietly burrowing Kraye.

Mr. Fotherton might have been worried, as he said, but he had done little except mention it in passing to Charles in his capacity as Steward at some other meeting. Charles, looking for something to divert my mind from my stomach, and perhaps genuinely anxious about Seabury, had tossed the facts to me. In his own peculiar way, naturally.

The casualness of the whole situation was horrifying. I basely wondered whether Fotherton himself had a large holding in Seabury shares and therefore a vested interest in its demise. Planning a much closer scrutiny of the list of shareholders, I followed Lord Hagbourne and Captain Oxon round the end of the stands, and we walked the three hundred yards or so through the racecourse gates and down the road to where Captain Oxon's flat was situated above the canteen in the stable block.

On Lord Hagbourne's suggestion he rang up a firm of local contractors while we were still there, and arranged for the urgent earth-moving to be done the following morning. His manner was still ruffled, and it didn't improve things when I declined the well-filled ham and chutney sandwiches he offered, though I would have adored to have eaten them, had he but known. I had been out of hospital for a fortnight, but I had another fortnight to go before things like new bread, ham, mustard and chutney were due back on the agenda. Very boring.

After the sandwiches Lord Hagbourne decided on a tour of inspection, so we all three went first round the stable block, into the lads' hostel, through the canteen to the kitchen, and into all the stable administrative offices. Everywhere the story was the same. Except for the rows of wooden boxes which had been thrown up cheaply after the old ones burned down, there was no recent maintenance and no new paint.

Then we retraced our steps up the road, through the main gate, and across to the long line of stands with the weighing room, dining rooms, bars and cloakrooms built into the back. At one end were the secretary's office, the press room and the Steward's room; at the other, the first-aid room and a store. A wide tunnel like a passage ran centrally through the whole length of the building, giving secondary access on one side to many of the rooms, and on the other to the steps of the stands themselves. We painstakingly covered the lot, even down to the boiler room and the oil bunkers, so I had my nostalgic look inside the weighing room and changing room after all.

The whole huge block was dankly cold, very drafty, and smelled of dust. Nothing looked new, not even the dirt. For inducing depression it was hard to beat, but the dreary buildings along in the cheaper rings did a good job of trying.

Captain Oxon said the general dilapidation was mostly due to the sea air, the racecourse being barely half a mile from the shore, and no doubt in essence he was right. The sea air had had a free hand for far too long.

Eventually we returned to where my car was parked inside the gate, and looked back to the row of stands: forlorn, deserted, decaying on a chilly early November afternoon, with a salt-laden drizzle just beginning to blur the outlines.

"What's to be done?" said Lord Hagbourne glumly, as we drove through the rows of bungalows on our way home.

"I don't know." I shook my head.

"The place is dead."

I couldn't argue. Seabury had suddenly seemed to me to be past saving. The Friday and Saturday fixtures could be held now, but as things stood the gate money would hardly cover expenses. No company could go on taking a loss indefinitely. Seabury could plug the gap at present by drawing on their reserve funds, but as I'd seen from their balance sheets at Company House, the reserves only amounted to a few thousands. Matters were bound to get worse. Insolvency waited round a close corner. It might be more realistic to admit that Seabury had no future and to sell the land at the highest price offered as soon as possible. People were, after all, crying out for flat land at the seaside. And there was no real reason why the shareholders shouldn't be rewarded for their long loyalty and recent poor dividends and receive eight pounds for each one they had invested. Many would gain if Seabury came under the hammer, and no one would lose. Seabury was past saving: best to think only of the people who would benefit.

My thoughts stopped with a jerk. This, I realized, must be the attitude of the clerk, Mr. Fotherton, and of the manager, Oxon, and of all the executives. This explained why they had made surprisingly little attempt to save the place. They had accepted defeat easily and seen it to be not only harmless but, to many, usefully profitable. As it had been with other courses, big courses like Hurst Park and Birmingham, so it should be with Seabury.

What did it matter that yet another joined the century's ghost ranks of Cardiff, Derby, Bournemouth, Newport? What did it matter if busy people like Inspector Cornish of Dunstable couldn't go racing much because their local course had vanished? What did it matter if Seabury's holidaymakers went to the bingo halls instead?

Chasing owners, I thought, should rise up in a body and demand that Seabury should be preserved, because no racecourse was better for their horses. But of course they wouldn't. You could tell owners how good it was, but unless they were horsemen themselves, it didn't register. They only saw the rotten amenities of the stands, not the splendidly sited well-built fences that positively invited their horses to jump. They didn't know how their horses relished the short springy turf underfoot, or found the arc and cambers of the bends perfect for maintaining an even speed. Corners at many other racecourses threw horses wide and broke up their stride, but not those at Seabury. The original course builder had been brilliant, and regular visits from the inspector of courses had kept his work fairly intact. Fast, true-run, unhazardous racing, that's what Seabury gave.

Or had given, before Kraye.

Kraye and the executive's inertia between them. . . . I stamped on the accelerator in a surge of anger and the car swooped up the side of the South Downs like a bird. I didn't often drive fast any more: I did still miss having two hands on the wheel. At the top, out of consideration for my passenger's nerves, I let the speedometer ribbon slide back to fifty.

He said, "I feel like that about it too."

I glanced at him in surprise.

"The whole situation is infuriating," he said. "Such a good course basically, and nothing to be done."

"It could be saved," I said.

"How?"

"A new attitude of mind. . . ." I trailed off.

"Go on," he said. But I couldn't find the words to tell him politely that he ought to chuck out all the people in power at Seabury; too many of them were probably his ex-school chums or personal friends.

"Suppose," he said after a few minutes, "that you had a free hand, what would you do?"

"One would never get a free hand. That's half the trouble. Someone makes a good suggestion, and someone else squashes it. They end up, often as not, by doing nothing."

"No, Sid, I mean you personally. What would you do?"

"I?" I grinned. "What I'd do would have the National Hunt Committee swooning like Victorian maidens."

"I'd like to know."

"Seriously?"

He nodded. As if he could ever be anything else but serious.

I sighed. "Very well, then. I'd pinch every good crowd-pulling idea that any other course has thought of and put them all into operation on the same day."

"What, for instance?"

"I'd take the whole of the reserve fund and offer it as a prize for a big race. I'd make sure the race was framed to attract the really top chasers.

Then I'd go round to their trainers personally and explain the situation, and beg for their support. I'd go to some of the people who sponsor Gold Cup races and cajole them into giving five-hundred-pound prizes for all the other races on that day. I'd make the whole thing into a campaign. I'd get Save Seabury discussed on television, and in the sports columns of newspapers. I'd get people interested and involved. I'd make helping Seabury the smart thing to do. I'd get someone like the Beatles to come and present the trophies. I'd advertise free car-parking and free race cards, and on the day I'd have the whole place bright with flags and bunting and tubs of flowers to hide the lack of paint. I'd make sure everyone on the staff understood that a friendly welcome must be given to the customers. And I'd insist that the catering firm use its imagination. I'd fix the meeting for the beginning of April, and pray for a sunny spring day. That," I said, running down, "would do for a start."

"And afterwards?" He was noncommittal.

"A loan, I suppose. Either from a bank or from private individuals. But the executive would have to show first that Seabury could be a success again, like it used to be. No one falls over himself to lend to a dying business. The revival has to come before the money, if you see what I mean."

"I do see," he agreed slowly, "but . . ."

"Yes. But. It always comes to 'but.' But no one at Seabury is going to bother."

We were silent for a long way.

Finally I said, "This meeting on Friday and Saturday—it would be a pity to risk another last-minute disaster. Hunt Radnor Associates could arrange for some sort of guard on the course. Security patrols, that kind of thing."

"Too expensive," he said promptly. "And you've not yet proved that it is really needed. Seabury's troubles still look like plain bad luck to me."

"Well, a security patrol might prevent any more of it."

"I don't know. I'll have to see." He changed the subject then, and talked firmly about other races on other courses all the way back to London.

10

DOLLY LENT me her telephone with resignation on Tuesday morning, and I buzzed the switchboard for an internal call to Missing Persons.

"Sammy?" I said. "Sid Halley, down in Racing. Are you busy?"

"The last teenager has just been retrieved from Gretna. Fire away. Who's lost?"

"A man called Smith."

Some mild blasphemy sped three stories down the wire.

I laughed. "I think his name really is Smith. He's a driver by trade. He's been driving a tanker for Intersouth Chemicals for the last year. He left his job and his digs last Wednesday; no forwarding address." I told him about the crash, the suspected concussion and the revelry by night.

"You don't think he was planted on purpose on the job a year ago? His name likely wouldn't be Smith in that case . . . make it harder."

"I don't know. But I think it's more likely he was a bona fide Intersouth driver who was offered a cash payment for exceptional services rendered."

"O.K., I'll try that first. He might give Intersouth as a reference, in which case they'll know if he applies for another job somewhere, or I might trace him through his union. The wife might have worked, too. I'll let you know."

"Thanks."

"Don't forget, when the old man buys you a gold-plated executive desk I want my table back."

"You'll want forever," I said, smiling. It had been Sammy's lunch.

On the table in question lay the slim file on the Andrews case that Jones-boy had unearthed from the basement. I looked round the room.

"Where's Chico?" I asked.

Dolly answered. "Helping a bookmaker to move house."

"He's doing *what?*" I goggled.

"That's right. Long-standing date. The bookmaker is taking his safe with him and wants Chico to sit on it in the furniture van. It had to be Chico, he said. No one else would do. The paying customer is always right, so Chico's gone."

"Damn."

She reached into a drawer. "He left you a tape," she said.

"Undamn, then."

She grinned and handed it to me, and I took it over to the recorder, fed it through onto the spare reel, and listened to it in the routine office way, through the earphones.

"After wearing my plates down to the ankles," said Chico's cheerful voice, "I found out that the worst things your clerk of the course did at Dunstable were to frame a lot of races that did the opposite of attract any decent runners, and be stinking rude to all and sundry. He was quite well liked up to the year before he killed himself. Then everyone says he gradually got more and more crazy. He was so rude to people who worked at the course that half of them wouldn't put up with it and left. And the local tradesmen practically spat when I mentioned his name. I'll fill you in when I see you, but there wasn't anything like Seabury—no accidents or damage or anything like that."

Sighing, I wiped the tape clean and gave it back to Dolly. Then I opened the file on my table and studied its contents.

A Mr. Mervyn Brinton of Reading, Berkshire, had applied to the agency for personal protection, having had reason to believe that he was in danger of being attacked. He had been unwilling to say why he might be attacked, and refused to have the agency make inquiries. All he wanted was a bodyguard. There was a strong possibility, said the report, that Brinton had tried a little amateurish blackmail, which had backfired. He had at length revealed that he possessed a certain letter, and was afraid of being attacked and having it stolen. After much persuasion by Chico Barnes, who pointed out that Brinton could hardly be guarded for the rest of his life, Brinton had agreed to inform a certain party that the letter in question was lodged in a particular desk drawer in the Racing Section of Hunt Radnor Associates. In fact it was not; and had not at any time been seen by anyone working for the agency. However, Thomas Andrews came, or was sent, to remove the letter, was interrupted by J. S. Halley (whom he wounded by shooting), and subsequently made his escape. Two days later Brinton telephoned to say he no longer required a bodyguard, and as far as the agency was concerned the case was then closed.

The foregoing information had been made available to the police in their investigation into the shooting of Halley.

I shut the file. A drab little story, I thought, of a pathetic little man playing out of his league.

Brinton.

The clerk of the course at Dunstable had also been called Brinton.

I sat gazing at the short file. Brinton wasn't an uncommon name. There was probably no connection at all. Brinton of Dunstable had died a good two years before Brinton of Reading had asked for protection. The only visible connection was that at different ends of the scale both the Dunstable Brinton and Thomas Andrews had earned their living on the racecourse. It wasn't much. Probably nothing. But it nagged.

I went home, collected the car, and drove to Reading.

A nervous, gray-haired elderly man opened the front door on a safety chain, and peered through the gap.

"Yes?"

"Mr. Brinton?"

"What is it?"

"I'm from Hunt Radnor Associates. I'd be most grateful for a word with you."

He hesitated, chewing an upper lip adorned with an untidy pepper-and-salt mustache. Anxious brown eyes looked me up and down and went past me to the white car parked by the curb.

"I sent a check," he said finally.

"It was quite in order," I assured him.

"I don't want any trouble . . . it wasn't my fault that the man was shot." He didn't sound convinced.

"Oh, no one blames you for that," I said. "He's perfectly all right now. Back at work, in fact."

His relief showed, even through the crack. "Very well," he said, and pushed the door shut to take off the chain.

I followed him into the front room of his tall terrace house. The air smelled stale and felt still, as if it had been hanging in the same spot for days. The furniture was of the hard-stuffed and brown shellacked substantial type that in my plywood childhood I had thought the peak of living, unobtainable; and there were cases of tropical butterflies on the walls, and carved ornaments from somewhere like Java or Borneo on several small tables. A life abroad, retirement at home, I thought. From color and heat to suburban respectability in Reading.

"My wife has gone out shopping," he said, still nervously. "She'll be back soon." He looked hopefully out of the lace-curtained window, but Mrs. Brinton didn't oblige him by coming to his support.

I said, "I just wanted to ask you, Mr. Brinton, if you were by any chance related to a William Brinton, one-time clerk of Dunstable race-course."

He gave me a long agonized stare, and to my consternation sat down on his sofa and began to cry, his shaking hands covering his eyes and the tears splashing down onto his tweed-clad knees.

"Please . . . Mr. Brinton . . . I'm so sorry," I said awkwardly.

He snuffled and coughed, and dragged a handkerchief out to wipe his eyes. Gradually the paroxysm passed, and he said indistinctly, "How did you find out? I told you I didn't want anyone asking questions."

"It was quite accidental. Nobody asked any questions, I promise you. Would you like to tell me about it? Then I don't think any questions will need to be asked at all, from anyone else."

"The police . . . ," he said doubtfully, on a sob. "They came before. I refused to say anything, and they went away."

"Whatever you tell me will be in confidence."

"I've been such a fool. I'd like to tell someone, really."

I pictured the strung-up, guilt-ridden weeks he'd endured, and the crying fit became not only understandable but inevitable.

"It was the letter, you see," he said, sniffling softly. "The letter William began to write to me, though he never sent it. I found it in a whole trunk of stuff that was left when he . . . killed himself. I was in Sarawak then, you know, and they sent me a cable. It was a shock . . . one's only brother doing such a . . . a terrible thing. He was younger than me. Seven years. We weren't very close, except when we were children. I wish . . . but it's too late now. Anyway, when I came home I fetched all his stuff round from where it had been stored and put it up in the attic here, all his racing books and things. I didn't know what to do with them, you see. I wasn't interested in them, but it seemed . . . I don't know . . . I couldn't just burn them. It was months before I bothered to sort them out, and then I found the letter. . . ." His voice faltered and he looked at me appealingly, wanting to be forgiven.

"Kitty and I had found my pension didn't go anywhere near as far as we'd expected. Everything is so terribly expensive. The rates . . . we decided we'd have to sell the house again though we'd only just bought it, and Kitty's family are all close. And then . . . I thought . . . perhaps I could sell the letter instead."

"And you got threats instead of money," I said.

"Yes. It was the letter itself which gave me the idea." He chewed his mustache.

"And now you no longer have it," I said matter-of-factly, as if I knew for certain and wasn't guessing. "When you were first threatened you thought you could still sell the letter if Hunt Radnor kept you safe, and then you got more frightened and gave up the letter, and then canceled the protection because the threats had stopped."

He nodded unhappily. "I gave them the letter because that man was shot. . . . I didn't realize anything like that would happen. I was horrified. It was terrible. I hadn't thought it could be so dangerous, just selling a letter. . . . I wish I'd never found it. I wish William had never written it."

So did I, as it happened.

"What did the letter say?" I asked.

He hesitated, his fear showing. "It might cause more trouble. They might come back."

"They won't know you've told me," I pointed out. "How could they?"

"I suppose not." He looked at me, making up his mind. There's one thing about being small: no one is ever afraid of you. If I'd been big and commanding I don't think he'd have risked it. As it was, his face softened and relaxed and he threw off the last threads of reticence.

"I know it by heart," he said. "I'll write it down for you, if you like. It's easier than saying it."

I sat and waited while he fetched a ball-point pen and a pad of large writing paper and got on with his task. The sight of the letter materializing again in front of his eyes affected him visibly, but whether to fear or remorse or sorrow, I couldn't tell. He covered one side of the page, then tore it off the pad and shakily handed it over.

I read what he had written. I read it twice. Because of these short desperate sentences, I reflected unemotionally, I had come within spitting distance of St. Peter.

"That's fine," I said. "Thank you very much."

"I wish I'd never found it," he said again. "Poor William."

"Did you see this man?" I asked, indicating the letter as I put it away in my wallet.

"No, I wrote to him . . . he wasn't hard to find."

"And how much did you ask for?"

Shamefaced, he muttered, "Five thousand pounds."

Five thousand pounds had been wrong, I thought. If he'd asked fifty thousand, he might have had a chance. But five thousand didn't put him among the big-power boys, it just revealed his mediocrity. No wonder he had been stamped on, fast.

"What happened next?" I asked.

"A big man came for the letter, about four o'clock one afternoon. It was awful. I asked him for the money and he just laughed in my face and pushed me into a chair. No money, he said, but if I didn't hand over the letter at once he'd . . . he'd teach me a thing or two. That's what he said, teach me a thing or two. I explained that I had put the letter in my box at the bank and that the bank was closed and that I couldn't get it until the next morning. He said that he would come to the bank with me the next day, and then he went away."

"And you rang up the agency almost at once? Yes. What made you choose Hunt Radnor?"

He looked surprised. "It was the only one I knew about. Are there any others? I mean, most people have heard of Hunt Radnor, I should think."

"I see. So Hunt Radnor sent you a bodyguard, but the big man wouldn't give up."

"He kept telephoning . . . then your man suggested setting a trap in his office, and in the end I agreed. Oh, I shouldn't have let him, I was such a fool. I knew all the time, you see, who was threatening me, but I couldn't tell your agency because I'd have to admit I'd tried to get money . . . illegally."

"Yes. Well, there's only one more thing. What was he like, the man who came and threatened you?"

Brinton didn't like even the memory of him. "He was very strong. Hard. When he pushed me it was like a wall. I'm not . . . I mean, I've never been good with my fists, or anything like that. If he'd started hitting me I couldn't have stopped him."

"I'm not blaming you for not standing up to him," I pointed out. "I just want to know what he looked like."

"Very big," he said vaguely. "Huge."

"I know it's several weeks ago now, but can't you possibly remember more than that? How about his hair? Anything odd about his face? How old? What class?"

He smiled for the first time, the sad wrinkles folding for a moment into some semblance of faded charm. If he'd never taken his first useless step into crime, I thought, he might still have been a nice gentle innocuous man, fading without rancor toward old age, troubled only by how to make a little pension go a long way. No tearing, destructive guilt.

"It's certainly easier when you ask questions like that. He was beginning to go bald, I remember now. And he had big blotchy freckles on the backs of his hands. It's difficult to know about his age. Not a youth, though; more than thirty, I think. What else did you ask? Oh yes, class. Working class, then."

"English?"

"Oh yes, not foreign. Sort of cockney, I suppose."

I stood up, thanked him, and began to take my leave. He said, begging me still for reassurance, "There won't be any more trouble?"

"Not from me or the agency."

"And the man who was shot?"

"Not from him either."

"I tried to tell myself it wasn't my fault . . . but I haven't been able to sleep. How could I have been such a fool? I shouldn't have let that young man set any trap. . . . I shouldn't have called in your agency . . . and it cost another chunk of our savings. . . . I ought never to have tried to get money for that letter."

"That's true, Mr. Brinton, you shouldn't. But what's done is done, and I don't suppose you'll start anything like that again."

"No, no," he said with pain. "I wouldn't. Ever. These last few weeks have been . . ." His voice died. Then he said more strongly, "We'll have to sell the house now. Kitty likes it here, of course. But what I've always wanted myself is a little bungalow by the sea."

When I reached the office I took out the disastrous letter and read it again, before adding it to the file. Being neither the original nor a photocopy, but only a reproduction from memory, it wasn't of the slightest use as evidence. In the elder Brinton's small tidy script, a weird contrast to the heartbroken contents, it ran:

> Dear Mervy, dear big brother,
>
> I wish you could help me, as you did when I was little. I have spent fifteen years building up Dunstable Racecourse, and a man called Howard Kraye is making me destroy it. I have to frame races which nobody likes. Very few horses come now, and the gate receipts are falling fast. This week I must see that the race-card goes to the printers too late, and the press-room telephones will all be out of order. There will be a terrible muddle. People must think I am mad. I can't escape him. He is paying me as well, but I must do as he says. I can't help my nature, you know that. He has found out about a boy I was living with, and I could be prosecuted. He wants the racecourse to sell for housing. Nothing can stop him getting it. My racecourse, I love it.
>
> I know I shan't send this letter. Mercy, I wish you were here. I haven't anyone else. Oh dear God, I can't go on much longer, I really can't.

At five to six that afternoon I opened the door of Zanna Martin's office. Her desk was facing me and so was she. She raised her head, recognized me, and looked back at me in a mixture of pride and embarrassment.

"I did it," she said. "If you didn't, I'll kill you."

She had combed her hair even further forward, so that it hung close round her face, but all the same one could see the disfigurement at first glance. I had forgotten, in the days since Friday, just how bad it was.

"I felt the same about you," I said, grinning.

"You really did keep your promise?"

"Yes, I did. All day Saturday and Sunday, most of yesterday and most of today, and very nasty it is, too."

She sighed with relief. "I'm glad you've come. I nearly gave it up this morning. I thought you wouldn't do it, and you'd never come back to see if I had, and that I was being a proper idiot."

"Well, I'm here," I said. "Is Mr. Bolt in?"

She shook her head. "He's gone home. I'm just packing up."

"Finished the envelopes?" I said.

"Envelopes? Oh, those I was doing when you were here before? Yes, they're all done."

"And filled and sent?"

"No, the leaflets haven't come back from the printers yet, much to Mr. Bolt's disgust. I expect I'll be doing them tomorrow."

She stood up, tall and thin, put on her coat and tied the scarf over her hair.

"Are you going anywhere this evening?" I asked.

"Home," she said decisively.

"Come out to dinner," I suggested.

"Aunty's legacy won't last long, the way you spend. I think Mr. Bolt has already invested your money. You'd better save every penny until after settlement day."

"Coffee, then, and the flicks?"

"Look," she said hesitantly, "I sometimes buy a hot chicken on my way home. There's a fish-and-chips shop next to the station that sells them. Would you . . . would you like to come and help me eat it? In return, I mean, for Friday night."

"I'd enjoy that," I said, and was rewarded by a pleased, half-incredulous laugh.

"Really?"

"Really."

As before, we went to Finchley by underground, but this time Miss Martin sat boldly where her whole face showed. To try to match her fortitude, I rested my elbow on the seat arm between us. She looked at my hand and then at my face, gratefully, almost as if we were sharing an adventure.

As we emerged from the tube station she said, "You know, it makes a great deal of difference if one is accompanied by a man, even—" she stopped abruptly.

"Even," I finished, smiling, "if he is smaller than you and also damaged."

"Oh dear . . . and much younger, as well." Her real eye looked at me with rueful amusement. The glass one stared stonily ahead. I was getting used to it again.

"Let me buy the chicken," I said, as we stopped outside the shop. The smell of hot chips mingled with diesel fumes from a passing lorry. Civilization, I thought. Delightful.

"Certainly not." Miss Martin was firm and bought the chicken herself. She came out with it wrapped in newspaper. "I got a few chips and a packet of peas," she said.

"And I," I said firmly, as we came to an off-license, "am getting some brandy." What chips and peas would do to my digestion I dared not think.

We walked round to the house with the parcels and went through into her room. She moved with a light step.

"In that cupboard over there," she said, pointing, as she peeled off her coat and scarf, "there are some glasses and a bottle of sherry. Will you pour me some? I expect you prefer brandy, but have some sherry if you'd like. I'll just take these things into the kitchen and put them to keep hot."

While I unscrewed the bottles and poured the drinks I heard her lighting her gas stove and unwrapping the parcels. There was dead quiet as I walked across the room with her sherry, and when I reached the door I saw why. She held the chicken in its piece of greaseproof paper absently in one hand; the bag of chips lay open on the table with a box of peas beside it; and she was reading the newspaper they had all been wrapped in.

She looked up at me in bewilderment.

"You," she said. "It's you. This is you."

I looked down where her finger pointed. The fish-and-chips shop had wrapped up her chicken in the Sunday *Hemisphere*.

"Here's your sherry," I said, holding it out to her.

She put down the chicken and took the glass without appearing to notice it.

"Another Halley," she said. "It caught my eye. Of course I read it. And it's your picture, and it even refers to your hand. You are Sid Halley."

"That's right." There was no chance of denying it.

"Good heavens. I've known about you for years. Read about you. I saw you on television, often. My father loved watching the racing, we always had it on when he was alive—" She broke off and then said with increased puzzlement, "Why on earth did you say your name was John and that you worked in a shop? Why did you come to see Mr. Bolt? I don't understand."

"Drink your sherry, put your chicken in the oven before it freezes and I'll tell you." There was nothing else to do: I didn't want to risk her brightly passing on the interesting tidbit of news to her employer.

Without demur she put the dinner to heat, came to sit on the sofa, opposite to where I apprehensively waited in an armchair, and raised her eyebrows in expectation.

"I don't work in a shop," I admitted. "I am employed by a firm called Hunt Radnor Associates."

Like Brinton, she had heard of the agency. She stiffened her whole body and began to frown. As casually as I could, I told her about Kraye and the Seabury shares; but she was no fool and she went straight to the heart of things.

"You suspect Mr. Bolt too. That's why you went to see him."

"Yes, I'm afraid so."

"And me? You took me out simply and solely to find out about him?" Her voice was bitter.

I didn't answer at once. She waited, and somehow her calmness was more piercing than tears or temper could have been. She asked so little of life.

At last I said, "I went to Bolt's office as much to take out his secretary as to see Bolt himself, yes."

The peas boiled over, hissing loudly. She stood up slowly. "At least that's honest."

She went into the tiny kitchen and turned out the gas under the saucepan.

I said, "I came to your office this afternoon because I wanted to look at those leaflets Bolt is sending to Seabury shareholders. You told me at once that they hadn't come from the printers. I didn't need to accept your invitation to supper after that. But I'm here."

She stood in the kitchen doorway, holding herself straight with an all too apparent effort.

"I suppose you lied about that too," she said in a quiet rigidly controlled voice, pointing to my arm. "Why? Why did you play such a cruel game with me? Surely you could have got your information without that. Why did you make me change my desk round? I suppose you were laughing yourself sick all day Saturday thinking about it."

I stood up. Her hurt was dreadful.

I said, "I went to Kempton races on Saturday."

She didn't move.

"I kept my promise."

She made a slight gesture of disbelief.

"I'm sorry," I said helplessly.

"Yes. Good night, Mr. Halley. Good night."

I went.

11

RADNOR HELD a Seabury conference the next morning, Wednesday, consisting of himself, Dolly, Chico and me; the result, chiefly, of my having the previous afternoon finally wrung grudging permission from Lord Hagbourne to arrange a twenty-four-hour guard at Seabury for the coming Thursday, Friday and Saturday.

The bulldozing had been accomplished without trouble, and a call to the course that morning had established that the tan was arriving in regular lorry loads and was being spread. Racing, bar any last-minute accidents, was now certain. Even the weather was cooperating. The glass was rising; the forecast was dry, cold and sunny.

Dolly proposed a straight patrol system, and Radnor was inclined to agree. Chico and I had other ideas.

"If anyone intended to sabotage the track," Dolly pointed out, "they would be frightened off by a patrol. Same thing if they were planning something in the stands themselves."

Radnor nodded. "Safest way of making sure racing takes place. I suppose we'll need at least four men to do it properly."

I said, "I agree that we need a patrol tonight, tomorrow night and Friday night, just to play safe. But tomorrow, when the course will be more or less deserted . . . what we need is to pinch them at it, not frighten them off. There's no evidence yet that could be used in a court of law. If we could catch them in mid-sabotage, so to speak, we'd be much better off."

"That's right," said Chico. "Hide and pounce. Much better than scaring them away."

"I seem to remember," said Dolly with a grin, "that the last time you two set a trap the mouse shot the cheese."

"Oh God, Dolly, you slay me," said Chico, laughing warmly and for once accepting her affection.

Even Radnor laughed. "Seriously, though," he said, "I don't see how you can. A racecourse is too big. If you are hiding you can only see a small part of it. And surely if you show yourself your presence would act like any other patrol to stop anything plainly suspicious being done? I don't think it's possible."

"Um," I said. "But there's one thing I can still do better than anyone else in this agency."

"And what's that?" said Chico, ready to argue.

"Ride a horse."

"Oh," said Chico. "I'll give you that, chum."

"A horse," said Radnor thoughtfully. "Well, that's certainly an idea. Nobody's going to look suspiciously at a horse at a racecourse, I suppose. Mobile, too. Where would you get one?"

"From Mark Witney. I could borrow his hack. Seabury's his local course. His stables aren't many miles away."

"But can you still—?" began Dolly, and broke off. "Well, don't glare at me like that, all of you. I can't ride with two hands, let alone one."

"A man called Gregory Philips had his arm amputated very high up," I said, "and went on racing in point-to-points for years."

"Enough said," said Dolly. "How about Chico?"

"He can wear a pair of my jodhpurs. Protective coloring. And lean nonchalantly on the rails."

"Stick insects," said Chico cheerfully.

"That's what you want, Sid?" said Radnor.

I nodded. "Look at it from the worst angle: we haven't anything on Kraye that will stand up. We might not find Smith, the tanker driver, and even if we do, he has everything to lose by talking and nothing to gain. When the racecourse stables burned down a year ago, we couldn't prove it wasn't an accident; an illicit cigarette end. Stable lads do smoke, regardless of bans.

"The so-called drain which collapsed—we don't know if it was dug a day, a week, or six weeks before it did its work. That letter William Brinton of Dunstable wrote to his brother, it's only a copy from memory that we've got, no good at all for evidence. All it proves, to our own satisfaction, is that Kraye is capable of anything. We can't show it to Lord Hagbourne, because I obtained it in confidence, and he still isn't a hundred per cent convinced that Kraye has done more than buy shares. As I see it, we've just got to give the enemy a chance to get on with their campaign."

"You think they will, then?"

"It's awfully likely, isn't it? This year there isn't another Seabury meeting until February. A three months' gap. And if I read it right, Kraye is in a hurry now because of the political situation. He won't want to spend fifty thousand buying Seabury and then find building land has been nationalized overnight. If I were him, I'd want to clinch the deal and sell to a developer as quickly as possible. According to the photographs of the share transfers, he already holds twenty-three per cent of the shares. This is almost certainly enough to swing the sale of the company if it comes to a vote. But he's greedy. He'll want more. But he'll only want more if he can get it soon. Waiting for February is too risky. So yes, I do think if we give him a chance that he will organize some more damage this week."

"It's a risk," said Dolly. "Suppose something dreadful happens and we neither prevent it nor catch anyone doing it?"

They kicked it round among the three of them for several more minutes, the pros and cons of the straight patrols versus cat and mouse. Finally Radnor turned back to me and said, "Sid?"

"It's your agency," I said seriously. "It's your risk."

"But it's your case. It's still your case. You must decide."

I couldn't understand him. It was all very well for him to have given me a free hand so far, but this wasn't the sort of decision I would have ever expected him to pass on.

Still . . . "Chico and I, then," I said. "We'll go alone tonight and stay all day tomorrow. I don't think we'll let even Captain Oxon know we're there. Certainly not the foreman, Ted Wilkins, or any of the other men. We'll come in from the other side from the stands, and I'll borrow the horse for mobility. Dolly can arrange official patrol guards with Oxon for tomorrow night—suggest he gives them a warm room, Dolly. He ought to have the central heating on by then."

"Friday and Saturday?" asked Radnor, noncommittally.

"Full guards, I guess. As many as Lord Hagbourne will sub for. The race-going crowds make cat-and-mouse impossible."

"Right," said Radnor, decisively. "That's it, then."

When Dolly, Chico and I had got as far as the door he said, "Sid, you wouldn't mind if I had another look at those photographs? Send Jones-boy down with them if you're not needing them."

"Sure," I agreed. "I've pored over them till I know them by heart. I bet you'll spot something at once that I've missed."

"It often works that way," he said, nodding.

The three of us went back to the Racing Section, and via the switchboard I traced Jones-boy, who happened to be in Missing Persons. While he was on his way down I flipped through the packet of photographs yet again. The share transfers, the summary with the list of bank accounts, the letters from Bolt, the ten-pound notes, and the two sheets of dates, initials and figures from the very bottom of the attaché case. It had been clear all along that these last were lists either of receipts or expenditures, but by now I was certain they were the latter. A certain W.L.B. had received regular sums of fifty pounds a month for twelve months, and the last date for W.L.B. was four days before William Leslie Brinton, clerk of Dunstable Racecourse, had taken the quickest way out. Six hundred pounds and a threat; the price of a man's soul.

Most of the other initials meant nothing to me, except the last one, J.R.S., which looked as if they could be the tanker driver's. The first entry for J.R.S., for one hundred pounds, was dated the day before the tanker overturned at Seabury, the day before Kraye went to Aynsford for the weekend.

In the next line, the last of the whole list, a further sum of one hundred and fifty pounds was entered against J.R.S. The date of this was that of the following Tuesday, three days before I had taken the photographs. Smith had packed up and vanished from his job and his digs on that Tuesday.

Constantly recurring among the other varying initials were two Christian names, Leo and Fred. Each of these was on the regular payroll, it seemed. Either Leo or Fred, I guessed, had been the big man who had visited the frightened Mervyn Brinton. Either Leo or Fred was the "big chap" who had sent Andrews with a gun to Cromwell Road.

I had a score to settle with either Leo or Fred.

Jones-boy came in for the photographs. I tapped them together back into their box and gave them to him.

"Where, you snotty-nosed little coot, is our coffee?" said Chico rudely.

We had been downstairs when Jones-boy did his rounds.

"Coots are bald," observed Dolly coyly, eyeing Jones-boy's luxuriant locks.

Jones-boy unprintably told Chico where he could find his coffee.

Chico advanced a step, saying, "You remind me of the people sitting on the walls of Jerusalem." He had been raised in a church orphanage, after all.

Jones-boy knew the more basic bits of Isaiah. He said callously, "You did it on the doorstep of Barnes cop shop, I believe."

Chico furiously lashed out a fist to Jones-boy's head. Jones-boy jumped back, laughed insultingly, and the box he was holding flew high out of his hand, opening as it went.

"Stop it you two, damn you," shouted Dolly, as the big photographs floated down onto her desk and onto the floor.

"Babes in the wood," remarked Jones-boy, in great good humor from having got the best of the slinging match. He helped Dolly and me pick up the photographs, shuffled them back into the box in no sort of order, and departed grinning.

"Chico," said Dolly severely, "you ought to know better."

"The bossy-mother routine bores me sick," said Chico violently.

Dolly bit her lip and looked away. Chico stared at me defiantly, knowing very well he had started the row and was in the wrong.

"As one bastard to another," I said mildly, "pipe down."

Not being able to think of a sufficiently withering reply fast enough Chico merely scowled and walked out of the room. The show was over. The office returned to normal. Typewriters clattered, someone used the tape recorder, someone else the telephone. Dolly sighed and began to draw up her list for Seabury. I sat and thought about Leo. Or Fred. Unproductively.

After a while I ambled upstairs to Bona Fides, where the usual amount of telephone shouting filled the air. George, deep in a mysterious conversation about moth balls, saw me and shook his head. Jack Copeland, freshly attired in a patchily faded green sleeveless pullover, took time out between calls to say that they were sorry, but they'd made no progress with Kraye. He had, Jack said, very craftily covered his tracks about ten years back. They would keep digging, if I liked. I liked.

Up in Missing Persons Sammy said it was too soon for results on Smith.

When I judged that Mark Witney would be back in his house after exercising his second lot of horses, I rang him up and asked him to lend me his hack, a pensioned-off old steeplechaser of the first water.

"Sure," he said. "What for?"

I explained what for.

"You'd better have my horse box as well," he commented. "Suppose it pours with rain all night? Give you somewhere to keep dry, if you have the box."

"But won't you be needing it? The forecast says clear and dry anyway."

"I won't need it until Friday morning. I haven't any runners until Seabury. And only one there, I may say, in spite of being so close. The owners just won't have it. I have to go all the way to Banbury on Saturday. Damn silly with another much better course on my doorstep."

"What are you running at Seabury?"

He told me, at great and uncomplimentary length, about a half-blind, utterly stupid, one-paced habitual non-jumper with which he proposed to win the novice chase. Knowing him, I guessed he would. We agreed that Chico and I should arrive at his place about eight that evening, and I rang off.

After that I left the office, went across London by underground to Company House in the city, and asked for the files of Seabury Racecourse. In a numbered chair at a long table, surrounded by earnest men and women clerks pouring over similar files and making copious notes, I studied the latest list of investors. Apart from Kraye and his various aliases, which I now recognized on sight from long familiarity with the share-transfer photographs, there were no large blocks in single ownership. No one else held more than 3 per cent of the total: and as 3 per cent meant that roughly £2500 was lying idle and not bringing in a penny in dividends, it was easy to see why no one wanted a larger holding.

Fotherton's name was not on the list. Although this was not conclusive, because a nominee name like "Mayday Investments" could be anyone at all, I was more or less satisfied that Seabury's clerk was not gambling on Seabury's death. All the big share movements during the past year had been to Kraye, and no one else.

A few of the small investors, holding two hundred or so shares each, were people I knew personally. I wrote down their names and addresses, intending to let me see Bolt's circular letter when it arrived. Slower than via Zanna Martin, but surer.

My mind shied away from Miss Martin. I'd had a bad night thinking about her. Her and Jenny, both.

Back in the office I found it was the tail end of the lunch hour, with nearly all the desks still empty. Chico alone was sitting behind his, biting his nails.

"If we're going to be up all night," I suggested, "we'd better take the afternoon off for sleep."

"No need."

"Every need. I'm not as young as you."

"Poor old grandpa." He grinned suddenly, apologizing for the morning. "I can't help it. That Jones-boy gets on my wick."

"Jones-boy can look after himself. It's Dolly—"

"It's not my bloody fault she can't have kids."

"She wants kids like you want a mother."

"But I don't—" he began indignantly.

"Your own," I said flatly. "Like you want your own mother to have kept you and loved you. Like mine did."

"You had every advantage, of course."

"That's right."

He laughed. "Funny thing is I like old Dolly, really. Except for the hen bit."

"Who wouldn't?" I said amicably. "You can sleep on my sofa."

He sighed. "You're going to be less easy than Dolly to work for, I can see that."

"Eh?"

"Don't kid yourself, mate. Sir, I mean." He was lightly ironic.

The other inmates at the office drifted back, including Dolly, with whom I fixed for Chico to have the afternoon free. She was cool to him and unforgiving, which I privately thought would do them both good.

She said, "The first official patrol will start on the racecourse tomorrow at six A.M. Shall I tell them to find you and report?"

"No," I said defiantly. "I don't know where I'll be."

"It had better be the usual then," she said. "They can report to the old man at his home number when they start the job, and again at six A.M. when they go off and the next lot take over."

"And they'll ring him in between if anything happens?" I said.

"Yes. As usual."

"It's as bad as being a doctor," I said smiling.

Dolly nodded, and half to herself she murmured, "You'll find out."

Chico and I walked round to my flat, pulled the curtains, and did our best to sleep. I didn't find it easy at two-thirty in the afternoon: it was the time for racing, not rest. It seemed to me that I had barely drifted off when the telephone rang. I looked at my watch on the way to answer it in the sitting room and found it was only ten to five. I had asked for a call at six.

It was not the telephone exchange, however, it was Dolly.

"A message has come for you by hand, marked 'very urgent.' I thought you might want it before you go to Seabury."

"Who brought it?"

"A taxi driver."

"Shunt him round here, then."

"He's gone, I'm afraid."

"Who's the message from?"

"I've no idea. It's in a plain brown envelope, the size we use for interim reports."

"Oh, all right, I'll come back."

Chico had drowsily propped himself up on one elbow on the sofa.

"Go to sleep again," I said. "I've got to go and see something at the office. Won't be long."

When I reached the Racing Section again I found that whatever had come for me, something else had gone. The shaky lemon-colored table. I was deskless again.

"Sammy said he was sorry," explained Dolly, "but he has a new assistant and nowhere to park him."

"I had things in the drawer," I complained. Shades of Sammy's lunch, I thought.

"They're here," Dolly said, pointing to a corner of her desk. "There was only the Brinton file, a half bottle of brandy, and some pills. Also I found this on the floor." She held out a flat, crackly cellophane packet.

"The negatives of those photographs are in here," I said, taking it from her. "They were in the box, though."

"Until Jones-boy dropped it."

"Oh, yes." I put the packet of negatives inside the Brinton file and pinched a large rubber band from Dolly to snap round the outside.

"How about that mysterious very urgent message?" I asked.

Dolly silently and considerately slit open the envelope in question, drew out the single sheet of paper it contained and handed it to me. I unfolded it and stared at it in disbelief.

It was a circular, headed Charing, Street and King Stockbrokers, dated with the following day's date, and it ran:

> Dear Sir or Madam,
>
> We have various clients wishing to purchase small parcels of shares in the following lists of minor companies. If you are considering selling your interests in any of these, we would be grateful if you would get in touch with us. We would assure you of a good fair price, based on today's quotation.

There followed a list of about thirty companies, of which I had heard of only one. Tucked in about three-quarters of the way down was Seabury Racecourse.

I turned the page over. Zanna Martin had written on the back in a hurried hand.

> This is only going to Seabury shareholders. Not to anyone owning shares in the other companies. The leaflets came from the printers this morning, and are to be posted tomorrow. I hope it is what you want. I'm sorry about last night.
>
> Z.M.

"What is it?" asked Dolly.

"A free pardon," I said lightheartedly, slipping the circular inside the Brinton file along with the negatives. "Also confirmation that Ellis Bolt is not on the side of the angels."

"You're a nut," she said. "And take these things off my desk. I haven't room for them."

I put the pills and brandy in my pocket and picked up the Brinton file.

"Is that better?"

"Thank you, yes."

"So long, then, my love. See you on Friday."

On the walk back to the flat I decided suddenly to go and see Miss Martin. I went straight down to the garage for my car without going up and waking Chico again, and made my way eastward to the city for the second time that day. The rush-hour traffic was so bad that I was afraid I would miss her, but in fact she was ten minutes late in leaving the office and I caught her up just before she reached the underground station.

"Miss Martin," I called. "Would you like a lift home?"

She turned round in surprise.

"Mr. Halley!"

"Hop in."

She hopped. That is to say, she opened the door, picked up the Brinton file which was lying on the passenger seat, sat down, tidily folded her coat over her knees, and pulled the door shut again. The bad side of her face was toward me, and she was very conscious of it. The scarf and the hair were gently pulled forward.

I took a pound of ten-shilling notes out of my pocket and gave them to her. She took them smiling.

"The taxi man told our switchboard girl you gave him that for bringing the leaflet. Thank you very much." I swung out through the traffic and headed for Finchley.

She answered obliquely. "That wretched chicken is still in the oven, stone cold. I just turned the gas out yesterday, after you'd gone."

"I wish I could stay this evening instead," I said, "but I've got a job on for the agency."

"Another time," she said tranquilly. "Another time, perhaps. I understand that you couldn't tell me at first who you worked for, because you didn't know whether I was an . . . er, an accomplice of Mr. Bolt's, and afterwards you didn't tell me for fear of what actually happened, that I would be upset. So that's that."

"You are generous."

"Realistic, even if a bit late."

We went a little way in silence. Then I asked, "What would happen to the shares Kraye owns if it were proved he was sabotaging the company? If he were convicted, I mean. Would his shares be confiscated, or would he still own them when he came out of jail?"

"I've never heard of anyone's shares being confiscated," she said, sounding interested. "But surely that's a long way in the future?"

"I wish I knew. It makes a good deal of difference to what I should do now."

"How do you mean?"

"Well . . . an easy way to stop Kraye buying too many more shares would be to tell the racing press and the financial press that a take-over is being attempted. The price would rocket. But Kraye already holds twenty-three per cent, and if the law couldn't take it away from him, he would either stick to that and vote for a sellout, or if he got cold feet he could unload his shares at the higher price and still make a fat profit. Either way, he'd be sitting pretty financially, in jail or out. And either way Seabury would be built on."

"I suppose this sort of thing's happened before?"

"Take-overs, yes, several. But only one other case of sabotage. At Dunstable. Kraye again."

"Haven't any courses survived a take-over bid?"

"Only Sandown, publicly. I don't know of any others, but they may have managed it in secrecy."

"How did Sandown do it?"

"The local council did it for them. Stated loudly that planning permission would not be given for building. Of course the bid collapsed then."

"It looks as though the only hope for Seabury, in that case, is that the council there will act in this same way. I'd try a strong lobby, if I were you."

"You're quite a girl, Miss Martin," I said smiling. "That's a very good idea. I'll go and dip a toe into the climate of opinion at the Town Hall."

She nodded approvingly. "No good lobbying against the grain. Much better to find out which way people are likely to move before you start pushing!"

Finchley came into sight. I said, "You do realize, Miss Martin, that if I am successful at my job, you will lose yours?"

She laughed. "Poor Mr. Bolt. He's not at all bad to work for. But don't worry about my job. It's easy for an experienced stockbroker's secretary to get a good one, I assure you."

I stopped at her gate, looking at my watch. "I'm afraid I can't come in. I'm already going to be a bit late."

She opened the door without ado and climbed out. "Thank you for coming at all." She smiled, shut the door crisply, and waved me away.

I drove back to my flat as fast as I could, fuming slightly at the traffic. It wasn't until I switched off the engine down in the garage and leaned over to pick it up that I discoverd the Brinton file wasn't there. And then remembered Miss Martin holding it on her lap during the journey, and me hustling her out of the car. Miss Martin still had Brinton's file. I hadn't time to go back for it, and I couldn't ring her up because I didn't know the name of the owner of the house she lived in. But surely, I reassured myself, surely the file would be safe enough where it was until Friday.

12

CHICO AND I sat huddled together for warmth in some gorse bushes and watched the sun rise over Seabury Racecourse. It had been a cold clear night with a tingle of naught degrees centigrade about it, and we were both shivering.

Behind us, among the bushes and out of sight, Revelation, one-time winner of the Cheltenham Gold Cup, was breakfasting on meager patches of grass. We could hear the scrunch when he bit down close to the roots, and the faint chink of the bridle as he ate. For some time Chico and I had been resisting the temptation to relieve him of his nice warm rug.

"They might try something now," said Chico hopefully. "First light, before anyone's up."

Nothing had moved in the night, we were certain of that. Every hour I had ridden Revelation at a careful walk round the whole of the track itself, and Chico had made a plimsollshod inspection of the stands at one with the shadows. There had been no one about. Not a sound but the stirring breeze, not a glimmer of light but from the stars and a waning moon.

Our present spot, chosen as the sky lightened and some concealment became necessary, lay at the furthest spot from the stands, at the bottom of the semicircle of track cut off by the road which ran across the course. Scattered bushes and scrub filled the space between the track and boundary fence, enough to shield us from all but closely prying eyes. Behind the boundary fence were the little back gardens of the first row of bungalows. The sun rose bright and yellow away to our left and the birds sang around us. It was half past seven.

"It's going to be a lovely day," said Chico.

At ten past nine there was some activity up by the stands and the tractor rolled onto the course pulling a trailer. I unshipped my race glasses, balanced them on my bent-up knees, and took a look. The trailor was loaded with what I guessed were hurdles, and was accompanied by three men on foot.

I handed the glasses to Chico without comment, and yawned.

"Lawful occasions," he remarked, bored.

We watched the tractor and trailer lumber slowly round the far end of the course, pause to unload, and return for a refill. On its second trip it came close enough for us to confirm that it was in fact the spare hurdles that were being dumped in position, four or five at each flight, ready to be used if any were splintered in the races. We watched for a while in silence. Then I said slowly, "Chico, I've been blind."

"Huh?"

"The tractor," I said. "The tractor. Under our noses all the time."

"So?"

"So the sulfuric acid tanker was pulled over by a tractor. No complicated lifting gear necessary. Just a couple of ropes or chains slung over the top of the tanker and fastened round the axles. Then you unscrew the hatches and stand well clear. Someone drives the tractor at full power up the course, over goes the tanker and out pours the juice. And Bob's your uncle!"

"Every racecourse has a tractor," said Chico thoughtfully.

"That's right."

"So no one would look twice at a tractor on a racecourse. Quite. No one would remark on any tracks it left. No one would mention seeing one on the road. So if you're right, and I'd say you certainly are, it wouldn't necessarily have been that tractor, the racecourse tractor, which was used."

"I'll bet it was, though." I told Chico about the photographed initials and payments. "Tomorrow I'll check the initials of all the workmen here from Ted Wilkins downwards against that list. Any one of them might have been paid just to leave the tractor on the course, lying handy. The tanker went over on the evening before the meeting, like today. The tractor would have been in use then too. Warm and full of fuel. Nothing easier. And afterwards, straight on up the racecourse, and out of sight."

"It was dusk," agreed Chico. "As long as no one came along the road in the minutes it took to unhitch the ropes or chains afterwards, they were clear. No traffic diversions, no detours, nothing."

We sat watching the tractor lumbering about, gloomily realizing we couldn't prove a word of it.

"We'll have to move," I said presently. "There's a hurdle just along there, about fifty yards away, where those wings are. They'll be down here over the road soon."

We adjourned with Revelation back to the horse box half a mile away down the road to the west and took the opportunity to eat our own breakfast. When we had finished Chico went back first, strolling along confidently in my jodhpurs, boots and polo-necked jersey, the complete horseman from head to foot. He had never actually sat on a horse in his life.

After a while I followed on Revelation. The men had brought the hurdles down into the semicircular piece of track and had laid them in place. They were now moving further away up the course, unloading the next lot. Unremarked, I rode back to the bushes and dismounted. Of Chico there was no sign for another half hour, and then he came whistling across from the road with his hands in his pockets.

When he reached me he said, "I had another look round the stands. Rotten security, here. No one asked me what I was doing. There are some women cleaning here and there, and some are working in the stable block, getting the lads' hostel ready, things like that. I said good morning to them, and they said good morning back." He was disgusted.

"Not much scope for saboteurs," I said morosely. "Cleaners in the stands and workmen on the course."

"Dusk tonight," nodded Chico. "That's the most likely time now."

The morning ticked slowly away. The sun rose to its low November zenith and shone straight into our eyes. I passed the time by taking a photograph of Revelation and another of Chico. He was fascinated by the tiny camera and said he couldn't wait to get one like it. Eventually I put it back into my breeches pocket, and shading my eyes against the sun took my hundredth look up the course.

Nothing. No men, no tractor. I looked at my watch. One o'clock. Lunch hour. More time passed.

Chico picked up the race glasses and swept the course.

"Be careful," I said idly. "Don't look at the sun with those. You'll hurt your eyes."

"Do me a favor."

I yawned, feeling the sleepless night catch up.

"There's a man on the course," he said. "One. Just walking."

He handed me the glasses and I took a look. He was right. One man was walking alone across the racecourse; not round the track but straight across the rough grass in the middle. He was too far away for his features to be distinguishable and in any case he was wearing a fawn duffel coat with the hood up. I shrugged and lowered the glasses. He looked harmless enough.

With nothing better to do we watched him reach the far side, duck under the rails, and move along until he was standing behind one of the fences with only his head and shoulders in our sight.

Chico remarked that he should have attended to nature in the gents' before he left the stands. I yawned again, smiling at the same time. The man went on standing behind the fence.

"What on earth is he doing?" said Chico, after about five minutes.

"He isn't doing anything," I said, watching through the glasses. "He's just standing there looking this way."

"Do you think he's spotted us?"

"No, he couldn't. He hasn't any binocs, and we are in the bushes."

Another five minutes passed in inactivity.

"He must be doing *something,*" said Chico, exasperated.

"Well, he isn't," I said.

Chico took a turn with the glasses. "You can't see a damn thing against the sun," he complained. "We should have camped up the other end."

"In the car park?" I suggested mildly. "The road to the stables and the main gates runs along the other end. There isn't a scrap of cover."

"He's got a flag," said Chico suddenly. "Two flags. One in each hand. White on the left, orange on the right. He seems to be waving them alternately. He's just some silly nit of a racecourse attendant practicing calling up the ambulance and the vet." He was disappointed.

I watched the flags waving, first white, then orange, then white, then orange, with a gap of a second or two between each wave. It certainly wasn't any form of recognizable signaling: nothing like semaphore. They were, as Chico had said, quite simply the flags used after a fall in a race: white to summon the ambulance for the jockey, orange to get attention for a horse. He didn't keep it up very long. After about eight waves altogether he stopped, and in a moment or two began to walk back across the course to the stands.

"Now what," said Chico, "do you think all that was in aid of?"

He swept the glasses all around the whole racecourse yet again. "There isn't a soul about except him and us."

"He's probably been standing by a fence for months waiting for a chance to wave his flags, and no one has been injured anywhere near him. In the end, the temptation proved too much."

I stood up and stretched, went through the bushes to Revelation, undid the halter with which he was tethered to the bushes, unbuckled the surcingle and pulled off his rug.

"What are you doing?" said Chico.

"The same as the man with the flags. Succumbing to an intolerable temptation. Give me a leg up." He did what I asked, but hung on to the reins.

"You're mad. You said in the night that they might let you do it after this meeting, but they'd never agree to it before. Suppose you smash the fences?"

"Then I'll be in almighty trouble," I agreed. "But here I am on a super jumper looking at a heavenly course on a perfect day, with everyone away at lunch." I grinned "Leave go."

Chico took his hand away. "It's not like you," he said doubtfully.

"Don't take it to heart," I said flippantly, and touched Revelation into a walk.

At this innocuous pace the horse and I went out into the track and proceeded in the direction of the stands. Counter-clockwise, the way the races were run. Still at a walk we reached the road and went across its uncovered Tarmac surface. On the far side of the road lay the enormous dark brown patch of tan, spread thick and firm where the burnt turf had been bulldozed away. Horses would have no difficulty in racing over it.

Once on the other side, on the turf again, Revelation broke into a trot. He knew where he was. Even with no crowds and no noise the fact of being on a familiar racecourse was exciting him. His ears were pricked, his step springy. At fourteen he had been already a year in retirement, but he moved beneath me like a four-year-old. He too, I guessed fancifully, was feeling the satanic tug of a pleasure about to be illicitly snatched.

Chico was right, of course. I had no business at all to be riding on the course so soon before a meeting. It was indefensible. I ought to know better. I did know better. I eased Revelation gently into a canter.

There were three flights of hurdles and three fences more or less side-by-side up the straight, and the water jump beyond that. As I wasn't sure that Revelation would jump the fences in cold blood on his own (many horses won't), I set him at the hurdles.

Once he had seen these and guessed my intention I doubt if I could have stopped him, even if I'd wanted to. He fairly ate up the first flight and stretched out eagerly for the second. After that I gave him a choice, and of the two obstacles lying ahead, he opted for the fence. It didn't seem to bother him that he was on his own. They were excellent fences and he was a Gold Cup winner, born and bred for the job and being given an unexpected, much-missed treat. He flew the fence with all his former dash and skill.

As for me, my feelings were indescribable. I'd sat on a horse a few times since I'd given up racing, but never found an opportunity of doing more than riding out quietly at morning exercise with Mark's string. And here I was, back in my old place, doing again what I'd ached for in the two and a half years. I grinned with irrepressible joy and got Revelation to lengthen his stride for the water jump.

He took it with feet to spare. Perfect. There were no irate shouts from the stands on my right, and we swept away on round the top bend of the course, fast and free. Another fence at the end of the bend—Revelation floated it—and five more stretching away down the far side. It was at the third of these, the open ditch, that the man had been standing and waving the flags.

It's an undoubted fact that emotions pass from rider to horse, and Revelation was behaving with the same reckless exhilaration which gripped me, so after two spectacular leaps over the next two fences we both sped onward with arms open to fate. There ahead was the guard rail, the four-foot-wide open ditch and the four-foot-six fence rising on the far side of it. Revelation, knowing all about it, automatically put himself right to jump.

It came, the blinding flash in the eyes, as we soared into the air. White, dazzling, brain-shattering light, splintering the day into a million fragments and blotting out the world in a blaze as searing as the sun.

I felt Revelation falling beneath me and rolled instinctively, my eyes open and quite unable to see. Then there was the rough crash on the turf and the return of vision from light to blackness and up through gray to normal sight.

I was on my feet before Revelation, and I still had hold of the reins. He struggled up, bewildered and staggering, but apparently unhurt. I pulled him forward into an unwilling trot to make sure of his legs, and was relieved to find them whole and sound. It only remained to remount as quickly as possible, and this was infuriatingly difficult. With two hands I could have jumped up easily; as it was I scrambled untidily back into the saddle at the third attempt, having lost the reins altogether and bashed my stomach on the pommel of the saddle into the bargain. Revelation behaved very well, all things considered. He trotted only fifty yards or so in the wrong direction before I collected myself and the reins into a working position and turned him round. This time we by-passed the fence and all subsequent ones: I cantered him first down the side of the track, slowed to a trot to cross the road, and steered then not on round the bottom semicircle but off to the right, heading for where the boundary fence met the main London road.

Out of the corner of my eye I saw Chico running in my direction across the rough grass. I waved him toward me with a sweep of the arm and reined in and waited for him where our paths converged.

"I thought you said you could bloody well ride," he said, scarcely out of breath from the run.

"Yeah," I said, "I thought so once."

He looked at me sharply. "You fell off. I was watching. You fell off like a baby."

"If you were watching . . . the horse fell, if you don't mind. There's a distinction. Very important to jockeys." Traffic Whizzed along the London road only ten yards away.

"Nuts," he said. "You fell off."

"Come on," I said, walking Revelation toward the boundary fence. "There's something to find," I told Chico what. "In one of those bungalows, I should think. At a window or on the roof, or in a garden."

"Sods," said Chico forcefully. "The dirty sods."

I agreed with him.

It wasn't very difficult, because it had to be within a stretch of only a hundred yards or so. We went methodically along the boundary fence toward the London road, stopping to look carefully into every separate little garden, and at every separate little house. A fair number of inquisitive faces looked back.

Chico saw it first, propped into a high leafless branch of a tree growing well back in the second-to-last garden. Traffic whizzed along the London road only ten yards ahead, and Revelation showed signs of wanting to retreat.

"Look," said Chico, pointing upward.

I looked, fighting a mild battle against the horse. It was five feet high, three feet wide, and polished to a spotless brilliance. A mirror.

"Sods," said Chico again.

I nodded, dismounted, led Revelation back to where the traffic no longer fretted him, and tied the reins to the fence. Then Chico and I walked along to the London road and round into the road of bungalows. Napoleon Close, it said. Napoleon wasn't *that* close, I reflected, amused.

We rang the door of the second bungalow. A man and a woman both came to the door to open it, elderly, gentle, inoffensive and inquiring.

I came straight to the point, courteously. "Do you know you have a mirror in your tree?"

"Don't be silly," said the woman, smiling as at an idiot. She had flat wavy gray hair and was wearing a sloppy black cardigan over a brown wool dress. No color sense, I thought.

"You'd better take a look," I suggested.

"It's not a mirror, you know," said the husband, puzzled. "It's a placard. One of those advertisement things."

"That's right," said his wife contrapuntally. "A placard."

"We agreed to lend our tree—"

"For a small sum, really . . . only our pension—"

"A man put up the framework—"

"He said he would be back soon with the poster—"

"A religious one, I believe. A good cause—"

"We wouldn't have done it otherwise—"

Chico interrupted. "I wouldn't have thought it was a good place for a poster. Your tree stands further back than the others. It isn't conspicuous."

"I did think—" began the man doubtfully, shuffling in his checked, woolly bedroom slippers.

"But if he was willing to pay rent for your particular tree, you didn't want to put him off," I finished. "An extra quid or two isn't something you want to pass on next door."

They wouldn't have put it so bluntly, but they didn't demur.

"Come and look," I said.

They followed me round along the narrow path beside their bungalow wall and into their own back garden. The tree stood halfway to the racecourse boundary fence, the sun slanting down through the leafless branches. We could see the wooden back of the mirror, and the ropes which fastened it to the tree trunk. The man and his wife walked round to the front, and their puzzlement increased.

"He said it was for a poster," repeated the man.

"Well," I said as matter-of-factly as I could, "I expect it is for a poster, as he said. But at the moment, you see, it is a mirror. And it's pointing straight out over the racecourse; and you know how mirrors reflect the sunlight? We just thought it might not be too safe, you know, if anyone got dazzled, so we wondered if you would mind us moving it?"

"Why, goodness," agreed the woman, looking with more awareness at our riding clothes, "no one could see the racing with light shining in their eyes."

"Quite. So would you mind if we turned the mirror round a bit?"

"I can't see that it would hurt, Dad," she said doubtfully.

He made a nondescript assenting movement with his hand, and Chico asked how the mirror had been put up in the tree in the first place. The man had brought a ladder with him, they said, and no, they hadn't one themselves. Chico shrugged, placed me beside the tree, put one foot on my thigh, one on my shoulder, and was up in the bare branches like a squirrel. The elderly couple's mouths sagged open.

"How long ago?" I asked. "When did the man put up the mirror?"

"This morning," said the woman, getting over the shock. "He came back just now, too, with another rope or something. That's when he said he'd be back with the poster."

So the mirror had been hauled up into the tree while Chico and I had been obliviously sitting in the bushes, and adjusted later when the sun was at the right angle in the sky. At two o'clock. The time, the next day, of the third race, the handicap steeplechase. Some handicap, I thought, a smash of light in the eyes.

White flag: a little bit to the left. Orange flag: a little bit to the right. No flag: dead on target.

Come back tomorrow afternoon and clap a religious poster over the glass as soon as the damage was done, so that even the most thorough search wouldn't reveal a mirror. Just another jinx on Seabury Racecourse.

Dead horses, crushed and trampled jockeys. A jinx. Send my horses somewhere else, Mr. Witney, something always goes wrong at Seabury.

I was way out in one respect. The religious poster was not due to be put in place the following day.

13

"I THINK," I said gently to the elderly couple, "that it might be better if you went indoors. We will explain to the man who is coming what we are doing to his mirror."

Dad glanced up the path toward the road, put his arm protectively round his wife's woolly shoulders, and said gratefully, "Er . . . yes . . . yes."

They shuffled rapidly through the back door into the bungalow just as a large man carrying an aluminum folding ladder and a large rolled-up paper came barging through their front gate. There had been the squeak of his large, plain, dark blue van stopping, the hollow crunch of the handbrake being forcibly applied, the slam of the door and the scrape of the ladder being unloaded. Chico in the tree crouched quite still, watching.

I was standing with my back to the sun, but it fell full on the big man's face when he came into the garden. It wasn't the sort of face one would naturally associate with religious posters. He was a cross between a heavyweight wrestler and Mount Vesuvius. Craggy, brutally strong and not far off erupting.

He came straight toward me across the grass, dropped the ladder beside him, and said inquiringly, "What goes on?"

"The mirror," I said, "comes down."

His eyes narrowed in sudden awareness and his body stiffened. "There's a poster going over it," he began quite reasonably, lifting the paper roll. Then with a rush the lava burst out, the paper flew wide, and the muscles bunched into action.

It wasn't much of a fight. He started out to hit my face, changed his mind, and ploughed both fists in below the belt. It was quite a long way down for him. Doubling over in pain onto the lawn, I picked up the ladder, and gave him a swinging swipe behind the knees.

The ground shook with the impact. He fell on his side, his coat swinging open. I lunged forward, snatching at the pistol showing in the holster beside his ribs. It came loose, but he brushed me aside with an arm like a telegraph pole. I fell, sprawling. He rolled over into a crouch, picked up the gun from the grass and sneered down into my face. Then he stood up like a released spring and on the way with force and deliberation booted his toecap into my navel. He also clicked back the catch on his gun.

Up in the tree Chico yelled. The big man turned and took three steps toward him, seeing him for the first time. With a choice of targets, he favored the one still in a state to resist. The hand with the pistol pointed at Chico.

"Leo," I shouted. Nothing happened. I tried again.

"Fred!"

The big man turned his head a fraction back to me and Chico jumped down onto him from ten feet up.

The gun went off with a double crash and again the day flew apart in shining splintering fragments. I sat on the ground with my knees bent up, groaning quietly, cursing fluently, and getting on with my business.

Drawn by the noise, the inhabitants of the bungalows down the line came out into their back gardens and looked in astonishment over the fences. The elderly couple stood palely at their window, their mouths again open. The big man had too big an audience now for murder.

Chico was overmatched for size and nearly equaled in skill. He and the big man threw each other round a bit while I crept doubled up along the path into the front garden as far as the gate, but the battle was a foregone conclusion, bar the retreat.

He came alone, crashing up the path, saw me hanging on to the gate and half raised the gun. But there were people in the road now, and more people peering out of opposite windows. In scorching fury he whipped at my head with the barrel, and I avoided it by letting go of the gate and collapsing on the ground again. Behind the gate, with the bars nice and comfortingly between me and his boot.

He crunched across the pavement, slammed into the van, cut his cogs to ribbons and disappeared out onto the London road in a cloud of dust.

Chico came down the garden path staggering, with blood sloshing out of a cut eyebrow. He looked anxious and shaken.

"I thought you said you could bloody well fight," I mocked him.

He came to a halt beside me on his knees. "Blast you." He put his fingers to his forehead and winced at the result.

I grinned at him.

"You were running away," he said.

"Naturally."

"What have you got here?" He took the little camera out of my hand. "Don't tell me," he said, his face splitting into an unholy smile. "Don't tell me."

"It's what we came for, after all."

"How many?"

"Four of him. Two of the van."

"Sid, you slay me, you really do."

"Well," I said, "I feel sick." I rolled over and retched what was left of my breakfast onto the roots of the privet hedge. There wasn't any blood. I felt a lot better.

"I'll go and get the horse box," said Chico, "and pick you up."

"You'll do nothing of the sort," I said, wiping my mouth on a handkerchief. "We're going back into the garden. I want that bullet."

"It's halfway to Seabury," he protested, borrowing my handkerchief to mop the blood off his eyebrow.

"What will you bet?" I said. I used the gate again to get up, and after a moment or two was fairly straight. We presented a couple of reassuring grins to the audience, and retraced our way down the path into the back garden.

The mirror lay in sparkling pointed fragments all over the lawn.

"Pop up the tree and see if the bullet is there, in the wood. It smashed the mirror. It might be stuck up there. If not, we'll have to comb the grass."

Chico went up the aluminum ladder that time.

"Of all the luck," he called. "It's here." I watched him take a penknife out of his pocket and carefully cut away at a section just off-center of the backboard of the ex-mirror. He came down and held the little misshapen lump out to me on the palm of his hand. I put it carefully away in the small waist pockets of my breeches.

The elderly couple had emerged like tortoises from their bungalow. They were scared and puzzled, understandably. Chico offered to cut down the remains of the mirror, and did, but we left them to clear up the resulting firewood.

As an afterthought, however, Chico went across the garden and retrieved the poster from a soggy winter rosebed. He unrolled it and showed it to us, laughing.

BLESSED ARE THE MEEK, FOR THEY SHALL INHERIT THE EARTH.

"One of them," said Chico, "has a sense of humor."

Much against his wishes, we returned to our observation post in the scrubby gorse.

"Haven't you had enough?" he said crossly.

"The patrols don't get here till six," I reminded him. "And you yourself said that dusk would be the likely time for them to try something."

"But they've already done it."

"There's nothing to stop them from rigging up more than one booby trap," I pointed out. "Especially as that mirror thing wouldn't have been one hundred per cent reliable, even if we hadn't spotted it. It depended on the sun. Good weather forecast, I know, but weather forecasts are as reliable as a perished hot-water bottle. A passing cloud would have wrecked it. I would think they have something else in mind."

"Cheerful," he said resignedly. He led Revelation away along the road to stow him in the horse box, and was gone a long time.

When he came back he sat down beside me and said, "I went all round the stables. No one stopped me or asked what I was doing. Don't they have *any* security here? The cleaners have all gone home, but there's a woman cooking in the canteen. She said I was too early, to come back at half past six. There wasn't anyone about in the stands block except an old geezer with snuffles mucking about with the boiler."

The sun was lower in the sky and the November afternoon grew colder. We shivered a little and huddled inside our jerseys.

Chico said, "You guessed about the mirror before you set off round the course."

"It was a possibility, that's all."

"You could have ridden along the boundary fence, looking into the gardens like we did afterwards, instead of haring off over all those jumps."

I grinned faintly. "Yes. As I told you, I was giving in to temptation."

"Screwy. You must have known you'd fall."

"Of course I didn't. The mirror mightn't have worked very effectively. Anyway, it's better to test a theory in a practical way. And I just wanted to ride round there. I had a good excuse if I were hauled up for it. So I went. And it was grand. So shut up."

He laughed. "All right." Restlesly he stood up again and said he would make another tour. While he was gone I watched the racecourse with and without the binoculars, but not a thing moved on it.

He came back quietly and dropped down beside me.

"As before," he said.

"Nothing here, either."

He looked at me sideways. "Do you feel as bad as you look?"

"I shouldn't be surprised," I said. "Do you?"

He tenderly touched the area round his cut eyebrow. "Worse. Much worse. Soggy bad luck, his slugging away at your belly like that."

"He did it on purpose," I said idly, "and it was very informative."

"Huh?"

"It showed he knew who I was. He wouldn't have needed to have attacked us like that if we'd just been people come over from the racecourse to see if we could shift the mirror. But when he spoke to me he recognized me, and he knew I wouldn't be put off by any poster eyewash. And his sort don't mildly back down and retreat without paying you off for getting in their way. He just hit where he knew it would have most effect. I actually saw him think it."

"But how did he know?"

"It was he who sent Andrews to the office," I said. "He was the man Mervyn Brinton described: big, going a bit bald, freckles on the back of his hands, cockney accent. He was strong-arming Brinton, and he sent Andrews to get the letter that was supposed to be in the office. Well, Andrews knew me, and I knew him. He must have gone back and told our big friend Fred that he had shot me in the stomach. My death wasn't reported in the papers, so Fred knew I was still alive and would put the finger on Andrews at once. Andrews wasn't exactly a good risk to Fred, just a silly spiv with no sense, so Fred, I guess, marched him straight off to Epping Forest and left him for the birds. Who did a fair job, I'll give them that."

"Do you think," said Chico slowly, "that the gun Fred had today . . . is that why you wanted the bullet?"

I nodded. "That's right. I tried for the gun too, but no dice. If I'm going on with this sort of work, pal, you'll have to teach me a spot of judo."

He looked down doubtfully. "With that hand?"

"Invent a new sport," I said. "One-armed combat."

"I'll take you to the club," he said, smiling. "There's an old Jap there who'll find a way if anyone can."

"Good."

Up at the far end of the racecourse a horse box turned in off the main road and trundled along toward the stables. The first of the next day's runners had apparently arrived.

Chico went to have a look.

I sat on in fading daylight, watching nothing happen, hugging myself against the cold and the reawakened grinding ache in my gut, and thinking evil thoughts about Fred. Not Leo. Fred.

There were four of them, I thought. Kraye, Bolt, Fred and Leo.

I had met Kraye: he knew me only as Sid, a despised hanger-on in the home of a retired admiral he had met at his club and had spent a weekend with.

I had met Bolt: he knew me as John Halley, a shop assistant wanting to invest a gift from an aunt.

I had met Fred: he knew my whole name, and that I worked for the agency, and that I had turned up at Seabury.

I did not know if I had met Leo. But Leo might know *me*. If he had anything to do with racing, he definitely did.

It would be all right, I thought, as long as they did not connect all the Halleys and Sids too soon. But there was my wretched hand, which Kraye had pulled out of my pocket, which Fred could have seen in the garden, and which Leo, whoever he was, might have noticed almost anywhere in the last six days, thanks to my promise to Miss Martin. Miss Martin, who worked for Bolt. A proper merry-go-round, I thought wryly.

Chico materialized out of the dusk. "It was Ping Pong, running in the first tomorrow. All aboveboard," he said. "And nothing doing anywhere, stand or course. We might as well go."

It was well after five. I agreed, and got up stiffly.

"That Fred," said Chico, casually giving me a hand, "I've been thinking. I've seen him before, I'm certain. At race meetings. He's not a regular. Doesn't work for a bookie, or anything like that. But he's about. Cheap rings, mostly."

"Let's hope he doesn't burrow," I said.

"I don't see why he should," he said seriously. "He can't possibly think you'd connect him with Andrews, or with Kraye. All you caught him doing was fixing a poster in a tree. If I were him, I'd be sleeping easy."

"I called him Fred," I said.

"Oh," said Chico glumly. "So you did."

We reached the road and started along it toward the horse box.

"Fred must be the one who does all the jobs," said Chico. "Digs the false drains, sets fire to stables, and drives tractors to pull over tankers. He's big enough for anything.

"He didn't wave the flag. He was up the tree at the time."

"Um. Yes. Who did?"

"Not Bolt," I said. "It wasn't fat enough for Bolt, even in a duffel coat. Possibly Kraye. More likely Leo, whoever he is."

"One of the workmen, or the foreman. Yes. Well, that makes two of them for overturning tankers and so on."

"It would be easier for two," I agreed.

Chico drove the horse box back to Mark's, and then, to his obvious delight, my Merc back to London.

14

CHIEF INSPECTOR Cornish was pleased but trying to hide it.

"I suppose you can chalk it up to your agency," he said as if it were debatable.

"He walked slap into us, to be fair."

"And slap out again," he said dryly.

I grimaced. "You haven't met him."

"You want to leave that sort to us," he said automatically.

"Where were you, then?"

"That's a point," he admitted, smiling.

He picked up the matchbox again and looked at the bullet. "Little beauty. Good clear markings. Pity he has a revolver, though, and not an automatic. It would have been nice to have had cartridge cases as well."

"You're greedy," I said.

He looked at the aluminum ladder standing against his wall, and at the poster on his desk, and at the rush-job photographs. Two clear prints of the van showing its number plates and four of Fred in action against Chico. Not exactly posed portraits, those, but four different, characteristic and recognizable angles taken in full sunlight.

"With all this lot to go on, we'll trace him before he draws breath."

"Fine," I said. And the sooner Fred was immobilized the better, I thought. Before he did any more damage to Seabury. "You'll need a tiger net to catch him. He's a very tough baby, and he knows judo. And unless he has the sense to throw it away, he'll still have that gun."

"I'll remember," he said. "And thanks." We shook hands amicably as I left.

It was results day at Radnor's, too. As soon as I got back Dolly said Jack Copeland wanted me up in Bona Fides. I made the journey.

Jack gleamed at me over the half-moons, pleased with his department. "George's got him. Kraye. He'll tell you."

I went over to George's desk. George was fairly smirking but after he'd talked for two minutes, I allowed he'd earned it.

"On the off-chance," he said, "I borrowed a bit of smooth quartz Kraye recently handled in the Geology Museum and got Sammy to do the prints on it. Two or three different sets of fingers came out, so we photographed the lot. None of them were on the British files, but I've given them the run-around with the odd pal in Interpol and so on, just in case. And brother, have we hit pay dirt or have we."

"We have?" I prompted, grinning.

"And how. Your friend Kraye is in the ex-con library of the state of New York."

"What for?"

"Assault."

"Of a girl?" I asked.

George raised his eyebrows. "A girl's father. Kraye had beaten the girl, apparently with her permission. She didn't complain. But her father saw the bruises and raised the roof. He said he'd get Kraye on a rape charge, though it seems the girl had been perfectly willing on that count too. But it looked bad for Kraye, so he picked up a chair and smashed it over the father's head and scampered. They caught him boarding a plane for South America and hauled him back. The father's brain was damaged. There are long medical details, but what it all boils down to is that he couldn't coordinate properly afterwards. Kraye got off on the rape charge, but served four years for attacking the father.

"Three years after that he turned up in England with some money and a new name, and soon acquired a wife. The one who divorced him for cruelty. Nice chap."

"Yes indeed," I said. "What was his real name?"

"Wilbur Potter," said George sardonically. "And you'll never guess. He was a geologist by profession. He worked for a construction firm, surveying. Always moving about. Character assessments: slick, a pusher, a good talker. Cut a few corners, always had more money than his salary, threw his weight about, but nothing indictable. The assault on the father was his first brush with the law. He was thirty-four at the time."

"Messy," I said. "The whole thing."

"Very," George agreed.

"But sex violence and fraudulent take-overs aren't much related," I complained.

"You might as well say it is impossible to have boils and cancer at the same time. Something drastically wrong with the constitution, and two separate symptoms."

"I'll take your word for it," I said.

Sammy up in Missing Persons had done more than photograph Kraye's fingerprints, he had almost found Smith.

"Intersouth rang us this morning," he purred. "Smith gave them as a reference. He's applied for a driving job in Birmingham."

"Good," I said.

"We should have his address by this afternoon."

Downstairs in Racing I reached for Dolly's telephone and got through to Charing, Street and King.

"Mr. Bolt's secretary speaking," said the quiet voice.

"Is Mr. Bolt in?" I asked.

"I'm afraid not . . . er, who is that speaking, please?"

"Did you find you had a file of mine?"

"Oh. . . . " She laughed. "Yes, I picked it up in your car. I'm so sorry."

"Do you have it with you?"

"No," she said, "I didn't bring it here. I thought it might be better not to risk Mr. Bolt seeing it, as it's got Hunt Radnor Associates printed on the outside along with a red sticker saying 'Ex Records, care of Sid Halley.' "

"Yes, it would have been a disaster," I agreed with feeling.

"I left it at home. Do you want it in a hurry?"

"No, not really. As long as it's safe, that's the main thing. How would it be if I came over to fetch it the day after tomorrow—Sunday morning? We could go for a drive, perhaps, and have some lunch."

There was a tiny pause. Then she said strongly, "Yes, please. Yes."

"Have the leaflets gone out?" I asked.

"They went yesterday."

"See you on Sunday, Miss Martin."

I put down Dolly's telephone to find her looking at me quizzically. I was again squatting on the corner of her desk, the girl from the typing pool having in my absence reclaimed her chair.

"The mouse got away again, I understand," she said.

"Some mouse."

Chico came into the office. The cut on his eyebrow looked red and sore, and all the side of his face showed grayish bruising.

"Two of you," said Dolly disgustedly, "and he knocked you about like kids."

Chico took this a lot better than if she had fussed maternally over his injury.

"It took more than two Lilliputians to peg down Gulliver," he said with good humor. (They had a large library in the children's orphanage.)

"But only one David to slay Goliath."

Chico made a face at her, and I laughed.

"And how are our collywobbles today?" he asked me ironically.

"Better than your looks."

"You know why Sid's best friends won't tell him?" said Chico.

"Why?" said Dolly, seriously.

"He suffers from halley-tosis."

"Oh God," said Dolly. "Take him away, someone. Take him away. I can't stand it."

On the ground floor I sat in a padded maroon armchair in Radnor's drawing-room office and listened to him saying there were no out-of-the-ordinary reports from the patrols at Seabury.

"Fison has just been on the telephone. Everything is normal for a race day, he says. The public will start arriving very shortly. He and Thom walked all round the course just now with Captain Oxon for a thorough check. There's nothing wrong with it, that they can see."

There might be something wrong with it that they couldn't see. I was uneasy.

"I might stay down there tonight, If I can find a room," I said.

"If you do, give me a ring at home, during the evening."

"Sure." I had disturbed his dinner, the day before, to tell him about Fred and the mirror.

"Could I have those photographs back, if you've finished with them?" I asked. I want to check that list of initials against the racecourse workmen at Seabury."

"I'm sorry, Sid, I haven't got them."

"Are they back upstairs?"

"No, no, they aren't here at all. Lord Hagbourne has them."

"But why?" I sat up straight, disturbed.

"He came here yesterday afternoon. I'd say on balance he is almost down on our side of the fence. I didn't get the usual caution about expenses, which is a good sign. Anyway, what he wanted was to see the proofs you told him we held which show it was Kraye who is buying the shares. Photographs of share transfer certificates. He knew about them. He said you'd told him."

"Yes, I did."

"He wanted to see them. That was reasonable, and I didn't want to risk tipping him back into indecision, so I showed them to him. He asked me very courteously if he could take them to show them to the Seabury executive. They held a meeting this morning, I believe. He thought they might be roused to some effective action if they could see for themselves how big Kraye's holding is."

"What about the other photographs? The others that were in the box."

"He took them all. They were all jumbled up, and he was in a hurry. He said he'd sort them out himself later."

"He took them to Seabury?" I said uneasily.

"That's right. For the executive meeting this morning." He looked at his watch. "The meeting must be on at this moment, I should think. If you want them you can ask him for them as soon as you get there. He should have finished with them by then."

"I wish you hadn't let him take them," I said.

"It can't do any harm. Even if he lost them we'd still have the negatives. You could get another print done tomorrow, of your list."

The negatives, did he but know it, were inaccessibly tucked into a mislaid file in Finchley. I didn't confess. Instead I said, unconvinced, "All right. I suppose it won't matter. I'll get on down there, then."

I packed an overnight bag in the flat. The sun was pouring in through the windows, making the blues and greens and blond wood furniture look warm and friendly. After two years the place was at last beginning to feel like home. A home without Jenny. Happiness without Jenny. Both were possible, it seemed. I certainly felt more myself than at any time since she left.

The sun was still shining, too, at Seabury. But not on a very large crowd. The poor quality of the racing was so obvious as to be pathetic: and it was in order that such a rotten gaggle of weedy quadrupeds could stumble and scratch their way round to the winning post, I reflected philosophically, that I had tried to pit my inadequate wits against Lord Hagbourne, Captain Oxon, the Seabury executive, Kraye, Bolt, Fred, Leo, old Uncle Tom Cobley and all.

There were no mishaps all day. The horses raced nonchalantly over the tan patch at their speedy crawl, and no light flashed in their eyes as they knocked hell out of the fences on the far side. Round one to Chico and me.

As the fine weather put everyone in a good mood, a shred of Seabury's former vitality temporarily returned to the place: enough, anyway, for people to notice the dinginess of the stands and remark that it was time something was done about it. If they felt like that, I thought, a revival shouldn't be impossible.

The Senior Steward listened attentively while I passed on Miss Martin's suggestion that Seabury council should be canvassed, and surprisingly said that he would see it was promptly done.

In spite of these small headways, however, my spine wouldn't stop tingling. Lord Hagbourne didn't have the photographs.

"They are only mislaid, Sid," he said soothingly. "Don't make such a fuss. They'll turn up."

He had put them down on the table round which the meeting had been held, he said. After the official business was over, he had chatted, standing up. When he turned back to pick up the box, it was no longer there. The whole table had been cleared. The ashtrays were being emptied. The table was required for lunch. A white cloth was being spread over it.

What, I asked, had been the verdict of the meeting, anyway? Er, um, it appeared the whole subject had been shelved for a week or two: no urgency was felt. Shares changed hands slowly, very slowly. But they had agreed that Hunt Radnor could carry on for a bit.

I hesitated to go barging into the executive's private room just to look for a packet of photographs, so I asked the caterers instead. They hadn't seen it, they said, rushing round me. I tracked down the man and woman who had cleared the table after the meeting and laid it for lunch.

Any amount of doodling on bits of paper, said the waitress, but no box of photographs, and excuse me love, they're waiting for these sandwiches. She agreed to look for it, looked, and came back shaking her head. It wasn't there, as far as she could see. It was quite big, I said despairingly.

I asked Mr. Fotherton, clerk of the course; I asked Captain Oxon; I asked the secretary and anyone else I could think of who had been at the meeting. None of them knew where the photographs were. All of them, busy with their racing jobs, said much the same as Lord Hagbourne.

"Don't worry, Sid, they're bound to turn up."

But they didn't.

I stayed on the racecourse until after the security patrols changed over at six o'clock. The in-comers were the same men who had been on watch the night before, four experienced and sensible ex-policemen, all middle-aged. They entrenched themselves comfortably in the press room, which had windows facing back and front, effective central heating, and four telephones; better headquarters than usual on their night jobs, they said.

Between the last race (three thirty) and six o'clock, apart from hunting without success for the photographs and driving Lord Hagbourne round to Napoleon Close for a horrified firsthand look at the smashed-up mirror, I persuaded Captain Oxon to accompany me on a thorough nook-and-cranny checkup of all the racecourse buildings.

He came willingly enough, his stiffness of earlier in the week having been thawed, I supposed, by the comparative success of the day; but we found nothing and no one that shouldn't have been there.

I drove into Seabury and booked into the Seafront Hotel, where I had often stayed in the past. It was only half full. Formerly, on racing nights, it had been crammed. Over a brandy in the bar the manager lamented with me the state of trade.

"Race meetings used to give us a boost every three weeks nearly all the winter. Now hardly anyone comes, and I hear they didn't even ask for the January fixtures this year. I tell you, I'd like to see that place blooming again, we need it."

"Ah," I said. "Then write to the Town Council and say so."

"That wouldn't help," he said gloomily.

"You never know. It might. Do write."

"All right, Sid. Just to please you then. For old time's sake. Let's have another brandy on the house."

I had an early dinner with him and his wife and afterward went for a walk along the seashore. The night was dry and cold and the onshore breeze smelled of seaweed. The banked pebbles scrunched into trickling hollows under my shoes and the winter sand was as hardpacked as rock. Thinking about Kraye and his machinations, I had strolled quite a long way eastward, away from the racecourse, before I remembered I had said I would ring Radnor at his home during the evening.

There was nothing much to tell him. I didn't hurry, and it was nearly ten o'clock when I got back to Seabury. The modernizations didn't yet run to telephones in all the bedrooms at the hotel, so I used the kiosk outside on the promenade, because I came to it first.

It wasn't Radnor who answered, but Chico, and I knew at once from his voice that things had gone terribly wrong.

"Sid . . . ," he said. "Sid . . . look, pal, I don't know how to tell you. You'll have to have it straight. We've been trying to reach you all the evening."

"What . . . ?" I swallowed.

"Someone bombed your flat."

"*Bombed,*" I said stupidly.

"A plastic bomb. It blew the street wall right out. All the flats round yours were badly damaged, but your . . . well, there's nothing there. Just a big hole with disgusting black sort of cobwebs. That's how they knew it was a plastic bomb. The sort the French terrorists used. . . . Sid, are you there?"

"Yes."

'I'm sorry, pal. I'm sorry. But that's not all. They've done it to the office, too." His voice was anguished. "It went off in the Racing Section. But the whole place is cracked open. It's . . . it's bloody ghastly."

"Chico."

"I know. I know. The old man's round there now, just staring at it. He made me stay here because you said you'd ring, and in case the racecourse patrols want anything. No one was badly hurt, that's the only good thing. Half a dozen people were bruised and cut, at your flats. And the office was empty, of course."

"What time . . . ?"

"The bomb in the office went off about an hour and a half ago, and the one in your flat was just after seven. The old man and I were round there with the police when they got the radio message about the office. The police seem to think that whoever did it was looking for something. The people who live underneath you heard someone moving about upstairs for about two hours shortly before the bomb went off, but they just thought it was you making more noise than usual. And it seems everything in your flat was moved into one pile in the sitting room and the bomb put in the middle. The police said it meant that they hadn't found what they were looking for and were destroying everything in case they had missed it."

"Everything . . . ," I said.

"Not a thing was left. God, Sid, I wish I didn't have to . . . but there it is. Nothing that was there exists any more."

The letters from Jenny when she loved me. The only photograph of my mother and father. The trophies I won racing. The lot. I leaned numbly against the wall.

"Sid, are you still there?"

"Yes."

"It was the same thing at the office. People across the road saw lights on and someone moving about inside, and just thought we were working late. The old man said we must assume they still haven't found what they were looking for. He wants to know what it is."

"I don't know," I said.

"You must."

"No. I don't."

"You can think on the way back."

"I'm not coming back, not tonight. It can't do any good. I think I'll go out to the racecourse again, just to make sure nothing happens there too."

"All right. I'll tell him when he calls. He said he'd be over in Cromwell Road all night, very likely."

We rang off and I went out of the kiosk into the cold night air. I thought that Radnor was right. It was important to know what it was that the bomb merchants had been looking for. I leaned against the outside of the box, thinking about it. Deliberately not thinking about the flat, the place that had begun to be home, and all that was lost. That had happened before in one way or another. The night my mother died, for instance. And I'd ridden my first winner the next day.

To look for something, you had to know it existed. If you used bombs, destroying it was more important than finding it. What did I have, which I hadn't had long (or they would have searched before) which Kraye wanted obliterated.

There was the bullet which Fred had accidentally fired into the mirror. They wouldn't find that, because it was somewhere in a police ballistics laboratory. And if they had thought I had it, they would have looked for it the night before.

There was the leaflet Bolt had sent out, but there were hundreds of those, and he wouldn't want the one I had, even if he knew I had it.

There was the letter Mervyn Brinton had rewritten for me, but if it were that it meant . . .

I went back into the telephone box, obtained Mervyn Brinton's number from the directory inquiries, and rang him up.

To my relief, he answered.

"You are all right, Mr. Brinton?"

"Yes, yes. What's the matter?"

"You haven't had a call from the big man? You haven't told anyone about my visit to you, or that you know your brother's letter by heart?"

He sounded scared. "No. Nothing's happened. I wouldn't tell anyone. I never would."

"Fine," I reassured him. "That's just fine. I was only checking."

So it was not Brinton's letter.

The photographs, I thought. They had been in the office all the time until Radnor gave them to Lord Hagbourne yesterday afternoon. No one outside the agency, except Lord Hagbourne and Charles, had known they existed. Not until this morning, when Lord Hagbourne took them to the Seabury executive meeting, and lost them.

Suppose they weren't lost, but stolen. By someone who knew Kraye, and thought he ought to have them. From the dates on all those documents Kraye would know exactly when the photographs had been taken. And where.

My scalp contracted. I must assume, I thought, that they had now connected all the Halleys and Sids.

Suddenly fearful, I rang up Aynsford. Charles himself answered, calm and sensible.

"Charles, please will you do as I ask, at once, and no questions? Grab Mrs. Cross, go out and get in the car and drive well away from the house, and ring me back at Seabury 79411. Got that? Seabury 79411."

"Yes," he said, and put down the telephone. Thank God, I thought, for a naval training. There might not be much time. The office bomb had exploded an hour and a half ago; London to Aynsford took the same.

Ten minutes later the phone began to ring. I picked up the receiver.

"They say you're in a call box," Charles said.

"That's right. Are you?"

"No, the pub down in the village. Now, what's it all about?"

I told him about the bombs, which horrified him, and about the missing photographs.

"I can't think what else it can be that they are looking for."

"But you said that they've got them."

"The negatives," I said.

"Oh. Yes. And they weren't in your flat or the office?"

"No. Quite by chance, they weren't."

"And you think if they're still looking, that they'll come to Aynsford?"

"If they are desperate enough, they might. They might think you would know where I keep things. . . . And even have a go at making you tell them. I asked you to come out quick because I didn't want to risk it. If they are going to Aynsford, they could be there at any minute now. It's horribly likely they'll think of you. They'll know I took the photos in your house."

"From the dates. Yes. Right. I'll get to the local police and ask for a guard on the house at once."

"Charles, one of them . . . well, if he's the one with the bombs, you'll need a squad." I described Fred and his van, together with its number.

"Right." He was still calm. "Why would the photographs be so important to them? Enough to use bombs, I mean?"

"I wish I knew."

"Take care."

"Yes," I said.

I did take care. Instead of going back into the hotel, I rang it up.

The manager said, "Sid, where on earth are you, people have been trying to reach you all the evening—the police too."

"Yes, Joe, I know. It's all right. I've talked to the police in London. Now, has anyone actually called at the hotel, wanting me?"

"There's someone up in your room, yes. Your father-in-law, Admiral Roland."

"Oh really? Does he look like an admiral?"

"I suppose so." He sounded puzzled.

"A gentleman?"

"Yes, of course." Not Fred, then.

"Well, he isn't my father-in-law. I've just been talking to him in his house in Oxfordshire. You collect a couple of helpers and chuck my visitor out."

I put down the receiver sighing. A man up in my room meant everything I'd brought to Seabury would very likely be ripped to bits. That left me with just the clothes I stood in, and the car—

I fairly sprinted round to where I'd left the car. It was locked, silent and safe. No damage. I patted it thankfully, climbed in, and drove out to the racecourse.

15

ALL WAS quiet as I drove through the gates and switched off the engine. There were lights on—one shining through the windows of the press room, one outside the weighing-room door, one high up somewhere on the stands. The shadows in between were densely black. It was a clear night with no moon.

I walked across to the press room, to see if the security patrols had anything to report.

They hadn't.

All four of them were fast asleep.

Furious, I shook the nearest. His head lolled like a pendulum, but he didn't wake up. He was sitting slumped into his chair. One of them had his arms on the table and his head on his arms. One of them sat on the floor, his head on the seat of the chair and his arms hanging down. The fourth lay flat, face downward, near the opposite wall.

The stupid fools, I thought. Ex-policemen letting themselves be put to sleep like infants. It shouldn't have been possible. One of their first rules in guard work was to take their own food and drink with them and not accept sweets from strangers.

I stepped round their heavily breathing hulks and picked up one of the press telephones to ring Chico for reinforcements. The line was dead. I tried the three other instruments. No contact with the exchange on any of them.

I would have to go back and ring up from Seabury, I thought. I went out of the press room but in the light pouring out before I shut the door I saw a dim figure walking toward me from the direction of the gate.

"Who's that?" he called imperiously, and I recognized his voice. Captain Oxon.

"It's only me, Sid Halley," I shouted back. "Come and look at this."

He came on into the light, and I stood aside for him to go into the press room.

"Good heavens. What on earth's the matter with them?"

"Sleeping pills. And the telephones don't work. You haven't seen anyone about who ought not to be?"

"No. I haven't heard anything except your car. I came down to see who had come."

"How many lads are there staying overnight in the hostel? Could we use some of those to patrol the place while I ring the agency to get some more men?"

"I should think they'd love it," he said. "There are about five of them. They shouldn't be in bed yet. We'll go over and ask them, and you can use the telephone from my flat to ring your agency."

"Thanks," I said. "That's fine."

I looked round the room at the sleeping men. "I think perhaps I ought to see if any of them tried to write a message. I won't be a minute."

He waited patiently while I looked under the head and folded arms of the man at the table and under the man on the floor, and all round the one with his head on the chair seat, but none of them had even reached for a pencil. Shrugging, I looked at the remains of their supper, lying on the table. Half-eaten sandwiches on greaseproof paper, dregs of coffee in cups and thermos flasks, a couple of apple cores, some cheese sections and empty wrappings, and an unpeeled banana.

"Found anything?" asked Oxon.

I shook my head in disgust. "Not a thing. They'll have terrible headaches when they wake up, and serve them right."

"I can understand you being annoyed. . . ." he began. But I was no longer really listening. Over the back of the chair occupied by the first man I had shaken was hanging a brown leather binoculars case, and on its lid were stamped three black initials: L.E.O. Leo. *Leo.*

"Something the matter?" asked Oxon.

"No." I smiled at him and touched the strap of the binoculars. "Are these yours?"

"Yes. The men asked if I could lend them some. For the dawn, they said."

"It was very kind of you."

"Oh. Nothing." He shrugged, moving out into the night. "You'd better make that phone call first. We'll tackle the boys afterwards."

I had absolutely no intention of walking into his flat.

"Right," I said.

We went out of the door, and I closed it behind us.

A familiar voice, loaded with satisfaction, spoke from barely a yard away. "So you've got him, Oxon. Good."

"He was coming—" began Oxon in anxious anger, knowing that "got him" was an exaggeration.

"No," I said, and turned and ran for the car.

When I was barely ten yards from it someone turned the lights on. The headlights of my own car. I stopped dead.

Behind me one of the men shouted and I heard their feet running. I wasn't directly in the beam, but silhouetted against it. I swerved off to the right, toward the gate. Three steps in that direction, and the headlights of a car turning in through it caught me straight in the eyes.

There were more shouts, much closer, from Oxon and Kraye. I turned, half-dazzled, and saw them closing in. Behind me now the incoming car rolled forward. And the engine of my Mercedes purred separately into life.

I ran for the dark. The two cars, moving, caught me again in their beams. Kraye and Oxon ran where they pointed.

I was driven across and back toward the stands like a coursed hare, the two cars behind inexorably finding me with their lights and the two men running with reaching, clutching hands. Like a nightmare game of "He," I thought wildly, with more than a child's forfeit if I were caught.

Across the parade ring, across the flat Tarmac stretch beyond it, under the rails of the unsaddling enclosure and along the inside of the door into the trainers' luncheon room and through there without stopping into the kitchen. And weaving on from there out into the members' lunch room, round acres of tables with upturned chairs, through the far door into the wide passage which cut like a tunnel along the length of the huge building, across it, and up a steep stone staircase emerging halfway up the open steps of the stands, and sideways along them as far as I could go. The pursuit was left behind.

I sank down, sitting with one leg bent to run, in the black shadow where the low wooden wall dividing the members from Tattersalls cut straight down the steps separating the stands into two halves. On top of the wall wire netting stretched up too high to climb: high enough to keep out the poorer customers from gate crashing the expensive ring.

At the bottom of the steps lay a large expanse of members' lawn stretching to another metal mesh fence, chest high, and beyond that lay the whole open expanse of racecourse. Half a mile across it to the London road to Seabury, with yet another barrier, the boundary fence, to negotiate.

It was too far. I knew I couldn't do it. Perhaps once, with two hands for vaulting, with a stomach which didn't already feel as if it were tearing into more holes inside. But not now. Although I always mended fast, it was only two weeks since I had found the short walk to Andrews' body very nearly too much; and Fred's well-aimed attentions on the previous day had not been therapeutic.

Looking at it straight: if I ran, it had to be successful. My kingdom for a horse, I thought. Any reasonable cowboy would have had Revelation hitched to the rails, ready for a flying leap into the saddle and a thundering exit. I had a hundred-and-fifty-mile-an-hour little white Mercedes, and someone else was sitting in it.

To run and be caught running would achieve nothing and be utterly pointless.

Which left just one alternative.

The security patrol hadn't been drugged for nothing. Kraye wasn't at Seabury for his health. Some more damage had been planned for this night. Might already have been done. There was just a chance, if I stayed to look, that I could find out what it was. Before they found *me*. Naturally.

If I ever have any children, they won't get me playing hide-and-seek.

Half an hour later the grim game was still in progress. My own car was now parked on the racecourse side of the stands, on the Tarmac in Tattersalls where the bookies had called that afternoon. It was facing the stands with the headlights full on. Every inch of the steps was lit by them, and since the car had arrived there I had not been able to use that side of the building at all.

The other car was similarly parked inside the racecourse gates, its headlights shining on the fronts of the weighing room, bars, dining rooms, cloakrooms and offices.

Presuming that each car still had a watching occupant, that left only Kraye and Oxon, as far as I could guess, to run me to ground; but I became gradually sure that there were three, not two, after me in the stands. Perhaps one of the cars was empty. But which? And it would be unlikely to have its ignition key in place.

Bit by bit I covered the whole enormous block. I didn't know what I was looking for, that was the trouble. It could have been anything from a plastic bomb downward, but if past form was anything to go by, it was something which could appear accidental. Bad luck. A jinx. Open, recognizable sabotage would be ruinous to the scheme.

Without a surveyor, I couldn't be certain that part of the steps would not collapse the following day under the weight of the crowd, but I could find no trace of any structural damage at all, and there hadn't been much time: only five or six hours since the day's meeting ended.

There were no large quantities of food in the kitchen: the caterers appeared to have removed what had been left over ready to bring fresh the next day. A large double-doored refrigerator was securely locked. I discounted the possibility that Kraye could have thought of large-scale food poisoning.

All the fire extinguishers seemed to be in their places, and there were no smoldering cigarette ends near tins of paraffin. Nothing capable of spontaneous combustion. I suppose another fire, so soon after the stables, might have been too suspicious.

I went cautiously, carefully, every nerve-racking step of the way, peering round corners, easing through doors, fearing that at any moment one of them would pounce on me from behind.

They knew I was still there, because everywhere they went they turned on lights, and everywhere I went I turned them off. Opening a door from a lighted room onto a dark passage made one far too easy to spot; I turned off the lights before I opened any door. There had been three lights in the passage itself, but I had broken them early on with a broom from the kitchen.

Once when I was in the passage, creeping from the men's lavatories to the Tattersalls bar, Kraye himself appeared at the far end, the members' end, and began walking my way. He came in through the faint glow from the car's headlights, and he hadn't seen me. One stride took me across the passage, one jump and a wriggle into the only cover available, the heap of equipment the bookmakers had left there out of the weather, overnight.

These were only their metal stands, their folded umbrellas, the boxes and stools they stood on: a thin spiky, precarious heap. I crouched down beside them, praying I wouldn't dislodge anything.

Kraye's footsteps scraped hollowly as he trod toward my ineffective hiding place. He stopped twice, opening doors and looking into the storerooms which were in places built back under the steps of the stands. They were mostly empty or nearly so, and offered nothing to me. They were too small, and all dead ends: if I were found in one of them, I couldn't get out.

The door of the bar I had been making for suddenly opened, spilling bright light into the passage between me and Kraye.

Oxon's voice said anxiously, "He can't have got away."

"Of course not, you fool," said Kraye furiously. "But if you'd had the sense to bring your keys over with you we'd have had him long ago." Their voices echoed up and down the passage.

"It was your idea to leave so much unlocked. I could go back and fetch them."

"He'd have too much chance of giving us the slip. But we're not getting anywhere with all this dodging about. We'll start methodically from this end and move down."

"We did that to start with," complained Oxon. "And we missed him. Let me go back for the keys. Then as you said before, we can lock all the doors behind us and stop him doubling back."

"No," said Kraye decisively. "There aren't enough of us. You stay here. We'll go back to the weighing room and start all together."

They began to walk away. The bar door was still open, lighting up the passage, which I didn't like. If anyone came in from the other end, he would see me for sure.

I shifted my position to crawl away along the wall for better concealment, and one of the bookmakers' metal tripods slid down and clattered off the side of the pile with an echoing noise like a dozen demented machine guns.

There were shouts from the two men down the passage.

"There he is."

"Get him."

I stood up and ran.

The nearest opening in the wall was a staircase up to a suite of rooms above the changing room and members' dining room. I hesitated a fraction of a second and then passed it. Up those steps were the executive's rooms and offices. I didn't know my way round up there, but Oxon did. He had a big enough advantage already in his knowledge of the building without my giving him a bonus.

I ran on, past the gents' cloaks, and finally in through the last possible door, that of a long, bare, dirty room smelling of beer. It was a sort of extra, subsidiary bar, and all it now contained was a bare counter backed by empty shelves. I nearly fell over a bucket full of crinkled metal bottle tops which someone had carelessly left in my way, and then wasted precious seconds to dart back to put the bucket just inside the door I'd come in by.

Kraye and Oxon were running. I snapped off the lights, and with no time to get clear through the far door out into the paddock, where anyway I would be lit by car headlights, I scrambled down behind the bar counter.

The door jerked open. There was a clatter of the bucket and a yell, and the sound of someone falling. Then the light snapped on again, showing me just how tiny my hiding place really was, and two bottle tops rolled across the floor into my sight.

"For God's sake," yelled Kraye in anger. "You clumsy, stupid fool. Get up. Get up." He charged down the room to the far door, the board floor bouncing slightly under his weight. From the clanking, cursing, and clattering of bottle tops I imagined that Oxon was extricating himself from the bucket and following. If it hadn't been so dangerous it would have been funny.

Kraye yanked the outside door open, stepped outside and yelled across to the stationary car to ask where I had gone. I felt rather than saw Oxon run down the room to join him. I crawled round the end of the counter, sprinted for the door I had come in by, flipped off the light again, slammed the door, and ran back up the passage. There was a roar from Kraye as he fumbled back into the darkened room; and long before they had emerged into the passage again, kicking bottle tops in all directions, I was safe in the opening of a little offshoot lobby to the kitchen.

The kitchens were safest for me because there were so many good hiding places and so many exits, but it wasn't much good staying there because I had searched them already.

I was fast running out of places to look. The boiler room had given me an anxious two minutes as its only secondary exit was into a dead-end storeroom containing, as far as I could see, nothing but vast oil tanks with pipes and gauges. They were hard against the walls: nowhere to hide. The boiler itself roared, keeping the central heating going all through the night.

The weighing room was even worse, because it was big and entirely without cover. It contained nothing it shouldn't have, just tables, chairs, notices pinned on the walls, and the weighing machine itself. Beyond, in the changing room, there were rows of pegs with saddles on, the warm, banked-up coke stove in the corner, and a big wicker basket full of helmets, boots, weight cloths and other equipment left by the valets overnight. A dirty cup and saucer. A copy of *Playboy*. Several raincoats. Racing colors on pegs. A row of washed breeches hanging up to dry. It was the most occupied-looking part of the stands, the place I felt most at home in and where I wanted to go to ground, like an ostrich in familiar sand. But on the far side of the changing room lay only the washroom, another dead end.

Opening out of the weighing room on the opposite side to the changing room was the Steward's room, where in the past like all jockeys I'd been involved in cases of objections-to-the-winner. It was a bare room: large table, chairs round it, sporting pictures, small threadbare carpet. A few of the Stewards' personal possessions lay scattered about, but there was no concealment.

A few doors here and there were locked, in spite of Oxon's having left the keys in his flat. As usual I had the bunch of lock pickers in my pocket; and with shortened breath I spent several sticky minutes letting myself into one well-secured room off the members' bar. It proved to be the liquor store: crates of spirits, champagne, wine and beer. Beer from floor to ceiling, and a porter's trolley to transport it. It was a temptation to lock myself in there, and wait for the caterers to rescue me in the morning. This was one door that Oxon would not expect to find me on the far side of.

In the liquor store I might be safe. On the other hand, if I were safe the racecourse might not be. Reluctantly I left again; but I didn't waste time locking up. With the pursuit out of sight, I risked a look upstairs. It was warm and quiet, and all the lights were on. I left them on, figuring that if the watchers in the cars saw them go out they would know too accurately where I was.

Nothing seemed to be wrong. On one side of a central lobby there was the big room where the executive held their meetings and ate their lunch. On the other side there was a sort of drawing room furnished with light armchairs, with two cloakrooms leading off it at the back. At the front, through double glass doors, it led out into a box high up on the stands. The private box for directors and distinguished guests, with a superb view over the whole course.

I didn't go there. Sabotage in the royal box wouldn't stop a race meeting to which royalty weren't going anyway. And besides, whoever was in my car would see me opening the door.

Retreating, I went back, right through the dining-board room and out into the service room on the far side. There I found a storeroom with plates, glass and cutlery, and in the storeroom also a second exit. A small service lift down to the kitchens. It worked with ropes like the one in the office on Cromwell Road . . . like the office lift *had* worked, before the bomb.

Kraye and Oxon were down in the kitchen. Their angry voices floated up the shaft, mingled with a softer murmuring voice which seemed to be arguing with them. Since for once I knew where they all were, I returned with some boldness to the ground again. But I was worried. There seemed to be nothing at all going wrong in the main building. If they were organizing yet more damage somewhere out on the course itself, I didn't see how I could stop it.

While I was still dithering rather aimlessly along the passage the kitchen door opened, the light flooded on, and I could hear Kraye still talking. I dived yet again for the nearest door and put it between myself and them.

I was, I discovered, in the ladies' room, where I hadn't been before, and there was no second way out. Only a double row of cubicles, all with the doors open, a range of washbasins, mirrors on the walls with a wide shelf beneath them, a few chairs, and a counter like that in the bar. Behind the counter there was a rail with coat hangers.

There were heavy steps in the passage outside. I slid instantly behind and under the counter and pressed myself into a corner. The door opened.

"He won't be in here," said Kraye. "The light's still on."

"I looked in here not five minutes ago, anyway," agreed Oxon.

The door closed behind them and their footsteps went away. I began to breathe again and my thudding heart slowed down. But for a couple of seconds only. Across the room, someone coughed.

I froze. I couldn't believe it. The room had been empty when I came in, I was certain. And neither Kraye nor Oxon had stayed. . . . I stretched my ears, tense, horrified.

Another cough. A soft, single cough.

Try as I could I could hear nothing else. No breathing. No rustle of clothing, no movement. It didn't make sense. If someone in the room knew I was behind the counter, why didn't they do something about it? If they didn't know, why were they so unnaturally quiet?

In the end, taking a conscious grip on my nerves, I slowly stood up.

The room was empty.

Almost immediately there was another cough. Now that my ears were no longer obstructed by the counter, I got a clearer idea of its direction. I swung toward it. There was no one there.

I walked across the room and stared down at the washbasin. Water was trickling from one of the taps. Even while I looked at it the tap coughed. Almost laughing with relief I stretched out my hand and turned it off.

The metal was very hot. Surprised, I turned the water on again. It came spluttering out of the tap, full of air bubbles and very hot indeed. Steaming. How stupid, I thought, turning it off again, to have the water so hot at this time of night. . . .

Christ, I thought. The boiler.

16

KRAYE AND Oxon's so-called methodical end-to-end search, which had just failed to find me in the ladies', was proceeding from the members' end of the stands toward Tattersalls. The boiler, like myself, was in the part they had already put behind them. I switched out the ladies'-room lights, carefully eased into the passage, and via the kitchen, the members' dining room, the gentlemen's cloaks and another short strip of passage returned to the boiler room.

Although there was no door through, I knew that the far side of the inside wall lay to the left of the weighing room and to the right the changing room, with the dividing wall between. From both those rooms, when it was quiet, as it was that night, one could quite clearly hear the boiler's muffled roar.

The light that I had switched off was on again in the boiler room. I looked round. It all looked as normal as it had before, except . . . except that away to the right there was a very small pool of water on the floor.

Boilers. We had had a lesson on them at school. Sixteen or seventeen years ago, I thought hopelessly. But I remembered very well the way the master had begun the lesson.

"The first thing to learn about boilers," he said, "is that they explode."

He was an excellent teacher: the whole class of forty boys listened from then on with avid interest. But since then the only acquaintance I'd had with boilers was down in the basement of the flats, where I sometimes drank a cup of orange tea with the caretaker. A tough ex-naval stoker, he was, and a confirmed student of racing form. Mostly we'd talked about horses, but sometimes about his job. There were strict regulations for boilers, he'd said, and regular official inspections every three months, and he was glad of it, working alongside them every day.

The first thing to learn about boilers is that they explode.

It's no good saying I wasn't frightened, because I was. If the boiler burst it wasn't simply going to make large new entrances into the weighing room and changing room, it was going to fill every cranny near it with scalding tornadoes of steam. Not a death I looked on with much favor.

I stood with my back against the door and tried desperately to remember that long-ago lesson, and to work out what was going wrong.

It was a big steam boiler. An enormous cylinder nine feet high and five feet in diameter. Thick steel, with dark red antirust paint peeling off. Fired at the bottom not by coke, which it had been built for, but by the more modern roaring jet of burning oil. If I opened the fire door I would feel the blast of its tremendous heat.

The body of the cylinder would be filled almost to the top with water. The flame boiled the water. The resulting steam went out of the top under its own fierce pressure in a pipe which—I followed it with my eye—led into a large yellow-painted round-ended cylinder slung horizontally near the ceiling. This tank looked rather like a zeppelin. It was, if I remembered right, a calorifier. Inside it, the steampipe ran in a spiral, like an immobile spring. The tank itself was supplied from the mains with the water which was to be heated, the water going to the central heating radiators, and to the hot taps in the kitchen, the cloakrooms and the jockeys' washrooms. The scorching heat from the spiral steampipe instantly passed into the water touching it, so that the cold water entering the calorifier was made very hot in the short time before it left at the other end.

The steam, however, losing its heat in the process, gradually condensed back into water. A pipe led down the wall from the calorifier into a much smaller tank, an ordinary square one, standing on the floor. From the bottom of this, yet another pipe tracked right back across the room and up near the boiler itself to a bulbous metal contraption just higher than my head. An electric pump. It finished the circuit by pumping the condensed water up from the tank on the floor and returning it to the boiler, to be boiled, steamed and condensed all over again. Round and round, continuously.

So far, so good. But if you interfered with the circuit so that the water didn't get back into the boiler, and at the same time kept the heat full on at the bottom, all the water inside the cylinder gradually turned to steam.

Steam, which was strong enough to drive a liner, or pull a twelve-coach train, but could in this case only get out at all through a narrow, closely spiraled pipe.

This type of boiler, built not for driving an engine but only for heating water, wasn't constructed to withstand enormous pressures. It was a tossup, I thought, whether when all the water had gone the fast-expanding air and steam found a weak spot to break out of before the flames burned through the bottom. In either case, the boiler would blow up.

On the outside of the boiler there was a water gauge, a foot-long vertical glass tube held in brackets. The level of water in the tube indicated the level of water in the boiler. Near the top of the gauge a black line showed what the water level ought to be. Two thirds of the way down a broad red line obviously acted as a warning. The water in the gauge was higher than the red line by half an inch.

To put it mildly, I was relieved. The boiler wasn't bulging. The explosion lay in the future, which gave me more time to work out how to prevent it. As long as it would take Oxon and Kraye to decide on a repeat search, perhaps.

I could simply have turned out the flame, but Kraye and Oxon would notice that the noise had stopped, and merely light it again. Nothing would have been gained. On the other hand, I was sure that the flame was higher than it should have been at night, because the water in the ladies' tap was nearly boiling.

Gingerly I turned the adjusting wheel on the oil line. Half a turn. A full turn. The roaring seemed just as loud. Another turn, and that time there was a definite change. Half a turn more. It was perceptibly quieter. Slowly I inched the wheel around more, until quite suddenly the roar turned to a murmur. Too far. Hastily I reversed. At that point where the murmur was again a roar, I left it.

I looked consideringly at the square tank of condensed water on the floor. It was this, overflowing, which was making the pool of water; and it was overflowing because the contents were not being pumped back into the boiler. If they've broken the pump, I thought despairingly, I'm done. I didn't know the first thing about electric pumps.

Another sentence from that faraway school lesson floated usefully through my mind. *For safety's sake, every boiler must have two sources of water.*

I chewed my lower lip, watching the water trickle down the side of the tank onto the floor. Even in the few minutes I had been there the pool had spread. One source of water was obviously knocked out. Where and what was the other?

There were dozens of pipes in the boiler room; not only oil pipes and water pipes, but all the electric cables were installed inside tubes as well. There were about six separate pipes with stopcocks on them. It seemed to me that all the water for the entire building came in through the boiler room.

Two pipes, apparently rising mains, led from the floor up the wall and into the calorifier. Both had stopcocks, which I tested. Both were safely open. There was no rising main leading directly into the boiler.

By sheer luck I was halfway round the huge cylinder looking for an inlet pipe when I saw the lever-type door handle move down. I leaped for the only vestige of cover, the space between the boiler and the wall. It was scorching hot there: pretty well unbearable.

Kraye had to raise his voice to make himself heard over the roaring flame.

"You're sure it's still safe?"

"Yes, I told you, it won't blow up for three hours yet. At least three hours."

"The water's running out already," Kraye objected.

"There's a lot in there." Oxon's voice came nearer. I could feel my heart thumping and hear the pulse in my ears. "The level's not down to the caution mark on the gauge yet," he said. "It won't blow for a long time after it goes below that."

"We've got to find Halley," Kraye said. "Got to." If Oxon moved another step he would see me. "I'll work from this end; you start again from the other. Look in every cupboard. The little rat has gone to ground somewhere."

Oxon didn't answer audibly. I had a sudden glimpse of his sleeve as he turned, and I shrank back into my hiding place.

Because of the noise of the boiler I couldn't hear them go away through the door, but eventually I had to risk that they had. The heat where I stood was too appalling. Moving out into the ordinarily hot air in the middle of the room was like diving into a cold bath. And Oxon and Kraye had gone.

I slipped off my jacket and wiped the sweat off my face with my shirt sleeves. Back to the problem: water supply.

The pump *looked* all right. There were no loose wires, and it had an undisturbed, slightly greasy, slightly dirty appearance. With luck, I thought, they hadn't damaged the pump, they'd blocked the pipe where it left the tank. I took off my tie and shirt as well, and put them with my jacket on the grimy floor.

The lid of the tank came off easily enough, and the water, when I tested it, proved to be no more than uncomfortably hot. I drank some in my cupped palm. The running and the heat had made me very thirsty, and although I would have preferred it iced, no water could have been purer, or more tasteless, though I was not inclined to be fussy on that point.

I stretched my arm down into the water, kneeling beside the tank. As it was only about two feet deep, I could touch the bottom quite easily, and almost at once my searching fingers found and gripped a loose object. I pulled it out.

It was a fine mesh filter, which should no doubt have been in place over the opening of the outlet pipe.

Convinced now that the pipe was blocked from this end, I reached down again into the water. I found the edge of the outlet, and felt carefully into it. I could reach no obstruction. Bending over further, so that my shoulder was half in the water, I put two fingers as far as they would go into the outlet. I could feel nothing solid, but there did seem to be a piece of string. It was difficult to get it between two fingers firmly enough to pull as hard as was necessary, but gradually with a series of little jerks I managed to move the plug backward into the tank.

It came away finally so suddenly that I nearly overbalanced. There was a burp from the outer pipe of the tank and on the other side of the room a sharp click from the pump.

I lifted my hand out of the water to see what had blocked the pipe, and stared in amazement. It was a large mouse. I had been pulling its tail.

Accidental sabotage, I thought. The same old pattern. However unlikely it was that a mouse should dive into a tank, find the filter conveniently out of place, and get stuck just inside the outlet pipe, one would have a hard job proving that it was impossible.

I carefully put the sodden little body out of sight in the small gap between the tank and the wall. With relief I noticed that the water level was already going down slightly, which meant that the pump was working properly and the boiler would soon be more or less back to normal.

I splashed some more water out of the tank to make a larger pool should Kraye or Oxon glance in again, and replaced the lid. Putting on my shirt and jacket I followed with my eyes the various pipes in and out of the boiler. The lagged steam exit pipe to the calorifier. The vast chimney flue for the hot gases from the burning oil. The inlet pipe from the pump. The water gauge. The oil pipe. There had to be another water inlet somewhere, partly for safety, partly to keep the steam circuit topped up.

I found it in the end running alongside and behind the inlet pipe from the pump. It was a gravity feed from a stepped series of three small unobtrusive tanks fixed high on the wall. Filters, I reckoned, so that the main's water didn't carry its mineral salts into the boiler and fur it up. The filter tanks were fed by a pipe which branched off one of the rising mains and had its own stopcock.

Reaching up, I tried to turn it clockwise. It didn't move. The main's water was cut off. With satisfaction, I turned it on again.

Finally, with the boiler once more working exactly as it should, I took a look at the water gauge. The level had already risen to nearly halfway between the red and black marks. Hoping fervently Oxon wouldn't come back for another check on it, I went over to the door and switched off the light.

There was no one in the passage. I slipped through the door, and in the last three inches before shutting it behind me stretched my hand back and put the light on again. I didn't want Kraye knowing I'd been in there.

Keeping close to the wall, I walked softly down the passage toward the Tattersalls end. If I could get clear of the stands there were other buildings out that way to give cover. The barn, cloakrooms and tote buildings in the silver ring. Beyond these lay the finishing straight, the way down to the tan patch and the bisecting road. Along that, bungalows, people and telephones.

That was when my luck ran out.

17

I WAS barely two steps past the door of the Tattersalls bar when it opened and the lights blazed out onto my tiptoeing figure. In the two seconds it took Oxon to realize what he was seeing I was six running paces down toward the way out.

His shouts echoed in the passage mingled with others further back, and I still thought that if Kraye too were behind me I might have a chance. But when I was within ten steps of the end another figure appeared there, hurrying, called by the noise.

I skidded nearly to a stop, sliding on one of the scattered bottle tops, and crashed through the only possible door, into the same empty bar as before. I raced across the board floor, kicking bottle tops in all directions, but I never got to the far door. It opened before I reached it, and that was the end.

Doria Kraye stood there, maliciously triumphant. She was dressed theatrically in white slender trousers and a shiny short white jacket. Her dark hair fell smoothly, her face was as flawlessly beautiful as ever, and she held rock-steady in one elegantly long-figured hand the little .22 automatic I had last seen in a chocolate box at the bottom of her dressing case.

"The end of the line, buddy boy," she said. "You stay just where you are."

I hesitated on the brink of trying to rush her.

"Don't risk it," she said. "I'm a splendid shot. I wouldn't miss. Do you want a kneecap smashed?"

There was little I wanted less. I turned round slowly. There were three men coming forward into the long room. Kraye, Oxon and Ellis Bolt. All three of them looked as if they had long ago got tired of the chase and were going to take it out on the quarry.

"Will you walk," said Doria behind me, "or be dragged?"

I shrugged. "Walk."

All the same, Kraye couldn't keep his hands off me. When, following Doria's instructions, I walked past him to go back out through the passage he caught hold of my jacket at the back of the neck and kicked my legs. I kicked back, which wasn't too sensible, as I presently ended up on the floor. There was nothing like little metal bottle tops for giving you a feeling of falling on little metal bottle tops, I thought, with apologies to Michael Flanders and Donald Swan.

"Get up," said Kraye. Doria stood beside him, pointing at me with the gun.

I did as he said.

"Right," said Doria. "Now, walk down the passage and go into the weighing room. And Howard, for God's sake wait till we get there, or we'll lose him again. Walk, buddy boy. Walk straight down the middle of the passage. If you try anything, I'll shoot you in the leg."

I saw no reason not to believe her. I walked down the center of the passage with her too close behind for escape, and with the two men bringing up the rear.

"Stop a minute," said Kraye, outside the boiler room.

I stopped. I didn't look round.

Kraye opened the door and looked inside. The light spilled out, adding to that already coming from the other open doors along the way.

"Well?" said Oxon.

"There's more water on the floor." He sounded pleased, and shut the door without going in for a further look. Not all of my luck had departed, it seemed.

"Move," he said. I obeyed.

The weighing room was as big and bare as ever. I stopped in the middle of it and turned round. The four of them stood in a row, looking at me, and I didn't at all like what I read in their faces.

"Go and sit there," said Doria, pointing.

I went on across the floor and sat where she said, on the chair of the weighing machine. The pointer immediately swung round the clock face to show my weight. Nine stone seven. It was, I was remotely interested to see, exactly ten pounds less than when I had last raced. Bullets would solve any jockey's weight problem, I thought.

The four of them came closer. It was some relief to find that Fred wasn't among them, but only some. Kraye was emitting the same livid fury as he had twelve days ago at Aynsford. And then, I had merely mildly insulted his wife.

"Hold his arms," he said to Oxon. Oxon was one of those thin wiry men of seemingly limitless strength. He came round behind me, clamped his fingers round my elbows and pulled them back. With concentration Kraye hit me several times in the face.

"Now," he said. "Where are they?"

"What?" I said indistinctly.

"The negatives."

"What negatives?"

He hit me again and hurt his own hand. Shaking it out and rubbing his knuckles, he said, "You know what negatives. The films you took of my papers."

"Oh, those."

"Those." He hit me again, but less hard.

"In the office," I mumbled.

He tried a slap to save his knuckles. "Office," I said.

He tried with his left hand, but it was clumsy. After that he sucked his knuckles and kept his hands to himself.

Bolt spoke for the first time, in his consciously beautiful voice. "Fred wouldn't have missed them, especially as there was no reason for them to be concealed. He's too thorough."

If Fred wouldn't have missed them, the bombs had been pure spite. I licked the inside of a split lip and thought about what I would like to do to Fred.

"Where in the office?" said Kraye.

"Desk."

"Hit him," said Kraye. "My hand hurts."

Bolt had a go, but it wasn't his sort of thing.

"Try with this," said Doria, offering Bolt the gun, but it was luckily so small he couldn't hold it effectively.

Oxon let go of my elbows, came round to the front, and looked at my face.

"If he's decided not to tell you, you won't get it out of him like that," he said.

"I told you," I said.

"Why not?" said Bolt.

"You're hurting yourselves more than him. And if you want my opinion, you won't get anything out of him at all."

"Don't be silly," said Doria scornfully. "He's so small."

Oxon laughed without mirth.

"If Fred said so, the negatives weren't at his office," asserted Bolt again. "Nor in his flat. And he didn't bring them with him. Or at least, they weren't in his luggage at the hotel."

I looked at him sideways, out of an eye which was beginning to swell. And if I hadn't been so quick to have him flung out of my hotel room, I thought sourly, he wouldn't have driven in through the racecourse gate at exactly the wrong moment. But I couldn't have foreseen it, and it was too late to help.

"They weren't in his car either," said Doria. "But this was." She put her hand into her shining white pocket and brought out my baby camera. Kraye took it from her, opened the case, and saw what was inside. The veins in his neck and temples became congested with blood. In a paroxysm of fury he threw the little black toy across the room so that it hit the wall with a disintegrating crash.

"Sixteen millimeter," he said savagely. "Fred must have missed them."

Bolt said obstinately, "Fred would find a needle in a haystack. And those films wouldn't have been hidden."

"He might have them in his pocket," suggested Doria.

"Take your coat off," Kraye said. "Stand up."

I stood up, and the base plate of the weighing machine wobbled under my feet. Oxon pulled my coat down over the back of my shoulders, gave a tug to get the sleeves off, and passed the jacket to Kraye. His own hand he thrust into my trouser pocket. In the right one, under my tie, he found the bunch of lock pickers.

"Sit down," he said. I did so, exploring with the back of my hand some of the damage to my face. It could have been worse, I thought resignedly, much worse. I would be lucky if that were all.

"What are those?" said Doria curiously, taking the jingling collection from Oxon.

Kraye snatched them from her and slung them after the camera. "Skeleton keys," he said furiously. "What he used to unlock my cases."

"I don't see how he could," said Doria, "with that . . . that . . . *claw*." She looked down where it lay on my lap.

A nice line in taunts, I thought, but a week too late. Thanks to Miss Martin, I was at last learning to live with the claw. I left it where it was.

"Doria," said Bolt calmly, "would you be kind enough to go over to the flat and wait for Fred to ring? He may already have found what we want at Aynsford."

I turned my head and found him looking straight at me, assessingly. There was a detachment in the eyes, an unmoved quality in the rounded features; and I began to wonder whether his stolid coolness might not in the end prove even more difficult to deal with than Kraye's rage.

"Aynsford," I repeated thickly. I looked at my watch. If Fred had really taken his bombs to Aynsford, he should by now be safely in the bag. One down, four to go. Five of them altogether, not four. I hadn't thought of

Doria being an active equal colleague of the others. My mistake.

"I don't want to," said Doria, staying put.

Bolt shrugged. "It doesn't matter. I see that the negatives aren't at Aynsford, because the thought of Fred looking for them there doesn't worry Halley one little bit."

The thought of what Fred might be doing at Aynsford or to Charles himself didn't worry any of them either. But more than that I didn't like the way Bolt was reasoning. In the circumstances, a clear-thinking opponent was something I could well have done without.

"We must have them," said Kraye intensely. "We must. Or be certain beyond doubt that they were destroyed." To Oxon he said, "Hold his arms again."

"No," I said, shrinking back.

"Ah, that's better. Well?"

"They were in the office." My mouth felt stiff.

"Where?"

"In Mr. Radnor's desk, I think."

He stared at me, eyes narrowed, anger half under control, weighing up whether I were telling the truth or not. He certainly couldn't go to the office and make sure.

"Were," said Bolt suddenly.

"What?" asked Kraye, impatiently.

"Were," said Bolt. "Halley said were. The negatives *were* in the office. Now that's very interesting indeed, don't you think?"

Oxon said, "I don't see why."

Bolt came close to me and peered into my face. I didn't meet his eyes, and anything he could read from my bruised features he was welcome to.

"I think he knows about the bombs," he said finally.

"How?" said Doria.

"I should think he was told at the hotel. People in London must have been trying to contact him. Yes, I think we can take it for granted he knows about the bombs."

"What difference does that make?" said Oxon.

Kraye knew. "It means he thinks he is safe saying the negatives were in the office, because we can't prove they weren't."

"They were," I insisted, showing anxiety.

Bolt pursued his full moist lips. "Just how clever is Halley?" he said.

"He was a jockey," said Oxon flatly, as if that automatically meant an I.Q. of 70.

Bolt said, "But they took him on at Hunt Radnor's."

"I told you before," said Oxon patiently, "I asked various people about that. Radnor took him on as an advisor, but never gave him anything special to do, and if that doesn't show that he wasn't capable of much, I don't know what does. Everyone knows that his job is only a face-saver. It sounds all right, but it means nothing really. Jobs are quite often given in that way to top jockeys when they retire. No one expects them to *do* much, it's just their name that's useful for a while. When their news value has gone, they get the sack."

This all-too-true summing up of affairs depressed me almost as deeply as my immediate prospects.

"Howard?" said Bolt.

"I don't know," said Kraye slowly. "He doesn't strike me as being in the least clever. Very much the opposite. I agree he did take those photographs, but I think you are quite right in believing he doesn't know why we want them destroyed."

That, too, was shatteringly correct. As far as I had been able to see, the photographs proved nothing conclusively except that Kraye had been buying Seabury shares under various names with Bolt's help. Kraye and Bolt could not be prosecuted for that. Moreover the whole of Seabury executive had seen the photographs at the meeting that morning, so their contents were no secret.

"Doria?" Bolt said.

"He's a slimy, spying little creep, but if he was clever he wouldn't be sitting where he is."

You couldn't argue with that, either. It had been fairly certain all along that Kraye was getting help from somebody working at Seabury, but even after knowing about clerk of the course Brinton's unwilling collaboration at Dunstable, I had gone on assuming that the helper at Seabury was one of the laborers. I hadn't given more than a second's flicker of thought to Oxon, because it didn't seem reasonable that it should be him. In destroying the racecourse he was working himself out of a job, and good jobs for forty-year-old ex-army captains weren't plentiful enough to be lost lightly. As he certainly wasn't mentally affected like Brinton, he wasn't being blackmailed into doing it against his will. I had thought him silly and self-important, but not a rogue. As Doria said, had I been clever enough to suspect him, I wouldn't be sitting where I was.

Bolt went on discussing me as if I weren't there, and as if the decision they would come to would have ordinary everyday consequences.

He said, "You may all be right, but I don't think so, because since Halley has been on the scene everything's gone wrong. It was he who persuaded Hagbourne to get the course put right, and he who found the mirror as soon as it was up. I took him without question for what he said he was when he came to see me—a shop assistant. You two took him for a wretched little hanger-on of no account. All that, together with the fact that he opened your locked cases and took good clear photographs on a miniature camera, adds up to just one thing to me. Professionalism. Even the way he sits there saying nothing is professional. Amateurs call you names and try to impress you with how much they know. All he has said is that the negatives were in the office. I consider we ought to forget every previous impression we have of him and think of him only as coming from Hunt Radnor."

They thought about this for five seconds. Then Kraye said, "We'll have to make sure about the negatives."

Bolt nodded. If reason hadn't told me what Kraye meant, his wife's smile would have. My skin crawled.

"How?" she said interestedly.

Kraye inspected his grazed knuckles. "You won't beat it out of him," said Oxon. "Not like that. You haven't a hope."

"Why not?" said Bolt.

Instead of replying, Oxon turned to me. "How many races did you ride with broken bones?"

I didn't answer. I couldn't remember anyway.

"That's ridiculous," said Doria scornfully. "How could he?"

"A lot of them do," said Oxon. "And I'm sure he was no exception."

"Nonsense," said Kraye.

Oxon shook his head. "Collarbones, ribs, forearms, they'll ride with cracks in any of those if they can keep the owners and trainers from finding out."

Why couldn't he shut up, I thought savagely. He was making things much much worse; as if they weren't appalling enough already.

"You mean," said Doria with sickening pleasure, "that he can stand a great deal?"

"No," I said. "No." It sounded like the plea it was. "You can only ride with cracked bones if they don't hurt."

"They must hurt," said Bolt reasonably.

"No," I said. "Not always." It was true, but they didn't believe it.

"The negatives were in the office," I said despairingly. "In the office."

"He's scared," said Doria delightedly. And that too was true.

It struck a chord with Kraye. He remembered Aynsford. "We know where he's most easily hurt," he said. "That hand."

"No," I said in real horror.

They all smiled.

My whole body flushed with uncontrollable fear. Racing injuries were one thing: they were quick, one didn't expect them, and they were part of the job.

To sit and wait and know that a part of one's self which had already proved a burden was about to be hurt as much as ever was quite something else. Instinctively I put my arm up across my face to hide from them that I was afraid, but it must have been obvious.

Kraye laughed insultingly. "So there's your brave clever Mr. Halley for you. It won't take much to get the truth."

"What a pity," said Doria.

They left her standing in front of me holding the little pistol in an unswerving pink-nailed hand while they went out and rummaged for what they needed. I judged the distance to the door, which was all of thirty feet, and wondered whether the chance of a bullet on the way wasn't preferable to what was going to happen if I stayed where I was.

Doria watched my indecision with amusement.

"Just try it, buddy boy. Just try it."

I had read that to shoot accurately with an automatic pistol took a great deal of skill and practice. It was possible that all Doria had wanted was the power feeling of owning a gun and that she couldn't aim it. On the other hand she was holding it high and with a nearly straight arm, close to where she could see along the sights. On balance, I thought her claim to be a splendid shot had too much probability to be risked.

It was a pity Doria had such a vicious soul inside her beautiful body. She looked gay and dashing in her white Courrèges clothes, smiling a smile which seemed warm and friendly and was as safe as the yawn of a python. She was the perfect mate for Kraye, I thought. Fourth, fifth, sixth time lucky, he'd found a complete complement to himself. If Kraye could do it, perhaps one day I too . . . but I didn't know if I would even see tomorrow.

I put the back of my hand up over my eyes. My whole face hurt, swollen and stiff, and I was developing a headache. I decided that if I ever got out of this I wouldn't try any more detecting. I had made a proper mess of it.

The men came back, Oxon from the Stewards' room lugging a wooden spoke-backed chair with arms, Kraye and Bolt from the changing room with the yard-long poker from the stove and the rope the wet breeches had been hung on to dry. There were still a couple of pegs clinging to it.

Oxon put the chair down a yard or two away and Doria waved the gun a fraction to indicate I should sit in it. I didn't move.

"God," she said disappointedly, "you really are a little worm, just like at Aynsford. Scared to a stand still."

"He isn't a shop assistant," said Bolt sharply. "And don't forget it."

I didn't look at him. But for him and his rejection of Charles's usefully feeble Halley image, I might not have been faced with quite the present situation.

Oxon punched me on the shoulder. "Move," he said.

I stood up wearily and stepped off the weighing machine. They stood close round me. Kraye thrust out a hand, twisted it into my shirt, and pushed me into the chair. He, Bolt and Oxon had a fine old time tying my arms and legs to the equivalent wooden ones with the washing line. Doria watched, fascinated.

I remembered her rather unusual pleasures.

"Like to change places?" I said tiredly.

It didn't make her angry. She smiled slowly, put her gun in a pocket, and leaned down and kissed me long and hard on the mouth. I loathed it. When at length she straightened up she had a smear of my blood on her lip. She wiped it off onto her hand, and thoughtfully licked it. She looked misty-eyed and languorous, as if she had had a profound sexual experience. It made me want to vomit.

"Now," said Kraye. "Where are they?" He didn't seem to mind his wife kissing me. He understood her, of course.

I looked at the way they had tied the rope tightly round and round my left forearm, leaving the wrist bare, palm downward. A hand, I thought. What good, anyway, was a hand that didn't work.

I looked at their faces, one by one. Doria, rapt. Oxon, faintly surprised. Kraye confident, flexing his muscles. And Bolt, calculating and suspicious. None of them within a mile of relenting.

"Where are they?" Kraye repeated, lifting his arm.

"In the office," I said helplessly.

He hit my wrist with the poker. I'd hoped he might at least try to be subtle, but instead he used all his strength and with that one first blow smashed the whole shooting match to smithereens. The poker broke through the skin. The bones cracked audibly like sticks.

I didn't scream only because I couldn't get enough breath to do it. Before that moment I would have said I knew everything there was to know about pain, but it seems one can always learn. Behind my shut eyes the world turned yellow and gray, like sun shining through mist, and every inch of my skin began to sweat. There had never been anything like it. It was too much, too much. And I couldn't manage any more.

"Where are they?" said Kraye again.

"Don't," I said. "Don't do it." I could hardly speak.

Doria sighed deeply.

I opened my eyes a slit, my head lolling weakly back, too heavy to hold up. Kraye was smiling, pleased with his efforts. Oxon looked sick.

"Well?" said Kraye.

I swallowed, hesitating still.

He put the tip of the poker on my shattered bleeding wrist and gave a violent jerk. Among other things it felt like a fizzing electric shock, up my arm into my head and down to my toes. Sweat started sticking my shirt to my chest and my trousers to my legs.

"Don't," I said. "Don't." It was a croak, a capitulation, a prayer.

"Come on, then," said Kraye, and jolted the poker again.

I told them. I told them where to go.

18

THEY DECIDED it should be Bolt who went to fetch the negatives.

"What is this place?" he said. He hadn't recognized the address.

"The home of . . . a . . . girl friend."

He dispassionately watched the sweat run in trickles down my face. My mouth was dry. I was very thirsty.

"Say . . . I sent you," I said, between jagged breaths. "I . . . asked her . . . to keep them safe. . . . They . . . are with . . . several other things. . . . The package . . . you want . . . has a name on it . . . a make of film . . . Jigoro . . . Kano."

"Jigoro Kano. Right," Bolt said briskly.

"Give me . . . ," I said, "some morphine."

Bolt laughed. "After all the trouble you've caused us? Even if I had any, I wouldn't. You can sit there and sweat it out."

I moaned. Bolt smiled in satisfaction and turned away.

"I'll ring you as soon as I have the negatives," he said to Kraye. "Then we can decide what to do with Halley. I'll give it some thought on the way up." From his tone he might have been discussing the disposal of a block of worthless stocks.

"Good," said Kraye. "We'll wait for your call over in the flat."

They began to walk toward the door. Oxon and Doria hung back, Doria because she couldn't tear her fascinated, dilated eyes away from watching me, and Oxon for more practical reasons.

"Are you just going to leave him here?" he asked in surprise.

"Yes. Why not?" said Kraye. "Come on, Doria darling. The best is over."

Unwillingly she followed him, and Oxon also.

"Some water," I said. "Please."

"No," said Kraye.

They filed past him out of the door. Just before he shut it he gave me a last look compounded of triumph, contempt and satisfied cruelty. Then he switched off all the lights and went away.

I heard the sound of a car starting up and driving off. Bolt was on his way. Outside the windows the night was black. Darkness folded round me like a fourth dimension. As the silence deepened I listened to the low hum of the boiler roaring safely on the far side of the wall. At least, I thought, I don't have to worry about that as well. Small, small consolation.

The back of the chair came only as high as my shoulders and gave no support to my head. I felt deathly tired. I couldn't bear to move: every muscle in my body seemed to have a private line direct to my left wrist, and merely flexing my right foot had me panting. I wanted to lie down flat. I wanted a long cold drink. I wanted to faint. I went on sitting in the chair, wide awake, with a head that ached and weighed a ton, and an arm which wasn't worth the trouble.

I thought about Bolt going to Zanna Martin's front door, and finding that his own secretary had been helping me. I wondered for the hundredth time what he would do about that: whether he would harm her. Poor Miss Martin, whom life had already hurt too much.

Not only her, I thought. In the same file was the letter Mervyn Brinton had written out for me. If Bolt should see that, Mervyn Brinton would be needing a bodyguard for life.

I thought about the people who had borne the beatings and brutalities of the Nazis and of the Japanese and had often died without betraying their secrets. I thought about the atrocities still going on throughout the world, and the ease with which man could break man. In Algeria, they said, unbelievable things had been done. Behind the Iron Curtain, brain-washing wasn't all. In African jails, who knew?

Too young for World War Two, safe in a tolerant society, I had had no thought that I should ever come to such a test. To suffer or to talk. The dilemma that stretched back to antiquity. Thanks to Kraye, I now knew what it was like at first hand. Thanks to Kraye, I didn't understand how anyone could keep silent unto death.

I thought: I wanted to ride round Seabury Racecourse again, and to go back into the weighing room, and to sit on the scales; and I've done all those things.

I thought: a fortnight ago I couldn't let go of the past. I was clinging to too many ruins, the ruins of my marriage and my racing career and my useless hand. They were gone for good now, all of them. There was nothing left to cling to. And every tangible memory of my life had blown away with a plastic bomb. I was rootless and homeless: and liberated.

What I refused to think about was what Kraye might still do during the next few hours.

Bolt had been gone for a good long time when at last Kraye came back. It had seemed half eternity to me, but even so I was in no hurry for it to end.

Kraye put the light on. He and Doria stood just inside the doorway, staring across at me.

"You're sure there's time?" said Doria.

Kraye nodded, looking at his watch. "If we're quick."

"Don't you think we ought to wait until Ellis rings?" she said. "He might have thought of something better."

"He's late already," said Kraye impatiently. They had clearly been arguing for some time. "He should have rung by now. If we're going to do this, we can't wait any longer."

"All right," she shrugged. "I'll go and take a look."

"Be careful. Don't go in."

"No," she said. "Don't fuss."

They both came over to where I sat. Doria looked at me with interest, and liked what she saw.

"He looks ghastly, doesn't he? Serves him right."

"Are you human?" I said.

A flicker of awareness crossed her lovely face, as if deep down she did indeed know that everything she had enjoyed that night was sinful and obscene, but she was too thoroughly addicted to turn back. "Shall I help you?" she said to Kraye, not answering me.

"No. I can manage. He's not very heavy."

She watched with a smile while her husband gripped the back of the chair I was sitting in and began to tug it across the floor toward the wall. The jerks were almost past bearing. I grew dizzy with the effort of not yelling my head off. There was no one close enough to hear me if I did. Not the few overnight stable lads fast asleep three hundred yards away. Only the Krayes, who would find it sweet.

Doria licked her lips, as if at a feast.

"Go on," said Kraye. "Hurry."

"Oh, all right," she agreed crossly, and went out through the door into the passage.

Kraye finished pulling me across the room, turned the chair round so that I was facing the wall with my knees nearly touching it and stood back, breathing deeply from the exertion.

On the other side of the wall the boiler gently roared. One could hear it more clearly at such close quarters. I knew I had no crashing explosion, no flying bricks, no killing steam to worry about. But the sands were running out fast, all the same.

Doria came back and said in a puzzled voice, "I thought you said there would be water all down the passage."

"That's right."

"Well, there isn't. Not a drop. I looked into the boiler room and it's as dry as a bone."

"It can't be. It's nearly three hours since it started over-flowing. Oxon warned us it must be nearly ready to blow. You must be wrong."

"I'm not," she insisted. "The whole thing looks perfectly normal to me."

"It can't be." Kraye's voice was sharp. He went off in a hurry to see for himself, and came back even faster.

"You're right. I'll go and get Oxon. I don't know how the confounded thing works." He went straight on out of the main door, and I heard his footsteps running. There was no urgency except his own anger. I shivered.

Doria wasn't certain enough of the boiler's safety to spend any time near me, which was about the first really good thing which had happened the whole night. Nor did she find the back of my head worth speaking to: she liked to see her worms squirm. Perhaps she had even lost her appetite, now things had gone wrong. She waited uneasily near the door for Kraye to come back, fiddling with the catch.

Oxon came with him, and they were both running. They charged across the weighing room and out into the passage.

I hadn't much left anyway, I thought. A few tatters of pride, perhaps. Time to nail them to the mast.

The two men walked softly into the room and down to where I sat. Kraye grasped the chair and swung it violently round. The weighing room was quiet, undisturbed. There was only blackness through the window. So that was that.

I looked at Kraye's face, and wished on the whole that I hadn't. It was white and rigid with fury. His eyes were two black pits.

Oxon held the mouse in his hand. "It must have been Halley," he said, as if he'd said it before. "There's no one else."

Kraye put his right hand down on my left, and systematically began to take his revenge. After three long minutes I passed out.

I clung to the dark, trying to hug it round me like a blanket, and it obstinately got thinner and thinner, lighter and lighter, noisier and noisier, more and more painful, until I could no longer deny that I was back in the world.

My eyes unstuck themselves against my will.

The weighing room was full of people. People in dark uniforms. Policemen. Policemen coming through every door. Bright yellow lights at long last shining outside the window. Policemen carefully cutting the rope away from my leaden limbs.

Kraye and Doria and Oxon looked smaller, surrounded by the dark blue men. Doria in her brave white suit instinctively and unsuccessfully tried to flirt with her captors. Oxon, disconcerted to his roots, faced the facts of life for the first time.

Kraye's fury wasn't spent. His eyes stared in hatred across the room.

He shouted, struggling in strong restraining arms, "Where did you send him? Bolt. Where did you send him?"

"Ah, Mr. Potter," I said into a sudden oasis of silence. "Mr. Wilbur Potter. Find out. But not from me."

19

Of course I ended up where I had begun, flat on my back in a hospital. But not for so long, that time. I had a pleasant sunny room with a distant view of the sea, some exceedingly pretty nurses and a whole stream of visitors. Chico came first, as soon as they would let him, on the Sunday afternoon.

He grinned down at me.

"You look bloody awful."

"Thanks very much."

"Two black eyes, a scabby lip, a purple and yellow complexion and a three-day beard. Glamorous."

"It sounds it."

"Do you want to look?" he asked, picking up a hand mirror from a chest of drawers.

I took the mirror and looked. He hadn't exaggerated. I would have faded into the background in a horror movie.

Sighing, I said, "X certificate, definitely."

He laughed, and put the mirror back. His own face still bore the marks of battle. The eyebrow was healing, but the bruise showed dark right down his cheek.

"This is a better room than you had in London," he remarked, strolling over to the window. "And it smells O.K. For a hospital, that is."

"Pack in the small talk and tell me what happened," I said.

"They told me not to tire you."

"Don't be an ass."

"Well, all right. You're a bloody rollicking nit in many ways, aren't you?"

"It depends how you look at it," I agreed peaceably.

"Oh sure, sure."

"Chico, give," I pleaded. "Come on."

"Well, there I was harmlessly snoozing away in Radnor's armchair with the telephone on one side and some rather good chicken sandwiches on the other, dreaming about a willing blonde and having a ball, when the front doorbell rang." He grinned. "I got up, stretched and went to answer it. I thought it might be you, come back after all and with nowhere to sleep. I knew it wouldn't be Radnor, unless he'd forgotten his key. And who else would be knocking on his door at two o'clock in the morning? But there was this fat geezer standing on the doorstep in his city pin-stripes, saying you'd sent him. 'Come in, then,' I said, yawning my head off. He came in, and I showed him into Radnor's sort of study place, where I'd been sitting.

" 'Sid sent you?' I asked him. 'What for?' He said he understood your girl friend lived here. God, mate, don't ever try snapping your mouth shut at the top of a yawn. I nearly dislocated my jaw. Could he see her, he said. Sorry it was so late, but it was extremely important.

" 'She isn't here,' I said. 'She's gone away for a few days. Can I help you?'

" 'Who are you?' he said, looking me up and down.

"I said I was her brother. He took a sharpish look at the sandwiches and the book I'd been reading, which had fallen on the floor, and he could see I'd been asleep, so he seemed to think everything was O.K., and he said, 'Sid asked me to fetch something she is keeping for him. Do you think you could help me find it?'

" 'Sure,' I said. 'What is it?'

"He hesitated a bit but he could see that it would look too weird if he refused to tell me, so he said, 'It's a packet of negatives. Sid said your sister had several things of his, but the packet I want has a name on it, a make of films. Jigoro Kano.'

" 'Oh?' I said innocently. 'Sid sent you for a packet marked Jigoro Kano?'

" 'That's right,' he said, looking round the room. 'Would it be in here?'

" 'It certainly would,' I said."

Chico stopped, came over beside the bed, and sat on the edge of it, by my right toe.

"How come you know about Jigoro Kano?" he said seriously.

"He invented judo," I said. "I read it somewhere."

Chico shook his head. "He didn't really invent it. In 1882 he took all the best bits of hundreds of versions of jujitsu and put them into a formal sort of order, and called it judo."

"I was sure you would know," I said, grinning at him.

"You took a very sticky risk."

"You had to know. After all, you're an expert. And there were all those years at your club. No risk. I knew you'd know. As long as I'd got the name right, that is. Anyway, what happened next?"

Chico smiled faintly.

"I tied him into a couple of knots. Armlocks and so on. He was absolutely flabbergasted. It was really rather funny. Then I put a bit of pressure on. You know. The odd thumb screwing down into a nerve. God, you should have heard him yell. I suppose he thought he'd wake the neighbors, but you know what London is. No one took a blind bit of notice. So then I asked him where you were, when you sent him. He didn't show very willing, I must say, so I gave him a bit more. Poetic justice, wasn't it, considering what they'd just been doing to you? I told him I could keep it up all night, I'd hardly begun. There was a whole bookful I hadn't touched on. It shook him, it shook him bad."

Chico stood up restlessly and walked about the room.

"You know?" he said wryly. "He must have had a lot to lose. He was a pretty tough cookie, I'll give him that. If I hadn't been sure that you'd sent him to me as a sort of S.O.S., I don't think I'd have had the nerve to hurt him enough to bust him."

"I'm sorry," I said.

He looked at me thoughtfully. "We both learned about it, didn't we? You on the receiving end, and me . . . I didn't like it. Doing it, I mean. I mean, the odd swipe or two and a few threats, that's usually enough, and it doesn't worry you a bit, you don't give it a second thought. But I've never hurt anyone like that before. Not seriously, on purpose, beyond bearing. He was crying, you see. . . ."

Chico turned his back to me, looking out of the window.

There was a long pause. The moral problems of being on the receiving end were not so great, I thought. It was easier on the conscience altogether.

At last Chico said, "He told me, of course. In the end."

"Yes."

"I didn't leave a mark on him, you know. Not a scratch. . . . He said you were at Seabury Racecourse. Well, I knew that was probably right, and that he wasn't trying the same sort of misdirection you had, because you'd told me yourself that you were going there. He said that you were in the weighing room and that the boiler would soon blow up. He said that he hoped it would kill you. He seemed half out of his mind with rage about you. How he should have known better than to believe you, he should have realized that you were as slippery as a snake, he'd been fooled once before. . . . He said he'd taken it for granted you were telling the truth when you broke down and changed your story about the negatives being in the office, because you . . . because you were begging for mercy and morphine and God knows what."

"Yes," I said. "I know all about that."

Chico turned away from the window, his face lightening into a near grin. "You don't say," he said.

"He wouldn't have believed it if I'd given in sooner, or less thoroughly. Kraye would have, but not him. It was very annoying."

"Annoying," said Chico. "I like that word." He paused, considering. "At what moment exactly did you think of sending Bolt to me?"

"About half an hour before they caught me," I admitted. "Go on. What happened next?"

"There was a ball of string on Radnor's writing desk, so I tied old Fatso up with that in an uncomfortable position. Then there was the dicey problem of who to ring up to get the rescue squads on the way. I mean, the Seabury police might think I was some sort of a nut, ringing up at that hour and telling such an odd sort of story. At the best, they might send a bobby or two out to have a look, and the Krayes would easily get away. And I reckoned you'd want them rounded up red-handed, so to speak. I couldn't get hold of Radnor on account of the office phones being plasticated. So, well, I rang Lord Hagbourne."

"You didn't!"

"Well, yes. He was O.K., he really was. He listened to what I told him about you and the boiler and the Krayes and so on, and then he said, 'Right,' he'd see that half the Sussex police force turned up at Seabury Racecourse as soon as possible."

"Which they did."

"Which they did," agreed Chico. "To find that my old pal Sid had dealt with the boiler himself, but was otherwise in a fairly ropey state."

"Thanks." I said. "For everything."

"Be my guest."

"Will you do me another favor?"

"Yes, what?"

"I was supposed to take someone out to lunch today. She'll be wondering why I didn't turn up. I'd have got one of the nurses to ring her, but I still don't know her telephone number."

"Are you talking about Miss Zanna Martin? The poor old duck with the disaster area on a face?"

"Yes," I said, surprised.

"Then don't worry. She wasn't expecting you. She knows you're here."

"How?"

"She turned up at Bolt's office yesterday morning, to deal with the mail apparently, and found a policeman waiting on the doorstep with a search warrant. When he had gone she put two and two together smartly and trailed over to Cromwell Road to find out what was going on. Radnor had gone down to Seabury with Lord Hagbourne, but I was there poking about in the ruins, and we sort of swapped info. She was a bit upset about you, mate, in a quiet sort of way. Anyhow, she won't be expecting you to take her out to lunch."

"Did she say anything about having one of our files?"

"Yes. I told her to hang on to it for a day or two. There frankly isn't anywhere in the office to put it."

"All the same, you go over to where she lives as soon as you get back, and collect it. It's the Brinton file. And take great care of it. The negatives Kraye wanted are inside it."

Chico stared. "You're not serious."

"Why not?"

"But everyone—Radnor, Lord Hagbourne, even Kraye and Bolt, and the police—everyone has taken it for granted that what you said first was right, that they were in the office and were blown up."

"It's lucky they weren't," I said. "Get some more prints made. We've still got to find out why they were so hellishly important. And don't tell Miss Martin they were what Kraye wanted."

The door opened and one of the pretty nurses came in.

"I'm afraid you'll have to go now," she said to Chico. She came close beside the bed and took my pulse. "Haven't you any sense?" she exclaimed, looking at him angrily. "A few quiet minutes was what we said. Don't talk too much, and don't let Mr. Halley talk at all."

"You try giving *him* orders," said Chico cheerfully, "and see where it gets you."

"Miss Martin's address," I began.

"No," said the nurse severely. "No more talking."

I told Chico the address.

"See what I mean?" he said to the nurse. She looked down at me and laughed. A nice girl behind the starch.

Chico went across the room and opened the door.

"So long, then, Sid. Oh, by the way, I brought this for you to read. I thought you might be interested."

He pulled a glossy booklet folded lengthwise out of an inner pocket and threw it over onto the bed. It fell just out of my reach, and the nurse picked it up to give it to me. Then suddenly she held on to it tight.

"Oh no," she said. "You can't give him that!"

"Why not?" said Chico. "What do you think he is, a baby?"

He went out and shut the door. The nurse clung to the booklet, looking very troubled. I held out my hand for it.

"Come on."

"I think I ought to ask the doctors. . . ."

"In that case," I said, "I can guess what it is. Knowing Chico. So be a dear and hand it over. It's quite all right."

She gave it to me hesitantly, waiting to see my reaction when I caught sight of the bold words on the cover: *Artificial Limbs. The Modern Development.*

I laughed. "He's a realist," I said. "You wouldn't expect him to bring fairy stories."

20

WHEN RADNOR came the next day he looked tired, dispirited and ten years older. The military jauntiness had gone from his bearing, there were deep lines around his eyes and mouth, and his voice was lifeless.

For some moments he stared in obvious distress at the white-wrapped arm which stopped abruptly four inches below the elbow.

"I'm sorry about the office," I said.

"For God's sake—"

"Can it be rebuilt? How bad is it?"

"Sid—"

"Are the outside walls still solid, or is the whole place a write-off?"

"I'm too old," he said, giving in, "to start again."

"It's only bricks and mortar that are damaged. You haven't got to start again. The agency is you, not the building. Everyone can work for you just as easily somewhere else."

He sat down in an armchair, rested his head back, and closed his eyes.

"I'm tired," he said.

"I don't suppose you've had much sleep since it happened."

"I am seventy-one," he said flatly.

I was utterly astounded. Until that day I would have put him in the late fifties.

"You can't be."

"Time passes," he said. "Seventy-one."

"If I hadn't suggested going after Kraye it wouldn't have happened," I said with remorse. "I'm so sorry . . . so sorry. . . ."

He opened his eyes. "It wasn't your fault. If it was anyone's it was my own. You wouldn't have let Hagbourne take those photographs to Seabury, if it had been left to you. I know you didn't like it, that I'd given them to him. Letting the photographs go to Seabury was the direct cause of the bombs, and it was my mistake, not yours."

"You couldn't possibly tell," I protested.

"I should have known better, after all these years. I think . . . perhaps I may not see so clearly . . . consequences, things like that." His voice died to a low, miserable murmur. "Because I gave the photographs to Hagbourne, you lost your hand."

"No," I said decisively. "It's ridiculous to start blaming yourself for that. For heaven's sake snap out of it. No one in the agency can afford to have you in this frame of mind. What are Dolly and Jack Copeland and Sammy and Chico and all the others to do if you don't pick up the pieces?"

He didn't answer.

"My hand was useless, anyway," I said. "And if I'd been willing to give in to Kraye I needn't have lost it. It had nothing whatever to do with you."

He stood up.

"You told Kraye a lot of lies," he said.

"That's right."

"But you wouldn't lie to me."

"Naturally not."

"I don't believe you."

"Concentrate on it. It'll come in time."

"You don't show much respect for your elders."

"Not when they behave like bloody fools," I agreed dryly.

He blew down his nostrils, smoldering inwardly. But all he said was, "And you? Will you still work for me?"

"It depends on you. I might kill us all next time."

"I'll take the risk."

"All right then. Yes. But we haven't finished this time, yet. Did Chico get the negatives?"

"Yes. He had two sets of prints done this morning. One for him, and he gave me one to bring to you. He said you'd want them, but I didn't think—"

"But you did bring them?" I urged.

"Yes, they're outside in my car. Are you sure—?"

"For heaven's sake," I said in exasperation. "I can hardly wait."

By the following day I had acquired several more pillows, a bedside telephone and a reputation for being a difficult patient.

The agency restarted work that morning, squeezing into Radnor's own small house. Dolly rang to say it was absolute hell, there was only one telephone instead of thirty, the blitz spirit was fortunately in operation, not to worry about a thing, there was a new word going round the office, it was Halley-lujah, and good-bye, someone else's turn now.

Chico rang a little later from a call box.

"Sammy found that driver, Smith," he said. "He went to see him in Birmingham yesterday. Now that Kraye's in jug Smith is willing to turn Queen's evidence. He agreed that he did take two hundred and fifty quid, just for getting out of his cab, unclipping the chains when the tanker had gone over, and sitting on the side of the road moaning and putting on an act. Nice easy money."

"Good," I said.

"But that's not all. The peach of it is he still has the money, most of it, in a tin box, saving it for a deposit on a house. That's what tempted him, apparently, needing money for a house. Anyway, Kraye paid him the second installment in tenners, from one of the blocks you photographed in his case. Smith still has one of the actual tenners in the pictures. He agreed to part with that for evidence, but I can't see anyone making him give the rest back, can you?"

"Not exactly!"

"So we've got Kraye nicely tied up on malicious damage."

"That's terrific," I said. "What are they holding him on now?"

"Gross bodily harm. And the others for aiding and abetting."

"Consecutive sentences, I trust."

"You'll be lucky."

I sighed. "All the same, he still owns twenty-three per cent of Seabury's shares."

"So he does," agreed Chico gloomily.

"How bad exactly is the office?" I asked.

"They're surveying it still. The outside walls look all right, it's just a case of making sure. The inside was pretty well gutted."

"We could have a better layout," I said. "And a lift."

"So we could," he said happily. "And I'll tell you something else which might interest you."

"What?"

"The house next door is up for sale."

I was asleep when Charles came in the afternoon, and he watched me wake up, which was a pity. The first few seconds of consciousness were always the worst: I had the usual hellish time, and when I opened my eyes, there he was.

"Good God, Sid," he said in alarm. "Don't they give you anything?"

I nodded, getting a firmer grip on things.

"But with modern drugs, surely . . . I'm going to complain."

"No."

"But Sid—"

"They do what they can, I promise you. Don't look so upset. It'll get better in a few days. Just now it's a bore, that's all. Tell me about Fred."

Fred had already been at the house when the police guard arrived at Aynsford. Four policemen had gone there, and it took all four to hold him, with Charles going back and helping as well.

"Did he do much damage?" I asked. "Before the police got there?"

"He was very methodical, and very quick. He had been right through my desk, and all the wardroom. Every envelope, folder and notebook had been ripped apart, and the debris was all in a heap, ready to be destroyed. He'd started on the dining room when the police arrived. He was very violent. And they found a box of plastic explosive lying on the hall table, and some more out in the van." He paused. "What made you think he would come?"

"They knew I took the photographs at Aynsford, but how would they know I got them developed in London? I was afraid they might think I'd had them done locally, and that they'd think you'd know where the negatives were, as it was you who inveigled Kraye down there in the first place."

He smiled mischievously. "Will you come to Aynsford for a few days when you get out of here?"

"I've heard that somewhere before," I said. "No thanks."

"No more Krayes," he promised. "Just a rest."

"I'd like to, but there won't be time. The agency is in a dicky state. And I've just been doing to my boss what you did to me at Aynsford."

"What's that?"

"Kicking him out of depression into action."

His smile twisted in amusement.

"Do you know how old he is?" I said.

"About seventy, why?"

I was surprised. "I'd no idea he was that age, until he told me yesterday."

Charles squinted at the tip of his cigar. He said, "You always thought I asked him to give you a job, didn't you? And guaranteed your wages."

I made a face at him, embarrassed.

"You may care to know it wasn't like that at all. I didn't know him personally, only by name. He sought me out one day in the club and asked me if I thought you'd be any good at working with him. I said yes, I thought you would. Given time."

"I don't believe it."

He smiled. "I told him you played a fair game of chess. Also that you had become a jockey simply through circumstances, because you were small and your mother died, and that you could probably succeed at something else just as easily. He said that from what he'd seen of you racing you were the sort of chap he needed. He told me then how old he was. That's all. Nothing else. Just how old he was. But we both understood what he was saying."

"I nearly threw it away," I said. "If it hadn't been for you—"

"Oh yes," he said wryly. "You have a lot to thank me for. A lot."

Before he went I asked him to look at the photographs, but he studied them one by one and handed them back shaking his head.

Chief Inspector Cornish rang up to tell me Fred was not only in the bag but sewn up.

"The bullets match all right. He drew the same gun on the men who arrested him, but one of them fortunately threw a vase at him and knocked it out of his hand before he could shoot."

"He was a fool to keep that gun after he had shot Andrews."

"Stupid. Crooks often are, or we'd never catch them. And he didn't mention his little murder to Kraye and the others, so they can't be pinched as accessories to that. Pity. But it's quite clear he kept it quiet. The Sussex force said that Kraye went berserk when he found out. Apparently he mostly regretted not having known about your stomach while he had you in his clutches."

"Thank God he didn't!" I exclaimed with feeling.

Cornish's chuckle came down the wire. "Fred was supposed to look for Brinton's letter at your agency himself, but he wanted to go to a football match up north or something, and sent Andrews instead. He said he didn't think there'd be a trap, or anything subtle like that. Just an errand, about on Andrews' level. He said he only lent him the gun for a lark, he didn't mean Andrews to use it, didn't think he'd be so silly. But then Andrews went back to him scared stiff and said he'd shot you, so Fred says he suggested a country ramble in Epping Forest and the gun went off by accident. I ask you, try that on a jury! Fred says he didn't tell Kraye because he was afraid of him."

"What! Fred afraid?"

"Kraye seems to have made an adverse impression on him."

"Yes, he's apt to do that," I said.

* * *

I read Chico's booklet from cover to cover. One had to thank the thalidomide children, it appeared, for the speed-up of modern techniques. As soon as my arm had properly healed I could have a versatile gas-powered tool-hand with a swiveling wrist, activated by small pistons and controlled by valves, and operated by my shoulder muscles. The main snag to that, as far as I could gather, was that one always had to carry the small gas cylinders about, strapped on, like a permanent skin diver.

Much more promising, almost fantastic, was the latest invention of British and Russian scientists, the myo-electric arm. This worked entirely by harnessing the tiny electric currents generated in one's own remaining muscles, and the booklet cheerfully said it was easiest to fit on someone whose amputation was recent. The less one had lost of a limb, the better were one's chances of success. That put me straight in the guinea seats.

Finally, said the booklet with a justifiable flourish of trumpets, at St. Thomas' Hospital they invented a miraculous new myo-electric hand which could do practically everything a real one could except grow nails.

I missed my real hand, there was no denying it. Even in its deformed state it had had its uses, and I suppose that any loss of so integral a part of oneself must prove a radical disturbance. My unconscious mind did its best to reject the facts: I dreamed each night that I was whole, riding races, tying knots, clapping—anything which required two hands. I awoke to the frustrating stump.

The doctors agreed to inquire from St. Thomas' how soon I could go there.

On Wednesday morning I rang up my accountant and asked when he had a free day. Owing to an unexpected cancellation of plans, he said, he would be free on Friday. I explained where I was and roughly what had happened. He said that he would come to see me, he didn't mind the journey, a breath of sea air would do him good.

As I put the telephone down my door opened and Lord Hagbourne and Mr. Fotherton came tentatively through it. I was sitting on the edge of the bed in a dark blue dressing gown, my feet in slippers, my arm in a cradle inside a sling, chin freshly shaved, hair brushed, and the marks of Kraye's fists fading from my face. My visitors were clearly relieved at these encouraging signs of revival, and relaxed comfortably into the armchairs.

"You're getting on well, then, Sid?" said Lord Hagbourne.

"Yes, thank you."

"Good, good."

"How did the meeting go?" I asked. "On Saturday?"

Both of them seemed faintly surprised at the question.

"Well, you did hold it, didn't you?" I said anxiously.

"Why, yes," said Fotherton. "We did. There was a moderately good gate, thanks to the fine weather." He was a thin, dry man with a long face molded into drooping lines of melancholy, and on that morning he kept smoothing three fingers down his cheek as if he were nervous.

Lord Hagbourne said, "It wasn't only your security men who were drugged. The stable lads all woke up feeling muzzy, and the old man who was supposed to look after the boiler was asleep on the floor in the canteen. Oxon had given them all a glass of beer. Naturally, your men trusted him."

I sighed. One couldn't blame them too much. I might have drunk with him myself.

"We had the inspector in yesterday to go over the boiler thoroughly," said Lord Hagbourne. "It was nearly due for its regular check anyway. They said it was too old to stand much interference with its normal working, and that it was just as well it hadn't been put to the test. Also that they thought that it wouldn't have taken as long as three hours to blow up. Oxon was only guessing."

"Charming," I said.

"I sounded out Seabury council," said Lord Hagbourne. "They're putting the racecourse down on their agenda for next month. Apparently a friend of yours, the manager of the Seafront Hotel, has started a petition in the town urging the council to take an interest in the racecourse on the grounds that it gives a seaside town prestige and free advertising and is good for trade."

"That's wonderful," I said, very pleased.

Fotherton cleared his throat, looked hesitantly at Lord Hagbourne, and then at me.

"It has been discussed . . . ," he began. "It has been decided to ask you if you . . . er . . . would be interested in taking on . . . in becoming clerk of the course at Seabury."

"Me?" I exclaimed, my mouth falling open in astonishment.

"It's getting too much for me, being clerk of two courses," he said, admitting it a year too late.

"You saved the place on the brink of the grave," said Lord Hagbourne with rare decisiveness. "We all know it's an unusual step to offer a clerkship to a professional jockey so soon after he's retired, but Seabury executive are unanimous. They want you to finish the job."

They were doing me an exceptional honor. I thanked them, and hesitated, and asked if I could think it over.

"Of course, think it over," said Lord Hagbourne. "But say yes."

I asked them then to have a look at the box of photographs, which they did. They both scrutinized each print carefully, one by one, but they could suggest nothing at the end.

Miss Martin came to see me the next afternoon, carrying some enormous, sweet-smelling bronze chrysanthemums. A transformed Miss Martin, in a smart dark-green tweed suit and shoes chosen for looks more than sturdy walking. Her hair had been restyled so that it was shorter and curved in a bouncy curl onto her cheek. She had even tried a little lipstick and powder, and had tidied her eyebrows into a shapely line. The scars were just as visible, the facial muscles as wasted as ever, but Miss Martin had come to terms with them at last.

"How super you look," I said truthfully.

She was embarrassed, but very pleased. "I've got a new job. I had an interview yesterday, and they didn't even seem to notice my face. Or at least they didn't say anything. In a bigger office, this time. A good bit more than I've earned before, too."

"How splendid," I congratulated her sincerely.

"I feel new," she said.

"I too."

"I'm glad we met." She smiled, saying it lightly. "Did you get that file back all right? Your young Mr. Barnes came to fetch it."

"Yes, thank you."

"Was it important?"

"Why?"

"He seemed very odd when I gave it to him. I thought he was going to tell me something about it. He kept starting to, and then he didn't."

I would have words with Chico, I thought.

"It was only an ordinary file," I said. "Nothing to tell."

On the off-chance, I got her to look at the photographs. Apart from commenting on the many examples of her own typing, and expressing surprise that anybody should have bothered to photograph such ordinary papers, she had nothing to say.

She rose to go, pulling on her gloves. She still automatically leaned forward slightly, so that the curl swung down over her cheek.

"Good-bye, Mr. Halley. And thank you for changing everything for me. I'll never forget how much I owe you."

"We didn't have that lunch," I said.

"No." She smiled, not needing me any more. "Never mind. Some other time." She shook hands. "Good-bye."

She went serenely out of the door.

"Good-bye, Miss Martin," I said to the empty room. "Good-bye, good-bye, good-bye." I sighed sardonically at myself, and went to sleep.

Noel Wayne came loaded on Friday morning with a bulging briefcase of papers. He had been my accountant ever since I began earning big money at eighteen, and he probably knew more about me than anyone else on earth. Nearly sixty, bald except for a gray fringe over the ears, he was a small, round man with alert black eyes and a slow-moving mills-of-God mind. It was his advice more than my knowledge which had turned my earnings into a modest fortune via the stock markets, and I seldom did anything of any importance financially without consulting him first.

"What's up?" he said, coming straight to the point as soon as he had taken off his overcoat and scarf.

I walked over to the window and looked out. The weather had broken. It was drizzling, and a fine mist lay over the distant sea.

"I've been offered a job," I said. "Clerk of the course at Seabury."

"No!" he said, as astonished as I had been. "Are you going to accept?"

"It's tempting," I said. "And safe."

He chuckled behind me. "Good. So you'll take it."

"A week ago I definitely decided not to do any more detecting."

"Ah."

"So I want to know what you think about me buying a partnership in Radnor's agency."

He checked.

"I didn't think you even liked the place."

"That was a month ago. I've changed since then. And I won't be changing back. The agency is what I want."

"But has Radnor *offered* a partnership?"

"No. I think he might have eventually, but not since someone let a bomb off in the office. He's hardly likely to ask me to buy a half share of the ruins. And he blames himself for this." I pointed to the sling.

"With reason?"

"No," I said rather gloomily. "I took a risk which didn't come off."

"Which was?"

"Well, if you need it spelled out, that Kraye would only hit hard enough to hurt, not to damage beyond repair."

"I see." He said it calmly, but he looked horrified. "And do you intend to take similar risks in future?"

"Only if necessary."

"You always said the agency didn't do much crime work," he protested.

"It will from now on, if I have anything to do with it. Crooks make too much misery in the world." I thought of the poor Dunstable Brinton. "And listen, the house next door is for sale. We could knock the two into one. Radnor's is bursting at the seams. The agency has expanded a lot even in the two years I've been there. There seems more and more demand for his sort of service. Then the head of Bona Fides, that's one of the departments, is a natural to expand as an employment consultant on the management level. He has a gift for it. And insurance—Radnor's always neglected that. We don't have an insurance investigation department. I'd like to start one. Suspect insurance claims, you know. There's a lot of work in that."

"You're sure Radnor will agree, if you suggest a partnership?"

"He may kick me out. I'd risk it though. What do you think?"

"I think you've gone back to how you used to be" he said thoughtfully. "Which is good. Nothing but good. But . . . well, tell me what you really think about that." He nodded at my chopped-off arm. "None of your flippant lies, either. The truth."

I looked at him and didn't answer.

"It's only a week since it happened," he said, "and as you still look the color of a grubby sheet I suppose it's hardly fair to ask. But I want to know."

I swallowed. There were some truths which really couldn't be told. I said instead, "It's gone. Gone, like a lot of other things I used to have. I'll live without it."

"Live, or exist?"

"Oh live, definitely. Live." I reached for the booklet Chico had brought, and flicked it at him. "Look."

He glanced at the cover and I saw the faint shock in his face. He didn't have Chico's astringent brutality. He looked up and saw me smiling.

"All right," he said soberly. "Yes. Invest your money in yourself."

"In the agency," I said.

"That's what I mean," he said. "In the agency. In yourself."

He said he'd need to see the agency's books before a definite figure could be reached, but we spent an hour discussing the maximum he thought I should prudently offer Radnor, what return I could hope for in salary and dividends, and what I should best sell to raise the sum once it was agreed.

When we had finished I trotted out once more the infuriating photographs.

"Look them over, will you?" I said. "I've shown them to everyone else without result. These photographs were the direct cause of the bombs in my flat and the office, and of me losing my hand, and I can't see why. It's driving me ruddy well mad."

"The police . . . ," he suggested.

"The police are only interested in the one photograph of a ten-pound note. They looked at the others, said they could see nothing significant, and gave them back to Chico. But Kraye couldn't have been worried about that bank note, it was ten thousand to one we'd come across it again. No, it's something else. Something not obviously criminal, something Kraye was prepared to go to any lengths to obliterate immediately. Look at the time factor. Oxon only pinched the photographs just before lunch, down at Seabury. Kraye lived in London. Say Oxon rang him and told him to come and look: Oxon couldn't leave Seabury, it was a race day. Kraye had to go to Seabury himself. Well, he went down and looked at the photographs and saw . . . what? What? My flat was being searched by five o'clock."

Noel nodded in agreement. "Kraye was desperate. Therefore there was something to be desperate about." He took the photographs and studied them one by one.

Half an hour later he looked up and stared blankly out the window at the wet, gray skies. For several minutes he stayed completely still, as if in a state of suspended animation: it was his way of concentrated thinking. Finally he stirred and sighed. He moved his short neck as if it were stiff, and lifted the top photograph off the pile.

"This must be the one," he said.

I nearly snatched it out of his hand.

"But it's only the summary of the share transfers," I said in disappointment. It was the sheet headed S.R., Seabury Racecourse, which listed in summary form all Kraye's purchases of Seabury shares. The only noticeable factor in what had seemed to me merely a useful at-a-glance view of his total holding, was that it had been typed on a different typewriter, and not by Miss Martin. This hardly seemed enough reason for Kraye's hysteria.

"Look at it carefully," said Noel. "The three left-hand columns you can disregard, because I agree they are simply a tabulation of the share transfers, and I can't see any discrepancies."

"There aren't," I said. "I checked that."

"How about the last column, the small one on the right?"

"The banks?"

"The banks."

"What about them?" I said.

"How many different ones are there?"

I looked down the long list, counting. "Five. Barclays, Piccadilly. Westminster, Birmingham. British Linen Bank, Glasgow. Lloyds, Doncaster. National Provincial, Liverpool."

"Five bank accounts, in five different towns. Perfectly respectable. A very sensible arrangement in many ways. He can move round the country and always have easy access to his money. I myself have accounts in three different banks: it avoids muddling my clients' affairs with my own."

"I know all that. I didn't see any significance in his having several accounts. I still don't."

"Hm," said Noel. "I think it's very likely that he has been evading income tax."

"Is that all?" I said disgustedly.

Noel looked at me in amusement, pursing his lips. "You don't understand in the least, I see."

"Well, for heaven's sake, you wouldn't expect a man like Kraye to pay up every penny he was liable for like a good little citizen."

"You wouldn't," agreed Noel, grinning broadly.

"I'll agree he might be worried. After all, they sent Al Capone to jug in the end for tax evasion. But over here, what's the maximum sentence?"

"He'd only get a year, at the most," he said, "but—"

"And he would have been sure to get off with a fine. Which he won't do now, after attacking me. Even so, for that he'll only get three or four years, I should think, and less for the malicious damage. He'll be out and operating again far too soon. Bolt, I suppose, will be struck off, or whatever it is with stockbrokers."

"Stop talking," he said, "and listen. While it's quite normal to have more than one bank account, an inspector of taxes, having agreed to your tax liability, may ask you to sign a document stating that you have disclosed to him *all* your bank accounts. If you fail to mention one or two, it constitutes a fraud, and if you are discovered you can then be prosecuted. So, suppose Kraye has signed such a document, omitting one or two or even three of the five accounts? And then he finds a photograph in existence of his most private papers, listing all five accounts as undeniably his?"

"But no one would have noticed," I protested.

"Quite. Probably not. But to him it must have seemed glaringly dangerous. Guilty people constantly fear their guilt will be visible to others. They're vibratingly sensitive to anything which can give them away. I see quite a lot of it in my job."

"Even so, bombs are pretty drastic."

"It would entirely depend on the sum involved," he said primly.

"Huh?"

"The maximum fine for income tax evasion is twice the tax you didn't pay. If, for example, you amassed ten thousand pounds but declared only two, you could be fined a sum equal to twice the tax on eight thousand pounds. With surtax and so on, you might be left with almost nothing. A nasty setback."

"To put it mildly," I said in awe.

"I wonder," Noel said thoughtfully, putting the tips of his fingers together, "just how much undeclared loot Kraye had got stacked away in his five bank accounts?"

"It must be a lot," I said, "for bombs."

"Quite so."

There was a long silence. Finally I said, "One isn't required either legally or morally to report people to the Inland Revenue."

He shook his head.

"But we could make a note of those five banks, just in case?"

"If you like," he agreed.

"Then I think I might let Kraye have the negatives and the new sets of prints," I said. "Without telling him I know why he wants them."

Noel looked at me inquiringly, but didn't speak.

I grinned faintly. "On condition that he makes a free, complete and outright gift to Seabury Racecourse Company of his twenty-three per cent holding."

FLYING FINISH

With my thanks to

THE BRITISH BLOODSTOCK AGENCY

BRUCE DAGLISH

OF LEP TRANSPORT

PETER PALMER,

AIRLINE CAPTAIN

JOHN MERCER

OF C.S.E. AVIATION,

OXFORD AIRPORT

I assure them that everyone
in this book is imaginary.

1

"YOU'RE A spoiled, bad-tempered bastard," my sister said, and jolted me into a course I nearly died of.

I carried her furious, unattractive face down to the station and into the steamed-up compartment of Monday gloom and half-done crosswords and all across London to my unloved office.

Bastard I was not; not with parents joined by bishop with half Debrett and Burke in the pews. And if spoiled, it was their doing, their legacy to an heir born accidentally at the last possible minute when earlier intended pregnancies had produced five daughters. My frail eighty-six-year-old father in his second childhood saw me chiefly as the means whereby a much hated cousin was to be done out of an earldom he had coveted; my father delighted in my existence and I remained to him a symbol.

My mother had been forty-seven at my birth and was now seventy-three. With a mind which had to all intents stopped developing round about Armistice Day 1918, she had been for as long as I could remember completely batty. Eccentric, her acquaintances more kindly said. Anyway, one of the first things I ever learned was that age had nothing to do with wisdom.

Too old to want a young child around them, they had brought me up and educated me at arm's length—nursemaids, prep school and Eton—and in my hearing had regretted the length of the school holidays. Our relationship was one of politeness and duty, but not of affection. They didn't even seem to expect me to love them, and I didn't. I didn't love anyone. I hadn't had any practice.

I was first at the office as usual. I collected the key from the caretaker's cubbyhole, walked unhurriedly down the long, echoing hall, up the gritty stone staircase, down a narrow, dark corridor, and at the far end of it unlocked the heavily brown varnished front door of the Anglia Bloodstock Agency. Inside, typical of the old London warren-type blocks of offices, comfort took over from barracks. The several rooms opening right and left from the passage were close carpeted, white painted, each with the occupant's name in neat black on the door. The desks ran to extravagances like tooled leather tops, and there were sporting prints on the wall. I had not yet, however, risen to this success bracket.

The room where I had worked, on and off, for nearly six years lay at the far end, past the reference room and the pantry. "Transport" it said on the half-open door. I pushed it wide. Nothing had changed from Friday. The three desks looked the same as usual: Christopher's, with thick uneven piles of papers held down by cricket balls; Maggie's, with the typewriter cover askew, carbons screwed up beside it, and a vase of dead chrysanthemums dropping petals into a scummy teacup; and mine, bare.

I hung up my coat, sat down, opened my desk drawers one by one and uselessly straightened the already tidy contents. I checked that it was precisely eight minutes to nine by my accurate watch, which made the office clock two minutes slow. After this activity I stared straight ahead unseeingly at the calendar on the pale green wall.

A spoiled, bad-tempered bastard, my sister said.

I didn't like it. I was not bad-tempered, I assured myself defensively. I was not. But my thoughts carried no conviction. I decided to break with tradition and refrain from reminding Maggie that I found her slovenly habits irritating.

Christopher and Maggie arrived together, laughing, at ten past nine.

"Hullo," said Christopher cheerfully, hanging up his coat. "I see you lost on Saturday."

"Yes," I agreed.

"Better luck next time," said Maggie automatically, blowing the sodden petals out of the cup on to the floor. I bit my tongue to keep it still. Maggie picked up the vase and made for the pantry, scattering petals as she went. Presently she came back with the vase, fumbled it, and left a dripping trail of Friday's tea across my desk. In silence I took some white blotting paper from the drawer, mopped up the spots, and threw the blotting paper in the wastebasket. Christopher watched in sardonic amusement, pale eyes crinkling behind thick spectacles.

"A short head, I believe?" he said, lifting one of the cricket balls and going through the motions of bowling it through the window.

"A short head," I agreed. All the same if it had been ten lengths, I thought sourly. You got no present for losing, whatever the margin.

"My uncle had a fiver on you."

"I'm sorry," I said formally.

Christopher pivoted on one toe and let go. The cricket ball crashed into the wall, leaving a mark. He saw me frowning at it and laughed. He had come straight into the office from Cambridge two months before, robbed of a cricket blue through deteriorating eyesight and having failed his finals into the bargain. He remained always in better spirits than I, who had suffered no similar reverses. We tolerated each other. I found it difficult, as always, to make friends, and he had given up trying.

Maggie came back from the pantry, sat down at her desk, took her nail varnish out of the stationery drawer and began brushing on the silvery pink. She was a large, assured girl from Surbiton with a naturally unkind tongue and a suspect talent for registering remorse immediately after the barbs were securely in.

The cricket ball slipped out of Christopher's hand and rolled across Maggie's desk. Lunging after it, he brushed one of his heaps of letters into a fluttering muddle on the floor, and the ball knocked over Maggie's bottle of varnish, which scattered pretty pink viscous blobs all over the "We have received yours of the fourtheenth ult."

"Goddamn," said Christopher with feeling.

Old Cooper, who dealt with insurance, came into the room at his doddery pace and looked at the mess with cross disgust and pinched nostrils. He held out to me the sheaf of papers he had brought.

"Your pigeon, Henry. Fix it up for the earliest possible."

"Right."

As he turned to go he said to Christopher and Maggie in a complaining voice certain to annoy them, "Why can't you two be as efficient as Henry? He's never late, he's never untidy, his work is always correct and always done on time. Why don't you try to be more like him?"

I winced inwardly and waited for Maggie's inevitable retaliation. She would be in good form; it was Monday morning.

"I wouldn't want to be like Henry in a thousand years," she said sharply. "He's a prim, dim, sexless *nothing*. He's not alive."

Not my day, definitely.

"He rides those races, though," said Christopher in mild defense.

"And if he fell off and broke both his legs, all he'd care about would be seeing they got the bandages straight."

"The bones," I said.

"What?"

"The bones straight."

Christopher blinked and laughed. "Well, well, what do you know? The still waters of Henry might just possibly be running deep."

"Deep, nothing," said Maggie. "A stagnant pond, more like."

"Slimy and smelly?" I suggested.

"No . . . oh dear . . . I mean, I'm sorry. . . ."

"Never mind," I said. "Never mind." I looked at the paper in my hand and picked up the telephone.

"Henry . . ." said Maggie desperately. "I didn't mean it."

Old Cooper tut-tutted and doddered away along the passage, and Christopher began sorting his varnished letters. I got through to Yardman Transport and asked for Simon Searle. "Four yearlings from the Newmarket sales to go to Buenos Aires as soon as possible," I said.

"There might be a delay."

"Why?"

"We've lost Peters."

"Careless," I remarked.

"Oh, ha-ha."

"Has he left?"

Simon hesitated perceptibly. "It looks like it."

"How do you mean?"

"He didn't come back from one of the trips. Last Monday. Just never turned up for the flight back, and hasn't been seen or heard of since."

"Hospitals?" I said.

"We checked those, of course. And the morgue, and the jail. Nothing. He just vanished. And as he hasn't done anything wrong the police aren't interested in finding him. No police would be; it isn't criminal to leave your job without notice. They say he fell for a girl, very likely, and decided not to go home."

"Is he married?"

"No." He sighed. "Well, I'll get on with your yearlings, but I can't give you even an approximate date."

"Simon," I said slowly. "Didn't something like this happen before?"

"Er . . . do you mean Ballard?"

"One of your liaison men," I said.

"Yes. Well . . . I suppose so."

"In Italy?" I suggested gently.

There was a short silence at the other end. "I hadn't thought of it," he said. "Funny coincidence. Well . . . I'll let you know about the yearlings."

"I'll have to get on to Clarksons if you can't manage it."

He sighed. "I'll do my best. I'll ring you back tomorrow."

I put down the receiver and started on a large batch of Customs declarations, and the long morning disintegrated toward the lunch hour. Maggie and I said nothing at all to each other and Christopher cursed steadily over his letters. At one sharp I beat even Maggie in the rush to the door.

Outside, the December sun was shining. On impulse I jumped onto a passing bus, got off at Marble Arch, and walked slowly through the park to the Serpentine. I was still there, sitting on a bench, watching the sun ripple on the water, when the hands on my watch read two o'clock. I was still there at half past. At a quarter to three I threw some stones with force into the lake, and a park keeper told me not to.

A spoiled, bad-tempered bastard. It wouldn't have been so bad if she had been used to saying things like that, but she was a gentle, see-no-evil person who had been made to wash her mouth out with soap for swearing as a child and had never taken the risk again. She was my youngest sister, fifteen years my elder, unmarried, plain, and quietly intelligent. She had reversed roles with our parents: she ran the house and managed them as her children. She also to a great extent managed me, and always had.

A repressed, quiet, "good" little boy I had been, and a quiet, withdrawn, secretive man I had become. I was almost pathologically tidy and methodical, early for every appointment, controlled alike in behavior, handwriting and sex. A prim dim nothing, as Maggie said. The fact that for some months now I had not felt in the least like that inside was confusing, and getting more so.

I looked up into the blue, gold-washed sky. Only there, I thought with a fleeting inward smile, only there am I my own man. And perhaps in steeplechases. Perhaps there too, sometimes.

She had been waiting for me as usual at breakfast, her face fresh from her early walk with the dogs. I had seen little of her over the weekend. I'd been racing on Saturday, and on Sunday I'd left home before breakfast and gone back late.

"Where did you go yesterday?" she asked.

I poured some coffee and didn't answer. She was used to that, however.

"Mother wanted to speak to you."

"What about?"

"She has asked the Filyhoughs to lunch next Sunday."

I tidily ate my bacon and egg. I said calmly, "That coy spotty Angela. It's a waste of time. I won't be here anyway."

"Angela will inherit half a million," she said earnestly.

"And we have beetles in the roof," I agreed dryly.

"Mother wants to see you married."

"Only to a very rich girl."

My sister acknowledged that this was true, but saw nothing particularly wrong in it. The family fortunes were waning. As my parents saw it, the swap of a future title for a future fortune was a suitable bargain. They didn't seem to realize that a rich girl nowadays had more sense than to hand over her wealth to her husband, and could leave with it intact if she felt like it.

"Mother told Angela you would he here."

"That was silly of her."

"Henry!"

"I do not like Angela," I said coldly. "I do not intend to be here for lunch next Sunday. Is that quite clear?"

"But you must. . . . You can't leave me to deal with them all alone."

"You'll just have to restrain Mother from issuing these stupid invitations. Angela is the umpteenth unattractive heiress she's invited this year. I'm fed up with it."

"We need. . . ."

"I am not," I said stiffly, "a prostitute."

She stood up, bitterly offended. "That's unkind."

"And while we are at it, I wish the beetles good luck. This damp decaying pile of a house eats up every penny we've got and if it fell down tomorrow we'd all be far better off."

"It's our home," she said, as if that was the final word.

When it was mine, I would get rid of it; but I didn't say that, and encouraged by my silence she tried persuasion. "Henry, please be here for the Filyhoughs."

"No," I said forcefully. "I won't. I want to do something else next Sunday. You can count me right out."

She suddenly and completely lost her temper. Shaking, she said, "I cannot stand much more of your damned autistic behavior. You're a spoiled, bad-tempered *bastard*. . . ."

Hell, I thought by the Serpentine, was I really? And if so, why?

At three, with the air growing cold, I got up and left the park, but the office I went to was not the elegant suite of Anglia Bloodstock in Hanover Square. There, I thought, they could go on wondering why the ever-punctual Henry hadn't returned from lunch. I went instead by taxi to a small, dilapidated, rubbish-strewn wharf down in the Pool, where the smell of Thames mud at low tide rose earthily into my nostrils as I paid the fare.

At one end of the wharf, on an old bombed site, a small square concrete building had been thrown up shortly after the war and shoddily maintained ever since. Its drab walls, striped by rust from leaking gutters, badly needed a coat of "Snowcem"; its rectangular metal windows were grimed and flaking, and no one had polished the brass door fittings since my previous visit six months ago. There was no need here to put on a plushy front for the customers; the customers were not expected to come.

I walked up the uncarpeted stairs, across the eight foot square of linoleumed landing and through the open door of Simon Searle's room. He looked up from some complicated doodling on a memo pad, lumbered to his feet and greeted me with a huge handshake and a wide grin. As he was the only person who ever gave me this sort of welcome I came as near to unbending with him as with anyone. But we had never done more than meet now and again on business and occasionally repair to a pub afterward. There he was inclined to lots of beer and bonhomie, and I to a single whisky, and that was that.

"You haven't trekked all the way down here about those yearlings?" he protested. "I told you . . ."

"No," I said, coming to the point abruptly. "I came to find out if Yardman would give me a job."

"*You,*" said Simon, "want to work *here?*"

"That's right."

"Well, I'm damned." Simon sat down on the edge of his desk and his bulk settled and spread comfortably around him. He was a vast shambling man somewhere in the doldrums between thirty-five and forty-five, bald on top, Bohemian in dress and broad of mind.

"Why, for God's sake?" he said, looking me up and down. A more thorough contrast than me in my charcoal worsted to him in his baggy green corduroys would have been hard to find.

"I need a change."

"For the worse?" He was sardonic.

"Of course not. And I'd like the chance of a bit of globe-trotting now and then."

"You can afford to do that in comfort. You don't have to do it on a horse transport."

Like so many other people, he took it for granted that I had money. I hadn't. I had only my salary from Anglia, and what I could earn by being frankly, almost notoriously, a shamateur jockey. Every penny I got was earmarked. From my father I took only my food and the beetle-infested roof over my head, and neither expected nor asked for anything else.

"I imagine I would like a horse transport," I said equably. "What are the chances?"

"Oh," Simon laughed. "You've only to ask. I can't see him turning you down."

But Yardman very nearly did turn me down, because he couldn't believe I really meant it.

"My dear boy, now think carefully, I do beg you. Anglia Bloodstock is surely a better place for you? However well you might do here, there isn't any power or any prestige. . . . We must face facts, we must indeed."

"I don't particularly care for power and prestige."

He sighed deeply. "There speaks one to whom they come by birth. Others of us are not so fortunate as to be able to despise them."

"I don't despise them. Also I don't want them. Or not yet."

He lit a dark cigar with slow care. I watched him, taking him in. I hadn't met him before, and as he came from a different mold from the top men at Anglia I found that I didn't instinctively know how his mind worked. After years of being employed by people of my own sort of background, where much that was understood never needed to be stated, Yardman was a foreign country.

He was being heavily paternal, which somehow came oddly from a thin man. He wore black-rimmed spectacles on a strong beaky nose. His cheeks were hollowed, and his mouth in consequence seemed to have to stretch to cover his teeth and gums. His lips curved downward strongly at the corners, giving him at times a disagreeable and at times a sad expression. He was bald on the crown of his head, which was not noticeable at first sight, and his skin looked unhealthy. But his voice and his fingers were strong, and as I grew to acknowledge, his will and character also.

He puffed slowly at the cigar, a slim, fierce-looking thing with an aroma to match. From behind the glasses his eyes considered me without haste. I hadn't a clue as to what he was thinking.

"All right," he said at last. "I'll take you on as an assistant to Searle, and we'll see how it goes."

"Well . . . thank you," I answered. "But what I really came to ask for was Peters's job."

"*Peters's. . . .*" His mouth literally fell open, revealing a bottom row of regular false teeth. He shut it with a snap. "Don't be silly, my boy. You can't have Peters's job."

"Searle says he has left."

"I dare say, but that's not the point, is it?"

I said calmly. "I've been in the Transport Section of Anglia for more than five years, so I know all the technical side of it, and I've ridden horses all my life, so I know how to look after them. I agree that I haven't any practical experience, but I could learn very quickly."

"Lord Grey," he said, shaking his head. "I don't think you realize just what Peters's job was."

"Of course I do," I said. "He traveled on the planes with the horses and saw they arrived safely and well. He saw that they passed the Customs all right at both ends and that the correct people collected them, and where necessary saw that another load of horses was brought safely back again. It is a responsible job and it entails a lot of traveling and I am seriously applying for it."

"You don't understand," he said with some impatience. "Peters was a traveling head groom."

"I know."

He smoked, inscrutable. Three puffs. I waited, quiet and still.

"You're not . . . er . . . in any trouble at Anglia?"

"No. I've grown tired of a desk job, that's all." I had been tired of it from the day I started, to be exact.

"How about racing?"

"I have Saturdays off at Anglia, and I take my three weeks annual holiday in separate days during the winter and spring. And they have been very considerate about extra half-days."

"Worth it to them in terms of trade, I dare say." He tapped off the ash absentmindedly into the inkwell. "Are you thinking of giving it up?"

"No."

"Mm . . . if you work for me, would I get any increase in business from your racing connections?"

"I'd see you did," I said.

He turned his head away and looked out of the window. The river tide was sluggishly at the ebb, and away over on the other side a row of cranes stood like red meccano toys in the beginnings of dusk. I couldn't even guess then at the calculations clicking away at high speed in Yardman's nimble brain, though I've often thought about those few minutes since.

"I think you are being unwise, my dear boy. Youth . . . youth. . . ." He sighed, straightened his shoulders and turned the beaky nose back in my direction. His shadowed greenish eyes regarded me steadily from deep sockets, and he told me what Peters had been earning; fifteen pounds a trip plus three pounds expenses for each overnight stop. He clearly thought that that would deter me, and it nearly did.

"How many trips a week?" I asked, frowning.

"It depends on the time of year. You know that, of course. After the yearling sales, and when the brood mares come over, it might be three trips. To France, perhaps even four. Usually two, sometimes none."

There was a pause. We looked at each other. I learned nothing.

"All right," I said abruptly. "Can I have the job?"

His lips twisted in a curious expression which I later came to recognize as an ironic smile.

"You can try it," he said. "If you like."

2

A JOB is what you make it. Three weeks later, after Christmas, I flew to Buenos Aires with twelve yearlings, the four from Anglia and eight more from different bloodstock agencies, all mustered together at five o'clock on a cold Tuesday morning at Gatwick. Simon Searle had organized their arrival and booked their passage with a charter company; I took charge of them when they unloaded from their various horseboxes, installed them in the plane, checked their papers through the Customs, and presently flew away.

With me went two of Yardman's traveling grooms, both of them fiercely resenting that I had been given Peters's job over their heads. Each of them had coveted the promotion, and in terms of human relationships the trip was a frostbitten failure. Otherwise, it went well enough. We arrived in Argentina four hours late, but the new owners' horseboxes had all turned up to collect the cargo. Again I cleared the horses and papers through the Customs, and made sure that each of the five new owners had got the right horses and the certificates to go with them. The following day the plane picked up a load of crated furs for the return journey, and we flew back to Gatwick, arriving on Friday.

On Saturday I had a fall and a winner at Sandown Races, Sunday I spent in my usual way, and Monday I flew with some circus ponies to Germany. After a fortnight of it I was dying from exhaustion; after a month I was acclimatized. My body got used to long hours, irregular food, nonstop coffee, and sleeping sitting upright on bales of hay ten thousand feet up in the sky. The two grooms, Timmie and Conker, gradually got over the worst of their anger, and we developed into a quick, efficient, laconic team.

My family were predictably horrified by my change of occupation and did their best to pry me away from it. My sister anxiously retracted the words I knew I'd earned, my father foresaw the earldom going to the cousin after all, airplanes being entirely against nature and usually fatal, and my mother had hysterics over what her friends would say.

"It's a laborer's job," she wailed.

"A job is what you make it."

"What will the Filyhoughs think?"

"Who the hell cares what they think?"

"It isn't a *suitable* job for you." She wrung her hands.

"It's a job I like. It suits me, therefore it *is* suitable."

"You know that isn't what I mean."

"I know exactly what you mean, Mother, and I profoundly disagree with you. People should do work they like doing; that's all that should decide them. Whether it is socially O.K. or not shouldn't come into it."

"But it does," she cried, exasperated.

"It has for me for nearly six years," I admitted, "but not any more. And ideas change. What I am doing now may be the top thing next year. If I don't look out half the men I know will be muscling in on the act. Anyway, it's right for me, and I'm going on with it."

All the same she couldn't be won over, and could only face her own elderly convention-bound circle by pretending my job was "for the experience, you know," and by treating it as a joke.

It was a joke to Simon Searle too, at first.

"You won't stick it, Henry," he said confidently. "Not you and all that dirt. You with your spotless dark suits and your snowy-white shirts and not a hair out of place. One trip will be enough."

After a month, looking exactly the same, I turned up for my pay packet late on Friday afternoon, and we sauntered along to his favorite pub, a tatty place with stained glass doors and a chronic smell of fog. He oozed on to a bar stool, his bulk drooping around him. A pint for him, he said. I bought it, and a half for me, and he drank most of his off with one much practiced swallow.

"How's the globe-trotting, then?" He ran his tongue over his upper lip for the froth.

"I like it."

"I'll grant you," he said, smiling amicably, "that you haven't made a mess of it yet."

"Thanks."

"Though of course since I do all the spade work for you at both ends, you bloody well shouldn't."

"No," I agreed. He was, in truth, an excellent organizer, which was mainly why Anglia often dealt with Yardman Transport instead of Clarkson Carriers, a much bigger and better known firm. Simon's arrangements were clear, simple, and always twice confirmed: agencies, owners and airlines alike knew exactly where they stood and at what hours they were expected to be where. No one else in the business, that I had come across at any rate, was as consistently reliable. Being so precise myself, I admired his work almost as a work of art.

He looked me over, privately amused. "You don't go on trips dressed like that?"

"I do, yes, more or less."

"What does more or less mean?"

"I wear a sweater instead of my jacket, in and around the aircraft."

"And hang up your jacket on a hanger for when you land?"

"Yes, I do."

He laughed, but without mockery. "You're a rum sort of chap, Henry." He ordered more beer, shrugged when I refused, and drank deep again. "Why are you so methodical?"

"It's safer."

"Safer." He choked on his beer, coughing and laughing. "I suppose it doesn't strike you that to many people steeplechasing and air transport might not seem especially safe?"

"That wasn't what I meant."

"What, then?"

But I shook my head, and didn't explain.

"Tell me about Yardman," I said.

"What about him?"

"Well, where he came from . . . anything."

Simon hunched his great shoulders protectively around his pint, and pursed his lips.

"He joined the firm after the war, when he left the Army. He was a sergeant in an infantry regiment, I think. Don't know any details; never asked. Anyway he worked his way up through the business. It wasn't called Yardman Transport then, of course. Belonged to a family, the Mayhews, but they were dying out . . . nephews weren't interested, that sort of thing. Yardman had taken it over by the time I got there; don't know how really, come to think of it, but he's a bright lad, there's no doubt of that. Take switching to air, for instance. That was him. He was pressing the advantages of air travel for horses while all the other transport agencies were going entirely by sea."

"Even though the office itself is on a wharf," I remarked.

"Yes. Very handy once. It isn't used much at all now since they clamped down on exporting horses to the Continent for meat."

"Yardman was in that?"

"Shipping agent," he nodded. "There's a big warehouse down the other end of the wharf where we used to collect them. They'd start being brought in three days before the ship came. Once a fortnight, on average.

I can't say I'm sorry it's finished. It was a lot of work and a lot of mess and noise, and not much profit, Yardman said."

"It didn't worry you, though, that they were going to be slaughtered?"

"No more than cattle or pigs." He finished his beer. "Why should it? Everything dies sometime." He smiled cheerfully and gestured to the glasses. "Another?"

He had one, I didn't.

"Has anyone heard any more of Peters?" I asked.

He shook his head. "Not a murmur."

"How about his cards?"

"Still in the office, as far as I know."

"It's a bit odd, isn't it?"

Simon shrugged. "You never know, he might have wanted to duck someone, and did it thoroughly."

"But did anyone ever come looking for him?"

"Nope. No police, no unpaid bookies, no rampaging females, no one."

"He just went to Italy and didn't come back?"

"That's the size of it," Simon agreed. "He went with some brood mares to Milan and he should have come back the same day. But there was some trouble over an engine or something, and the pilot ran out of time and said he'd be in dead trouble if he worked too many hours. So they stayed there overnight and in the morning Peters didn't turn up. They waited nearly all day, then they came back without him."

"And that's all?"

"That's the lot," he agreed. "Just one of life's little mysteries. What's the matter, are you afraid Peters will reappear and take back his job?"

"Something like that."

"He was an awkward bastard," he said thoughtfully. "Stood on his rights. Always arguing; that sort of chap. Belligerent. Never stood any nonsense from foreign Customs officers." He grinned. "I'll bet they're quite glad to see you instead."

"I dare say I'll be just as cussed in a year or two."

"A year or two?" He looked surprised. "Henry, it's all very well you taking Peters's job for a bit of a giggle but you surely can't mean to go on with it permanently?"

"You think it would be more suitable if I was sitting behind a nice solid desk at Anglia?" I asked ironically.

"Yes," he said seriously. "Of course it would."

I sighed. "Not you too. I thought you at least might understand. . . ." I stopped wryly.

"Understand what?"

"Well . . . that who one's father is has nothing to do with the sort of work one is best suited for. And I am not fitted for sitting behind a desk. I came to that conclusion my first week at Anglia, but I stayed there because I'd kicked up a fuss and insisted on getting an ordinary job, and I wasn't going to admit I'd made a mistake with it. I tried to like it. At any rate I got used to it, but now . . . now . . . I don't think I could face that nine-to-five routine ever again."

"Your father's in his eighties, isn't he?" Simon said thoughtfully.

I nodded.

"And do you think that when he dies you will be allowed to go on carting horses round the world? And for how long *could* you do it without becoming an eccentric nut? Like it or not, Henry, it's easy enough to go up the social scale, but damn difficult to go down. And still be respected, that is."

"And I could be respected sitting behind a desk at Anglia, transferring horses from owner to owner on paper, but not if I move about and do it on airplanes?"

He laughed. "Exactly."

"The world is mad," I said.

"You're a romantic. But time will cure that." He looked at me in a large tolerant friendship, finished his beer, and flowed down from the stool like a green corduroy amoeba.

"Come on," he said, "there's time for another along the road at the Saracen's Head."

At Newbury Races the following afternoon I watched five races from the stands and rode in one.

This inactivity was not mine by choice, but thrust upon me by the Stewards. They had, by the time I was twenty, presented me with their usual ultimatum to regular amateur riders: either turn professional, or ride in only fifty open races each season. In other words, don't undercut the trade; stop taking the bread and butter out of the professionals' mouths. (As if jockeys *ate* much bread and butter, to start with.)

I hadn't turned professional when I was twenty because I had been both too conventional and not really good enough. I was still not good enough to be a top rank professional, but I had long been a fully employed amateur. A big fish in a small pond. In the new-found freedom of my Yardman's job I regretted that I hadn't been bolder at twenty. I liked steeplechasing enormously, and with full-time professional application I might just have made a decent success. Earth-bound on the stands at Newbury I painfully accepted that my sister had brought me to my senses a lot too late.

The one horse I did ride was in the "amateurs only" race. As there were no restrictions on the number of amateur events I could ride in, few were run without me. I rode regularly for many owners who grudged paying professional jockeys' fees, for some who reckoned their horses stood more chance in amateur races, and for a few who genuinely liked my work.

All of them knew very well that if I won either amateur or open races I expected ten per cent of the prize. The word had got around. Henry Grey rode for money, not love. Henry Grey was the shamateur to end all shamateurs. Because I was silent and discreet and they could trust my tongue, I had even been given cash presents by stewards; and solely because my father was the Earl of Creggan, my amateur permit survived.

In the changing room that afternoon I found that however different I might feel, I could not alter my long-set pattern. The easy bantering chat flowed round me and as usual it was impossible to join in. No one expected me to. They were used to me. Half of them took my aloofness to be arrogant snobbery, and the rest shrugged it off as "just Henry's way." No one was actively hostile, and it was I, I, who had failed to belong. I changed slowly into my racing clothes and listened to the jokes and the warm earthy language, and I could think of nothing, not one single thing, to say.

I won the race. The well-pleased owner gave me a public clap on the shoulder and a drink in the members' bar, and surreptitiously, round a private corner, forty pounds.

On the following day, Sunday, I spent the lot.

I started my little Herald in the garage in the predawn dark, and as quietly as possible opened the doors and drifted away down the drive. Mother had invited yet another well-heeled presumptive virgin for the weekend, together with her slightly forbidding parents, and having dutifully escorted them all to Newbury Races the day before and tipped them a winner—my own—I felt I had done quite enough. They would be gone, I thought coolly, before I got back late that evening, and with a bit of luck my bad manners in disappearing would have discouraged them forever.

A steady two and a half hours driving northward found me at shortly before ten o'clock turning in through some inconspicuously signposted gates in Lincolnshire. I parked the car at the end of the row of others, climbed out, stretched, and looked up into the sky. It was a cold, clear morning with maximum visibility. Not a cloud in sight. Smiling contentedly I strolled over to the row of white painted buildings and pushed open the glass door into the main hall of the Fenland Flying Club.

The hall was a big room with several passages leading off it and a double door on the far side opening to the airfield itself. Round the walls hung framed charts, Air Ministry regulations, a large map of the surrounding area, do's and don'ts for visiting pilots, a thumbtacked weather report, and a list of people wanting to enter for a ping-pong tournament. There were several small wooden tables and hard chairs at one end, half occupied, and across the whole width of the other end stretched the reception-cum-operations-cum-everything-else desk. Yawning behind it and scratching between his shoulder blades stood a plump sleepy man of about my own age, sporting a thick sloppy sweater and a fair-sized hangover. He held a cup of strong coffee and a cigarette in his free hand, and he was talking lethargically to a gay young spark who had turned up with a girl friend he wanted to impress.

"I've told you, old chap, you should have given us a ring. All the planes are booked today. I'm sorry, no can do. You can hang about if you like, in case someone doesn't turn up. . . ."

He turned toward me, casually.

"Morning, Harry," he said. "How's things?"

"Very O.K.," I said. "And you?"

"Ouch," he grinned, "don't cut me. The gin would run out." He turned round and consulted the vast timetable charts covering most of the wall behind him. "You've got Kilo November today, it's out by the petrol pumps, I think. Cross country again; is that right?"

"Uh-huh," I nodded.

"Nice day for it." He put a tick on his chart where it said H. Grey, solo cross.

"Couldn't be better."

The girl said moodily, "How about this afternoon, then?"

"No dice. All booked. And it gets dark so early. . . . There'll be plenty of planes tomorrow."

I strolled away, out of the door to the airfield and round to the petrol pumps.

There were six single-engined aircraft lined up there in two rows of three, with a tall man in white overalls filling one up through the opening on the upper surface of the port wing. He waved when he saw me coming, and grinned.

"Just doing yours next, Harry. The boys have tuned her up special. They say you couldn't have done it better yourself."

"I'm delighted to hear it," I said, smiling.

He screwed on the cap and jumped down.

"Lovely day," he said, looking up. There were already two little planes in the air, and four more stood ready in front of the control tower. "Going far?" he asked.

"Scotland," I said.

"That's cheating." He swung the hose away and began to drag it along to the next aircraft. "The navigation's too easy. You only have to go west till you hit the A.1 and then fly up it."

"I'm going to Islay," I smiled. "No roads, I promise."

"Islay. That's different."

"I'll land there for lunch and bring you back a bit of heather."

"How far is it?"

"Two seventy nautical miles, about."

"You'll be coming back in the dark." It was a statement, not a question. He unscrewed the cap of Kilo November and topped up the tanks.

"Most of the way, yes."

I did the routine checks all round the aircraft, fetched my padded jacket and my charts from the car, filed my flight plan, checked with the control tower for taxi clearance, and within a short while was up in the sky and away.

Air is curious stuff. One tends to think that because it is invisible it isn't there. What you can't see doesn't exist, sort of thing. But air is tough, elastic and resistant; and the harder you dig into it the more solid it becomes. Air has currents stronger than tides and turbulences that would make Charybdis look like bath water running away.

When I first went flying I rationalized the invisibility thing by thinking of an aircraft being like a submarine; in both one went up and down and sideways in a medium one couldn't see but which was very palpably around. Then I considered that if human eyes had been constructed differently it might have been possible to see the mixture of nitrogen and oxygen we breathe as clearly as the hydrogen and oxygen we wash in. After that I took the air's positive plastic existence for granted, and thought no more about it.

The day I went to Islay was pure pleasure. I had flown so much by then that the handling of the little aircraft was as normal as driving a car, and with the perfect weather and my route carefully worked out and handy on the empty passenger seat behind me, there was nothing to do but enjoy myself. And that I did, because I liked being alone. Specifically I liked being alone in a tiny noisy efficient little capsule at 2,500 revs a minute, four thousand five hundred feet above sea level, speed over the ground one hundred and ten miles an hour, steady on a course 313 degrees, bound northwest toward the sea and a Scottish island.

I found Islay itself without trouble, and tuned my radio to the frequency—118.5—of Port Ellen airfield.

I said, "Port Ellen tower, this is Golf Alpha Romeo Kilo November, do you read?"

A Scots accent crackled back, "Golf Kilo November, good afternoon, go ahead."

"Kilo November is approaching from the southeast, range fifteen miles, request joining instructions, over."

"Kilo November is cleared to join right base for runway zero four, QFE 998 millibars. Surface wind zero six zero, ten knots, call field in sight."

Following his instructions I flew in and round the little airfield on the circuit, cut the engine, turned into wind, glided in at eighty, touched down, and taxied across to the control tower to report.

After eating in a snack bar I went for a walk by the sea, breathing the soft Atlantic air, and forgot to look for some heather to take back with me. The island lay dozing in the sun, shut up close because it was Sunday. It was peaceful and distant and slowed the pulse; soul's balm if you stayed three hours, devitalizing if you stayed for life.

The gold had already gone from the day when I started back, and I flew contentedly along in the dusk and the dark, navigating by compass and checking my direction by the radio beacons over which I passed. I dropped down briefly at Carlisle to refuel, and uneventfully returned to Lincolnshire, landing gently and regretfully on the well-known field.

As usual on Sundays the club room next to the main hall was bursting with amateur pilots like myself all talking at once about stalls and spins and ratings and slide slips and allowances for deviations. I edged round the crowd to the bar and acquired some whisky and water, which tasted dry and fine on my tongue and reminded me of where I had been.

Turning round I found myself directly beside the reception-desk man and a red-haired boy he was talking to. Catching my eye he said to the boy, "Now here's someone you ought to have a word with. Our Harry here, he's dead quiet, but don't let that fool you. . . . He could fly the pants off most of that lot." He gestured round the room. "You ask Harry, now. He started just like you, knowing nothing at all, only three or four years ago."

"Four," I said.

"There you are, then. Four years. Now he's got a commercial license and enough ratings to fill a book and he can strip an engine down like a mechanic."

"That's enough," I interrupted mildly. The young man looked thoroughly unimpressed anyway, as he didn't understand what he was being told. "I suppose the point is that once you start, you go on," I said. "One thing leads to another."

"I had my first lesson today," he said eagerly, and gave me a rev by rev account of it for the next fifteen minutes. I ate two thick ham sandwiches while he got it off his chest, and finished the whisky. You couldn't really blame him, I thought, listening with half an ear; if you liked it, your first flight took you by the throat and you were hooked good and proper. It had happened to him. It had happened to me, one idle day when I passed the gates of the airfield and then turned back and went in, mildly interested in going up for a spin in a baby aircraft just to see what it was like.

I'd been to visit a dying great-aunt, and was depressed. Certainy Mr. . . ? "Grey," I said. Certainly Mr. Grey could go up with an instructor, the air people said; and the instructor, who hadn't been told I only wanted a sight-seeing flip, began as a matter of course to teach me to fly. I stayed all day and spent a week's salary in fees; and the next Sunday I went back. Most of my Sundays and most of my money had gone the same way since.

The redhead was brought to a full stop by a burly tweed-suited man who said "Excuse me," pleasantly but very firmly, and planted himself between us.

"Harry, I've been waiting for you to come back."

"Have a drink?"

"Yes . . . all right, in a minute."

His name was Tom Wells. He owned and ran a small charter firm which was based on the airfield, and on Sundays, if they weren't out on jobs, he allowed the flying club to hire his planes. It was one of his that I had flown to Islay.

"Have I done something wrong?" I asked.

"Wrong? Why should you, for God's sake? No, I'm in a spot and I thought you might be able to help me out."

"If I can, of course."

"I've overbooked next weekend and I'm going to be a pilot short. Will you do a flight for me next Sunday?"

"Yes," I said. I'd done it before, several times.

He laughed. "You never waste words, Harry boy. Well, thanks. When can I ring you to give you a briefing?"

I hesitated. "I'd better ring you, as usual."

"Saturday morning, then."

"Right."

We had a drink together, he talking discontentedly about the growing shortage of pilots and how it was now too expensive for a young man to take it up on his own account; it cost at least three thousand pounds to train a multiengine pilot, and only the airlines could afford it. They trained their own men and kept them, naturally. When the generation who had learned flying in the R.A.F. during the war got too old, the smaller charter firms were going to find themselves in very sticky straits.

"You now," he said, and it was obviously what he'd been working round to all along. "You're an oddity. You've got a commercial license and all the rest, and you hardly use it. Why not? Why don't you give up that boring old desk job and come and work for me?"

I looked at him for a long, long moment. It was almost too tempting, but apart from everything else, it would mean giving up steeplechasing, and I wasn't prepared to do that. I shook my head slowly, and said not for a few years yet.

Driving home I enjoyed the irony of the situation. Tom Wells didn't know what my desk job was, only that I worked in an office. I hadn't got around to telling him that I no longer did, and I wasn't going to. He didn't know where I came from or anything about my life away from the airfield. No one there did, and I liked it that way. I was just Harry who turned up on Sundays and flew if he had any money and worked on the engines in the hangars if he hadn't.

Tom Wells had offered me a job on my own account, not, like Yardman, because of my father, and that pleased me very much. It was rare for me to be sure of the motive behind things which were offered to me. But if I took the job my anonymity on the airfield would vanish pretty soon, and all the old problems would crowd in, and Tom Wells might very well retract, and I would be left with nowhere to escape to on one day a week to be myself.

My family did not know I was a pilot. I hadn't told them I had been flying that first day because by the time I got home my great-aunt had died and I was ashamed of having enjoyed myself while she did it. I hadn't told them afterward because I was afraid that they would make a fuss and stop me. Soon after that I realized what a release it was to lead two lives and I deliberately kept them separate. It was quite easy, as I had always been untalkative; I just didn't answer when asked where I went on Sundays, and I kept my books and charts, slide rules and computers securely locked up in my bedroom. And that was that.

3

It was on the day after I went to Islay that I first met Billy.

With Conker and Timmie, once they had bitten down their resentment at my pinching their promotion, I had arrived at a truce. On trips they chatted exclusively to each other, not to me, but that was as usual my fault; and we had got as far as sharing things like sandwiches and chocolate—and the work—on a taken-for-granted level basis.

Billy at once indicated that with him it would be quite, quite different. For Billy the class war existed as a bloody battlefield upon which he was the most active and tireless warrior alive. Within five seconds of our first meeting he was sharpening his claws.

It was at Cambridge Airport at five in the morning. We were to take two consignments of recently sold racehorses from Newmarket to Chantilly near Paris, and with all the loading and unloading at each end it would be a long day. Locking my car in the car park I was just thinking how quickly Conker and Timmie and I were getting to be able to do things when Yardman himself drove up alongside in a dark Jaguar Mark 10. There were two other men in the car, a large indistinct shape in the back, and in front, Billy.

Yardman stepped out of his car, yawned, stretched, looked up at the sky, and finally turned to me.

"Good morning, my dear boy," he said with great affability. "A nice day for flying."

"Very," I agreed. I was surprised to see him; he was not given to early rising or to waving us bon voyage. Simon Searle occasionally came if there were some difficulty with papers, but not Yardman himself. Yet here he was with his black suit hanging loosely on his too thin frame and the cold early-morning light making uncomplimentary shadows on his stretched coarsely pitted skin. The black-framed spectacles as always hid the expression in his deep-set eyes. After a month in his employ, seeing him at the wharf building two or three times a week on my visits for instructions, reports and pay, I knew him no better than on that first afternoon. In their own way his defense barriers were as good as mine.

He told me between small shut-mouthed yawns that Timmie and Conker weren't coming, they were due for a few days' leave. He had brought two men who obligingly substituted on such occasions and he was sure I would do a good job with them instead. He had brought them, he explained, because public transport wasn't geared to five-o'clock rendezvous at Cambridge Airport.

While he spoke the front passenger climbed out of his car.

"Billy Watkins," Yardman said casually, nodding between us.

"Good morning, Lord Grey," Billy said. He was about nineteen, very slender, with round cold blue eyes.

"Henry," I said automatically. The job was impossible on any other terms and these were in any case what I preferred.

Billy looked at me with eyes wide, blank and insolent. He spaced his words, bit them out and hammered them down.

"Good . . . morning . . . Lord . . . Grey."

"Good morning then, Mr. Watkins."

His eyes flickered sharply and went back to their wide stare. If he expected any placatory soft soaping from me, he could think again.

Yardman saw the instant antagonism and it annoyed him.

"I warned you, Billy," he began swiftly, and then as quickly stopped. "You won't, I am sure, my dear boy," he said to me gently, "allow any personal . . . er . . . clash of temperaments to interfere with the safe passage of your valuable cargo."

"No," I agreed.

He smiled, showing his grayish regular dentures back to the molars. I wondered idly why, if he could afford such a car, he didn't invest in more natural-looking teeth. It would have improved his unprepossessing appearance one hundred per cent.

"Right then," he said in brisk satisfaction. "Let's get on."

The third man levered himself laboriously out of the car. His trouble stemmed from a paunch which would have done a pregnant mother of twins proud. About him flapped a brown storeman's overall which wouldn't do up by six inches, and under that some bright red braces over a checked shirt did a load-bearing job on some plain dark trousers. He was about fifty, going bald, and looked tired, unshaven and sullen, and he did not then or at any time meet my eyes.

What a crew, I thought resignedly, looking from him to Billy and back. So much for a day of speed and efficiency. The fat man, in fact, proved to be even more useless than he looked, and treated the horses with the sort of roughness which is the product of fear. Yardman gave him the job of loading them from their own horseboxes up the long matting-covered side-walled ramp into the aircraft, while Billy and I inside fastened them into their stalls.

John, as Yardman called him, was either too fat or too scared of having his feet trodden on to walk side by side with each horse up the ramp; he backed up it, pulling the horse after him, stretching its head forward uncomfortably. Not surprisingly they all stuck their toes in hard and refused to budge. Yardman advanced on them from behind, shouting and waving a pitchfork, and prodded them forward again. The net result was some thoroughly upset and frightened animals in no state to be taken flying.

After three of them had arrived in the plane sweating, rolling their eyes and kicking out, I went down the ramp and protested.

"Let John help Billy, and I'll lead the horses," I said to Yardman. "I don't suppose you'll want them to arrive in such an unnerved state that their owners won't use the firm again? Always supposing that they don't actually kick the aircraft to bits en route."

He knew very well that this had really happened once or twice in the history of bloodstock transport. There was always the risk that a horse would go berserk in the air at the best of times. Taking off with a whole planeload of het-up thoroughbreds would be a fair way to commit suicide.

He hesitated only a moment, then nodded.

"All right. Change over."

The loading continued with less fuss but no more speed. John was as useless at installing the horses as he was at leading them.

Cargo on airplanes has to be distributed with even more care than on ships. If the center of gravity isn't kept to within fairly close specific limits the plane won't fly at all, just race at high speed to the end of the runway and turn into scrap metal. If the cargo shifts radically in mid-air it keels the plane over exactly as it would a ship, but with less time to put it right, and no lifeboats handy as a last resort.

From the gravity point of view, the horses had to be stowed down the center of the plane, where for their own comfort and balance they had to face forward. This meant, in a medium-sized aircraft such as Yardman's usually chartered, four pairs of horses standing behind each other. From the balance point of view, the horses had to be fairly immobile, and they also had to be accessible, as one had to be able to hold their heads and soothe them at take-off and landing. Each pair was therefore boxed separately, like four little islands down the center of the plane. There were narrow gangways between the boxes and up both sides the whole length of the aircraft so that one could easily walk round and reach every individual horse to look after him.

The horses stood on large trays of peat which were bolted to the floor. The boxes of half-inch-thick wood panels had to be built up round the horses when each pair was loaded; one erected the forward end wall and the two sides, led in the horses and tied them up, added the back wall, and made the whole thing solid with metal bars banding the finished box. The bars were joined at each corner by lynch pins. There were three bars, at the top, center and bottom. To prevent the boxes from collapsing inward, each side of each box had to be separately fixed to the floor with chains acting as guy ropes. When the loading was complete, the result looked like four huge packing cases chained down, with the horses' backs and heads showing at the open tops.

As one couldn't afford to have a box fall apart in the air, the making of them, though not difficult, demanded attention and thoroughness. John conspicuously lacked both. He was also unbelievably clumsy at hooking on and tightening the guy chains, and he dropped two lynch pins which we couldn't find again. We had to use wire instead, which wouldn't hold if a strong-minded horse started kicking. By the end Billy and I were doing the boxes alone, while John stood sullenly by and watched; and Billy throughout made my share as difficult as he could.

It all took such a time that at least the three frightened horses had calmed down again before the pilot climbed aboard and started the engines. I closed the first of the big double doors we had loaded the horses through, and had a final view of Yardman on the tarmac, the slipstream from the propellers blowing his scanty hair up round the bald patch like a black sea anemone. The light made silver window panes of his glasses. He lifted his hand without moving his elbow, an awkward little gesture of farewell. I put my own hand up in acknowledgment and reply, and fastened the second door as the plane began to move.

As usual there was a crew of three flying the aircraft, pilot, copilot and engineer. The engineer, on all the trips I had so far made, was the one who got landed with brewing the coffee and who could also reasonably be asked to hold a pair of horses' heads during take-off. This one did so with far more familiarity than John.

The trip was a relatively short one and there was a helpful following wind, but we were over an hour late at the French end. When we had landed the airport staff rolled another ramp up to the doors and I opened them from inside. The first people through them were three unsmiling businesslike Customs officials. With great thoroughness they compared the horses we had brought against our list and their own. On the papers for each horse were details of its physical characteristics and color. The Customs men checked carefully every star, blaze and sock, guarding against the possibility that some poorer animal had been switched for the good one bought. France proved more hard to satisfy and more suspicious than most other countries.

Content at length that no swindle had been pulled this time, the chief Customs man politely gave me back the papers and said that the unloading could begin.

Four horseboxes from French racing stables had turned up to collect the new purchases. The drivers, phlegmatically resigned to all delays, were engaged in digging round their mouths with toothpicks in a solid little group. I went down the ramp and across to them and told them in which order the horses would be unloaded. My French vocabulary, which was shaky on many subjects, covered at least all horse jargon and was fairly idiomatic when it came to racing or bloodstock. At Anglia I had done quite a bit of work on French horses, and after six years I knew my way round the French stud book as well as I did the British.

The drivers nodded, sucked their teeth and drove up the boxes in the right order. The first horse off (the last loaded at Cambridge) was a nondescript brown filly who was led into the waiting horsebox by the driver himself. He took her casually from my hand, slapped her rump in a friendly fashion, and by the time I led out the second horse he had already loaded her up and was on his way.

The other drivers had, more usually, brought one or two grooms with them, as they were to collect more than one horse. Billy took over leading the horses from the ramp, and I dismantled the boxes with John. This very nearly meant, in effect, doing it by myself. He dropped the bars, tripped over the anchorages on the floor, caught his fingers in the chains, and because of the paunch could do nothing which entailed bending down. Why Yardman employed him at all, I thought in irritation, was an unfathomable mystery.

We were supposed to be taking four horses back on the return trip, but by the time the last of our cargo had departed, not one of the four had turned up. When they were more than half an hour overdue, I walked over to the airport buildings and rang up one of the trainers concerned. Certainly he was sending two horses today he said, two four-year-old hurdlers which he had sold to an English stable, but they were not due at the airport until three o'clock. Fifteen hundred hours; it was typed clearly on his notice from Yardman Transport. A second trainer, consulted, said the same, and although I had no phone number for the third, I took it for granted that his notice had been identical. Either Simon, or more likely his typist, had written five instead of nought on all three. It was a bore, as it meant unloading at the end of the last trip when we would all be tired.

The day's troubles, however, had barely warmed up. On my way back to the plane I saw Billy and John standing beside it engaged in a furious argument, but they broke off before I was close enough to hear what they were saying. John turned his back and kicked moodily at the bottom of the ramp and Billy gave me his best insulting stare.

"What's the matter?" I said.

Billy pursed his lips into an expression which said clearly that it was none of my business, but after a visible inner struggle he did answer.

"He's got a headache," he said, nodding at John. "From the noise."

A headache. That hardly explained the fat man's hopeless inefficiency, his sullenness, his shifty manner or his row with Billy. Nor, I realized in some surprise, did it explain why he hadn't spoken a single word to me the whole trip. But as repeating the question was unlikely to get a more fruitful answer, I shrugged and didn't bother.

"Get on board," I said instead. "We're going back empty. There's been a mix-up and we'll have to take the French horses back next time."

"——" said Billy calmly. He used a word so obscene that I wondered what he used for when he was annoyed.

"I dare say," I said dryly. "Let's not waste any more time."

John lumbered unwillingly and morosely up the ramp. Billy followed him after a pause, and I too let Billy get well ahead before I started after him. The spaces between us, I thought sardonically, were symbolic.

The airport staff removed the ramp, the plane's crew returned from their coffee break, and we proceeded back to Cambridge. On the way we sat on three separate bales of straw along the length of the aircraft and didn't even look at each other. John put his elbows on his knees and held his head in his hands, and Billy looked steadily and sightlessly at the cloud-dotted sky.

With all the sides of the boxes lying flat and strapped down on the peat trays the body of the aircraft seemed large and empty. In that state it echoed and was much noisier than usual, and I had some small sympathy for John's head. The plane was adapted, by the charter company who owned it, for any purpose that was required. The regularly spaced anchorages on the floor were as often used for fastening passenger seats as boxes for animals, and the airline would fly sixty people on a coach tour type holiday to Europe one day and a load of pigs or cattle the next. In between they merely bolted or unbolted the rows of seats and swept out the relevant debris, either farmyard manure and straw or cigarette packets and bags full of vomit.

One was not allowed to sweep out manure onto foreign soil. The whole lot had to be solemnly carted back to England to comply with quarantine regulations. The odd thing was, I reflected again, that the peat trays never seemed to smell. Not even now that there was no live horse smell to mask it. Of course this plane was unpressurized, so that fresh air continually found its way in, but all the same it smelled less than an ordinary stable, even after a whole day in a hot climate.

The first person on the plane at Cambridge was a cheerful underworked bareheaded excise officer who had come there especially to clear the horses. He bounced in as soon as the cockpit ladder was in position, made a loud rude comment to the pilot and came back through the galley into the main cabin.

"What have you done with them, then?" he said, looking round at the emptiness. "Dumped them in the Channel?"

I explained the situation.

"Damn," he said. "I wanted to get off early. Well, did any of you buy anything in France?"

John didn't answer. I shook my head. Billy said offensively, "We weren't given a sodding minute to get off the sodding plane."

The Customs man in his navy blue suit glanced at me sideways in amusement. I gathered that he had met Billy before.

"O.K.," he said. "See you this afternoon, then."

He opened the big double doors, beckoned to the men outside who were wheeling up the ramp, and as soon as it was in position walked jauntily down it and back across the tarmac toward the airport building. As we were now more or less up to schedule through not having to load and unload the French hurdlers, John and Billy and I followed him in order to have lunch. I sat at one table and Billy and John ostentatiously moved to another as far away as they could get. But if Billy thought he could distress me in that way, he was wrong. I felt relieved to be alone, not shunned.

By one o'clock the horseboxes bringing the next consignment had arrived, and we started the loading all over again. This time I got the groom who had brought the horses to lead them up to the plane. Billy and I made the boxes, and John belched and got in the way.

When I had finished I went into the airport building, checked the horses' export papers with the Customs man and persuaded the pilot away from his fourth cup of coffee. Up we went again into the clear wintry sky, across the gray sea, and down again in France. The same French Customs men came on board, checked every horse as meticulously as before, and as politely let it go. We took down the boxes, led out the horses, saw them loaded into their horseboxes, and watched them depart.

This time the French hurdlers for the return journey had already arrived and without a pause we began getting them on board. As there were only four we had only two boxes to set up, which by that point I found quite enough. John's sole contribution toward the fourth journey was to refill and hang the haynets for the hurdlers to pick from on their way, and even at that he was clumsy and slow.

With the horses at length unconcernedly munching in their boxes we went across to the airport buildings, Billy and John ahead, I following. The only word I heard pass between them as they left down the ramp was "beer."

There was a technical delay over papers in one of the airport offices. One of the things I had grown to expect in the racehorse export business was technical delays. A journey without one of some sort was a gift. With up to twenty horses sometimes carried on one airplane there only had to be a small query about a single animal for the whole load to be kept waiting for hours. Occasionally it was nothing to do with the horses themselves but with whether the airlines owed the airport dues for another plane or another trip, in which case the airport wouldn't clear the horse plane to leave until the dues were paid. Sometimes the quibbling was enough to get one near to jumping out of the window. I was growing very good indeed at keeping my temper when all around were losing theirs and blaming it on me. Kipling would have been proud.

This time it was some question of insurance which I could do nothing to smooth out as it involved the owner of one of the hurdlers, who was fighting a contested claim on a road accident it had been slightly hurt in. The insurance company didn't want the horse to leave France. I said it was a bit late, the horse was sold, and did the insurance company have the right to stop it anyway. No one was quite sure about that. A great deal of telephoning began.

I was annoyed, mainly because the horse in question was in the forward of the two boxes; if we had to take it off the plane it meant dismantling the rear box and unloading the back pair first in order to reach it, and then reloading those two again once we had got it off. And with Billy and John full of all the beer they were having plenty of time to ship, this was likely to be a sticky maneuver. The horses' own grooms and motor boxes had long gone home. The hurdlers were each worth thousands. Who, I wondered gloomily, was I going to trust not to let go of them if we had to have them standing about on the tarmac.

The pilot ran me to earth and said that if we didn't take off soon we would be staying all night as after six o'clock he was out of time. We had to be able to be back at Cambridge at six, or he couldn't start at all.

I relayed this information to the arguing officials. It produced nothing but some heavy Gallic shrugs. The pilot swore and told me that until twenty to five I would find him having coffee and after that he'd be en route for Paris. And I would have to get another pilot as he had worked the maximum hours for a long spell and was legally obliged now to have forty-eight hours' rest.

Looking morosely out of the window across to where the plane with its expensive cargo sat deserted on the apron, I reflected that this was the sort of situation I could do without. And if we had to stay all night, I was going to have to sleep with those horses. A delightful new experience every day, I thought in wry amusement. Join Yardman Transport and see the world, every discomfort thrown in.

With minutes to spare, the insurance company relented. The hurdler could go. I grabbed the papers, murmuring profuse thanks, raced to dig out the pilot, and ran Billy to earth behind a large frosty glass. It was clearly far from his first.

"Get John," I said shortly. "We've got to be off within ten minutes."

"Get him yourself," he said with sneering satisfaction. "If you can."

"Where is he?"

"Halfway to Paris." He drank unconcernedly. "He's got some whore there. He said he'd come back tomorrow on a regular airline. There isn't a sodding thing you can do about it, so put that in your pipe and smoke it."

John's presence, workwise, made little difference one way or another. I really cared not a bent sou if he wanted to pay his own fare back. He was free enough. He had his passport in his pocket, as we all did. Mine was already dog-eared and soft from constant use. We had to produce them whenever asked, though they were seldom stamped, as we rarely went into the passengers' immigration section of airports. We showed them more like casual passes than weighty official documents, and most countries were so tolerant of people employed on aircraft that one pilot told me he had left his passport in a hotel bedroom in Madrid and had been going unhindered round the world for three weeks without it while he tried to get it back.

"Ten minutes," I said calmly to Billy. "Fifteen, and you'll be paying your own fare back too."

Billy gave me his wide-eyed stare. He picked up his glass of beer and poured it over my foot. The yellow liquid ran away in a pool on the glossy stone floor, froth bubbles popping round the edges.

"What a waste," I said, unmoving. "Are you coming?"

He didn't answer. It was too much to expect him to get up meekly while I waited, and as I wanted to avoid too decisive a clash with him if I could I turned away and went back alone, squelching slightly, to the aircraft. He came as I had thought he would, but with less than two minutes in hand to emphasize his independence. The engines were already running when he climbed aboard, and we were moving as soon as the doors were shut.

As usual during take-off and landing, Billy stood holding the heads of two horses and I of the other two. After that, with so much space on the half-loaded aircraft, I expected him to keep as far from me as he could, as he had done all day. But Billy by then was eleven hours away from Yardman's restraining influence and well afloat on airport beer. The crew were all up forward in the cockpit, and fat useless John was sex-bent for Paris.

Billy had me alone, all to himself.

Billy intended to make the most of it.

4

"YOUR KIND ought not to be allowed," he said, with charming directness. He had to say it very loudly, also, on account of the noise of the aircraft.

I sat on a hay bale with my back against the rear wall of the cabin and looked at him as he stood ten feet in front of me with his legs apart for balance.

"Your kind, of course," I shouted back, "are the salt of the earth."

He took a step forward and the plane bumped hard in an air pocket. It lurched him completely off his balance and he fell rolling onto his side. With sizzling fury, though it wasn't I who had pushed him, he raised himself up on one knee and thrust his face close to mine.

"—— you," he said.

At close quarters I could see how very young he was. His skin was still smooth like a child's and he had long thick eyelashes round those vast pale blue-gray searchlight eyes. His hair, a fairish brown, curled softly close to his head and down the back of his neck, cut short and in the shape of a helmet. He had a soft, full-lipped mouth and a strong straight nose. A curiously sexless face. Too unlined to be clearly male, too heavily boned to be female.

He wasn't so much a man, not even so much a person, as a force. A wild, elemental, poltergeist force trapped barely controllably in a vigorous steel-spring body. You couldn't look into Billy's cold eyes from inches away and not know it. I felt a weird unexpected primitive tingle away down somewhere in my gut, and at the same time realized on a conscious level that friendliness and reason couldn't help, that there would be no winning over, ever, of Billy.

He began mildly enough.

"Your sort," he yelled. "You think you own the bloody earth. You soft lot of out-of-date nincompoops, you and your lah-di-dah bloody Eton."

I didn't answer. He put his sneering face even nearer.

"Think yourself something special, don't you? You and your sodding ancestors."

"They aren't very usual," I yelled in his ear.

"What aren't?"

"Sodding ancestors."

He had no sense of humor. He looked blank.

"You didn't spring from an acorn," I said resignedly. "You've had as many ancestors as I have."

He stood up and took a step back. "Bloody typical," he shouted, "making fun of people you look down on."

I shook my head, got to my feet, and went along the plane to check the horses. I didn't care for useless arguments at the best of times, let alone those which strained the larynx. All four hurdlers were standing quiet in the boxes, picking peacefully at the haynets, untroubled by the noise. I patted their heads, made sure everything was secure, hesitated about going forward to the galley and cockpit for more friendly company, and had the matter settled for me by Billy.

"Hey," he shouted. "Look at this." He was pointing downward with one arm and beckoning me with sweeps of the other. There was anxiety on his face.

I walked back between the last box and the side wall of the aircraft, into the open space at the back, and across to Billy. As soon as I got near enough to see what he was pointing at, the anxiety on his face changed to spite.

"Look at this," he shouted again, and jabbed his clenched fist straight at my stomach.

The only flicker of talent I had shown in a thoroughly mediocre and undistinguished career at Eton had been for boxing. I hadn't kept it up afterward, but all the same the defense reflex was still there even after eight years. Billy's unexpected blow landed on a twisting target and my head did not go forward to meet a punch on the jaw. Or more likely in this case, I thought fleetingly, a chop on the back of the neck. Instead, I gave him back as good as I got, a short hard jolt to the lower ribs. He was surprised, but it didn't stop him. Just the reverse. He seemed pleased.

There are better places for fighting than the back of an aircraft. The floor of that one was banded by the rows of seat anchorages, so that it was only a matter of time before one of us caught his foot in them and overbalanced, and it happened to be me, dodging away from a hand stretched at my throat. I went down flat on my back, unable to stop myself.

Billy fell deliberately and heavily on top of me, grinning fiercely with his own private pleasure, stabbing his elbows sharply into my chest and pressing me down hard on to the rigid anchorages. It hurt, and he meant it to. I kicked and rolled over, trying to get him underneath for a taste of it, but he was off like a cat at the crucial point and already aiming his boot as I stood up. I took that on the thigh and lunged accurately in return at his head. He just shook it briefly and went on punching, hard, quick, and with no respect for convention; but the pleasure left his face when he continued to get everything back with interest.

Thankful at least that he had produced no flick knife or bicycle chain I battled on, knowing in a cold detached part of my brain that I would gain nothing even if I won. Billy's resentment would be greater, not less, for being slogged by what he despised.

I did win in the end, if anyone did, but only because he had a belly full of beer and I hadn't. We were both very near to a standstill. I hit him finally very hard just below the navel, my fist sinking in deep, and he fell against the aft box retching and clutching himself and sliding down onto his knees. I caught hold of one of his wrists and twisted his arm up across his back.

"Now you listen, Billy," I said loudly in his ear, panting to get enough breath, "I don't see any point in fighting you, but I will if you make me. You can forget I'm an earl's son, Billy, and take me as I am, and this is what I am. . . ." I jerked his arm. "Hard, Billy, not soft. As tough as necessary. Remember it."

He didn't answer, perhaps because he was showing signs of being sick. I yanked him to his feet, pushed him across to the lavatory compartment in the tail, opened the door for him, and shoved him through. As the only lock was on the inside I couldn't make sure he stayed there, but from the sounds which presently issued from the open door, he was in no state to leave.

My own body ached from head to foot from his punches and kicks and from brisk contact with many sharp and knobbed edges, not the least those spaced regularly on the floor. I sat down weakly on a straw bale and rubbed at a few places which didn't do much good, and was suddenly struck by something very odd indeed.

My face was completely unmarked.

I had bashed my head against one of the metal bars on the rear box and there was a tender swelling a little above my right ear. But Billy, I remembered distinctly, had not once even aimed at my face; not at any point higher than my throat.

For someone in the grip of obsessive fury, surely that was extraordinary, I thought. The usual impulse in such a case was to "smash his face in." Billy had actually taken pains not to. I didn't understand why. I thought about it all the way to Cambridge.

It was dark when we landed and the cabin lights were on. The cheerful Customs man made his way through the plane, raised his eyebrows, and asked where my two mates were.

"Billy is in there," I nodded toward the lavatory, "and John stayed in France. He said he was coming back tomorrow."

"O.K." He checked through the horses' papers perfunctorily. "All clear," he said, and as an afterthought, "Buy anything?"

I shook my head, and he grinned, helped me open the double doors, and whistled away down the ramp as soon as it was in position.

Billy had locked himself into the lavatory and refused to come out, so I had to get one of the box drivers who had arrived to collect the cargo to help me unload the horses. Unloading was always quicker and easier than loading, but I had begun to stiffen up all over with bruises, and I was glad when it was done. The helpful box driver led out the last horse, an undistinguished brown mare, and before turning back to tidy up I watched them step and slither down the ramp. That mare, I thought idly, was very like the one we had taken across in the morning, though the rug she wore might be misleading. But it couldn't of course be the same. No one would ship a horse out in the morning and back in the afternoon.

I turned away and began slowly to stack the box sides and the bars, wished painfully that Billy hadn't been quite so rough, and forgot about it.

* * *

The following day I went down to the wharf building and hooked Simon out for a liquid lunch. We shambled down the road to the usual hideous pub and he buried his face in a pint like a camel at an oasis.

"That's better," he said, sighing, when a scant inch remained. "How did yesterday's trip go?"

"All right."

His eyes considered me thoughtfuly. "Did you have a fall on Saturday?"

"No. A winner. Why?"

"You're moving a bit carefully, that's all."

I grinned suddenly. "You should see the other fellow."

His face melted in comprehension and he laughed. "I imagine I have," he said. "Billy has a sunset of a black eye."

"You've seen him?" I was surprised.

Simon nodded. "He was in the office this morning, talking to Yardman."

"Getting his version in first, I suppose."

"What happened?" he asked interestedly.

"Billy picked a fight." I shrugged. "He resents my existence. It's ridiculous. No one can help what his father is. You can't choose your birth."

"You feel strongly about it," Simon observed, ordering another pint. I shook my head to his invitation.

"So would you, if you had to live with it. I mostly get treated as a villain or a nit or a desirable match, and not much else." I was exaggerating, but not unduly.

"That last doesn't sound too bad," he grinned.

"You haven't had half the debs' mums in London trying to net you for their daughters," I said gloomily, "with your own mother egging them on."

"It sounds a wow." He had no sympathy for such a fate.

"It isn't me they want," I pointed out. "It's only my name. Which is no fun at all. And on the other end from the wedding ring I get bashed around for exactly the same reason."

"Very few can feel as strongly as Billy."

I looked at him. "There were the French in seventeen eighty-nine, remember? And the Russians in nineteen-seventeen. They all felt as strongly as Billy."

"The English like their aristocrats."

"Don't you believe it. They don't mind them from the social point of view because titles make the scandal sheets juicier. But they make damn sure they have no effective power. They say we are a joke, an anachronism, out-of-date, and weak and silly. They pretend we are these things so that we are kept harmless, so that no one will take us seriously. Think of the modern attitude to the House of Lords, for example. And you— you still think it funny that I want this sort of job, but you wouldn't think so if my father was a . . . a farmer, or a pubkeeper, or a schoolmaster. But I'm me, here and now, a man of now, not of some dim glorious past. I am not an anachronism. I'm Henry Grey, conceived and born like everyone else, into this present world. Well, I insist on living in it. I am not going to be shoved off into an unreal playboy existence where my only function is to sire the next in line, which is what my parents want."

"You could renounce your title, when you get it," Simon pointed out calmly. He spotted a pin on the bar counter and absentmindedly tucked it into his lapel. It was such a habit with him that he sported a whole row of them, like a dressmaker.

"I could," I said, "but I won't. The only good reason for doing that is to stay in the House of Commons, and I'll never be a politician, I'm not the type. Renouncing for any other reason would be just a retreat. What I want is for people to acknowledge that an earl is as good as the next man, and give him an equal chance."

"But if you get on, they say it's because of your title, not because you have talent."

"You are so right. But there's a prince or two, a few dukes' sons, and some others like me, all in the same boat just now, and I reckon that our generation, if we try hard enough, might in the end be treated on our own terms. Have some more beer."

He laughed and agreed.

"I've never heard you say so much," he said, smiling.

"It's Billy's fault. Forget it."

"I don't think I will."

"You know something odd? I'm covered with bruises, and there isn't a single one on my face."

He considered, drinking.

"He'd have got into trouble if he'd marked you for all to see."

"I suppose so."

"I gather you haven't told Yardman?"

"No."

"Why not?"

I shrugged. "I think he expected it, or something like it. He was ironic when he gave me the job. He must have known that sooner or later I would come up against Billy. And yesterday, he knew Billy would be after me. He warned me, in his way."

"What are you going to do about it?"

"Nothing."

"But what if you find yourself on another trip with Billy? I mean, you're bound to, sometime."

"Yes, I know. Well, it's up to him entirely. I wouldn't start anything. I didn't yesterday. But I did tell him plainly that I'd fight back any time. And I am not, repeat *not,* leaving here because of him."

"And you look so quiet and mild." He smiled one-sidedly, looking down into his again empty glass. "I think," he said slowly, almost it seemed to me sadly, "that one or two people in Yardman Transport have miscalculated about you, Henry."

But when I pressed him to explain, he wouldn't.

With no more export trips to be flown until Thursday, I went the next day, Wednesday, to the races. Someone offered me a spare ride in the novice chase and for some reason it fretted me more than ever to have to refuse. "I can't," I said, explaining thoroughly so that he wouldn't think I was being rude. "I'm only allowed to ride in fifty open races a season, and I'm already over the forty mark, and I've got mounts booked for Cheltenham and the Whitbread and so on. And if I ride too much now I'll be out of those, but thank you very much for asking me."

He nodded understandingly and hurried off to find someone else, and in irritation two hours later I watched his horse canter home to a ten lengths win. It was some consolation, however, when immediately afterward I was buttonholed by a large shrewd-faced man I knew very slightly, the father of another well-occupied amateur jockey. Between them, father and son owned and trained half a dozen good hunter 'chasers which they ran only in amateur events with notoriously satisfactory results. But on this particular afternoon Mr. Thackery, a large-scale farmer from Shropshire, showed signs both of worry and indecision.

"Look," he said, "I'll not beat about the bush, I'm a blunt man, so I'm told. Now, what do you say to riding all my horses until the end of the season?"

I was astonished. "But surely Julian . . . I mean, he hasn't had a bad fall or anything, has he?"

He shook his head. The worry stayed in place. "Not a fall. He's got jaundice. Got it pretty badly, poor chap. He won't be fit again for weeks. But we've a grand lot of horses this year and he won't hear of them not running just because he can't ride them. He told me to ask you, it's his idea."

"It's very good of him," I said sincerely. "And thank you, I'd like to ride for you very much, whenever I can."

"Good, then." He hesitated, and added, "Er . . . Julian told me to tell you, to ask you, if ten per cent of the prize money would be in order?"

"Thank you," I said. "That will be fine."

He smiled suddenly, his heavy face lightening into wrinkles which made him look ten years younger. "I wasn't sure about asking you, I'll tell you that, only Julian insisted on it. There's no nonsense about Henry, he said, and I can see he's right. He said Henry don't drink much, don't talk much, gets on with the job and expects to be paid for it. A pro at heart, he says you are. Do you want expenses?"

I shook my head. "Ten per cent for winning. Nothing else."

"Fair enough." He thrust out his hand and I shook it.

"I'm sorry about Julian's jaundice," I said.

Mr. Thackery's lips twitched. "He said if you said that, that he hoped for the sake of our horses you were being hypocritical."

"Oh, subtle stuff." I pondered. "Tell him to get up too soon and have a relapse."

The next afternoon I went on a flight to New York.

With Billy.

The ice between us was as cold as the rarefied air outside the pressurized stratocruiser which took us. Yardman, I reflected, wasn't showing much sense in pushing us off together so soon, and on a two-day journey at that.

The wide cold stare was somewhat marred by the blackish streaks and yellow smudges left by my fist, and Billy was distinctly warier than he had been on the French journeys. There were no elementary taunts this time; but at the end of everything he said to me he tacked on the words "Lord Grey," and made them sound like an insult.

He tried nothing so crude as punching to make my trip memorable; instead he smashed down one of the metal bars as I was fixing a guy chain during the loading. I looked up angrily, squeezing four squashed right fingers in my left hand, and met his watchful waiting eyes. He was looking down at me with interest, with faintly sneering calculation, to see what I would do.

If anyone else had dropped the bar, I would have known it was accidental. With Billy, apart from the force with which it had landed, I knew it wasn't. But the day had barely begun, and the cargo was much too valuable to jeopardize for personal reasons, which I dare say he was counting on. When he saw that I was not going to retaliate, or at least not instantly, he nodded in satisfaction, picked up the bar with a small cold private smile, and calmly began putting it into place.

The loading was finished and the plane took off. There were thick dark red marks across my fingers an inch below the nails, and they throbbed all the way to America.

With us on that trip, looking after a full load of twelve horses, we took two other grooms, an elderly deaf one supplied by Yardman, and another man traveling privately with one particular horse. Owners occasionally sent their own grooms instead of entrusting their valued or difficult animals entirely to Yardman's, and far from resenting it I had learned from Timmie and Conker to be glad of the extra help.

The horse involved on this occasion had come from Norway, stayed in England overnight, and was bound for a racing stable in Virginia. The new owner had asked for the Norwegian groom to go all the way, at his expense, so that the horse should have continuous care on the journey. It didn't look worth it, I reflected, looking over at it idly while I checked the horses in the next box. A weak-necked listless chestnut, it had a straggle of hair round the fetlocks which suggested there had been a cart horse not far enough back in its ancestry, and the acute-angled hocks didn't have the best conformation for speed. Norway was hardly famed for the quality of its racing any more, even though it was possibly the Vikings who had invented the whole sport. They placed heaps of valued objects (the prizes) at varying distances from the starting point; then all the competitors lined up, and with wild whoops the race began. The prizes nearest the start were the smallest, the farthest away the richest, so each rider had to decide what suited his mount best, a quick sprint or a shot at stamina. Choosing wrong meant getting no prize at all. Twelve hundred years ago fast sturdy racing horses had been literally worth a fortune in Norway, but the smooth-skinned long-legged descendants of those tough shaggy ponies didn't count for much in the modern thoroughbred industry. It was sentiment, I supposed, which caused an American to pay for such an inferior looking animal to travel so far from home.

I asked the middle-aged Norwegian groom if he had everything he wanted, and he said, in halting, heavily accented English, that he was content. I left him sitting on his hay bale staring mindlessly into space, and went on with my rounds. The horses were all traveling quietly, munching peacefully at their haynets, oblivious to rocketing round the world at six hundred miles an hour. There is no sensation of speed if you can't see an environment rushing past.

We arrived without incident at Kennedy Airport, where a gumchewing Customs man came on board with three helpers. He spoke slowly, every second word an "uh," but he was sharply thorough with the horses. All their papers were in order, however, and we began the unloading without more ado. There was the extra job of leading all the horses through a tray of disinfectant before they could set foot on American soil, and while I was seeing to it I heard the Customs man asking the Norwegian groom about a work permit, and the halting reply that he was staying for a fortnight only, for a holiday, the kindness of the man who owned the horse.

It was the first time I too had been to the States, and I envied him his fortnight. Owing to the five hours' time difference, it was only six in the evening, local time, when we landed at Kennedy, and we were due to leave again at six next morning; which gave me about nine free hours in which to see New York. Although to my body mechanism it was already bedtime, I didn't waste any of them in sleeping.

The only snag to this was having to start another full day's work with eyes requiring matchsticks. Billy yawned over making the boxes as much as I did and only the third member of the team, the deaf elderly Alf, had had any rest. Since even if one shouted he could hear very little, the three of us worked in complete silence like robots, isolated in our own thoughts, with gaps as unbridgeable between us as between like poles of magnets. Unlike poles attract, like poles repel. Billy and I were a couple of cold Norths.

There was a full load going back again, as was usual on Yardman trips from one continent to another. He hated wasting space, and was accustomed to telephone around the studs when a long flight was on the books, to find out if they had anything to send or collect. The customers all liked it, for on full long distance loads Yardman made a reduction in the fares. Timmie and Conker had less cheerful views of this practice, and I now saw why. One's body didn't approve of tricks with the clock. But at the point of no return way out over the Atlantic I shed my drowsiness in one leaping heartbeat, and with horror had my first introduction to a horse going berserk in mid-air.

Old Alf shook my shoulder, and the fright in his face brought me instantly to my feet. I went where he pointed, up toward the nose of the aircraft.

In the second to front box a solidly-muscled three-year-old colt had pulled his head collar to pieces and was standing free and untied in the small wooden square. He had his head down, his forelegs straddled, and he was kicking out with his hind feet in a fixed, fearful rhythm. White foamy sweat stood out all over him, and he was squealing. The companion beside him was trying in a terrified way to escape, his eyes rolling and his body pushing hard against the wooden side of the box.

The colt's hooves thudded against the back wall of the box like battering rams. The wooden panels shook and rattled and began to splinter. The metal bars banding the sides together strained at the corner lynch pins, and it only needed one to break for the whole thing to start disintegrating.

I found the copilot at my elbow, yelling urgently.

"Captain says how do you expect him to fly the aircraft with all this thumping going on. He says to keep that horse still, it's affecting the balance."

"How?" I asked.

"That's your affair," he pointed out. "And for God's sake do something about it quickly."

The back wall of the colt's box cracked from top to bottom. The pieces were still held in place by the guy chains, but at the present rate they wouldn't hold more than another minute, and then we should have on our minds a maddened animal loose in a pressurized aircraft with certain death to us all if he got a hoof through a window.

"Have you got a humane killer on board?" I said.

"No. This is usually a passenger craft. Why don't you bring your own?"

There were no rules to say one had to take a humane killer in animal transport. There should be. But it was too late to regret it.

"We've got drugs in the first-aid kit," the copilot suggested.

I shook my head. "They're unpredictable. Just as likely to make him worse." It might even have been a tranquilizer which started him off, I thought fleetingly. They often backfired with horses. And it would be quite impossible in any case to inject even a safe drug through a fine needle designed for humans into a horse as wild as this.

"Get a carving knife or something from the galley," I said. "Anything long and sharp. And quick."

He turned away, stumbling in his haste. The colt's hind feet smashed one broken half of the back wall clean out. He turned round balefully, thrust his head between the top and center banding bars, and tried to scramble through. The panic in his eyes was pitiful.

From inside his jerkin Billy calmly produced a large pistol and pointed it toward the colt's threshing head.

"Don't be a bloody fool," I shouted. "We're thirty thousand feet up."

The copilot came back with a white-handled saw-edged bread knife, saw the gun, and nearly fainted.

"D . . . don't," he stuttered. "D . . . d . . . don't."

Billy's eyes were very wide. He was looking fixedly at the heaving colt and hardly seemed to hear. All his mind seemed to be concentrated on aiming the gun that could kill us all.

The colt smashed the first of the lynch pins and lunged forward, bursting out of the remains of the box like flood water from a dam. I snatched the knife from the copilot and as the horse surged toward me stuck the blade into the only place available, the angle where the head joined the neck.

I hit by some miracle the carotid artery. But I couldn't get out of his way afterwards. The colt came down solidly on top of me, pouring blood, flailing his legs and rolling desperately in his attempts to stand up again.

His mane fell in my mouth and across my eyes, and his heaving weight crushed the breath in and out of my lungs like some nightmare form of artificial respiration. He couldn't right himself over my body, and as his struggles weakened he eventually got himself firmly wedged between the remains of his own box and the one directly aft of it. The copilot bent down and put his hands under my armpits and in jerks dragged me out from underneath.

The blood went on pouring out, hot sticky gallons of it, spreading down the gangways in scarlet streams. Alf cut open one of the hay bales and began covering it up, and it soaked the hay into a sodden crimson-brown mess. I don't know how many pints of blood there should be in a horse; the colt bled to death and his heart pumped out nearly every drop.

My clothes were soaked in it, and the sweet smell made me feel sick. I stumbled down the plane into the lavatory compartment and stripped to the skin, and washed myself with hands I found to be helplessly trembling. The door opened without ceremony, and the copilot thrust a pair of trousers and a sweater into my arms. His overnight civvies.

'Here,'' he said. ''Compliments of the house.''

I nodded my thanks, put them on, and went back up the plane, soothing the restive frightened cargo on the way.

The copilot was arguing with Billy about whether Billy would really have pulled the trigger and Billy was saying a bullet from a revolver wouldn't make a hole in a metal aircraft. The copilot cursed, said you couldn't risk it, and mentioned ricochets and glass windows. But what I wanted to know, though I didn't ask, was what was Billy doing carrying a loaded pistol round with him in an underarm holster as casually as a wallet.

5

I SLEPT like the dead when I finally got home, and woke with scant time the next morning to reach Kempton for the amateurs' chase. After such a mangling week I thought it highly probable I would crown the lot by falling off the rickety animal I had in a weak moment promised to ride. But though I misjudged where it was intending to take off at the last open ditch and practically went over the fence before it while it put in an unexpected short one, I did in fact cling sideways like a limpet to the saddle, through sheer disinclination to hit the ground.

Though I scrambled back on top, my mount, who wouldn't have won anyway, had lost all interest, and I trotted him back and apologized to his cantankerous owner, who considered I had spoiled his day and was churlish enough to say so. As he outranked my father by several strawberry leaves he clearly felt he had the right to be as caustic as he chose. I listened to him saying I couldn't ride in a cart with a pig-net over it and wondered how he treated the professionals.

Julian Thackery's father caught the tail end of these remarks as he was passing, and looked amused; and when I came out of the weighing room after changing he was leaning against the rails waiting for me. He had brought the list of entries of his horses, and at his suggestion we adjourned to the bar to discuss them. He bought me some lemon squash without a quiver, and we sat down at a small table on which he spread out several sheets of paper. I realized, hearing him discussing his plans and prospects, that the year by year success of his horses was no accident; he was a very able man.

"Why don't you take out a public license?" I said finally.

"Too much worry," he smiled. "This way it's a hobby. If I make mistakes, I have no one on my conscience. No one to apologize to or smooth down. No need to worry about owners whisking their horses away at an hour's notice. No risk of them not paying my fees for months on end."

"You know the snags," I agreed dryly.

"There's no profit in training," he said. "I break even most years, maybe finish a little ahead. But I work the stable in with the farm, you see. A lot of the overheads come into the farm accounts. I don't see how half these public trainers stay in business, do you? They either have to be rich to start with, or farmers like me, or else they have to bet, if they want a profit."

"But they don't give it up," I pointed out mildly. "And they all drive large cars. They can't do too badly."

He shook his head and finished his whisky. "They're good actors, some of them. They put on a smiling not-a-care-in-the-world expression at the races when they've got the bank manager camping on their doorstep back home. Well, now," he shuffled the papers together, folded them, and tucked them into a pocket, "you think you can get next Thursday off to go to Stratford?"

"I'm pretty sure of it, yes."

"Right. I'll see you there, then."

I nodded and we stood up to go. Someone had left an *Evening Standard* on the next table, and I glanced at it casually as we passed. Then I stopped and went back for a closer look. A paragraph on the bottom of the front page started "Derby Hope Dead," and told in a few bald words that Okinawa, entered for the Derby, had died on the flight from the United States, and was consequently scratched from all engagements.

I smiled inwardly. From the lack of detail or excitement, it was clear the report had come from someone like the trainer to whom Okinawa had been traveling, not from airport reporters sniffing a sensational story. No journalist who had seen or even been told of the shambles on that plane could have written so starkly. But the horse had been disposed of now, and I had helped wash out the plane myself, and there was nothing to see any more. Okinawa had been well insured, a vet had certified that destroying him was essential, and I had noticed that my name on the crew list was spelled wrongly: H. Gray. With a bit of luck, and if Yardman himself had his way, that was the end of it. "My dear boy," he'd said in agitation when hurriedly summoned to the airport, "it does business no good to have horses go crazy on our flights. We will not broadcast it, will we?"

"We will not," I agreed firmly, more for my sake than for his.

"It was unfortunate. . . ." he sighed, and shrugged, obviously relieved.

"We should have a humane killer," I said, striking the hot iron.

"Yes. Certainly. All right. I'll get one."

I would hold him to that, I thought. Standing peacefully in the bar at Kempton I could almost feel the weight of Okinawa and the wetness of his blood, the twenty-four hour old memory of lying under a dying horse still much too vivid for comfort. I shook myself firmly back into the present and went out with Julian's father to watch a disliked rival ride a brilliant finish.

Saturday night I did my level best to be civil to Mother's youngest female weekend guest, while avoiding all determined maneuvers to leave me alone with her, and Sunday morning I slid away before dawn northward to Lincolnshire.

Tom Wells was out on the apron when I arrived, giving his planes a personal check. He had assigned me, as I had learned on the telephone the previous morning, to fly three men to Glasgow for a round of golf. I was to take them in an Aztec and do exactly what they wanted. They were good customers. Tom didn't want to lose them.

"Good morning, Harry," he said as I reached him. "I've given you Quebec Bravo. You planned your route?"

I nodded.

"I've put scotch and champagne on board, in case they forget to bring any," he said. "You're fetching them from Coventry—you know that—and taking them back there. They may keep you late at Gleneagles until after dinner. I'm sorry about that."

"Expensive game of golf," I commented.

"Hm," he said shortly. "That's an alibi. They are three tycoons who like to compare notes in private. They stipulate a pilot who won't repeat what he hears, and I reckon you fit that bill, Harry my lad, because you've been coming here for four years and if a word of gossip has passed your lips in that time I'm a second-class gas fitter's mate."

"Which you aren't."

"Which I'm not." He smiled, a pleasant solid sturdy man of forty plus, a pilot himself who knew chartering backward and ran his own little firm with the minimum of fuss. Ex-R.A.F., of course, as most flyers of his age were; trained on bombers, given a love for the air, and let down with a bang when the service chucked them out as redundant. There were too many pilots chasing too few jobs in the postwar years, but Tom Wells had been good, persistent and lucky, and had converted a toe-hole copilot's job in a minor private airline into a seat on the board, and finally, backed by a firm of light aircraft manufacturers, had started his present company on his own.

"Give me a ring when you're leaving Gleneagles," he said, "I'll be up in the tower myself when you come back."

"I'll try not to keep you too late."

"You won't be the last." He shook his head. "Joe Wilkins is fetching three couples from a weekend in Le Touquet. A dawn job, that'll be, I shouldn't wonder. . . ."

I picked up the three impressive businessmen as scheduled and conveyed them to Scotland. On the way up they drank Tom Wells' Black and White and talked about dividend equalization reserves, unappropriated profits, and contingent liabilities, none of which I found in the least bit interesting. They moved on to exports and the opportunities available in the European market. There was some discussion about "whether the one and three-quarters was any positive inducement," which was the only point of their conversation I really understood.

The one and three-quarters, as I had learned at Anglia Bloodstock, was a percentage one could claim from the Government on anything one sold for export. The three tycoons were talking about machine tools and soft drinks, as far as I could gather, but the mechanism worked for bloodstock also. If a stud sold a horse abroad for say twenty thousand pounds, it received not only that sum from the buyer but also one and three-quarters per cent of it—three hundred and fifty pounds—from the Government. A carrot before the export donkey. A bonus. A pat on the head for helping the country's economy. In effect, it did influence some studs to prefer foreign buyers. But racehorses were simple to export; they needed no after sales service, follow-up campaign or multilingual advertising, which the tycoons variously argued were or were not worth the trouble. Then they moved on to taxation and I lost them again, the more so as there were some lowish clouds ahead over the Cheviots and at their request I was flying them below three thousand feet so that they could see the countryside.

I went up above the cloud into the quadrantal system operating above three thousand feet, where to avoid collision one had to fly on a steady regulated level according to the direction one was heading; in our case, going northwest, four thousand five hundred or six thousand five hundred or eight thousand five hundred, and so on up.

One of the passengers commented on the climb and asked the reason for it, and wanted to know my name.

"Grey."

"Well, Grey, where are we off to? Mars?"

I smiled. "High hills, low clouds."

"My God," said the weightiest and oldest tycoon, patting me heavily on the shoulder. "What wouldn't I give for such succinctness in my boardroom."

They were in good form, enjoying their day as well as making serious use of it. The smell of whisky in the warm luxurious little cabin overcame even that of hot oil, and the expensive cigar smoke swirled huskily in my throat. I enjoyed the journey, and for Tom's sake as well as my own pride, knowing my passengers were connoisseurs of private air travel, put them down on the Gleneagles strip like a whisper on a lake.

They played golf and drank and ate; and repeated the program in the afternoon. I walked on the hills in the morning, had lunch, and in the late afternoon booked a room in the hotel, and went to sleep. I guess it was a satisfactory day all round.

It was half-past ten when the reception desk woke me by telephone and said my passengers were ready to leave, and eleven before we got away. I flew back on a double dog-leg, making for the St. Abbs radio beacon on the Northumberland coast and setting a course of one sixty degrees south southeast from there on a one five two nautical mile straight course to Ottringham and then southwest across country to Coventry, coming in finally on their 122.70 homer signal.

The tycoons, replete, talked in mellow, rumbling, satisfied voices, no longer about business but about their own lives. The heaviest was having trouble over currency regulations with regard to a villa he had bought on the Costa del Sol. The Government had slapped a two-thousand-pound ceiling on investment spending abroad, and two thousand would hardly buy the bath taps. . . .

The man sitting directly behind me asked about decent yachts available for charter in the Aegean, and the other two told him. The third said it was really time his wife came back from Gstaad, she had been there for two months, and they were due to go to Nassau for Easter. They made me feel poverty-stricken, listening to them.

We landed safely at Coventry, where they shook my hand, yawning, thanked me for a smooth trip, and ambled off to a waiting Rolls, shivering in the chilly air. I made the last small hop back to Fenland and found Tom, as good as his word, on duty in the control tower to help me down. He yelled out of the window to join him, and we drank coffee out of a thermos jug while he waited for his Le Touquet plane to come back. It was due in an hour, earlier than expected. Apparently the client had struck a losing streak and the party had fizzled out.

"Everything go all right with your lot?" Tom said.

"They seemed happy," I nodded, filling in the flight details on his record chart and copying them into my own logbook.

"I suppose you want your fee in flying hours, as usual?"

I grinned. "How did you guess?"

"I wish you'd change your mind and work for me permanently."

I put down the pen and stretched, lolling back on the wooden chair with my hands laced behind my head. "Not yet. Give it three or four years; perhaps then."

"I need you now."

Need. The word was sweet. "I don't know. . . . I'll think it over again, anyway."

"Well, that's something, I suppose." He ruffled his thinning light brown hair and rubbed his hands down over his face, his skin itching with tiredness. "Sandwich?"

"Thanks." I took one. Ham, with French mustard, made in their bungalow by Tom's capable wife Janie, not from the airport canteen. The ham was thick and juicy, home-cooked in beer. We ate in silence and drank the hot strong coffee. Outside the glass-walled high-up square room the sky grew a thick matte black, with clouds drifting in to mask the stars. The wind was slowly backing, the atmospheric pressure falling. It was getting steadily colder. Bad weather on its way.

Tom checked his instruments, frowned, leaned back on his chair and twiddled his pencil. "The forecast was right," he said gloomily, "Snow tomorrow."

I grunted sympathetically. Snow grounded his planes and caused a hiatus in his income.

"Have to expect it in February, I suppose," he sighed.

I nodded in agreement. I wondered if Stratford Races would be snowed off on Thursday. I wondered if weather interfered much with Yardman's trips. I reflected that Janie Wells made good coffee, and that Tom was a sound sensible man. Untroubled, organized surface thoughts. And it was the last night I ever spent in my calm emotional deepfreeze.

The sky was a sullen orange-gray when we took off at eight the next morning from Gatwick, the as yet unshed snow hanging heavily as spawn in a frog's belly. We were carrying eight brood mares in an old unpressurized DC-4, flying away from the incoming storm, en route to Milan. Timmie and Conker were back, to my relief, but neither had had a scintillating holiday, by the sound of it. I overheard Conker, a much harassed small father of seven large hooligans, complaining as he loaded the cargo that he'd done nothing but cook and wash up while his wife curled up in bed with what was, in his opinion, opportunist malingering influenza. Timmie showed his sympathy in his usual way; a hearty gear-changing sniff. A thick-set black-haired square little Welshman, he suffered from interminable catarrh and everyone around him suffered also. It had been his sinuses, he unrepentantly said after one particularly repulsive spitting session, which had stopped him going down the mines like his pa. The February holiday, Timmie agreed, was not much cop.

"How many holidays do you have?" I asked, fixing chains.

"A week off every two months," Conker said. "Blimey, mate, don't tell me you took this job without asking that."

"I'm afraid I did."

"You'll be exploited," Conker said seriously. "When you start a job, you want your terms cut and dried, wages, overtime, holidays with pay, bonuses, superannuation, the lot. If you don't stand up for your rights, no one else will, there isn't a union for us, you know, bar the agricultural workers, if you care for that which I don't. And old Yardman, he don't give nothing away you know. You want to make sure about your weeks off, mate, or you won't get any. I'm telling you."

"Well . . . thank you. I'll ask him."

"Aw, look, man," said Timmie in his soft Welsh voice, "we get other times off too. You don't want to work yourself to death. Mr. Yardman don't hold you to more than two trips a week, I'll say that for him. If you don't want to go, that is."

"I see," I said. "And if you don't go, Billy and Alf do?"

"That's about it," agreed Conker. "I reckon." He fitted the last lynch pin on the last box and rubbed his hands down the sides of his trousers.

I remembered Simon saying that my predecessor Peters had been a belligerent stand-on-your-rights man, and I supposed that Conker had caught his anti-exploitation attitude from him, because it seemed to me, from what they'd said, that Conker and Timmie both had free time positively lavished upon them. A day's return trip certainly meant working a continuous stretch of twelve hours or more, but two of those in seven days wasn't exactly penal servitude. Out of interest I had added up my hours on duty some weeks, and even at the most they had never touched forty. They just don't know when they are well off, I thought mildly, and signaled to the airport staff to take the ramp away.

The DC-4 was noisy and very cramped. The gangways between and alongside the horses were too narrow for two people to pass, and in addition one had to go forward and backward along the length of the plane bent almost double. It was, as usual, normally a passenger ship, and it had low-hung luggage shelves along its length on both sides. There were catches to hold the racks up out of the way, but they were apt to shake open in flight and it was more prudent to start with all the racks down than have them fall on one's head. This, added to the angled guy chains cutting across at shin level, made walking about a tiresome process and provided the worst working conditions I had yet struck. But Conker, I was interested to notice, had no complaints. Peters, maybe, hadn't been with him on a DC-4.

After take-off, the horses all being quiet and well behaved, we went forward into the galley for the first cup of coffee. The engineer, a tall thin man with a habit of raising his right eyebrow five or six times rather fast when he asked a question, was already dispensing it into disposable mugs. Two full ones had names penciled on: Patrick and Bob. The engineer picked them up and took them forward to the pilot and copilot in the cockpit. Coming back, the engineer asked our names and wrote us each a mug.

"There aren't enough on board for us to throw them away every time," he explained, handing me "Henry." "Sugar?" He had a two-pound bag of granulated, and a red plastic spoon. "I know the way your lot drinks coffee. The skipper, too."

We drank the scalding brown liquid. It didn't taste of coffee, but if you thought of it as a separate unnamed thirst quencher, it wasn't too bad. In the galley the engine noise made it necessary to shout loudly to be heard, and the vibration shook concentric ripples in the coffee. The engineer sipped his gingerly over the scrawled word "Mike."

"You've got a right load there," he commented. "A ship full of expectant mums, aren't they?"

Conker, Timmie and I nodded in unison.

"Are they Italian?"

Together we shook our heads. Music hall stuff.

"What are they going for, then?"

"They are English mares going to be mated with Italian sires," explained Conker, who had once worked in a stud and would be positively happy if one of the mares foaled down prematurely on the flight.

"Pull the other one, it's got bells on," said the engineer.

"No, it's right," said Conker. "They have to have the foals they are carrying now in the stud where their next mate is."

"Why?" The agile eyebrow worked overtime.

"Ah," said Conker seriously. "The gestation period for horses is eleven months, right? And a brood mare has a foal every twelve months, right? So there's only four weeks left between production and—er—reproduction, do you see? And in those four weeks the new foal isn't fit for traveling hundreds of miles in the freezing cold, so the mares have to have the foals in the stud of their next mate. Get?"

"I get," agreed the engineer. "I get indeed."

"That one," said Conker admiringly, pointing out in the foremost box an elegant brown silky head which owing to the general lack of space was almost in the galley, "that one's going to Molvedo."

"How do you know?" asked Timmie interestedly.

"Horsebox driver told me."

The copilot came back from the cockpit and said the skipper wanted a refill.

"Already? That man's a tank." The engineer poured into the Patrick mug.

"Here," said the copilot, handing it to me. "Take it to him, will you? I'm off to see a man about a dog." He brushed under Molvedo's future wife's inquisitive nose and bent down for the obstructed walk down to the john.

I took the steaming mug forward into the cockpit. The pilot, flying in whiter-than-white shirtsleeves despite the zero temperature outside, stretched out a languid hand and nodded his thanks. I stayed for a second looking round at the banked instruments, and he glanced up at me and gestured to me to put my ear down to his mouth. The noise there made even ordinary shouting impossible.

"Are you the head chap with the horses?"

"Yes."

"Like to sit there for a bit?" He pointed to the empty copilot's seat.

"Yes, I would." He gestured permissively, and I edged sideways into the comfortable bucket seat beside him. The cockpit was tiny, considering how much had to be packed into it, and battered and dented with age. It was also, to me, very much my home.

I studied the instruments with interest. I had never flown a four-engined craft, only one and two, for the excellent reason that there were no four-engined planes at Fenland. As even small two-engined jobs like the Aztec I had taken to Gleneagles the day before cost nearly thirty-five pounds per flying hour to hire from Tom, I thought it unlikely I would ever raise enough cash for a course on the really big stuff, even if I could use the qualification once I got it. You couldn't just go up alone for an afternoon's jolly in an airliner; they simply weren't to be had. None of which stopped me for a moment being intent on learning everything I could.

The pilot, Patrick, indicated that I should put on the combined set of earphones and mouthpiece which was hanging over the semicircular wheel. I slid it on to my head, and through it he began to explain to me what all the switches and dials were for. He was the first pilot I'd flown with on Yardman's trips who had taken such trouble, and I listened and nodded and felt grateful, and didn't tell him I knew already most of what he was saying.

Patrick was a big striking-looking man of about thirty, with straight dark auburn hair cut a bit theatrically in duck tails, and light amber eyes like a cat's. His mouth turned naturally up at the corners so that even in repose he seemed to be smiling, as if everything in the world was delightful, with no evil to be found anywhere. Nor, I later proved, did the implication of that curve lie; he persisted in believing the best of everybody, even with villainy staring him in the face. He had the illogical faith in human goodness of a probation officer, though in that first half hour all I learned about him was that he was a gentle, careful, self-assured and eminently safe pilot.

He tuned in to the frequency of the radio beacon at Dieppe, explaining it to me as he went, and took a weather report there before turning on to the course to Paris.

"We'll go down to the Med and fly along the coast," he said. "There's too much cloud over the Alps to go straight across. Not being pressurized we ought not to go above ten thousand feet but fourteen thousand or so doesn't hurt unless you've got a bad heart. Even that doesn't give us enough in hand over the Alps in the present conditions, so I'm going the long way round."

I nodded, thoroughly approving.

He checked the de-icing equipment for a second time in ten minutes and said, "This bird won't fly with more than a quarter of a ton of ice on her, and the de-icers were U.S. last week." He grinned. "It's O.K., I've checked them six times since they were repaired, they're doing all right."

He peeled and ate one of a large bunch of bananas lying on the ledge over the instrument panel, then calmly unhinged the window beside him a few inches and threw the skin out. I laughed to myself in appreciation and began to like Patrick a good deal.

The copilot returned to claim his place, and I went back to the horses for the rest of the journey. Uneventfully we went down across France to Dijon, turned south down the Rhone valley, east at Saint-Tropez, and north again at Albenga, landing at Malpensa Airport, Milan, in exactly four hours from Gatwick.

Italy was cold. Shivering as the open doors let in air thirty degrees below the cabin temperature we watched about ten airport men in royal blue battle dress push the wide top-class ramp into position, and waited while three Customs men made their way over from the building. They came up the ramp, and the eldest of them said something in his own language.

"Non parlo italiano," I said apologetically, which useful sentence was all I knew.

"Non importa," he said. He took from me the mares' temporary import permits which had been made out in both English and Italian, and his two assistants began going from horse to horse calling out their descriptions.

All was in order. He gave me back the papers with a courteous nod of the head, and led his shadows away down the ramp. Again we went through the familiar routine of transferring the cargo from the plane to the waiting horseboxes, Conker making a great fuss of the mare going to Molvedo.

With an hour to spare before we set about loading another cargo of mares bound in the opposite direction for the same reason, Conker, Timmie and I walked across a quarter of a mile of tarmac to the airport building to have lunch. We were met at the door by Patrick, looking very official with gold-braided shoulder tabs on his navy uniform jacket, and wearing an expression of resignation.

"We can't go back today," he said, "so you chaps don't need to hurry over your beer."

"What's up, then?" asked Timmie, sniffing loudly.

"A blizzard. Came down like a burst eiderdown in a wind tunnel after we left this morning. It's raging all over the south and halfway across the channel, and snowing clear up to John o' Groats. The bottom's dropped out of the barometer and . . . well, anyway, my instructions are not to go back."

"All that pasta," said Conker philosophically. "It does my tripes no good."

He and Timmie went off to the snack bar and Patrick showed me the telegraph office to send "no go" messages to Yardman and the expectant studs. After that we went back to the aircraft, where he collected his overnight bag and I turned homeward the arriving convoy of Italian mares. He waited for me to finish and helped me shut the big double doors from inside at the top of the ramp, and we walked forward across the flattened dismantled boxes, through the galley, and down the staircase which had been wheeled up to the door just behind the cockpit.

"Where will you stay?" he said.

"Hotel, I suppose," I said vaguely.

"If you like, you could come with me. There's a family in Milan I berth with when I'm stranded, and there's room for two."

I had a strong inclination, as usual, to be by myself, but principally because I couldn't even ask for a hotel room in Italian let alone find entertainment except looking at architecture for the rest of the day, I accepted his offer, and thanked him.

"You'll like them," he said.

We went two hundred yards in silence.

"Is it true," he said, "that you're a viscount?"

"No," I said casually. "A Boeing 707."

He chuckled. "A bleeding viscount, that little Welshman said you were, to be precise."

"Would it make any difference to you if I were?"

"None whatever."

"That's all right, then."

"So you are?"

"On and off."

We went through the glass doors into the hall of the airport. It was spacious, airy, glass-walled, stone-floored. Along one side stretched a long gift counter with souvenir presents crowded in a row of display cases and stacked on shelves at the back. There were silk ties on a stand, and dolls in local dress scattered on the counter, and trays of paper-backed books and local view postcards. In charge of this display stood a tall dark-haired girl in a smooth black dress. She saw us coming and her coolly solemn face lit into a delicious smile.

"Patrick," she said. "Hullo, Patrick, come sta?"

He answered her in Italian, and as an afterthought waved his hand at me and said "Gabriella, . . . Henry." He asked her a question, and she looked at me carefully and nodded.

"Si," she said. "Henry anche."

"That's fixed, then," said Patrick cheerfully.

"You mean," I said incredulously, "that we are going to stay with—er—Gabriella?"

He stiffened slightly. "Do you object?"

I looked at Gabriella, and she at me.

"I think," I said slowly, "that it is too good to be true."

It wasn't for another ten minutes, during which time she talked to Patrick while looking at me, that I realized that I spoke no Italian and the only English word that she knew was "Hullo."

6

YOU COULDN'T say it was reasonable, it was just electric. I found out between one heartbeat and the next what all the poets throughout the ages had been going on about. I understood at last why Roman Antony threw away his honor for Egyptian Cleopatra, why Trojan Paris caused a ten years' war abducting Greek Helen, why Leander drowned on one of his risky nightly swims across the Dardanelles to see Hero. The distance from home, the mystery, the unknownness, were a part of it; one couldn't feel like that for the girl next door. But that didn't explain why it hadn't happened before; why it should be this girl, this one alone who fizzed in my blood.

I stood on the cool stone airport floor and felt as if I'd been struck by lightning; the world had tilted, the air was crackling, the gray February day blazed with light, and all because of a perfectly ordinary girl who sold souvenirs to tourists.

The same thing, fantastically, had happened to her as well. Perhaps it had to be mutual, to happen at all. I don't know. But I watched the brightness grow in her eyes, the excitement and gaiety in her manner, and I knew that against all probability it was for me. Girls were seldom moved to any emotion by my brown-haired, tidy, unobtrusive self, and since I rarely set out to make an impression on them, I even more rarely did so. Even the ones who wanted to marry my title were apt to yawn in my face. Which made Gabriella's instant reaction doubly devastating.

"For God's sake," said Patrick in amusement, when she didn't answer a twice repeated question, "will you two stop gawping at each other?"

"Gabriella," I said.

"Si?"

"Gabriella. . . ."

Patrick laughed. "You're not going to get far like that."

"Parla francese?" she said anxiously.

Patrick translated. "Do you speak French."

"Yes." I laughed with relief. "Yes, more or less."

"E bene," she sighed, smiling. "E molto molto bene."

Perhaps because we were unburdened by having to observe any French proprieties and because we both knew already that we would need it later on, we began right away using the intimate form tu instead of vous, for "you." Patrick raised his eyebrows and laughed again and said in three languages that we were nuts.

I *was* nuts, there was no getting away from it. Patrick endured the whole afternoon sitting at a table in the snack bar drinking coffee and telling me about Gabriella and her family. We could see her from where we sat, moving quietly about behind her long counter, selling trinkets to departing travelers. She was made of curves, which after all the flat hips, flat stomachs, and more or less flat chests of the skinny debs at home, was as warming as a night watchman's fire on a snowy night. Her oval pale olive-skinned face reminded me of medieval Italian paintings, a type of bone structure which must have persisted through centuries, and her expression, except when she smiled, was so wholly calm as to be almost unfriendly.

It struck me after a while, when I had watched her make two or three self-conscious customers nervous by her detached manner, that selling wasn't really suited to her character, and I said so, idly, to Patrick.

"I agree," he said dryly. "But there are few places better for a smuggler to work than an airport."

"A . . . *smuggler?* I don't believe it." I was aghast.

Patrick enjoyed his effect. "Smuggler," he nodded. "Definitely."

"No," I said.

"So am I," he added, smiling.

I looked down at my coffee, very disturbed. "Neither of you is the type."

"You're wrong, Henry. I'm only one of many who brings . . . er . . . goods . . . in to Gabriella."

"What," I said slowly, fearing the answer, "are the goods?"

He put his hand into his jacket pocket pulled out a flat bottle about five inches high, and handed it to me. A printed chemist's label on the front said "Two hundred aspirin tablets B.P.," and the brown glass bottle was filled to the brim with them. I unscrewed the top, pulled out the twist of cotton wool, and shook a few out on to my hand.

"Don't take one," said Patrick, still smiling. "It wouldn't do you any good at all."

"They're not aspirins." I tipped them back into the bottle and screwed on the cap.

"No."

"Then what?"

"Birth control pills," he said.

"*What?*"

"Italy is a Roman Catholic country," he observed. "You can't buy these pills here. But that doesn't stop women wanting to avoid being in a constant state of baby production, does it? And the pills are marvelous for them, they can take them without the devoutest husbands knowing anything about it."

"Good God," I said.

"My brother's wife collects them at home from her friends and so on, and when she has a bottle full I bring it to Gabriella and she passes them on at this end. I know for a fact that at least four other pilots do the same, not to mention a whole fleet of air hostesses, and she admitted to me once that a day seldom goes by without some supplies flying in."

"Do you . . . well . . . sell . . . them to Gabriella?"

He was quite shocked, which pleased me. "Of course not. She doesn't sell them, either. They are a gift, a service if you like, from the women of one country to the women of another. My sister-in-law and her friends are really keen on it; they don't see why any woman in the world should have to risk having a child if she doesn't want one."

"I've never thought about it," I said, fingering the bottle.

"You've never had a sister who's borne six children in six years and collapsed into a shattering nervous breakdown when she started the seventh."

"Gabriella's sister?"

He nodded. "That's why she got some pills, in the first place. And the demand just grew and grew."

I gave him back the bottle and he put it in his pocket. "Well?" he said, with a hint of challenge.

"She must be quite a girl," I said, "to do something like this."

His curving mouth curved wider. "If she smuggled the Crown Jewels you'd forgive her. Confess it."

"Whatever she did," I said slowly.

The amusement died right out of his face and he looked at me soberly. "I've heard of this sort of thing," he said. "But I've never seen it happen before. And you didn't even need to speak to each other. In fact, it's just damn lucky you *can* speak to each other. . . ."

Three times during the afternoon I made sure of that. She would get into trouble, she said, if she just talked to me when she should be working, so I bought presents, separately, for my father, mother and sister, taking a long time over each choice. Each time she spoke and looked at me in a kaleidoscopic mixture of excitement, caution and surprise, as if she too found falling helplessly in love with a complete stranger an overwhelming and almost frightening business.

"I like that one."

"It costs six thousand lire."

"That is too dear."

"This one is cheaper."

"Show me some others."

We began like that, like school day textbooks, in careful stilted French, but by the end of the afternoon, when she locked the display cases and left with Patrick and me through the employees' entrance, we could talk with some ease. I perhaps knew the most French of the three of us, then Gabriella, then Patrick; but his Italian was excellent, so between us everything could in one language or another be understood.

We left the airport in a taxi, and as soon as we were on the move Patrick gave her the aspirin bottle. She thanked him with a flashing smile and asked him if they were all the same sort. He nodded, and explained they'd come from some R.A.F. wives whose husbands were away on a three-months overseas course.

From her large shoulder-sling bag of black leather she produced some of the bright striped wrapping paper from her airport gift shop and a large packet of sweets. The sweets and the aspirin bottle were expertly whisked into a ball-shaped parcel with four corners sticking up on top like leaves on a pineapple, and a scrap of sticky tape secured them.

The taxi stopped outside a dilapidated narrow terrace house in a poor-looking street. Gabriella climbed out of the taxi, but Patrick waved me back into my seat.

"She doesn't live here," he said. "She's just delivering the sweets."

She was already talking to a tired-looking young woman whose black dress accentuated the pallor of her skin, and whose varicose veins were the worst I had seen, like great dark blue knobbed worms networking just under the surface of her legs. Round her clung two small children with two or three more behind in the doorway, but she had a flat stomach in her skimpy dress and no baby in her arms. The look she gave Gabriella and her pretty present were all the reward that anyone would need. The children knew that there were sweets in the parcel. They were jumping up trying to reach it as their mother held it above their heads, and as we left she went indoors with them, and she was laughing.

"Now," said Patrick, turning away from the window, "we had better show Henry Milan."

It was getting dark and was still cold, but not for us. I wouldn't have noticed if it had been raining ice. They began by marching me slowly around the Piazza del Duomo to see the great Gothic cathedral and the Palazzo Reale, and along the high glass arcade into the Piazza della Scala to gaze at the opera house, which Gabriella solemnly told me was the second-largest theater in Europe, and could hold three thousand six hundred people.

"Where is the largest?" said Patrick.

"In Naples," she said smiling. "It is ours too."

"I suppose Milan has the biggest cathedral, then," he teased her.

"No," she laughed, showing an unsuspected dimple, "Rome."

"An extravagant nation, the Italians."

"We were ruling the world while you were still painting yourselves blue."

"Hey, hey," said Patrick.

"Leonardo da Vinci lived in Milan," she said.

"Italy is undoubtedly the most beautiful country in the world and Milan is its pearl."

"Patrick, you are a great idiot," she said affectionately. But she was proud indeed of her native city, and before dinner that evening I learned that nearly a million and a half people lived there and that there were dozens of museums, and music and art schools, and that it was the best manufacturing town in the country, and the richest, and its factories made textiles and paper and railway engines and cars. And, in fact, airplanes.

We ate in a quiet warmly lit little restaurant which looked disconcertingly like Italian restaurants in London but smelled quite different, spicy and fragrant. I hardly noticed what I ate. Gabriella chose some sort of veal for us all, and it tasted fine, like everything else that evening. We drank two bottles of red local wine which fizzed slightly on the tongue, and unending little gold cups of black coffee. I knew even then that it was because we were all speaking a language not our own that I felt liberated from my usual self. It was so much easier to be uninhibited away from everything which had planted the inhibitions; another sky, another culture, a time out of time. But that only made the way simpler, it didn't make the object less real. It meant I didn't have chains on my tongue; but what I said wasn't said loosely, it was still rooted in some unchanging inner core. On that one evening in Milan I learned what it was like to be gay deep into the spirit, and if for nothing else I would thank Gabriella for that all my life.

We talked for hours, not profoundly, I dare say, but companionably; at first about the things we had done and seen that day, then of ourselves, our childhood. Then of Fellini's films, and a little about travel, and then, in ever-widening ripples, of religion, and our own hopes, and the state the world was in. There wasn't an ounce of natural reforming zeal among the three of us, as perhaps there ought to have been when so much needed reforming; but faith didn't move mountains any more, it got bogged down by committees, Patrick said, and the saints of the past would be smeared as psychological misfits today.

"Could you imagine the modern French army allowing itself to be inspired and led into battle by a girl who saw visions?" he said. "You could not."

It was true. You could not.

"Psychology," Patrick said, with wine and candlelight in his yellow eyes, "is the death of courage."

"I don't understand," protested Gabriella.

"Not for girls," he said. "For men. It is now not considered sensible to take physical risks unless you can't avoid them. Ye gods, there's no quicker way to ruin a nation than to teach its young men it's foolish to take risks. Or worse than foolish, they would have you believe."

"What do you mean?" she said.

"Ask Henry. He'll cheerfully go out and risk his neck on a racehorse any day of the week. Ask him why."

"Why?" she said, half-serious, half-laughing, the glints of light in her dark eyes outpointing the stars.

"I like it," I said. "It's fun."

Patrick shook his red head. "You look out, pal, you mustn't go around admitting that sort of thing these days. You've got to say you do it only for the money, or you'll be labeled as a masochistic guilt complex before you can say . . . er . . . masochistic guilt complex."

"Oh yeah?" I said, laughing.

"Yeah, damn it, and it's not funny. It's deadly serious. The knockers have had so much success that now it's fashionable to say you're a coward. You may not *be* one, mind, but you've got to *say* so, just to prove you're normal. Historically, it's fantastic. What other nation ever went around saying on television and in the press and at parties and things that cowardice is normal and courage is disgusting? Nearly all nations used to have elaborate tests for young men to prove they were brave. Now in England they are taught to settle down and want security. But bravery is built in somewhere in human nature and you can't stamp it out any more than the sex urge. So if you outlaw ordinary bravery it bursts out somewhere else, and I reckon that's what the increase in crime is due to. If you make enjoying danger seem perverted, I don't see how you can complain if it becomes so."

This was too much for his French; he said it to me in hot English, and repeated it, when Gabriella protested, in cooler Italian.

"But," she said wonderingly, "I do not like a man to say he is a coward. Who wants that? A man is for hunting and for defending, for keeping his wife safe."

"Back to the caves?" I said.

"Our instincts are still the same," agreed Patrick. "Basically good."

"And a man is for loving," Gabriella said.

"Yes, indeed," I agreed with enthusiasm.

"If you like to risk your neck, I like that. If you risk it for me, I like it better."

"You mustn't say so," said Patrick smiling. "There's probably some vile explanation for that too."

We all laughed, and some fresh coffee came, and the talk drifted away to what girls in Italy wanted of life as opposed to what they could have. Gabriella said the gap was narrowing fast, and that she was content, particularly as she was an orphan and had no parental pressure to deal with. We discussed for some time the pros and cons of having parents after adolescence, and all maintained that what we had was best; Gabriella her liberty, Patrick a widowed mother who spoiled him undemandingly, and I, free board and lodging. Patrick looked at me sharply when I said that, and opened his mouth to blow the gaff.

"Don't tell her," I said in English. "Please don't."

"She would like you even more."

"No."

He hesitated, but to my relief he left it, and when Gabriella asked, told her we had been arguing as to who should pay the bill. We shared it between us, but we didn't leave for some time after that. We talked, I remember, about loyalty; at first about personal loyalty, and then political.

Gabriella said that Milan had many Communists, and she thought that for a Roman Catholic to be a Communist was like an Arab saying he wanted to be ruled by Israel.

"I wonder who they would be loyal to, if Russia invaded Italy?" Patrick said.

"That's a big if," I said smiling. "Pretty impossible with Germany, Austria and Switzerland in between, not to mention the Alps."

Gabriella shook her head. "Communists begin at Trieste."

I was startled and amused at the same time, hearing an echo of my die-hard father. "Wogs begin at Calais."

"Of course they do," Patrick said thoughtfully. "On your doorstep."

"But cheer up," she said laughing. "Yugoslavia also has mountains, and the Russians will not be arriving that way either."

"They won't invade any more countries with armies," I agreed mildly. "Only with money and technicians. Italian and French and British Communists can rely on never having to choose which side to shoot at."

"And can go on undermining their native land with a clear conscience," Patrick nodded, smiling.

"Let's not worry about it," I said, watching the moving shadows where Gabriella's smooth hair fell across her cheek. "Not tonight."

"It will never touch us, anyway," Patrick agreed. "And if we stay here much longer Gabriella's sister will lock us out."

Reluctantly we went out into the cold street. When we had gone ten paces Patrick exclaimed that he had left his overnight bag behind, and went back for it, striding quickly.

I turned to Gabriella, and she to me. The street lights were reflected in her welcoming eyes, and the solemn mouth trembled on the edge of that transfiguring smile. There wasn't any need to say anything. We both knew. Although I stood with my body barely brushing hers and put my hands very gently on her arms just below the shoulders, she rocked as if I'd pushed her. It was the same for me. I felt physically shaken by a force so primitive and volcanic as to be frightening. How could just touching a girl, I thought confusedly, just touching a girl I'd been longing to touch all afternoon and all evening, sweep one headlong into such an uncivilized turbulence? And on a main street in Milan, where one could do nothing about it.

She let her head fall forward against my shoulder, and we were still standing like that, with my cheek on her hair, when Patrick came back with his bag. Without a word, smiling resignedly, he pulled her round, tucked her arm into his, and said briefly, "Come on. You'll get run in if you stay here much longer like that." She looked at him blindly for a moment, and then laughed shakily. "I don't understand why this has happened," she said.

"Struck by the gods," said Patrick ironically. "Or chemistry. Take your pick."

"It isn't sensible."

"You can say that again."

He began to walk down the road, pulling her with him. My feet unstuck themselves from the pavement and reattached themselves to my watery legs and I caught them up. Gabriella put her other arm through mine, and we strolled the mile and a half to where her sister lived, gradually losing the heavy awareness of passion and talking normally and laughing, and finally ending up on her doorstep in a fit of giggles.

Lisabetta, Gabriella's sister, was ten years older and a good deal fatter, though she had the same smooth olive skin and the same shaped fine dark eyes. Her husband, Giulio, a softly flabby man approaching forty, with a black mustache, bags under his eyes, and less hair than he'd once had, lumbered ungracefully out of his armchair when we went into his sitting room and gave us a moderately enthusiastic welcome.

Neither he nor Lisabetta spoke English or French so while the two girls made yet more coffee, and Patrick talked to Giulio, I looked around with some interest at Gabriella's home. Her sister had a comfortable four-bedroomed flat in a huge recently-built tower, and all the furnishings and fabrics were uncompromisingly modern. The floors were some sort of reconstituted stone heated from underneath and without carpet or rugs, and there were blinds, not curtains, to cover the windows. I thought the total effect rather stark, but reflected idly that Milan in midsummer must be an oven, and the flat had been planned for the heat.

Several children came and went, all indistinguishable to my eyes. Seven of them, there should be, I remembered. Four boys, three girls, Patrick had said. Although it was nearly midnight, none of them seemed to have gone to bed. They had all been waiting to see Patrick and tumbled about him like puppies.

When Lisabetta had poured the coffee and one of the children had handed it round Giulio asked Patrick a question, looking at me.

"He wants to know what your job is," Patrick said.

"Tell him I look after the horses."

"Nothing else?"

"Nothing else."

Giulio was unimpressed. He asked another question.

Smiling faintly, Patrick said, "He wants to know how much you earn?"

"My pay for a single trip to Milan is about one fifth of yours."

"He won't like that."

"Nor do I."

He laughed. When he translated Giulio scowled.

Patrick and I slept in a room which normally belonged to two of the boys, now doubling with the other two. Gabriella shared a third bedroom with the two elder girls, while the smallest was in with her parents. There were toys all over the place in our room, and small shoes kicked off and clothes dumped in heaps, and the unchanged sheets on the boys' beds were wrinkled like elephant skins from their restless little bodies. Patrick had from long globe-trotting habit come equipped with pajamas, slippers, washing things, and a clean shirt for the morning. I eyed this splendor with some envy, and slept in my underpants.

"Why," said Patrick in the dark, "won't you tell them you have a title?"

"It isn't important."

"It would be to Giulio."

"That's the best reason for not telling him."

"I don't see why you're so keen to keep it a secret."

"Well, you try telling everyone you're an earl's son, and see what happens."

"I'd love it. Everyone would be bowing and scraping in all directions. Priorities galore. Instant service. A welcome on every mat."

"And you'd never be sure if anyone liked you for yourself."

"Of course you would."

"How many head grooms have you brought here before?" I asked mildly.

He drew in a breath audibly and didn't answer.

"Would you have offered me this bed if Timmie had kept his big mouth shut?"

He was silent.

I said, "Remind me to kick your teeth in in the morning."

But the morning, I found, was a long way off. I simply couldn't sleep. Gabriella's bed was a foot away from me on the far side of the wall, and I lay and sweated for her with a desire I hadn't dreamed possible. My body literally ached. Cold, controlled Henry Grey, I thought helplessly. Grey by name and gray by nature. Cold, controlled Henry Grey lying in a child's bed in a foreign city biting his arm to stop himself crying out. You could laugh at such hunger; ridicule it away. I tried that, but it didn't work. It stayed with me hour after wretched hour, all the way to the dawn, and I would have been much happier if I'd been able to go to sleep and dream about her instead.

She had kissed me good night in the passage outside her door, lightly, gaily, with Patrick and Lisabetta and about six children approvingly looking on. And she had stopped and retreated right there because it was the same as in the street outside the restaurant; even the lightest touch could start an earthquake. There just wasn't room for an earthquake in that crowded flat.

Patrick lent me his razor without a word, when we got up.

"I'm sorry," I said.

"You were quite right. I would not have offered to take you with me if the Welshman hadn't said . . ."

"I know." I put on my shirt and buttoned the cuffs.

"All the same I still wouldn't have asked you if I hadn't thought you looked all right."

I turned toward him, surprised.

"What you need, Henry, is a bit more self-confidence. Why ever shouldn't people like you for yourself? Gabriella obviously does. So do I."

"People often don't." I pulled on my socks.

"You probably don't give them half a chance." With which devastatingly accurate shot he went out of the door, shrugging his arms into his authoritative captain's uniform.

Subdued by the raw steely morning, the three of us went back to the airport. Gabriella had dark shadows under her eyes and wouldn't look at me, though I could think of nothing I had done to offend her. She spoke only to Patrick, and in Italian, and he, smiling briefly, answered her in the same language. When we arrived at the airport, she asked me, hurriedly, not to come and talk to her at the gift counter, and almost ran away from me without saying good-by. I didn't try to stop her. It would be hours before we got the horses loaded, and regardless of what she asked, I intended to see her again before I left.

I hung around the airport all the morning with Conker and Timmie, and about twelve Patrick came and found me and with a wide grin said I was in luck, traffic at Gatwick was restricted because of deep snow, and unessential freight flights were suspended for another day.

"You'd better telephone the studs again, and tell them we are taking the mares to England tomorrow at eight," he said. "Weather permitting."

Gabriella received the news with such a flash of delight that my spirits rose to the ionosphere. I hesitated over the next question, but she made it easy for me.

"Did you sleep well?" she asked gravely, studying my face.

"I didn't sleep at all."

She sighed, almost blushing. "Nor did I."

"Perhaps," I said tentatively, "if we spent the evening together, we could sleep tonight."

"Henry!" She was laughing. "Where?"

Where proved more difficult than I had imagined. She would not consider a hotel, as we must not sleep there, but go back to her sister's before midnight. One must not be shameless, she said. She could not stay out all night. We ended up, of all unlikely places, inside the DC-4, lying in a cozy nest hollowed in a heap of blankets stacked in the luggage bay alongside the galley.

There, where no one would ever find us, and with a good deal of the laughter of total happiness, we spent the whole of the evening in the age-old way, and were pleased and perhaps relieved to find that we suited each other perfectly.

Lying quietly cradled in my arms, she told me hesitantly that she had had a lover before, which I knew anyway by then, but that it was odd making love anywhere except in bed. She felt the flutter in my chest and lifted her head up to peer at my face in the dim reflected moonlight.

"Why are you laughing?" she said.

"It so happens that I have never made love *in* bed."

"Where then?"

"In the grass."

"Henry! Is that the custom in England?"

"Only at the end of parties in the summer."

She smiled and put her head down contentedly again, and I stroked her hair and thought how wholesome she was, and how dreadful in comparison seemed the half-drunk nymphs taken casually down the deb-dance garden path. I would never do that again, I thought. Never again.

"I was ashamed, this morning," she said, "of wanting this so much. Ashamed of what I had been thinking all night."

"There is no shame in it."

"Lust is one of the seven deadly sins."

"Love is a virtue."

"They get very mixed up. Are we this evening being virtuous or sinful?" She didn't sound too worried about it.

"Doing what comes naturally."

"Then it's probably sinful."

She twisted in my arms, turning so that her face was close to mine. Her eyes caught a sheen in the soft near-darkness. Her teeth rubbed gently against the bare skin on the point of my shoulder.

"You taste of salt," she said.

I moved my hand over her stomach and felt the deep muscles there contract. Nothing, I thought, shaken by an echoing ripple right down my spine, nothing was so impossibly potent as being wanted in return. I kissed her, and she gave a long soft murmuring sigh which ended oddly in a laugh.

"Sin," she said, with a smile in her voice, "is O.K."

We went back to her sister's and slept soundly on each side of the wall. Early in the morning, in her dressing gown, with tousled hair and dreaming eyes, she made coffee for Patrick and me before we set off for the airport.

"You'll come back?" she said almost casually, pouring my cup.

"As soon as I can."

She knew I meant it. She kissed me good-by without clinging, and Patrick also. "For bringing him," she said.

In the taxi on the way to the airport Patrick said, "Why don't you just stay here with her? You easily could."

I didn't answer him until we were turning into the airport road.

"Would you? Stay, I mean."

"No. But then, I need to keep my job."

"So do I. For different reasons, perhaps. But I need to keep it just the same."

"It's none of my business," he said, "but I'm glad."

We loaded the Italian mares and flew them to snowy England without another hitch. I soothed them on their way and thought about Gabriella, who seemed to have established herself as a warming knot somewhere under my diaphragm.

I thought about her with love and without even the conventional sort of anxiety, for she had said with a giggle, it would be a poor smuggler who couldn't swallow her own contraband.

7

STRATFORD RACES were off because of snow, which was just as well as Yardman squeezed in an extra trip on that day at very short notice. Seven three-year-olds to France, he said; but at loading time there were eight.

I was held up on the way to Cambridge by a lorry which had skidded sideways and blocked the icy road, and when I reached the airport all the cargo had already arrived, with the box drivers stamping their feet to keep warm and cursing me fluently. Billy, and it was Billy again, not Conker and Timmie, stood about with his hands in his pockets and a sneer permanently fixed like epoxy resin, enjoying the disapproval I had brought on myself. He had not, naturally, thought of beginning the work before I arrived.

We loaded the horses, he, I, and deaf old Alf, whom Billy had brought with him, and we worked in uncompanionable silence. There was a fourth groom on the trip, a middle-aged characterless man with a large straggly mustache and a bad cold, but he had come with one particular horse from an upper crust stud, and he refrained from offering to help with any others. Neither did he lend a hand on the journey, but sat throughout beside his own protégée, guarding it carefully from no visible danger. Billy dropped a handful of peat in my coffee and later poured his own, which was half-full of sugar, over my head. I spent the rest of the journey in the wash-room, awkwardly rinsing the stickiness out of my hair and vowing to get even with Billy one day when I hadn't thousands of pounds' worth of bloodstock in my care.

During the unloading I looked closely at one inconspicuous brown mare, trying to memorize her thoroughly unmemorable appearance. She was definitely not a three-year-old, like all the others on the trip, and she was, I was sure, almost identical to the one we had taken to France the first day I flew with Billy. And very like the one we had brought back that afternoon on the second trip. Three mares, all alike . . . well, it was not impossible, especially as they had no distinct markings between them, none at all.

The special groom left us in Paris, escorting his own horse right through to its new home. He had been engaged, he said, to bring another horse back, a French stallion which his stud had bought, and we would be collecting him again the next week. We duly did collect him, the next Tuesday, complete with the stallion, a tight-muscled butty little horse with a fiery eye and a restless tail. He was squealing like a colt when we stored him on board, and this time there was some point in his straggly mustached keeper staying beside him all the way.

Among the cargo there was yet another undistinguished brown mare. I was leaning on the starboard side of her box, gazing over and down at her, not able to see her very clearly against the peat she stood on and the brown horse on her other side, when Billy crept up behind me and hit me savagely across the shoulders with a spare tethering chain. I turned faster than he expected and got in two hard quick kicks on his thigh. His lips went back with the pain and he furiously swung his arm, the short chain flickering and bending like an angry snake. I dodged it by ducking into one of the crossway alleys between the boxes, and the chain wrapped itself with a vicious clatter round the corner where I had been standing. Unhesitatingly I skipped through to the port side of the plane and went forward at top speed to the galley. Hiding figuratively under the engineer's skirts may not have been the noblest course, but in the circumstances by far the most prudent, and I stayed with him, drinking coffee, until we were on the final approach to Cambridge.

I did a good deal of hard thinking that night and I didn't like my thoughts.

In the morning I waited outside Yardman's office, and fell into step with Simon as he shambled out to lunch.

"Hullo," he said, beaming. "Where did you spring from? Come and have a warmer up at the Angel."

I nodded and walked beside him, shuffling on the thawing remains of the previous week's snow. Our breaths shot out in small sharp clouds. The day was misty and overcast; the cold, raw, damp and penetrating, exactly matched my mood.

Simon pushed the stained glass and entered the fug; swam on to his accustomed stool, tugged free his disreputable corduroy jacket and hustled the willing barmaid into pouring hot water onto rum and lemon juice, a large glass each. There was a bright new modern electric fire straining at its kilowatts in the old brick fireplace, and the pulsating light from its imitation coal base lit warmly the big smiling face opposite me, and shone brightly on the friendliness in his eyes.

I had so few friends. So few.

"What's the matter then?" he said, sipping his steaming drink. "You're excessively quiet today, even for you."

I watched the fake flames for a while, but it couldn't be put off forever.

"I have found out," I said slowly, "about the brown mare."

He put down his glass with a steady hand but the smile drained completely away.

"What brown mare?"

I didn't answer. The silence lengthened hopelessly.

"What do you mean?" he said at last.

"I escorted a brown mare to France and back twice in a fortnight. The same brown mare every time."

"You must be mistaken."

"No."

There was a pause. Then he said again, but without conviction, "You are mistaken."

"I noticed her the day she went over in the morning and came back the same afternoon. I wondered when she went over again last Thursday . . . and I was certain it was the same horse yesterday, when she came back."

"You've been on several other trips. You couldn't remember one particular mare out of all those you dealt with. . . ."

"I know horses," I said.

"You're too quick," he said, almost to himself. "Too quick."

"No." I shook my head. "You were. You shouldn't have done it again so soon; then I might not have realized. . . ."

He shook himself suddenly, the bulk quivering in folds. "Done what?" he said more firmly. "What if a horse did go over and back twice? And what's it got to do with me?"

"There's no point in telling you what you already know."

"Henry." He leaned forward. "I know what I know, but I don't know what you think you know. You've got some damn-fool notion in your head and I want to hear what it is."

I watched the steam rise gently from my untouched drink and wished I hadn't come.

"Nice little fiddle," I sighed. "A sweet, neat little fraud. Easy as shelling peas. A few hundred quid every time you send the mare to France."

He looked at me without speaking, waiting, making me say it all straight out.

"All right then. You sell a horse—the brown mare—to an accomplice in France. He arranges for his bank to transfer the purchase price to England and the bank over here certifies that it has been received. You put in a claim to the Government that one thoroughbred has been exported for x thousand francs; part of the great bloodstock industry. The grateful Government pays you the bonus, the one and three-quarters per cent bonus on exports, and you put it in your pocket. Meanwhile you bring the horse back here and smuggle the money back as cash to France and you're ready to start again."

Simon sat like a stone, staring at me.

"All you really need is the working capital," I said. "A big enough sum to make the one and three-quarters per cent worth the trouble. Say twenty thousand pounds, for argument's sake. Three hundred and fifty pounds every time the mare goes across. If she went only once a month that would make an untaxed dividend of over 20 per cent on the year. Four thousand or more, tax free. You'd have a few expenses, of course, but even so . . ."

"Henry!" his voice was low and stunned.

"It's not a big fraud," I said. "Not big. But pretty safe. And it had to be you, Simon, because it's all a matter of filling up the right forms, and you fill the forms at Yardman's. If anyone else, an outsider, tried it, he'd have to pay the horse's air passage each way, which would make the whole business unprofitable. No one would do it unless he could send the horse for nothing. You can send one for nothing, Simon. You just put one down on the flying list, but not on the office records. Every time there's room on a flight to France, you send the mare. Yardman told me himself there would be seven three-year-olds going over last Thursday, but we took eight horses, and the eighth wasn't a three-year old, it was the brown mare.

"The day we did two trips, when we took her over in the morning and brought her back in the afternoon, that day it was no accident the return horses weren't at the airport to come back on the first trip. Not even you could risk unloading the mare and promptly loading her up again straight away. So you made a 'mistake' and put fifteen hundred hours on the trainers' traveling instructions instead of ten hundred hours, you, who never make such mistakes, whose accuracy is so phenomenal usually that no one queries or checks up on what you do. . . ."

"How," he said dully. "How did you work it out?"

"I came from Anglia Bloodstock," I said gently. "Don't you remember? I used to fill up the same export forms as you do. I used to send them to you from the transport section. But I might not have remembered about the Government bonus if I hadn't heard three businessmen discussing it ten days ago, and last night while I was wondering how anyone could gain from shuffling that mare over and back, the whole thing just clicked."

"Clicked," he said gloomily.

I nodded. "No markings on the mare, either. You couldn't keep sending her in her own name, someone would have noticed at once. I would have, for a start. But all you had to do was go through the stud book, and choose other unmarked mares of approximately the same age and fill up the export forms accordingly. The Customs certify a brown mare was actually exported from here, and the French Customs certify it was imported there. No trouble at all. No one bothers to check with an owner that he has sold his horse. Why ever should they? And coming back, you go through the same process with the French stud book, only this time you have to be a bit careful your faked mare isn't too well bred because you can't spend more than two thousand in sterling abroad without searching inquiries, which you couldn't risk."

"Got it all buttoned up, haven't you?" he said bitterly.

"I was thinking about it nearly all night."

"Who are you going to tell?"

I glanced at him and away, uncomfortably.

"Yardman?" he asked.

I didn't answer.

"The police?"

I looked at the flickering fire. I wouldn't have told anyone had it not been for . . .

"Did you," I said painfully, "did you *have* to get Billy to knock me about?"

"Henry!" He looked shattered. "I didn't. How can you think I did that?"

I swallowed. "He's been on all the trips with the mare, and he's never given me a moment's peace on any of them, except perhaps the first. He's punched me and poured sirupy coffee on my hair, and yesterday when I was looking at the mare he hit me with a chain. He's not doing it because he dislikes me . . . or not only. It's a smoke screen to keep me away from looking too closely at the horses. That's why he didn't smash my face in . . . he was fighting for a purpose, not from real fury."

"Henry, I promise you, it isn't true." He seemed deeply distressed. "I wouldn't hurt you, for God's sake."

He put out his hand for his drink and took a long swallow. There was no more steam; drink and friendship were both cold.

"Don't look like that," he said, shivering. "Like an iceberg." He drank again. "All right, you've got it right about the mare. I'll admit that, but as God's my judge, I didn't put Billy on to you. I can't stand him. He's a young thug. Whatever he's been doing to you, it's from his own bloody nature. I promise you, Henry, I promise you. . . ."

I looked at him searchingly, wanting very much to believe him, and feeling I'd merely be fooling myself if I did.

"Look," he said anxiously, leaning forward, "would you have sicked him on to me?"

"No."

"Well, then." He leaned back again. "I didn't either."

There was a long, long pause.

"What do you do with the money?" I asked, shelving it.

He hesitated. "Pay my gambling debts."

I shook my head. "You don't gamble."

"I do."

"No."

"You don't know everything."

"I know that," I said tiredly. "I know that very well. You're not interested in racing. You never ask me for tips, never even ask me if I expect to win myself. And don't say you gamble at cards or something feeble like that . . . if you gambled enough to have to steal to pay your debts, you'd gamble on anything, horses as well. Compulsively."

He winced. "Steal is a hard word." He leaned forward, picked up my untasted drink, and swallowed the lot.

"There's no pension at Yardman's," he said.

I looked into his future, into his penurious retirement. I would have the remains of the Creggan fortune to keep me in cars and hot rums. He would have what he'd saved.

"You've banked it?"

"Only a third," he said. "A third is my cousin's. He's the one who keeps the mare on his small holding and drives her to the airport at this end. And a third goes to a chap with a horse-dealing business in France. He keeps the mare when she is over there, and drives her back and forth to the planes. They put up most of the stake, those two, when I thought of it. I hadn't anything like enough on my own."

"You don't really make much out of it, then, yourself, considering the risks."

"Double my salary," he observed dryly. "Tax free. And you underestimate us. We have two horses, and they each go about fifteen times a year."

"Have I seen the other one?"

"Yes," he nodded. "There and back."

"Once?"

"Once."

"And how do you get the money back to France?"

"Send it in magazines. Weeklies. The *Horse and Hound,* things like that."

"English money?"

"Yes. The chap in France has a contact who exchanges it."

"Risky, sending it by post."

"We've never lost any."

"How long have you been doing it?"

"Since they invented the bonus. Shortly after, anyway."

There was another long silence. Simon fiddled with his empty glass and didn't look like an embezzler. I wondered sadly if it was priggish to want one's friends to be honest, and found that I did still think of him as a friend, and could no longer believe that he had paid Billy to give me a bad time. Billy quite simply hated my pedigreed guts, and I could live with that.

"Well," he said in the end, "what are you going to do about it?"

He knew as well as I did that he'd have no chance in an investigation. Too many records of his transactions would still exist in various Government and banking files. If I started any inquiry he would very likely end up in jail. I stood up stiffly off the bar stool and shook my head.

"Nothing. . . ." I hesitated.

"Nothing . . . as long as we stop?"

"I don't know."

He gave me a twisted smile. "All right, Henry. We'll pack it in."

We went out of the pub and walked together through the slush back to the office, but it wasn't the same. There was no trust left. He must have been wondering whether I would keep my mouth shut permanently, and I knew, and hated the knowledge, that he could probably go on with his scheme in spite of saying he wouldn't. The brown mare wouldn't go again, but he could change her for another, and there was his second horse, which I hadn't even noticed. If he was careful, he could go on. And he was a careful man.

The travel schedules in the office, checked again, still showed no more trips to Milan till the Wednesday of the following week. Nor, as far as I could see, were there any flights at all before then; only a couple of sea passages booked for polo ponies, which weren't my concern. I knocked on Yardman's door, and went in and asked him if I could have the rest of the week off; my rights, Conker would have said.

"Milan next Wednesday," he repeated thoughtfully. "And there's nothing before that? Of course, my dear boy, of course you can have the time off. If you don't mind if I bring you back should an urgent trip crop up?"

"Of course not."

"That's good, that's good." The spectacles flashed as he glanced out of the window, the tight skin around his mouth lifting fleetingly into a skeletal smile. "You still like the job, then?"

"Yes, thank you," I said politely.

"Well, well, my dear boy, and I won't say that you're not good at it, I won't say that at all. Very reliable, yes, yes. I admire you for it, dear boy, I do indeed."

"Well . . . thank you, Mr. Yardman." I wasn't sure that underneath he wasn't laughing at me, and wondered how long it would be before he understood that I didn't look on my job as the great big joke everyone else seemed to think it.

I wrote to Gabriella to tell her I would be coming back the following week, and drove moderately home, thinking alternately of her and Simon in an emotional seesaw.

There was a message for me at home to ring up Julian Thackery's father, which I did. The weather forecast was favorable, he said, and it looked as though there would be racing on Saturday. He was planning to send a good hunter 'chaser up to Wetherby, and could I go and ride it.

"I could," I said. "Yes."

"That's fine. She's a grand little mare, a real trier, with the shoulders of a champion and enough behind the saddle to take you over the best."

"Wetherby fences are pretty stiff," I commented.

"She'll eat them," he said with enthusiasm. "And she's ready. We gave her a mile gallop this morning, thinking she'd be backward after the snow, and she was pulling like a train at the end of it. Must thrive on being held up."

"Sounds good."

"A snip," he said. "I'll see you in the weighing room, just before the first. Right?"

I assured him I would be there, and was glad to be going, as I learned from a letter of acceptance lying beside the telephone that the Filyhoughs were again expected for the weekend. My sister Alice came along while I held the letter in my hand.

"I'm going up to Wetherby on Saturday," I said, forestalling her.

"Sunday . . ." she began.

"No, Alice dear, no. I have no intention whatsoever of marrying Angela Filyhough and there's no point in seeing her. I thought that we had agreed that Mother should stop this heiress hunting."

"But you must marry someone, Henry," she protested.

I thought of Gabriella, and smiled. Maybe her, once I was sure she'd be a friend for life, not just a rocket passion with no embers.

"I'll marry someone, don't you worry."

"Well," Alice said, "if you're going as far north as Wetherby you might as well go on and see Louise and cheer her up a bit."

"Cheer her up?" I said blankly. Louise was the sister just older than Alice. She lived in Scotland, nearly twice as far from Wetherby, as it happened, as Wetherby from home, but before I could point that out Alice replied.

"I told you yesterday evening," she said in exasperation. "Weren't you listening?"

"I'm afraid not." I'd been thinking about brown mares.

"Louise has had an operation. She goes home from hospital today and she'll be in bed for two or three weeks more."

"What's wrong with her?" But Alice either didn't know or wouldn't tell me, and though I hardly knew Louise in any deep sense I thought she would be far preferable to Angela Filyhough, and I agreed to go. Deciding, as I would be driving a long way after the races, to go up to Yorkshire on the Friday and spend the Saturday morning lazily, I set off northward at lunchtime and made a detour out of habit to Fenland.

"Hey, Harry, you're just the man I want. A miracle." Tom Wells grabbed my arm as I walked in. "Do me a short flight tomorrow? Two trainers and a jockey from Newmarket to Wetherby races."

I nearly laughed. "I'm awfully sorry. I can't, Tom. I really called in to cancel my booking for Sunday. I can't come then either. Got to go and visit a sick sister in Scotland. I'm on my way now."

"Blast," he said forcibly. "Couldn't you put it off?"

"Afraid not."

"You can have a plane to fly up, on Sunday." He was cunning, looking at me expectantly. "Free."

I did laugh then. "I can't."

"I'll have to tell the trainers I can't fix them up."

"I'm really sorry."

"Yeah. Damn it all. Well, come and have a cup of coffee."

We sat in the canteen for an hour and talked about aircraft, and I continued my journey to Wetherby thinking in amusement that my life was getting more and more like a juggling act, and that it would need skill to keep the racing, flying, horse-ferrying and Gabriella all spinning round safely in separate orbits.

At Wetherby the struggling sunshine lost to a fierce east wind, but the going was perfect, a surprise after the snow. Mr. Thackery's mare was all that he had promised, a tough workmanlike little chestnut with a heart as big as a barn, a true racer who didn't agree with giving up. She took me over the first two fences carefully, as she'd not been on the course before, but then with confidence attacked the rest. I'd seldom had a more solid feeling ride and enjoyed it thoroughly, finding she needed the barest amount of help when meeting a fence wrong and was not too pigheaded to accept it. Coming round the last bend into the straight she was as full of running as when she started, and with only a flicker of encouragement from me she began working her way up smoothly past the four horses ahead of us. She reached the leader coming into the last, pecked a bit on landing, recovered without breaking up her stride, and went after the only horse in sight with enviable determination. We caught him in time, and soared past the winning post with the pleasure of winning coursing like wine in the blood.

"Not bad," said Julian's father, beaming. "Not bad at all," and he gave me a sealed envelope he'd had the faith to prepare in advance.

With about three hundred and fifty miles to go I left soon after the race, and on the empty northern roads made good time to Scotland. My sister Louise lived in a dreary baronial hall near Elgin, a house almost as big as ours at home and just as inadequately heated. She had pleased our parents by marrying for money, and hadn't discovered her husband's fanatical tightfistedness until afterward. For all she'd ever had to spend since, she'd have been better off in a semidetached in Peckham. Her Christmas gifts to me as a child had been Everyman editions of the classics. I got none at all now.

Even so, when I went in to see her in the morning, having arrived after she was sleeping the night before, it was clear that some of her spirit had survived. We looked at each other as at strangers. She, after a seven-year gap, was much older looking than I remembered, older than forty-three, and pale with illness, but her eyes were bright and her smile truly pleased.

"Henry, my little brother, I'm so glad you've come. . . ."

One had to believe her. I was glad too, and suddenly the visit was no longer a chore. I spent all day with her, looking at old photographs and playing Chinese checkers, which she had taught me as a child, and listening to her chat about the three sons away at boarding school and how poor the grouse had been this winter and how much she would like to see London again, it was ten years since she had been down. She asked me to do various little jobs for her, explaining that "dear James" was apt to be irritated, and the maids had too much else to do, poor things. I fetched things for her, packed up a parcel, tidied her room, filled her hot water bottle and found her some more toothpaste. After that she wondered if we couldn't perhaps turn out her medicine drawer while we had the opportunity.

The medicine drawer could have stocked a dispensary. Half of them, she said with relief, she would no longer need. "Throw them away." She sorted the bottles and boxes into two heaps. "Put all those in the wastepaper basket." Obediently I picked up a handful. One was labeled "Conovid," with some explanatory words underneath, and it took several seconds before the message got through. I picked that box out of the rubbish and looked inside. There was a strip of foil containing pills, each packed separately. I tore one square open and picked out the small pink tablet.

"Don't you want these?" I asked.

"Of course not. I don't need them any more, after the operation."

"Oh . . . I see. No, of course not. Then may I have them?"

"What on earth for?"

"Don't be naïve, Louise."

She laughed. "You've got a girl friend at last? Of course you can have them. There's a full box lying around somewhere too, I think. In my top drawer, perhaps? Maybe some in the bathroom too."

I collected altogether enough birth control pills to fill a bottle nearly as big as the one Patrick had given Gabriella, a square-cornered brown bottle four inches high, which had held a prescription for penicillin sirup for curing the boys' throat infections. Louise watched with amusement while I rinsed it out, baked it dry in front of her electric fire, and filled it up, stuffing the neck with cotton wool before screwing on the black cap.

"Marriage?" she said. As bad as Alice.

"I don't know." I put the drawer she had tidied back into the bedside table. "And don't tell Mother."

* * *

Wednesday seemed a long time coming, and I was waiting at Gatwick a good hour before the first horses turned up. Not even the arrival of Billy and Alf could damp my spirits, and we loaded the horses without incident and faster than usual, as two of the studs had sent their own grooms as well, and for once they were willing.

It was one of the mornings that Simon came with last minute papers, and he gave them to me warily in the charter airline office when the plane was ready to leave.

"Good morning, Henry."

"Good morning."

One couldn't patch up a friendship at seven-thirty in the morning in front of yawning pilots and office staff. I took the papers with a nod, hesitated, and went out across the tarmac, bound for the aircraft and Milan.

There were running steps behind me and a hand on my arm.

"Lord Grey? You're wanted on the telephone. They say it's urgent."

I picked up the receiver and listened, said "All right," and slowly put it down again. I was not, after all, going to see Gabriella. I could feel my face contract into lines of pain.

"What is it?" Simon said.

"My father . . . my father has died . . . sometime during the night. They have just found him . . . he was very tired, yesterday evening. . . ."

There was a shocked silence in the office. Simon looked at me with great understanding, for he knew how little I wanted this day.

"I'm sorry," he said, his voice thick with sincerity.

I spoke to him immediately, without thinking, in the old familiar way. "I've got to go home."

"Yes, of course."

"But the horses are all loaded, and there's only Billy. . . ."

"That's easy, I'll go myself," he fished in his brief case and produced his passport.

It was the best solution. I gave him back the papers and took the brown bottle of pills out of my pocket. With a black ballpoint I wrote on the label, "Gabriella Barzini, Souvenir Shop, Malpensa Airport."

"Will you give this to the girl at the gift counter, and tell her why I couldn't come, and say I'll write?"

He nodded.

"You won't forget?" I said anxiously.

"No, Henry." He smiled as he used to. "I'll see she gets it, and the message. I promise."

We shook hands, and after a detour through the passport office he shambled across the tarmac and climbed up the ramp into the plane. I watched the doors shut. I watched the aircraft fly away, taking my job, my friend and my gift, but not me.

Simon Searle went to Italy instead of me, and he didn't come back.

8

It was over a week before I found out. I went straight up to his room when I reached the wharf, and it was empty and much too tidy.

The dim teen-age secretary next door, in answer to my questions, agreed that Mr. Searle wasn't in today, and that no one seemed to know when he would be in at all . . . or whether.

"What do you mean?"

"He hasn't been in for a week. We don't know where he's got to."

Disturbed, I went downstairs and knocked on Yardman's door.

"Come in."

I went in. He was standing by the open window, watching colliers' tugs pulling heavy barges up the river. A Finnish freighter, come up on the flood, was maneuvering alongside across the river under the vulture-like meccano cranes. The air was alive with hooter signals and the bang and clatter of dock work, and the tide was carrying the garbage from the lower docks steadily upstream to the Palace of Westminster. Yardman turned, saw me, carefully closed the window, and came across the room with both hands outstretched.

"My dear boy," he said, squeezing one of mine. "My condolences on your sad loss, my sincere condolences."

"Thank you," I said awkwardly. "You are very kind. Do you . . . er . . . know where Simon Searle is?"

"Mr. Searle?" He raised his eyebrows so that they showed above the black spectacle frames.

"He hasn't been in for a week, the girl says."

"No . . ." He frowned. "Mr. Searle, for reasons best known to himself, chose not to return to this country. Apparently he decided to stay in Italy, the day he went to Milan in your place."

"But why?" I said.

"I really have no idea. It is very inconvenient. Very. I am having to do his work until we hear from him."

He shook his head. "Well, my dear boy, I suppose our troubles no longer concern you. You'd better have your cards, though I don't expect you'll be needing them." He smiled the twisted ironic smile and stretched out his hand to the inter-office phone.

"You're giving me the sack, then?" I said bluntly.

He paused, his hand in mid-air. "My dear boy," he protested. "My dear boy. It simply hadn't occurred to me that you would want to stay on."

"I do."

He hesitated, and then sighed. "It's against my better judgment, it is indeed. But with Searle and you both away, the agency has had to refuse business, and we can't afford much of that. No, we certainly can't. No, we certainly can't. Very well then, if you'll see us through at least until I hear from Searle, or find someone to replace him, I shall be very grateful, very grateful indeed."

If that was how he felt, I thought I might as well take advantage of it.

"Can I have three days off for Cheltenham races in a fortnight? I've got a ride in the Gold Cup."

He nodded calmly. "Let me have the exact dates, and I'll avoid them."

I gave them to him then and there, and went back to Simon's room thinking that Yardman was an exceptionally easy employer, for all that I basically understood him as little as on our first meeting. The list of trips on Simon's wall showed that the next one scheduled was for the following Tuesday, to New York. Three during the past and present week had been crossed out, which as Yardman had said, was very bad for business. The firm was too small to stand much loss of its regular customers.

Yardman confirmed on the intercom that the Tuesday trip was still on, and he sounded so pleased that I guessed that he had been on the point of canceling it when I turned up. I confirmed that I would fetch the relevant papers from the office on Monday afternoon, and be at Gatwick on the dot on Tuesday morning. This gave me a long weekend free and unbeatable ideas on how to fill it. With some relief the next day I drove determinedly away from the gloomy gathering of relations at home, sent a cable, picked up a stand-by afternoon seat with Alitalia, and flew to Milan to see Gabriella.

Three weeks and three days apart had changed nothing. I had forgotten the details of her face, shortened her nose in my imagination and lessened the natural solemnity of her expression, but the sight of her again instantly did its levitation act. She looked momentarily anxious that I wouldn't feel the same, and then smiled with breathtaking brilliance when she saw that I did.

"I got your cable," she said. "One of the girls has changed her free day with me, and now I don't have to keep the shop tomorrow or Sunday."

"That's marvelous."

She hesitated, almost blushing. "And I went home at lunch time to pack some clothes, and I have told my sister I am going to stay for two days with a girl friend near Genoa."

"Gabriella!"

"Is that all right?" she asked anxiously.

"It's a miracle," I said fervently, having expected only snatched unsatisfactory moments by day, and nights spent each side of a wall. "It's unbelievable."

When she had finished for the day we went to the station and caught a train, and on the principle of not telling more lies than could be helped, we did in fact go to Genoa. We booked separately into a large impersonal hotel full of incurious businessmen, and found our rooms were only four doors apart.

Over dinner in a warm obscure little restaurant she said, "I'm sorry about your father, Henry."

"Yes. . . ." Her sympathy made me feel a fraud. I had tried to grieve for him, and had recognized that my only strong emotion was an aversion to being called by his name. I wished to remain myself. Relations and family solicitors clearly took it for granted, however, that having sown a few wild oats I would now settle down into his pattern of life. His death, if I wasn't careful, would be my destruction.

"I was pleased to get your letter," Gabriella said, "because it was awful when you didn't come with the horses. I thought you had changed your mind about me."

"But surely Simon explained?"

"Who is Simon?"

"The big fat bald man who went instead of me. He promised to tell you why I couldn't come, and to give you a bottle . . ." I grinned, "a bottle of pills."

"So they were from you!"

"Simon gave them to you. I suppose he couldn't explain why I hadn't come, because he doesn't know Italian. I forgot to tell him to speak French."

She shook her head.

"One of the crew gave them to me. He said he'd found them in the toilet compartment just after they had landed, and he brought them across to see if I had lost them. He is a tall man, in uniform. I've seen him often. It was not your bald, fat Simon."

"And Simon didn't try to talk to you at all?"

"No." She shook her head. "I don't think so. I see hundreds of bald fat travelers, but no one tried to speak to me about you."

"A friendly big man, with kind eyes," I said. "He was wearing a frightful old green corduroy jacket, with a row of pins in one lapel. He has a habit of picking them up."

She shook her head again. "I didn't see him."

Simon had promised to give her my message and the bottle. He had done neither, and he had disappeared. I hadn't liked to press Yardman too hard to find out where Simon had got to because there was always the chance that too energetic spadework would turn up the export bonus fraud, and I had vaguely assumed that it was because of the fraud that Simon had chosen not to come back. But even if he had decided on the spur of the moment to duck out, he would certainly have kept his promise to see Gabriella. Or didn't a resuscitated friendship stretch that far?

"What's the matter?" Gabriella asked.

I explained.

"You are worried about him?"

"He's old enough to decide for himself. . . ." But I was remembering like a cold douche my predecessor Peters hadn't come back from Milan, and before him the liaison man Ballard.

"Tomorrow morning," she said firmly, "you will go back to Milan and find him."

"I can't speak Italian."

"Undoubtedly you will need an interpreter," she nodded. "Me."

"The best," I agreed, smiling.

We walked companionably back to the hotel.

"Were the pills all right?" I asked.

"Perfect, thank you very much. I gave them to the wife of our baker. . . .She works in the bakery normally, but when she gets pregnant she's always sick for months, and can't stand the sight of dough, and he gets bad-tempered because he has to pay a man to help him instead. He is not a good Catholic." She laughed. "He makes me an enormous cake oozing with cream when I take the pills."

No one took the slightest notice of us in the hotel. I went along the empty passage in my dressing gown and knocked on her door, and she opened it in hers to let me in. I locked it behind me.

"If my sister could see us," she said smiling, "she'd have a fit."

"I'll go away . . . if you like."

"Could you?" She put her arms round my neck.

"Very difficult."

"I don't ask it."

I kissed her. "It would be impossible to go now," I said.

She sighed happily. "I absolutely agree. We will just have to make the best of it."

We did.

We went back to Milan in the morning sitting side by side in the railway carriage and holding hands surreptitiously under her coat, as if by this tiny area of skin contact we could keep alive the total union of the night. I had never wanted to hold hands with anyone before; never realized it could feel like being plugged into a small electric current, warm, comforting, and vibrant, all at the same time.

Apart from being together, it was a depressing day. No one had seen Simon.

"He couldn't just vanish," I said in exasperation, standing late in the afternoon in a chilly wind outside the last of the hospitals. We had drawn a blank there as everywhere else, though they had gone to some trouble to make sure for us. No man of his description had been admitted for any illness or treated for any accident during the past ten days.

"Where else can we look?" she said, the tiredness showing in her voice and in the droop of her rounded body. She had been splendid all day, asking questions unendingly from me and translating the replies, calm and businesslike and effective. It wasn't her fault the answers had all been negative. Police, Government departments, undertakers, we had tried them all. We had rung up every hotel in Milan and asked for him; he had stayed in none.

"I suppose we could ask the taxi drivers at the airport," I said finally.

"There are so many . . . and who would remember one passenger after so long?"

"He had no luggage," I said as I'd said a dozen times before. "He didn't know he was coming here until fifteen minutes before he took off. He couldn't have made any plans. He doesn't speak Italian. He hadn't any Italian money. Where did he go? What did he do?"

She shook her head dispiritedly. There was no answer. We took a tram back to the station and with half an hour to wait made a few last inquiries from the station staff. They didn't remember him. It was hopeless.

Over dinner at midnight in the same café as the night before we gradually forgot the day's frustration; but the fruitless grind, though it hadn't dug up a trace of Simon, had planted foundations beneath Gabriella and me.

She drooped against me going back to the hotel, and I saw with remorse how exhausted she was. "I've tired you too much."

She smiled at the anxiety in my voice. "You don't realize how much energy you have."

"Energy?" I repeated in surprise.

"Yes. It must be that."

"What do you mean?"

"You don't look energetic. You're quiet, and you move like machinery, oiled and smooth. No effort. No jerks. No awkwardness. And inside somewhere is a dynamo. It doesn't run down. I can feel its power. All day I've felt it."

I laughed. "You're too fanciful."

"No. I'm right."

I shook my head. There were no dynamos ticking away inside me. I was a perfectly ordinary and not too successful man, and the smoothness she saw was only tidiness.

She was already in bed and half asleep when I went along to her room. I locked the door and climbed in beside her, and she made a great effort to wake up for my sake.

"Go to sleep," I said, kissing her lightly. "There is always the morning."

She smiled contentedly and snuggled into my arms, and I lay there cradling her sweet soft body, her head on my chest and her hair against my mouth, and felt almost choked by the intensity with which I wanted to protect her and share with her everything I had. Henry Grey, I thought in surprise in the dark, was suddenly more than halfway down the untried track to honest-to-goodness love.

Sunday morning we strolled aimlessly round the city, talking and looking at the mountains of leatherwork in the shops in the arcades; Sunday afternoon we went improbably to a football match, an unexpected passion of Gabriella's; and Sunday night we went to bed early because, as she said with her innocent giggle, we would have to be up at six to get her back to start work in the shop on time. But there was something desperate in the way she clung to me during that night, as if it were our last forever instead of only a week or two, and when I kissed her there were tears on her cheeks.

"Why are you crying?" I said, wiping them away with my fingers. "Don't cry."

"I don't know why." She sniffed, half laughing. "The world is a sad place. Beauty bursts you. An explosion inside. It can only come out as tears."

I was impossibly moved. I didn't deserve her tears. I kissed them away in humility and understood why people said love was painful, why Cupid was invented with arrows. Love did pierce the heart, truly.

It wasn't until we were on the early train to Milan the next morning that she said anything about money, and from her hesitation in beginning I saw that she didn't want to offend me.

"I will repay you what you lent me for my bill," she said matter-of-factly, but a bit breathlessly. I had pushed the notes into her hand on the way downstairs, as she hadn't wanted me to pay for her publicly, and she hadn't enough with her to do it herself.

"Of course not," I said.

"It was a much more expensive place than I'd thought of. . . ."

"Big hotels ignore you better."

She laughed. "All the same . . ."

"No."

"But you don't earn much. You can't possibly afford it all. The hotel and the train fares and the dinners."

"I earned some money winning a race."

"Enough?"

"I'll win another race . . . then it will be enough."

"Giulio doesn't like it that you work with horses." She laughed. "He says that if you were good enough to be a jockey you'd do it all the time instead of being a groom."

"What does Guilio do?"

"He works for the Government in the taxation office."

"Ah," I said, smiling. "Would it help if you told him my father has left me some money? Enough to come to see you, anyway, when I get it."

"I'm not sure I'll tell him. He judges people too much by how much money they've got."

"Do you want to marry a rich man?"

"Not to please Giulio."

"To please yourself?"

"Not rich necessarily. But not too poor. I don't want to worry about how to afford shoes for the children."

I smoothed her fingers with my own.

"I think I will have to learn Italian," I said.

She gave me the flashing smile. "Is English very difficult?"

"You can practice on me."

"If you come back often enough. If your father's money should not be saved for the future."

"I think," I said slowly, smiling into her dark eyes, "that there will be enough left. Enough to buy the children's shoes."

I went to New York with the horses the following day in the teeth of furious opposition from the family. Several relatives were still staying in the house, including my three sharp-tongued eldest sisters, none of whom showed much reserve in airing their views. I sat through a depressing lunch, condemned from all sides. The general opinion was, it seemed, that my unexplained absence over the weekend was disgraceful enough, but that continuing with my job was scandalous. Mother cried hysterical tears and Alice was bitterly reproving.

"Consider your *position*," they all wailed, more or less in chorus.

I considered my position and left for Yardman's and Gatwick three hours after returning from Milan.

Mother had again brought up the subject of my early marriage to a suitable heiress. I refrained from telling her I was more or less engaged to a comparatively penniless Italian girl who worked in a gift shop, smuggled birth control pills, and couldn't speak English. It wasn't exactly the moment.

The outward trip went without a hitch. Timmie and Conker were along, together with a pair of grooms with four Anglia Bloodstock horses, and in consequence the work went quickly and easily. We were held up for thirty-six hours in New York by an engine fault, and when I rang up Yardman to report our safe return on the Friday morning he asked me to stay at Gatwick, as another bunch of brood mares was to leave that afternoon.

"Where for?"

"New York again," he said briskly. "I'll come down with the papers myself, early in the afternoon. You can send Timms and Chestnut home. I'm bringing Billy and two others to replace them."

"Mr. Yardman. . . ." I said.

"Yes?"

"If Billy tries to pick a fight, or molests me at all on the way, my employment with you ceases the instant we touch down in New York, and I will not help unload the horses or accept any responsibility for them."

There was a short shocked silence. He couldn't afford to have me do what I threatened, in the present sticky state of the business.

"My dear boy . . ." he protested sighing. "I don't want you to have troubles. I'll speak to Billy. He's a thoughtless boy. I'll tell him not everyone is happy about his little practical jokes."

"I'd appreciate it," I said with irony at his view of Billy's behavior.

Whatever Yardman said to him worked. Billy was sullen, unhelpful, and calculatingly offensive, but for once I completed a return trip with him without a bruise to show for it.

On the way over I sat for a time on a hay bale beside Alf and asked him about Simon's last trip to Milan. It was hard going, as the old man's deafness was as impenetrable as seven-eighths cloud.

"Mr. Searle," I shouted. "Did he say where he was going?"

"Eh?"

After about ten shouts the message got through, and he nodded.

"He came to Milan with us."

"That's right, Alf. Where did he go then?"

"Eh?"

"Where did he go then?"

"I don't rightly know," he said. "He didn't come back."

"Did he *say* where he was going?"

"Eh?"

I yelled again.

"No. He didn't say. Perhaps he told Billy. He was talking to Billy, see?"

I saw. I also saw that it was no use my ever asking Billy anything about anything. Yardman would have asked him, anyway, so if Simon had told Billy where he was going Yardman would have known. Unless, of course, Simon had asked Billy not to tell, and he hadn't. But Simon didn't like Billy and would never trust him with a secret.

"Where did Mr. Searle go, when you left the plane?"

I was getting hoarse before he answered.

"I don't know where he went. He was with Billy and the others. I went across on my own, like, to get a beer. Billy said they were just coming. But they never came."

"None of them came?"

There had been the two grooms from the stud besides Simon and Billy, on that trip.

Eventually Alf shook his head. "I finished my beer and went back to the plane. There was no one there as I ate my lunch."

I left it at that because my throat couldn't stand any more.

Coming back we were joined by some extra help in the shape of a large pallid man who didn't know what to do with his hands and kept rubbing them over the wings of his jodhpurs as if he expected to find pockets there. He was ostensibly accompanying a two-year-old, but I guessed tolerantly he was some relation of the owner or trainer traveling like that to avoid a transatlantic fare. I didn't get around to checking on it, because the double journey had been very tiring, and I slept soundly nearly all the way back. Alf had to shake me awake as we approached Gatwick. Yawning I set about the unloading—it was by then well into Sunday morning—and still feeling unusually tired, drove home afterward in a beeline to bed. A letter from Gabriella stopped me in the hall, and I went slowly upstairs reading it.

She had, she said, asked every single taxi driver and all the airport bus drivers if they had taken anywhere a big fat Englishman who couldn't speak Italian, had no luggage, and was wearing a green corduroy jacket. None of them could remember anyone like that. Also, she said, she had checked with the car hire firms which had agencies at the airport, but none of them had dealt with Simon. She had checked with all the airlines' passenger lists for the day he went to Milan, and the days after; he had not flown off to anywhere.

I lay in a hot bath and thought about whether I should go on trying to find him. Bringing in any professional help, even private detectives, would only set them searching in England for a reason for his disappearance, and they'd all too soon dig it up. A warrant out for his arrest was not what I wanted. It would effectively stop him coming back at all. Very likely he didn't want to be found in the first place, or he wouldn't have disappeared so thoroughly, or stayed away so long. But supposing something had happened to him . . . though what, I couldn't imagine. And I wouldn't have thought anything could have happened at all, were it not for Peters and Ballard.

There were Simon's partners in the fraud. His cousin, and the man in France. Perhaps I could ask them if they had heard from him. . . . I couldn't ask them, I thought confusedly; I didn't know their names. Simon had an elderly aunt somewhere, but I didn't know her name either . . . the whole thing was too much . . . and I was going to sleep in the bath.

I went to the wharf building the next morning at nine-thirty to collect my previous week's pay and see what was on the schedule for the future. True to his word, Yardman had arranged no air trips for the following three days of Cheltenham Races. There was a big question mark beside a trip for six circus horses for Spain that same afternoon, but no question mark, I was glad to see, about a flight to Milan with brood mares on Friday.

Yardman, when I went down to see him, said the circus horses were postponed until the following Monday owing to their trainer having read in his stars that it was a bad week to travel. Yardman was disgusted. Astrology was bad for business.

"Milan on Friday, now," he said, sliding a pencil to and fro through his fingers. "I might come on that trip myself, if I can get away. It's most awkward, with Searle's work to be done. I've advertised for someone to fill his place . . . anyway, as I was saying, if I can get away I think I'd better go and see our opposite numbers out there. It always pays, you know, my dear boy. I go to all the countries we export to. About once a year. Keeps us in touch, you know."

I nodded. Good for business, no doubt.

"Will you ask them . . . our opposite numbers . . . if they saw Simon Searle any time after he landed?"

He looked surprised, the taut skin stretched over his jaw.

"I could, yes. But I shouldn't think he told them where he was going, if he didn't have the courtesy to tell me."

"It's only an outside chance," I agreed.

"I'll ask, though." He nodded. "I'll certainly ask."

I went upstairs again to Simon's room, shut his door, sat in his chair, and looked out of his window. His room, directly over Yardman's, had the same panoramic view of the river, from a higher angle. I would like to live there, I thought idly. I liked the shipping, the noise of the docks, the smell of the river, the coming and going. Quite simply, I supposed, I liked the business of transport.

The Finnish ship had gone from the berth opposite and another small freighter had taken her place. A limp flag swung fitfully at her masthead, red and white horizontal stripes with a navy blue triangle and a white star. I looked across at the nationality chart on Simon's wall. Puerto Rico. Well, well, one lived and learned. Three alphabetical flags lower down, when checked, proved to be E, Q and M. Mildly curious, I turned them up in the international code of signals. "I am delivering." Quite right and proper. I shut the book, twiddled my thumbs, watched a police launch swoop past doing twenty knots on the ebb, and reflected not for the first time that the London river was a fast, rough waterway for small boats.

After a while I picked up the telephone and rang up Fenland to book a plane for Sunday.

"Two o'clock?"

"That'll do me fine," I said. "Thanks."

"Wait a minute, Harry. Mr. Wells said if you rang that he wanted a word with you."

"O.K."

There were some clicks, and then Tom's voice.

"Harry? Look, for God's sake, what is this job of yours?"

"I work for . . . a travel agency."

"Well, what's so special about it? Come here, and I'll pay you more." He sounded worried and agitated, not casually inviting as before.

"What's up?" I said.

"Everything's up except my planes. I've landed an excellent contract with a car firm in Conventry ferrying their executives, technicians, salesmen and so on all round the shop. They've a factory in Lancashire and tie-ups all over Europe, and they're fed-up with the airfield they've been using. They're sending me three planes. I'm to maintain them, provide pilots and have them ready when wanted."

"Sounds good," I said. "So what's wrong?"

"So I don't want to lose them again before I've started. And not only can I not find any out-of-work pilots worth considering, but one of my three regulars went on a skiing holiday last week and broke his leg, the silly bastard. So how about it?"

"It's not as easy as you make it sound," I said reluctantly.

"What's stopping you?"

"A lot of things . . . if you'll be around on Sunday, anyway, we could talk it over."

He sighed in exasperation. "The planes are due here at the end of the month, in just over a fortnight."

"Get someone else, if you can," I said.

"Yeah . . . if I can." He was depressed. "And if I can't?"

"I don't know. I could do a day a week to help out, but even then . . ."

"Even then, what?"

"There are difficulties."

"Nothing to mine, Harry. Nothing to mine. I'll break you down on Sunday."

Everyone had troubles, even with success. The higher the tougher, it seemed. I wiggled the button, and asked for another number, the charter airline which Patrick worked for. The Gatwick office answered, and I asked them if they could tell me how to get hold of him.

"You're in luck. He's actually here, in the office. Who's speaking?"

"Henry Grey, from Yardman Transport."

I waited, and he came on the line.

"Hullo . . . how's things? How's Gabriella?"

"She," I said, "is fine. Other things are not. Could you do me a favor?"

"Shoot."

"Could you look up for me the name of the pilot who flew a load of horses to Milan for us a fortnight last Thursday? Also the names of the copilot and engineer, and could you also tell me how or when I could talk to one or all of them?"

"Trouble?"

"Oh, no trouble for your firm, none at all. But one of our men went over on that trip and didn't come back, and hasn't got in touch with us since. I just wanted to find out if the crew had any idea what became of him. He might have told one of them where he was going . . . anyway, his work is piling up here and we want to find out if he intends to come back."

"I see. Hang on then. A fortnight last Thursday?"

"That's it."

He was away several minutes. The cranes got busy on the freighter from Puerto Rico. I yawned.

"Henry? I've got them. The pilot was John Kyle, copilot G. L. Rawlings, engineer V. N. Brede. They're not here, though; they've just gone to Arabia, ferrying mountains of luggage from London after some oil chieftain's visit. He brought about six wives, and they all went shopping."

"Wow," I said. "When do they get back?"

He consulted someone in the background.

"Sometime Wednesday. They have Thursday off, then another trip to Arabia on Friday."

"Some shopping," I said gloomily. "I can't get to see them on Wednesday or Thursday. I'm racing at Cheltenham. But I could ring them up on Wednesday night, if you can give me their numbers."

"Well . . . ," said Patrick slowly. "John Kyle likes his flutter on the horses."

"You don't think he'd come to Cheltenham, then?"

"He certainly might, if he isn't doing anything else."

"I'll get him a member's badge, and the others too, if they'd like."

"Fair enough. Let's see. I'm going to Holland twice tomorrow. I should think I could see them on Wednesday, if we all get back reasonably on schedule. I'll tell them what you want, and ring you. If they go to Cheltenham you'll see them, and if not you can ring them. How's that?"

"Marvelous. You'll find me at the Queen's Hotel at Cheltenham. I'll be staying there."

"Right . . . and oh, by the way, I see I'm down for a horse transport flight on Friday to Milan. Is that your mob, or not?"

"Our mob," I agreed. "What's left of it."

We rang off, and I leaned back in Simon's chair, pensively biting my thumbnail and surveying the things on his desk; telephone, tray of pens, blank notepad, and a pot of paper clips and pins. Nothing of any help. Then slowly, methodically, I searched through the drawers. They were predictably packed with export forms of various sorts, but he had taken little of a personal nature to work. Some indigestion tablets, a screwdriver, a pair of green socks, and a plastic box labeled "spare keys." That was the lot. No letters, no bills, no private papers of any sort.

I opened the box of keys. There were about twenty or more, the silt of years. Suitcase keys, a heavy old iron key, car keys. I stirred them up with my finger. A Yale key. I picked it out and looked at it. It was a duplicate, cut for a few shillings from a blank, and had no number. The metal had been dulled by time, but not smoothed, from use. I tapped it speculatively on the edge of the desk, thinking that anyway there would be no harm in trying.

9

SIMON'S HOME address, obtained off his insurance card via the dim typist, proved to be located in a dingy block of flats in the outer reaches of St. John's Wood. The grass on patchy lawns had remained uncut from about the previous August, which gave the graceless building a mournful look of having been thoughtlessly dumped in a hayfield. I walked through spotted glass entrance doors, up an uninspiring staircase, met no one, and came to a halt outside number fifteen in white twopenny plastic letters screwed on to cheap green-painted deal.

The Yale key slid raspingly into the lock as if it had never been there before, but it turned under my pressure and opened the door. There was a haphazard foot-high pile of newspapers and magazines just inside. When I pushed the door against them they slithered away, and I stepped in and round them, and shut the door behind me.

The flat consisted only of a tiny entrance hall, a small bedroom, poky kitchen and bathroom and a slightly larger sitting room. The prevailing color was maroon, which I found depressing, and the furniture looked as if it had been bought piece by piece from second-class second-hand shops. The total effect could have been harmonious, but it wasn't, not so much through lack of taste as lack of imagination. He had spent the minimum of trouble on his surroundings, and the result was gloomy. Cold dead air and a smell of mustiness seeped up my nose. There were unwashed, mold-growing dishes on the drainboard in the kitchen, and crumpled thrown-back bedclothes on the bed. He had left his shaving water in the washbasin and the scum had dried into a hard gray line round the edge. Poor Simon, I thought forlornly, what an existence. No wife, no warmth; no wonder he liked pubs.

One wall in the sitting room was lined with bookcases, and the newest, most obviously luxurious object in the flat was a big stereophonic radio standing behind the door. No television. No pictures on the dull coffee walls. Not a man of visual pleasures. Beside a large battered armchair, handy to perpetual reach, stood a wooden crate of bottled beer.

Wandering round his flat I realized what a fearful comment it was on myself that I had never been there before. This big tolerant dishonest man I would have counted my only real friend, yet I'd never seen where he lived. Never been asked; never thought of asking him to my own home. Even where I had wanted friendship, I hadn't known how to try. I felt as cold inside as Simon's flat; as uninhabited. Gabriella seemed very far away.

I picked up the heap of papers inside the front door and carried them into the sitting room. Sorted into piles, they consisted of sixteen dailies three Sundays, three *Horse and Hounds,* three *Sporting Life* weeklies and one *Stud and Stable*. Several letters in brown unstuck envelopes looked unpromising, and with very little hesitation I opened all the rest. There were none from France, and none from the accomplice cousin. The only one of any help was written in a spiky black hand on dark-blue paper. It began "Dear Simon," thanked him for a birthday present, and was signed "your loving aunt Edna." The handwritten address at the top said 3 Gordon Cottages, East Road, Potter's Green, Berks., and there was no telephone number.

There was no desk as such in his flat. He kept his bills and papers clipped into labeled categories in the top drawer of a scratched chest in his bedroom, but if his cousin's name and address was among them, I couldn't recognize them. Alongside the papers lay a *Horse and Hound* rolled tightly into a tube and bound with wide brown sticky paper, ready to be posted. I picked it up and turned it round in my hands. It bore no address. The thick layers of brown sticky paper were tough, and even though I was careful with my penknife it looked as though a tiger had been chewing it when I finally hacked my way through. The magazine unrolled reluctantly, and I picked it up and shook it. Nothing happened. It wasn't until one looked at it page by page that the money showed, five-pound notes stuck on with plastic tape. They were used notes, not new, and there were sixty of them. I rolled the *Horse and Hound* up again and laid it back in the drawer, seeing a vivid mental picture, as I picked up the brown pieces of gummed strips and put them in the wastebasket, of Simon listening to his radio and sticking his money into the journals, night after night, an endless job, working for his old age.

Potter's Green turned out to be a large village spreading out into tentacles of development around the edges. East Road was a new one, and Gordon Cottages proved to be one of several identical strips of council-built bungalows for old people. Number three like all the rest still looked clean and fresh, with nothing growing yet in the bathmat-sized flower bed under the front window. There was bright yellow paint clashing with pale pink curtains and a bottle of milk standing on the concrete doorstep.

I rang the bell. The pink curtains twitched, and I turned my head to see myself being inspected by a pair of mournful, faded eyes set in a large pale face. She flapped a hand at me in a dismissing movement, shooing me away, so I put my finger on the bell and rang again.

I heard her come round to the other side of the door.

"Go away," she said. "I don't want anything."

"I'm not selling," I said through the letter box. "I'm a friend of Simon's, your nephew Simon Searle."

"Who are you? I don't know you."

"Henry Grey. . . . I work with Simon at Yardman's. Could I please talk to you inside, it's very difficult like this, and your neighbors will wonder what's going on." There were in truth several heads at the front windows already, and it had its effect. She opened the door and beckoned me in.

The tiny house was crammed with the furniture she must have brought with her from a much larger place, and every available surface was covered with useless mass-produced ornaments. The nearest to me as I stood just inside the doorway was a black box decorated with "A present from Brighton" in shells. And next to that a china donkey bore panniers of dried everlasting flowers. Pictures of all sorts crowded the walls, interspersed by several proverbs done in poker-work on wood. "Waste not, Want not" caught my eye, and farther round there was "Take care of the pence and the pounds will take care of you"; an improvement on the original.

Simon's stout aunt had creaking corsets and wheezing breath and smelled of mentholated cough pastilles. "Simon isn't here, you know. He lives in London, not here."

"I know, yes." Hesitatingly, I told her about Simon going away and not coming back. "I wondered," I finished, "if by any chance he has written to you. Sent you a picture postcard. That sort of thing."

"He will. He's sure to." She nodded several times. "He always does, and brings me a little souvenir when he's been away. Very considerate is Simon."

"But you haven't had a postcard yet."

"Not yet. Soon, I expect."

"If you do, would you write to me and let me know? You see, he hasn't said when he'll be back, and Mr. Yardman is advertising for someome to fill his job."

"Oh, dear." She was troubled. "I hope nothing has happened to him."

"I don't expect so; but if you hear from him, you will let us know?"

"Yes, yes, of course. Dear oh dear, I wonder what he is up to."

Her choice of phrase reminded me of what in fact he was up to, and I asked her if she knew Simon's cousin's name and address. Unhesitatingly she reeled it off. "He's my poor dead sister's son," she said. "But a surly man. I don't get on with him at all. Not easy, like Simon, now. Simon stayed with me a lot when he was little, when I kept the village shop. He never forgets my birthday, and always brings me nice little mementos like these." She looked proudly round her overflowing possessions. "Simon's very kind. I've only my old age pension, you know, and a little bit put by, and Simon's the only one who bothers with me much. Oh I've got my two daughters, of course, but one's married in Canada and the other's got enough troubles of her own. Simon's given me a hundred pounds for my birthday every year for the last three years; what do you think of that?"

"Absolutely splendid." A hundred pounds of taxpayers' money. Robin Hood stuff. Oh well.

"You'll let me know, then," I said, turning to go. She nodded, creaking as she moved round me to open the street door. Facing me in the little hall hung more timeworn poker-work. "See a pin and pick it up, all the day you'll have good luck. See a pin and let it lie, you will want before you die." So there, I thought, smiling to myself, was the origin of Simon's pin tidying habit, a proverb stretching back to childhood. He didn't intend to want before he died.

The accomplice cousin farmed in Essex, reasonably handy for Cambridge Airport, but a long haul for Gatwick. It was evident at once, however, that I could expect no easy help from him.

"You," he said forcefully, "you're the interfering bastard who's fouled up the works, aren't you? Well you can damn well clear off, that's what you can do. It's no business of yours where Simon's gone and in the future you keep your bloody nose out of things that don't concern you."

"If," I said mildly, "you prefer me to ask the police to find him, I will."

He looked ready to explode, a large red-faced man in khaki clothes and huge gum boots, standing foursquare in a muddy yard. He struggled visibly between the pleasure of telling me to go to hell and fear of the consequences if he did so. Prudence just won.

"All right. All right. I don't know where he is and that's straight. He didn't tell me he was going, and I don't know when he's coming back."

Depressed, I drove home to Bedfordshire. The bulk and grandeur of the great house lay there waiting as I rolled slowly up the long drive. History in stone; the soul of the Creggans. Earl upon earl had lived there right back to the pirate who brought Spanish gold to Queen Bess, and since my father died I had only to enter to feel the chains fall heavily on me like a net. I stopped in the sweep of gravel in front instead of driving round to the garages as usual, and looked at what I had inherited. There was beauty, I admitted, in the great façade with its pillars and pediments and the two wide flights of steps sweeping up to meet at the door. The Georgian Palladian architect who had grafted a whole new mansion on to the Elizabethan and Stuart one already existing had produced a curiously satisfactory result, and as a Victorian incumbent had luckily confined his Gothic urges to a ruined folly in the garden, the only late addition had been a square red-bricked block of Edwardian plumbing. But for all its splendid outer show it had those beetles in the roof, miles of drafty passages, kitchens in the basement, and twenty bedrooms moldering into dust. Only a multimillionaire could maintain and fill such a place now with servants and guests, whereas after death duties I would be hard put to it to find a case of champagne once the useless pile had voraciously gulped what it cost just to keep standing.

Opening it to the public might have been a solution if I had been any sort of a showman. But to someone solitary by nature that way meant a lifetime of horrifying square-peggery. Slavery to a building. Another human sacrifice on the altar of tradition. I simply couldn't face it. The very idea made me wilt.

Since it was unlikely anyone would simply let me pull the whole thing down, the National Trust, I thought, was the only hope. They could organize the sight-seeing to their heart's content and they might let Mother live there for the rest of her life, which she needed.

Mother usually used the front entrance while Alice and I drove on and went in through one of the doors at the side, near the garages. That early evening, however, I left my little car on the gravel and walked slowly up the shallow steps. At the top I leaned against the balustrade and looked back over the calm wide fields and bare-branched trees just swelling into bud. I didn't really own all this, I thought. It was like the baton in a relay race, passed on from one, to be passed on to the next, belonging to none for more than a lap. Well, I wasn't going to pass it on. I was the last runner. I would escape from the track at a tangent and give the baton away. My son, if I ever had one, would have to lump it.

I pushed open the heavy front door and stepped into the dusk-filled house. I, Henry Grey, descendant of the sea pirate, of warriors and explorers and empire builders and of a father who'd been decorated for valor on the Somme, I, the least of them, was going to bring their way of life to an end. I felt one deep protesting pang for their sakes, and that was all. If they had anything of themselves to pass on to me, it was already in my genes. I carried their inheritance in my body, and I didn't need their house.

Not only did John Kyle and his engineer come to Cheltenham, but Patrick as well.

"I've never been before," he said, his yellow eyes and auburn hair shining as he stood in the bright March sun. "These two are addicts. I just came along for the ride."

"I'm glad you did," I said, shaking hands with the other two. John Kyle was a bulky battered-looking young man going prematurely thin on top. His engineer, tall and older, had three racing papers and a form sheet tucked under his arm.

"I see," he said, glancing down at them, "th . . . that you won the United Hunts Ch . . . Challenge Cup yesterday." He managed his stutter unself-consciously. "W . . . w . . . well done."

"Thank you," I said. "I was a bit lucky. I wouldn't have won if Century hadn't fallen at the last."

"It d . . . d . . . d . . . does say that, in the p . . . p . . . paper," he agreed disarmingly.

Patrick laughed and said, "What are you riding in today?"

"The Gold Cup and the Mildmay of Flete Challenge Cup."

"Clobber and Boathook," said John Kyle readily.

"I'll back you," Patrick said.

"M . . . m . . . money down the drain b . . . backing Clobber," said the engineer seriously.

"Thanks very much," I said with irony.

"F . . . form's all haywire. V . . . v . . . very inconsistent," he explained.

"Do you think you've got a chance?" Patrick asked.

"No, not much. I've never ridden him before. The owner's son usually rides him, but he's got jaundice."

"N . . . not a b . . . betting proposition," nodded the engineer.

"For God's sake, don't be so depressing, man," protested Kyle.

"How about Boathook?" I asked, smiling.

The engineer consulted the sky. The result wasn't written there, as far as I could see.

"B . . . B . . . Boathook," he remarked, coming back to earth, "m . . . m . . . might just do it. G . . . good for a p . . . place anyway."

"I shall back both, just the same," said Patrick firmly.

I took them all to lunch and sat with them while they ate.

"Aren't you having any?" said Patrick.

"No. It makes you sick if you fall after eating."

"How often do you fall, then?" asked Kyle curiously, cutting into his cold red beef.

"On average, once in a dozen rides, I suppose. It varies. I've never really counted."

"When did you fall last?"

"Day before yesterday."

"Doesn't it bother you?" asked Patrick, shaking salt. "The prospect of falling?"

"Well, no. You never think you're going to, for a start. And a lot of falls are easy ones; you only get a bruise, if that. Sometimes when the horse goes right down you almost step off."

"And sometimes you break your bones," Kyle said dryly.

I shook my head. "Not often."

Patrick laughed. I passed him the butter for his roll, looked at my watch, and said, "I'll have to go and change soon. Do you think we could talk about the day you took Simon Searle to Milan?"

"Shoot," said Kyle. "What do you want to know?"

"Everything you can think of that happened on the way there and after you landed."

"I don't suppose I'll be much help," he said apologetically. "I was in the cockpit most of the time, and I hardly spoke to him at all. I went aft to the karzy once, and he was sitting in one of those three pairs of seats that were bolted on at the back."

I nodded. I'd bolted the seats on to the anchorages myself, after we had loaded all the horses. There was usually room for a few seats, and they made a change from hay bales.

"Was he alone?"

"No, there was a young fellow beside him. Your friend Searle was on the inside by the window, I remember, because this young chap had his legs sprawled out in the gangway and I had to step over them. He didn't move."

"Billy." I nodded.

"After I came out I asked them if they were O.K. and said we'd be landing in half an hour. The young one said 'thanks, Dad' as if he was bored to death, and I had to step over his legs again to get past. I can't say I took to him enormously."

"You surprise me," I said sardonically. "Did Simon say anything?"

He hesitated. "It's three weeks ago. I honestly can't remember, but I don't think so. Nothing special, anyway."

I turned to the engineer. "How about you?"

He chewed, shook his head, swallowed, and took a sip of beer.

"D . . . d . . . don't think I'm much better. I w . . . w . . . was talking to him q . . . q . . . quite a lot at the beginning. In the g . . . g . . . galley. He said he'd come at the l . . . l . . . last minute instead of you. He t . . . t . . . talked about you quite a lot."

The engineer took a mouthful of salad and stuttered through it without embarrassment. A direct man, secure in himself. "He s . . . said you were ice on a v . . . volcano. I said th . . . th . . . that didn't make sense, and he said it w . . . was the only w . . . way to describe you."

Without looking up from his plate Patrick murmured, "In a nutshell."

"That's no help at all," I said, disregarding him. "Didn't he say anything about where he was going, or what he might do, when you got to Milan?"

The engineer shook his head. "He m . . . m . . . meant to come straight back with us, in the afternoon, I'm sure of th . . . th . . . that."

"We didn't come straight back, of course," said Kyle matter-of-factly.

"You didn't?" I was surprised. "I didn't know that."

"We were supposed to. They got the return load of horses loaded up and then discovered there were no papers for one of the two they'd put in first. They had to get the whole lot out again, and they weren't very quick because there were only two of them, and by the time I said it was pointless loading again, as it would be too late to start, I'd be out of hours."

"They should have checked; they had all the papers before they loaded," I said.

"Well, they didn't."

"Only two of them," I said, frowning.

"That's right. The young one—Billy, did you say?—and one other. Not your friend Simon. A deaf old fellow."

"Alf," I said. "That's Alf. What about the two others who went over? They were two specials going with horses from the studs they worked in."

"From what I could make out from the old man, those two were going on with their horses right to the destination, somewhere farther south."

I thought it over. Simon obviously hadn't intended to come back at all, and it hadn't been the unexpected overnight stop which had given him the idea.

"You didn't see where Simon was headed, I suppose, when you got to Milan?" I spoke without much hope, and they both shook their heads.

"We got off the plane before him," Kyle said.

I nodded. The crew didn't have Customs and unloading to see to.

"Well . . . that's that. Thank you for coming today, anyway. And thank you," I said directly to the engineer, "for delivering that bottle of pills to the girl in the souvenir shop."

"P . . . pills? Oh yes, I remember." He was surprised. "How on earth d . . . d . . . did you know about that?"

"She told me a tall crew member brought them over for her."

"I f . . . f . . . found them on the plane, standing on the w . . . w . . . washbasin in the k . . . k . . . karzy. I th . . . th . . . thought I might as well give them to her, as I was g . . . going across anyway. I did . . . didn't see how they got there, b . . . b . . . but they had her name on them."

"Simon was taking them to her from me," I explained.

"Oh, I s . . . see."

Patrick said, grinning, "Were they . . . ?"

"Yes, they were."

"He didn't go over to the airport building at all, then," said Patrick flatly. "He left the pills on board, hoping they would get to Gabriella somehow, and scooted from there."

"It looks like it," I agreed gloomily.

"You can get off that end of the airfield quite easily, of course. It's only that scrubland and bushes, and if you walk down that road leading away from the unloading area, the one the horseboxes often use, you're off the place in no time. I should think that explains pretty well why no one saw him."

"Yes," I sighed, "that's what he must have done."

"But it doesn't explain why he went," said Patrick gently.

There was a pause.

"He had . . . troubles," I said at last.

"*In* trouble?" said Kyle.

"Looming. It might be because of something I discovered, that he went. I wanted to find him, and tell him it was . . . safe . . . to come back."

"On your conscience," said Patrick.

"You might say so."

They all nodded, acknowledging their final understanding of my concern for a lost colleague. The waiter brought their cheese and asked whether they would like coffee. I stood up.

"I'll see you again," I said. "How about after the fifth, outside the weighing room? After I've changed."

"Sure thing," said Patrick.

I ambled off to the weighing room and later got dressed in Mr. Thackery's red and blue colors. I'd never ridden in the Gold Cup before, and although I privately agreed with the engineer's assessment of the situation, there was still something remarkably stirring in going out in the best class race of the season. My human opponents were all hand-picked professionals and all Clobber's bunch looked to have the beating of him, but nevertheless my mouth grew dry and my heart thumped.

I suspected Mr. Thackery had entered Clobber more for the prestige of having a Gold Cup runner than from any thought that he would win, and his manner in the parade ring confirmed it. He was enjoying himself enormously, untouched by the sort of anxious excitement characteristic of the hopeful.

"Julian's regards," he said, beaming and shaking hands vigorously. "He'll be watching on TV."

TV. There was always the fair chance that one of the people I knew at Fenland might be watching television, though none that I'd heard of was interested in racing. I turned my back on the cameras, as usual.

"Just don't disgrace me," said Mr. Thackery happily. "Don't disgrace me, that's all I ask."

"You could have got a professional," I pointed out.

"Oh, eh, I could. But frankly, it hasn't done me any harm, here and there, for folks to know you're riding my horses."

"A mutually satisfactory arrangement, then," I said dryly.

"Yes," said Mr. Thackery contentedly. "That's about it."

I swung up on his horse, walked out in the parade, and cantered down to the start. Clobber, an eight-year-old thoroughbred chestnut hunter, had only once won (thanks to being low in the handicap) in the company he was taking on now at level weights, but he shone with condition and his step was bursting with good feeling. Like so many horses, he responded well to spring air and sun on his back and my own spirits lifted with his. It was not, after all, going to be a fiasco.

We lined up and the tapes went up, and Clobber set off to the first fence pulling like a train. As he hadn't a snowball's hope in hell of winning, I thought Mr. Thackery might as well enjoy a few moments in the limelight, and I let Clobber surge his way to the front. Once he got there he settled down and stopped trying to run away with me and we stayed there, surprisingly leading the distinguished field for over two and a half of the three and a quarter miles.

Clobber had never been run in front before, according to the form book, but from his willingness it was evidently to his liking. Holding him up against his inclination, I thought, probably accounted for his inconsistency; he must have lost interest on many occasions when thwarted, and simply packed up trying.

The others came up to him fast and hard going into the second last fence, and three went ahead before the last; but Clobber jumped it cleanly and attacked the hill with his ears still pricked good-temperedly, and he finished fourth out of eight with some good ones still behind him. I was pleased with the result myself, having thoroughly enjoyed the whole race, and so it appeared was Mr. Thackery.

"By damn," he said, beaming, "that's the best he's ever run."

"He likes it in front."

"So it seems, yes. We've not tried that before, I must say."

A large bunch of congratulating females advanced on him and I rolled the girths round my saddle and escaped to the weighing room to change for the next race. The colors were those of Old Strawberry Leaves, who had commented sourly that it was disgraceful of me to ride in public only three weeks after my father's death, but had luckily agreed not to remove me from his horse. The truth was that he begrudged paying professionals when he could bully the sons of his friends and acquaintances for nothing. Boathook was his best horse, and for the pleasure of winning on him I could easily put up with the insults I got from losing on the others. On that day, however, there was one too good for him from Ireland, and for being beaten by half a length I got the customary bawling out. Not a good loser by any means, Old Strawberry Leaves.

All in all I'd had a good Cheltenham, I thought, as I changed into street clothes; a winner, a second, an also ran, one harmless fall, and fourth in the Gold Cup. I wouldn't improve on it very easily.

Patrick and the other two were waiting for me outside, and after we'd watched the last race together, I drove them down to the station to catch the last train to London. They had all made a mint out of the engineer's tips and were in a fine collective state of euphoria.

"I can see why you like it," Patrick said on the way. "It's a magnificent sport. I'll come again."

"Good," I said, stopping at the station to let them out. "I'll see you tomorrow, then."

He grinned. "Milan first stop."

"Arabia again for us," said Kyle resignedly, shutting the door.

They waved their thanks and began to walk away into the station. An elderly man tottered slowly across in front of my car, and as I was waiting for him to pass the engineer's voice floated back to me, clear and unmistakable.

"It's f . . . funny," he said, "you qu . . . quite forget he's a L . . . Lord."

I turned my head round to them, startled. Patrick looked over his shoulder and saw that I had heard, and laughed. I grinned sardonically in return, and drove off reflecting that I was much in favor of people like him who could let me forget it too.

10

FIRE CAN'T burn without air. Deprived of an oxygen supply in a sealed space, it goes out. There existed a state of affairs like a smoldering room which had been shuttered and left to cool down in safety. Nothing much would have happened if I hadn't been trying to find Simon, but when I finally came on a trace of him, it was like throwing wide the door. Fresh air poured in and the whole thing banged into flames.

The fine Cheltenham weather was still in operation on the Friday, the day after the Gold Cup. The met reports in the charter company's office showed clear skies right across Europe, with an extended high-pressure area almost stationary over France. No breakup of the system was expected for at least twenty-four hours. Someone tapped me on the shoulder and I half turned to find Patrick reading over my shoulder.

"Trouble-free trip," he commented with satisfaction. "Piece of cake."

"We've got that old DC-4 again, I see," I said, looking out of the window across to where it stood on the tarmac.

"Nice reliable old bus."

"Bloody uncomfortable old bus."

Patrick grinned. "You'll be joining a union next."

"Workers unite," I agreed.

He looked me up and down. "Some worker. You remind me of Fanny Cradock."

"Of *who?*" I said.

"That woman on television who cooks in a ball gown without marking it."

"Oh." I looked down at my neat charcoal worsted, my black tie, and the fraction of white showing at the cuffs. Beside me, in the small overnight bag I now carried everywhere, was the high-necked black jersey I worked in, and a hanger for my jacket. Tidiness was addictive; one couldn't kick it, even when it was inappropriate.

"You're no slouch yourself," I pointed out defensively. He wore his navy gold-braided uniform with an air of authority, his handsome good-natured face radiating confidence. A wonderful bedside manner for nervous passengers, I thought. An inborn conviction that one only had to keep to the rules for everything to be all right. Fatal.

"Eight each way today?" he said.

"Eight out, four back. All brood mares."

"Ready to drop?"

"Let's hope not too ready."

"Let's indeed." He grinned and turned away to check over his flight plan with one of the office staff. "I suppose," he said over his shoulder, "you'd like me to organize an overnight delay at Milan?"

"You suppose correctly."

"You could do it yourself."

"How?"

"Load up all the horses and then 'lose' the papers for a front one. Like John Kyle said, by the time they'd unloaded and reloaded, it was too late to take off."

I laughed. "An absolutely brilliant idea. I shall act on it immediately."

"That'll be the day." He smiled over his papers, checking the lists.

The door opened briskly and Yardman came in, letting a blast of cold six-thirty air slip past him.

"All set?" he said, impressing on us his early hour alertness.

"The horses haven't arrived yet," I said mildly. "They're late again."

"Oh." He shut the door behind him and came in, putting down his brief case and rubbing his thin hands together for warmth. "They were due at six." He frowned and looked at Patrick. "Are you the pilot?"

"That's right."

"What sort of trip are we going to have?"

"Easy," said Patrick. "The weather's perfect."

Yardman nodded in satisfaction. "Good, good." He pulled out a chair and sat down, lifting and opening his brief case. He had brought all the brood mares' papers with him, and as he seemed content to check them with the airline people himself I leaned lazily against the office wall and thought about Gabriella. The office work went steadily on, regardless of the hour. No nine-to-five about an airline. As usual, some of the flying staff were lying there fast asleep, one on a canvas bed under the counter Patrick was leaning on, another underneath the big table where Yardman sat, and a third on my right, stretched along the top of a row of cupboards. They were all wrapped in blankets, heads and all, and were so motionless that one didn't notice them at first. They managed to sleep solidly through the comings and goings and telephoning and typing, and even when Yardman inadvertently kicked the one under the table he didn't stir.

The first of the horseboxes rolled past the window and drove across to the waiting plane. I peeled myself off the wall, temporarily banished Gabriella, and touched Yardman's arm.

"They're here," I said.

He looked round and glanced through the window. "Ah, yes. Well here you are, my dear boy, here's the list. You can load the first six, they are all checked. There's just one more to do . . . it seems there's some query of insurance on this one . . . ." He bent back to his work, riffling through his brief case for more papers.

I took the list and walked across to the plane. I had expected Timmie and Conker to arrive in a horsebox as they lived near the stud one lot of horses had come from, but when I got over there I found it was to be Billy and Alf again. They had come with Yardman, and were already sitting on the stacked box sides in the plane, eating sandwiches. With them sat a third man in jodhpurs and a grubby tweed jacket a size too small. He was wearing an old greenish cap and he didn't bother to look up.

"The horses are here," I said.

Billy turned his wide insolent glare full on and didn't answer. I bent down and touched Alf's knee, and pointed out of the oval window. He saw the horseboxes, nodded philosophically, and began to wrap up his remaining sandwiches. I left them and went down the ramp again, knowing very well that Billy would never obey an instruction of mine if I waited over him to see he did it.

The horsebox drivers said they'd had to make a detour because of roadworks. A detour into a transport café, more like.

Two grooms who had traveled with the mares gave a hand with the loading, which made it easy. The man who had come with Billy and Alf, whose name was John, was more abstracted than skillful, but with six of us it was the quickest job I had done when Billy was along. I imagined that it was because he knew Yardman was within complaining distance that he left me alone.

Yardman came across with the all clear for the other two mares, and we stowed them on board. Then as always we trooped along to the Immigration Office in the main passenger building where a bored official collected our dog-eared passports, flipped through them, and handed them back. Mine still had Mr. on it, because I'd originally applied for it that way, and I intended to put off changing it as long as possible.

"Four grooms and you," he said to Yardman. "That's the lot?"

"That's the lot." Yardman stifled a yawn. Early starts disagreed with him.

A party of bleary-eyed passengers from a cut-rate night flight shuffled past in an untidy crocodile.

"O.K. then." The passport man flicked the tourists a supercilious glance and retired into his office. Not everyone was at his best before breakfast.

Yardman walked back to the plane beside me.

"I've arranged to meet our opposite numbers for lunch," he said. "You know what business lunches are, my dear boy. I'm afraid it may drag on a little, and that you'll be kicking your heels about the airport for a few hours. Don't let any of them get . . . er . . . the worse for wear."

"No," I agreed insincerely. The longer his lunch, the better I'd be pleased. Billy drunk couldn't be worse than Billy sober, and I didn't intend to waste my hours at Malpensa supervising his intake.

Patrick and his crew were ready out by the plane, and had done their checks. The mobile battery truck stood by the nose cone with its power lead plugged into the aircraft. Patrick liked always to start his engines from the truck, so that he took off with the plane's own batteries fully charged.

Yardman and I followed Billy, Alf and John up the ramp at the rear, and Patrick with his copilot Bob, and the engineer, Mike, climbed the forward stairs into the nose. The airport staff wheeled away the stairs and unfastened and removed the two long sections of ramp. The inner port propeller began to grind slowly round as I swung shut the double doors, then sparked into life with a roar, and the plane came alive with vibration. The moment of the first engine firing gave me its usual lift of the spirits and I went along the cabin checking the horses with a smile in my mind.

Patrick moved down the taxi track and turned onto the apron set aside for power checks, the airframe quivering against the brakes as he pushed the throttles open. Holding two of the horses by their head collars I automatically followed him in imagination through the last series of checks before he closed the throttles, released the brakes and rolled round on to Gatwick's large single runway. The engine's note deepened and the plane began to move, horses and men leaning against the thrust as the speed built up to a hundred over the tarmac. We unstuck as per schedule and climbed away in a great wheeling turn, heading toward the Channel on course to the radio beacon at Dieppe. The heavy mares took the whole thing philosophically, and having checked round the lot of them I went forward into the galley, bending under the luggage racks and stepping over the guy chains as always in the cramped DC-4.

Mike, the engineer, was already writing names on disposable cups with a red felt pen.

"All O.K.?" he asked, the eyebrow going up and down like a yo-yo.

"All fine," I said.

He wrote "Patrick" and "Bob" and "Henry" and asked me the names of the others. "Mr. Y," "Billy," "Alf" and "John" joined the roll. He filled the crew's cups and mine, and I took Patrick's and Bob's forward while he went back to ask the others if they were thirsty. The rising sun blazed into the cockpit, dazzling after the comparative gloom of the cabin. Both pilots were wearing dark glasses, and Patrick already had his jacket off, and had started on the first of his attendant bunch of bananas. The chart lay handy, the usual unlikely mass of half-inch circles denoting radio stations connected by broad pale-blue areas of authorized airlines, with the normal shape of the land beneath only faintly drawn in and difficult to distinguish. Bob pulled a tuft of cotton wool off a shaving cut, made it bleed again, and swore, his exact words inaudible against the racket of the engines. Both of them were wearing headsets, earphones combined with a microphone mounted on a metal band which curved round in front of the mouth. They spoke to each other by means of a transmitting switch set into the wheel on the control column, since normal speech in that noise was impossible. Giving me a grin and a thumbs-up sign for the coffee, they went on with their endless attention to the job in hand. I watched for a bit, then strolled back through the galley, picking up "Henry" en route, and relaxed on a hay bale to drink, looking down out of the oval window and seeing the coast of France tilt underneath as we passed the Dieppe beacon and set course for Paris.

A day like any other day, a flight like any other flight. And Gabriella waiting at the other end of it. Every half hour or so I checked round the mares, but they were a docile lot and traveled like veterans. Mostly horses didn't eat much in the air, but one or two were picking at their haynets, and a chestnut in the rearmost box was fairly guzzling. I began to untie her depleted net to fill it again for her from one of the bales when a voice said in my ear, "I'll do that."

I looked round sharply and found Billy's face two feet from my own.

"You?" The surprise and sarcasm got drowned by the engine noise.

He nodded, elbowed me out of the way, and finished untying the haynet. I watched with astonishment as he carried it away into the narrow starboard gangway and began to stuff it full again. He came back pulling the drawstring tight round the neck, slung it over to hang inside the box, and retied its rope onto the cleat. Wordlessly he treated me to a wide sneering glare from the searchlight eyes, pushed past, and flung himself with what suddenly looked like pent-up fury into one of the seats at the back.

In the pair of seats immediately behind him Yardman and John sat side by side. Yardman was frowning crossly at Billy, though to my mind he should have been giving him a pat on the head and medal for self-control.

Yardman turned his head from Billy to me and gave me his graveyard smile. "What time do we arrive?" he shouted.

"About half an hour."

He nodded and looked away through the window. I glanced at John and saw that he was dozing, with his grubby cap pushed back on his head and his hands lying limp on his lap. He opened his eyes while I was looking at him, and his relaxed facial muscles sharply contracted so that suddenly he seemed familiar to me, though I was certain I hadn't met him before. It puzzled me for only a second because Billy, getting up again, managed to kick my ankle just out of Yardman's sight. I turned away from him, lashed backward with my heel, and felt a satisfactory clunking jar as it landed full on his shin. One day, I thought, smiling to myself as I squeezed forward along the plane, one day he'll get tired of it.

We joined the circuit at Malpensa four hours from Gatwick; a smooth, easy trip. Holding the mares' heads I saw the familiar red and white checkered huts near the edge of the airfield grow bigger and bigger as we descended, then they were suddenly behind us at eye level as Patrick leveled out twenty feet from the ground at about a hundred and ten miles an hour. The bump from the tricycle undercarriage as we touched down with full flaps at a fraction above stalling speed wasn't enough to rock the mares on their feet. Top of the class, I thought.

The Customs man with his two helpers came on board, and Yardman produced the mares' papers from his brief case. The checking went on without a hitch, brisk but thorough. The Customs man handed the papers back to Yardman with a small bow and signed that the unloading could begin.

Yardman ducked out of any danger of giving a hand with that by saying that he'd better see if the opposite numbers were waiting for him inside the airport. As it was barely half-past eleven, it seemed doubtful, but all the same he marched purposefully down the ramp and away across the tarmac, a gaunt black figure with sunshine flashing on his glasses.

The crew got off at the sharp end and followed him, a navy-blue trio in peaked caps. A large yellow Shell tanker pulled up in front of the aircraft, and three men in white overalls began the job of refueling.

We unloaded into the waiting horseboxes in record time, Billy seemingly being as anxious as me to get it done quickly, and within half an hour of landing I had changed my jersey for my jacket and was pushing open the glass doors of the airport. I stood just inside, watching Gabriella. She was selling a native doll, fluffing up the rich dark skirt to show the petticoats underneath, her face solemn and absorbed. The heavy dark club-cut hair swung forward as she leaned across the counter, and her eyes were cool and quiet as she shook her head gently at her customer, the engineer Mike. My chest constricted at the sight of her, and I wondered how I was possibly going to bear leaving again in three hours' time. She looked up suddenly as if she felt my gaze, and she saw me and smiled, her soft mouth curving sweet and wide.

Mike looked quite startled at the transformation and turned to see the reason.

"Henry," said Gabriella, with welcome and gaiety shimmering in her voice. "Hullo, darling."

"Darling?" exclaimed Mike, the eyebrow doing its stuff.

Gabriella said in French, "I've doubled my English vocabulary, as you see. I know two words now."

"Essential ones, I'm glad to say."

"Hey," said Mike. "If you can talk to her, Henry, ask her about this doll. It's my elder girl's birthday tomorrow, and she's started collecting these things, but I'm damned if I know whether she'll like this one."

"How old is she?"

"Twelve."

I explained the situation to Gabriella, who promptly produced a different doll, much prettier and more colorful, which she wrapped up for him while he sorted out some lire. Like Patrick's his wallet was stuffed with several different currencies, and he scattered a day's pay in deutschmarks over the merchandise before finding what he wanted. Collecting his cash in an untidy handful he thanked her cheerfully in basic French, picked up his parcel and walked off upstairs into the restaurant. There were always lunches provided for us on the planes, tourist-class lunches packed in boxes, but both Mike and Bob preferred eating on the ground, copiously and in comfort.

I turned back to Gabriella and tried to satisfy my own sort of hunger by looking at her and touching her hand. And I could see in her face that to her too this was like a bowl of rice to the famine of India.

"When do you go?" she said.

"The horses arrive at two-thirty. I have to go then to load them. I might get back for a few minutes afterward, if my boss dallies over his coffee."

She sighed, looking at the clock. It was ten past noon. "I have an hour off in twenty minutes. I'll make it two hours . . . ." She turned away into swift chatter with the girl along on the duty-free shop, and came back smiling. "I'm doing her last hour today, and she'll do the gift shop in her lunch hour."

I bowed my thanks to the girl and she laughed back with a flash of teeth, very white against the gloom of her bottle shop.

"Do you want to have lunch up there?" I suggested to Gabriella, pointing where Mike and Bob had gone.

She shook her head. "Too public. Everyone knows me so well. We've time to go in to Milan, if you can do that?"

"If the horses get here early, they can wait."

"Serve them right." She nodded approvingly, her lips twitching.

A crowd of outgoing passengers erupted into the hall and swarmed round the gift counter. I retired to the snack bar at the far end to wait out the twenty minutes, and found Yardman sitting alone at one of the small tables. He waved me to join him, which I would just as soon not have done, and told me to order myself a double gin and tonic, like his.

"I'd really rather have coffee."

He waved a limp hand permissively. "Have whatever you like, my dear boy."

I looked casually round the big airy place, at the glass, the polished wood, the terrazza. Along one side, next to a stall of sweets and chocolates, stretched the serving counter with coffee and beer rubbing shoulders with milk and gin. And down at the far end, close-grouped round another little table and clutching pint glasses, sat Alf and Billy, and with his back to us, John. Two and a half hours of that, I thought wryly, and we'd have a riotous trip home.

"Haven't your people turned up?" I asked Yardman.

"Delayed," he said resignedly. "They'll be here about one, though."

"Good," I said, but not for his sake. "You won't forget to ask them about Simon?"

"Simon?"

"Searle."

"Searle . . . oh yes. Yes, all right, I'll remember."

Patrick walked through the hall from the office department, exchanged a greeting with Gabriella over the heads of her customers and came on to join us.

"Drink?" suggested Yardman, indicating his glass. He only meant to be hospitable, but Patrick was shocked.

"Of course not."

"Eh?"

"Well . . . I thought you'd know. One isn't allowed to fly within eight hours of drinking alcohol."

"Eight hours," repeated Yardman in astonishment.

"That's right. Twenty-four hours after a heavy party, and better not for forty-eight if you get paralytic."

"I didn't know," said Yardman weakly.

"Air Ministry regulations," Patrick explained. "I'd like some coffee, though."

A waitress brought him some, and he unwrapped four sugars and stirred them in. "I enjoyed yesterday," he said, smiling at me with his yellow eyes. "I'll go again. When do you race next?"

"Tomorrow."

"That's out for a start. When else?"

I glanced at Yardman. "It depends on the schedules."

Patrick turned to him in his usual friendly way. "I went to Cheltenham yesterday and saw our Henry here come fourth in the Gold Cup. Very interesting."

"You know each other well, then?" Yardman asked. His deep-set eyes were invisible behind the glasses, and the slanting sunlight showed up every blemish in his sallow skin. I still had no feeling for him either way, not liking, not disliking. He was easy to work for. He was friendly enough. He was still an enigma.

"We know each other," Patrick agreed. "We've been on trips together before."

"I see."

Gabriella came down toward us, wearing a supple brown suede coat over her black working dress. She had flat black round-toed patent-leather shoes and swung a handbag with the same shine. A neat, composed, self-reliant, nearly beautiful girl who took work for granted and a lover for fun.

I stood up as she came near, trying to stifle a ridiculous feeling of pride, and introduced her to Yardman. He smiled politely and spoke to her in slow Italian, which surprised me a little, and Patrick translated for me into one ear.

"He's telling her he was in Italy during the war. Rather tactless of him, considering her grandfather was killed fighting off the invasion of Sicily."

"Before she was born," I protested.

"True." He grinned. "She's pro-British enough now, anyway."

"Miss Barzini tells me you are taking her to lunch in Milan," Yardman said.

"Yes," I agreed. "If that's all right with you? I'll be back by two-thirty when the return mares come."

"I can't see any objection," he said mildly. "Where do you have in mind?"

"Trattoria Romana," I said promptly. It was where Gabriella, Patrick and I had eaten on our first evening together.

Gabriella put her hand in mine. "Good. I'm very hungry." She shook hands with Yardman and waggled her fingers at Patrick. "Arrivederci."

We walked away up the hall, the voltage tingling gently through our joined palms. I looked back once, briefly, and saw Yardman and Patrick watching us go. They were both smiling.

11

NEITHER OF us had much appetite, when it came to the point. We ate half our lasagna and drank coffee, and needed nothing else but proximity. We didn't talk a great deal, but at one point, clairvoyantly reading my disreputable thoughts, she said out of the blue that we couldn't go to her sister's flat as her sister would be in, complete with two or three kids.

"I was afraid of that," I said wryly.

"It will have to be next time."

"Yes." We both sighed deeply in unison, and laughed.

A little later, sipping her hot coffee, she said, "How many pills were there in the bottle you sent with Simon Searle?"

"I don't know. Dozens. I didn't count them. The bottle was over three-quarters full."

"I thought so." She sighed. "The baker's wife rang up last night to ask me whether I could let her have some more. She said the bottom of the bottle was all filled up with paper, but if you ask me she's given half of them away to a friend, or something, and now regrets it."

"There wasn't any paper in the bottle. Only cotton wool on top."

"I thought so." She frowned, wrinkling her nose in sorrow. "I wish she'd told me the truth."

I stood up abruptly. "Come on," I said. "Leave the coffee."

"Why?" She began to put on her coat.

"I want to see that bottle."

She was puzzled. "She'll have thrown it away."

"I hope to God she hasn't," I said urgently, paying the bill. "If there's paper in the bottle, Simon put it there."

"You mean . . . it could matter?"

"He thought I was giving the pills to you. He didn't know they'd go to someone else. And I forgot to tell him you didn't speak English. Perhaps he thought when you'd finished the pills you'd read the paper and tell me what it said. Heaven knows. Anyway, we must find it. It's the first and only trace of him we've had."

We hurried out of the restaurant, caught a taxi, and sped to the bakery. The baker's wife was fat and motherly and looked fifty, though she was probably only thirty-five. Her warm smile for Gabriella slowly turned anxious as she listened, and she shook her head and spread her hands wide.

"It's in the dustbin," Gabriella said. "She threw it away this morning."

"We'll have to look. Ask her if I can look for it."

The two women consulted.

"She says you'll dirty your fine suit."

"Gabriella. . . ."

"She says the English are mad, but you can look."

There were three dustbins in the backyard, two luckily empty and one full. We turned this one out and I raked through the stinking contents with a broom handle. The little brown bottle was there, camouflaged by wet coffee grounds and half a dozen noodles. Gabriella took it and wiped it clean on a piece of newspaper while I shoveled the muck back into the dustbin and swept the yard.

"The paper won't come out," she said. She had the cap off and was poking down the neck of the bottle with her finger. "It's quite right. There is some in there." She held it out to me.

I looked and nodded, wrapped the bottle in newspaper, put it on the ground, and smashed it with the shovel. She squatted beside me as I unfolded the paper and watched me pick out from the winking fragments of brown glass the things which had been inside.

I stood up slowly, holding them. A strip torn off the top of a piece of Yardman's stationery. A banknote of a currency I did not recognize, and some pieces of hay. The scrap of writing paper and the money were pinned together, and the hay had been folded up inside them.

"They are nonsense," said Gabriella slowly.

"Do you have any idea where this comes from?" I touched the note. She flicked it over to see both sides.

"Yugoslavia. One hundred dinars."

"Is that a lot?"

"About five thousand one hundred lire."

Three pounds. Wisps of hay. A strip of paper. In a bottle.

Gabriella took the money and paper out of my hands and removed the pin which joined them.

"What do they mean?" she asked.

"I don't know."

A message in a bottle.

"There are some holes in the paper."

"Where he put the pin."

"No. More holes than that. Look." she held it up to the sky. "You can see the light through."

The printed heading said in thick red letters "Yardman Transport Ltd., Carriers." The strip of paper was about six inches across and two inches deep from the top smooth edge to the jagged one where it had been torn off the page. I held it up to the light.

Simon had pinpricked four letters. S.M.E.N. I felt the first distant tremor of cold apprehension.

"What is it?" she asked. "What does it say?"

"Yardman Transport." I showed her. "See where he has added to it. If you read it with the pin hole letters tacked on, it says: 'Yardman Transports MEN.' "

She looked frightened by the bleakness in my voice, as if she could feel the inner coldness growing. "What does it mean?"

"It means he didn't have a pencil," I said grimly, evading the final implication. "Only pins in his coat."

A message in a bottle, washed ashore.

"I've got to think it out," I said. "I've got to remember."

We perched on a pile of empty boxes stacked in one corner of the baker's yard, and I stared sightlessly at the whitewashed wall opposite and at the single bush in a tub standing in one corner.

"Tell me," Gabriella said. "Tell me. You look so . . . so terrible."

"Billy," I said. "Billy put up a smoke screen, after all."

"Who is Billy?"

"A groom. At least, he works as one. Men. . . . Every time Billy has been on a trip, there has been a man who didn't come back."

"Simon?" she said incredulously.

"No, I don't mean Simon, though he went with Billy. . . . No. Someone who went as a groom, but wasn't a groom at all. And didn't come back. I can't remember any of their faces, not to be sure, because I never talked to any of them much. Billy saw to that."

"How?"

"Oh, by insults and . . ." I stopped, concentrating back. "The first time I went with Billy, there was a very fat man called John. At least, that was what I was told he was called. He was absolutely useless. Didn't know how to handle horses at all. We did two trips to France that day, and I think he wanted to vanish after the first. I saw him arguing furiously with Billy just before we came back the first time. But Billy made him do the double journey . . . and when he told me John had gone to Paris instead of coming back with us, he poured beer over my foot, so that I'd think about that, and not about John. And he made sure of it by picking a fight on the plane coming back. . . ."

"But who was this John?"

I shook my head. "I've no idea."

"And were there others?"

"Yes . . . we went to New York next, he and I. There was a groom traveling with a half-bred Norwegian horse. He hardly talked at all, said he didn't speak English much. I understood he was staying in the States for a fortnight; but who knows if he came back? And on that trip Billy smashed a bar across my fingers so that they hurt all the way across, and I thought about them, not the Norwegian groom."

"Are you sure?" She was frowning.

"Oh yes, I'm sure. I thought once before that Billy had done it for a purpose. I just got the purpose wrong." I pondered. "There was a day we took a man with a large bushy mustache to France, and a fortnight later we brought a man with a large bushy mustache back again. I never looked beyond the mustache. . . . I think it could have been two different men."

"What did Billy do, those times?"

"On the way over he poured sirupy coffee on my head, and I spent nearly all the time in the washroom getting it out. And on the way back he hit me with a chain, and I went up into the galley all the way with the engineer to avoid any more."

She looked at me very gravely. "Is that . . . is that the lot?"

I shook my head. "We went to New York last week. I told Yardman if Billy didn't leave me alone I'd quit. The journey out went quite all right, but coming back . . . there was a man who was plainly not a horseman. He wasn't even comfortable in the riding clothes he had on. I thought at the time he was the owner's nephew or something, cadging a free ride, but again I didn't talk to him much. I slept all the way back. All ten hours . . . I don't usually get tired like that, but I thought it was only because it was my fourth Atlantic crossing in six days. . . ."

"A sleeping pill?" she said slowly.

"It might have been. Alf brought some coffee back for me soon after we left. There was a restive colt in the aft box and I was trying to soothe him. . . . It could have been in that."

"Alf?"

"An old deaf man, who always goes with Billy."

"Do you think it *was* a sleeping pill?"

"It could have been. . . . I was still tired long after I got home. I even went to sleep in the bath."

"It's serious," she said.

"Today," I said. "There's a stranger with us today. His name is John too. I've never met him before, but there's something about him. . . . I was looking at him on the plane and wondering what it was, and Billy kicked me on the ankle. I kicked him back, but I went away, and stopped thinking about that man."

"Can you think now?"

"Well . . . his hands are wrong for one thing. Stablemen's hands are rough and chafed from being wet so often in cold weather, with washing tack and so on, but his are smooth, with well-shaped nails."

She picked up one of my hands and looked at it, running the tips of her fingers over the roughnesses which had developed since I left my desk job.

"They are not like yours, then."

"Not like mine. But it's his expression really. I watched him wake up. It was what came into his face with consciousness. . . ." I could remember that moment vividly, in spite of Billy's kick. I knew that expression very well . . . so what was it? "Oh," I exclaimed in enlightenment, half laughing at my own stupidity, "I know what it is . . . he went to the same school as I did."

"You do know him then, I mean, you've seen him before, if you were at school together."

"Not together. He's older. He must have left about five years before I went. No, I've never seen him before, but the look he has is typical of some of the boys there. Not the nicest ones . . . only the ones who think they are God's gift to mankind and everyone else is a bit inferior. He's one of those. Definitely *not* a groom. He looked as if wearing the grubby riding clothes he's got on was a kick in the dignity."

"But you don't wear riding clothes," she pointed out. "It isn't necessary for him if he doesn't like them."

"It is though. Alf wears jodhpurs, Billy wears jeans. The two grooms who travel turn about with these two, Timmie and Conker, they both wear breeches to work in. It's a sort of office. . . . No one would think twice about a man arriving on a horse transport dressed in breeches or jodhpurs."

"No, I see that."

"No one bothers much about our passports," I said. "Look how simply I came out into Milan today, through the airport staff door. Hardly any airports, especially the very small ones, take much notice of you, if you work on airplanes. It's dead easy just to walk off most airfields round at the loading bays without ever being challenged. The Americans are strictest, but even they are used to our comings and goings."

"But people do look at your passports sometimes, surely," she protested.

I produced mine, battered and dog-eared in the last three months after several years of dark-blue stiffness. "Look at it. It gets like that from always being in my pocket, but it doesn't get stamped much." I turned through the pages. "American visa, certainly. But look, the only stamp from Milan is the time I came on a scheduled flight and went through immigration with the other passengers. Hardly a mark for France, and I've been over there several times. . . . Of course it gets looked at, but never very thoroughly. It must be easy to fake one in this condition, and even traveling without one wouldn't be impossible. A pilot told me he'd done it for three weeks once, all over the world."

"People who work on aircraft would go mad if everyone started checking their passports thoroughly every time they walked in or out."

"Well . . . normally there's no need for it. It isn't all that easy to get on a single one-way flight as a worker. Impossible, if you haven't a strong pull somewhere or other. Just any odd person who fancies a quiet trip to foreign parts wouldn't have a hope of getting himself into a horse transport. But if the transport agency itself, or someone working for it, is ready to export people illegally along with the horses, then it's easy."

"But . . . what people?"

"What indeed! Billy can hardly advertise his service in the daily press. But he has no shortage of customers."

"Crooks, do you think?" Gabriella asked, frowning.

I fingered the banknote and twisted the small pieces of hay.

"Hay," I said. "Why hay?"

Gabriella shrugged. "Perhaps he found the money in some hay."

"Of course!" I exclaimed. "You're dead right. Haynets. Carried openly on and off the planes and never searched by Customs officers. Perhaps they're transporting currency as well as men." I told her about Billy refilling the net for me on the trip over, and how astonished I had been.

"But, Henry darling, what I really do not understand is why you were not astonished all along at the unpleasant things Billy has been doing to you. I would have thought it utterly extraordinary, and I would have made a very big fuss about it." She looked solemn and doubtful.

"Oh, I thought it was simply because I . . ." I stopped.

"Because you what?"

I smiled slightly. "Because I belong to a sort of people he thinks should be exterminated."

"Henry!" Her mouth lost its severity. "What sort of people?"

"Well . . . you have counts and countesses still in Italy. . . ."

"But you're not . . . you're not, are you . . . a count?"

"Sort of. Yes."

She looked at me doubtfully, halfway to laughing, not sure that I was not teasing her.

"I don't believe you."

"The reason I wasn't astonished at Billy knocking me about was that I knew he hated my guts for having a title."

"That makes sense, I suppose." She managed to frown and smile at the same time, which looked adorable. "But if you have a title, Henry, why are you working in a horse transport?"

"You tell me why," I said.

She looked at me searchingly for a moment, then she put her arms round my neck and her cheek on mine, with her mouth against my ear.

"It isn't enough for you to have a title," she said. "It isn't enough for anyone. It is necessary to show also that you are . . ." She fished around in her French vocabulary, and came up with a word: ". . . véritable. Real."

I took a deep breath of relief and overspilling love, and kissed her neck where the dark hair swung below her ear.

"My wife will be a countess," I said. "Would you mind that?"

"I could perhaps bear it."

"And me? Could you bear me? For always?"

"I love you," she said in my ear. "Yes. For always. Only, Henry . . ."

"Only what?"

"You won't stop being real?"

"No," I said sadly.

She pulled away from me, shaking her head.

"I'm stupid. I'm sorry. But if even I can doubt you . . . and so quickly . . . you must always be having to prove . . ."

"Always," I agreed.

"Still, you don't have to go quite so far."

My heart sank.

"It's not everyone," she said, "who gets proposed to in a baker's backyard surrounded by dustbins." Her mouth trembled and melted into the heart-wrenching smile.

"You wretch, my love."

"Henry," she said, "I'm so happy I could burst."

I kissed her and felt the same, and lived another half minute of oblivion before I thought again of Simon.

"What is it?" she said, feeling me straighten.

"The time. . . ."

"Oh."

"And Simon. . . ."

"I fear for him," she said, half under her breath.

"I too."

She took the piece of paper out of my hand and looked at it again.

"We've been trying to avoid realizing what this means."

"Yes," I said softly.

"Say it, then."

"This was the only message he had a chance of sending. The only way he could send it." I paused, looking into her serious dark eyes. After ten silent seconds I finished it. "He is dead."

She said in distress, "Perhaps he is a prisoner."

I shook my head. "He's the third man who's disappeared. There was a man called Ballard who used to arrange trips from this end, and the man who used to have my own job, a man called Peters. They both vanished, Ballard over a year ago, and no one's heard of them since."

"This Billy . . ." she said slowly, her eyes anxious.

"This Billy," I said, "is young and heartless, and carries a loaded revolver under his left arm."

"Please . . . don't go back with him."

"It will be quite safe as long as I keep quiet about this." I took the hurried, desperate, pinpricked message back, folded it up with the banknote and the hay, and put them all in my wallet. "When I get back to England, I'll find out who I have to tell."

"The police," she said, nodding.

"I'm not sure. . . ." I thought about the Yugoslav currency and remembered Gabriella saying on our first evening, "Communists begin at Trieste." I felt like someone who had trodden through a surface into a mole run underneath, and had suddenly realized that it was part of a whole dark invisible network. I thought it very unlikely that the men I'd flown with were ordinary crooks. They were couriers, agents . . . heaven knew what. It seemed fantastic to me to have brushed so closely with people I had known must exist but never expected to see; but I supposed the suburban people who had lived next door to Peter and Helen Kroger in Cranley Drive, Ruislip, had been pretty astonished too.

"Billy must have unloaded whatever he brought over in the haynets today," I said. "But going back . . ."

"No," Gabriella said vehemently. "Don't look. That's what Simon must have done. Found the money. And Billy saw him."

It might have been like that. And there had been two extra grooms on that trip, men I'd never seen before. Somehow, on the way, Simon had come across something I'd been blind to, perhaps because there was one more man than he'd arranged for, perhaps because Billy couldn't distract his attention by the methods he'd used on me, perhaps because of other happenings in the past which I didn't know about. In any case, Simon had found Billy out, and had let Billy know it. I thought drearily of Simon suddenly realizing toward the end of that flight that Ballard and Peters had never come back, and that he wouldn't get a chance to put Billy in jail. Billy, the young thug, with his ready gun. A few minutes in the lavatory, that was all the time he'd had. No pencil. Only his pins, and the little bottle I'd given him in the privacy of the airline office; the bottle Billy didn't know existed, with Gabriella's name on it. Pills into loo. Banknote and paper with its inadequate message into bottle. Simon into eternity.

"Please don't search the haynets," Gabriella said again.

"No," I agreed. "Someone official had better do it, next time Billy goes on a trip."

She relaxed with relief. "I'd hate you to disappear."

I smiled. "I won't do that. I'll go back most of the way up front with the crew, with Patrick and the man who bought the doll. And when I get to England I'll telephone you to let you know I arrived safely. How's that?"

"It would be wonderful. I could stop worrying."

"Don't start," I said confidently. "Nothing will go wrong."

How the local gods must have laughed their Roman heads off.

12

WE WENT through the baker's shop and out into the street. I looked somewhat anxiously at my watch and calculated a dead heat with the brood mares.

"We need a taxi," I said.

Gabriella shook her head. "Very unlikely to find one in this quarter. We'd better catch a tram back to the center, and take one on from there."

"All right," I agreed. "Tram or taxi, whichever comes first."

The trams ran along the busy street at the end of the quiet empty road where the baker lived, and we began to walk toward them with some dispatch.

"I didn't realize how late it is," Gabriella said, catching sight of a clock with the hands together pointing northeast.

"And that one's slow. It's a quarter past."

"Oh dear."

One of the long green and cream single-decker trams rolled across the end of the road, not far ahead.

"Run," Gabriella said. "The stop's just round the corner. We must catch it."

We ran, holding hands. It couldn't have been more than ten strides to the corner. Not more.

Gabriella cried out suddenly and stumbled, whirling against me as I pulled her hand. There was a sharp searing stab in my side and we fell down on the pavement, Gabriella's weight pulling me over as I tried to save her from hurting herself.

Two or three passers-by stopped to help her up, but she didn't move. She was lying face down, crumpled. Without belief, I stared at the small round hole near the center of the back of her coat. Numbly, kneeling beside her, I put my left hand inside my jacket against my scorching right side, and when I brought it out it was covered in blood.

"Oh no," I said in English. "Oh dear God, no."

I bent over her and rolled her up and on to her back in my arms. Her eyes were open. They focused on my face. She was alive. It wasn't much.

"Henry," her voice was a whisper. "I can't . . . breathe."

The three passers-by had grown to a small crowd. I looked up desperately into their inquiring faces.

"Doctor," I said. "Medico." That was Spanish. "Doctor."

"Si si," said a small boy at my elbow. "Un dottore, si."

There was a stir in the crowd and a great deal of speculation of which I understood only one word. "Inglese," they said, and I nodded. "Inglese."

I opened gently the front of Gabriella's brown suede coat. There was a jagged tear in the right side, nearest me, and the edges of it were dark. Underneath, the black dress was soaking. I waved my arm wildly round at the people to get them to stand back a bit, and they did take one pace away. A motherly-looking woman produced a pair of scissors from her handbag and knelt down on Gabriella's other side. She pointed at me to open the coat again, and when I'd tucked it back between Gabriella's body and my own she began to cut away the dress. Gentle as she was, Gabriella moved in my arms and gave a small gasping cry.

"Hush," I said, "my love, it's all right."

"Henry . . . ." She shut her eyes.

I held her in anguish while the woman with the scissors carefully cut and peeled away a large piece of dress. When she saw what lay underneath her big face filled with overwhelming compassion, and she began to shake her head. "Signor," she said to me, "mi dispiace molto. Molto."

I took the clean white handkerchief out of my top pocket, folded it inside out, and put it over the terrible wound. The bullet had smashed a rib on its way out. There were splinters of it showing in the bleeding area just below her breast. The bottom edge of her white bra had a new scarlet border. I gently untucked the coat and put it over her again to keep her warm and I thought in utter agony that she would die before the doctor came.

A carabiniere in glossy boots and greenish khaki breeches appeared beside us, but I doubt if I could have spoken to him even if he'd known the same language. The crowd chattered to him in subdued voices and he left me alone.

Gabriella opened her eyes. Her face was gray and wet with the sweat of appalling pain.

"Henry. . . ."

"I'm here."

"I can't . . . breathe."

I raised her a little more so that she was half sitting, supported by my arm and my bent knee. The movement was almost too much for her. Her pallor became pronounced. The short difficult breaths passed audibly through her slackly open mouth.

"Don't . . . leave me."

"No," I said. "Hush, my dearest love."

"What . . . happened?"

"You were shot," I said.

"Shot. . . ." She showed no surprise. "Was it . . . Billy?"

"I don't know. I didn't see. Don't talk, my sweet love, don't talk. The doctor will be here soon."

"Henry. . . ." She was exhausted, her skin the color of death. "Henry . . . I love you."

Her eyes flickered shut again, but she was still conscious, her left hand moving spasmodically and restlessly on the ground beside her and the lines of suffering deepening in her face.

I would have given anything, anything on earth, to have had her whole again, to have taken that pain away.

The doctor, when at last he came, was young enough to have been newly qualified. He had thick black curly hair and thin clever hands; this was what I most saw of him as he bent over Gabriella, and all I remember. He looked briefly under my white handkerchief and turned to speak to the policeman.

I heard the words "auto ambulanza" and "pallota," and eager information from the crowd.

The young doctor went down on one knee and felt Gabriella's pulse. She opened her eyes, but only a fraction.

"Henry. . . ."

"I'm here. Don't talk."

"Mm. . . ."

The young doctor said something soothing to her in Italian, and she said faintly "Si." He opened his case beside him on the ground and with quick skillful fingers prepared an injection, made a hole in her stocking, swabbed her skin with surgical spirit, and pushed the needle firmly into her thigh. Again he spoke to her gently, and again felt her pulse. I could read nothing but reassurance in his manner, and the reassurance was for her, not me.

After a while she opened her eyes wider and looked at me, and a smile struggled on to her damp face.

"That's better," she said. Her voice was so weak as to be scarcely audible, and she was growing visibly more breathless. Nothing was better, except the pain.

I smiled back. "Good. You'll be all right soon, when they get you to hospital."

She nodded a fraction. The doctor continued to hold her pulse, checking it on his watch.

Two vehicles drove up and stopped with a screech of tires. A Citroën police car and an ambulance like a large estate car. Two carabinieri of obvious seniority emerged from one, and stretcher bearers from the other. These last, and the doctor, lifted Gabriella gently out of my arms and on to the stretcher. They piled blankets behind her to support her, and I saw the doctor take a look at what he could see of the small hole in her back. He didn't try to take off her coat.

One of the policemen said, "I understand you speak French."

"Yes," I said, standing up. I hadn't felt the hardness of the pavement until that moment. The leg I'd been kneeling on was numb.

"What are the young lady's name and address?"

I told him. He wrote them down.

"And your own?"

I told him.

"What happened?" he said, indicating the whole scene with a flickering wave of the hand.

"We were running to catch the tram. Someone shot at us, from back there." I pointed down the empty street toward the baker's.

"Who?"

"I didn't see." They were lifting Gabriella into the ambulance. "I must go with her," I said.

The policeman shook his head. "You can see her later. You must come with us, and tell us exactly what happened."

"I said I wouldn't leave her. . . ." I couldn't bear to leave her. I took a quick stride and caught the doctor by the arm. "Look," I said, pulling open my jacket.

He looked. He tugged my bloodstained shirt out of my trousers to inspect the damage more closely. A ridged furrow five inches long along my lowest rib. Not very deep. It felt like a burn. The doctor told the policeman who also looked.

"All right," said the one who spoke French, "I suppose you'd better go and have it dressed." He wrote an address on a page of his notebook, tore it off and gave it to me. "Come here, afterwards."

"Yes."

"Have you your passport with you?"

I took it out of my pocket and gave it to him, and put the address he'd given me in my wallet. The doctor jerked his head toward the ambulance to get in, and I did.

"Wait," said the policeman as they were shutting the door. "Did the bullet go through the girl into you?"

"No," I said. "Two bullets. She was hit first, me after."

"We will look for them," he said.

Gabriella was still alive when we reached the hospital. Still alive when they lifted her, stretcher and all, onto a trolley. Still alive while one of the ambulance men explained rapidly to a doctor what had happened, and while that doctor and another took in her general condition, left my handkerchief undisturbed, and whisked her away at high speed.

One doctor went with her. The other, a thickset man with the shoulders of a boxer, stayed behind and asked me a question.

"Inglese." I shook my head. "Non parlo italiano."

"Sit down," he said in English. His accent was thick, his vocabulary tiny, but it was a relief to be able to talk to him at all. He led me into a small white cubicle containing a hard, high narrow bed and a chair. He pointed to the chair and I sat on it. He went away and returned with a nurse carrying some papers.

"The name of the miss?"

I told him. The nurse wrote it all down, name, address and age, gave me a comforting smile, took the papers away and came back with a trolley of equipment and a message.

She told it to the doctor, and he translated, as it was for me.

"Telephone from carabinieri. Please go to see them before four."

I looked at my watch, blank to the time. It was still less than an hour since Gabriella and I had run for the tram. I had lived several ages.

"I understand," I said.

"Please now, remove the coat," the doctor said.

I stood up, took off my jacket and slid my right arm out of my shirt. He put two dressings over the bullet mark, an impregnated gauze one and a slightly padded one with adhesive tape. He pressed the tapes firmly into my skin and stood back. I put my arm back into my shirt sleeve.

"Don't you feel it?" he said. He seemed surprised.

"No."

His rugged face softened. "E sua moglie?"

I didn't understand.

"I am sorry . . . is she your wife?"

"I love her," I said. The prospect of losing her was past bearing. There were tears suddenly in my eyes and on my cheeks. "I love her."

"Yes." He nodded, sympathetic and unembarrassed, one of a nation who saw no value in stiff upper lips. "Wait here. We will tell you. . . ." He left the sentence unfinished and went away, and I didn't know whether it was because he didn't want to tell me she was dying or because he simply didn't know enough English to say what he meant.

I waited an hour I couldn't endure again. At the end of it another doctor came, a tall gray-haired man with a fine-boned face.

"You wish to know about Signora Barzini?" His English was perfect, his voice quiet and very precise.

I nodded, unable to ask.

"We have cleaned and dressed her wound. The bullet passed straight through her lung, breaking a rib on the way out. The lung was collapsed. The air from it, and also a good deal of blood, had passed into the chest cavity. It was necessary to remove the air and blood at once so that the lung would have room to inflate again, and we have done that." He was coolly clinical.

"May I . . . may I see her?"

"Later," he said, without considering it. "She is unconscious from the anesthetic and she is in the postoperative unit. You may see her later."

"And . . . the future?"

He half smiled. "There is always danger in such a case, but with good care she could certainly recover. The bullet itself hit nothing immediately fatal; none of the big blood vessels. If it had, she would have died soon, in the street. The longer she lived, the better were her chances."

"She seemed to get worse," I said, not daring to believe him.

"In some ways that was so," he explained patiently. "Her injury was very painful, she was bleeding internally, and she was suffering from the onset of shock, which as you may know is a physical condition often as dangerous as the original damage."

I nodded, swallowing.

"We are dealing with all those things. She is young and healthy, which is good, but there will be more pain and there may be difficulties. I can give you no assurances. It is too soon for that. But hope, yes definitely, there is considerable hope."

"Thank you," I said dully, "for being so honest."

He gave his small smile again. "Your name is Henry?"

I nodded.

"You have a brave girl," he said.

If I couldn't see her yet, I thought, I would have to go and talk to the police. They had said to be with them by four and it was already twenty past; not that that mattered a jot.

I was so unused to thinking in the terms of the strange half-world into which I had stumbled that I failed to take the most elementary precautions. Distraught about Gabriella, it didn't even cross my mind that if I had been found and shot at in a distant back street I was equally vulnerable outside the hospital.

There was a taxi standing in the forecourt, the driver reading a newspaper. I waved an arm at him, and he folded the paper, started the engine and drove over. I gave him the paper with the address the policeman had written out for me, and he looked at it in a bored sort of way and nodded. I opened the cab door and got in. He waited politely till I was settled, his head half turned, and then drove smoothly out of the hospital gates. Fifty yards away he turned right down a tree-lined secondary road beside the hospital, and fifty yards down there he stopped. From a tree one yard from the curb a lithe figure peeled itself, wrenched open the nearest door, and stepped inside.

He was grinning fiercely, unable to contain his triumph. The gun with the silencer grew in his hand as if born there. I had walked right into his ambush.

Billy the Kid.

"You took your bloody time, you stinking bastard," he said.

I looked at him blankly, trying to keep the shattering dismay from showing. He sat down beside me and shoved his gun into my ribs, just above the line it had already drawn there.

"Get cracking, Vittorio," he said. "His effing Lordship is late."

The taxi rolled smoothly away and gathered speed.

"Four o'clock we said," said Billy, grinning widely. "Didn't you get the message?"

"The police. . . ." I said weakly.

"Hear that, Vittorio?" Billy laughed. "The hospital thought you were the police. Fancy that. How extraordinary."

I looked away from him, out of the window on my left.

"You just try it," Billy said. "You'll have a bullet through you before you get the door open."

I looked back at him.

"Yeah," he grinned. "Takes a bit of swallowing, don't it, for you to have to do what I say. Sweet, I call it. And believe me, matey, you've hardly bloody started."

I didn't answer. It didn't worry him. He sat sideways, the gloating grin fixed like a rictus.

"How's the bird . . . Miss what's her name?" He flicked his fingers. "The girl friend."

I did some belated thinking.

I said stonily, "She's dead."

"Well, well," said Billy gleefully. "How terribly sad. Do you hear that, Vittorio? His Lordship's bit of skirt has passed on."

Vittorio's head nodded. He concentrated on his driving, mostly down side streets, avoiding heavy traffic. I stared numbly at the greasy back of his neck and wondered what chance I had of grabbing Billy's gun before he pulled the trigger. The answer to that, I decided, feeling its steady pressure against my side, was none.

"Come on now, come on," said Billy. "Don't you think I'm clever?"

I didn't answer. Out of the corner of my eye I sensed the grin change from triumph to vindictiveness.

"I'll wipe that bloody superior look off your face," he said. "You sodding blue-arsed——"

I said nothing. He jerked the gun hard into my ribs.

"You just wait, your high and mighty Lordship, you just bloody well wait."

There didn't in fact seem to be much else I could do. The taxi bowled steadily on, leaving the city center behind.

"Hurry it up, Vittorio," said Billy. "We're late."

Vittorio put his foot down and we drove on away from the town and out into an area of scrubland. The road twisted twice and then ran straight, and I stared in astonishment and disbelief at what lay ahead at the end of it. It was the broad open sweep of Malpensa Airport. We had approached it from the side road leading away from the loading bay, the road the horseboxes sometimes took.

The DC-4 stood there on the tarmac less than a hundred yards away, still waiting to take four mares back to England. Vittorio stopped the taxi fifty yards from the loading area. "Now," said Billy to me, enjoying himself again, "you listen and do as you are told, otherwise I'll put a hole in you. And it'll be in the breadbasket, not the heart. That's a promise." I didn't doubt him. "Walk down the road, straight across to the plane, up the ramp and into the toilet. Get it? I'll be two steps behind you, all the way."

I was puzzled, but greatly relieved. I had hardly expected such a mild end to the ride. Without a word I opened the door and climbed out. Billy wriggled agilely across and stood up beside me, the triumphant sneer reasserting itself on his babyish mouth.

"Go on," he said.

There was no one about at that side of the airfield. Four hundred yards ahead there were people moving round the main building, but four hundred yards across open tarmac looked a very long way. Behind lay scrubland and the taxi. Mentally shrugging, I followed Billy's instructions, walked down the short stretch of road, across to the plane, and up the ramp. Billy stalked a steady two paces behind me, too far to touch, too near to miss.

At the top of the ramp stood Yardman. He was frowning heavily, though his eyes were as usual inscrutable behind the glasses, and he was tapping his watch.

"You've cut it very fine," he said in annoyance. "Another quarter of an hour and we'd have been in trouble."

My chief feeling was still of astonishment and unreality. Billy broke the bubble, speaking over my shoulder.

"Yeah, he was dead late coming out of the hospital. Another five minutes, and we'd have had to go in for him."

My skin rose in goose pimples. The ride had after all led straight to the heart of things. The pit yawned before me.

"Get in then," Yardman said. "I'll go and tell the pilot our wandering boy has at last returned from lunch and we can start back for England." He went past us and down the ramp, hurrying.

Billy sniggered. "Move, your effing Lordship," he said. "Open the toilet door and go in. The one on the left." The pistol jabbed against the bottom of my spine. "Do as you're told."

I walked the three necessary steps, opened the left-hand door, and went in.

"Put your hands on the wall," said Billy. "Right there in front of you, so that I can see them."

I did as he said. He swung the door shut behind him and leaned against it. We waited in silence. He sniggered complacently from time to time, and I considered my blind stupidity.

Yardman. Yardman transports men. Simon had fought through to a conclusion, where I had only gone halfway. Billy's smoke screen had filled my eyes. I hadn't seen beyond it to Yardman. And instead of grasping from Simon's message and my own memory that it had to be Yardman too, I had kissed Gabriella and lost the thread of it. And five minutes later she had been bleeding on the pavement. . . .

I shut my eyes and rested my forehead momentarily against the wall. Whatever the future held it meant nothing to me if Gabriella didn't live.

After a while Yardman returned. He rapped on the door and Billy moved over to give him room to come in.

"They're all coming across, now," he said. "We'll be away shortly. But before we go . . . how about the girl?"

"Croaked," said Billy laconically.

"Good," Yardman said. "One less job for Vittorio."

My head jerked.

"My dear boy," said Yardman. "Such a pity. Such a nice girl too." In quite a different voice he said to Billy, "Your shooting was feeble. You are expected to do better than that."

"Hey," there was a suspicion of a whine in Billy's reply. "They started running."

"You should have been closer."

"I *was* close. Close enough. Ten yards at the most. I was waiting in a doorway, ready to pump it into them just after they'd passed me. And then they just sudddenly started running. I got the girl all right, though, didn't I? I mean, I got her, even if she lingered a bit, like. As for him, well, granted I did miss him, but she sort of swung round and knocked him over just as I pulled the trigger."

"If Vittorio hadn't been with you . . . " Yardman began coldly.

"Well, he was with me, then, wasn't he?" Billy defended himself. "After all, it was me that told him to worm into that crowd round the girl and keep his ears flapping. Granted it was Vittorio who heard the police telling this creep to go and see them straight from the hospital, but it was me that thought of ringing up the hospital and winkling him out. And anyway, when I rang you up the second time, didn't you say it was just as well, you could do with him back here alive as you'd got a use for him?"

"All right," said Yardman. "It's worked out all right, but it was still very poor shooting."

He opened the door, letting in a brief murmur of people moving the ramp away, and closed it behind him. Billy sullenly delivered a long string of obscenity, exclusively concerned with the lower part of the body. Not one to take criticism sweetly.

The aircraft trembled as the engines started one after the other. I glanced at my watch, on a level with my eyes. If it had been much later, Patrick would have refused to take off that day. As it was, there was little enough margin for him to get back to Gatwick within fifteen hours of going on duty that morning. It was the total time which mattered, not just flying hours, with inquiries and fines to face for the merest minutes over.

"Kneel down," Billy said, jabbing me in the spine. "Keep your hands on the wall. And don't try lurching into me acccidental like when we take off. It wouldn't do you an effing bit of good."

I didn't move.

"You'll do as you're ruddy well told, matey," said Billy, viciously kicking the back of one of my knees. "Get down."

I knelt down on the floor. Billy said, "There's a good little earl," with a pleased sneer in his voice, and rubbed the snout of his pistol up and down the back of my neck.

The plane began to taxi, stopped at the perimeter for power checks, rolled forward on to the runway, and gathered speed. Inside the windowless lavatory compartment it was impossible to tell the exact moment of unstick, but the subsequent climb held me close anyway against the wall, as I faced the tail, and Billy stopped himself from overbalancing onto me by putting his gun between my shoulder blades and leaning on it. I hoped remotely that Patrick wouldn't strike an air pocket.

Up in the cockpit, as far away in the plane as one could get and no doubt furious with me for coming back so late, he would be drinking his first coffee, and peeling his first banana, a mile from imagining I could need his help. He completed a long climbing turn and after a while leveled off and reduced power. We were well on the first leg south to the Mediterranean.

The Mediterranean. A tremor as nasty as the one I'd had on finding Yardman at the heart of things fluttered through my chest. The DC-4 was unpressurized. The cabin doors could be opened in flight. Perhaps Billy had simply opened the door and pushed Simon out.

The traceless exit. Ten thousand feet down to the jewel-blue sea.

13

YARDMAN CAME back, edging round the door.

"It's time," he said.

Billy sniggered. "Can't be too soon."

"Stand up, stand up, my dear boy," Yardman said. "You look most undignified down there. Face the wall all the time."

As I stood up he reached out, grasping my jacket by the collar, and pulled it backward and downward. Two more jerks and it was off.

"I regret this, I do indeed," he said. "But I'm afraid we must ask you to put your hands together behind your back."

I thought that if I did I was as good as dead. I didn't move. Billy squeezed round into the small space between me and the washbasin and put the silencer against my neck.

Yardman's unhurried voice floated into my ear. "I really must warn you, my dear boy, that your life hangs by the merest thread. If Billy hadn't clumsily missed you in the street, you would be in the Milan morgue by now. If you do not do as we ask, he will be pleased to rectify his mistake immediately."

I put my hands behind my back.

"That's right," Yardman said approvingly. He tied them together with a rough piece of rope.

"Now, my dear boy," he went on. "You are going to help us. We have a little job for you."

Billy's searchlight eyes were wide and bright, and I didn't like his smile.

"You don't ask what it is," Yardman said. "So I will tell you. You are going to persuade your friend the pilot to alter course."

Alter course. Simple words. Premonition shook me to the roots. Patrick wasn't strong enough.

I said nothing. After a moment Yardman continued conversationally, "We were going to use the engineer originally, but as I find you and the pilot are good friends I am sure he will do as you ask."

I still said nothing.

"He doesn't understand," Billy sneered.

I understood all right. Patrick would do what they told him. Yardman opened the washroom door. "Turn round," he said.

I turned. Yardman's eyes fell immediately to the dried bloodstains on my shirt. He reached out a long arm, pulled the once white poplin out of my trousers and saw the bandage underneath.

"You grazed him," he said to Billy, still critical.

"Considering he was running and falling at the same time that isn't bad, not with a silencer."

"Inefficient." Yardman wasn't letting him off the hook.

"I'll make up for it," Billy said viciously.

"Yes, you do that."

Yardman turned his head back to me. "Outside, dear boy."

I followed him out of the washroom into the cabin, and stopped. It looked utterly normal. The four mares stood peacefully in the two middle boxes, installed, I presumed, by Yardman and Alf. The foremost and aft boxes were strapped down flat. There were the normal bales of hay dotted about. The noise was the normal noise, the air neither hotter nor colder than usual. All familiar. Normal. As normal as a coffin.

Yardman walked on.

"This way," he said. He crossed the small area at the back of the plane, stepped up onto the shallow platform formed by the flattened rear box, walked across it, and finished down again on the plane's floor, against the nearest box containing mares. Billy prodded his gun into my back. I joined Yardman.

"So wise, my dear boy," nodded my employer. "Stand with your back to the box."

I turned round to face the tail of the aircraft. Yardman took some time fastening my tied hands to the center banding bar round the mares' box. Billy stood up on the flattened box and amused himself by pointing his gun at various parts of my anatomy. He wasn't going to fire it. I took no notice of his antics but looked beyond him, to the pair of seats at the back. There was a man sitting there, relaxed and interested. The man who had flown out with us, whose name was John. Milan hadn't been the end of his journey, I thought. Yardman wanted to land him somewhere else.

He stood up slowly, his pompous manner a complete contradiction to his grubby ill-fitting clothes.

"Is this sort of thing really necessary?" he asked, but with curiosity, not distress. His voice was loud against the beat of the engine.

"Yes," said Yardman shortly. I turned my head to look at him. He was staring gravely at my face, the bones of his skull sharp under the stretched skin. "We know our business."

Billy got tired of waving his gun about to an unappreciative audience. He stepped off the low platform and began dragging a bale of hay into the narrow alleyway between the standing box and the flattened one, settling it firmly longwise between the two. On top of that bale he put another, and on top of that another and another. Four bales high. Jammed against these, on top of the flattened box, he raised three more, using all the bales on the plane. Together, they formed a solid wall three feet away on my left. Yardman, John and I watched him in silence.

"Right," Yardman said when he'd finished it. He checked the time and looked out of the window. "Ready?"

Billy and John said they were. I refrained from saying that I wasn't, and never would be.

All three of them went away up the plane, crouching under the luggage racks and stumbling over the guy chains. I at once discovered by tugging that Yardman knew his stuff with a rope. I couldn't budge my hands.

Jerking them in vain, I suddenly discovered Alf watching me. He had come back from somewhere up front, and was standing on my right with his customary look of missing intelligence.

"Alf," I shouted. "Untie me."

He didn't hear. He simply stood and looked at me without surprise. Without feeling. Then he slowly turned and went away. Genuinely deaf; but it paid him to be blind too, I thought bitterly. Whatever he saw he didn't tell. He had told me nothing about Simon.

I thought achingly of Gabriella hanging on to life in Milan. She must still be alive, I thought. She must. Difficulties, the doctor had said. There might be difficulties. Like infection. Like pneumonia. Nothing would matter if she died . . . but she wouldn't . . . she couldn't. Anxiety for her went so deep that it pretty well blotted out the hovering knowledge that I should spare some for myself. The odds on her survival were about even; I wouldn't have taken a hundred to one on my own.

After ten eternal minutes Yardman and Billy came back, with Patrick between them. Patrick stared at me, his face tight and stiff with disbelief. I knew exactly how he felt. Billy pushed him to the back with his gun, and Yardman pointed to the pair of seats at the back. He and Patrick sat down on them, side by side, fifteen feet away. A captive audience, I reflected sourly. Front row of the stalls.

Billy put his mouth close to my ear. "He doesn't fancy a detour, your pilot friend. Ask him to change his mind."

I didn't look at Billy, but at Patrick. Yardman was talking to him unhurriedly, but against the engine noise I couldn't hear what he said. Patrick's amber eyes looked dark in the gauntness of his face, and he shook his head slightly, staring at me beseechingly. Beseech all you like, I thought, but don't give in. I knew it was no good. He wasn't tough enough.

"Ask him," Billy said.

"Patrick," I shouted.

He could hear me. His head tilted to listen. It was difficult to get urgency and conviction across when one had to shout to be heard at all, but I did my best. "Please . . . fly back to Milan."

Nothing happened for three seconds. Then Patrick tried to stand up and Yardman pulled him back, saying something which killed the beginning of resolution in his shattered face. Patrick, for God's sake, I thought, have some sense. Get up and go.

Billy unscrewed the silencer from his gun and put it in his pocket. He carefully unbuttoned my shirt, pulled the collar back over my shoulders, and tucked the fronts round into the back of my trousers. I felt very naked and rather silly. Patrick's face grew, if anything, whiter.

Billy firmly clutched the dressing over the bullet mark and with one wrench pulled the whole thing off.

"Hey," he shouted to Yardman. "I don't call that a miss."

Yardman's reply got lost on the way back.

"Want to know something?" Billy said, thrusting his sneering face close to mine. "I'm enjoying this."

I saved my breath.

He put the barrel of his revolver very carefully against my skin, laying it flat along a rib above the existing cut. Then he pushed me round until I was half facing the wall he had made of the hay bales. "Keep still," he said. He drew the revolver four inches backward with the barrel still touching me and pulled the trigger. At such close quarters, without the silencer, the shot was a crashing explosion. The bullet sliced through the skin over my ribs and embedded itself in the wall of hay. The spit of flame from the barrel scorched in its wake. In the box behind me, the startled mares began making a fuss. It would create a handy diversion, I thought, if they were frightened into dropping their foals.

Patrick was on his feet, aghast and swaying, I heard him shouting something unintelligible to Billy, and Billy shouting back, "Only you can stop it, mate."

"Patrick," I yelled. "Go to Milan."

"That's bloody enough," Billy said. He put his gun back on my side, as before. "Keep still."

Yardman couldn't afford me dead until Patrick had flown where they wanted. I was all for staying alive as long as possible, and jerking around under the circumstances could cut me off short. I did as Billy said, and kept still. He pulled the trigger.

The flash, the crash, the burn, as before.

I looked down at myself, but I couldn't see clearly because of the angle. There were three long furrows now, parallel and fiery. The top two were beginning to bleed.

Patrick sat down heavily as if his knees had given way and put his hands over his eyes. Yardman was talking to him, clearly urging him to save me any more. Billy wasn't for waiting. He put his gun in position, told me to keep still, and shot.

Whether he intended it or not, that one went deeper, closer to the bone. The force of it spun me round hard against the mares' box and wrenched my arms, and my feet stumbled as I tried to keep my balance. The mares whinnied and skittered around, but on the whole they were getting less agitated, not more. A pity.

I had shut my eyes, that time. I opened them slowly to see Patrick and Yardman much nearer, only eight feet away on the far side of the flattened box. Patrick was staring with unreassuring horror at Billy's straight lines. Too softhearted, I thought despairingly. The only chance we had was for him to leave Billy to get on with it and go and turn back to Milan. We weren't much more than half an hour out. In half an hour we could be back. Half an hour of this. . . .

I swallowed and ran my tongue round my dry lips.

"If you go where they say," I said urgently to Patrick, "they will kill us all."

He didn't believe it. It wasn't in his nature to believe it. He listened to Yardman instead.

"Don't be silly, my dear boy. Of course we won't kill you. You will land, we will disembark, and you can all fly off again, perfectly free."

"Patrick," I said desperately. "Go to Milan."

Billy put his gun along my ribs.

"How long do you think he can keep still?" he asked, as if with genuine interest. "What'll you bet?"

I tried to say, "They shot Gabriella," but Billy was waiting for that. I got the first two words out but he pulled the trigger as I started her name, and the rest of it got lost in the explosion and my own gasping breath.

When I opened my eyes that time, Patrick and Yardman had gone.

For a little while I clung to a distant hope that Patrick would turn back, but Billy merely blew across the top of his hot revolver and laughed at me, and when the plane banked it was to the left, and not a one-eighty-degree turn. After he had straightened out I looked at the acute angle of the late afternoon sun as it sliced forward in narrow slivers of brilliance through the row of oval windows on my right.

No surprise, I thought drearily.

We were going east.

Billy had a pocket full of bullets. He sat on the flattened box, feeding his gun. The revolving cylinder broke out sideways with its axis still in line with the barrel, and an ejector rod, pushed back toward the butt, had lifted the spent cartridges out into his hand. The empty cases now lay beside him in a cluster, rolling slightly on their rims. When all the chambers were full again he snapped the gun shut and fondled it. His eyes suddenly switched up to me, the wide stare full of malice.

"Stinking earl," he said.

A la lanterne, I thought tiredly. And all that jazz.

He stood up suddenly and spoke fiercely, with some sort of inner rage.

"I'll make you," he said.

"What?"

"Ask."

"Ask what?"

"Something . . . anything. I'll make you bloody well ask me for something."

I said nothing.

"Ask," he said savagely.

I stared past him as if he wasn't there. Fights, I thought with some chill, weren't always physical.

"All right," he said abruptly. "All right. You'll ask in the end. You bloody sodding well will."

I didn't feel sure enough to say I bloody sodding well wouldn't. The taunting sneer reappeared on his face, without the same infallible confidence perhaps, but none the less dangerous for that. He nodded sharply, and went off along the alleyway toward the nose, where I hoped he'd stay.

I watched the chips of sunshine grow smaller and tried to concentrate on working out our course, more for distraction than from any hope of needing the information for a return journey. The bullets had hurt enough when Billy fired them, but the burns, as burns do, had hotted up afterwards. The force generated inside the barrel of a pistol was, if I remembered correctly, somewhere in the region of five tons. A bullet left a revolver at a rate of approximately seven hundred feet per second and if not stopped carried about five hundred yards. The explosion which drove the bullet spinning on its way also shot out flames, smoke, hot propulsive gases and burning particles of gunpowder, and at close quarters they made a very dirty mess. Knowing these charming facts was of no comfort at all. The whole ruddy area simply burned and went on burning, as if someone had stood an electric iron on it and had forgotten to switch off.

After Billy went away it was about an hour before I saw anyone again, and then it was Alf. He shuffled into my sight round the corner of the box I was tied to, and stood looking at me with one of the disposable mugs in his hand. His lined old face was, as usual, without expression.

"Alf," I shouted. "Untie me."

There wasn't anywhere to run to. I just wanted to sit down. But Alf either couldn't hear, or wouldn't. He looked unhurriedly at my ribs, a sight which as far as I could see produced no reaction in him at all. But something must have stirred somewhere, because he took a slow step forward, and being careful not to touch me, lifted his mug. It had "Alf" in red where Mike had written it that morning, in that distant sane and safe lost world of normality.

"Want some?" he said.

I nodded, half afraid he'd pour it out on the floor, as Billy would have done; but he held it up to my mouth, and let me finish it all. Lukewarm, oversweet neo-coffee. The best drink I ever had.

"Thank you," I said.

He nodded, produced the nearest he could do to a smile, and shuffled away again. Not an ally. A noncombatant, rather.

More time passed. I couldn't see my watch or trust my judgment, but I would have guessed it was getting on for two hours since we had turned. I had lost all sense of direction. The sun had gone, and we were traveling into dusk. Inside the cabin the air grew colder. I would have liked to have had my shirt on properly, not to mention a jersey, but the mares behind my back provided enough warmth to keep me from shivering. On a full load in that cramped plane eight horses generated a summer's day even with icing conditions outside, and we seldom needed the cabin heaters. It was far too much to hope in the circumstances that Patrick would think of switching them on.

Two hours' flying. We must, I thought, have been down near Albenga when we turned, which meant that since then, if we were still going east and the winds were the same as in the morning, we could have been crossing Italy somewhere north of Florence. Ahead lay the Adriatic, beyond that, Yugoslavia, and beyond that, Roumania.

It didn't matter a damn where we went, the end would be the same.

I shifted wearily, trying to find some ease, and worried for the thousandth time whether Gabriella was winning, back in Milan. The police there, I supposed, wrenching my mind away from her, would be furious I hadn't turned up. They still had my passport. There might at least be a decent investigation if I never went back for it, and Gabriella knew enough to explain what I'd inadvertently got caught up in. If she lived. If she lived. . . .

The plane banked sharply in a steep turn to the left. I leaned against the roll and tried to gauge its extent. Ninety-degree turn, I thought. No; more. It didn't seem to make much sense. But if—if—we had reached the Adriatic I supposed it was possible we were now going up it, northwest, back toward Venice . . . and Trieste. I admitted gloomily to myself that it was utter guesswork; that I was lost, and in more than one sense.

Ten minutes later the engine note changed and the volume of noise decreased. We had started going down. My heart sank with the plane. Not much time left. Oncoming night and a slow descent, the stuff of death.

There were two rows of what looked like car headlights marking each end of a runway. We circled one so steeply that I caught a glimpse of them through the tipped window, and then we leveled out for the approach and lost speed, and the plane bumped down on to a rough surface. Grass, not tarmac. The plane taxied round a bit, and then stopped. One by one the four engines died. The plane was quiet and dark, and for three long deceptive minutes at my end of it there was peace.

The cabin lights flashed on, bright overhead. The mares behind me kicked the box. Farther along, the other pair whinnied restlessly. There was a clatter in the galley, and the noise of people coming back through the plane, stumbling over the chains.

Patrick came first, with Billy after. Billy had screwed the silencer back on his gun.

Patrick went past the flattened box into the small area in front of the two washroom doors. He moved stiffly, as if he couldn't feel his feet on the floor, as if he were sleepwalking.

Billy had stopped near me, on my right.

"Turn round, pilot," he said.

Patrick turned, his body first and his legs untwisting after. He staggered slightly, and stood swaying. If his face had been white before, it was leaden gray now. His eyes were stretched and glazed with shock, and his good-natured mouth trembled.

He stared at me with terrible intensity.

"He . . . shot . . . them," he said. "Bob . . . and Mike. Bob and Mike." His voice broke on the horror of it.

Billy sniggered quietly.

"You said . . . they would kill us all." A tremor shook him. "I didn't . . . believe it."

His eyes went down to my side. "I couldn't . . ." he said. "They said they'd go on and on. . . ."

"Where are we?" I said sharply.

His eyes came back in a snap, as if I'd kicked his brain.

"Italy," he began automatically. "Southwest of. . . ."

Billy raised his gun, aiming high for the skull.

"No." I yelled at him in rage and horror at the top of my voice. "No."

He jumped slightly, but he didn't even pause. The gun coughed through the silencer and the bullet hit its target. Patrick got both his hands halfway to his head before the blackness took him. He spun on his collapsing legs and crashed headlong, face down, his long body still and silent, the auburn hair brushing against the washroom door. The soles of his feet were turned mutely up, and one of his shoes needed mending.

14

YARDMAN AND John edged round Billy and the flattened box and stood in the rear area, looking down at Patrick's body.

"Why did you do it back here?" John said.

Billy didn't answer. His gaze was fixed on me.

Yardman said mildly, "Billy, Mr. Rous-Wheeler wants to know why you brought the pilot here to shoot him?"

Billy smiled and spoke to me. "I wanted you to watch," he said.

John—Rous-Wheeler—said faintly "My God," and I turned my head and found him staring at my ribs.

"Pretty good shooting," said Billy complacently, following the direction of his eyes and taking his tone as a compliment. "There's no fat on him and the skin over his ribs is thin. See where I've got every shot straight along a bone? Neat, that's what it is. A bit of craftsmanship I'd say. These lines are what I'm talking about," he was anxious to make his point, "not all that black and red around them. That's only dried blood and powder burn."

Rous-Wheeler, to do him justice, looked faintly sick.

"All right, Billy," Yardman said calmly. "Finish him off."

Billy lifted his gun. I had long accepted the inevitability of that moment, and I felt no emotion but regret.

"He's not afraid," Billy said. He sounded disappointed.

"What of it?" Yardman asked.

"I want him to be afraid."

Yardman shrugged. "I can't see what difference it makes."

To Billy it made all the difference in the world. "Let me take a little time over him, huh? We've got hours to wait."

Yardman sighed. "All right, Billy, if that's what you want. Do all the other little jobs first, eh? Shut all the curtains in the plane first, we don't want to advertise ourselves. And then go down and tell Giuseppe to turn those landing lights off; the stupid fool's left them on. He'll have ladders and paint waiting for us. He and you and Alf can start straight away on painting out the airline's name and the plane's registration letters."

"Yeah," said Billy. "O.K. And while I'm doing it I'll think of something." He put his face close to mine, mocking. "Something special for your effing Lordship."

He put the gun in its holster and the silencer in his pocket, and drew all the curtains in the back part of the plane, before starting forward to do the rest.

Rous-Wheeler stepped over Patrick's body, sat down in one of the seats, and lit a cigarette. His hands were shaking.

"Why do you let him?" he said to Yardman. "Why do you let him do what he likes?"

"He is invaluable," Yardman sighed. "A natural killer. They're not at all common, you know. That combination of callousness and enjoyment, it's unbeatable. I let him have his way if I can as a sort of reward, because he'll kill anyone I tell him to. I couldn't do what he does. He kills like stepping on a beetle."

"He's so young," Rous-Wheeler protested.

"They're only any good when they're young," Yardman said. "Billy is nineteen. In another seven or eight years, I wouldn't trust him as I do now. And there's a risk a killer will turn maudlin any time after thirty."

"It sounds," Rous-Wheeler cleared his throat, trying to speak as unconcernedly as Yardman, "it sounds rather like keeping a pet tiger on a leash."

He began to cross his legs and his shoes knocked against Patrick's body. With an expression of distaste he said, "Can't we cover him up?"

Yardman nodded casually and went away up the plane. He came back with a gray blanket from the pile in the luggage bay, opened it out, and spread it over, covering head and all. I spent the short time that he was away watching Rous-Wheeler refuse to meet my eyes and wondering just who he was, and why he was so important that taking him beyond Milan was worth the lives of three totally uninvolved and innocent airmen.

An unremarkable-looking man of about thirty-five, with incipient bags under his eyes, and a prim mouth. Unused to the violence surrounding him, and trying to wash his hands of it. A man with his fare paid in death and grief.

When Yardman had covered Patrick, he perched himself down on the edge of the flattened box. The overhead lights shone on the bald patch on his skull and the black spectacle frames made heavy bars of shadow on his eyes and cheeks.

"I regret this, my dear boy, believe me, I regret it sincerely," he said, eyeing the result of Billy's target practice. Like Rous-Wheeler he took out a cigarette and lit it. "He really has made a very nasty mess."

But only skin-deep, if one thought about it. I thought about it. Not much good.

"Do you understand what Billy wants?" Yardman said, shaking out his match.

I nodded.

He sighed. "Then couldn't you . . . er . . . satisfy him, my dear boy? You will make it so hard for yourself, if you don't."

I remembered the stupid boast I'd made to Billy the first day I'd met him, that I could be as tough as necessary. Now that I looked like having to prove it, I had the gravest doubts.

When I didn't answer Yardman shook his head sorrowfully. "Foolish boy, whatever difference would it make, after you are dead?"

"Defeat. . . ." I cleared my throat and tried again. "Defeat on all levels."

He frowned. "What do you mean?"

"Communists are greedy," I said.

"Greedy," he echoed. "You're wandering, my dear boy."

"They like to . . . crumble . . . people, before they kill them. And that's . . . gluttony."

"Nonsense," said Rous-Wheeler in a vintage Establishment voice.

"You must have read newspaper accounts of trials in Russia," I said, raising an eyebrow. "All those 'confessions.' "

"The Russians," he said stiffly, "are a great, warm-hearted simple people."

"Oh, sure," I agreed. "And some are like Billy."

"Billy is English."

"So are you," I said. "And where are you going?"

He compressed his lips and didn't answer.

"I hope," I said, looking at the blanket which covered Patrick, "that your travel agents have confirmed your belief in the greatness, warm-heartedness and simplicity of the hemisphere you propose to join."

"My dear boy," interrupted Yardman smoothly, "what eloquence!"

"Talking," I explained, "takes the mind off . . . this and that."

A sort of recklessness seemed to be running in my blood, and my mind felt clear and sharp. To have even those two to talk to was suddenly a great deal more attractive than waiting for Billy on my own.

"The end justifies the means," said Rous-Wheeler pompously, as if he'd heard it somewhere before.

"Crap," I said inelegantly. "You set yourself too high."

"I am . . ." he began angrily, and stopped.

"Go on" I said. "You are what? Feel free to tell me. Moriturus, and all that."

It upset him, which was pleasant. He said stiffly, "I am a civil servant."

"Were," I pointed out.

"Er, yes."

"Which ministry?"

"The Treasury," he said, with the smugness of those accepted in the inner of inner sanctums.

The Treasury. It was a stopper, that one.

"What rank?" I asked.

"Principal." There was a grudge in his voice. He hadn't risen.

"And why are you defecting?"

The forthcomingness vanished. "It's none of your business."

"Well it is rather," I said in mock apology, "since your change of allegiance looks like its having a fairly decisive effect on my future."

He looked mulish and kept silent.

"I suppose," I said with mild irony, "you are going where you think your talents will be appreciated."

For a second he looked almost as spiteful as Billy. A petty-minded man I thought, full of imagined slights, ducking the admission that he wasn't as brilliant as he thought he was. None of that lessened one jot the value of the information he carried in his head.

"And you," I said to Yardman. "Why do you do it? All this."

He looked back gravely, the tight skin pulling over his shut mouth.

"Ideology?" I suggested.

He tapped ash off his cigarette, made a nibbling movement with his lip, and said briefly, "Money."

"The brand of goods doesn't trouble you, as long as the carriage is paid?"

"Correct," he said.

"A mercenary soldier. Slaughter arranged. Allegiance always to the highest bidder?"

"That," he said, inclining his head, "is so."

It wasn't so strange, I thought inconsequentially, that I'd never been able to understand him.

"But believe me, my dear boy," he said earnestly, "I never really intended you any harm. Not you."

"Thanks," I said dryly.

"When you asked me for a job I nearly refused you . . . but I didn't think you'd stay long, and your name gave my agency some useful respectability, so I agreed." He sighed. "I must admit, you surprise me. You were very good at that job, if it's of any comfort to you. Very good. Too good. I should have stopped it when your father died, when I had the chance, before you stumbled on anything . . . it was selfish of me. Selfish."

"Simon Searle stumbled," I reminded him. "Not me."

"I fear so," he agreed without concern. "A pity. He too was invaluable. An excellent, accurate man. Very hard to replace."

"Would you be so good as to untuck my shirt?" I said. "I'm getting cold."

Without a word he stood up, came round, tugged the bunched cloth out of the back of my trousers and pulled the collar and shoulders back to their right place. The shirt fronts fell together edge to edge, the light touch of the cloth on the burns being more than compensated by the amount of cool air shut out.

Yardman sat down again where he had been before and lit another cigarette from the stub of the first, without offering one to Rous-Wheeler.

"I didn't mean to bring you on this part of the trip," he said. "Believe me, my dear boy, when we set off from Gatwick I intended to organize some little delaying diversion for you in Milan, so that you wouldn't embark on the trip back."

I said bleakly, "Do you call sh . . . shooting my girl a little diversion?"

He looked distressed. "Of course not. Of course not. I didn't know you had a girl until you introduced her. But then I thought it would be an excellent idea to tell you to stay with her for a day or two, that we could easily manage without you on the way back. He," he nodded at Patrick's shrouded body, "told me you were . . . er . . . crazy about her. Unfortunately for you, he also told me how assiduous you had been in searching for Searle. He told me all about that bottle of pills. Now, my dear boy, that was a risk we couldn't take."

"Risk," I said bitterly.

"Oh yes, my dear boy, of course. Risk is something we can't afford in this business. I always act on risk. Waiting for certain knowledge may be fatal. And I was quite right in this instance, isn't that so? You had told me yourself where you were going to lunch, so I instructed Billy to go and find you and follow you from there, and make sure it was all love's young dream and no excitement. But you went bursting out of the restaurant and off at high speed to an obscure little bakery. Billy followed you in Vittorio's cab and rang me up from near there." He spread his hands. "I told him to kill you both and search you under cover of helping, as soon as you came out."

"Without waiting to find out if there was anything in the bottle except pills?"

"Risk," he nodded. "I told you. We can't afford it. And that reminds me; where is Searle's message?"

"No message," I said wearily.

"Of course there was, my dear boy," he chided. "You've shown so little surprise, asked so few questions. It was clear to me at once that you knew far too much when Billy brought you back to the plane. I have experience in these things, you see.''

I shrugged a shoulder. ''In my wallet,'' I said.

He drew on his cigarette, gave me an approving look, stepped over Patrick, and fetched my jacket from the washroom. He took everything out of the wallet and spread the contents beside him on the flattened box. When he picked out the hundred-dinar note and unfolded it, the pieces of writing paper and hay fell out.

He fingered the note. ''It was plain carelessness on Billy's part,'' he said. ''He didn't hide the canisters properly.''

''There was a lot of money, then, on the plane?''

''Wheels have to be oiled,'' Yardman said reasonably, ''and it's no good paying Yugoslavs in sterling. All agents insist on being paid in the currency they can spend without arousing comment. I do, myself.''

I watched him turn the scrap of his stationery over and over, frowning. He saw the pin holes in the end, and held them up to the light. After a few seconds he put it down and looked from me to Rous-Wheeler.

''Men,'' he said without inflection. ''And when you read that, my dear boy, you understood a great deal.'' A statement, not a question.

Gabriella, I thought dumbly, for God's sake live. Live and tell. I shut my eyes and thought of her as she had been at lunch. Gay and sweet and vital. Gabriella my dearest love. . . .

''Dear boy,'' said Yardman in his dry unconcerned voice, ''are you feeling all right?''

I opened my eyes and shut Gabriella away out of reach of his frightening intuition.

''No,'' I said with truth.

Yardman actually laughed. ''I like you, my dear boy, I really do. I shall miss you very much in the agency.''

''Miss. . . .'' I stared at him. ''You are going back?''

''Of course.'' He seemed surprised, then smiled his bony smile. ''How could you know; I was forgetting. Oh yes, of course we're going back. My transport system . . . is . . . er . . . much needed, and much appreciated. Yes. Only the plane and Mr. Rous-Wheeler are going on.''

''And the horses?'' I asked.

''Those too,'' he nodded. ''They carry good blood lines, those mares. We expected to have to slaughter them, but we have heard they will be acceptable alive, on account of their foals. No, my dear boy, Billy and I go back by road, halfway with Giuseppe, the second half with Vittorio.''

''Back to Milan?''

''Quite so. And tomorrow morning we learn the tragic news that the plane we missed by minutes this afternoon has disappeared and must be presumed lost with all souls, including yours, my dear boy, in the Mediterranean.''

''There would be a radar trace. . . .'' I began.

''My dear boy, we are professionals.''

''Oiled wheels?'' I said ironically.

''So quick,'' he said nodding. ''A pity I can't tempt you to join us.''

''Why can't you?'' said Rous-Wheeler truculently.

Yardman answered with slightly exaggerated patience. "What do I offer him?"

"His life," Rous-Wheeler said with an air of triumph.

Yardman didn't even bother to explain why that wouldn't work. The Treasury, I thought dryly, really hadn't lost much.

Billy's voice suddenly spoke from the far end of the plane.

"Hey, Mr. Yardman," he called. "Can't you and Mr. Rous-flipping-Wheeler come and give us a hand? This ruddy airplane's bloody covered with names and letters. We're practically having to paint the whole sodding crate."

Yardman stood up. "Yes, all right," he said.

Rous-Wheeler didn't want to paint. "I don't feel . . ." he began importantly.

"And you don't want to be late," Yardman said flatly.

He stood aside to let the deflated Rous-Wheeler pass, and they both made their way up past the two boxes, through the galley, and down the telescopic ladder from the forward door.

Desperation can move mountains. I'd never hoped to have another minute alone to put it to the test, but I'd thought of a way of detaching myself from the mares' box, if I had enough strength. Yardman had had difficulty squeezing the rope down between the banding bar and the wooden box side when he'd tied me there; he'd had to push it through with the blade of his penknife. It wouldn't have gone through at all, I thought, if either the box side wasn't a fraction warped or the bar a shade bent. Most of the bars lay flat and tight along the boxes, with no space at all between them.

I was standing less than two feet from the corner of the box, and along at the corner the bar was fastened by a lynch pin.

I got splinters in my wrists, and after I'd moved along six inches I thought I'd never manage it. The bar and the box seemed to come closer together the farther I went, and jerking the rope along between them grew harder and harder, until at last it was impossible. I shook my head in bitter frustration. Then I thought of getting my feet to help, and bending my knee put my foot flat on the box as high behind me as I could get leverage. Thrusting back with my foot, pulling forward on the bar with my arms, and jerking my wrists sideways at the same time, I moved along a good inch. It worked. I kept at it grimly and finally arrived at the last three inches. From there, twisting, I could reach the lynch pin with my fingers. Slowly, agonizingly slowly, I pushed it up from the bottom, transferred my weak grip to the rounded top, slid it fraction by fraction up in my palm, and with an enormous sense of triumph felt it come free. The iron bands parted at the corner, and it required the smallest of jerks to tug the rope out through the gap.

Call that nothing, I said to myself with the beginnings of a grin. All that remained was to free my hands from each other.

Yardman had left my jacket lying on the flattened box, and in my jacket pocket was a small sharp penknife. I sat down on the side of the shallow platform, trying to pretend to myself that it wasn't because my legs were buckling at the knees but only the quickest way to reach the jacket. The knife was there, slim and familiar. I clicked open the blade, gripped it firmly, and sawed away blindly at some unseen point between my wrists. The friction of dragging the rope along had frayed it helpfully, and before I'd begun to hope for it I felt the strands stretch and give, and in two more seconds my hands were free. With stiff shoulders I brought them round in front of me. Yardman had no personal brutality and hadn't tied tight enough to stop the blood. I flexed my fingers and they were fine.

Scooping up wallet and jacket I began the bent walk forward under the luggage rack and over the guy chains, stepping with care so as not to make a noise and fetch the five outdoor decorators in at the double. I reached the galley safely and went through it. In the space behind the cockpit I stopped dead for a moment. The body of Mike the engineer lay tumbled in a heap against the left-hand wall.

Tearing both mind and eyes away from him I edged toward the way out. On my immediate right I came first to the luggage bay, and beyond that lay the door. The sight of my overnight bag in the bay made me remember the black jersey inside it. Better than my jacket, I thought. It had a high neck, was easier to move in, and wouldn't be so heavy on my raw skin. In a few seconds I had it on, and had transferred my wallet to my trousers.

Five of them round the plane, I thought. The exit door was ajar, but when I opened it the light would spill out, and for the time it took to get onto the ladder they would be able to see me clearly. Unless by some miracle they were all over on the port side, painting the tail. Well, I thought coldly, I would just be unlucky if the nearest to me happened to be Billy with his gun.

It wasn't Billy, it was the man I didn't know, Giuseppe. He was standing at the root of the starboard wing painting out the airline's name on the fuselage, and he saw me as soon as I opened the door not far below him. I pulled the door shut behind me and started down the ladder, hearing Giuseppe shouting and warning all the others. They had ladders to get down too, I thought. I could still make it.

Giuseppe was of the hard core, a practicing militant Communist. He was also young and extremely agile. Without attempting to reach a ladder he ran along the wing to its tip, put his hands down, swung over the edge, and dropped ten feet to the ground. Seeing his running form outlined on the wing against the stars I veered away to the left as soon as I had slid down the ladder, and struck out forward, more or less on the same axis as the plane.

My eyes weren't accustomed to the light as theirs were. I couldn't see where I was going. I heard Giuseppe shouting in Italian, and Yardman answering. Billy tried a shot which missed by a mile. I scrambled on, holding my arms up defensively and hoping I wouldn't run into anything too hard. All I had to do, I told myself, was to keep going. I was difficult to see in black and moved silently over the grass of the field. If I got far enough from the plane they wouldn't be able to find me, not five of them with Alf no better than a snail. Keep going and get lost. After that I'd have all night to search out a bit of civilization and someone who could speak English.

The field seemed endless. Endless. And running hurt. What the hell did that matter, I thought dispassionately, with Billy behind me. I had also to refrain from making a noise about it in case they should hear me, and with every rib-stretching breath that got more difficult. In the end I stopped, went down on my knees, and tried to get air in shallow silent gulps. I could hear nothing behind but a faint breeze, see nothing above but the stars, nothing ahead but the dark. After a few moments I stood up again and went on, but more slowly. Only in nightmares did fields go on forever. Even airfields.

At the exact second that I first thought I'd got away with it, bright white lights blazed out and held me squarely in their beams. A distant row of four in front, a near row of four behind, and I a black figure in the flarepath. Sick, devastating understanding flooded through me. I had been trying to escape down the runway.

Sharply, almost without missing a step, I wheeled left and sprinted; but Giuseppe wasn't very far behind after all. I didn't see or hear him until the last moment when he closed in from almost in front. I swerved to avoid him, and he threw out his leg at a low angle and tripped me up.

Even though I didn't fall very heavily, it was enough. Giuseppe very slickly put one of his feet on each side of my head and closed them tight on my ears. Grass pressed into my eyes, nose and mouth, and I couldn't move in the vise.

Billy came up shouting as if with intoxication, the relief showing with the triumph.

"What you got there then, my friend? A bleeding aristocrat, then? Biting the dust, too, ain't that a gas?"

I guessed with a split second to spare what he would do, and caught his swinging shoe on my elbow instead of my ribs.

Yardman arrived at a smart military double.

"Stop it," he said. "Let him get up."

Giuseppe stepped away from my head and when I put my hands up by my shoulders and began to push myself up, Billy delivered the kick I had avoided before. I rolled half over, trying not to care. The beams from the runway lights shone through my shut eyelids, and the world seemed a molten river of fire, scarlet and gold.

Without, I hoped, taking too long about it I again started to get up. No one spoke. I completed the incredibly long journey to my feet and stood there, quiet and calm. We were still on the runway between the distant lights, Yardman close in front of me, Giuseppe and Billy behind, with Rous-Wheeler struggling breathlessly up from the plane. Yardman's eyes, level with mine, were lit into an incandescent greenness by the glow. I had never clearly seen his eyes before. It was like drawing back curtains and looking into a soul.

A soldier without patriotism. Strategy, striking power and transport were skills he hired out, like any other craftsman. His pride was to exercise his skill to the most perfect possible degree. His pride overrode all else.

I think he probably meant it when he said he liked me. In a curious way, though I couldn't forgive him Gabriella, I felt respect for him, not hatred. Battle against him wasn't personal or emotional, as with Billy. But I understood that in spite of any unexpected warmth he might feel, he would be too prudent to extend foolish mercy to the enemy.

We eyed each other in a long moment of cool appraisal. Then his gaze slid past me, over my shoulder, and he paid me what was from his point of view a compliment.

"You won't crack him, Billy. Kill him now. One shot, nice and clean."

15

I OWED my life to Billy's greed. He was still hungry, still unsatisfied, and he shook his head to Yardman's request. Seeing the way Yardman delicately deferred to Billy's wishes it struck me that Rous-Wheeler's simile of a tiger on a leash might not be too far off the mark. In any case for the first time I was definitely glad of Billy's lust to spill my blue blood ounce by ounce, as I really was most averse to being shot down on the spot; and I acknowledged that I already had him to thank that I was still breathing at all. If I'd been anyone but who I was I would have died with the crew.

We walked back up the runway, I in front, the other four behind. I could hear Rous-Wheeler puffing, the only one not physically fit. Fit. . . . It was only yesterday, I thought incredulously, that I rode in the Gold Cup.

The plane was a faintly lit shape to the left of the end of the runway. A hundred yards short of it Yardman said, "Turn left, dear boy. That's it. Walk straight on. You will see a building. Go in."

There was, in fact, a building. A large one. It resembled an outsize prefabricated garage, made of asbestos sheets on a metal frame. The door was ajar and rimmed by light. I pushed it open, and with Billy's gun touching my back, walked in.

The right-hand two-thirds of the concrete floor space was occupied by a small four-seater single-engined airplane, a new-looking high-winged Cessna with an Italian registration. On its left stood a dusty black Citroën, its bonnet toward me. Behind the car and the plane the whole far wall consisted of sliding doors. No windows anywhere. Three metal girders rose from floor to ceiling on the left of the car, supporting the flat roof and dividing the left-hand part of the hangar into a kind of bay. In that section stood Alf.

"Right," said Yardman briskly. "Well done, Alf, turn them off now." His voice echoed hollowly in space.

Alf stared at him without hearing.

Yardman went up to him and shouted in his ear. "Turn the runway lights off."

Alf nodded, walked up to the wall on the left of the door I had come in by, and pushed up a heavy switch beside a black fuse box. A second similar box worked, I suppose, the fluorescent strips across the ceiling and the low-powered radiant heaters mounted high on both side walls. Beside the switches stood a mechanic's bench with various tools and a vise, and farther along two sturdy brackets held up a rack of gardening implements; spades, fork, rake, hoe and shears. Filling all the back of the bay was a giant motor mower with a seat for the driver, and dotted about there were some five-gallon petrol cans, funnels, tins of paint, an assortment of overalls and several greasy-looking metal chairs.

That Cessna, I thought briefly; I could fly it like riding a bicycle. And the car . . . if only I had known they were there.

Yardman searched among the clutter on the bench and produced a length of chain and two padlocks, one large, one small. Billy had shut the door and was standing with his back to it, the gun pointing steadily in my direction. Alf, Rous-Wheeler and Giuseppe had prudently removed themselves from his line of fire.

Yardman said, "Go over to that first girder, my dear boy, and sit down on the floor."

To say I was reluctant to be tied again is to put it mildly. It wasn't only that it was the end of any hope of escape, but I had a strong physical repugnance to being attached to things, the result of having been roped to a fir in a Scottish forest one late afternoon in a childhood game by some cousins I was staying with; they had run away to frighten me and got lost themselves, and it had been morning before the subsequent search had found me.

When I didn't obey at once, Yardman, Giuseppe and Billy all took a step forward as if moved by the same mind. There was no percentage in having them jump on me; I was sore enough already. I walked over to the girder and sat down facing them, leaning back idly against the flat metal surface.

"That's better," Yardman said. He came round and knelt down on the ground at my back. "Hands behind, my dear boy."

He twined the chain round my wrists and clicked on both padlocks. Tossing the keys on his palm he stood up and came round in front of me. All five of them stared down with varying degrees of ill-feeling and I stared glassily back.

"Right," said Yardman after a pause. "We'd better get out and finish the painting. But this time we must leave someone with him, just in case." He reviewed his available troops, and alighted on Rous-Wheeler. "You sit here," he said to him, picking up a chair and taking it over beside the switches, "and if he does anything you aren't sure about, switch on the runway lights and we'll come at once. Clear?"

Rous-Wheeler was delighted to avoid any more painting and accepted his new task with enthusiasm.

"Good." Yardman looked at his watch. "Go on then, Billy." Billy, Alf and Giuseppe filed out and Yardman stopped as he followed them to say to Rous-Wheeler, "The cargo will be arriving soon. Don't be alarmed."

"Cargo?" said Rous-Wheeler in surprise.

"That's right," Yardman said. "Cargo. The reason for this . . . um . . . operation."

"But I thought I . . ." began Rous-Wheeler.

"My dear Rous-Wheeler, no," said Yardman. "Had it been just you, I could have sent you down the usual discreet pipeline from Milan. Your journey would have been just as secret as it is now. No, we needed the plane for a rather special cargo, and as you know, my dear boy," he swung round to speak directly to me with a small ironic smile, "I do hate wasting space on flights. I always try to make up a full load, so as not to neglect an opportunity."

"What is this cargo, then?" asked Rous-Wheeler with a damaged sense of self-importance.

"Mm?" said Yardman, putting the padlock keys down on the bench. "Well now, it's the brain child of a brilliant little research establishment near Brescia. A sort of machine. An interesting little development, one might say. Broadly speaking, it's a device for emitting ultrasonic rays on the natural frequency of any chosen mineral substance."

"Ultrasonics have been extensively researched," Rous-Wheeler said testily.

Yardman smiled tightly. "Take it from me, dear fellow, this particular development has great possibilities. Our friends have been trying to arrange photographs of the drawings and specifications, but these have been too well guarded. It proved easier in the end to . . . er . . . remove some vital parts of the device itself. But that of course presented a transport problem, a difficult transport problem, requiring my own personal supervision." He was talking for my benefit as much as Rous-Wheeler's, letting me know how expert he was at his job. "Once we were committed to the plane, of course it was the easiest way to take you too."

No opportunity wasted. But he hadn't originally intended to take me as well, to give him his due.

Yardman went out of the hangar. Rous-Wheeler sat on his hard chair and I on the hard conrete and again my presence and/or predicament embarrassed him.

"Played any good wall games lately?" I said at length.

A hit, a palpable hit. He hadn't expected any needling school chums on his little trip. He looked offended.

"Have you been to . . . er . . . wherever you're going . . . before?" I asked.

"No," he said shortly. He wouldn't look at me.

"And do you speak the language?"

He said stiffly, "I am learning."

"What are they offering you?"

Some heavy smugness crept into his manner. "I am to have a flat and a car, and a better salary. I will of course be in an important advisory position."

"Of course," I said dryly.

He flicked me his first glance. Disapproving.

"I am to be a consultant interpreter of the British way of life. . . . I pride myself that in my own small way I shall be promoting better understanding between two great peoples and making a positive contribution to the establishment of fruitful relations."

He spoke as if he really meant it; and if he were as self-satisfied as that, he wouldn't consider turning round and going back. I tried again without success to do a Houdini on Yardman's chain job, and Rous-Wheeler watched me.

"What branch of the Treasury were you in?" I said, giving it up.

"Initial Finance," he replied stiffly.

"What does that mean?"

"Grants."

"You mean, your department settles who gets grants of public money, and how much?"

"That is so."

"Development, research, defense, and so on?"

"Precisely."

"So that you personally would know what projects are in hand . . . or contemplated?"

"Yes."

They wouldn't have bothered with him, I supposed, for any less.

After a pause, I said, "What about this ultrasonic transmitter?"

"What about it? It isn't a British project, if that's what you mean."

"Did I get it right . . . that it will emit waves on the natural frequency of any mineral substance?"

"I believe that's what Yardman said," he agreed stiffly.

"It would break things . . . like sound breaks glass?"

"I am not a scientist. I've no idea." And from the tone of his voice he didn't care.

I stared gloomily at the floor and wondered what made a man change his allegiance. Rous-Wheeler might have been self-important and disappointed and have refused to face his own limitations, but thousands of men were like that, and thousands of men didn't give away a slice of their nation's future in return for a flat, a car, and a pat on the back. There had to be more to it. Deep obsessive murky convoluted motives I couldn't guess at, pushing him irresistibly over. But he would be the same man wherever he went; in five years or less, again disgruntled and passed over. A useless, dispensable piece of flotsam.

He, it appeared, took as pessimistic a view of my future as I of his.

"Do you think," he cleared his throat. "Do you think Billy will really kill you?"

"Be your age," I said. "You saw what he did to the crew."

"He keeps putting it off," he said.

"Saving the icing till last."

"How can you be so frivolous?" he exclaimed. "Your position is very serious."

"So is yours," I said. "And I wouldn't swap."

He gave me a small pitying smile of contemptuous disbelief, but it was true enough. Everyone dies sometime, as Simon had once said, and one was probably as little eager at eighty as at twenty-six. And there really were, I reflected with a smile for Victorian melodramas, fates worse than death.

A heavy van or lorry of some sort pulled up with a squeak of brakes somewhere near the door and after a few moments its driver came into the hangar. He was like Giuseppe, young, hard, cold-eyed and quick. He looked at me without apparent surprise and spoke to Rous-Wheeler in rapid Italian, of which the only intelligible word as far as I was concerned was Brescia.

Rous-Wheeler held up a hand, palm toward the driver. "I don't understand you, my good fellow. Wait until I fetch Yardman."

This proved unnecessary as my ex-employer had already seen the lorry's arrival. Followed by his entourage carrying ladders, paint pots, brushes and overalls, Yardman came forward into the hangar and exchanged some careful salutations with the driver.

"Right,' Yardman said in English to Billy. "There should be several small light cases and one large heavy one. It will be easiest to load the light cases up through the forward door and stow them in the luggage bay. Then we will open the back doors, haul the heavy case in on the block and tackle, and stand it in the peat tray of the last box, the one that's now flattened. Clear?"

Billy nodded.

I opened my mouth to speak, and shut it again.

Yardman noticed. "What is it?" he said sharply.

"Nothing." I spoke listlessly.

He came over to me and looked down. Then he squatted on his haunches to peer on a level with my face.

"Oh yes, my dear boy, there is something. Now what, what?"

He stared at me as if he could read my thoughts while the calculations ticked over in his own. "You were going to tell me something, and decided not to. And I feel I really should know what it is. I feel it must be to my disadvantage, something definitely to my disadvantage, as things stand between us."

"I'll shoot it out of him," Billy offered.

"It'll be quicker if I guess it. . . . Now, what is wrong with stowing the cases the way I suggested? Ah yes, my dear boy, you know all about loading airplanes, don't you? You know what I said was wrong. . . ." He snapped his fingers and stood up. "The heavy case at the back is wrong. Billy, move the mares forward so that they occupy the two front boxes, and put the heavy case in the second to back box, and leave the rear one as it is."

"Move the mares?" Billy complained.

"Yes, certainly. The center of gravity is all-important, isn't that right, my dear boy?" He was pleased with himself, smiling. Quick as lightning. If I gave him even a thousandth of a second of suspicion that Gabriella was still alive . . .

Billy came over and stood looking down at me with a revoltingly self-satisfied smile.

"Not long now," he promised.

"Load the plane first," Yardman said. "The van has to go back as soon as possible. You can . . . er . . . have your fun when I go to fetch the pilot. And be sure he's dead by the time I get back."

"O.K.," Billy agreed. He went away with Alf, Giuseppe and the driver, and the van ground away on the short stretch to the DC-4.

"What pilot?" Rous-Wheeler asked.

"My dear Rous-Wheeler," Yardman explained with a touch of weary contempt. "How do you think the plane is going on?"

"Oh . . . Well, why did you kill the other one? He would have flown on to wherever you said."

Yardman sighed. "He would have done no such thing without Billy at hand to shoot pieces off our young friend here. And frankly, my dear fellow, quite apart from the problem of Billy's and my return journey, it would have been embarrassing for us to kill the crew in your new country. Much better here. Much more discreet, don't you think?"

"Where exactly . . . where are we?" asked Rous-Wheeler. A good question if ever there was one.

"A private landing field," Yardman said. "An elderly and respected nobelman lets us use it from time to time."

Elderly and respected; Yardman's voice held some heavy irony.

"The usual sort of blackmail?" I asked. "Filmed in a bed he had no right in?"

Yardman said "No," unconvincingly.

"What's he talking about?" Rous-Wheeler asked testily.

"I'm talking about the methods employed by your new friends," I said. "If they can't get help and information by bamboozling and subverting people like you, they do it by any form of blackmail or intimidation that comes to hand."

Rous-Wheeler was offended. "I haven't been bamboozled."

"Nuts," I said. "You're a proper sucker."

Yardman took three threatening steps toward me with the first anger he had shown. "That's enough."

"Nothing's enough," I said mildly. "What the hell do you think I have to lose?"

Yardman's glasses flashed in the light, and he looked from me to Rous-Wheeler with a taut mouth. "I have to go over to the plane, Mr. Rous-Wheeler, and I think it would be best if you came with me." He came behind me and bent down to check that his chains were still effective, which unfortunately they were. "You look so gentle, dear boy," he said into my ear. "So misleading, isn't it?"

They went away and left me alone. I had another go at the chains, tantalized by the Cessna standing so close behind me; but this time Yardman had been more careful. The girder was rooted in concrete, the chain wouldn't fray like rope, and try as I might I couldn't slide my hands out.

Little time to go, I thought. And no questions left. There wasn't much profit in knowing the answers, since in a very short while I would know nothing at all. I thought about that too. I didn't believe in any form of afterlife. To die was to finish. I'd been knocked out several times in racing falls, and death was just a knockout from which one didn't awake. I couldn't honestly say that I much feared it. I never had. Undoubtedly on my part a defect of the imagination, a lack of sensitivity. All I felt was a strong reluctance to leave the party so soon when there was so much I would have liked to do. But there was the messy business of Billy to be got through first . . . and I admitted gloomily to myself that I would have avoided that if I could have dredged up the smallest excuse.

Alf shuffled into the hangar, went across to the rack of gardening tools and took down a spade. I shouted to him, but he showed no sign of having heard, and disappeared as purposefully as he'd come.

More minutes passed. I spent them thinking about Gabriella. Gabriella alive and loving, her solemnity a crust over depths of warmth and strength. A girl for always. For what was left of always.

The lorry came back, halted briefly outside, and rumbled away into the distance. Yardman and all his crew except Alf trooped into the hangar. Giuseppe walked past me across to the sliding doors at the back and opened a space behind the Citroën. A cool draft blew in and sent the dust round in little swirls on the concrete floor, and outside the sky was an intense velvety black.

Yardman said, "Right, Billy. If the new crew are on time, we'll be back with them in a little over an hour. I want you ready to go then, immediately the plane has taken off. All jobs done. Understood?"

"O.K." Billy nodded. "Relax."

Yardman walked over and paused in front of me, looking down with a mixture of regret and satisfaction.

"Good-by, my dear boy."

"Good-by," I answered politely.

His taut mouth twisted. He looked across at Billy. "Take no chances, Billy, do you understand? You underestimate this man. He's not one of your fancy nitwits, however much you may want him to be. You ought to know that by now. And Billy, I'm warning you, I'm warning you, my dear Billy, that if you should let him escape at this stage, knowing everything that he does, you may as well put one of your little bullets through your own brain, because otherwise, rest assured, my dear Billy, I will do it for you."

Even Billy was slightly impressed by the cold menace in Yardman's usually uninflected voice. "Yeah," he said uneasily. "Well, he won't bloody escape, not a chance."

"Make sure of it." Yardman nodded, turned, and went and sat in the front passenger seat on the Citroën. Giuseppe beside him started the engine, reversed the car out of the hangar, and drove smoothly away, Yardman facing forward and not looking back. Billy slid the door shut again behind them and came slowly across the concrete, putting his feet down carefully and silently like a stalker. He stopped four paces away, and the silence slowly thickened.

Rous-Wheeler cleared his throat nervously, and it sounded loud.

Billy flicked him a glance. "Go for a walk," he said.

"A . . . walk?"

"Yeah, a walk. One foot in the front of the other." He was offensive. "Down the runway and back should just about do it."

Rous-Wheeler understood. He wouldn't meet my eyes and he hadn't even enough humanity to plead for me. He turned his back on the situation and made for the exit. So much for the old school tie.

"Now," said Billy. "Just the two of us."

16

HE WALKED cat-footed round the hangar in his quiet shoes, looking for things. Eventually he came back toward me carrying an old supple broken bicycle chain and a full flat five-gallon tin of petrol. I looked at these objects with what I hoped was fair impassiveness and refrained from asking what he intended to do with them. I supposed I would find out soon enough.

He squatted on his haunches and grinned at me, his face level with mine, the bicycle chain in one hand and the petrol can on the floor in the other. His gun was far away, on the bench.

"Ask me nicely," he said. "And I'll make it easy."

I didn't believe him anyway. He waited through my silence and sniggered.

"You will," he said. "You'll ask all right, your sodding Lordship."

He brought forward the bicycle chain, but instead of hitting me with it as I'd expected he slid it round my ankle and tied it there into two half-hitches. He had difficulty doing this but once the knots were tied the links looked like holding forever. The free end he led through the handle of the petrol can and again bent it back on itself into knots. When he had finished there was a stalk of about six inches between the knots on my ankle and those on the can. Billy picked up the can and jerked it. My leg duly followed, firmly attached. Billy smiled, well satisfied. He unscrewed the cap of the can and let some of the petrol run out over my feet and make a small pool on the floor. He screwed the cap back on, but looser.

Then he went round behind the girder and unlocked both the padlocks on my wrists. The chain fell off, but owing to a mixture of surprise and stiffened shoulders I could do nothing toward getting my hands down to undo the bicycle chain before Billy was across the bay for his gun and turning with it at the ready.

"Stand up," he said. "Nice and easy. If you don't, I'll throw this in the petrol." This, in his left hand, was a cigarette lighter, a gas lighter with a top which stayed open until one snapped it shut. The flame burned bright as he flicked his thumb.

I stood up stiffly, using the girder for support, the sick and certain knowledge of what Billy intended growing like a lump of ice in my abdomen. So much for not being afraid of death. I had changed my mind about it. Some forms were worse than others.

Billy's mouth curled. "Ask, then," he said.

I didn't. He waved his pistol slowly toward the floor. "Outside, matey. I've a little job for you to do. Careful now, we don't want a bleeding explosion in here if we can help it." His face was alight with greedy enjoyment. He'd never had such fun in his life. I found it definitely irritating.

The can was heavy as I dragged it along with slow steps to the door and through onto the grass outside. Petrol slopped continuously in small amounts through the loosened cap, leaving a highly inflammable trail in my wake. The night air was sweet and the stars were very bright. There was no moon. A gentle wind. A beautiful night for flying.

"Turn right," Billy said behind me. "That's Alf along there where the light is. Go there, and don't take too bloody long about it, we haven't got all night." He sniggered at his feeble joke.

Alf wasn't more than a tennis court away, but I was fed up with the petrol can before I got there. He had been digging, I found. A six- or seven-foot square of grass had been cut out, the turf lying along one edge in a tidy heap, and about a foot of earth had been excavated into a crumbling mound. A large torch standing on the pile of turf shone on Alf's old face as he stood in the shallow hole. He held the spade loosely and looked at Billy inquiringly.

"Go for a walk," Billy said loudly. Alf interpreted the meaning if not the words, nodded briefly, leaned the spade against the turf, stepped up on to the grass and shuffled away into the engulfing dark.

"O.K., then," said Billy. "Get in there and start digging. Any time you want to stop, you've only got to ask. Just ask."

"And if I do?"

The light shone aslant on Billy's wide bright eyes and his jeering delighted mouth. He lifted the pistol a fraction. "In the head," he said. "And I'll have bloody well beaten you, your effing bloody Lordship. And it's a pity I haven't got the whole lot like you here as well."

"We don't do any harm," I said, and wryly knew that history gave me the lie. There'd been trampling enough done in the past, and resentment could persist for centuries.

"Keep both hands on the spade," he said. "You try and untie the bicycle chain, and you've had it."

He watched me dig, standing safely out of reach of any slash I might make with the spade and snapping his lighter on and off. The smell of petrol rose sharply into my nostrils as it oozed drop by drop through the leaking cap and soaked into the ground I stood on. The earth was soft and loamy, not too heavy to move, but Billy hadn't chosen this task without careful malice aforethought. Try as I might, I found I could scarcely shift a single spadeful without in some way knocking or rubbing my arm against my side. Jersey and shirt were inadequate buffers, and every scoop took its toll. The soreness increased like a geometrical progression.

Billy watched and waited. The hole grew slowly deeper. I told myself severely that a lot of other people had had to face far worse than this, that others before me had dug what they knew to be their own graves, that others had gone up in flames for a principle . . . that it was possible, even if not jolly.

Billy began to get impatient. "Ask," he said. I threw a spadeful of earth at him in reply and very nearly ended things there and then. The gun barrel jerked up fiercely at my head, and then slowly subsided. "You'll be lucky," he said angrily. "You'll have to go down on your bloody knees."

When I was sure my feet must be below his line of sight I tugged my foot as far away from the petrol can as the chain would allow, and jammed the spade down hard on the six inches of links between the knots. It made less noise than I'd feared on the soft earth. I did it again and again with every spadeful, which apart from being slightly rough on my ankle produced no noticeable results.

"Hurry up," Billy said crossly. He flicked the lighter. "Hurry it up."

Excellent advice. Time was fast running out and Yardman would be back. I jammed the spade fiercely down and with a surge of long dead hope felt the battered links begin to split. It wasn't enough. Even if I got free of the petrol can I was still waist deep in a hole, and Billy still had his revolver; but even a little hope was better than none at all. The next slice of the spade split the chain further. The one after that severed it, but I had hit it with such force that when it broke I fell over, sprawling on hands and knees.

"Stand up," Billy said sharply. "Or I'll . . ."

I wasn't listening to him. I was acknowledging with speechless horror that the grave which was big enough for Patrick and Mike and Bob as well as myself was already occupied. My right hand had closed on a piece of cloth which flapped up through the soil. I ran my fingers along it, burrowing, and stabbed them into something sharp. I felt, and knew. A row of pins.

I stood up slowly and stared at Billy. He advanced nearly to the edge of the hole, looked briefly down, and back at me.

"Simon," I said lifelessly. "It's . . . Simon."

Billy smiled. A cold, terrible, satisfied smile.

There was no more time. Time was only the distance from his gun to my head, from his gas lighter to my petrol-soaked shoes and the leaking can at my feet. He'd only been waiting for me to find Simon. His hunger was almost assuaged.

"Well," he said, his eyes wide. "Ask. It's your last chance."

I said nothing.

"Ask," he repeated furiously. "You must."

I shook my head. A fool, I thought. I'm a bloody fool. I must be mad.

"All right," he said, raging. "If I had more time you'd ask. But if you won't . . ." His voice died, and he seemed suddenly almost as afraid as I was at what he was going to do. He hesitated, half lifting the gun instead; but the moment passed and his nerve came back, renewed and pitiless.

He flicked the lighter. The flame shot up, sharp and blazing against the night sky. He poised it just for a second so as to be sure to toss it where I couldn't catch it on the way; and in that second I bent down, picked up the petrol can, and flung it at him. The loose cap unexpectedly came right off on the way up, and the petrol splayed out in a great glittering volatile stream, curving round to meet the flame.

A split second for evasion before the world caught fire.

The flying petrol burned in the air with a great rushing noise and fell like a fountain over both the spots where Billy and I had just been standing. The can exploded with a gust of heat. The grave was a square blazing pit and flames flickered over the mound of dug-out soil like brandy on an outsize plum pudding. Five gallons made dandy pyrotechnics.

I rolled out on my back over the lip of the grave with nothing to spare before it became a crematorium, and by some blessed miracle my feet escaped becoming part of the general holocaust. More than I had hoped.

Billy was running away screaming with his coat on fire along the left shoulder and down his arm. He was making frantic efforts to get it off but he was still clinging to his gun and this made it impossible. I had to have the gun and would have fought for it, but as I went after him I saw him drop it and stagger on, tearing at his jacket buttons in panic and agony, and my spine and scalp shuddered at the terror I had escaped.

With weak knees I half stumbled, half ran for the place where the revolver had fallen. The light of the flames glinted on it in the grass, and I bent and took it into my hand, the bulbous silencer heavy on the barrel and the butt a good fit in my palm.

Billy had finally wrenched his jacket off and it lay on the ground ahead in a deserted smoldering heap. Billy himself was still on his feet and making for the hangar, running and staggering and yelling for Alf.

I went after him.

Alf wasn't in the hangar. When I reached it Billy was standing with his back to me in the place where the car had been, rocking on his feet and still yelling. I stepped through the door and shut it behind me.

Billy swung round. The left sleeve of his shirt had burned into ribbons and his skin was red and glistening underneath. He stared unbelievingly at me and then at his gun in my hand. His mouth shut with a snap; and even then he could still raise a sneer.

"You won't do it," he said panting.

"Earls' sons,' I said, "learn to shoot."

"Only birds." He was contemptuous. "You haven't the guts."

"You're wrong, Billy. You've been wrong about me from the start."

I watched the doubt creep in and grow. I watched his eyes and then his head move from side to side as he looked for escape. I watched his muscles bunch to run for it. And when I saw that he finally realized in a moment of stark astonishment that I was going to, I shot him.

17

THE CESSNA had full tanks. Hurriedly I pressed the master switch in the cockpit and watched the needles swing round the fuel gauges. All the instruments looked all right, the radio worked, and the latest date on the maintenance card was only three days old. As far as I could tell from a cursory check, the little aircraft was ready to fly. All the same . . .

Alf and Rous-Wheeler came bursting in together through the door, both of them startled and wild looking and out of breath. Back from their little walks and alarmed by the bonfire. Alf gave an inarticulate cry and hurried over to Billy's quiet body. Rous-Wheeler followed more slowly, not liking it.

"It's Billy," he said, as if stupefied. "Billy."

Alf gave no sign of hearing. They stood looking down at Billy as he lay on his back. There was a small scarlet star just left of his breastbone, and he had died with his eyes wide open, staring sightlessly up to the roof. Alf and Rous-Wheeler looked lost and bewildered.

I climbed quickly and quietly out of the Cessna and walked round its tail. They turned after a moment or two and saw me standing there not six paces away, holding the gun. I wore black. I imagine my face was grim. I frightened them.

Alf backed away two steps, and Rous-Wheeler three. He pointed a shaking arm at Billy.

"You . . . you killed him."

"Yes." My tone gave him no comfort. "And you too, if you don't do exactly as I say."

He had less difficulty in believing it than Billy. He made little protesting movements with his hands, and when I said, "Go outside; take Alf," he complied without hesitation.

Just outside the door I touched Alf's arm, pointed back at Billy and then down to where the grave was. The flames had burned out.

"Bury Billy," I shouted in his ear.

He heard me, and looked searchingly into my face. He too found no reassurance, and he was used to doing what I said. Accepting the situation with only a shade more dumb resignation than usual he went slowly back across the concrete. I watched him shut the glazing eyes with rough humane fingers, and remembered the cup of coffee he'd given me when I badly needed it. He had nothing to fear from me as long as he stayed down by the grave. He picked Billy up, swung him over his shoulder in a fireman's lift, and carried him out and away across the grass, a sturdy old horseman who should never have got caught up in this sort of thing. Any more than I should.

I stretched an arm back into the hangar and pulled down the lever which controlled the runway lights. At each end of the long strip the four powerful beams sprang out, and in that glow Alf could see where he was going and what he was going to do.

That Cessna, I thought, glancing at it, probably had a range of about six or seven hundred miles. . . .

"You," I said abruptly to Rous-Wheeler. "Go and get into the plane we came in. Go up the forward steps, back through the galley, right back through the cabin, and sit down on those seats. Understand?"

"What . . . ?" he began nervously.

"Hurry up."

He gave me another frightened glance and set off to the plane, a lumbering gray shape behind the runway lights. I walked three steps behind him and unsympathetically watched him stumble in his fear.

"Hurry," I said again, and he stumbled faster. The thought of the Citroën returning was like a devil on my tail. I was just not going to be taken again. There were five bullets left in the gun. The first for Rous-Wheeler, the next for Yardman, and after that . . . he would have Giuseppe with him, and at least two others. Not nice.

"Faster," I said.

Rous-Wheeler reached the ladder and stumbled up it, tripping over half the steps. He went awkwardly back through the plane just as I had said and flopped down panting on one of the seats. I followed him. Someone, Alf I supposed, had given the mares some hay, and one of the bales from Billy's now dismantled wall had been clipped open and split. The binding wire from it lay handy on the flattened aft box. I picked it up to use on Rous-Wheeler, but there was nothing on the comfortable upholstered double seat I could tie him to.

He made no fuss when I bound his wrists together. His obvious fear made him flabby and malleable, and his eyes looked as if he could feel shock waves from the violence and urgency which were flowing through me.

"Kneel down," I said, pointing to the floor in front of the seats. He didn't like that. Too undignified.

"Kneel," I said. "I haven't time to bother about your comfort."

With a pained expression that at any other time would have been funny he lowered himself onto his knees. I slid the ends of the wire through one of the holes in the seat anchorages on the floor, and fastened him there securely by the wrists.

"I ss . . . say," he protested.

"You're bloody lucky to be alive at all, so shut up."

He shut up. His hands were tied only a couple of feet away from the blanket which covered Patrick. He stared at the quiet mound and he didn't like that either. Serve him right, I thought callously.

"What . . . what are you going to do?" he said.

I didn't answer. I went back up the cabin, looking at the way they'd restored the cargo. Aft box still flat. The walls of the next one, dismantled, had been stacked in the starboard alley. On the peat tray now stood a giant packing case six feet long, four feet wide, and nearly five feet tall. Chains ran over it in both directions, fastening it down to the anchorages. It had rope handles all the way round, and Yardman had said something about using a block and tackle, but all the same maneuvering it into its present position must have been a tricky sweaty business. However, for the sake of forwarding the passage of this uninformative crate Yardman had also been prepared to steal a plane and kill three airmen. Those who had no right to it wanted it very badly.

I went up farther. The four mares were unconcernedly munching at full haynets and paid me scant attention. Through the galley and into the space behind the cockpit, where Mike's body still lay. Burial had been the last of the jobs. Uncompleted.

The luggage compartment held four more crates, the size of tea chests. They all had rope handles and no markings.

Beyond them was the open door. It represented to me a last chance of not going through with what I had in mind. Yardman hadn't yet come back, and the Cessna was ready. If I took it, with its radio and full tanks, I would undoubtedly be safe, and Yardman's transport business would be busted. But he'd still have the DC-4 and the packing cases. . . .

Abruptly I pulled up the telescopic ladder and shut the door with a clang. Too much trouble, I told myself, to change my mind now. I'd have to take Rous-Wheeler all the way back to the Cessna or shoot him, and neither course appealed. But the situation I found in the cockpit nearly defeated me before I began.

Billy had shot Bob as he sat, through the back of the head. The upper part of him had fallen forward over the wheel, the rest held firmly in the seat by the still fastened safety strap across his thighs. In the ordinary way even stepping into the copilot's seat in the cramped space was awkward enough, and lifting a dead man out of it bodily was beyond me. Blacking my mind to the sapping thought that this was a man I had known, and considering him solely as an object which spelled disaster to me if I didn't move it I undid the seat belt, heaved the pathetic jackknifed figure round far enough to clear his feet and head from the controls, and fastened the belt tight across him again in his new position, his back half toward me.

With the same icy concentration I sat in Patrick's place and set about starting the plane. Switches. Dozens of switches everywhere. On the control panel, on the roof, in the left side wall and in the bank of throttles on my right. Each labeled in small metal letters, and too many having to be set correctly before the plane would fly.

Patrick had shown me how. Quite different from doing it. I pared the pre-starting checks down to the barest minimum; fuel supply on, mixture rich, propeller revs maximum, throttle just open, brakes on; trimmer central, direction indicator synchronized with the compass.

My boats were burned with the first ignition switch, because it worked. The three-bladed propeller swung and ground and the inner port engine roared into action with an earsplitting clatter. Throttle too far open. Gently I pulled the long lever with its black knob down until the engine fell back to warming-up speed, and after that in quick succession and with increasing urgency I started the other three. Last, I switched on the headlights. Alf might not have heard the engines, but he would certainly see the lights. It couldn't be helped. I had to be able to see where I was going. With luck he wouldn't know what to do, and do nothing.

I throttled back a bit and took the brakes off and the plane began to roll. Too fast. Too fast. I was heading straight for the runway lights and could smash them, and I needed them alight. I pulled the two starboard throttles back for a second and the plane slued round in a sort of skid and missed the lights and rolled forward on to the runway.

The wind was behind me, which meant taxiing to the far end and turning back to take off. No one ever taxied a DC-4 faster. And at the far end I skipped all the power checks and everything else I'd been taught and swung the plane round facing the way I'd come and without a pause pushed forward all the four throttles wide open.

The great heavy plane roared and vibrated and began to gather speed with what seemed to me agonizing slowness. The runway looked too short. Grass was slower than tarmac, the strip was designed for light aircraft, and heaven alone knew the weight of that packing case. . . . For short runways, lower flaps. The answer came automatically from the subconscious, not as a clear coherent thought. I put my hand on the lever and lowered the trailing edges of the wings. Twenty degrees. Just under halfway. Full flaps were brakes. . . .

Yardman came back.

Unlike Alf, he knew exactly what to do, and wasted no time doing it. Toward the far end the Citroën was driven straight out onto the center line of the runway, and my headlights shone on distant black figures scrambling out and running toward the hangar. Swerve wide enough to miss the car, I thought, and I'll get unbalanced on rough ground and pile up. Go straight up the runway and not be able to lift off in time, and I'll hit it either with the wheels or the propellers. . . .

Yardman did what Alf hadn't. He switched off the runway lights. Darkness clamped down like a sack over the head. Then I saw that the plane's bright headlights raised a gleam on the car now frighteningly close ahead and at least gave me the direction to head for. I was going far too fast to stop, even if I'd felt like it. Past the point of no return, and still on the ground. I eased gently back on the control column, but she wouldn't come. The throttles were wide; no power anywhere in reserve. I ground my teeth and with the car coming back to me now at a hundred miles an hour hung on for precious moments I couldn't spare, until it was then or never. No point in never. I hauled back on the control column and at the same time slammed up the lever which retracted the undercarriage. Belly flop or car crash; I wasn't going to be around to have second thoughts. But the DC-4 flew. Unbelievably there was no explosive finale, just a smooth roaring upward glide. The plane's headlights slanted skyward, the car vanished beneath, the friction of the grass fell away. Airborne was the sweetest word in the dictionary.

Sweat was running down my face; part exertion, part fear. The DC-4 was heavy, like driving a fully loaded pantechnicon after passing a test on empty minis, and the sheer muscle power needed to hold it straight on the ground and get it into the air was under the circumstances exhausting. But it was up, and climbing steadily at a reasonable angle, and the hands were circling reassuringly round the clock face of the altimeter. Two thousand, three thousand, four thousand feet. I leveled out at that and closed the throttles a little as the airspeed increased to two-twenty knots. A slow old plane, built in 1945. Two-twenty was the most it could manage.

The little modern Cessna I'd left behind was just about as fast. Yardman had brought a pilot. If he too took off without checks, he could be only scant minutes behind.

Get lost, I thought. I'd the whole sky to get lost in. The headlights were out, but from habit I'd switched on the navigation lights on the wing tips and tail and also the revolving beacon over the cockpit. The circling red beam from it washed the wings alternately with pale pink light. I switched it out, and the navigation lights too. Just one more broken law in a trail of others.

The runway had been laid out from due east to west. I had taken off to the west and flown straight on, urgent to get out, regardless of where. Too easy for them. I banked tentatively to the left and felt the plane respond cumbrously, heavy on my arms. Southwest, into the wind. I straightened up and flew on, an invisible shell in the darkness, and after five minutes knew they wouldn't find me. Not with the Cessna, anyway.

The tight-strung tension of my nerves relaxed a little, with most uncomfortable results. I was suddenly far too aware of the wicked square of burn over my ribs, and realized that I hadn't really felt it since the moment I found Simon. Under the pressure of events its insistent message hadn't got through. Now it proceeded to rectify that with enthusiasm.

Weakness seeped down my limbs. I shivered, although I was still sweating from exertion. My hands started trembling on the wheel, and I began to realize the extent to which I was unfit to fly anything, let alone take a first try at an airliner way out of my normal class. But far worse than the physical stress was the mental letdown which accompanied it. It was pride which had got me into that plane and up into the air. Nothing but pride. I was still trying to prove something to Billy, even though he was dead. I hadn't chosen the DC-4 because of any passionate conviction that the ultrasonic gadget needed saving at all costs, but simply to show them, Yardman and Billy's ghost, that there wasn't much I couldn't do. Childish, vainglorious, stupid, ridiculous: I was the lot.

And now I was stuck with it. Up in the air in thundering tons of metal, going I didn't know where.

I wiped the sleeve of my jersey over my face and tried to think. Direction and height were vital if I were ever to get down again. Four thousand feet, I thought, looking at the altimeter; at that height I could fly straight into a mountain . . . if there were any. Southwest steady, but southwest from where? I hunted round the cockpit for a map of any sort, but there wasn't one to be found.

Patrick had said we were in Italy, and Giuseppe was Italian, and so was the registration on the Cessna, and the ultrasonic device had been driven straight from Brescia. Conclusive, I thought. Northern Italy, probably somewhere near the east coast. Impossible to get closer than that. If I continued southwest, in the end I'd be over the Mediterranean. And before that . . . new sweat broke out on my forehead. Between the northern plain and the Mediterranean lay the Apennines, and I couldn't remember at all how high they were. But four thousand was much too low . . . and for all I knew they were only a mile ahead. . . .

I put the nose up and opened the throttles and slowly gained height. Five thousand, six thousand, seven thousand, eight. That ought to be enough. . . . The Alps only reached above twelve thousand at the peaks, and the Apennines were a good deal lower. I was guessing. They might be higher than I thought. I went up again to ten thousand.

At that height I was flying where I had no business to be, and at some point I'd be crossing the airways to Rome. Crossing a main road in the dark, without lights. I switched the navigation lights on again, and the revolving beacon too. They wouldn't give much warning to a jetliner on a collision course, but possibly better than none.

The thunderous noise of the engines was tiring in itself. I stretched out a hand for Patrick's headset and put it on, the padded earphones reducing the din to a more manageable level. I had taken it for granted from the beginning that Yardman would have put the radio out of order before ever asking Patrick to change course, and some short tuning with the knobs confirmed it. Not a peep or crackle from the air. There had been just a chance that he wouldn't have disconnected the V.O.R.—Very high frequency Omni-Range—by which one navigated from one radio beacon to the next; it worked independently of two-way ground-to-air communication, and he might have needed to use it to find the airfield we had landed on. But that too was dead.

Time, I thought. If I didn't keep track of the time I'd be more lost than ever. I looked at my watch. Half-past eleven. I stared at the hands blankly. If they'd said half nine or half one it would have felt the same. The sort of time one measured in minutes and hours had ceased to exist in a quiet street in Milan. I shook myself. Half-past eleven. From now on it was important. Essential. Without maps or radio, time and the compass were going to decide my fate. Like all modern pilots I had been taught to stick meticulously to using all the aids and keeping all the regulations. The "seat of the pants" stuff of the pioneers was held to be unscientific and no longer necessary. This was a fine time to have to learn it from scratch.

If I'd been up for a quarter of an hour, I thought, and if I'd started from the northern plain, and if I could only remember within a hundred miles how broad Italy was, then I might have some idea of when I'd be over the sea. Not yet, anyway. There were pinpricks of lights below me, and several small clusters of towns. No conveniently lit airports with welcoming runways.

If I'd taken the Cessna, I thought wretchedly, it would have been easy. Somewhere, by twiddling the knobs, I'd have raised radio contact with the ground. The international air language was English. A piece of cake. They'd have told me my position, what course to set, how to get down, everything. But if I'd taken the Cessna, I would have had to leave the DC-4 intact, because of the mares. I'd thought at first of piling a couple more five-gallon cans under the big plane and putting a match to it, and then remembered the living half of the cargo. Yardman might be cold-bloodedly prepared to kill three airmen, but I balked at roasting alive four horses. And I couldn't get them out, because the plane carried no ramp. With time I could have put the engines out of action . . . and with time they could have mended them again. But I hadn't had time. If I'd done that, I couldn't have got the Cessna out and away before Yardman's return.

The useless thoughts squirreled round and round, achieving nothing. I wiped my face again on the sleeve of my jersey and understood why Patrick had nearly always flown in shirt sleeves, even though it was winter.

Italy couldn't be much wider than England, if as wide. A hundred and twenty, a hundred and forty nautical miles. Perhaps more. I hadn't looked at the time when I took off. I should have. It was routine. I hadn't a hope if I couldn't concentrate better than that. A hundred and forty miles at two-twenty knots . . . say a hundred and sixty miles to be sure . . . it would take somewhere between forty and forty-five minutes. If I'd had the sense to look at my watch earlier I would have known how far I'd gone.

The lights below grew scarcer and went out. It was probably too soon to be the sea . . . it had to be mountains. I flew on for some time, and then checked my watch. Midnight. And still no lights underneath. The Apennines couldn't be so broad . . . but if I went down too soon, I'd hit them. I gave it another five minutes and spent them wishing Billy's burns would let up again. They were a five-star nuisance.

Still no lights. I couldn't understand it. I couldn't possibly still be over the narrow Apennines. It was no good. I'd have to go down for a closer look. I throttled back, let the nose go down, and watched the altimeter hands go anticlockwise through seven, six, five, four. At four thousand feet I leveled out again, and the night was as black as ever. I'd certainly hit no mountains, but for all I could see I was a lost soul in Limbo. It wasn't a safe feeling, not at all.

When at last I saw lights ahead I was much more uneasy than reassured. It was twelve-fifteen by my watch, which meant I had come nearly two hundred miles already, and Italy couldn't be as wide as that. Or at least I wouldn't have thought so.

The lights ahead resolved themselves into little clusters strung out in a horizontal line. I knew the formation too well to mistake it. I was approaching a coastline. Incredulity swamped me. I was approaching *from the sea.*

Nightmares weren't in it. I felt a great sense of unreality, as if the world had spun and rearranged its face, and nothing was ever going to be familiar again. I must be somewhere, I thought, taking a fierce grip on my escaping imagination. But where on earth, where literally on earth, was I?

I couldn't go on flying blindly southwest forever. The coastline must have a shape. About three miles short of it I banked to the right, wheeling northward, guided by nothing more rational than instinct, and flew along parallel with the few and scattered lights on the shore. The sea beneath was black but the land was blacker. The line where they met was like ebony against coal, a shadowy change of texture, a barely perceptible rub of one mass against another.

I couldn't, I thought, bullying my mind into some sort of order, I couldn't possibly have flown straight across the Gulf of Genoa and now be following the Italian coast northward from Alassio. There weren't enough lights, even for that time of night. And I knew that coastline well. This one, I didn't. Moreover, it ran due north for far too long. I had already been following it for fifteen minutes; fifty-five miles.

It had to be faced that I'd been wrong about where I started from. Or else the directional gyro was jammed. It couldn't be. . . . I'd checked it twice against the remote reading compass, which worked independently. I checked again: they matched. They couldn't both be wrong. But I *must* have started in Italy. I went right back in my mind to the flight out, when Patrick had first turned east. It had been east. I was still sure of that, and that was all.

There was a flashing light up ahead, on the edge of the sea. A lighthouse. Very useful if I'd had a nautical chart, which I hadn't. I swept on past the lighthouse and stopped dead in my mental tracks. There was no land beyond.

I banked the plane round to the left and went back. The lighthouse stood at the end of a long narrow finger of land pointing due north. I flew southward along the western side of it for about twenty miles until the sporadic lights spread wider and my direction swung again to the southwest. A fist pointing north.

Supposing I'd been right about starting from Italy, but wrong about being so far east. Then I would have been over the sea when I thought I was over the mountains. Supposing I'd been going for longer than a quarter of an hour when I first looked at my watch; then I would have gone farther than I guessed. All the same, there simply wasn't any land this shape in the northern Mediterranean, not even an island.

An island of this size. . . .

Corsica.

It couldn't be, I thought. I couldn't be so far south. I wheeled the plane round again and went back to the lighthouse. If it was Corsica and I flew northwest I'd reach the south of France and be back on the map. If it was Corsica I'd started from right down on the southern edge of the northern plain, not near Trieste or Venice as I'd imagined. It wasn't impossible. It made sense. The world began to fall back into place. I flew northwest over the black invisible sea. Twenty-seven minutes. About a hundred miles.

The strings and patterns of lights along the French coast looked like lace sewn with diamonds, and were just as precious. I turned and followed them westward, looking for Nice Airport. It was easy to spot by day; the runways seemed to be almost on the beach, as the airfield had been built on an outward curve of the shoreline. But either I was farther west than I thought, or the airport had closed for the night, because I missed it. The first place I was sure of was Cannes with its bay of embracing arms, and that was so close to Nice that if the runway had been lit I must have seen it.

A wave of tiredness washed through me, along with a numb feeling of futility. Even if I could find one, which was doubtful, I couldn't fly into a major airport without radio, and all the minor ones had gone to bed. I couldn't land anywhere in the dark. All I looked like being able to do was fly around in circles until it got light again and land at Nice . . . and the fuel would very likely give out before then.

It was at that depressing point that I first thought about trying to go all the way to England. The homing instinct in time of trouble. Primitive. I couldn't think of a thing against it except that I was likely to go to sleep from tiredness on the way, and I could do that even more easily going round in circles outside Cannes.

Committed from the moment I'd thought of it, I followed the coast until it turned slightly north again and the widespread lights of Marseilles lay beneath. The well-known way home from there lay up the Rhone Valley over the beacons at Montélimar and Lyons, with a left wheel at Dijon to Paris. But though the radio landmarks were unmistakable the geographical ones weren't, and I couldn't blindly stumble into the busy Paris complex without endangering every other plane in the area. North of Paris was just as bad, with the airlanes to Germany and the east. South, then. A straight line across France south of Paris. It would be unutterably handy to have known where Paris lay; what precise bearing. I had to guess again . . . and my first guesses hadn't exactly been a riotous triumph.

Three-twenty degrees, I thought. I'd try that. Allow ten degrees for wind drift from the southwest. Three ten. And climb a bit . . . the center of France was occupied by the Massif Central and it would be fairly inefficient to crash into it. I increased the power and went back up to ten thousand feet. That left fuel, the worst problem of all.

I'd taken off on the main tanks and the gauges now stood at half full. I switched over to the auxiliaries and they also were half full. And half empty, too. The plane had been refueled at Milan that morning, ten centuries ago. It carried . . . I thought searchingly back to Patrick's casually thrown out snippets of information the first day I flew with him . . . it carried twelve hundred United States gallons, giving a range of approximately eighteen hundred miles in normal conditions with a normal load. The load, though unconventional, was normal enough in weight. The condition of the weather was perfect, even if the condition of the pilot wasn't. Nine hundred miles from Marseilles would see me well over England, but it wouldn't take much more than four hours at the present speed until the tanks ran dry and it would still be too dark. . . .

There was just one thing to be done about that. I put my hand on the throttle levers and closed them considerably. The airspeed fell back from two-twenty, back through two hundred, one-eighty, steadied on one-fifty. I didn't dare go any slower than that because one thing Patrick hadn't told me was the stalling speed, and a stall I could do without. The nose wanted to go down heavily with the decreased airspeed and I was holding it up by brute strength, the wheel of the control column lodged against my whole left forearm. I stretched my right hand up to the trimmer handle in the roof and gave it four complete turns, and cursed as a piece of shirt which was sticking to the furrows and burns unhelpfully unstuck itself. The nose of the plane steadied; ten thousand feet at one-fifty knots; and blood oozed warmly through my jersey.

A hundred and fifty knots should reduce the petrol consumption enough for me to stay in the air until long enough after dawn to find an airfield. I hoped. It also meant not four hours ahead, but more than five, and I'd had enough already. Still, now that I knew roughly where I was going, the plane could fly itself. I made small adjustments to the trimmer until the needle on the instrument which showed whether she was climbing or descending pointed unwaveringly to level, and then switched in the automatic pilot. I took my hands off the wheel and leaned back. The DC-4 flew straight on. Very restful.

Nothing happened for several minutes except that I developed a thirst and remembered Rous-Wheeler for the first time since takeoff. Still on his knees, I supposed, and extremely uncomfortable. His bad luck.

There was water in the galley only five or six steps behind me, cold and too tempting. Gingerly I edged out of my seat. The plane took no notice. I took two steps backward. The instruments didn't quiver. I went into the galley and drew a quick cup of water, and went back toward the cockpit drinking it. Clearly the plane was doing splendidly without me. I returned to the galley for a refill of the cold delicious liquid, and when I'd got it, nearly dropped it.

Even above the noise of the engines I could hear Rous-Wheeler's scream. Something about the raw terror in it raised the hair on my neck. That wasn't pain, I thought, not the sort he'd get from cramp anyway. It was fear.

He screamed again, twice.

One of the horses, I thought immediately. If Billy hadn't boxed them properly . . . My newly irrigated mouth went dry again. A loose horse was just too much.

I went back to the cockpit, hurrying. Nothing had moved on the instrument panel. I'd have to risk it.

The plane had never seemed longer, the chains and racks more obstructing. And none of the mares was loose. They weren't even fretting, but simply eating hay. Half relieved, half furious, I went on past the packing case. Rous-Wheeler was still there, still kneeling. His eyes protruded whitely and his face was wet. The last of his screams hung like an echo in the air.

"What the hell's the matter?" I shouted to him angrily.

"He . . ." his voice shrieked uncontrollably. "He . . . moved."

"Who moved?"

"Him." His eyes were staring fixedly at the blanket covering Patrick.

He couldn't have moved. Poor, poor Patrick. I went across and pulled the rug off and stood looking down at him, the tall silent body, the tumbled hair, the big pool of blood under his down-turned face.

Pool of blood.

It was impossible. He hadn't had time to bleed as much as that. I knelt down beside him and rolled him over, and he opened his yellow eyes.

18

HE'D BEEN out cold for six hours and he was still unconscious. Nothing moved in his eyes, and after a few seconds they fell slowly shut again.

My fingers were clumsy on his wrist and for anxious moments I could feel nothing; but his pulse was there. Slow and faint, but regular. He was on his way up from the depths. I was so glad that he wasn't dead that had Rous-Wheeler not been there I would undoubtedly have wept. As it was, I fought against the flooding back of the grief I'd suppressed when Billy shot him. Odd that I should be tumbled into such intense emotion only because the reason for it was gone.

Rous-Wheeler stuttered "What . . . what is it?" with a face the color and texture of putty, and I glanced at him with dislike.

"He's alive," I said tersely.

"He can't be."

"Shut up."

Billy's bullet had hit Patrick high, above the hairline and at a rising angle, and instead of penetrating his skull had slid along outside it. The long, swollen and clotted wound looked dreadful, but was altogether beautiful in comparison with a neat, round hole. I stood up and spread the blanket over him again, to keep him warm. Then, disregarding Rous-Wheeler's protest, I went away up the plane.

In the cockpit nothing had changed. The plane roared steadily on its three-ten heading and all the instruments were like rocks. I touched the back of the copilot, awake again to his presence. The silence in him was eternal; he wouldn't feel my sympathy, but he had it.

Turning back a pace or two, I knelt down beside Mike. He too had been shot in the head, and about him too there was no question. The agile eyebrow was finished. I straightened him out from his crumpled position and laid him flat on his back. It wouldn't help any, but it seemed to give him more dignity. That was all you could give the dead, it seemed; and all you could take away.

The four packing cases in the luggage bay were heavy and had been thrust in with more force than finesse, pushing aside and crushing most of the things already there. Shifting the first case a few inches I stretched a long arm past it and tugged out a blanket, which I laid over Mike. Armed with a second one I went back into the galley. Sometime in the past I'd seen the first-aid box in one of the cupboards under the counter, and to my relief it was still in the same place.

Lying on top of it was a gay parcel wrapped in the striped paper of Malpensa Airport. The doll for Mike's daughter. I felt the jolt physically. Nothing could soften the facts. I was taking her a dead father for her birthday.

And Gabriella . . . anxiety for her still hovered in my mind like a low cloud ceiling, thick, threatening and unchanged. I picked up the parcel she had wrapped and put it on the counter beside the plastic cups and the bag of sugar. People often did recover from bullets in the lungs; I knew they did. But the precise Italian doctor had only offered hope, and hope had tearing claws. I was flying home to nothing if she didn't live.

Taking the blanket and the first-aid kit I went back to Patrick. In the lavatory compartment I washed my filthy hands and afterward soaked a chunk of cotton wool with clean water to wipe his blood-streaked face. Dabbing dry with more cotton wool I found a large hard lump on his forehead where it had hit the floor; two heavy concussing shocks within seconds, his brain had received. His eyelids hadn't flickered while I cleaned him, and with a new burst of worry I reached for his pulse; but it was still there, faint but persevering.

Sighing with relief I broke open the wrapping of a large sterile wound dressing, laid it gently over the deep gash in his scalp, and tied it on with the tape. Under his head I slid the second blanket, folded flat, to shield him a little from the vibration in the aircraft's metal skin. I loosened his tie and undid the top button of his shirt and also the waistband of his trousers, and beyond that there was no help I could give him. I stood up slowly with the first-aid kit and turned to go.

With anxiety bordering on hysteria Rous-Wheeler shouted, "You aren't going to leave me like this again, are you?"

I looked back at him. He was half sitting, half kneeling, with his hands still fastened to the floor in front of him. He'd been there for nearly three hours, and his flabby muscles must have been cracking. It was probably too cruel to leave him like that for the rest of the trip. I put the first-aid kit down on the flattened box, pulled a bale of hay along on the starboard side and lodged it against the ultrasonic packing case. Then with Alf's cutter I clipped through the wire round his wrists and pointed to the bale.

"Sit there."

He got up slowly and stiffly, crying out. Shuffling, half falling, he sat where I said. I picked up another piece of wire and in spite of his protests bound his wrists together again and fastened them to one of the chains anchoring the crate. I didn't want him bumbling all over the plane and breathing down my neck.

"Where are we going?" he said, the pomposity reawakening now that he'd got something from me.

I didn't answer.

"And who is flying the plane?"

"George," I said, finishing his wrists with a twirl he'd never undo. "Naturally."

"George who?"

"A good question," I said, nodding casually.

He was beautifully disconcerted. I left him to stew in it, picked up the first-aid kit, checked again that Patrick's pulse was plodding quietly along, and made my way back to the galley.

There were a number of dressings in the first-aid box, including several especially for burns, and I wasn't keen on my shirt sticking and tearing away again. Gingerly I pulled my jersey up under my arms and tucked the side of the shirt away under it. No one except Billy would have found the view entertaining, and the air at once started everything going again at full blast. I opened one of the largest of the burn dressings and laid it in place with that exquisite kind of gentleness you only give to yourself. Even so, it was quite enough. After a moment I fastened it on and pulled my shirt and jersey down on top. It felt so bad for a bit that I really wished I hadn't bothered.

I drank another cup of water, which failed to put out the fire. The first-aid kit, on further inspection, offered a three-way choice in pain killers: a bottle each of aspirin and codeine tablets, and six ampoules of morphine. I shook out two of the codeines, and swallowed these. Then I packed everything back into the box, shut the lid, and left it on the counter.

Slowly I went up to the cockpit and stood looking at the instruments. All working fine. I fetched a third blanket from the luggage bay and tucked it over and round the body of Bob. He became immediately less of a harsh reality, and I wondered if that was why people always covered the faces of the dead.

I checked the time. An hour from Marseilles. Only a hundred and fifty miles, and a daunting way still to go. I leaned against the metal wall and shut my eyes. It was no good feeling the way I did with so much still to do. Parts of Air Ministry regulations drifted ironically into my mind. . . . "Many flying accidents have occurred as a result of pilots flying while medically unfit . . . and the more exacting the flying task the more likely are minor indispositions to be serious . . . so don't go up at all if you are ill enough to need drugs . . . and if coffee isn't enough to keep you awake you are not fit to fly."

Good old Air Ministry, I thought; they'd hit the nail on the head. Where they would have me be was down on the solid earth, and I wholeheartedly agreed.

The radio, I thought inconsequentially. Out of order. I opened my eyes, pushed myself off the wall, and set about finding out why. I hadn't far to look. Yardman had removed all the circuit breakers, and the result was like an electric light system with no fuses in the fuse box. Every plane carried spares, however. I located the place where the spares should have been, and there weren't any. The whole lot in Yardman's pockets, no doubt.

Fetching a fresh cup of water, I climbed again into Patrick's seat and put on the headset to reduce the noise. I leaned back in the comfortable leather upholstery and rested my elbows on the stubby arms, and after a while the codeine and the bandage turned in a reasonable job.

Outside the sky was still black and dotted with brilliant stars, and the revolving anti-collision beacon still skimmed pinkly over the great wide span of the wings, but there was also a new misty grayish quality in the light. Not dawn. The moon coming up. Very helpful of it, I thought appreciatively. Although it was well on the wane I would probably be able to see what I was doing the next time I flew out over the coastline. I began to work out what time I would get there. More guesses. Northwest across France coast to coast had to be all of five hundred miles. It had been one-forty when I left Marseilles; was three-ten now. E.T.A. English Channel, somewhere about five.

Patrick's being alive made a lot of difference to everything. I was now thankful without reservation that I had taken the DC-4 however stupid my motive at the time, for if I'd left it, and Yardman had found him alive, they would simply have pumped another bullet into him, or even buried him as he was. The tiring mental merry-go-round of whether I should have taken the Cessna troubled me no more.

I yawned. Not good. Of all things I couldn't afford to go to sleep. I shouldn't have taken those pills, I thought; there was nothing like the odd spot of agony for keeping you awake. I rubbed my hand over my face and it felt as if it belonged to someone else.

I murdered Billy, I thought.

I could have shot him in the leg and left him to Yardman, and I'd chosen to kill him myself. Choice and those cold-blooded seconds of revenge . . . they made it murder. An interesting technical point, where self-defense went over the edge into something else. Well . . . no one would ever find out; and my conscience didn't stir.

I yawned again more deeply, and thought about eating one of Patrick's bananas. A depleted bunch of them lay on the edge by the windscreen, with four blackening stalks showing where he had fended off starvation on the morning trip. But I imagined the sweet pappiness of them in my mouth, and left them alone. I wasn't hungry enough. The last thing I'd eaten had been the lasagna with Gabriella.

Gabriella. . . .

After a while I got up and went through the plane to look at Patrick. He lay relaxed and unmoving, but his eyes were open again. I knelt beside him and felt his pulse. Unchanged.

"Patrick," I said. "Can you hear?"

There was no response of any sort.

I stood up slowly and looked at Rous-Wheeler sitting on the bale of hay. He seemed to have shrunk slightly as if the gas had leaked out, and there was a defeated sag to his whole body which showed that he realized his future was unlikely to be rosy. I left him without speaking and went back to the cockpit.

Four o'clock. France had never seemed so large. I checked the fuel gauges for the hundredth time and saw that the needles on the auxiliary tanks were knocking uncomfortably near zero. The plane's four engines used a hundred and fifty gallons an hour at normal speed and even with the power reduced they seemed to be drinking the stuff. Fuel didn't flow automatically from the main tanks when the auxiliaries were empty; one had to switch over by hand. And I simply couldn't afford to use every drop in the auxiliaries, because the engines would stop without warning the second the juice dried up. My fingers hovered on the switch until I hadn't the nerve to wait any longer, and then flipped it over to the mains.

Time passed, and the sleeping country slipped by underneath. When I got to the coast, I thought wearily, I was going to have the same old problem. I wouldn't know within two hundred miles where I was, and the sky was ruthless to the lost. One couldn't stop to ask the way. One couldn't stop at all. A hundred and fifty an hour might be slow in terms of jetliners, but it was much too fast in the wrong direction.

In Patrick's brief case there would be not only a thick book of radio charts but also some topographical ground maps. They weren't needed for ordinary aerial navigation, but they had to be carried in case of radio failure. The brief case was almost certainly somewhere under or behind the four packing cases in the luggage bay. I went to have a look, but I already knew. The heavy cases were jammed in tight, and even if there had been room to pull them all out into the small area behind the cockpit I hadn't enough strength to do it.

At about half-past four I went back for another check on Patrick, and found things very different. He had thrown off the blanket covering him and was plucking with lax uncoordinated hands at the bandage on his head. His eyes were open but unfocused still, and his breath came out in short regular groans.

"He's dying," Rous-Wheeler shouted unhelpfully.

Far from dying, he was up close to the threshold of consciousness, and his head was letting him know it. Without answering Rous-Wheeler I went back along the alley and fetched the morphine from the first-aid kit.

There were six glass ampoules in a flat box, each with its own built-in hypodermic needle enclosed in a glass cap. I read the instruction leaflet carefully and Rous-Wheeler shouted his unasked opinion that I had no right to give an injection; I wasn't a doctor, I should leave it for someone who knew how.

"Do you?" I said.

"Er, no."

"Then shut up."

He couldn't. "Ask the pilot, then."

I glanced at him. "I'm the pilot."

That did shut him up. His jaw dropped to allow a clear view of his tonsils and he didn't say another word.

While I was rolling up his sleeve Patrick stopped groaning. I looked quickly at his face and his eyes moved slowly round to meet mine.

"Henry," he said. His voice didn't reach me, but the lip movement was clear.

I bent down and said, "Yes, Patrick. You're O.K. Just relax."

His mouth moved. I put my ear to his lips, and he said, "My bloody head hurts."

I nodded, smiling. "Not for long."

He watched me snap the glass to uncover the needle and didn't stir when I pushed it into his arm, though I'd never been on the delivering end of an injection before and I must have been clumsy. When I'd finished he was talking again. I put my head down to hear.

"Where . . . are . . . we?"

"On your way to a doctor. Go to sleep."

He lay looking vaguely at the roof for a few minutes and then gradually shut his eyes. His pulse was stronger and not so slow. I put the blanket over him again and tucked it under his legs and arms and with barely a glance for Rous-Wheeler went back to the cockpit.

A quarter to five. Time to go down. I checked all the gauges, found I was still carrying the box of ampoules, and put it up on the ledge beside the bananas and the cup of water. I switched out the cockpit lights so that I could see better outside, leaving the round dial faces illuminated only by rims of red, and finally unlocked the automatic pilot.

It was when I'd put the nose down and felt again the great weight of the plane that I really doubted that I could ever land it, even if I found an airfield. I wasn't a mile off exhaustion and my muscles were packing up, and not far beyond this point I knew the brain started missing on a cylinder or two, and haze took the place of thought. If I couldn't think in crystalline terms and at reflex speed I was going to make an irretrievable mistake, and for Patrick's sake, quite apart from my own, I couldn't afford it.

Four thousand feet. I leveled out and flew on, looking down through the moonlit blackness, searching for the sea. Tiredness was insidious and crept up like a tide, I thought, until it drowned you. I shouldn't have taken that codeine, it was probably making me sleepy . . . though I'd had some at other times after racing injuries, and never noticed it. But that was on the ground, with nothing to do but recover.

There. There was the sea. A charcoal change from black, the moonlight just reflecting enough to make it certain. I flew out a little way, banked the plane to the right and began to follow the shore. Compass heading, east southeast. This seemed extraordinary, but it certainly had to be the northeast coast of France somewhere, and I wasn't going to lose myself again. There were lighthouses, flashing their signals. No charts to interpret them. The biggest port along the coast, I thought, was Le Havre. I couldn't miss that. There would be a lot of lights even at five in the morning. If I turned roughly north from there, I couldn't help but reach England. Roughly was just the trouble. The map in my head couldn't be trusted. Roughly north could find me barging straight into the London Control Zone, which would be even worse than Paris.

It wouldn't be light until six at the earliest. Sunrise had been about a quarter to seven, the day before.

The lights of Le Havre were ahead and then below me before I'd decided a thing. Too slow, I thought numbly, I was already too slow. I'd never get down.

The coast swung northward, and I followed. Five-twenty A.M. The fuel gauges looked reasonable with dawn not far ahead. But I'd got to decide where I was going. I'd got to.

If I simply went on for a bit I'd reach Calais. It still wouldn't be light. Somewhere over in Kent were Lympne, Lydd and Manston airports. Somewhere. My mind felt paralyzed.

I went on and on along the French coast like an automaton until at last I knew I'd gone too far. I hadn't watched the compass heading closely enough and it had crept round from north to nearly east. That light I'd passed a while back, I thought vaguely, the light flashing at five-second intervals, that must have been Gris Nez. I'd gone past Calais. I was nearly round to Belgium. I'd simply got to decide. . . .

The sky was definitely lighter. With surprise I realized that for several minutes the coastline had been easier to see, the water beneath lightening to a flat dark gray. Soon I could look for an airport, but not in Belgium. The explanations would be too complicated. Back to Kent, perhaps. . . .

In a way, the solution when it came was simple. I would go to the place I knew best. To Fenland. In daylight I could find my way unerringly there from any direction, which meant no anxious circling around, and familiarity would cancel out a good deal of the tiredness. The flying club used grass runways which were nothing like long enough for a DC-4, but its buildings had once been part of an old Air Force base, and the concrete runways the bombers had used were still there. Grass grew through the cracks in them and they weren't maintained, but they were marked at the ends with a white cross over a white bar, air traffic signal for a safe enough landing in an emergency.

My mental fog lifted. I banked left and set off north seaward, and only after five decisive minutes remembered the fuel.

The burns were hurting again and my spirits fell to zero. Would I never get it right? I was an amateur, I thought despairingly. Still an amateur. The jockey business all over again. I had never achieved anything worthwhile and I certainly hadn't built the solid life I wanted. Simon had been quite right, I couldn't have gone on carting racehorses all my life; and now that Yardman Transport no longer existed I wouldn't look for the same job again.

It was a measure of my exhausted state that having once decided to go to Fenland I hadn't the will to plunge back into uncertainty. The fuel margin was far too small for it to be prudent to go so far. Prudence in the air was what kept one alive. If I went to Fenland I'd be landing on a thimbleful, and if the engines stopped five miles away it would be too late to wish I hadn't.

Streaks of faint red crept into the sky and the sea turned to gray pearl. The sky wasn't so clear any more; there were layers of hazy cloud on the horizon, shading from dark gray-blue to a wisp of silver. The moment before dawn had always seemed to me as restoring as sleep, but that time when I really needed it, it had no effect. My eyes felt gritty and my limbs trembled under every strain. And the codeine had worn off.

The coast of East Anglia lay like a great gray blur ahead on my left. I would follow it round, I thought, and go in over the Wash. . . .

A swift dark shape flashed across in front of the DC-4 and my heart jumped at least two beats. A fighter, I thought incredulously. It had been a jet fighter. Another came over the top of me ridiculously close and screamed away ahead leaving me bumping horribly in the turbulence he left in his wake. They both turned a long way ahead and roared back toward me, flying level together with their wing tips almost touching. Expert formation pilots, and unfriendly. They closed at something like the speed of sound and swept over the DC-4 with less than a hundred feet between. To them I must have seemed to be standing still. To me, the trail they left me was very nearly the clincher.

Yardman couldn't have found me, I thought desperately. Not after the wavering roundabout route I'd taken. They couldn't have followed me and wouldn't have guessed I'd go up the North Sea . . . it couldn't be Yardman's doing. So who?

I looked out at East Anglia away on my left, and didn't know whether to laugh or die of fear. Americans. East Anglia was stiff with American air bases. They would have picked me up on their radar, an unidentified plane flying in at dawn and not answering to radio. Superb watchdogs, they would send someone to investigate . . . and they'd found a plane without registration numbers or markings of any sort. A plane like that couldn't be up to any good . . . had to be hostile. One could almost hear them think it.

They wouldn't start shooting, not without making sure . . . not yet. If I just went straight on and could deal with the buffeting, what would they do? I wouldn't let them force me down . . . I had only to plod straight on. . . . They swept past on each side and threw the DC-4 about like a cockleshell.

I couldn't do it, I thought, not this on top of everything else. My hands were slipping on the wheel with sweat. If the fighters went on much longer the sturdy old plane would shake to bits. They came past twice more and proved me wrong. They also reduced me to a dripping wreck. But after that they vanished somewhere above me, and when I looked up I saw them still circling overhead like angry bees. They were welcome to accompany me home, I thought weakly, if that was only where they'd stay.

I could see the lightship off Cromer still flashing its group of four every fifteen seconds. The first real sign of home. Only sixty miles to go. Fifteen minutes to the lightship in the Wash, and the sun rose as I went over it. I turned the plane on to the last leg to Fenland, and up above the escorts came with me.

The fuel gauges looked horrible. I drove what was left of my mind into doing some vital checks. Pitch fully fine, brakes off, mixture rich, fuel pumps on. There must have been a list somewhere, but heaven knew where. I had no business to be flying the plane at all, I didn't know its drill. . . . The Air Ministry could take away my license altogether and I was liable for a prison sentence as well. Except, I thought suddenly with a flicker of amusement, that Patrick was qualified to fly it, and he might be said to be technically in charge. Resident, anyway.

I throttled back and began to go down. If I managed it, I thought, I would be a professional. The decision was suddenly standing there full blown like a certainty that had been a long time growing. This time it wasn't too late. I would take Tom Wells' job and make him stick to it when he inevitably found out my name. I would fly his car firm executives around and earn the sort of life I wanted, and if it meant giving up racing . . . I'd do that too.

The airspeed indicator stood at a hundred and thirty knots on the slow descent, and I could see the airfield ahead. The fighters were there already, circling high. The place would be crawling with investigators before my wheels stopped rolling. Questions, when I could do with sleep.

The distant orange wind sock blew out lazily, still from the southwest. There wasn't enough fuel for frills like circuits, the gauges registered empty. I'd have to go straight in, and get down first time . . . get down. If I could.

I was close now. The club building developed windows, and there was Tom's bungalow. . . .

A wide banking turn to line up with the old concrete runway. . . . It looked so narrow, but the bombers had used it. Six hundred feet. My arms were shaking. I pushed down the lever of the undercarriage and the light went green as it locked. Five hundred . . . I put on full flap, maximum drag . . . retrimmed . . . felt the plane get slower and heavier, soft on the controls . . . I could stall and fall out of the sky . . . a shade more power . . . still some fuel left . . . the end of the runway ahead with its white cross coming up to meet me, rushing up . . . two hundred feet . . . I was doing a hundred and twenty . . . I'd never landed a plane with a cockpit so high off the ground . . . allow for that. . . . One hundred . . . lower . . . I seemed to be holding the whole plane up. . . . I closed the throttles completely and leveled out as the white cross and the bar slid underneath, and waited an agonized few seconds while the airspeed fell down and down until there was too little lift to the wings and the whole mass began to sink. . . .

The wheels touched and bounced, touched and stayed down, squeaking and screeching on the rough surface. With muscles like jelly, with only tendons, I fought to keep her straight. I couldn't crash now . . . I wouldn't. The big plane rocketed along the bumpy concrete . . . I'd never handled anything so powerful . . . I'd misjudged the speed and landed too fast and she'd never stop. . . .

A touch of brake . . . agonizing to be gentle with them and fatal if I wasn't. . . . They gripped and tugged and the plane stayed straight . . . more brake, heavier . . . it was making an impression . . . she wouldn't flip over onto her back, she had a tricycle undercarriage with a nose wheel . . . I'd have to risk it. . . . I pulled the brakes on hard and the plane shuddered with the strain, but the tires didn't burst and I hadn't dipped and smashed a wing or bent the propellers and there wasn't going to be a scratch on the blessed old bus. . . . She slowed to taxiing speed with a hundred yards to spare before the runway tapered off into barbed wire and gorse bushes. Anything would have been enough. A hundred yards was a whole future.

Trembling, feeling sick, I wheeled round in a circle and rolled slowly back up the runway to where it ran closest to the airport buildings. There I put the brakes full on and stretched out a hand which no longer seemed part of me, and stopped the engines. The roar died to a whisper, and to nothing. I slowly pulled off the headset and listened to the cracking noises of the hot metal cooling.

It was done. And so was I. I couldn't move from my seat. I felt disembodied. Burned out. Yet in a sort of exhausted peace I found myself believing that as against all probability I had survived the night, so had Gabriella . . . that away back in Milan she would be breathing safely through her damaged lung. I had to believe it. Nothing else would do.

Through the window I saw Tom Wells come out of his bungalow, staring first up at the circling fighters and then down at the DC-4. He shrugged his arms into his old sheepskin jacket and began to run toward me over the grass.

BLOOD SPORT

1

I AWOKE with foreboding. My hand closed in a reflex on the Luger under the pillow. I listened, acutely attentive. No sound. No quick surreptitious slither, no rub of cloth on cloth, no half-controlled pulse-driven breath. No enemy hovering. Slowly, relaxing, I turned half over and squinted at the room. A quiet, empty, ugly room. One third of what for want of a less cozy word I called home.

Bright sunshine bypassed the thin pink curtains, spilling a gold slash on the faded brown Wilton. I didn't like pink. Also I didn't have the energy it would take to argue the landlord into changing to blue. After eight months I knew he never renewed anything until it had fallen to bits.

In spite of the prevailing calm the feeling of foreboding deepened and then identified itself and dissolved into a less threatening, more general state of gloom. Sunday morning, June 20. The beginning of three weeks' leave.

I rolled back onto my stomach and shut my eyes against the sun, and took my hand six inches from the Luger, which was far enough, and wondered how long a man could sleep if he really put his mind to it. Even a man who never slept soundly to start with. Three weeks, the three obligatory overdue weeks, could be got through more easily asleep.

Three millenniums of sleep lay under the pillow. The nine-millimeter equalizer, my inseparable friend. It went with me everywhere, to beaches, to bathrooms, to other beds than my own. It was there to save my life. Not to take it. I had lived through a lot of temptations, and I lived with that too.

The telephone bell put paid to the three weeks before they had gone half an hour.

" 'Lo," I said blearily, balancing the receiver on the pillow.

"Gene?"

"Uh-huh."

"You haven't gone away then." There was relief in the voice, the voice of my boss. I looked at my watch. Ten o'clock.

"No," I said unnecessarily. He knew I wasn't going away. I didn't understand his relief. It was missing when he spoke again.

"How about a day on the river?"

He had a motor cruiser somewhere on the upper Thames. I'd never seen it. Hadn't been asked before.

"Invitation or order?" I said, yawning.

He hesitated. "Whichever you'll accept."

What a man. You did more for him than you believed you would, every time.

"Where do I go, and when?"

"My daughter will fetch you," he said. "She'll be there in about half an hour. Family party. Boating clothes. Come as you are."

"Sure," I said. Complete with stubble, Luger and shorts. A riot. I never wore pajamas. They slowed you up too much.

Boating clothes, I decided, were grayish brown cotton trousers and an olive green nylon jersey shirt. I carried the Luger with me in the left-hand pocket when the doorbell rang. One never really knew. But a look through the wide-angled spyhole showed it was only Keeble's daughter, as arranged. I opened up.

"Mr. Hawkins?" she said hesitantly, looking from me to the dingy brass six screwed onto the solid dark-stained wood.

"That's right." I smiled. "Come in."

She walked past me and I shut the door, interested to notice that four flights of stairs hadn't left her breathless, as they did most visitors. I lived high up for that purpose.

"I was just finishing my coffee," I said. "Would you like some?"

"It's very kind of you, but Daddy said not to waste time, he wants to be off upriver as soon as possible."

Keeble's daughter was just like her photograph on Daddy's desk. Half woman, still at school. Short bouncy dark hair and watchful dark eyes, a rounded body slimming down, a self-possessed touch-me-not expression, and an endearing gaucheness in her present situation.

She looked cautiously round the sitting room which neither she nor I nor anyone else would have classed as elegant living. The landlord's furniture was junk-shop stuff and I had made no effort to improve it. My total contributions to the scene were two rows of books on the shelves and in one corner a tin trunk of oddments which I had never bothered to unpack. A drawn-back curtain revealed the kitchen alcove and its entire contents: cupboard, refrigerator, sink, and stove, all of them showing their age.

One went through the sitting room to the bedroom, through the bedroom to the bathroom, and through the bathroom to the fire escape. The flat had everything but a drawbridge and a moat, and it had taken me weeks to find it. Only the tiny spyhole had been lacking, and the landlord had been furious when he finally noticed I had installed it. It had cost me three months' rent in advance to convince him it wasn't there for the sole purpose of being out when he came.

I watched Keeble's daughter search for something nice to say about my living quarters and give up the struggle with a defeated shake of her young head. I could have told her that I had once had a better flat, a spacious comfortable first-floor front with a balcony overlooking a tree-dotted square. It had proved too accessible to unwanted guests. I had vacated it on a stretcher.

"I'll fetch my jacket," I said, finishing the coffee. "And then we'll go."

She nodded, looking relieved, oppressed already by the emptiness of my home life. Five minutes of it had been enough, for her.

I went into the bedroom, picked the jacket off the bed, and transferred the Luger from my trousers into its built-in underarm holster, fastening it there with a press stud on a strap. Then, coat over arm, I dumped the dirty coffee cup in the sink, pulled the curtain across the kitchen, opened the front door, and let myself and Miss Keeble out.

Four uneventful stories down we emerged into the quiet sunlit Putney street, and she looked back and up at the solid old converted house. It needed paint and oozed respectability, exactly like its row of neighbors.

"I wasn't sure I'd come to the right place. Daddy just said the fourth house along."

"He gives me a lift home, sometimes."

"Yes, he said so." She turned to the white Austin standing at the curb and paused with the key in her hand. "Do you mind if I drive?"

"Of course not."

She smiled for the first time since she'd arrived, a quick flashing affair which verged on friendliness. She unlocked her door, climbed in, and reached over to unlatch the opposite one for me. The first thing I noticed as I bent to get in were the L plates lying on the back seat.

"When did you pass the test?" I said mildly.

"Well . . ." the smile lingered, "as a matter of fact, yesterday."

For all that, she drove very well, careful but confident, quiet with the gears though a bit heavy with the hand signals. She crept somewhat tentatively around the Chiswick circle and up the slope to the M4. The big blue motorway sign said no L drivers and her nose twitched mischievously as we passed it.

"Did you come this way to fetch me?" I asked idly.

She edged into the slow lane and hit forty.

"Er, no. I live in a hostel with about sixty other girls in South Ken. Daddy just rang me and said as I'd got the car up in London this weekend I could collect you and meet him in Henley. Sort of spur-of-the-moment thing."

"I see."

We came to the end of the fifty-mile-an-hour limit and her foot went down with determination.

"Do I scare you?" The needle quivered on sixty-five.

I smiled wryly. "No."

"Actually . . ." Her hands gripped the wheel with the tension of inexperience. "Actually, you don't look as if you'd scare easily."

I glanced at her in surprise. I look ordinary. Quiet and ordinary. And very useful it is, too.

"Anyway," she went on frankly, "I asked Daddy about coming this way, and he said he guessed your nerves would stand it. He seemed to find it very funny, for some reason or other."

"He has his own brand of humor."

"Mm." She drove for several miles in silence, concentrating on the road. The speed dropped slowly down to fifty again, and I guessed she was finding the motorway not such pure fun as she'd imagined. The usual number of Sunday Jim Clarks were showing off in the fast lane and family outings with Grandma driving from the back seat were bumbling about in the slow. We went down the center and pulled out bravely now and then to pass an airport bus.

Eventually, in thinner traffic after Windsor, she said doubtfully, "You do . . . er . . . work for Daddy?"

"Yes. Why not?"

"Well, no reason why not. I mean," she looked embarrassed, "I mean, I can't remember him ever asking anyone from work . . . Well, he just doesn't usually, that's all." She looked as if she wished she hadn't started.

"A kind thought," I suggested; and wondered what he wanted. Not just to give me a sunny day out. As his daughter said, he didn't do that sort of thing.

We made it to Henley with the paint intact, and she parked neatly in a large graveled enclosure by the railway station. Her hands trembled slightly as she locked the doors, and I realized that it must have been her longest drive, as well as the fastest.

"You drove beautifully," I said sincerely. "Like a veteran."

"Oh." She gave a laugh which was half a cough and looked relieved and pleased. "Well, thank you." She would be more relaxed, I knew, on the way back, and less strung up when she got there. To give and to remove confidence were tools of my trade, and there was no union to say I couldn't use them on Sundays.

"*Flying Linnet*—that's our boat—will be somewhere along the bank," she said. "It isn't." She smiled again and gestured, "That way."

We walked down to the river and along the neatly built broad tarmac towpath, where half the town seemed to be out feeding the ducks. The sun sparkled on the dark-green water and there was a queue at the boatyard for rowing boats and punts. There were gardens and lawns and seats, and a bowling green, and a playground with a slide and swings, all of them sprinkled with sunny Sunday faces and murmuring summer voices. Families and couples and groups: few alone. Three weeks alone, I thought bleakly. I could spend them beside the deep green river feeding ducks, and just jump in when I couldn't stand any more of it.

"There's Daddy," said Keeble's daughter, pointing. The sun lay along her light-brown arm and shifted in burned toffee shadows on the curves of her orange-tan dress. Too young for me, I thought inconsequentially. Or, rather, I was too old. Aeons too old. Forty still lay a couple of years ahead but I could have told Methuselah a thing or two.

Keeble had stepped ashore from one of the boats moored top to tail along the towpath and was walking toward us, hand outstretched, welcoming smile on face. My boss, except for an open-necked shirt, looked his usual weekday self, a short slightly chubby man with a mild manner and a faintly anxious expression. The light blue-gray eyes blinked freely as usual behind the unimpressive spectacles and as usual he had missed a patch while shaving. Premature baldness had made him look fifty at thirty-five but, far from regretting this, he believed it was the cause of his rapid promotion over well-thatched contemporaries. He may have been right. He looked harmless, cautious, unambitious, one of nature's safest plodders. It was eight years since he had inherited me along with the rest of the setup, and to discern the cutting brain behind the waffle had taken me two minutes flat.

"Gene," he said. "Glad you could come." He pumped my hand up and down perfunctorily, the social gesture as meaningless to him as to me, and we exchanged smiles to match. For his daughter the warmth came from the heart. She kissed him affectionately on the cheek and his eyes held a glimmering pride I had never seen in him before.

"Well, Lynnie my love, you got here safely. Or did you let Gene do the driving?"

"Do me a favor," she said. "He didn't even flinch."

Keeble flicked me an amused glance, and I repeated the compliment to her skill, with her father nodding his thanks to me over her head, knowing exactly why I said it.

They turned and began to walk back along the path, gesturing to me to come. Keeble's boat, the one they stopped at, was a graceful neat-looking fiberglass cruiser with a cabin forward and a large open cockpit at the back, the decks spotless and the chromium shining. Sitting casually side by side on the pale-blue plastic upholstery were a man and a woman, both of whom raised smiling faces at our approach and neither of whom got up.

Lynnie jumped down into the boat and kissed the woman, and Keeble stepped carefully after.

"Come aboard," he said to me, and again in his tone there was a choice. An invitation or an order, whichever I would accept. I opted for the invitation, and embarked on more than the *Flying Linnet*.

"My wife Joan," said Keeble, stretching a hand to the seated woman. "Gene Hawkins, honey."

Joan Keeble was a frail birdlike woman with a coyness of manner left over from the time when she was pretty. She twinkled her eyes at me, inviting admiration. I scraped some up, and exchanged the necessary platitudes about weather, boating, and driving daughters. Keeble waded into this with a wave towards the man sitting beside her.

"You two haven't met . . ." He hesitated a fraction. "Dave . . . Gene, this is Dave Teller."

Teller stood up, shook hands economically, and said he was glad to know me. He wore a sloppy wrinkled pale-blue shirt hanging out over patched cotton trousers, battered plimsolls on his feet, and a dirty old baseball cap on his head. American, well educated, prosperous, assured: the categories clicked over from habit in my assessing mind. Also he was a lean man nearing fifty, with a strong beaky nose, straightforward eyes, and a marvelous dentist.

Keeble offered no information beyond the bald introduction, but bustled about getting his ship ready to put to sea. His yell into the cabin for a certain Peter to come and help produced no results. I stuck my head through the door and saw a boy of about twelve engrossed in fitting a new roll of film into a small simple camera.

"Peter!" his father yelled.

Peter heaved a martyred sigh, scrambled the back of the camera shut, and went out past me with his eyes down and his fingers winding the knob. Sure-footed, he stepped without looking onto the narrow side of the boat and from there to the towpath.

"He'll fall in one day," Lynnie said to the world in general. Her brother didn't even hear. Still concentrating on his camera with one hand he was slowly untying the rope from the mooring ring with the other, crouching down on the tarmac in his clean black jeans and getting up with two large dusty patches on the knees. Pointing his viewfinder at a passing formation of ducks he clicked the shutter and with a serious, absorbed expression wound on the film.

Farther up the path Keeble and Teller were undoing the bow rope, talking amicably in the sun. Lynnie and her mother straightened the cushions and coiled the ropes and fussed around over a lot of nothing, chatting trivialities. I wondered what the hell I was doing there and felt out of contact with everything around me. Not a new feeling, but recurring more often. The two levels of living were growing farther apart. The day-to-day social level had lost all meaning, and underneath, where there should have been rock, had opened a void of shriveling loneliness. It was getting worse. The present was bad enough: the future an abyss. Only work brought my splintering self into any sort of whole, and I knew well enough that it was the work itself which had started the process. That and Caroline. Or, to be more accurate, Caroline's husband.

"I say, hold this rope, will you?" Peter said. I took the wet snake he offered. "Hi," he added, seeing me properly for the first time, "who are you?"

"Anybody's guess," I said with more truth than sense, and his mother stared at me with astonishment and told him my name.

Keeble came back on board and started the engine. Teller stood up on the small forward deck and cast off the bow rope when Keeble told him, and Peter left it until almost too late to leap on board with the stern rope. The camera bounced on the cord round his neck. "Birthday present from Gran," he said to Lynnie with pride. "Super, isn't it?"

"You'll drop it in the river, if you aren't careful."

"This is only my second film. I used the first one up on the boys at school. Do you think those ducks will come out all right?"

"I expect you had your finger over the shutter."

"I've got a book in there." He nodded toward the cabin, expertly sifting out the affection behind her sarcasm and showing no resentment. "It tells you about exposures and focuses. I think I'll just check what it says about sunny days. It was cloudy dull all week at school."

I don't belong here, I thought. I wished I was asleep.

The *Flying Linnet* nosed upstream through a scatter of rowboats, Keeble at the wheel, Teller sitting forward still on the cabin roof, and Peter trying to get past Lynnie teasing him in the cabin doorway. Joan Keeble sat down on the wide seat across the back and patted the place next to her for me to join her. With an effort I did so, but after a minute or two, in the middle of apparently idle hostessy chat, she pulled me back to attention by trying delicately to find out who I was and why I had been invited, while not wanting to have me realize that she didn't know.

I could play that sort of game forever. Inference on inference. I didn't know the answer to why was I there, but that she needed to ask it, that indeed she had asked it, told me a great deal about noncontact between Keeble and his wife, and opened new doors into Keeble himself. I knew then why he'd never before asked me home. It was one thing to employ a microscope, but another to put oneself under the lens. I thought it all the odder that he'd done it now.

As if he could feel my mind on the back of his neck he turned round and said, "The lock's just ahead." I stood up and joined him, and Peter gave up his struggle and went back to his duty with the stern rope.

"Marsh Lock," Lynnie said, standing beside me and looking forward through the windshield. "Not an easy one, from this side, going upstream."

When we got nearer I saw what she meant. The broad stretch of river narrowed abruptly to the lock gates on the left and the weir on the right, alongside. Baby whirlpools and trails of bubbles met us fifty yards away with larger eddies and convolutions bubbling up as we went on. The boat tended to swing sideways under their power, and Keeble spun the wheel rapidly to keep her straight. Ahead of us water in tons tumbled over the weir, green and brown and splashing white, thundering down in great curving leaps, smelling of mustiness and mud.

A low wooden wall divided the lock approach from the turbulent weir water, and to the calm side of the barrier Keeble neatly steered his boat. Teller standing at the bow threw his rope over the hook on a mooring post there, and Peter slung a loop over a bollard at the stern.

I looked idly over the side of the boat, over the wall, up to the weir. Bouncing, tumbling, foaming, sweeping away back into the width of the river, the rough water looked superb in the sun. I felt the warmth and the fine spray mixed on my face and wondered whether if someone fell in there he would ever come up.

The lock gates opened, the downcoming boats chugged out, and the *Flying Linnet* went in. Teller and Peter did their stuff mooring us to the side and Peter took a photograph of the boat in the lock. Water surged through the sluices in the upper gates, lifting us up, and in ten minutes we were going out of the lock onto another broad calm stretch of river, six feet higher than the one below.

"There are fifty locks on the Thames," Keeble said. "Lechlade is as far up as you can go except in a rowing boat, and that's about 300 feet above sea level."

"Quite a staircase," I commented.

"The Victorians," he nodded, "were a brilliant lot. They built them."

Teller stood on the foredeck holding the coil of rope, the peak of his baseball cap pointing forward like an attentive bird. I watched him, speculating, and Keeble followed the direction of my eyes and gave me only silence to work on.

Less than half a mile upstream from the lock we made an obviously prearranged stop at a riverside pub, Teller jumping ashore with his rope and fending the boat off the concrete edges as we drifted toward it. He and Peter tied expert knots, and everyone followed them ashore.

We drank sitting on a ring of uncomfortable metal chairs round a table with a sun umbrella spiked through its center. Lynnie and Peter had Cokes and without consultation Keeble bought Scotch for the rest of us. Joan sipped hers with a pursed mouth and screwed eyes, as if it were a mite too strong for fragile little her, but I noticed she finished a long way first. Teller left his untouched for several minutes and then tossed it back in king-sized gulps. Keeble drank in pauses, revolving his glass in his hand and squinting through it at the sun. They were talking about the river, and other days on it, and other weather. On either side of us, round more umbrellas, sat more family parties much the same; Sunday morning drinks, Sunday lunch, Sunday snooze, Sunday *Express,* Sunday supper, Sunday Night at the London Palladium . . .; safe little families in a sheltered routine, well intentioned and more or less content. Even Keeble fitted in. Whereas I . . . was apart.

"Drink," Keeble said. "You're on holiday."

Faced with instant sharp curiosity from the rest of his family I meekly picked up my glass, still full when theirs were empty. It felt wrong to drink in the morning; it raised subconscious bells of alarm. I liked the taste of alcohol all right, but couldn't afford its effects. Alcohol encouraged you to put your trust in luck, and I was better off trusting a clear head. Consequently I sometimes didn't touch the stuff for weeks on end and on that morning had had none for nearly a month.

Keeble watched me swallow, the whiskey as vivid and familiar as a long-lost friend. The extent to which I was ever on holiday lay in the jacket across my knees, a pound of deadly mechanism in an underarm holster; but it did seem most unlikely that I would need it on the Thames. When Teller ordered a refill, I drank that too. And then, since it was my turn, a third.

Peter lasted the course to three Cokes, and then wandered away with his camera poised, looking for excuses to use it. Next door a boatyard, like the one at Henley, was doing a roaring trade in punts. Four of the pub's more enthusiastic customers were having trouble stepping aboard, and Teller said, chuckling, "What's the fine for punting under the influence . . . ?"

"A soaking," Lynnie said. "Silly nits."

The punt pole waved recklessly as they set off but the four men didn't fall in. The punt skidded ten feet up the river and hit the pub's landing stage with a thump that tumbled them into a leg-waving heap. I tried to laugh with everyone else and only succeeded in feeling more remote than ever.

We finished the drinks, re-embarked, and went up through the next lock, Harbour, to an unpopulated green pasture stretch of river, where we moored for lunch. Peter swam, jumping off the boat repeatedly in glittering splashes, and Lynnie helped her mother in the cabin, preparing the food. Teller sprawled lazily on the back seat, and Keeble sat down with a Sunday newspaper and unfolded it, and I wearily began to wonder just when he would come to the point.

The point, however, was the newspaper. We had arrived.

"Read that," he said, tapping a small paragraph on an inside page.

I read it.

> There is still no sign of Chrysalis, free in Kentucky, U.S., since Tuesday. Anxiety mounts for the safety of the £500,000 stallion, sire of this year's Derby winner, Moth.

"Is this what you mean?" I asked, puzzled, making sure I'd read the right section. I had. He nodded vigorously.

"Didn't you know about it?" he asked.

"That Chrysalis had got lost? Yes, I suppose so. It was on all the news bulletins on Wednesday."

"And it didn't mean a damn thing to you," Teller said, with a trace of controlled and civilized bitterness under his smile.

"Well . . ."

"I have a share in that horse," Teller said. "A one-eighth share—200,000 dollars' worth."

"Wow," I said blankly. It seemed a lot of money to invest in one eighth of a horse.

"What is more," he said, sighing, "I spent all of last month negotiating the sale, and was lucky to beat out another syndicate that was bidding for him. And now as soon as he gets over there, this has to happen."

"I'm sorry," I said, conventionally polite.

"I can't expect you to understand." He shook his head excusingly. "It isn't the money which matters, it's the horse. He's irreplaceable."

"They'll find him." I had no doubt of it, and I didn't care one way or the other.

"I'm not so sure," he said. "And I would like you to get out there and look for him."

For five seconds no one twitched a muscle, least of all me. Then Teller turned his head to Keeble and smiled his glossy smile. "I wouldn't play poker with him," he said. "O.K., I'll buy what you say about him being all that good."

I glanced at Keeble and he gave me raised eyebrows, a tiny shrug, and a slightly embarrassed expression. I wondered just how complete his testimonial had been.

Teller turned back to me. "Sim here and I, we were in the same business, way back in World War II."

"I see," I said. And I did see. Quite a lot.

"It was just a war job for me, though," he said. "I got out of the Army in '47 and went back home to Pappy, and a couple of years later he died and left me his race horses and a few bucks on the side." The beautiful teeth flashed.

I waited. The story had hardly begun.

After a pause he said, "I'll pay your fare and expenses, of course, and a fee."

"I don't hunt horses," I protested mildly.

"I can guess what you hunt." He glanced again at Keeble. "Sim says you're on vacation."

I didn't need reminding.

"Chrysalis," he said, "is the third stallion of international status to have disappeared in the last ten years."

2

THEY TRIED pretty hard in their subtle way, but it seemed ridiculous to me.

"You know about horses," Keeble said. "Your father trained them for racing."

"There's the police," I pointed out. "Also the insurance company. Also every man, woman and child with an eye for a horse in the state of Kentucky. And I presume there's a reward?"

Teller nodded.

"So why me?"

"No one found the other two."

"There's a lot of land in America," I said. "They're both probably free on a prairie somewhere having a high old time siring herds of wild horses."

Teller said grudgingly, "The first one was found dead in a gully two years after he disappeared."

"That's it, then."

"But the second one . . . I bought that one too. I had a one-tenth share. This is second time around for me."

I stared at him. "Were any of the circumstances the same?"

Reluctantly he shook his head. "No . . . except that they both got free. Allyx was never found. That's why I want something special done about Chrysalis."

I was silent.

Keeble stirred. "You've got nothing else to do, Gene. Why not take your holiday in the States? What will you do with yourself if you stay in Putney?"

His eyes had stopped blinking, as they always did when he was intent. It was the surest guide I had to the complex calculations which sometimes lay beneath his most casual remarks. He couldn't have guessed, I thought in alarm. He was a manipulator but not clairvoyant. I shrugged and answered him on the surface.

"Walk round Kew Gardens and smell the orchids."

"They have no scent," said Teller, pointing out the obvious.

"He knows that." Keeble nodded, still unblinking. "Any fruitless way of passing the time is what he meant."

"I guess you two operate on your own private wavelength," Teller said with a sigh. "But I'd like you to come back with me, Gene, and at least take a look. What's the harm in that?"

"And what's the good in it? It's not my sort of job." I looked away, down into the green water. "And . . . I'm tired."

They hadn't a quick answer to that. I thought it would have been simple if all that was the matter with me was the straightforward tiredness of overwork, not the deadly fatigue of a struggle I wasn't sure I could win. Chasing some crazy colt over a thousand square miles didn't look like any sort of cure.

Joan came out of the cabin into their defeated silence with a bowl of salad and a string of bright fussing chatter. A folding table was erected and the dishes put on it, and we sat around in the sun eating cold chicken and hot French bread. There was a pleasant pink wine to drink and strawberries and cream afterwards, and Peter, still in wet bathing trunks despite orders from his mother, took mouthfuls and photographs by turn.

Lynnie, sitting beside me, told Dave Teller an amusing story about the finishing school she attended, her warm bare arm brushing unselfconsciously against mine. I should have enjoyed that placid Sunday picnic on the river. I tried to. I smiled and answered when I was spoken to and concentrated carefully on the taste and texture of what I was eating, and all that happened was that the fat black slug of depression flexed its muscles and swelled another notch.

At four o'clock, after dishwashing and dozing, we started back toward Henley. My refusal to go to America hadn't basically disturbed Teller or Keeble an ounce. I concluded that whatever had prompted the suggestion it wasn't a burning conviction that I and only I could find the missing horse. I put the whole thing out of my mind. It wasn't hard.

There was a punt in difficulties at the approach to Harbour Lock. Teller, again standing on the bow with rope at the ready, shouted back to Keeble and pointed ahead. We looked, all of us, following his finger.

Where the river divided, going slowly into the left fork round the bend to the lock and fast on the right straight to the weir, a sturdy square post in midstream bore a large notice, a single word: DANGER.

A girl lying flat half in and half out of the punt with her arms round the post was trying to tie up to it by passing a rope from one hand to the other, and making a poor job of it. On the stern, watching anxiously, punt pole in hand, stood a young man in a red and yellow shirt. He waved his arms when he saw us coming and as Keeble throttled back and drifted near he shouted across the water.

"Could you help us, sir?"

Since the punt was full in the weir stream with only the girl's slender arms keeping it from floating straight to destruction, he seemed remarkably cool. Keeble cursed about ignorant nitwits and edged nearer with his engine in slow reverse. The *Flying Linnet,* unlike the punt, was too big to go through this particular weir, a long row of separately openable gates: but the summer current was quite strong enough to crash her nastily against the thick concrete supports and pin her there for someone else humiliatingly to rescue.

Keeble shouted to the girl that we would tow them away, and to hand the mooring rope to me or Lynnie, whichever she could reach, as soon as we were nearer. The girl nodded, her arms still stretched forward round the big post, her long fair hair nearly brushing the water, her body quivering with the strain.

"Hold on!" Lynnie shouted urgently. "Oh, do hold on. Just a little longer, that's all." She leaned over the side as if trying to shorten the few yards of water which still lay between, her worry and fright growing as we drew nearer. With the engine doing little more than tick over, the noise of the water on the far side of the weir began to fill our ears with its threat, but Keeble at any rate remained calm and sure of himself, an easy master of his boat and the situation. With six feet still to go the girl took one arm off the post and held out the rope toward Lynnie's groping hand. Then, disastrously, she dropped it. Crying out, beating in big splashes on the water, she struggled to get her arm back round the post. Lynnie yelled to her to get hold of the rope again, it was fastened to the punt under her chest, to get hold of it again and hand it over. But the girl was now far too frightened either to listen or to let go of the post again, and the panic was rising to screams in her voice.

Out of the side of my vision I saw the young man start forward to help her, apparently at last realizing that their position was serious. The punt pole swung awkwardly in his hands, curved through the air in a clumsy arc, and hit Dave Teller on the head. With buckling knees the American fell forward off the bows and straight down into the water.

I was up on the cabin roof, out of my shoes and into the river after him almost before any of the others realized what had happened. I heard Keeble's despairing voice shouting "Gene" in the second before I went under, but I was thinking simply that speed was the only chance of finding Teller, since anything that sank in a river the size of the Thames was instantly out of sight. Algae made the water opaque.

Diving in as near to where he had gone as I could judge, I kicked downward, arms wide. I was going faster than Teller, I had to be. I had a strong impression that the punt pole had knocked him out, that he was on a slow one-way trip to the bottom.

About eight feet down my fingers hooked almost immediately into cloth. Even with my eyes open I could see nothing and with my right hand I felt for his face while I tried to kick us both to the surface. I found his face, clamped his nose between my fingers and the heel of my hand on his mouth, and turned him so that I held his head against my chest. He didn't struggle; couldn't feel.

From that point on the rescue operation failed to go as per schedule. I couldn't get back to the surface. The current underneath was much stronger, very cold, sweeping us downward, clinging round our bodies with irresistible force. I thought, We'll hit the weir and be pinned there down deep, and that will be that. For a treacherous instant I didn't even care. It would solve all my problems. It was what I wanted. But not really with another life in my arms, for which I was literally the only hope.

My chest began hurting with the lack of air. When we hit the weir, I thought, I would climb my way up it. Its face might not be slippery smooth. It had to be possible . . .

There was a sudden tug as if some fisherman had us hooked. I felt us change direction slightly and then a tug again, stronger and continuing and stronger still. No miraculous rescue. The water had us, gripping tighter, sucking us fast, inexorably, into the weir. The sheer overwhelming weight and power of it made nonsense of human strength, reduced my efforts to the fluttering of a moth in a whirlwind. The seizing speed suddenly accelerated further still, and we hit. Or, rather, Teller hit, with a jar that nearly wrenched him away from me. We spun in the current and my shoulder crashed into concrete and we spun again and crashed, and I couldn't get hold of any surface with my free hand. The tumbling and crashing went on, and the pain in my chest went deeper, and I knew I wasn't going to be climbing up any weir, I could only find it when it hit me, and when I reached for it it hit me somewhere else.

The crashing stopped, but the tumbling went on. My ears were roaring to bursting point. There was a sword embedded in my chest. The searing temptation came back more strongly just to open my mouth and be finished with it. But by my own peculiar rules I couldn't do that, not with someone else involved, not when what I was doing was in a way what I'd been trained for. Some other time, I thought lightheartedly, some other time I'd drown myself. This time I'll just wait until my brain packs up from lack of oxygen, which won't be long now, and if I haven't any choice in the matter then I haven't any guilt either.

The tumbling suddenly died away and the clutching current relaxed and loosened and finally unlocked itself. I was only seconds this side of blackout and at first it didn't register: then I gave a feeble kick with legs half entwined round Teller and we shot upward as if on springs. My head broke the surface into the sun and the air went down into the cramp of my lungs like silver fire.

The weir, the killing weir, was fifty yards away. Fifty yards *upstream*. We had come right through it under the water.

I took my freezing stiffened fingers off Teller's face, and held his head up to mine, and blew into his flaccid mouth. The current, gentle again and comparatively warm, carried us slowly along, frothy bubbles bursting with little winks against our necks. I trod water with my legs, and held Teller up, and went on pushing into him all my used-up breath. He showed no response. It would be exceedingly inconsiderate of him, I thought resignedly, if he had died right at the beginning and I had gone to all that trouble for nothing.

There were shouts from the banks suddenly and people pointing, and someone came after us in a dinghy with an outboard motor. It puttered noisily past my ear and hands stretched over the side to grasp.

I shook my head. "A rope," I said, and breathed into Teller. "Give me a rope. And pull slowly."

One of the two men argued, but the other did as I asked. I wound the rope round my arm twice and held it, and when I nodded they let the boat drift away until we were a safe distance from its propeller and slowly began to pull us toward the bank. Teller got ten more of my ex-breaths on the way. They didn't seem to be doing him a bit of good.

The dinghy towed us out of the weir stream side of the river and landed on the same side as the lock. People appeared in a cluster to help, and there was little doubt it was needed, but even so I was loath to part with Teller until one large calm man lay on his stomach on the grass and stretched his arms down under the American's armpits.

"Don't worry," he said. "We'll go straight on with the breathing."

I nodded, took my mouth away from Teller's, and transferred his weight into the stranger's arms. He began to pull him out of the water as fast as he could. I put a steadying hand on Teller's chest and felt it heave suddenly under the clinging blue shirt. I hadn't enough breath left myself to tell the man who was lifting him, and while I was still trying to, Teller half out, gave a choking cough and opened his eyes. There was some water in his lungs, racking him. The stranger pulled him even more quickly out onto the grass, and as his ankles bumped over the edge his returning consciousness flooded into a stark sort of awareness which had nothing to do with a release from drowning. Somewhere between a cough and a groan he said, "Jesus," and again went completely limp.

Another couple of strong wrists hauled me up onto the bank in his wake, and I knelt there beside him feeling the reassuringly small swelling on the side of his head but anxiously listening to the dragging breath bubbling in his throat.

"Roll him over," I said. "Carefully . . . just so his tongue isn't choking him."

We put him on his side and his breathing eased immediately, but I wouldn't let them pick him up and carry him to the lock. Almost any injury was bound to be made worse by moving, and he'd been moved too much already. The calm man agreed and went briskly off to fetch a doctor.

The lockkeeper arrived along the towpath, followed at a rush by Keeble and all his family. Their faces were all strained with shock, and Lynnie had been crying.

"Thank God," Keeble said, crouching beside me. "You're both all right." His voice held almost more incredulity than relief.

I shook my head. "He's hurt, somewhere."

"Badly?"

"Don't know. . . . He crashed into the weir."

"We didn't see you go over. We were watching . . ."

"They must have gone under," said the lockkeeper. "Through one of the gates. Those gates wind upward, same as a sash window. We've got two of them a couple of feet open at the bottom today, with the river a bit full after all that rain."

I nodded. "Under."

Dave Teller choked and woke up again, coughing uncontrollably through the puddle in his lungs, every cough jerking him visibly into agony. From his fluttering gesture it was clear where the trouble lay.

"His leg," Keeble said. "He's not bleeding . . . could he have broken it?"

The jar when he hit the weir had been enough. I said so. "We can't do anything for him," said Keeble, watching him helplessly.

The crowd around us waited, murmuring in sympathy but enjoying the disaster, listening to Teller coughing, watching him clutch handfuls of grass in rigid fingers. Not a scrap of use begging them to go away.

"What happened to the punt?" I asked Keeble.

"We towed it ashore. Lynnie got hold of the rope. Those kids were terribly shocked." He looked round for them vaguely, but they weren't in the crowd. "I suppose they've stayed back at the lock. The girl was nearly hysterical when you and Dave didn't come up." A remembering bleakness came into his face. "We towed them into the lock cut and moored there. Then we ran along to the lock to get the lockkeeper . . . and he was already down here." He looked up across the river to the pretty weir. "How long were you under the water?"

"A couple of centuries."

"Seriously."

"Can't tell. Maybe three minutes."

"Long enough."

"Mm."

He looked me over objectively, boss to employee. One shoulder of my green jersey shirt was ripped in a jagged tear.

"Bruised," he said matter-of-factly.

"The weir," I agreed, "has knobs on."

"It's like a flight of steps under there," said the lockkeeper solemnly. "Going down from the top level to this one, you see. The current would have rolled you right down those steps, I reckon. In fact it's a bleeding miracle you ever came up, if you ask me. There's some every year fall in this river and never get seen again. Current takes them along the bottom all the way to the sea."

"Charming," Keeble said under his breath.

Dave Teller stopped coughing, rolled slightly onto his back and put his wrist in his mouth. His strong beaky nose stuck uncompromisingly up to the sky, and the wetness on his face wasn't from the Thames. After a while he moved his hand and asked Keeble what had happened. Keeble briefly explained, and the screwed-up eyes slid round to me.

"Lucky you were with us," he said weakly, the smile in his voice making no progress on his face. He moved his hand apprehensively behind his ear, and winced when it reached the bump. "I don't remember a thing."

"Do you remember asking me to look for your horse?"

He nodded a fraction, slowly. "Yuh. You said no."

"I've changed my mind," I said. "I'll go."

In the cabin of the *Flying Linnet* Keeble watched me slowly strip off my sodden clothes. I had never, as far as I remembered, felt so weak. I'd left half my muscles under the weir. Buttons would no longer come out of their holes.

"You heard what the man said," Keeble remarked. "It was lucky you were with us."

I didn't answer.

"Make a note of it," Keeble said. "Stick around. You never know when you'll be needed."

"Sure," I said, refusing to acknowledge that I understood what he was talking about.

He wouldn't be deterred. "You're like Dave's horse. Irreplaceable."

My lips twitched. That was the crunch, all right. His job would be a little harder if he lost his head cook and bottlewasher. Personal regard didn't come into it.

I struggled out of my jersey. He handed me a towel, glancing noncommittally at the marks of this and previous campaigns.

"I'm serious, Gene."

"Yeah." I sighed. "Well . . . I'm still here."

It was too much of an admission, but at least it seemed to reassure him enough to change the subject.

"Why are you going to the States?"

"Maybe I owe it to him."

"Who? Dave?"

I nodded.

"I don't follow," he said frowning. "Surely he owes you? If anyone owes anything."

"No. If I'd been quicker, he wouldn't have gone in, wouldn't now have a smashed thigh. Too much whiskey and wine and sleeping in the sun. I was much too slow. Abysmally, shamefully slow."

He made a gesture of impatience. "Don't be ridiculous, Gene. No speed on earth could have prevented an accident like that."

I put the towel round my neck and started to take off my trousers.

"That accident," I said briefly, "was attempted murder."

He gazed at me, eyes blinking slowly behind the mild spectacles. Then he turned, opened the cabin door, and stepped up into the cockpit. I heard him shouting to Peter.

"Get out of that punt at once, there's a good chap. And don't let anyone else get in it. It's important."

"Not even Lynnie?"

"Not even Lynnie."

"I don't want to," said Lynnie's voice in a wail from the cockpit. "I never want to go in a punt again."

She wasn't much her father's daughter. His mind was as tough as old boots. The chubby body which contained it came back into the cabin and shut the door.

"Convince me," he said.

"The boy and girl have scarpered."

He raised his eyebrows and protested. "They were frightened."

"They didn't stop to answer questions. They may quite possibly think Dave and I are dead, because they didn't even wait to make sure. I should say they never even intended to appear at any inquest."

He was silent, thinking about it. The boy and girl had gone from the lock when we had eventually returned to it: gone unnoticed, leaving the punt behind. No one had given them a thought until after the doctor had splinted Teller's leg and seen him carried on a stretcher a hundred yards to an ambulance. When the doctor asked how the accident had happened, the causes of it weren't around.

"We don't know," Keeble said. "They may very likely have come down the towpath and seen you were all right, and they might have dozens of personal reasons for not wanting to stay."

I finished kicking my legs out of the clammy cotton trousers and peeled off my socks.

"The boy stood on the stern too long. He should have been helping with the rope."

Keeble frowned. "Certainly he seemed unconcerned, but I don't think he realized quite what a jam they were in. Not like the girl did."

"The first time he moved, he hit Dave straight on the head."

"Punt poles are clumsy if you aren't careful . . . and he couldn't have counted on Dave standing in so vulnerable a spot."

"He'd been standing there most of the way, seeing to the bow rope."

"The boy and girl couldn't know that."

"He was certainly standing there when we approached the punt."

"And," Keeble said in a demolishing voice, "no one would deliberately put himself into so much danger just to bait a trap."

I dried my legs and wondered what to do about my underpants.

Keeble sighed down his nose and fluttered his fingers. "No one except you."

He reached into a locker and produced a bundle of clothes.

"Emergency falling-in kit," he explained, giving them to me. "I don't suppose anything will fit."

As there was a mixture of his own cast-offs, which were too wide, and Lynnie's, which were too narrow, he was right. Everything, besides, was too short.

"In addition," he went on, "how did the boy and girl know we were on the river at all and would be coming down through Harbour Lock? How long did you expect them to wait there clinging to the post? How did they know exactly which boat to hail, and how did they avoid being rescued by any other boat?"

"The best accidents always look as if they couldn't possibly be anything else."

"I grant you that," he said, nodding. "I just think that this one literally couldn't be set up."

"Yes, it could. With a safe get-out, in that if it didn't work according to plan, if for instance Peter had been on the bows instead of Dave, they had no need to go into the act of yelling for help, because of course they waited to make sure it was us before they started."

"They were in danger," Keeble protested.

"Maybe. I'd like to take a close look at that post."

"And there might have been other boats around, helping. Or watching."

"If Dave never came within range of the punt pole, they lost nothing but an opportunity. If other boats had been watching, there would simply have been more people to cry accident. The girl was screaming and splashing and dramatically dropping her rope when the boy hit Dave. We were all watching her, not him. Any sized audience would have been doing the same."

"And how could boy and girl have known where Dave would be this Sunday, in the first place? And why on God's earth should anyone want to kill him?"

I stepped into some aged gray trousers of Keeble's and found them a foot too generous round the waist. My boss wordlessly held out a short striped elastic schoolboy belt, which took care of the problem by gripping like a tourniquet.

"It was a simple accident, Gene. It had to be."

The trousers ended four inches above my ankles, and the socks I slowly fumbled my way into made no effort to bridge the gap.

"Gene!" said Keeble, exasperated.

I sighed. "You'll agree I'm a sort of specialist in arranging accidents?"

"Not usually fatal ones," he protested.

"Not often." And no more, if I could wriggle out of it. "Just a general stage-managing of events, so that the victim believes that what has happened to him is the merest mischance."

Keeble smiled. "You've sprung more hares that way . . ."

"So," I said reasonably. "I'm apt to spot a rig-up when I see one."

The smile half faded and changed into speculation.

"And no," I said, "I was not concussed in the recent boating party and I haven't got water on the brain."

"Keep your telepathy to yourself," he said uncomfortably. "I just think you are mistaken."

"O.K., then I'll spend my holiday in Putney."

He said, "No," so vehemently, so explosively, that there was no subtlety left in the situation. From his naked alarm I saw unmistakably how much he understood of my depressed mental state and how convinced he was that I wouldn't survive three weeks of my own company. Shocked, I realized that his relief when I answered his telephone call had not been at finding me at home, but at finding me alive. He had dug me out onto the river to keep an eye on me and was prepared to send me off on any old wild-goose chase so long as it kept me occupied. Then maybe, I supposed, he thought I would snap out of it.

"The blues," I said gently, "have been with me for a long time."

"Not like this."

I had no answer.

After a pause he said persuasively, "Three world-class stallions disappearing . . . isn't that also the sort of accident you don't believe in?"

"Yes, it is. Especially when someone tries to get rid of the man who bought two of them."

He opened his mouth and shut it again. I almost smiled.

"It was a craftsman's accident," I said. "It could hardly have been done better. All they didn't bargain for was interference from someone like me."

He still didn't believe it, but as he was now happy that I should, since it meant that I would go to the States, he raised no more objections. With a shrug and a rueful smile he tossed me a darned brown sweater, which hung round me like a tent; and I picked up my own wet clothes and followed him out into the sunshine.

Peter and Lynnie both giggled at my baggy appearance, the nervous shock still sharp in their voices, especially Lynnie's. I grinned at her and ruffled her hair, and made as if to kick Peter overboard, and some of the tension loosened in their eyes. In another half hour they would have reached the compulsive talking stage and an hour after that they would be back to normal. Nice ordinary kids, with nice ordinary reactions.

I climbed wearily up onto the cabin roof and spread out my clothes to dry. My shoes were still there where I had stepped out of them, and absentmindedly I put them on. Then, standing up, I looked across to the weir, and back to the hefty post with its notice DANGER, and at the innocent empty punt tied up behind the *Flying Linnet:* and I found myself thinking about the legend of the Sirens, the sea nymphs who sat on a rock near a whirlpool and with their pretty voices drew passing sailors toward them, to lure them to their death.

3

THE PUNT had the name of the owner screwed onto the stern on a small metal plate. The lockkeeper, consulted, said that it came from a boatyard about a mile down the river, next to a pub; you couldn't miss it.

"That," I murmured to Keeble, "is where we had our drinks this morning."

His eyelids flickered. He said to the lockkeeper, "I suppose a lot of punts from there come up through your lock?"

"They sure do, on a fine Sunday like this," he agreed.

"Did you happen to notice this one, with a girl and a young man in it? The girl had long fair hair, white trousers, and a pink shirt, and the boy was wearing tight pale-blue jeans and a red and yellow check shirt."

"I should say they came up before my dinner break. I can't remember anyone like that this afternoon."

The lockkeeper eased the white-topped hat back on his head and eyed the boats lining up to go into the lock. He was a youngish man with an air of long-suffering patience, the occupational result, no doubt, of a life spent watching an endless procession of incompetence. People, he had said matter-of-factly, fell into his lock every day of the week. Near-drownings, however, were of no special interest to him: he too often had to deal with the unsaved.

"Would you know them again?" Keeble asked.

The lockkeeper shook his head decisively. "Not a chance. And if I don't get back to my lock there'll be a lot of bad tempers coming through the gates and as like as not we'll be fishing out another one."

He gave me a sketchy farewell salute as one of the few who had gone down his weir and walked away, and strolled unhurriedly back to deal with his Sunday going-home traffic problem.

"We may as well tow the punt back to the boatyard," Keeble said thoughtfully. "We've got to go down past there anyway, and they won't be able to spare anyone to come and fetch it on a busy day like this. And maybe they'll know where the boy and girl came from."

And maybe they wouldn't, I thought: but even the most hopeless questions have to be asked.

"I'd like to look at the post," I said.

Keeble was agreeable, but Lynnie and Peter and their mother were horrified when they found where we were proposing to go, and said they would wait on the bank. In a row, with anxious faces, they stood guard over the punt, while Keeble neatly maneuvered the *Flying Linnet* upstream a little way through the downcoming cruisers and then drifted gently across toward the post. I, standing on the stern seat, caught hold of the crossbar with its emphatic warning and clung to it while Keeble put the boat into reverse against the drag of the weir stream.

Once the engine was thrusting hard enough to hold its own, so that the tension on my arms slackened, I knelt down on the seat and tried to do what the girl had been doing, to pass a rope around the post from one hand to the other. The tendency of the two-ton *Flying Linnet* to drift away couldn't have been much less to deal with than the weight of the punt, but even allowing almost for the fact that my arms were longer and stronger, it was easy. I secured the rope and gave a thumbs-up to Keeble, who stopped the engine. Then with one toe wedged and the narrow side of the boat under my pelvis, I shoved up the sleeves of the brown sweater and leaned down and over to inspect the scenery.

"For God's sake be careful," Keeble said, his voice sharp over the noise of the weir.

I turned my head and laughed at him.

"We haven't any more dry clothes," he pointed out, scowling. "None that you can get into. If you fall in again you'll have to go home wet."

Smiling, I turned back to the post. But feel and look how I might, there was nothing out of the ordinary about the square sturdy white-painted balk of timber set rocklike up on end in the Thames bed.

Keeble shrugged and said, "I told you so," and steered his boat back to the bank.

"How about fingerprinting the punt?" I said.

"You never let up."

"You should be glad of it."

The long line of past occasions when not letting up had led to a useful harvest rose up between us, and I saw his conviction waver.

"All right, Gene, if you're sure."

"Get Raben to do it. He's the best."

"All right. Tomorrow."

"How about the police?"

He pursed his lips. "It's not our usual territory. More theirs, I agree. But they're not likely to take your theory seriously, or to act on it, unless we tell them what your job is . . . and impress them with it. No, I'm not in favor of that. We could just go along with this quietly on our own for a little while, I think."

"So that if nothing turns up, we won't have made bloody fools of ourselves?"

All his facial muscles contracted for a second. "You are not paid to turn your perceptions on your boss."

"I probably am."

"That's a point."

The boat grounded gently against the bank, and I helped Joan and Lynnie back on board. Peter, on his father's directions, stepped into the punt and handed him up the mooring rope, which Keeble fastened to the cleat on the *Flying Linnet*'s stern. Then, towing the punt, we took our turn into the lock, explained what we were doing to the lockkeeper, and cruised downstream to the pub and its next-door boatyard.

A flustered middle-aged boatman there was trying to cope with returning family picnic parties and a bunch of youths and girls who wanted to fill in the half hour before the pub opened at seven o'clock. The late afternoon sun shone redly on his big sweating face and his freckled bald head, and we had to wait while he juggled his customers precariously in and out of skiffs and punts and took their money and warned the young couples that it was an offense to be on the river without lights after dark and that the boatyard closed at nine-thirty anyway.

When Keeble at last had a chance he asked the boatman if he had seen the girl with fair hair and the boy in a red and yellow check shirt who had hired a punt that morning.

"Seen 'em? I suppose so, I've been here all day."

"I mean, do you remember them," Keeble said patiently.

"Where are they then?" The boatman looked round suspiciously.

"They've gone," Keeble began.

"Then who's going to settle up?" said the boatman belligerently, this last problem looking to be just one too many for his temper.

"Oh, I will," said Keeble soothingly. He took his wallet out of his back pocket and unfolded it to show the usual thickish wad. Keeble didn't have to live on Her Majesty's pay and worked from conviction, not need; his beer money represented a week's wage to me and his boat a year's.

"How much do they owe you?" He handed over what the boatman asked and offered a fiver on top. "I'd like to hire this punt for this evening and tomorrow." He said. "Is that all right?"

The boatman took the money without hesitation and made a few half-hearted efforts to appear cautious.

"Where'll you be taking it?"

"Henley," Keeble said.

"You won't leave the cushions out if it rains?"

Keeble shook his head.

"All right then." The boatman had already tucked the notes away. "And you'll bring it back tomorrow?"

"Tomorrow afternoon," Keeble agreed. "Now, about those young people who took it this morning . . ."

Unexpectedly the boatman suddenly leered. "I remember 'em," he said, "come to think of it, they was the two who had no business to be out together."

"What do you mean?" Keeble asked.

"Well, see, this girl, she said, like, what if her old man had put detectives on her, what would they say if she went off all day with him in a punt, and how she'd said she'd only come out as long as it was nothing anyone could use in a divorce. And the fellow in the check shirt turned round and said old moneybags, meaning her old man, see, would never find out where they'd been, he was in France on business wasn't he, or some such, and then they took note that I was standing there hearing and they sort of nudged each other and shut up. But I reckon as they were off for a bit on the side, see, and didn't want no one to catch 'em."

"Exactly," said Keeble to me with another touch of I-told-you-so.

"And very nicely done," I agreed. "Artistic."

"You haven't seen them since then, since this morning, I suppose?" Keeble said to the boatman. "Do you happen to know how they got here?"

"Car," said the boatman, waving an arm. "They came from the car park back there."

"Which car, do you know?"

He gave Keeble a pitying stare. "Look, there's cars in and out all day, what with the pub and us. And I'm looking at the river, see, with my hands full an' all, and I couldn't tell you no one who's come and gone nor what they came in, but they must have come in a car, because they come in the morning, and there's no buses along here on Sundays before half-past two in the afternoon."

"Thank you anyway," said Keeble, sighing. "You've been very helpful." He added another pound to his overpayment and the boatman's eyes swiveled rapidly from the pub to the clock over the boathouse door. Still ten minutes until the bar opened. I proceeded to fill them.

"Did the young man, or the girl, or both of them, speak with any special type of accent?" I asked.

Since he spoke broad Berkshire himself, the boatman's hesitation was understandable. "They talked," he said, considering, "like they do on the telly."

"Not much help," Keeble commented.

"How do you lash the end of your punts' mooring ropes?" I asked.

"Eh?" said the boatman, puzzled.

"Do you lash the end of the ropes to stop them unraveling?"

"Oh, I get you. No, we splice 'em. Turn the ends back and sort of weave them in. Lashing's no good as it comes undone too easily."

I unwound the punt's mooring rope from the *Flying Linnet*'s stern cleat. "This one is coming undone, though."

"Let's see that," he said suspiciously, and I gave it to him. He twisted the frayed unraveling strands in his strong dirty fingers and hovered in what I guessed to be a fairly usual mixture of fury and resignation.

"These bleeding vandals . . . excuse me, ma'am," he apologized to Joan, "these so-and-sos, they tie up to a tree, see, or something, and come they want to push on, they can't undo the knots if the rope's wet, and they just don't bother, they cut through the rope and off they go."

"Does that often happen?"

"Every summer we has this trouble now and then." He pulled the rope up straight, measuring its length with his eye. "There's a good four or five feet gone off this one, I shouldn't wonder. We've been talking of switching to chains, but they can get into holy terrors of knots, chains can. Here," he added to Keeble, "you'd better have another punt, one with a better rope."

"This one will be fine," Keeble said, fastening it on again. "We'll see you tomorrow."

He towed the punt down to Henley and right into the garage-like boathouse which kept the English summer off the *Flying Linnet*. The punt was secured alongside by Peter and his father and everyone disembarked along a narrow boardwalk carrying things like the remains from lunch, newspapers, bathing towels, and in my case wet clothes and a loaded jacket, out through the boathouse and into Keeble's Rover, which was parked on a neat square of grass at the back.

Peter's main care was for his precious camera, again hanging round his neck on its cord.

"I suppose," I said idly, "you didn't happen to take a photograph up there by the weir? You didn't happen to get a shot of those people in the punt?"

He shook his head, blinking like his father.

"Gosh, no, I didn't. I don't suppose actually I would have thought of taking one, not when everything was happening, do you think? I mean, it would have looked a bit off if you and Mr. Teller had been drowning and I was just standing there taking pictures and so on."

"You'll never be a newspaperman," I said, grinning at him.

"Wouldn't you have minded, then?"

"I don't think so."

"But anyway," he said mournfully, "I couldn't, you see, because I finished the film at lunchtime and I didn't have another one, so even if there had been a fire or something I couldn't have taken it." He looked at his camera thoughtfully. "I won't finish up any more films in the middle of the day, just in case."

"A fire," I agreed seriously, "would anyway make a much better picture than just people drowning, which they mostly do out of sight."

Peter nodded, considering me. "You know, you're quite sensible, aren't you?"

"Peter!" exclaimed his mother in unnecessary apology. "That's not the way to talk." And she wasn't much pleased when I said that as far as I was concerned he could say what he liked.

Keeble drove round to the station car park, where Lynnie and I transferred to the Austin.

"I'll ring in the morning," Keeble said, standing half out of his respectable car.

"Right."

"Take care of Lynnie."

"I'll do that."

Lynnie kissed her parents good-by, but her father more warmly, and made a face at Peter as the Rover rolled away out of the gate. Then she climbed into the Austin, waited until I was sitting beside her, and stretched out her hand to the ignition.

She was trembling again.

"Shall I drive?" I said mildly, making it absolutely her own choice.

She put both her hands in her lap and looked straight out through the windshield. Her face was pale above the orange dress.

"I thought you were both dead."

"I know."

"I still feel churned up. It's silly."

"It's not silly. And I expect you're fond of Dave Teller."

"He's sent us presents and things since we were little."

"A nice man."

"Yes." She sighed deeply and after a pause said calmly, "I think it would be better, if you really don't mind, if you drive back."

"Of course I will."

We changed places, and went back to London with more cars passing us than we passed. At the Chiswick circle I said I would drive her to her flat and go on home by taxi, but with a sideways laughing glance she said no taxi would stop for me in her father's clothes, and that she was feeling better and could quite easily do the last lap herself: so I rolled round the few corners to Putney and stopped outside my own front door.

Summer dusk filled the quiet street. No one about. Lynnie looked out of her window upwards at the tall house, and shivered.

"You're cold," I said, concerned for her bare arms.

"No . . . I have a cardigan in the back. I was just thinking about your flat."

"What about it?"

"It's so . . . empty." She gave a half-laugh, shrugging it off. "Well, I hope you won't have nightmares, after today."

"No . . ." I collected my things and got out of the car, and she moved over into the driver's seat.

"Will they have saved any dinner for you at the hostel?" I asked.

"Not a hope," she said cheerfully. "But I expect there'll be some cake and milk about, there usually is."

"Would you care to eat with me? Not up there," I added hastily, seeing the beginnings of well-brought-up suspicion. "In a restaurant, I mean."

"I've my mother to thank for my beastly mind," she said unexpectedly. "I really am rather hungry, and I don't see at all why I shouldn't have supper in your flat, if you've got any food." And without more ado she got out of the car and locked it, and stood expectantly beside me on the pavement.

"There are some tins," I said, reflecting. "Wait here just a second, would you? I just want to have a look round the back."

"Round the back?"

"For burglars," I said sardonically. But I went to look, as usual, at the powder-coated bottom flight of the fire escape. No one had been up or down all day.

Lynnie climbed the stairs to the fourth floor as easily as before, and having checked via a well-placed paper clip that my door hadn't been opened since I had shut it that morning, I put the key in the lock and let us in.

The green plastic lampshade in my sitting room scattered its uncozy glare over the tidy room, switching the soft gray light outside into sudden black and evoking the forlornness of institution buildings on winter afternoons. It wouldn't be much trouble, I thought, to go out and buy myself a red shade in the morning, and see if it propagated rosy thoughts instead.

"Sit down," I suggested. "Are you warm enough? Switch the electric fire on if you'd like it. I think I'll go and change, and then we can decide about going out."

Lynnie nodded, but took things into her own hands. When I came out of the bedroom she had already investigated my meager cupboard and had lined up a packet of soup, some eggs, and a tin of anchovies.

"Soup, and anchovies on scrambled egg," she said.

"If you'd really like that," I said doubtfully.

"I can't cook much else."

I laughed. "All right. I'll do the coffee."

There were burnt specks in the eggs when she had finished, which harmonized nicely with the scraped-off overdone toast and the brown anchovy strips, and there had been a slight over-emphasis on pepper.

"No one," she sighed, "is going to marry me for my cordon bleu."

There were plenty of other reasons why she'd be fending off suitors knee-deep in a year or two: a curvy figure, delicate neck, baby skin; the touch-me-not expression, the awakening social courage, the quick compassion. No one was going to care if she couldn't cook. But she wasn't secure enough to be told so at that moment.

"When were you seventeen?" I asked.

"The week before last."

"You didn't waste much time passing the driving test."

"I've been able to drive since I was twelve. Peter can, too." She finished her eggs and stirred two heaped teaspoonfuls of sugar into her coffee. "I was hungry. Funny, that."

"It's a long time since lunch."

"A terribly long time . . ." She suddenly looked me straight in the face, which she had mostly been avoiding, and with devastating innocence said, "I'm so glad you're alive."

I turned a hopeless wince into a laugh. "I'm so glad Dave Teller is."

"Both of you," she said. "It was the worst thing in my whole life when you didn't come up."

A child untouched by tragedy, I thought. A pity the world was such a rough place, would catch her by her pretty neck one day and tear her guts apart. No one ever escaped. To have got to seventeen unlacerated was merely a matter of luck.

When we had finished the coffee she insisted on doing the dishes, but when she hung up the tea towel I saw all her mother's warnings pour back, and she glanced at me and quickly away, and stood stiffly in the center of the room, looking nervous and embarrassed.

"Why don't you have any pictures on your walls?" she said jerkily.

I gestured to the trunk in the corner. "There are some in there, but I don't like them very much. Not enough to bother with hanging them up. . . . Do you know it's after ten? I'd better take you home or the hostel will shut you out."

"Oh, yes," she said in great relief, and then hearing her own voice, added in confusion: "I mean . . . I didn't know if you would think me very rude, dashing off as soon as we'd finished eating."

"Your mother is quite right to tell you to be cautious," I said lightly. "Little Red Riding Hood couldn't tell a wolf from her grandmother . . . and you can never rely on a woodcutter turning up in the nick of time."

The rigidity dissolved like mist. "You do say some extraordinary things," she said. "As if you could read my mind."

"I could." I smiled. "You'd better put that cardigan on. It will be cold outside."

"O.K." She pulled a dark-brown jersey out of her bucket-shaped tote bag and put it on. I bent to pick up a clean folded handkerchief which had fallen out with it, and when she was ready, handed it to her.

"Thanks," she said, looking at it casually. "That's the one Peter found in the punt."

"In the punt?"

"Yes, down a crack between two of the cushions. He gave it to me because it was too small for him, he said. Too sissy."

"Did he find anything else?"

"I don't think so. I mean it isn't stealing or anything, is it, to keep her handkerchief? I'll give it to her of course if she comes back, but by the time Peter was sitting in the punt, they had been gone already for ages."

"No, it's not stealing," I reassured her, though technically it was doubtful. "But may I have a look at it?"

"Of course."

She gave it back and I unfolded it: a white square of thin gauzy material. In one corner a stylized bear in a flat straw hat.

"Is that out of Walt Disney?" I asked.

She shook her head and said with surprise at my ignorance, "Yogi Bear."

"Who is Yogi Bear?"

"I can't believe it! Well, he's a character in a lot of cartoon films. Like Top Cat and Atom Ant and the Flintstones."

"I've seen the Flintstones," I agreed.

"Like them, then. The same people make Yogi Bear."

"Do you mind if I keep it for a day or two?"

"Of course, if you really want to," she said, puzzled. "But it surely hasn't any value."

Down in the street I said I might as well finish the job and drive her to her hostel.

"I'm really all right now," she protested. "You don't need to come."

"Yes, I do. Your father said to look after you, and I'm seeing you safe to your door."

She raised her eyebrows and gave me a comical look, but compliantly went round to the passenger seat. I started the car, switched on the lights, and started toward Kensington.

"Do you always do what Daddy tells you?" she asked, smiling.

She was feeling much surer of herself, I thought.

"Yes, when I want to."

"That's a contradiction in terms."

"So it is."

"Well, what do you actually *do?* What does *anyone* do in the Civil Service?"

"I interview people."

"What sort of people?"

"People who want jobs in government departments."

"Oh!" She laughed. "A sort of Personnel Officer?"

"Sort of."

"It sounds a bit drizz."

"The sun shines occasionally."

"You're pretty quick. We only made up drizz yesterday."

"A very useful word."

"Yes, we thought so too. Covers a lot of things nicely."

"Like wet boyfriends?"

She laughed. "Actually, it's pretty drizz to *have* a wet boyfriend." She pointed. "The hostel's down there, but we have to drive around and find somewhere to park the car all night. One or two squares down here don't have meters yet."

The nearest empty space was a good quarter of a mile from the hostel, so I walked her back.

"You don't need to . . ." she began. "Well, don't say it. Daddy said."

"Right," I agreed.

She sniffed resignedly and walked beside me out of step, the leather bag swinging and her flat shoes silent on the pavement. At the hostel's glossy black well-lit front door she came to a stop and hovered on one foot, her half-anxious uncertain expression saying clearer than words that she wasn't sure how to part from me. I wasn't old enough for uncle terms or young enough for a casual contemporary brush-off. I worked for her father, but wasn't his servant. Lived alone, looked respectable, asked nothing: I didn't fit into any of the categories she had yet learned how to deal with. I put out my hand and smiled.

"Good night, Lynnie."

Her clasp was brief, warm, relieved.

"Good night . . ." There was a pause while she made up her mind to it; and even then it was little more than a breath. "Gene."

"I wish you," I said, "blind traffic wardens and foam rubber bumpers."

"Good night." The chuckle rolled spontaneously in her throat. "Good night." She turned on one toe and jumped the two steps up to the door, then looked over her shoulder and waved as she went inside.

Little Lynnie, I thought, whistling to a passing taxi, little Lynnie, right at the beginning of it. Flying half consciously, half unconsciously, the notice-me flags of the pretty young female; and it was no use pretending that she didn't make me hungry; that she wasn't absolutely what I would have liked as an oasis in my too continent life. But if I had learned anything in thirty-eight years it was who not to go to bed with.

And, more drearily, how not to.

4

THE BUTTRESS Life offices on Thirty-third Street were high on customer appeal on the sixth floor. On the fifth and seventh they tucked the computers and electric typewriters into functional plasterboard cubicles. I sat three inches deep in black leather and considered that of all American craftsmen I admired the chair designers most: in no other country in the world could one sit on the same seat for several hours without protest from the sacroiliac.

I had waited forty pleasantly cool minutes already. Long enough to discover that the rows of potted plants along the low wall dividing the 40-foot square hall into five smaller bays were made of plastic. Long enough to admire the pinewood walls, the ankle-deep carpet, the carefully lowered ceiling with its inset lights. In each bay there was a large desk, with one large chair behind it, one at the side, one in front. Nearly all occupied. Dividing each bay neatly in two stood a second, smaller desk; for the secretary-receptionist with his back discreetly to his boss. In front of him, in each bay, the long black leather bench for waiting on.

I waited. There was still someone for the big man to see before me. Very sorry, said the secretary apologetically, but the schedule had been crowded even before Mr. Teller's cable arrived. Could I possibly wait?

So why not? I had three weeks to spare.

The light was dim and piped music poured over everything like syrup. That and the built-in deadness of the acoustics made the earnest consultations going on at the five big desks completely inaudible to the waiting benches, while at the same time giving the customers a comforting illusion that they weren't alone in their troubles. Everyone, at the core of things, was alone. Just some more than others.

I hadn't slept all night after leaving Lynnie; but not her fault. It had been one long stupid struggle between a craving for oblivion and conviction that appeasing it wasn't so much morally wrong as a thoroughgoing defeat. I had never learned to accept defeat. Obstinacy had given me what success I had had in my job, and it alone seemed to be keeping me alive, since all other props were as much use as toothpicks in an avalanche. Enthusiasm for finding Dave Teller's horse burned in me as brightly as wet coal dust: and the nation would hardly collapse if I left its employ.

Caroline had crowded like a flood tide through my head and down my body. Caroline . . . whom I would have married had it not been for the husband who would not divorce her.

Caroline had left him to live with me, and had felt guilty about it. A mess. An ordinary, everyday mess. Her fine passion had fretted away over six frustrating years of will-he won't-he?—and to the end he wouldn't. Not that he'd ever got her back. In the year since she had left me she had returned to nursing and was working in a Nairobi hospital, impervious to come-back letters from either of us.

The sharp pain of her departure had dulled to the extent that I no longer felt it through every waking minute: it came stabbing back at longer and longer intervals. But when it did, I remembered her as she'd been at the beginning, and the hunger was pretty well unbearable. It was easy enough to find different girls to talk to, to work with, to take to bed: hard to find a match on all levels: and Caroline had been a match. In the past year, instead of receding, the loneliness had closed in. My work, of its nature, set me apart. And I had no one to go home to, to share with, to care for. The futility and emptiness had gone down to my roots, and nothing seemed to lie ahead but years and years more of what I was already finding intolerable.

The clients at the big desk stood up, shook hands, and left. The secretary ushered the man with the earlier appointment into the presence. I went on waiting, without impatience. I was accustomed to it.

The punt, investigated in Henley that morning, had produced nothing but ten different sets of smudged fingerprints, of which the topmost and stickiest were Peter's. The Yogi Bear handkerchief was on its way round the manufacturers, in the distant hope that someone could tell where it had been sold. Dave Teller, briefly visited, had said wanly to charge everything to him. The super VC 10 which lifted off at 3 P.M. British summertime from Heathrow had landed at Kennedy at 3:10. Buttress Life closed its doors at six, which gave it still a half hour to go. And outside in the canyon streets the 100-degree heat wave crept up a notch to 101.

My turn came for the big desk. The big man, on his feet behind it, held out a large dry flabby hand and produced the sincere smile of the professional insurance man. Having settled me into the large comfortable chair alongside, he sat down himself and picked up the cable discreetly placed to hand by the secretary. A polished chunk of wood sat on the desk between us. On it, neat gold letters facing me said helpfully: PAUL M. ZEISSEN.

"We received this cable from Mr. Teller," he said. A slight, very slight, undertone of disapproval.

I nodded. I had sent it myself.

"Our own investigators are experts." He didn't like me coming: but he wouldn't want to lose the Teller policies. His politeness had effort behind it.

I soothed him down, more from habit than anything else.

"Of course. Please think of me simply as an auxiliary. Mr. Teller persuaded me to come over because he has unfortunately broken a leg in England and will be immobilized in hospital for a few weeks. He sent me very much on impulse, as a personal friend, to kind of represent him. To see if there was anything I could do. There was no suggestion that he wasn't satisfied with your firm." I paused delicately. "If he criticized anyone, it was the police."

Paul M. Zeissen's smile warmed up a fraction from within: but he hadn't risen to high executive status in his tough profession without disbelieving half that everyone said. That was all right with me. Half of what I'd said was true. Or half true, anyway.

"Mr. Teller understands of course," he said, "that it is for our own sakes that we are looking for the horse?"

"Naturally," I agreed. "Mr. Teller is also most anxious that you should succeed, as the horse is irreplaceable. He would infinitely prefer his return to any amount of insurance money."

"A million and a half," said Zeissen reverently.

"Worth more on the hoof," I said.

He glanced at me with a first gleam of real welcome. Once he'd swallowed the firm's affronted pride, it was quite clear that they'd nothing to lose by letting me in.

"One of our best men, Walt Prensela, is in charge of the Chrysalis case," he said. "He'll give you the picture. He knows you're coming, I sent him a memo with a copy of the cable." He pressed the switch on his desk intercom.

"Walt? We have Mr. Hawkins from England here. Shall I have him come up to you now?"

The polite question was, as so often in American affairs, an equally polite order. The affirmative duly came. Zeissen flipped the switch and stood up.

"Walt's office is one floor up, number four-seven. Anyone will direct you. Would you like to go up now?"

I would; and I went.

I'd expected to have to deal with the same ruffled feathers in 47, but I didn't, because Walt had done his homework though I wasn't sure of that at first. He greeted me with businesslike casualness, shook hands, waved me to the spare chair, and sat down himself, all in five smooth seconds. Much my age, I judged, but shorter and a good deal thicker. His hands were square and powerful with nails so brief that the fingertip pads seemed to be boiling over backwards. There were middle European origins in the bone structure of the skull, topped by roughly cropped wiry gray-brown hair, and his deep-socketed brown eyes were set permanently into the I-don't-believe-a-word-of-it expression of his boss downstairs, only more so.

"So, Gene," he said, neither with nor without much friendliness, "you've come a long way."

"Dave Teller's idea, Walt," I said mildly.

"Looking for horses. . . . Do you do much of that?" His voice was flat, uninformative.

"Practically none. How about you?"

His nostrils twitched. "If you mean, was it I who didn't find the other two, then, no, it wasn't."

I tried a smile: didn't get one back.

He said: "Buttress Life had to pay up for Allyx three years ago. One million six hundred and forty-three thousand seven hundred and twenty-nine dollars, give or take a nickel. Showman, the first one, was insured with another company."

"Accident?" I murmured. "Or design."

He rubbed his left thumb over the top of the round-ended fingers, the first of a hundred times I saw that gesture.

"Now that you've come, design. Before, I wasn't sure."

"I'm officially on holiday," I protested. "I came only because Teller asked me. You should read no meaning into it."

He gave me a level, half-sardonic stare.

"I checked you out," he said, flicking at the copy of the cable, which lay on his desk. "I wanted to know just what sort of limey busybody was being wished onto me."

I didn't say anything, and he made a clicking noise at the side of his mouth, expressive of understanding, resignation and acceptance, all in one.

"A screener," he said. "How come Teller found you?"

"How come you found me?" I asked instead.

"I mentioned your name in two places," he said complacently. "The FBI, and the CIA. And got a positive reaction from both. A couple of useful pals there filled me in. It seems you're a major stumbling block in the way of the planting of spies in certain government departments and places like biological warfare research laboratories; and you've passed on some useful warnings on that subject to our people at Fort Detrick. They say the other side have tried to deter you, a little roughly, once or twice." He sighed. "You have a clean bill with our boys. And how."

"And with you?"

"They said you didn't like limelight."

"It's all yours."

"Just so as I stand in right with Buttress."

My decisive nod satisfied him. If we found the horse, he was welcome to the handshakes.

"Fill me in, then," I said. "How did Chrysalis get lost?"

Walt glanced at his watch and checked it against the electric clock on the wall. The little boxlike office had no windows, as the single glass panel faced out onto the corridor; and although it was cool and comfortable enough, it was no place to talk if one didn't have to.

"Five after six," Walt said. "Do you have any other engagements?"

"Know any good bars?" I suggested.

"A mind reader." He raised eyes to heaven. "There's Delaney's a block up Broadway."

We stepped out of the air conditioning into the sweltering street, up 30 degrees in two paces. With the humidity running also at 98 percent, walking as little as a hundred yards left one damp to the skin. I never minded it: New York in a heat wave was always preferable to New York in a snowstorm, or anywhere hot to anywhere cold, for that matter. Cold seeped farther than into the bones, numbed the mind, drained the will. If the depression deepened toward winter, defeat would come with the snow.

Delaney's was spilling out onto the pavement with a business convention let out of school. An oblong name tab sat on each neat seersucker lapel, a confident smile hid the anxiety behind every face; they stretched from the substantial group outside into the deep cool gloom of the bar. Pushing through them looked a problem; conversation in their company an impossibility.

"How about your hotel? Where are you staying?" Walt said.

"The Gotham."

Walt's eyebrows rose two clear inches.

"Teller's paying," I said. "He has an account there."

"What did you do then? Save his life?"

"Six times," I agreed, matching his sarcasm.

"He must really think," Walt said reflectively, "that you might get his horse back."

"We," I said.

"Nope. You. There's no trail. I've looked."

A colored cab driver in rolled-up shirt sleeves took us to the hotel, hot air blowing in gusts through the open window each time he accelerated. The city moved sluggishly under the brazen sun and there was more rubbish than usual littering the streets.

"This is a filthy town," said Walt, seeing it through my eyes. "Give me Chicago."

"Too cold," I said automatically. "Beautiful, but too cold. That freezing wind off the lake . . ."

"Are you guys from Chicago?" said the cab driver. "I was born there, in the Loop."

Walt talked to him about that. I drifted away into the disoriented state of not caring a jot about the cab driver, or Walt, or Dave Teller, or Caroline, or anyone on earth. We went up to my hotel room and I dragged through the host motions of ringing down for a bottle of Scotch and ice and seeing to temperature, light and ashtrays. Walt loosened his tie and took a first appreciative swallow.

"You look pooped," he said.

"Natural state."

"I guess it's midnight already, to you."

"I guess."

There was a considerable drinking pause. Then he said, shifting his sturdy body in the leather chair, "Well, do you want to know about this horse, or don't you?"

"Sure." The boredom in my answer came over shockingly strong, even to me. He looked faintly startled and then speculative, but when he spoke it was strictly business.

"They were taking him in a horse van from Kennedy airport to Lexington, Kentucky. He'd spent the compulsory twenty-four hours' immigration quarantine in the airport stable, along with six other horses which came over on the same flight. All normal at that time. They loaded Chrysalis and four others into the van, and drove westward from New York on the Pennsylvania Turnpike."

"Time?" I asked.

"Left Kennedy 4 P.M. Monday. Last Monday, that is. A week today. Estimated Lexington midday Tuesday. Seven hundred miles."

"Stops?"

"Yeah," Walt said. "Stops. That's where the trouble started." He swirled the clinking ice round in his glass. "They took their first meal stop at a diner near Allentown, ninety-three miles from New York. There were four men in the van, two drivers and two grooms. Drivers in the cab, grooms in back with the cargo. At the first stop they took turns to eat, drivers first, grooms after. The drivers chivvied the grooms, and gave them too short a time to eat a good meal. There was an unfriendly argument."

"They all say so?"

"Yeah. I've talked to all four, one at a time. They're all trying their hardest to pin the blame on the others. They left the diner and went about two hundred miles to their next stop at Bedford. That was no better. Far from cooling off, they had begun to scuffle.

"They turned off the turnpike onto the interstate highway—70—south of Pittsburgh, and left that again at Zanesville, taking the southwest fork to Cincinnati. About fifty miles farther on they turned due south to cross the Ohio River into Kentucky, and go on through Paris and down the Paris Pike to Lexington."

"I'll need to see it on a map," I said.

He nodded. "From Zanesville to Paris they took secondary routes, though all paved roads, of course. Right? Now, it was in Ohio that the van was hijacked, and it was over the state border in Kentucky when it was found, which has caused a couple of arguments here and there."

"Hijacked! That's the first I've heard of that."

"It was hijacked all right."

"How did it happen?"

"By that time, Tuesday morning, the drivers and the grooms were all eating at the same time, though at each end of the lunch counter. They left the horses unguarded for a full quarter hour, and during that time someone simply drove off with the whole works."

"Surely the drivers locked up, and took the keys, at least?"

"Oh, sure. It was a good job though. A direct wire contact from the battery terminals to the starter motor."

"So then what?"

"When they found the van gone the drivers called the police, but it wasn't until Wednesday morning that the van was found off the road and out of sight around a hill in Kentucky. But—no horses. The ramps were down, and all the horses had been let loose."

"Deliberately."

"Sure. United. All the halters were still in the van. Those race horses were all free with no bridle or anything to catch them by. The Kentucky boys reckon the horses were let out to create a diversion, to get the cops off the tails of the hijackers by making them chase horses all over."

"And it worked."

"Yeah," said Walt gloomily. "The owners kicked up stink. All the horses were valuable, not only Chrysalis. But only Chrysalis was insured with Buttress."

"Did they get all the others back?"

"Yeah. But Chrysalis has as good as disappeared off the face of the earth."

"Fingerprints?"

"Gloves."

Walt had talked himself dry. I refueled his glass and felt like sleep.

"What do you think?" he said.

I shrugged. "It was Chrysalis they really wanted."

"But why? Why should anyone want to steal a stallion? That's what's got us all floored. I don't know much about horses, I'm a false claims man really. I just got pitched into this between cripple cases, if you get me. But even I know that it's the stallion's name that brings in the stud fee. Say someone's stolen Chrysalis, what's the point? They can't advertise him for stud, so he isn't worth a dime. We figured someone might be nutty enough to want him all to themselves, like some world famous painting, but you can hide a painting quietly in a cellar, which you can't do with a horse. The whole thing doesn't make sense."

I had my own views on that, but I said only, "What happened to Allyx?"

"I only know about that from the files. I got the case out and looked it up this morning. Allyx was a French horse, apparently one of the best young sires in Europe. He was nine when he came over here, and already his get had won a list of races as long as your arm. Dave Teller was head of the syndicate which bought him; that's why he was insured with us, as we do all the Teller estate work. Allyx was delivered safely to the Teller stud farm. No trouble in transit that time. But he was there only four days. Then there was a fire in the stables one night and they took all the horses out of the barn and turned them loose into a small corral."

"And when they came to fetch them—no horses?"

He nodded. "There was a broken rail over the far side, which no one knew about. All the horses had got through it, including Allyx. They caught all the others, though some were free for days. No sign ever of Allyx. The company had to face that he probably got into the foothills of the Appalachian Mountains and maybe broke his neck, and in the end they had to pay up."

"What about the fire?"

"There was apparently nothing suspicious about it at the time. One of our very best men found no evidence of fire being set. Still, stable fires can be started so easily . . . a cigarette butt in a pile of straw leaves no trace. This one didn't do much damage before they put it out. No question of kerosene, for instance. The whole chain of events was agreed to be accidental."

I smiled thinly.

"What about Showman?"

Walt shook his head. "I don't know how he got loose. But they found him. Dead, of course. He'd been dead some time, I think."

"Where?"

"Oh, in the Appalachians. He came from that area, same as the others. But then Lexington has more stud farms than anywhere else in the States, so there's no significance in that really."

"You went down to Lexington last week?"

He nodded. "Flew there Wednesday, when Mrs. Teller called us."

"Mrs. Dave Teller?"

"Uh-huh." Something moved obscurely in Walt's face. Dave's wife had made an impression. "She's English, like you."

"I'll go down there tomorrow," I said. I watched him waver and decide not to tell me about her. Instead, he looked at his watch, put down his glass firmly, and stood up.

"Must be off," he said. "It's our anniversary, and my wife's fixed something special."

"Give her my apologies for keeping you."

"That's all right. It fitted in fine. I go home from Grand Central, not far. Walk it fast. Twenty minutes to traintime."

I walked him to the door.

"Walt, would you be free to come down to Lexington in the morning?" As he hesitated, I added, "There's no point in my covering all the ground twice. I'd appreciate having you along."

"Be glad to, Gene," he said too politely, and I thought to hell with you, Walt, to hell with everything on earth, including me, but I'm stuck with this horse nonsense for the next three weeks, and if I say go to Lexington, you go. I hid the violent moment of irritation in turning from him to open the door, and I understood his reluctance anyway, as who likes to be dragged down to do the same piece of work twice, especially under the critical eye of an imported limey busybody?

He shook my hand. "I'll call you in the morning," he said, his feelings under better control than mine.

"Seven-thirty?"

"All right." He loosened his jaw muscles into what looked like going to be a smile but didn't quite make it, sketched a salute with the thick-topped fingers, and ambled unhurriedly away down the passage.

I had dinner in the hotel restaurant. A steak. Never eat steak west of Nebraska, they used to say. The beef was bred on the prairie and walked eastward to the markets: when it got to eastern Nebraska it hit the corn belt and only after that was it fat enough to kill. New York steaks were mostly superb, but I didn't suppose they'd walked in through the New Jersey Tunnel. Long distance haulage took care of that . . . and whoever had removed Allyx and Chrysalis had had a haulage problem too. You couldn't ride a stallion along state highways. For one thing, they no longer took kindly to a saddle after years at stud, even if they had been reasonable to handle in the first place.

Nightclubs attract me like wet Mondays in Manchester, and apathy kept me from even reading the list of shows. I went straight upstairs after dinner to catch up on a lot of lost sleep and woke again infuriatingly at two, dead tired and with a restless brain.

From habit, the Luger lay under my pillow.

It was another long night.

5

WE FLEW down in the morning, Walt's puffed eyes showing that the anniversary had been duly celebrated and mine feeling as if they'd been rolled in grit.

The two drivers, reached by telephone, met us by appointment in the entrance hall of a motel near the center of Lexington, where Walt had stayed on his previous trip. He booked rooms for us both, and we took the drivers up to his, which proved a mile short of Gotham standards but hot on cleanliness and Kleenex.

Walt switched on the air conditioning, shuffled chairs around, and promised beer later. The drivers, very much on the defensive, went sullenly through the disastrous tale again, aware beyond any doubt that they should never have left the horses unwatched and were more than likely to lose their jobs. Nothing they said added much to what Walt had already told me.

"Do you know each other well?" I asked.

The thin birdlike one said they did.

"And the grooms. Do you know them? And do they know each other?"

"Seen them around," said the heavy one. "The lazy so-and-sos."

The thin one said, "One of them came from the Midway Farm."

That was Dave Teller's. "He came specially for Chrysalis. It's him ought to be blamed for the whole thing."

"Did the boys know each other before the trip?"

"Sure," said the heavy one. "Way they talked they both been in the horse game all their lives."

Walt sniffed and nodded. He'd checked all this, his resigned face said. Routine.

To the drivers I said, "I want you to think back and make a list of all the cars and trucks you can remember seeing on the road, all the way from Kennedy to the place you lost the horses."

They looked aghast and as if I were crazy.

"Look," I said, "on those turnpikes you sometimes see the same cars over and over. The ones going your way, that is. You see them at the rest stops, and maybe you start off first, and then they pass you, and then you see them again maybe stopped at another diner while you go on to the next one, and then they come past you again. Right?"

They nodded.

"So maybe you still remember some of the cars and trucks you saw on that trip? Especially any you saw on both days."

They stared at me. The heavy one said, "It's impossible. It was a week ago."

"I know. Try, anyway. Think it over. See if you can remember any at all, between you. Then write them down and leave the list here for us, sometime this evening."

I took out my wallet and tried twenty dollars each for size. It went down well enough. They said they would try.

"Don't invent anything," I said. "I'd rather pay for nothing than a lot of hogwash."

They nodded and went, with the beer postponed to their return.

"What are you looking for?" Walt asked curiously.

"Another horse van, I suppose."

He thought it over. "They could just have planned to rendezvous where the empty van was found. They didn't need to be seen on the road."

"I don't think they can have been sure when they would be able to do the hijacking. They wouldn't know where the drivers would stop for meals. No good fixing a rendezvous in Kentucky if the opportunity came earlier, up near Wheeling."

"They wouldn't want to drive too far with a hot truck," Walt agreed. "In fact, it was twenty-five miles, mostly back roads. They made straight for the hills, where it would take longest to round up loose horses."

"Any tracks?"

"No tire tracks of any use. The nearest road was gravel, dry and dusty this time of year. There were the tracks of the van going off the road round behind a hillock, but on the road itself they were just a jumble. Every car which passed raised a cloud of dust and wiped out all tracks which were there before."

I grunted. "Hoof prints?"

"Dozens of those. In all directions."

"Back onto the gravel road?"

He shook his head resignedly. "Impossible to tell. None on top of the van's tire tracks, anyway. But we took a lot of soil samples, on the outside chance something would turn up later."

"You did it pretty thoroughly."

The smile almost came. "A million and a half," he said briefly, "is a lot of insurance."

Midway Farm had prosperity printed on its gateposts, and I went through them alone, as Walt had said he felt the onset of a migraine headache.

A middle-aged Hungarian woman opened the door to me and in halting English asked me my business. Diagnosing her accent from long practice, I replied in her own language, as it was simpler, and presently, having consulted in the drawing room, she showed me in there.

Dave's wife stood in the center of a quarter acre of deep green carpet, surrounded by deep green walls, white paint, and tomato-red upholstery. She flicked my card with one thumb and said, "You're the man who fished Dave out of the river."

"Yes," I said, surprised.

"He telephoned to me yesterday," she explained. "He says I am to trust you entirely."

She was a slim small-boned creature with the rounded tight little bottom which comes from riding horses a great deal in early girlhood. Her jawline was delicately square, nose narrow, eyes wide and bright. Gray speckled the mouse-brown springy hair, and if she was wearing cosmetics one would have needed to be nearer than I was to be certain of it. Decisive assurance showed from every crisp gesture, and from her tone I gathered that taking her husband's word for things was not her habit.

"Sit down," she said, pointing to a tomato chair. "Drink?" It was two o'clock on a hot afternoon. "Scotch," she said without waiting for an answer, making it a statement, not a choice.

I watched her splash the pale golden liquid onto ice cubes in two tall glasses, and add a token drop of water. She came across and held out one of them with a graceful sun-tanned arm. A heavy gold chain bracelet loaded with fobs and charms clinked from her wrist, and into my nostrils floated a trace of Joy.

I tasted the whiskey. Hedges and Butler's Royal, I thought. Too fine and light for anything else. The flavor from one sip lasted a long time on my tongue.

"Eva says you speak Hungarian," she said, moving away, picking up her own glass, and taking an adult swallow.

"Mm, yes."

"She was most impressed."

"I came about Chrysalis," I began.

"Do you speak any other languages?" Her voice veered more to American than English and had the abrupt, inconsequential lurch of two drinks too many; but it didn't show in her face.

"German," I said, raising a dutiful social smile.

The way I'd been taught languages, it took a week for a smattering, three months for fluency, and two years to bring one to the point of reorganizing typical speech and thought patterns when one heard them translated back into perfect English. In one period of seven years, in my twenties, I'd been crammed with German, Hungarian, and five Slavonic languages, from Russian and Czech to Serbo-Croat. None of them was likely to come in handy for finding stallions, and in any case they were almost out of date. The new boys were learning Swahili, Arabic and Chinese.

"And French, I suppose?" she said.

"A little," I agreed.

"Enough for the necessities of life, I expect." Her expression and emphasis gave the word "necessities" a precise meaning, which wasn't food and drink.

"Absolutely," I agreed, acknowledging her definition.

She laughed. Nothing frail or fine-boned about that.

"Chrysalis," she said, "is a right bloody nuisance. He wouldn't have been my choice in the first place; that Purple Emperor strain is as soft as an old man's pencil and he's passing it on, they always do. Moth won the Derby in a shockingly bad year and if anything had given him half a race he'd have folded like a wet sheet." She took a deep swallow. "Do you know the first bloody thing about horses?"

"What *is* the first bloody thing about horses?"

She gave me a startled stare which turned into an incredulous laugh. "The first bloody thing about horses is that they make bloody fools of men."

I smiled back spontaneously, amused by the contrast between her robustness of thought and language and her delicacy of frame.

"I'm going for a swim," she said. "Bring your drink."

She mixed herself a new one in passing, and without looking back crossed the green carpet, pulled open a sliding glass door, pushed through the screen outside it, and walked with rocklike steadiness across a paved terrace and onto a deep green lawn. Sighing, I got to my feet and followed her. The grass was thick and resilient, a different species altogether from English turf, and a sprinkler on one side threw out diamond sprays.

She stopped on another paved area around a kidney-shaped pool and unfastened some clips on her yellow dress, which came off in one piece and left two more in view underneath. Her body was slender and well cared for, but not at all a young girl's. Middle to late forties, I thought: and the sort of woman who would have been uninteresting under thirty.

She slipped into the water and floated and I watched the sun make watered-silk ripples over her brown stomach.

"Come on in," she said. "There are plenty of swimsuits in the hut."

I smiled and shook my head, and sat down on one of the soft plastic poolside chairs. She took her time, humming and splashing gently with her hands. The sun was hot, but not like in the city. I took my jacket off and felt heat baking into my skin through the white cotton shirt. Peacefulness gradually seeped in too. I was in no hurry for her to rejoin me, which she presently did, the water drops shining singly on her oiled skin.

"You've hardly touched your drink," she observed accusingly. "Surely you're not one of those soft buggers who can't hold their liquor?" She picked up her own glass and went on proving that she, at any rate, wasn't.

"Chrysalis . . ." I began.

She interrupted immediately. "Do you ride?"

"I can," I said, "but I don't."

"Why not?"

"I haven't a horse. Nor a kingdom to give for one."

"Drink your whiskey," she said, smiling.

"In a while."

"Then strip off and get in the pool."

I shook my head.

"Why not?"

"I like it as I am." And I had too many bruises from the weir.

She shrugged, half annoyed. "Don't you do any bloody thing?"

"How many people knew at what hour Chrysalis would leave Kennedy Airport?"

"God," she said, "you're a bloody bore."

"Don't you want the horse back?"

"No," she said vehemently. "As far as I'm concerned, we'd be far better off with the insurance."

"Two hundred thousand dollars," I agreed, "is a heck of a gamble. Supposing he never sired another like Moth?"

"There's no stopping Dave when he's set his mind on something." She sat on the edge of a full-length chair and smoothed cream onto her face from a dusky pink tube. "And he had meant to sell off a bit of that, when he got back. God knows what will happen now he's strung up on those goddam pulleys."

"He'll be home in about four weeks."

"Yes. So he said." She lay down flat and closed her eyes. "I told him to take his time. It's too bloody expensive being ill over here."

Five quiet minutes passed. A single jet plane flew across, a silver streak so high up one couldn't hear it until it had gone. The air was still. The oiled brown body in the yellow bikini took in a hefty dose of ultraviolet and the ice cubes melted in the drinks.

"Take your clothes off, for God's sake," she said, without opening her eyes. "Or are you ashamed of that pink-white slug of a body the English usually bring over here?"

"I'd better be going."

"Do what you damn well like." She fluttered a lax wrist in a double gesture which said equally well, stay or good-by.

I stood up and walked over to the hut, a large beautifully made pine-wood structure with a protruding front roof, for shade. Inside were a bathroom and two changing rooms, and in the tiny lobby some shelves in a cupboard held bright-colored towels and swimsuits. I took a pair of blue shorts and put them on. The bruises on my legs very nearly matched. I left my shirt on, picked up a towel for a pillow, and went back and lay down on the next chair to hers.

She merely grunted with her eyes still shut, but after another minute she said, "If you want to know about the timetable for Chrysalis, you'd better ask Sam Hengelman in Lexington. He fixed the van. He runs a private service from here. Dave called me and told me the date the horse was being shipped over, and I called Sam Hengelman. And he took it from there."

"Who else did you tell the shipping date to?"

"It wasn't any goddam secret, for God's sake. I called six or seven of the syndicate to let them know. Dave asked me to. Half Kentucky knew about it, I guess."

She suddenly sat up straight and opened her eyes.

"Why the hell does it matter how many people knew when Chrysalis was coming? How do you know it was him the hijackers wanted?"

"Supposing they got just what they wanted?"

"Were you born yesterday? The bloodline is what breeders pay stud fees for. Chrysalis isn't worth a sou to anyone if they can't use his pedigree. No one's going to even send a decent mare to a stallion someone just happens to have handy, which has no name in the studbook, no history, and no papers; let alone pay fifteen thousand dollars for the privilege."

"Buttress Life have been looking for an insurance swindle."

"They can look till they're blue in the face." She picked up her glass, swallowed, and grimaced. "This drink's as warm as that pool and just as sodden. Mix me another, will you?" She held out the glass and I unwound myself and took it and my own back into the house. I mixed her the same size dose as before, concocted a different one for myself, and took them both back, the ice clinking coolly as I walked.

"Thanks." She sank almost half. "That's better."

I stood beside the pool and put one toe in the water. It was blood warm, or more.

"What's the matter with your legs?" she said.

"The same as your husband's, only mine didn't break."

"What's under the shirt?"

"The sun's too hot. I can do without a sunburn."

"Yes." She lay flat again. "Pink-white slug."

Smiling, I sat down on the edge of the pool with my back toward her and dangled my feet in the water. I ought, I supposed, to go away and do something more useful, like interviewing Sam Hengelman. But Walt would no doubt have thought of that, and done it, since his threatening migraine would only have lasted until the car we had rented had taken me out of sight. Walt and Dave's wife hadn't exactly clicked.

"Mr. Hawkins," she said from behind me.

"Mm?"

"What do you do for a living?"

"I'm a civil servant."

"With this?"

There was a sharp metallic click, the one sound guaranteed to raise the hairs on my neck as if I'd never left the jungle.

"Do you know what you're doing with that thing?" I asked, as conversationally as I could.

"Yes."

"Then put the safety on."

She didn't answer, and I stood up and turned round, and looked straight into the barrel of my own gun.

I deserve it, I thought. Slow, careless and stupid, I was anything one cared to mention.

She was sitting with her legs curled underneath her, the Luger lodged unwaveringly in her fist. The gap between us, five yards at least, was too great for anything constructive in the way of action, so I simply stood still.

"You're a cool bastard, I'll say that for you."

"You won't shoot me," I said, smiling.

"Why not?"

"I'm not insured for a million and a half."

Her eyes widened. "Does that mean that you think that I . . . I . . . *shot Chrysalis?*"

"It's possible."

She stared. "You're a goddam fool."

"So are you, if I may say so. That gun goes off very easily."

She looked down at it vaguely and before I could stop her she threw it away from her onto the paving stones. The jar as it hit the ground inevitably fired it. Flame streaked out of the barrel, and the bullet smashed through the whiskey glass which stood on the ground beside her long chair, nine inches from her body.

It took her a second to realize what had happened, then she shuddered heavily and put her hands over her face. I walked across to fetch the gun, and put the safety on, and then perched on the chair facing her.

"Games," she said in a shattered voice. "What do I have but games? Bridge and golf. All games."

"This too?" I put the Luger back in the underarm niche and buttoned the strap.

"I just thought I'd make you sweat."

"Why?"

"That's a bloody good question. A bloody good question. All games. Life is all bloody games."

"And we're all poor bloody losers," I agreed sardonically.

She put her hands down and looked at me. Her eyes were dry, but half her assurance had drained away.

"It was only a game. I didn't mean you any harm."

She thought she was telling the truth, but I'd met too many of the tricks the unconscious mind gets up to. Perhaps because I'd saved her husband, or was looking for his horse, or merely represented some obscure form of male challenge, she'd had an undoubted urge to destroy me. And she was a very troubled lady in far more obvious ways than that.

"Give me your drink," she said abruptly.

"I'll get you some more whiskey," I said.

"Yours will do," she insisted.

I gave her the glass, but one sip was enough. Dry ginger ale. On the rocks.

"Do you cheat all along the line?"

"Whenever it's kinder, or safer, or gets better results."

I walked away across the lawn and brought her back another glass. She took a moderate pull and put it down amid the ruins of the first one.

"Stay to dinner," she said. She made it a casual suggestion rather than a warm invitation, and I answered her need, not her tone.

"All right."

She nodded briefly and flattened herself face down, to roast her back. I lay with one arm over my eyes to shield them from the direct sun, and thought about all the things she hadn't asked, like how was Dave when I saw him and how bad was the broken thigh.

After a while she went back to floating.

"Come on in," she called.

I shook my head.

"Don't be so prissy," she said. "I'm not a swooning virgin. If your legs are like that, the rest of you must be the same. Take that bloody shirt off and give yourself a break."

It was indeed very hot, and the clear blue water looked good. I sighed, stood up, took the shirt off, and slid down into the pool. Its lukewarm antigravitational gentleness unlocked knots and tensions in my nerves and muscles that I hadn't even realized were there, and I swam and floated tranquilly for nearly an hour. When finally I hauled myself out over the edge she was smoothing on another coating of oil. Her glass was empty.

"Is Dave in that state too?" she asked, eying me.

"Pretty much."

She grimaced slightly and said nothing when I put my shirt back on.

The sun had begun to lose its height in the sky and shadows were fanning out from the trees. A golden sheen lay on the big cream colonial-type house across the green lawn. The pool water stilled, and the quietness of the place crept subtly into all the senses.

"It's so beautiful here," I said. A banal enough phrase for the promise of peace.

She looked round casually. "I suppose it is. But we're moving, of course."

"Moving?"

"Yes. To California."

"Moving the stud? Horses, and everything?"

"That's right. Dave's just bought a farm down near Santa Barbara, and we're moving over there in the fall."

"I would have thought you were settled here for life. Wasn't this Dave's father's place?"

"Oh, no. We moved here about ten years ago. The old farm was on the other side of Lexington, out on the Versailles Road."

"California is a long way," I commented. But she didn't respond with a reason for the move, and after a pause I said, "If it wouldn't be much trouble to you, I'd like very much to see the horses and stables you have here."

She narrowed her eyes. "Business or pleasure?"

"Both," I smiled.

She shrugged. "Help yourself. But get me another drink first."

A poolside icebox, I reflected, would save a lot of walking: but maybe she still needed the illusion that she didn't drink in the afternoon. I fetched her a refill, changed into my clothes, and found her still face down in the bikini.

"Say I sent you," she said.

Before I could move, however, Dave rang from England, and Eva brought a portable telephone out and plugged the long cord into a socket in the hut. Dave's wife made three or four unanxious inquiries about her husband's condition, and then said, "Yes, he's here right now." She held out the receiver to me. "He wants to talk to you."

"Gene?" His voice was as clear as if he'd been in Lexington, and much stronger than it had been the previous morning.

"Hi," I said.

"Look, fella, Sim and I want you back here for a conference. Can you get a plane tomorrow?"

"But the fare . . ." I protested mildly.

"To hell with the fare. You've got a return ticket."

"All right."

"You haven't found the horse yet?"

"No."

"Do you think you will?"

"I don't know yet."

He sighed. "See you Thursday, then," and the line went dead.

The stables lay some distance away on the far side of the house. I walked round there and was shortly talking to the stud groom, Chub Lodovski, a large good-natured man with slow speech, a bird head, and great hamlike hands. He showed me round the whole setup with unlimited patience and an obvious pride in his job. The state of the place was his testimonial. The mares and foals ate peacefully in neatly railed paddocks reached by impeccable narrow drives with sharply cut grass edges. The stallions lived in a short row of six large airy box stalls in a spacious barn, with a wooden railed exercise paddock in front, flanked by two high-walled mating compounds.

Only five of these stalls were occupied. The vacancy was for Chrysalis.

"Is this where you kept Allyx?" I asked.

"That's right. Second stall from the end. He was only in it four days."

"And where was the fire?"

He frowned. "It started in some straw one night, just about here." We were fairly central. "It wasn't much. Mostly smoke."

"And you turned the horses out into the exercise paddock in front here?"

"That's right. Just as a precaution. But one of those doggone animals got scared and broke a rail on the far side, and the whole bunch got out across that stretch of grass onto that dirt road over there. We never did find Allyx. There hasn't been sight nor sound of him since."

We talked for a while about the search they'd made next morning, but, Lodovski said, the whole of Kentucky was plastered with horses, and no one thought much about it if they saw one loose, and although a reward had been offered, and the insurance people had swarmed around like bloodhounds, they'd never found him.

"And now Chrysalis." I sighed sympathetically.

"Sure. And they say lightning never strikes the same place twice!"

He was moderately upset that the stud looked like losing another major attraction, but it wasn't his money that was involved, and besides that he was proud enough of the stallions remaining in residence. I asked him if he'd ever been to California.

"The farm's moving out there, did you know?" he said.

"Are you going, yourself?"

"Mebbe, mebbe not. Depends on the missus, and she can't make up her mind." He grinned comfortably and accepted the note I gave him with dignity.

When I got back to the pool Dave's wife had got her dress on again and Eva was brushing the splinters of glass into a dustpan, which she carried carefully away across the lawn.

"Well, what did you think of the place?"

"The horses all looked very well. The stallions especially."

"So would you, if all you had to do was—" she began, and then stopped and shrugged. "So would you."

Apart from an occasional "bloody" which crept in from habit, that was the last of her verbal squibs for the day. But my lack of scandalized reaction didn't have the same effect on her drinking, and she kept up a slow but steady intake right through dusk and dinner. Her mental brakes remained half on, half off, as before.

Over thick slices of rare beef she said, "Are you married?"

"No." I shook my head.

"Divorced?"

"No," I said. "I've never been married at all."

"Are you queer?" she asked, as simply as if she'd said "Are you comfortable?"

I smiled slightly. "No."

"Then why aren't you married?"

"I haven't found anyone who will marry me."

"Don't be ridiculous. You must have women lying down for you in droves."

"It's not the same thing."

She looked at me broodingly over the rim of her glass. "So you live all alone?"

"That's right."

"No parents?"

"They're both dead," I said. "And I've no brothers, no sisters, no uncles, aunts or cousins." I smiled. "Anything else?"

"Stay the night."

She said it abruptly, as if it came from a deeper level than her fairly harmless interrogation, and there was an element of surprise and alarm on her face afterwards.

"I'm sorry," I said matter-of-factly, "but I can't."

She looked at me without expression for about ten seconds.

"I have a mother," she said. "And sisters, and brothers, and dozens of relations. And a husband, and a son, and all this." She waved a hand around the millionaire-bracket walls. "I have everything." Her eyes filled with tears, but she went on looking straight across the table, without blinking.

"I have . . . bloody . . . everything."

6

THERE WAS an envelope from Walt in my room at the motel containing a short note and a list.

> Gene,
>
> This is all the drivers came up with. I think it's safe to bet that they actually did see these vehicles. The top three, they both remembered. The others, only one of them remembered. No horse vans, though.
>
> Walt

The list read:

> Impala, lilac, 2 years old, California number plates. Pas-

sengers included a fat child who made faces out of the rear window. Both days.

Gray station wagon trailing a load of furniture. Both days.

Dark green Ford Mustang, Nevada plates. Young couple, no description. The horse van drivers remember this one because they were discussing whether the Mustang was a good car or not. Second day only.

White convertible: young woman with blonde hair wound on rollers. Second day only.

Army green pickup truck with white lettering on the doors. Second day only.

The pickup, one of the drivers thinks, was probably on Interstate 70, after Zanesville and before they turned off south. He doesn't remember clearly.

I read the list through three times while I undressed. The load of furniture looked the most promising, but none of it exactly inspired.

Walt, driving to the airport in the morning, damped even the furniture. "It was only one of those Snail Express trailers."

"Like the U-Haul," I said.

"That's right. 'Carry your house on your back, but let us take the weight,' " he said, quoting the Snail Express advertising slogan. "The drivers said it wasn't big enough to put a horse in."

"How about the pickup?" I asked.

"Much too small for a horse," Walt said gloomily.

He came back with me to New York and rubbed his thumb continuously over the finger pads while I went through the file we had made on the case.

There was a batch of photographs of the missing horse, mostly taken from studbook advertisements by the look of them. Not a very remarkable creature on paper, I thought.

Sam Hengelman had sent his two most careful drivers to fetch Chrysalis. He had had a call from Mrs. Teller informing him of the date fixed for the horse to fly over, and also a cable from England when he was on his way. Hengelman had telephoned Kennedy Airport and been told the horses would be through the 24-hour immigration regulations at noon on Monday. He had sent the van as soon as he got the cable, on Sunday. There was, he agreed, a system like the U-Haul in operation among horse vans, to avoid the need for long empty journeys, but some folks liked personal service, and Mr. Teller was one of them.

The Buttress Life insurance covered transport. Sam Hengelman had not had to take out a policy for the trip, and stood neither to lose nor to gain from the hijacking.

Both drivers had clean records going far back.

Both grooms had been in their present jobs for more than three years. One of them came from Midway Farm; the other from another farm which had a horse coming in on the same trip.

An interview with Mrs. Eunice Teller had produced no helpful information.

I shut the folder with a smile and gave it back to Walt.

"How about checking with Snail Express, on the off chance?"

He looked skeptical. "The drivers said the trailer wasn't high enough."

"They're used to thinking in terms of ordinary horse vans. And they were looking down from their cab. You could squeeze a racehorse into a box about seven feet by four, by six feet high, if you were ruthless enough. Find out how many trailers that size or larger Snail Express had out last Monday or Tuesday, which might conceivably have been on the turnpike."

"All right," he said expressionlessly. "If you say so."

With the time lag working in reverse it was 3 A.M. Thursday morning when I landed at Heathrow, and noon before I walked into Dave Teller's room in a Reading hospital. Flaming June had come and gone: it was raining again.

If one discounted the ropes, pulleys, slings and plaster suspending his leg in mid-air, the patient looked healthy enough. He greeted me without fuss, the direct eyes steady and bright.

"Tiring trip?"

"So-so."

"You've eaten?" He waved vaguely at a collection of chocolates and grapes.

"I had breakfast over Ireland, at two o'clock."

He laughed, eased himself on the pillows, and stretched out a hand for a cigarette.

"How's my wife?"

"Very well."

He lit his cigarette and flicked shut the lighter.

"What was she doing when you called?" His apprehension was pretty well concealed.

"Sunbathing. Swimming. There's a heat wave coast to coast."

A couple of muscles relaxed in his forearm and he inhaled deeply. "She gave you a drink . . . I hope?"

"Sure. And a swim. And I stayed to dinner."

He looked at me directly for some time without speaking. Then he said merely, "A good one?"

"Very, thank you. And I saw your horses. Chub Lodovski showed me round."

He talked much more naturally about the horses: no problems there.

"I hear you're moving to California," I said after a while.

The tenseness instantly came back; the small give-away tightening of eye, neck and respiratory muscles that I looked for every day in my job and couldn't be blind to in my friends.

"Yes," he said, tapping off ash. "Eunice loves the ocean, and in Kentucky we're as far from it as can be . . . and of course, the horse-breeding business in California is every bit as profitable. We will do very well out there, I've no doubt."

Eunice would take her problems right along with her, I thought: though with a bit of luck they would recede for a year or two. Perhaps Teller considered the upheaval worth it.

"What's the new place like?" I asked.

"It's good land, pretty well irrigated. And the stable and general layout are as good as Midway. Better even in some respects. It's Davis L. Davis's old place."

I looked blank, and he explained. "Made his money out of roadside hamburger stands. Well, he died early this year, and last month they held a dispersal sale of his brood mares and stallions, to divide up his estate for inheritance. I put in a bid for the farm to his executors before I came over here this time, and they wrote me a week or so back to say they're accepting it. The contracts are in hand right now, but I don't foresee any difficulties. I'm sure glad to have got it settled at last."

"At last?"

"Been looking for a farm in southern California for over a year now, but there were too many snags to most of them. Eunice and I took a trip over in March of this year, and we saw the Davis farm then, and liked it. So . . ." He waggled his fingers to finish the sentence.

The door opened and Keeble came in, mild spectacles reflecting the pallid light from the window, eyes blinking rapidly, and the usual patch of bristle growing gray where he had short-sightedly missed with the razor. He said hellos all round and settled himself comfortably into the spare armchair.

"Well, how's it with the States?" he said, and I told them everything Walt had told me. They thought it over for a while in silence.

"So what do you think now?" Keeble said.

I glanced doubtfully at Teller, but he tapped ash off his cigarette and remarked simply, "Sim says you were convinced I was pushed into the river on purpose. I guess what he's asking you is, have you changed your mind?"

"No, I haven't."

Keeble and Teller looked at each other. Then Teller said, sighing, "We've come up with one or two things which makes it almost certain you are right."

Keeble nodded. "I went to Dave's hotel in London to collect his luggage and pay his bill, and explained where he was if anyone wanted him. The young man at the reception desk asked me if the lady journalist from *Stud and Stable* had found Dave all right on Saturday. She had, he said, been most insistent, owing to a deadline on the magazine, and he had given her my address and telephone number, which Dave had left with him in case he was wanted hurriedly in connection with Chrysalis."

"And that," I remarked, "is how boy and girl knew where to find you."

"Quite," Keeble agreed. "From the house to the river was no doubt a simple piece of following. Incidentally, I checked with *Stud and Stable*. They didn't want Dave, and their deadline is the first of each month."

"Nice," I said.

Keeble took an envelope from his pocket and fished out some three-by-three inch black and white photographs. "These are Peter's snaps," he said. "Take a look."

I took them from him and looked. The ducks had come out splendidly; better than one of Lynnie, who had been moving. The picnic lunch was there, and the *Flying Linnet* in Marsh Lock, and one of Dave Teller standing on the bows, and a rather grim one of myself staring down into the water. There was one of the four men fallen in a heap in the punt at the pub where we'd had our morning drinks, and another, taken with the photographer's back to the river, of Keeble, Joan, Dave, Lynnie and myself sitting round the little table under the sun umbrella, with glasses in our hands.

Keeble waited without blinking. With this in mind I started through the pile again, and found what he had seen. I looked up at him. He nodded, and from an inside pocket produced a magnifying lens, which he threw over to me. With the help of that, the two figures were clear. A girl with long hair and white trousers, a young man with pale trousers and a checked shirt, standing side by side in the background of the photograph of us all drinking at the pub.

"It's them," I nodded.

"Yes," Keeble agreed. "They were there in the morning. So I'll grant you they could have followed us by car from Henley—you can see the river from several places along the road—and also that they saw Dave standing on the bows when we left Henley and when we left the pub. And possibly also when we arrived at the pub, and at Marsh Lock. They would know there was a good chance of him being there again when we came back through Harbour."

I smiled. "And the five feet which was missing from the punt's mooring rope had been used to tie it securely to the danger post while they waited for us."

"I agree," Keeble said. "We took that punt right out of the water after you'd gone on Monday, and we found that the cleat for the stern rope had been unscrewed from the stern, and screwed on again under the waterline at the bow end."

"So both mooring points were at one end," Teller said. "The safe rope was underwater all the time, hidden by the punt itself and the girl's body and arms. And, of course, we weren't looking for anything like that at the time, so we'd never have seen it."

Keeble finished it. "Once they'd got the visible rope safely in Joan's hands, and we were all looking anxiously for you and Dave to surface, the girl had only to pull some sort of quick release knot, and the punt was free. So I'll agree, Gene, that that was an accident which could be staged, and was staged, and you were right and I was wrong. Which, I seem to remember vaguely, has happened once or twice before."

He smiled at me with irony, and I reflected that there were few superior officers who would say that sort of thing so utterly ungrudgingly.

A nurse clattered in with Teller's lunch, which proved to be chicken salad and tinned mandarin oranges. The patient poured the oranges onto the salad and ate the combined course with resignation.

"The food is lousy," he said mildly. "I've forgotten what a good steak looks like."

We watched him eat without envy, and I asked Keeble if he'd had any results with the handkerchief.

"Only negative ones. None of the Yogi Bear concessionists in this country imported it. They say, from the material and the sort of paint used for the bear, that it was probably made in Japan. And some of them had doubts it was done by the Hanna-Barbera artists. Not well enough drawn, they said.''

"I'll take it back to the States and try there," I said. "After all, the boy and girl were very possibly American."

Teller raised his eyebrows with his mouth full.

"The boy shouted 'Can you help us, sir?' and that 'sir' comes a great deal more commonly from Americans than from the English. Also, the boatman said their accent was 'same as on the telly' and there's as much American as English on our television."

"The same argument might apply to public school boys," Keeble said casually. "But they might well be Americans, I agree."

"So all we need to know now, apart from who were they," I said to Teller, "is why they wanted you dead."

No one had any constructive ideas on that point. Teller drank his coffee and a maid in a green uniform came to take the tray.

"You're guarding against them having another go?" I said to Keeble, watching the maid's back disappear through the door.

Keeble followed my eyes. "All precautions," he nodded. "The works. I got the Radnor-Halley Agency. Only the best for Dave!"

"They won't let me open any packages," Teller complained. "I think they take them outside, dunk them in a bucket, and wait for the ticking to start. And the only chocolates I have were bought by Sim personally. You'd never believe the half of what goes on in here."

I laughed. "It's when you get out of here you'll notice it."

"He'll stay here till you've wrapped it up," remarked Keeble; and he wasn't joking.

I stared. "I'm in anti-infiltration, remember? Not the C.I.D."

"Oh, sure. But the same motivation, I imagine. Just let your hunter instincts loose . . . and tell us what you plan to do next."

I stood up restlessly and went to the window. Still raining. Two nurses ran from one building to another, clutching capes around them and spattering mud up the backs of their stockings. Useful people, nurses. Needed people. Constructive, compassionate, tough people . . .

"Well?" said Keeble, behind me.

I turned and leaned against the wall. "How's the exchequer?"

Teller answered. "Look, Gene, I've enough to launch a minor space program. And, as I said before, if it weren't for you I wouldn't be here at all. So spend what you need to, and I'll pick up the bills."

"Right. Then I think it would be best to let the Radnor-Halley Agency deal with anything that crops up here. . . . I suppose they did the handkerchief inquiry?"

Keeble nodded.

"And I'll go back to the States tomorrow. I can't believe the attempted murder isn't tied in with the horse theft, so the springboard for everything must be in America. Unless some Irish fanatic disapproves of you skinning off the cream of British bloodstock!"

"Is Chrysalis Irish, then?" Keeble asked seriously.

"Irish bred dam," I said. "That's all. His sire was Purple Emperor, in the Read Stud at Newmarket."

"How do you know?" Teller asked, surprised.

"I looked it up," I said briefly. "Also his markings. And that is important." I paused. "Whoever took Allyx and Chrysalis knew a lot about horses. Allyx was one of six stallions loose in a paddock at night. Chrysalis was one of five horses in a horse box. Yet each time the right horse was singled out for removal. We have to believe it was the right horse, not just chance, because each time it was by far the most valuable one of the collection which disappeared. Well, Chrysalis is a dark bay with no distinguishing marks. No socks, no blaze, no star. One color all over. And Allyx was exactly the same. There are literally thousands of horses like that."

The two men didn't stir.

I went on. "This means that if we ever do find Chrysalis, there will be an enormous problem of identification. English horses have no tattoed numbers, like American."

"Christ," Teller said.

"I wouldn't know him if he came up and ate sugar out of my hand. Would you?" He shook his head. I went on: "The only people at all likely to be able to pick him out for us with any certainty are those who handled him in England. And that's where we hit a very big snag. The stud groom at Read's died of a heart attack two months ago and the new man couldn't be sure of knowing Chrysalis again. Read himself is too shortsighted, apparently, to be of any help. This means we have to go back nearly five years, to the season when Chrysalis last raced. To his owner at that time, and his trainer. Though the only one I'd pin any faith on would be the lad who looked after him. And it's the lad, I think, who we'll need to take to the States if we find a horse which might be Chrysalis."

"We could easily find out who the lad is," Keeble nodded, "and shunt him over."

"His name is Sam Kitchens, and he'll be at Ascot at this moment, as one of his horses is running in the four-thirty. It's Gold Cup Day today." I smiled faintly. "I thought I might just drift along to the races when I leave here."

"Just tell me," Teller said in a small voice, "how and when you found out all this?" He spread his fingers. "I only ask."

"I spent an hour this morning at the British Bloodstock Agency. I was practically camped on their doorstep at nine o'clock. And then I did some telephoning. That's all."

"When do you sleep, fella?"

"Between meals. Very bad for the appetite."

"He's mad," Teller said to Keeble.

"You get used to it," Keeble assured him. "The first eight years are the worst."

"And this is the guy you'd trust your daughter to?"

"Hm," said Keeble. "We haven't mentioned that."

"What?" I said suspiciously.

"We'd . . . er . . . like you to take Lynnie back with you to the States," Teller said. "She's going to visit with Eunice for a while."

I glanced at Keeble and saw that he knew what I was inevitably thinking: that Eunice's special need for company was more compelling than the rest of Lynnie's finishing school term.

"I'd be glad to," I said to them both with formality. "On a slow boat via New Zealand, if you like."

"She's too young for you," said Keeble without anxiety.

"She is indeed." I pushed myself away from the wall and stood upright. "Where will I collect her?"

Keeble handed me an envelope. "Air tickets for you both. She'll be at the Victoria Air Terminal at eight-thirty tomorrow morning. Is that all right?"

I took the tickets and nodded. "Can I have the handkerchief?"

He obligingly produced it, in another envelope. I put that and the air tickets away, and picked up Peter's snaps. Holding the negatives up to the light I singled out the drinking group and put it in my wallet.

"I'll get it blown up tomorrow in New York," I said. "Then it'll only be a matter of sifting through two hundred million inhabitants."

Drizzle was wilting the fluffy hats when I got to Ascot, but the turf looked greener for it and the horses glossier. I spotted the trainer I wanted and walked across to where he was talking to a large woman in a creased pink dress under a dripping pink umbrella. He caught sight of me over her shoulder, and I watched the initial memory job pass through mind search to recognition. He smiled warmly at his success.

"Gene Hawkins!"

The large woman turned round, saw she didn't know me, decided she didn't want to, and departed.

"Mr. Arkwright." We shook hands, and I thought how little age had changed him. Still the upright, brisk, gray-headed neighbor from my father's days in Yorkshire.

"Come and have a drink," he said, "and let's get out of this rain." There were misty beads of water fuzzing his tall gray hat. "Though it's much better than it was an hour ago, isn't it?"

"I've only just come."

He led the way up the staircase into the Balcony Bar and ordered vodka and tonic. I asked if I could have the tonic without the vodka and he remarked that my father, an enthusiastic alcoholic, would have turned in his grave.

"What are you doing now, then?" he said, sipping the clear mixture. "Still in the Civil Service?"

"Yes." I nodded. "But I'm on leave at present."

"It always seemed rum to me, you doing something so . . . so tame," he said. "Considering the sort of boy you were." He shrugged. "Never would have thought it. Your old father always thought you'd do something in racing, you know. You rode well enough, you knew your way around. Can't understand it." He looked at me accusingly. "Those two years in the Army did you no good."

I smiled. "It was while I was in the Army that they offered me this job."

"Safe, I suppose," he said, making allowances. "Prospects, pension, and all that."

"Mm," I said noncommittally. "Actually, I really came here today to see you, to ask you about Chrysalis."

"Have they found him, do you know?" he said.

"Not yet, no. The American who bought him is a friend of my boss, and they've asked me, as I know you, to see if you would do them a favor."

"If I can," he said promptly. "If I can."

"Their problem is," I explained, "that if and when a loose horse is found, especially if he's some distance from where he was lost, how are they to be sure it is Chrysalis."

He looked startled and then amused, "That certainly is a problem. But Chrysalis hasn't been in my yard since . . . let's see . . . four years last October. I don't know whether I'd be certain of him, not absolutely certain, if I saw him, for instance, among twenty others rather like him. And you'd want it to be more positive than that."

"Yes," I agreed. "Actually I rang your home this morning and your secretary said I'd find you here. And he also said Chrysalis' old lad would be here. Sam Kitchens. Would you mind if I had a word with him?"

"That's right, he came with Milkmaid for the four-thirty. No, I don't mind, you ask him what you like."

"Mr. Dave Teller, who bought Chrysalis, wonders whether you would let Sam Kitchens go over to the States for a few days, if and when the horse turns up, to identify him. Mr. Teller will pay his fare and expenses."

Arkwright laughed. "Sam will like that. He's not a bad chap. Pretty reliable."

"Then if he's needed, you'll get a cable saying which flight he's to go on, and so on. Will that be all right?"

He nodded, "You tell the American I'll let him go."

I thanked him. "They'll be very grateful." I bought him another vodka and tonic and we talked about horses.

Sam Kitchens walked his fair young Milkmaid around the parade ring and I risked ten bob on her, but she turned out to be a cow. I joined Arkwright while he ran his hand down the filly's legs and listened to the jockey explaining forcefully that it wasn't down there that the trouble lay, but up in her pea-sized brain.

Lads usually resent criticism of their charges, but from his expression Kitchens, a short stocky man of about thirty, held much the same view. I asked him, after introductions from Arkwright, whether he would know Chrysalis again with enough certainty to testify if necessary in a court of law.

"Sure," he said without hesitation. "I'd know the boy. I had him three years. Sure I'd know him. Maybe I couldn't pick him out of a herd, now, but I'd know him close to. The way his hide grows, and little nicks in his skin, I wouldn't have forgotten those."

"That's fine," I said, nodding. "Was there . . . is there . . . anything special about him which might help someone who'd never seen him before to recognize him?"

He thought it over for several minutes. "It's four years. More, nearly five, see. The only thing I remember is, we had trouble with his off hind hoof. It was thin, used to crack at the same place every time. But the stud he went to might have cured it, as he wasn't racing any more. Or he might just have grown out of it, being older now." He paused. "Tell you something, he liked sardines. He's the only horse I know of who had a taste for sardines."

I smiled. "That's pretty odd. How did you find out?"

"Took my tea into his box once. Sardines on toast. I put it down for a minute on the window sill, and when I looked round he'd scoffed the lot. It tickled me, it did. I used to share a tinful with him sometimes after that. He always liked them."

I stayed for the last race and picked another loser. I would have made a lousy trainer, anyway.

7

I REACHED the air terminal at 8:15, but Lynnie was there first.

"I couldn't sleep much," she said. "I've never been to America before."

I'd been to America a dozen times. I hadn't slept much either.

Lynnie's clothes, a deep pink shiny PVC raincoat over the orange-tan dress, were having an antisoporific effect on everyone in sight. Resisting an urge to grope for dark glasses I felt an uncommon lift to the spirits, which lasted to mid-Atlantic. There Lynnie went to sleep and a strong wave of nonenthusiasm for finding Chrysalis invaded my mind like one enormous yawn. I wouldn't mind, I thought idly, I really wouldn't mind lazing around that swimming pool with Eunice and Lynnie, doing nothing at all but drink in sunshine, peace, Scotch, and an uninterrupted view of two well-shaped females in bikinis. Peace most of all. Lie like a log, and not think, not feel. And sleep. Sleep for sixteen hours a day and mindlessly laze away the other eight: a program as near to death as dammit. A very small step from there to eternity, to make the peace permanent. . . .

"What are you thinking about?" Lynnie said.

She had opened her eyes and was watching my face.

"Heaven," I said.

She shook her head slightly. "Hell, more like." She sat up briskly. "How long before we land?"

"About an hour."

"Will I like Mrs. Teller?"

"Haven't you met her before?" I asked.

"Once, when I was little. I don't remember her."

I smiled. "She isn't easy to forget."

"Exactly," Lynnie said. "There's something odd about me going to stay with her. Of course I said I'd love to, and who wouldn't go off on any trip to get away from school, let alone a super one like this, but I distinctly think that Daddy and Mr. Teller have an ulterior motive and I want to know what it is."

"They want her to have company, to stop her drinking too much alone."

"Wow!" She looked surprised. "You're not serious?"

"They didn't say so. I'm only guessing."

"But I can't stop her drinking," she protested.

"Don't try. She doesn't get drunk. And you'll like her all right, as long as your ears don't fall off."

She laughed. "My mother wouldn't approve of her?"

"Quite rightly not."

"I expect that's why I've only met her once." She grinned at me mischievously without a shred of self-consciousness, Joan's influence waning visibly with every hundred miles.

It was late morning, local time, when we checked in at the Gotham. From there Lynnie departed on foot for a private tour of New York, and I cabbed down to Buttress Life. The heat wave was still in position, the air still saturated. Lethargy and haze hung over the city, and buildings shivered like mirages through the blue exhausts of the cars. Once over the Buttress building's threshold the temperate zone took over: I rode up to the seventh floor with the humidity in my clothes condensing into water, and sagged damply into Walt's spare chair in 47.

"Good trip?" he said. "You look . . ." he hesitated.

"Yeah," I said. "Pooped."

He smiled. It was worth waiting for. There's a load to be read in a smile, and Walt's was a good one.

"How's it with the Snail Express?" I asked.

He picked a list off his desk. "They were very cooperative. Only trouble is, they had about thirty-five trailers out on those dates which just might have been going west on the turnpike." He handed me the paper sympathetically. "It was a pretty long shot, of course."

"Hm." I looked at the list of names and addresses, and at my watch. "I think we'd better check them."

"I had a feeling you'd say that." A touch of gloom.

I smiled at him. "I'll start it, if you like. Do you know where we can get good enlargements of a snapshot done quickly?" He nodded and mentioned a name, and I gave him the negative. "The top left-hand corner. A couple. Man and girl." He nodded again. "And there's this handkerchief." I produced it. "Would you mind making a tour of all the offices on this floor, and perhaps the fifth as well, and finding out what everyone associates with it?"

Walt took the small white square curiously.

"Yogi Bear," he said. 'What's the point?"

"It belonged to a girl who may know more than she ought about Chrysalis. The girl on the negative."

"Find her, find the horse?" He was half incredulous, a fraction excited.

"Maybe."

"Right, then," he said at the door. "See you."

I studied the list. Snail Express had done their best. Most names had two addresses, the old and the new. All were followed by a place and a date, the depot where the trailer had been checked in after its trip. There were several telephone numbers for the Eastern addresses, few for the West.

Working stolidly down the list, with long pauses while new inhabitants went to find the new telephone numbers of the old, I said I was calling from Snail Express, wanting to know that the service had been satisfactory, or if the customers had any suggestions or complaints. I listened to more praise than criticism, and eventually checked off twenty-seven genuine hirings.

Walt came back while I was biting the end of one of his pencils and wondering what to do next. It was three o'clock. He'd added lunch to his itinerary but he carried a large white package, which he opened carefully. Six enlargements of the corner of Peter's negative. Various sizes, from postcard to 9 by 7. The faces were clearest on the smallest print, too fuzzy on the largest.

"He says he'll run off as many as you want by this evening, if you let him know at once."

"Ask him for six, then. Postcard size."

"O.K." He picked up the receiver, pressed the buttons, and asked.

The boy and girl stood side by side, their heads turned slightly to the left, toward where we had sat under the sun umbrella. Their faces were calm, good-looking, and somewhat alike. The boy's hair was darker. They were of almost the same height. The checks of the boy's shirt stood out clearly, and one of its buttons was either undone or missing. The girl had a watch with an extra-wide strap on her left wrist. She hadn't been wearing it while she hung onto the post.

"All-American kids," Walt commented. "So what?"

"So how did you get on with the handkerchief?"

Walt produced it. A little limper, a little grubbier than before.

"Fifteen Yogi Bears, ten don't-bother-me-nows, six lewd suggestions, and one Yellowstone Park."

"One where?"

"Yellowstone Park."

"Why Yellowstone Park?"

"That's where Yogi Bear lives. At least, it's called Jellystone in the cartoons, but it's Yellowstone really."

"Real live bears still in Yellowstone?"

"Oh sure."

"A natural beauty spot . . . holiday place, isn't it?" I remembered vaguely.

Walt nodded.

"With souvenirs?" I suggested.

"Great lot of help that would be to us."

I agreed. It would only narrow the field down to one of the thousands who'd been to Yellowstone sometime, or one of the other thousands who knew someone who'd been to Yellowstone sometime. But I remembered a Jamaican would-be assistant to the Biological Warfare Defense Laboratory at Porton who'd been turned down because of a Russian-made bust of Castro in his bedroom. Souvenirs sometimes had their uses.

"The handkerchief probably came from Japan. Do you have a leg man who can check who imported it, and where it was sold over here?"

"Leg man?" Walt echoed dismally. "That's me." He put the handkerchief away in its envelope, chased up a few answers on the telephone, and heaved himself reluctantly to his feet. "I may as well go see a man about a Yogi, then. How're the trailers?"

"Twenty-seven are O.K. Of the other eight, five don't answer, and three have no telephone."

I tried two of the nonanswerers yet again. Still no reply. Walt looked through the shorter list I'd made of the unchecked.

"They sure went all over, didn't they?" he said. "Nebraska, Kentucky, New Mexico, California, Wyoming, Colorado, Texas and Montana. Just don't ask me to leg it around all those places!" He drifted out and his solid footsteps diminuendoed down the hall.

I went on trying the numbers now and then. After two hours I had crossed Texas off the list, bitten the end right off Walt's pencil, and started on it an inch farther down, decided I couldn't work many days in his rabbit hutch of an office, and wondered how Eunice was making out beside her pool.

The telephone buzzed.

"Are you staying at the Gotham again?" Walt said.

"Yes."

"Meet me in the bar there?" he suggested. "I'm nearer there than to you."

"Sure," I said. "I'm on my way."

Lynnie wasn't back. I left a message at the desk for her and joined Walt. His pale-blue suit looked as if it had just come out of a spin dryer and there was a damp translucent look to his skin. Repentant, I bought him a large Scotch on the rocks and waited until he had it where it would do the most good. He sighed, rubbed the back of one wrist across his eyes, fished a crumpled piece of paper out of his pocket, and spread it open on the bar.

"To start with," he said disgustedly, "it's not Yogi Bear."

I waited in sympathetic silence and beckoned to the barman for a refill. On the paper a list of about eight souvenir manufacturers and distributors had been crossed out, a single line through each. The top lines were neat and straight, the last three a great wild slash across the paper. Walt had had a very bad day.

"The handkerchief came from Japan, like you said." He took a swallow of his second drink and began to revive. "Several of the firms phoned their West Coast offices for me. No dice. It seems as if at least half the souvenirs sold in the West are made in Japan, but all these Yogi Bear concessionists say that this isn't Yogi Bear at all, it's the wrong-shaped head."

He pulled out of the by now battered envelope a very bedraggled-looking handkerchief and looked at it with loathing.

"If it was sold at or near Yellowstone Park, it could have come from any two-bit import business. As it's not Yogi Bear, no one will have had to pay a commission to use the picture, and there isn't any way that I know of finding who brought it into the country and who sold it to where."

After ten seconds I suggested diffidently, "We could start from the other end."

He glared at me incredulously. "Are you plumb nuts? You can't mean what I think you mean."

The rocks in my drink had melted to pebbles. I tasted the drowned whiskey and put the glass back on the bar.

I said, "One of the Snail Express trailers was checked in at Rock Springs, Wyoming. It's still there: They haven't had another customer for it yet. I've asked them to hold it until I've had a look at it."

"Why that one? Why that one particularly?" Walt asked. Irritation only half repressed sharpened his voice.

"Because it's one of the three with no phone number. Because it's in the same state as Yellowstone. And because it gives me an itch."

"Yellowstone is all the way north from Rock Springs," he said. "Must be four hundred miles."

"Three hundred. I looked at a map."

He drank and rubbed his thumb over his fingers much faster than usual. Tired lines had appeared around his eyes.

"I think it's a futile waste of time," he said abruptly.

"I've no time to waste."

"And I haven't."

He put his glass down with a thump, reached into an inner pocket and brought out another white package which he tossed down in front of me.

"These are your photographs."

"Thanks."

The look he gave me was a long way from the smile of that morning. I wondered whether I would have let him go looking for answers if I'd known he was short on stamina, and decided I probably would. He hadn't given up halfway: only at the end.

Lynnie appeared in the bar doorway and the tired-looking men straightened their spines in a hurry. She wouldn't come in. I eased Walt with me across the heavy carpet and introduced him to her in the hall outside. He made only a few perfunctory remarks and left in a short time with a glowering face and solid back.

"Whatever's bitten him?" said Lynnie, looking after him.

"He's had a tiring day and he's going home to his wife."

She looked at me quickly, half laughing. "Do you always know what you're saying?"

"Frequently."

She chuckled. "Anyway, you look a lot tireder than he does." We started to walk over to the desk to collect our keys.

"That's most encouraging."

"What shall we do this evening? Or do you want to sleep?" She was unselfish enough to keep anxiety entirely out of her voice, but when I said we'd go wherever she wanted there was an extra bounce in her stride. She decided on a two-hour taxi ride to everywhere in the city she'd ever heard of that she hadn't managed to see that afternoon, followed by dinner in a second-floor glass-walled restaurant, looking down and across the lights of Broadway and Times Square. At eleven-thirty, when we got back to the Gotham, she was still wide awake.

"What a fabulous, fantastic day," she said in the lift.

"Good."

"I'll remember it as long as I live."

I smiled at her enthusiasm. It was a thousand years since I'd been as happy as that, but sometimes I could still imagine how it felt. That evening it had been quite easy.

"You are far from drizz," she said, contentedly grinning.

"You'd be no great drag to be stuck in a lift with, yourself."

But the car stopped unimaginatively at the eighth floor as scheduled and we walked along to our rooms. Her door opposite mine.

I kissed her cheek. "Good night, little Lynnie."

Her brown eyes smiled serenely back. "Good night, Gene. Sleep well."

"You too," I said. "Kentucky first stop in the morning."

It took four more days to find the girl in the photograph, though maybe I could have done it in two if it hadn't been for Lynnie. Privately aware that it wasn't necessary for me to do the job myself, I dredged up a cast-iron-sounding reason for having to accompany her to Lexington, and we flew down via Washington, which involved another quick taxi tour instead of a lengthy wait at the airport. Lynnie didn't intend to miss a thing.

Eunice met us at the Lexington airfield and drove us to Midway, and after a prawn and avocado lunch lent me her car to go on my errand. I greased Chrysalis' ex-groom into going with me with twenty dollars of his employer's money, and took him off to Sam Hengelman's. The horse van, Sam said out of the corner of his mouth as he watched an old movie on a color set, was still in care of the police department. If I wanted to look at it, go talk to them.

At the police department a state trooper listened to what I had to say, said, "Yeah," several times, consulted higher authority, and sorted out some keys. Higher authority turned out to be a good-looking detective in his twenties, and we all four repaired to the parking lot behind the police building, where the horse van stood in one corner.

Chrysalis' lad pointed out the stall the stallion had inhabited, and the state trooper came up with a successful conclusion to the expedition: four long shining bay hairs.

"From his mane," said the groom authoritatively.

The detective kept two for the state and sent off the other two special delivery to Walt at Buttress Life, and the groom and I drove back to Midway.

Eunice and Lynnie were both in the pool, and the rest of that day and night came close enough to my daydream on the plane, except that the sixteen hours' sleep shrank to six, but even that was spectacular by recent standards.

When Lynnie said over large cups of breakfast coffee the next morning that she wished I wasn't going, I very nearly didn't. If I'd stayed, Buttress Life would have paid the insurance and a load of grief would never have happened. Yet if I could go back to that crossroads moment again I know I would inevitably make the same decision. Once a hunter always a hunter: the inner compulsion hadn't loosened its grip: the quality they'd hauled me out of the Army for was too basic in my nature, and being what I was, what I am, slopping out of the chase was impossible. Keeble had known, I admitted wryly, that he had only to get me hooked.

"I must go," I said, "if I'm to find the horse."

"Damn the horse," Lynnie said.

I laughed at her. "You've learned quickly."

"I like Eunice," she said defensively. "She doesn't shock me."

I gathered from that that she certainly did, but that Lynnie would never admit it.

"But you will come back here? Before you go home, I mean."

"I expect so," I said.

She fiddled with her coffee cup, looking down. "It's only a week since I picked you up at your flat, last Sunday."

"And you've aged a year."

She looked up quickly, startled. "Why did you say that?"

"It was what you were thinking."

"I know," she said, puzzled, "but I don't know how you do."

"Crystal set in the attic. Intermittent though, unfortunately."

"Just as well, if you ask me." There was a healthy mockery on her laughing face. "How would you like to be tuned in permanently to Eunice?"

Eunice herself trailed through the doorway at that moment wearing an electric-blue wrapper and a manageable hangover. With both still in place, after two cups of coffee and a cigarette, she trundled Lynnie and me to the airport.

"Good-by, you son of a bitch," she said to me, as I stood beside her window. "I guess you can come back any time you want to."

Lynnie glanced at her sharply, with sudden speculation: growing up in front of one's eyes. I smiled good-by to them both and walked into the airport. From there I bus-stopped twelve hundred miles to Denver, and chartered a twin-engine Piper from a local firm for the last three hundred to Rock Springs. The pilot chewed his nails savagely beside me all the way as if he were a dedicated autocannibal, and I arrived feeling sick.

On the hot late Sunday afternoon the little desert town looked lifeless. Shimmering air rose endlessly over the dump of abandoned rusting motorcars, a Greyhound bus rolled past with passengers staring like fish through its green glass windows, and sprinklers on the richer front lawns kept the parching heat at bay. At the bus station I learned that old man Hagstrom's boy was the agent for Snail Express, but when I found old man Hagstrom, fanning himself in a rocker on the front porch of his small frame house, he said that his boy was out calling.

Hagstrom himself seemed to be glad to have company and told me to go inside and bring two beers out of the icebox. The icebox was in the living room, just through the screen door. It was a shambles of a room with sagging broken-spring chairs, dirty worn-out rag rugs, a scattered assortment of cups, glasses and bottles, all unwashed, and a vast new television set. I took the beer out to the porch, sat on the top step, and drank from the bottle, like my host.

The old man rocked, scratched himself, drank, and said vaguely that his boy would be right along, I could bet on it. I looked up and down the hot empty street. There were other shapes rocking gently in the shade of the porches, half invisible because many had screens round the outside rails. From behind them they watched the world go by: Only thing was, the world rolled past in automobiles and didn't stop to talk.

Two beers later, while old man Hagstrom was telling me how he personally would deal with the Saigon situation, his boy rolled up in a pockmarked Chrysler. His boy was literally a boy, not more than eighteen: old man Hagstrom's grandson. He rubbed his hands down his grease-marked T shirt and jeans, and held one out to me with as easygoing a welcome as his grandfather's. I explained what I wanted.

"Sure you can look at the trailer," he said amiably. "Now?"

"If you don't mind."

"You're welcome."

He waved me into his baking car and whirled it casually around a few corners, drawing up with a jerk outside a rickety-looking gate set in a head-high wall. Through the gate, in a dusty area, stood four Snail Express trailers, all different sizes.

"That one," I said, pointing to the largest.

"Came in last Saturday, I think. I'll look it up." He unlocked a small brick office on one side, and I followed him in. Hot enough in there to please Satan.

"That's right. Saturday," he said, consulting the ledger. "Came from New York State, renting charge paid in advance for one week. The week wasn't up until Monday."

"Do you remember who brought it here?"

"Uh, let's see. Oh, yes. An old guy. Can't remember much about him. He had white hair, I guess."

"What sort of car did he have, to pull the trailer?"

"I helped him unhitch . . . a station wagon, I think. Gray, mebbe."

"It wasn't these two?" I showed him the photograph.

"Nope." He was definite. As far as he knew, he'd never seen them. Had I asked his grandfather? I had.

He said he'd swept out the trailer, but I could look inside if I wanted to.

"Why did you sweep it?" I asked.

"Usually do. It was pretty clean already, though."

I looked anyway. There were no bay hairs. Nothing at all to suggest that Chrysalis had ever been squeezed into it. The only suggestive thing about it was the way it was built: the roof opened outward right along the center line, to make the loading of tall objects easier. It had been worrying me that Chrysalis would not have walked into a tiny dark trailer: but one open to the sky was a different matter.

Old man Hagstrom's boy obligingly dug out the Hertz agent, who rented me an air-conditioned black Chevrolet with only 5,000 miles on the clock. Overnight I added 334 more, and drove into Gardiner for breakfast.

The road there had led through Yellowstone Park itself, where the dawn had crept in mistily between the pine trees, and glimpses of lakes had looked like flat puddles of quicksilver. I had seen an ugly great moose, but no bears. Yogi was asleep.

I spent all morning walking round the town. None of the shops were selling the handkerchief, or had ever stocked any like it. The photograph produced no reactions at all. After a toasted bacon, tomato and lettuce sandwich at a lunch counter I left Gardiner and went about fifty-four miles to West Yellowstone.

The afternoon's trudge produced exactly the same absence of results. Hot, tired, and frustrated, I sat in the Chevrolet and wondered what to do next. No trace of Chrysalis in the trailer, even though it seemed likely it was the one the drivers had seen. No matching handkerchiefs at Yellowstone Park. Walt had been right. The trip was one pointless waste of time.

I thought of the long forest drive back through the park, the canyon gradients at midway, and the final hundred miles of desert to Rock Springs, and decided to put it off until the next day. Sighing, I found the best-looking motel and booked the best room they had, stood under the shower until the day's aches had run down the drain with the dust, and stretched out for a couple of hours on the king-sized Slumberland.

The waitress who brought my steak at dinner was large, loosely upholstered, kind-natured, and with an obvious conviction that a man alone liked a bit of gossip. I wanted her to go away and let me eat in peace, but business was slack and I learnt more than I cared about her complicated home life. In the end, simply to stop the flow, I pulled out the crumpled handkerchief and asked if she knew where I could get a new one like it.

She thought "the girls" might know, and went off to ask them. Relieved, I finished my steak. Then she came back and doubtfully put the white square down beside me on the tablecloth.

"They say you might get one in Jackson. They do have bears on ashtrays and things down there. Down in the Tetons. Just over a hundred sixty miles. It's a holiday town, Jackson."

I'd driven straight through Jackson the night before on the way up from Rock Springs, and seen only a small Western town fast asleep. When I went back on Tuesday morning it was buzzing with holidaymakers and local inhabitants, dressed all alike in cowboy clothes. Dude ranch country, I learned. The main street was lined with souvenir shops, and the first one I went into had a whole pile of small white handkerchiefs with bears on them.

8

THE GIRL in the punt opened the ranch house door, walked halfway to meet me from the car, and greeted me with professional instant welcome.

"Mr. Hochner? How nice to have you with us."

"I'm glad you could take me at such short notice, with the Fourth coming up next weekend." I shook her hand, putting a slight touch of German accent into my voice because it was easier for me than American if I had to keep it up for any length of time. It didn't seem altogether wise to be English. Also, I was wearing thick-rimmed, slightly smoky sunglasses I didn't really need.

"We're seldom full this early in the season." She smiled as far up her face as her cheek bones while her eyes skimmed my clothes, car and luggage. Only a hotelkeeper's checkup: it hadn't occurred to her that she'd seen me before; the accent and the sunglasses helped, too.

"I'll show you straight to your cabin, if you like? Then you can freshen up and come along here to the ranch house for dinner later on. There will be a bell, to let you know when."

I parked the car, and carrying my two suitcases, the old one and the new one from Jackson, followed her along a grassy woodland track toward one of several small log cabins scattered among the trees.

She was tall and strong, and older than she had seemed on the river: twenty-six or twenty-seven, I guessed. The fair hair no longer hung childishly loose, but was combed up into a round topknot, leaving her neck cool and uncluttered. She wore dark-blue Levi's instead of the white trousers, but the pink shirt on top looked identical. One of the storekeepers in Jackson, the fifth I tried, had known her immediately when I had artistically let the photograph drop face up in front of him as I took money for a local map out of my wallet.

"Yola Clive," he said casually, picking it up. "And Matt. Friends of yours?"

"I'd thought of looking them up," I agreed, sorting out bills. "How do I get there, do you know? I haven't been to their place before."

He obligingly gave me clear directions for a 15-mile drive, finishing, "and the High Zee Ranch is the only place along there, so you can't miss it. But if you're planning on staying, I'd give them a call and make a reservation. It's a mighty popular place they run."

"I sure will," I said: and I did. I also bought some Levi's and shirts and a pair of riding boots, and the suitcase to put them in. In cowboy country guns passed without comment: I added a heavy black tooled leather belt with a silver buckle, and the clerk didn't show any surprise at my wanting to make sure that the small-of-the-back holster I sometimes used would slot onto it.

Jackson preserved its own Wild Western flavor to the extent of a small authentic stagecoach waiting in front of the drugstore: but the sleepy disillusioned horses between the shafts looked a poor prospect against galloping redskins. Broad raised boardwalks edged with hitching rails ran along in front of the stores in the short main street, though the mud they had been built to avoid had long been paved over. Motels with signs saying "air-conditioning and central heating" were called Covered Wagon and Rustlers' Hideout. Jackson was an uneasy mixture of evolution and make-believe, and clearly a success.

I sat in the sun on a hitching rail most of the afternoon: did a bit of thinking, and made two calls to Walt at Buttress Life.

Yola Clive led me round a neat stack of sawn logs, up two steps, across a minimal porch and through a screen door and a wooden door into the cabin.

"Bathroom through there," she said, pointing. "And you'll probably need to light the stove in the evenings. The snows only melted here two or three weeks ago, and the nights are cold." She smiled briefly and indicated a small tubful of a crumbly mixture which stood beside the squat black stove. "Light the logs with two or three handfuls of that."

"What is it?" I asked.

"Pep," she said. "A mixture of diesel oil and sawdust." Her eyes glanced professionally round the room, checking that everything was in order. "There's an ice machine out back of the kitchen, if you want to make drinks. Most guests bring their own liquor. We don't sell it ourselves. I expect you'll want to go riding tomorrow. We usually fix that up over dinner." The half-smile came and went, and Yola walked quietly away along the track.

Sighing, I investigated my quarters. There had been a reasonable compromise between age-old materials and modern construction, resulting in a sturdy two-roomed cabin with a pitched roof and varnished tree trunk walls. Two single beds stood on the polished wood floor in the main room, covered with patchwork quilts. A curtain across a half-shelved recess acted as closet, and the two upright chairs and the table were all home built. So too, I discovered, were the towel rail, stool and shelf in the bathroom. But the backwoods stopped short of the plumbing: and the lighting was ranch-generated electric.

I unpacked onto the shelves and hangers, and changed from town clothes into Levi's and a blue and white checked shirt. The complete vacationer, I thought sourly: and buckled the gun belt round my waist.

After that for an hour I sat on the porch and looked at the view, which was good enough for a chocolate box. The Teton Range of the Rocky Mountains stretched north and south, with dark-green pine forests washing up from the valley to meet spotless snow-capped peaks. Along the bottom ran a sparkling thread of blue and silver, a tributary to the upper reaches of the thousand-mile Snake River: and between the river and the woods on whose edge my cabin stood, a wide stretch of sagebrush and scrub was dotted with yellow weedlike flowers.

The woods around the cabin stood on the lower slopes of another ridge of peaks which rose sharp and high behind the ranch, shutting it in, close and private. The stream ran right along, in and out, but the only road into the narrow valley stopped dead in the parking area of the High Zee.

A bell clanged loudly up at the ranch house. I went back into the cabin and put on a sloppy black sweater which hid the Luger and looked reasonable at 9,200 feet above sea level, though the still-persisting heat wave was doing a good job in the mountains too. Walking slowly along the dusty grass track I wondered if Matt Clive would know me. The accent and the glasses were aids, and I certainly had no clear memory of his face on the punt, though I now knew it well from the photograph. It was unlikely, since his full attention must have been concentrated on Dave Teller, that he had taken much notice of me; but he might possibly have a sharper impression than Yola, as I had been close to him when I went in after Dave. I needn't have wondered. He wasn't there.

Yola sat at one end of a long golden wood table flanked by chattering well-dug-in ranch guests. Family groups, mostly, and three married couples. No singles except me. A bright well-coiffured mother invited me to sit beside her, and her hearty husband opposite asked if I'd had a long drive. On the other side of me a small boy told his parents loudly that he didn't like stuffed pancakes, and every face round the table looked sunburned, vital and overflowing with holiday spirits. I battened down a fierce urge to get up and go out, to get away from all that jollity. I didn't see how I was ever going to make the effort to look as if I were enjoying myself.

By the end of the meal it felt as if my smile were set in plaster, rigid and mechanical to the extent that my face ached with producing it. But the hearty man opposite, Quintus L. Wilkerson III, "Call me Wilkie," seemed pleased to have a practically nonspeaking audience, and made the most of it. I endured a splash-by-splash account of his day's fishing. His wife Betty-Ann had ridden to the lake with him, and then gone on into the hills in a party containing her two children, Samantha and Mickey. I heard about that too, from all three of them. They asked me to ride with their party the next day, and I wrenched my tongue into saying I'd be glad to.

I lasted out the coffee. The Wilkersons promised to see me at breakfast, and Yola asked if I was comfortable in the cabin.

"Thank you, yes." Remember the German accent. Smile.

"That's fine," she said brightly, her eyes sliding past. "Ask if there's anything you need."

I walked stiffly out of the ranch house and along the dark track to the empty cabin; leaned wearily against one of the posts holding up the porch roof and looked at the row of peaks glimmering palely in shifting moonlight, with streaky clouds across the sky. My head ached with a feeling of compression, as if my brain wanted to expand and fill up with air.

How can I go on like this? I thought. Dinner had been about as much as I could manage. I didn't know what to do about it. No use praying: no faith. If I went to a doctor I'd get a bottle of tonic and a homily about pulling myself together. There was absolutely nothing to be done but endure it and go on with that until it got better. If I could only convince myself that it would in the end get better, at least I would have something to cling to.

Somewhere in the valley a stallion shrieked.

Maybe it was Chrysalis. If he wasn't actually on the High Zee Ranch, I thought the chances very high that he was somewhere near. Maybe Keeble did know what he was doing sending me to find him, because it was evident that I could still function normally on the work level: concentration acted like a switch which cut out the personal chaos. If I concentrated twenty-four hours a day, life would be simple.

One trouble with that. It was impossible.

The ranch held upward of a hundred and twenty horses. About forty of them were penned in a big corral near the main ranch house, saddle horses for the ranch guests to ride.

Breakfast had been early, but the fitting of guests to horses took some time, even though everyone except me had been there two or three days and knew which animal they wanted. The head wrangler asked me if I could ride, and if so, how well.

"I haven't been on a horse for nine or ten years," I said.

He gave me a dead quiet one with U-shaped hocks. The western saddle seemed like an armchair after the postage stamp I'd been teethed on; and there were no newfangled things like buckles for raising and lowering stirrups. The head wrangler unlaced the thong holding the three-inch-wide leathers to the saddle, slid them down two or three holes, and laced them up again. Good soft leather, which could go all day and not rub the horse.

Over to one side of the ranch house, past its green watered lawn, there was a smallish sturdily railed paddock of not more than an acre. I'd spent all breakfast looking out the window at the seven horses in it. Three mares, two small foals, two stallions. Both the stallions were bays, but one had a white blaze and was no thoroughbred.

"What are those horses over there?" I asked the wrangler, pointing.

He paused a second while he worked out how to put it delicately to an ignorant dude, and a foreigner into the bargain, and then said, "We breed most of the horses, on this ranch."

"Oh, I see," I said. "Do you have many stallions?"

"Three or four. Most of these," he glanced round the patiently waiting mounts, "are geldings."

"That's a nice-looking bay," I commented.

He followed my direction over to the small paddock again. "He's new," he said. "A half-bred Matt bought in Laramie two or three weeks back." There was disapproval in his tone.

"You don't like him?" I said.

"Not enough bone for these hills," he said briefly, finishing the second stirrup. "Now, is that comfortable?"

"Fine," I said. "Thank you."

He nodded with casual friendliness and went to see to someone else. The wranglers differed from the dudes only in the matter of age and dress. They were all boys or young men between eighteen and thirty, several of them college boys working their vacation. The dudes were either parents or children; scarcely one in the twenties. No one, Betty-Ann Wilkerson told me knowledgeably, called cowboys cowboys anywhere except in films. Cowhand was possible, but the right word was wrangler. There were no cattle on the High Zee. The wranglers herded the horses, and the horses were there for the dudes to ride.

In the matter of clothes the wranglers were less flamboyant, less well pressed, altogether dustier. They had been up since 5:30 and other people's holidays were their hard work.

"They turn the horses out on the hills every night," Wilkie explained, "and go up and herd them down in the morning."

We set off from the ranch in two parties, about twelve guests and two wranglers in each. Down over a flat wooden bridge across the narrow river, and up into the main Teton Range opposite. Wilkie rode in front of me and Betty-Ann behind as we wound upward through the woods in single file; and neither of them tired of talking.

"They turn the horses out on the hills over here because there isn't enough pasture in the valley to feed them." Wilkie turned half around in his saddle to make sure I could hear. "They go miles away, most nights. The wranglers fix a bell onto some of them, like cowbells in Switzerland, so that they can find them in the morning. The ones they put bells on are the sort of natural leaders, the horses other horses like to be with." He smiled heartily. "It's sure difficult to see them sometimes, with the sun shining through the trees and making shadows."

What he said was true because we passed a group of three in a hollow later on, and I didn't see them until one moved his head and clinked his bell.

"They only bring in the number they need," Betty-Ann filled in. "They just leave the rest out, and maybe bring some of them in tomorrow, if they come across them first."

"So sometimes a horse could be out for a week at a time?" I suggested.

"I guess so," Wilkie said vaguely. He didn't really know. "Of course, if they want one particular horse, the wranglers will go right up the mountain to find him, I do know that."

"Anyone who can ride well enough can go up with the wranglers in the morning," Betty-Ann said. "But they *canter* up and down here instead of walk."

The path was steep and also rocky.

"These horses are born to it, honey," said Wilkie kindly. "Not like the riding school horses back home."

At 11,000 feet the path leveled out onto a small tree-shaded plateau overlooking a breath-taking pine-wooded valley with a big brilliant blue lake in its depths. The cameras came out and clicked excitedly. The chattering voices exclaimed over an order of beauty that demanded silence. And eventually we rode down again.

Yola asked me at lunch if I had enjoyed my morning, and I said without difficulty that I had. The Wilkerson children were calling me Hans and asked me to swim in the stream with them in the afternoon. Wilkie clapped me heartily on the shoulder and told me I was a good guy, and Betty-Ann had irritatingly begun looking at me in a way which would change her husband's mind about that instantly if he noticed.

I left the lunch table last and whisked away a large slice of bread in a paper napkin. Along in my cabin I unpacked some specially acquired groceries, filled one pocket with sugar cubes, and onto the bread scooped out a whole tin of sardines. With the bread held still in the napkin I walked down through the sagebrush and along to the mares' and foals' paddock, reaching it on the far side from the ranch house.

There I offered sugar in one hand and sardines in the other. The mares came and sniffed, and all chose sugar. The foals chose sugar. The bay with the white blaze chose sugar. The dusty half-bred that Matt had bought two or three weeks ago in Laramie came last, less curious than the rest.

He sniffed at the sardines and raised his head with his ears pricked, staring across at the high Tetons as if hearing some far-off sound, smelling some distant scent. His nostrils quivered gently. I looked at the splendid lines of bone in the skull, the gracefully slanted eye, the perfect angle of head on neck. He had the crest of a thoroughbred stallion, and the hocks of a race horse. He bent his head down to the sardines and ate the lot.

Yola and Matt Clive lived in a cabin of their own, separate from the main ranch house, which contained only the dining room, kitchens, sitting room, and wet-day games room for the guests.

Yola backed an olive-drab pickup with small white lettering on its doors out of a shady carport beside her cabin, and drove away down the dusty road. I stared after her, half amazed, half smiling. Full marks to the horse van drivers, I thought. They'd seen both the Snail Express van and the pickup. They must have seen them both several times, but even so, they'd remembered.

Guests were allowed to use the one telephone, which was located in the Clives' cabin. I strolled over there, knocked on the door, and found the place empty. Not locked, though in this case there was a key. There were no locks on any of the guest cabin doors: one could only bolt them on the inside, with a simple wooden wedge slotted into the latch.

A quick tour of the Clives' cabin revealed two separate single bedrooms, living room, kitchen, bathroom and office. I planted three hypersensitive listening devices as invisibly as possible, and unhurriedly left.

After that I climbed into the Chevrolet and drove myself back to Jackson, where the telephone was more private. My call to Buttress Life lasted a long time, and Walt's contribution to the second part of the conversation consisted of gasps and protests of "You can't."

"Listen, Walt," I said in the end. "We're not policemen. I imagine your company would settle for the property back and no questions asked? And my brief is to restore Chrysalis to Dave Teller. Just that. Nothing more. If we start things the way you want, we'll end up with a lot of smart lawyers and most probably a dead horse."

There was a long pause. "All right," he said slowly. "O.K. You win."

He wrote down a long list of instructions. "This is Wednesday," I said, thinking aloud. "Sunday morning. That gives you three clear days. Should be enough."

"Only just."

"Never mind," I said soothingly. "You can do most of it sitting down."

Walt wasn't amused. "And you, what exactly will you be doing?" he asked sarcastically.

"On a dude ranch," I said reasonably, "one dudes."

At the post office I mailed off to him by express delivery six hairs from the mane of the sardine horse, and motored back to the grim business of acting the holiday I'd feared from the start.

The three days seemed eternal. Riding took up the mornings and most afternoons and that was the best of it. Meals continued to be a desperate trial. The nights were long. I wished that Lynnie could have come with me, because in her company the depression seemed to retreat, but she was Eunice's crutch, not mine. And her father, trust me as he might, would have found it hard to believe I would only ask for her daytime closeness. And maybe I couldn't have done it. So no props. No props at all.

Yola ran the ranch with a sort of superefficiency which looked easy, juggling staff and guests into harmony without a single wrinkle of anxiety and without any show of aggression. The fair hair continued to be worn tidily on top. Her clothes were jeans and shirt and soft flat shoes. No boots: no masculinity. She radiated friendliness and confidence, and her smile never once reached her eyes.

She didn't go riding with her guests, and I never sat next to her at meals because most of the husbands and many of the wives conducted a dignified scramble for her favors; but on Thursday evening, when with several others I was drinking after-dinner coffee out in the open on the long porch, she dropped gracefully down into the empty chair beside me and asked if I was enjoying my holiday and was finding my cabin comfortable.

I answered with half-true platitudes, to which she half listened.

"You are young," I said next, with great politeness, "to own so beautiful a place."

She replied to this small probe with frank ease. "It belonged to my grandfather and then to my mother. She died a year or two back."

"Has it always been a dude ranch? I mean, it seems a bit hilly for cattle . . ."

"Always a dude ranch," she agreed. "My grandfather built it about forty years ago. How did you hear of us?"

I glanced at her unhurriedly, but she was merely curious, not suspicious.

"I asked in Jackson for somewhere good and fairly quiet, out in the mountains."

"Who recommended us?"

"Just a man in the street."

She nodded, satisfied.

"What do you do in the winter?" I asked.

There was a flicker in the eyes and a quick private smile on the mouth: whatever she did in the winter pleased her more than hotelkeeping.

"We move down south. Snow completely blocks this valley from November through March. Most years it's May before we come back. . . . We usually open the ranch the second week in June, but the canyons are often impassable then."

"What do you do with the horses?"

"Oh, they go down to the plain, on a friend's ranch."

Her voice was as strong and capable as the rest of her. I watched her eyes slide round toward the paddock with the mares and foals, and pause there calmly, and return to me. Expressionless.

I smiled her a force five version of an adults-only smile, and asked if she ever found it lonely, so far out in the wilds. To this mild but unmistakable come-on there was no reaction beyond a crisp shake of the head. I was the only man there not guarded by a watchful wife: Yola wasn't in the least bit interested.

I complimented her on the ranch food, and on the helpfulness of the wranglers. She said she was glad I was pleased. I yawned and apologized, and said it must be all the fresh air . . . she'd heard it all dozens of times a year, said everything she'd said so often that she no longer had to think. No use on this occasion using any jolting technique to force out an unguarded phrase: jolting her was roughly the last thing I wanted to do.

After a while I stood up lazily and said I would turn in, and she gave me the usual meaningless half-way-up smile. She hadn't really seen me at all: wouldn't remember me in another month. Unless I inadvertently gave her cause.

The three bugs in her cabin worked on the audio-switch principle: any noise, and speech especially, which they picked up automatically started the recording machine which occupied the back half of the ordinary-looking transistor radio standing beside my bed. But there was little to overhear. Yola slept alone, and apart from one evening when she invited four of the guests in for a drink, the only conversations were telephone calls.

In my cabin each evening, warmed by the squat black stove, I played back the day's "take." Nearly all the calls were to do with business: grocery orders, laundry, blacksmith's supplies, and future bookings. But one call, on Friday evening, was worth all the trouble.

"Uncle Bark?" Yola's voice said, low and clear. One of the bugs was behind a picture of drooping roses on the wall over the telephone table.

". . . honey." The occasional word escaped from the receiver in return, but Yola must have been holding it close to her ear.

"Sure. Everything's just fine here," she said. "Absolutely no kind of trouble."

". . . Matt? . . ."

"That's what I called about, Uncle Bark. Matt wrote me he's having to give up in Europe. He says he can't get near to you-know-who, they've got him holed up as tight as Fort Knox. So I guess we'll just have to keep everything under wraps for a while longer."

". . . ."

"It sure is a nuisance, yeah. But as long as we get him to you before the snows come again . . ."

"..."

"How can we? You know it isn't built for that."

". . . stay . . ."

"We certainly can't send him down to Clint's with the others. We'd waste a whole year and he might break a leg or something."

". . . desert."

"We don't want him at Pitts, it isn't built for it, but there's a good long time for Matt to arrange something."

". . . hadn't started."

"Yeah, I'm sure you would. But it's too late now. How were we to know that something so goddam stupid would happen? Matt will probably be home sometime tomorrow. I'll have him call you."

She put down the receiver soon after that: and I wound back the tape and played the conversation over again. Two unsubstantial points emerged. If Dave Teller had been too obviously guarded, Matt would have realized that the punt episode was not considered to be an accident. And the something "goddam stupid" which had somewhere or other upset the Clives' original plans might be that I'd been there to fish Dave out of the river, or might be something else quite different; something which had made the removal of Dave necessary in the first place. The horse had been stolen on June 15, Tuesday, and Yola had asked the London hotel for Dave's weekend address on June 19, Saturday. So what, if anything, had happened in the four days between? Something goddam stupid . . .

I told Yola after breakfast on Saturday morning that I had enjoyed my stay immensely and would be leaving the following day. She smiled the regulation smile without clearly focusing, and thanked me for letting her know.

"So if I could have my bill at breakfast tomorrow?" I suggested.

"Sure," she said. "But you can't stay over Monday for the Fourth?"

"I'm afraid not."

She nodded, not caring one way or the other. "I'll get it ready for you then."

The Wilkersons exclaimed over my going. "You'll miss the barbecue," Samantha said. "And the float trip down the river."

A local man took parties down the fast-flowing Snake on black inflated rubber raft dinghies: one of the area's attractions, like the rodeo and the ski lift. The Wilkersons had asked me to join them. "Maybe I'll come back next year," I said. And maybe I wouldn't.

I looked after the children that afternoon while Betty-Ann went to the hairdresser and Wilkie drove to a distant lake for the fishing. They swam in the stream, where I refused to join them in case my head in the water jogged Yola's sleeping memory, and we fed sugar and handfuls of grass through the rails to the leggy foals in the little paddock. The rails were solid young tree trunks dovetailed and nailed into even sturdier posts, and the gate was just as substantial. Its hinges were bolted through the gate-post, and a heavy padlock fastened it through two strong hasps. None of this strength was new.

Samantha and Mickey didn't think much of the sardine bay.

"Too spindly," Mickey said. "His legs would snap if he went up the mountain." I looked across at the Teton Range, the tops shining white in the hot sun. The sure-footed born-to-it ranch horses picked their way easily up and down the steep rocky paths over there, through the woods growing with flat huckleberry leaves, across the screes left from landslips, and onto the bare stony patches above the snowline.

"Why don't you stay till Monday night?" asked Mickey. "If you go tomorrow, you'll miss the fireworks."

9

AT ONE o'clock, early Sunday morning, I stood on the porch of my cabin, my glasses in my pocket this time, waiting for my eyes to dilate and listening to the night.

A slight wind, riffling the trees. A car horn, very distant. The faint hum of the electric generator in its special house. No sound from Yola's cabin. None all evening. Matt hadn't yet come home.

With some misgivings I had left my riding boots in the cabin, and wore only thin rubber-soled plimsolls, with a pair of socks over them. I walked quietly through the sagebrush on the long way around to the little paddock, the spicy fragrance rising into my nose as I disturbed the silver-gray leaves. The half-moonlight was enough to see by without a flashlight and streaky clouds made shifting shadows across the ground: it couldn't have been better if I'd sent in an order.

The padlock's strength was illusory. It had a simple lever movement inside which took me less than five minutes to fiddle open. No one could have heard the click of success. Nor the tiny squeak of the gate opening. I slipped through and distributed sugar to the mares and foals. The bay with the white blaze greeted this with a trumpeting whinny; but no lights went on in Yola's cabin or the wranglers' bunkhouse.

The sardine horse flared his nostrils at me but ate the sugar and let me slip over his head the simple rope halter I had come armed with. I spent some time rubbing his nose and patting his neck, and when I walked toward the gate he came with me docilely enough. I opened the gate and led him through, and the mares and foals quietly followed, their unshod hoofs making dull little clops on the loamy ground.

The gentle procession went slowly across toward the river, over the flat bridge with hollow thuds, and up into the darkness of the pine woods. The mares soon stopped to graze, and the foals with them, but the bay stallion with the blaze suddenly realized he was free again, and crashed past me at high speed, squealing and cantering up the path and making as much noise as a trainload of football fans. Anxious, heart-quickened moments passed: but still no reaction from below.

The sardine bay tugged hard to follow. I soothed him and steadied him, and we presently walked on. He picked his way too cautiously over the stones and corners of rocks sticking up in the narrow path, but I couldn't hurry him without risk; my neck prickled at the thought of being slung into a Wyoming jail for horse stealing; but it was nothing to the fear I had that Mickey might be right about those spindly legs.

In places all the way up the width of the path dwindled to two feet, with a wall of rock on one side and a steep slope on the other. Riding along them by day one simply had to trust that one's horse wouldn't tumble over the edge, as nothing could then have stopped a rock-strewn rolling descent of two or three hundred feet. At these points there wasn't room to walk side by side with a horse one was leading: I inched up the path ahead of him, and slowly, cautiously, he put his feet delicately down between the bigger stones, and scrunched after me.

Two or three times we passed small groups of horses from the ranch, the cowbell clanking gently round the neck of the leader and betraying their presence. Their dark shapes melted into the jumbled background of woods and rocks, and the moonlight picked out only an eye, a rump, a swishing tail. The wranglers found them each morning by tracking, as the bells were audible for only a furlong. I'd had a long talk with one of the boys about tracking, and he'd shown me how they did it. They were going to be able to follow my way up the mountain as clearly as if I'd given them directions, and to tell the time I went by the amount of dew which formed in the hoofprints. The boy had shown me hoofprints, told me how many horses had gone by and when, and all I had seen were some scattered dusty marks. They read the ground like a book. If I tried to obliterate the sardine horse's hoof prints, I obliterated also any chance of the Clives believing he had wandered off by accident. The fuzzy outline of plimsolls under socks was, I hoped, going to pass unnoticed: nothing less was worth the discomfort of wearing them on such jagged going.

It took two hours to reach 12,000 feet and to come to the end of the tracks I'd learned in the past four days. From there it was a case of trusting my own nose. The drifting streaks of cloud made black shadows like pits across the rocks and several times I stood still and felt ahead with one toe to make sure that the ground was in fact still there and I was not stepping straight off a precipice. The moon itself, and the cold mountain air moving against my right cheek, kept me going in the right general direction, but the dotted-line trail I had studied on the map proved more optimistic than actual.

The horse's legs stood up to it remarkably well. Mine had already had enough. Mountaineering was not among Civil Service requirements.

The peak of the Grand Teton rose to 13,700 feet. The summit loomed very close. Patches of snow, half melted, exposed black-looking banks of scree. I came suddenly across a narrow trail winding past them like an eel: people had walked along there recently, scraping into the snow. I had, with some luck, come the right way. The cold bit down under my black jersey and through the thin shirt underneath, and I wished I had had the sense to bring gloves. But it couldn't be a great deal farther: through the short canyon pass, and out the other side. I looked at my watch. The climb had taken nearly three hours, and I was late.

It was darker in the canyon, but also invisible from the valley below. I took the small flashlight out of my jeans pocket, and shone it in front of my feet. Because of that, the whole expedition came unstuck.

A man suddenly rounded a corner a short way ahead and stood four-square in the center of the trail. Startled even more than I was, the horse backed instantly away, tore the rope out of my hand, pulled me flat over as I tried to hang on, and skipped sharply away along a narrow ridge branching off to the left.

Sick and furious I got back on my feet and turned to go after him. The man took a tentative step down the trail and called out:

"Gene?"

It was Walt.

I bit my tongue literally to stop the rage in my mind from spilling over him. There wasn't time for it.

"I saw you coming. The light," he explained. "I thought I'd come along to meet you. You're later than you said."

"Yes." I shut my mouth. There was half a million pounds loose in a death trap. My responsibility, and my fault.

The moon pushed out a feeble twenty watts. I couldn't see the horse. The path he had taken in panic was a ledge eighteen inches wide with sheer rock on the left and a fierce slope of scree on the right. A gradient so steep that it was as dangerous as a straight downdrop: and in its black invisible depths there would be the usual big slabs with upjutting edges.

"Stay here," I said to Walt. "And keep quiet."

He nodded without speaking, understanding that the situation was beyond apology. His instructions had been expressly to wait for me at one arranged spot.

The ledge was thirty feet long with a bend to the left. I walked along it slowly, not using the light, my left hand trailing along the rock wall, the gray light just enough to show the crumbly uneven outer edge.

After thirty feet the ledge widened into a saucer-shaped bowl three quarters surrounded by towering rocks. The sloping floor of the bowl led directly into the sharper slope of the scree. On the floor of the bowl were patchy snow and rough black pebble.

The horse was standing there, sweating. Quivering in every rigid limb.

There was no way out except back along the ledge.

I stroked his muzzle and gave him four lumps of sugar, speaking gently to him in a voice much calmer than my feelings. It took ten minutes for the excessive tension to leave his body, and another five before he would move. Then I turned him carefully round until he was facing the way he had come.

Horses react instantly to human fear. The only chance I had of getting him safely back was to walk around there as if it were a broad concrete path across his own stable yard. If he smelled fear he wouldn't come.

Where the ledge began he balked. I gave him more sugar and more sweet talk. Then I turned my back on him and with the halter rope leading over my left shoulder, walked slowly away. There was the faintest of protesting backward tugs, then he came.

Thirty feet had never seemed so interminable. But an animal's sixth sense kept him from putting a foot over the edge, and the slithering clop of his hoofs on the broken ground came steadily after me all the way.

Walt, this time, made no sound at all. I came across him standing motionless several yards up the intended trail and he turned without speaking and went on ahead.

Less than half a mile farther the path descended and widened into a broad sweeping basin: and there, where Walt had been supposed to meet me, waited another man, stamping his feet to keep warm.

Sam Kitchens. Holding another horse.

With a powerful flashlight he inspected every inch of the one I'd brought, while I held his.

"Well?" I said.

He nodded. "It's Chrysalis, all right. See that tiny scar up here, under his shoulder? He cut himself on a metal gatepost one day when he was a two-year-old and a bit full of himself. And these black dots, sort of freckles, along that patch of his belly. And the way his hide grows in a whirl just there inside his hock. He always had clean legs. There's a mark or two on them now that wasn't there when I had him. But apart from knowing him from his general shape, like, I'd certainly swear to those other things in any court you'd like to mention."

"Was the cut from the gatepost bad enough to be treated by a vet?"

He nodded. "Five or six stitches."

"Good," I said. "Then off you go with him. And take good care."

Sam Kitchens grinned. "Who'd have thought I'd have seen him again up the Rocky Mountains in the middle of the night? Never you mind, I'll take care, all right."

He turned Chrysalis expertly round, clicking his tongue affectionately, and began the mile-long walk down to the Teton camping ground, to where he and Walt and Sam Hengelman had come in a horse box.

Walt said, "It's too late for you to go back. Come with us."

I shook my head. "I'll meet you in Idaho Falls as we arranged."

Walt moved uncomfortably. "It's not safe to go back."

"I'll be fine. You just get the two Sams cracking. They've got to be well on their way before dawn. They've got that bill of sale?"

Walt nodded, looking at the big mountain pony beside me.

"He cost five hundred dollars. One bay horse, no markings, entire, aged seven or eight. As ordered. That's what the bill of sale says, and that's what we've got in the van, if anyone asks. Sam Kitchens chose it. Said it was as near as you would get, without actually paying thousands for a blood horse."

"This one looks fine. See you, then, Walt."

He stood in silence while I levered myself onto the new horse's bare back and gathered up the reins. I nodded to him, turned away, and started back up the trail to the canyon.

Late, I thought. Almost too late now. The wranglers would be high up in the hills by six, rounding up the horses. Dudes rode as usual on Sunday mornings. It was already five, and the first grayness of dawn had crept in as the moon faded. If they saw me out so early, I was in trouble.

At a jog trot, his sturdy legs absolutely at home on the terrain, the new horse took me back up into the canyon, past the fearful little ridge that Chrysalis had taken, and out onto the Clive valley side of the Tetons. From there down I looked out for a bunch of High Zee horses, but I was well below the snowline before I heard any of the bells.

There was a little group in a tree-filled hollow. They moved away at my approach, but slowly, and when I was among them and stopped, they stopped also. I slid off the horse I was riding, threaded my fingers through the mane of one of the High Zee group, and transferred the bridle from one to the other. Then, leaving Dave Teller's five-hundred-dollar purchase free on the hill, I pointed my new mount's nose homeward, and gave him a kick.

He knew the way, and he consequently could go much faster. The Wilkersons had told me the wranglers cantered down those steep rocky inclines, but until I did it I hadn't imagined what a hair-raising business it would be. The horse put his feet where I would have said no man could balance, let alone a quadruped, and when I turned him off the regular path he hardly slackened his pace. We went headlong down through pines and alders and groves of silver-trunked dead trees, back to the thicker woods with patches of grass underfoot, and more undergrowth of huckleberry and sapling. There was one sticky incline of black bog where a mountain stream had spilled out sideways onto a slope of earth, but my pony staggered across it, tacking downward, sinking in to his knees at every step. Farther on, he crossed the tumbling stream itself, picking his way through a mass of underwater rocks, and lower still he went straight down a bare pebbly slope where the normal path ran from side to side in easier zigzags. Whippy branches caught at us under the trees, but I laid my head flat beside his ear, and where he could go I went too.

The gentle dude rides had been no preparation for this reckless descent, and the one or two point-to-points I'd tried in my teens were distant memories and milksop stuff in comparison. But skills learned in childhood stay forever: balance still came instinctively. I didn't fall off.

We kept up the pace until there was less than a mile to go, then I veered the pony along to the right, up along the valley and away from the bridge to the ranch.

The wranglers would no doubt follow him up there to round him up, but I hadn't time to do the whole detour on foot. It was too light and too late to get back into the ranch across the bridge. I was going to have to cross the stream higher up and go down to my cabin through the woods on the far side.

I slid off the pony nearly half a mile upstream, and took off the bridle. The rough brown hide was streaked dark with sweat, and he didn't look at all like an animal who had spent a peaceful night grazing. I gave him a slap and he trotted away, wheeling around and upward, back onto the hill. With luck the wranglers wouldn't find him until he'd cooled down, especially as it wouldn't be him they'd be looking for.

I could hear the panic going on down by the ranch house as soon as I stepped cautiously out of the woods and began the freezing-cold traverse of the stream. The stones dug into my feet, and the water splashed my rolled-up trouser legs. But as from where I was I couldn't see any of the buildings, I trusted that no one there could see me. The shouts came up clearly, and then the thud of several horses cantering across the bridge. By the time I was across the stream and sitting down to put on my shoes again, they were going up toward the woods, and I could see them. Six wranglers, moving fast. If they looked back, they could see my head and shoulders sticking up out of the stretch of sagebrush.

A hundred yards of it between me and the safety of the trees on the ranch house side of the valley. I lay down flat on the ground for a few exhausted minutes, looking up at the dawn-filled sky: a high clear pale blue taking over from gray. The tracks of the mares and foals and both the stallions led straight uphill. I gave the wranglers time to go some way after them, and then quietly got to my feet and slipped unhurriedly across the sagebrush and down through the trees to my cabin.

It was ten past six. Broad daylight.

I pulled off my filthy sweaty clothes and ran a deep hot bath. Tiredness had gone down to the bone, and the water tingled like a friction rub on my skin. Relaxing, reviving, I stayed in it for half an hour.

The tape played back for me the heavy knocking on Yola's door and the head wrangler telling her that the mares and stallions were out.

"What do you mean, out?"

"The tracks lead down to the bridge. They're out on the hills."

"What?" Yola's voice screeched as the full meaning hit her. "They can't be."

"They sure are." The wrangler's voice was much calmer. He didn't know the size of the disaster: wasn't in the game. "But I can't understand it. The padlock was fastened like you said it must be, when I checked around yesterday evening."

"Get them back," said Yola sharply. "Get them back." Her voice rose hysterically. "That new stallion. Get him. Get him back."

There were sounds after that of drawers being pulled roughly open, and a door slamming, and silence. Yola was out looking for Chrysalis. And Chrysalis was on his way to Kentucky.

The ranch guests knew all about it at breakfast.

"What a fuss," Wilkie said. "You'd think they'd lost the deeds to a gold mine." They had.

"I'm glad they found the dear little foals anyway," Samantha said.

"They've found them?" I asked. The small paddock was still empty.

"They've put them in the barn," said Mickey, "with their mothers."

"Someone left the gate unlocked," Betty-Ann told me. "Isn't it a shame? Yola's obviously in a fearful state."

Yola had been in the dining room when I strolled in to breakfast, standing silent and rigid by the kitchen door, checking that all the guests were there, looking for signs of guilt.

Poise had deserted her. Her hair was roughly tied with a ribbon at the nape of her neck and the lipstick was missing. There had been no professional reassuring smiles. A muscle twitched in the strong jaw and she hadn't been in control of the wildness in her eyes.

I ate a double order of bacon and buckwheat cakes with maple syrup, and drank three cups of coffee.

Betty-Ann opposite me lit a cigarette and said did I have to leave, couldn't I stay another few days. Wilkie gruffly said they shouldn't try to keep a feller. Wilkie had cottoned on, and was glad to see me go.

Strong footsteps came into the room from the door behind me, Betty-Ann looked over my head and her eyes widened.

"Why, hello there!" she exclaimed warmly, transferring her attentions. "How good to see you."

Wilkie, I thought in amusement, should be used to it by now. But the Wilkersons' problems blinked out of my mind forever when someone else called the new man by his name.

Matt.

Matt Clive spoke from behind my shoulder; a drawling bass voice under strict control.

"Listen, folks. I guess you know we've had little trouble here this morning. Someone let out the mares and horses from their paddock over there. Now if it was any of you kids, we'd sure like to know about it."

There was a short silence. The various children looked uncomfortable and their parents' eyebrows peaked into question marks.

"Or if anyone knows that the gate wasn't properly fastened yesterday at any time?"

More silence.

Matt Clive walked tentatively round the long table, into my line of sight. About Yola's age, Yola's height. Same jawline. Same strong body, only more so. I remembered the two bedrooms in their cabin: the ringless fingers of Yola's hand. Yola's brother, Matt. I drank my coffee and avoided meeting his eyes.

One or two of the guests laughingly mentioned rustlers, and someone suggested calling in the police. Matt said they were seriously thinking of it. One of the stallions was quite valuable. But only, of course, if it was absolutely certain that none of the guests had left the gate open by accident.

Sympathetic murmurs were all he got. He might indeed be brave enough, or desperate enough, to call in the police. But if he did, they wouldn't recover Chrysalis, who should by now be hundreds of miles away on a roundabout route, accompanied by a strictly legal bill of sale.

Matt eventually went away, trailing a thunderous aura leaving the guests unsettled and embarrassed.

I asked the girl who waited at table if she could fetch my account for me, as I wanted to pay up before leaving, and after an interval she returned with it. I gave her cash, and waited while she wrote a receipt.

The Wilkerson family said their good-bys, as they were hoping to go riding if any of the wranglers had come back from searching for the missing horse, and I walked unhurriedly back to my cabin to finish packing. Up the two steps, across the porch, through the two doors, and into the room.

Yola came out of the bathroom carrying a rifle. The way she handled it showed she knew how to use it. Matt stepped from behind the curtained closet, between me and the way out. No rifle for him. A shotgun.

I put on the puzzled act, German accent stronger.

"Excuse me. I do not understand."

"It's the same man," Matt said. "Definitely."

"Where's our horse?" said Yola furiously.

"I do not know," I said truthfully, spreading my hands out in a heavy shrug. "Why do you ask such a question?"

Both the guns were pointing steadfastly my way.

"Excuse me," I said, "I have my packing to finish. I have paid the bill. I am leaving this morning."

"You're not going anywhere, friend," Matt said grimly.

"Why not?"

"You get that horse back here, and then you can go. Not before."

He was going to have a fine old time if he intended to keep a prisoner silent indefinitely on a ranch full of holiday guests.

"I can't get him back," I said. "I don't know where he is. Several friends of mine, however, do know where I am. They will be expecting me to be leaving here this morning."

They stared at me in silent fury. Children in crime, I thought, for all their ingenuity. They had walked straight in with their guns without thinking clearly through. They were, however, lethal children, ruled by impulse more than reason.

I said, "I am unlikely to go around saying 'I stole a horse from the Clives.' If you do nothing, and I now drive safely away, you may hear no more of it. That's the best I can offer. You will not, whatever you do, recover the horse."

The only sensible course open to them was to let me go. But Yola's finger tightened on the trigger, and I reluctantly decided it was time for the Luger. Watching her, I saw a split second too late in the looking-glass that Matt had taken a step behind me and was swinging his gun butt like a bludgeon.

He caught me solidly across the back of the skull and the patchwork quilt on the bed dazzled into kaleidoscopic fragments in my glazing eyes as I went down.

10

WHEN I woke up it was pretty clear that I wasn't intended to be a hostage, but a corpse.

The cabin was full of smoke and small flames rose in a long uneven swath across the floor. I couldn't remember anything at first. I looked at the scene muzzily, half sitting up, my head dizzy and splitting with pain. The Clives, I thought. They'd emptied the whole tub of pep out into a straggling line, and set it alight. Sawdust and diesel oil burning slowly and billowing out unbreathable gases.

They'd laid me against the stove so that it would seem as if I'd fallen and hit my head on it. The empty pep tin rolled away from my foot as I tried to get up, and my hand brushed against a cigarette and a book of matches.

Most deaths in fires weren't caused by burns but by asphyxia. The cabin wouldn't burn down from fire on the floorboards: fire never burned downward, only up. The Clives were staging my exit for no better motive than revenge. And as an accident it was one of their poorer efforts.

Having staggered its way through those useless random thoughts, my brain cleared enough for me to decide it was high time to move if I was going to do anything about living. And I supposed I would have to.

I stumbled onto my feet, pulled the quilt off one of the beds, tottered into the bathroom with it and soaked it under the taps in the bath. Smoke was well down in my lungs, thick and choking. It's bloody stupid, I thought groggily, it's damn bloody stupid that boy-and-girl keep trying to shove me where I want to go, and I keep trying not to let them. Ridiculous. Ridiculous . . .

I found myself on my knees, half unconscious. The bath water still running. Pulled myself up a little, hauled out the dripping quilt, flung it over the worst of the fire. Silly, I thought. Much better to go out the door. Tried that. Damn thing was stuck.

Window, then. Stuck.

Wrapped my hand in the curtain and pushed it through one of the panes of glass. Some air came in. The screen stopped more.

Down on my knees again. Terribly dizzy. A black hell in my head. Smelled the quilt burning, lifted it off one lot of fire, and onto the next. Damped it all out into a smelly black faintly smoldering path and felt old and weak from too much scrambling up and down mountains and deeply ill from the crash on the brain and too much smoke.

Opened the front of the fat black stove. Shapleigh, it said. Gradually the smoke began to clear away up its pipe while I lay in a poor state beside the cabin door and breathed the fresh air trickling in underneath.

Several eras later I stopped feeling like morgue material and the hammer in my head died to a brutal aching throb. I began to wonder how long it would be before Matt and Yola returned to make their horrified discovery of my death, and wearily decided it was time for action.

I stood up slowly and leaned against the door. They'd fastened it somehow from the outside, in spite of there being no lock: and it was simple enough to see when one's eyes weren't filled with smoke. The screen door opened outward, the wooden door inward. A small hook leading in through the latch was holding the two together. I pushed it up, and it slid away as the inner door opened.

My wallet lay on the table, not in my pocket. They'd been looking. Nothing for them to find, except their own photograph. They'd taken that. But they hadn't searched very far: the Luger was still in its holster at my back, under my outhanging shirt. I checked the magazine—still loaded—and put it back in place.

The only other thing I really wanted to take with me was my radio. I squashed down its extended antenna aerial and shoved it into my old suitcase on top of the things I'd packed before breakfast. Then, picking it up and fighting down the whirling chaos that resulted, I opened the screen door. Behind me the cabin lay in a singed shambles. Ahead, the comparatively short walk to the car seemed a marathon.

I might have made it in one if I hadn't felt any worse: but at the end of the woodland track, when all that was left to go was the open expanse of the car park, a wave of clammy sweating faintness seethed through me and I dropped the suitcase and leaned against a tree, waiting weakly for it to pass.

Yola came out the kitchen door and saw me. Her mouth fell open, then she turned on one heel and dived back into the ranch house. For the rifle. Or for Matt. My hands closed on the pistol at my back, but I was very loath to use it. Too many explanations to authority would be involved, and I preferred to avoid them at this stage.

"Hello," said a cheerful voice behind me. "We thought you'd gone ages ago."

I turned my wonky head and let my hand fall away from the gun. Mickey and Samantha were coming down the track from the branch which led to the Wilkersons' cabin.

"And I thought," I said, "that you'd gone riding."

"The wranglers haven't brought in enough horses," Mickey explained sadly.

"Are you sick or something?" asked his sister, coming to a halt and staring up into my face.

"A bit," I admitted. "I'd be awfully glad if you'd carry my suitcase for me, across to that black car."

"Sure," said Mickey importantly, and Samantha took my hand in motherly solicitude. With one child on each side I completed the trip.

It was the rifle Yola fetched. She stood with it stiffly in her hands and watched the children put the suitcase in the car and stand close to my window while I started the engine. An accidental drowning, an accidental smothering she could manage: but three public murders by shooting were outside her range. Just as well. If she'd lifted that rifle toward the children, I would have shot her.

"'Bye," they said, waving. Nice kids.

"'Bye."

I released the brakes and rolled away down the drive in a plume of dust, accelerating fast as soon as I hit the paved road, and taking the main branch down to Jackson. If Yola thought of following in the pickup, she didn't do it fast enough. Repeated inspection in the mirror showed no

Clives on my tail. The only things constantly before my eyes were bright dancing spots.

Through Jackson I turned north and west onto the winding road to Idaho Falls. Along there the Snake River and the Palisades Reservoir, sparkling blue against the dark pines, were stunningly beautiful. But my several stops weren't for appreciation: the cold sweating waves of dizziness kept recurring, like twenty-two over seven. I drove slowly, close to the side, never overtaking, ready to pull up. If I hadn't wanted to put a hundred miles or so between me and the Clives I wouldn't have started from Jackson. Most of the time I wished I hadn't.

Walt was pacing the motel lobby like a frenetic film producer when I finally showed up at 5:30 in the afternoon.

"You are four and a half hours late," he began accusingly. "You said . . ."

"I know," I interrupted. "Book us some rooms. We're staying here."

He opened his mouth and shut it tight.

"I'm sorry," I said, softening it, "but I feel ill."

"What's the matter?"

"Concussion."

Walt gave me a searching look, booked the rooms, and even went so far as to carry my suitcase. I lay down on the bed and he sat in an easy chair in my room and rubbed his fingers.

"Do you need a doctor?" he said.

"I don't think so. It's not getting any worse."

"Well . . . what happened?"

"I'll give you some free advice," I said. "Don't ever let Matt Clive come within bashing distance of your head."

The dizziness wasn't so bad lying down.

"Do you want a drink?" he asked.

"No. . . . Let's listen to a tape recording instead." I told him how to open the back of the radio and to rewind the reels.

"Neat little job," he commented. "Where did you get it?"

"Had it specially made two or three years ago."

Walt grunted, and switched on. The head wrangler banged on Yola's door and told her that the mares and stallions were out. Walt's face lifted into a half-grin.

The recorder played twenty seconds of silence after each take, and began again at the next sound. The next piece was very short.

"Yola?" A man's voice, very loud. "Yola! Where the hell is everybody?" A door slammed. Silence.

"That's Matt Clive," I told Walt. "He came back before breakfast."

The voices began again. Yola speaking, coming indoors. ". . . say the tracks go straight up the hill, but he turned back at the high patch of scree and came down again."

That was a bit of luck.

"They'll just have to go on looking," Matt said. "Yola, for God's sake, we can't lose that horse." His voice was strained and furious. "I'll go over to the house and see if any of those kids had a hand in it."

"I don't think so. Not a darned one of them looks nervous."

"I'll try, anyway." His footsteps receded.

Yola picked up the telephone and made a call.

"That you, Jim? Have you seen any horse vans coming through Pikelet since last night?"

"Well, no, I just wondered if you'd seen one. Not this morning, early? . . .

"No, it was just a chance. Sure. Yeah. Thanks anyway." She put down the receiver with a crash.

Walt raised his eyebrows. "Pikelet?"

"Couple of shops and a filling station where the Clives' own road joins the main road to Jackson."

"Just as well we didn't . . . " he began, and then changed it to, "Is that why you insisted on the long way around?"

"Partly," I agreed. "I wanted it to look as if Chrysalis had gone off by himself. I wanted to avoid them realizing he'd been deliberately stolen. Keep them guessing a bit, give us time to get well clear."

The tape began again. Matt came back running.

"Yola, that man. That damned man."

"What man?" She was bewildered.

"The man that pulled Teller out of the river. How long has he been here?"

Yola said almost in a whisper, "Here?"

Matt was shouting. "Here. Having breakfast. Staying here, you stupid bitch."

"I don't . . . I don't . . . "

"I saw him at Reading too," Matt said. "He called to see Teller in the hospital. They let him in past all the watchdogs. I saw him looking out the window. How the hell did he get here? Why, in God's name didn't you spot him, you stupid, stupid . . . He's the one that's taken the horse. And I'll damn well make him bring it back."

"How?" Yola said, wailing.

"Excuse me," said the voice of the girl who waited at table. "Excuse me Miss Clive. Mr. Hochner wants his bill."

"There on the desk," Yola said.

"Which is Hochner?" Matt, urgent.

"The German in cabin three."

"Where was he sitting at breakfast? What does he look like?"

"He had his back to the door from the hall," the girl said. "He's wearing a blue and white checked shirt, smoky glasses and he's quite tall and has dark-brown hair and a tired sort of face."

"Give him the bill then," Matt said, and waited until she had gone. "Hochner!" The voice was almost incoherent with rage. "How long has he been here?"

"Since . . . Tuesday." Yola's voice was faint.

"Get your rifle." Matt said. "If he won't give us that horse back . . . I'll kill him."

There were small moving-about sounds, and the tape went quiet. The time they had spent in my cabin telescoped into twenty seconds of silence; and the recording began again.

"He was right, Matt," Yola said. "We should have let him go." Her voice had gone quiet with despair, but Matt's still rode on anger.

"He had his chance. He should have told us what he'd done with Chrysalis."

After a pause Yola said, "He wasn't going to do that. He said so. Whatever you do, he said, you won't recover the horse."

"Shut up," Matt said violently.

"Matt." A wail in her voice. "He was right. We won't recover the horse, and his friends will come looking for him, like he said."

"They'll only find an accident."

"But they won't believe it."

"They won't be able to prove any different," Matt insisted.

After another pause Yola said almost without emotion, "If he got the horse clean away . . . if someone else has him now, and he's on his way back to Teller . . . they'll know we had Chrysalis here. We'll be arrested for that."

"Hochner wasn't going to say he'd stolen the horse from here."

"But you wouldn't listen." Yola suddenly flared into anger of her own. "He was right all the time. We should have let him go. We'd have lost Chrysalis . . . but this way we're in terrible trouble, they'll never believe he died by accident, we'll have the whole FBI here and we'll end up . . . we'll end up in . . . "

"Shut up," Matt said. "Shut up."

"He might not be dead yet . . . can't we go and stop it?" Her voice was urgent, beseeching.

"And have him accuse us of attempted murder? Don't be such a fool. No one can prove it isn't an accident, can they? Can they?"

"I suppose not . . . "

"So you leave him, Yola. You just leave him. He had his chance. I gave him his chance. . . . You just wait for some of the guests to see the smoke and come and tell you, like we said. Don't you try going up there. Just don't try it."

"No . . . "

"And I'm going back on the mountain with the wranglers. Chrysalis went across the bridge. His tracks are there. Well, I'm going tracking. Mr. Clever Hochner might be bluffing all along the line. He might have Chrysalis tied to some tree up there, and he might not have told anyone where he is, and no one will come asking." He convinced himself that this view of things was reasonable, and in the end Yola halfway agreed.

"We'll have to tell Uncle Bark," she said finally.

There was a blank pause while they considered this.

"He'll blow his top," Matt said gloomily. "After all that planning."

"He'll have to know," Yola said.

"I'll call him this evening, if we have to. But we might have found Chrysalis by then."

"I sure hope so . . . "

Matt went away then on his search, and presently, after Yola had left to go back to the ranch house, there was continued silence on the tape.

Walt switched the recorder off and looked across at me with a complete absence of expression.

"What did they do?"

I told him.

"Would it have passed as an accident?"

"I expect so. Neat little picture: man lighting cigarette, throws match absent-mindedly in tub of pep instead of wastebasket, panics, spills the stuff, steps wildly back from flames, trips over stove and knocks himself out. Bingo."

"Do you smoke, though?"

"Sometimes. They used my own pack, from the bedside table. And my own matches. It was impulsive, unpremeditated. They just looked around and used what came to hand. They're quite good at it."

"Lucky you woke up in time," Walt said.

"I suppose so." I shut my eyes and wondered how he would react if I asked him to go out for some codeine.

"I've worked with one or two people like you before," he said. "And I can't say I like it."

"Thanks," I said sardonically. No pills.

"With your kind," he said, "dying comes easy. It's living takes the guts."

I opened my eyes. He was watching me steadily, his sober face removing any possibility that he was intending to be funny.

"How are you on guts?" he asked.

"Fresh out."

He sighed deeply. "That figures."

"Walt . . . " I began.

"It struck me first last night, on the mountain. You were sure anxious about Chrysalis, but you didn't give a goddam about falling off the top yourself. It made me freeze just to watch you leading him along that ledge . . . and you came back as calm as if it had been your own back yard."

He was apologizing, in his indirect way, for his startling appearance on the path.

"Walt," I said, half-smiling. "Will you go get me something for a headache?"

11

EUNICE, LYNNIE, Sam Kitchens, and stud groom Chub Lodovski leaned in a row on the rail of the stallions' paddock at Midway and watched Chrysalis eat Kentucky grass, with opinions varying from Lodovski's enthusiasm to Eunice's resignation.

The one and a half million dollars' worth looked none the worse for his trip up the Tetons. Better than on the ranch, as Sam Kitchens had removed all the Wyoming dust from his coat on the journey back, and the bay hide shone with glittering good health in the sunshine. There wasn't, Lodovski assured me, the slightest chance of his going missing again.

Batteries of photographers and newsmen had come and gone: the stallion had been "found" straying on the land of a friend of Dave Teller's about thirty miles from where he had disappeared. All the excitement was over.

I walked back to Dave's house with Eunice and Lynnie, and Eunice poured me a drink which was four fifths whiskey and one fifth ice.

"Who put you through what meat grinder?" she said. "You look like a honeymoon couple on the tenth night."

Sam Hengelman had driven into Midway with Chrysalis at lunchtime (Tuesday). I had flown to New York with Walt the day before, and had just backtracked to Lexington in time to catch the tail end of Eunice interviewing the press. Several of that hard-bitten fraternity had tottered out past me with poleaxed expressions and Lynnie had been halfway through a fit of giggles. I made inroads into the hefty drink.

"I could do with a good long sleep," I admitted. "If you could give me a bed? Or there's the motel . . . "

"Stay here," Eunice said abruptly. "Of course you're staying here."

I looked from her to Lynnie. I couldn't stay in the house with one alone: perfectly proper with both. Silly.

"Thanks, then. And I must call Dave, in England."

Dave, still in the hospital, sounded incredulous.

"I heard it on a news flash not half an hour ago," he said. "Chrysalis just plain turned up."

"He sure did," I said dryly.

"Where had he been?"

"It's a long story," I said, "and wires have ears. But the expenses stand right now at somewhere near six thousand three hundred dollars. Is that enough for you, or do you want to go on for some answers?"

"To what questions, fella?" He sounded uncertain.

"To why Chrysalis was hijacked, and why you fell in the river. And another thing: do you want Allyx back?"

"For God's sake . . . do you know where he is?"

"No. But maybe I could find him. However, if I do, and we get as positive an identification as on Chrysalis, the insurance money on Allyx will have to be repaid to Buttress Life. That will be the equivalent of buying him all over again. He's three years older now, and you'll have lost three crops of foals. He may not be a good proposition for you or your syndicate any more. In which case you might prefer not to have him found. It's up to you."

"Jeez," he said.

"Will you think it over and call back?" I suggested. "Your wife and Lynnie are filling me up with food and drink, and I guess I'll be staying here tonight. But if you want me to go on, will you clear it with Keeble? I'm due back at my desk at nine next Monday morning, and I might not make it."

"Sure," he said, somewhat weakly, and I handed the receiver to Eunice.

"How's it going, honey?" she said, and I took a good swallow, put my head back on the chair, and listened to her long-married-wifely conversation with my eyes shut.

"Don't ask me how he did it, Dave, I don't know. All I know is he rang from New York yesterday afternoon and asked me for the name of any close friend of ours who was influential and respected, preferably high up in horse-breeding circles, and whose word would be taken as gospel by the press. So after a rake around I said I guessed Jeff Roots filled the bill; and lo and behold Chrysalis turned up on Jeff's land this morning . . . . Yup, the horse is as good as new; wherever he's been they've treated him right . . . . Look, Dave, surely enough's enough? I heard what Gene said about finding Allyx. Well, don't do it. We need Allyx like a dose of clap. And your boy here is no goddam Hercules, a puff of wind would knock him off, the way he's come back . . . . Lynnie's fine, sure. We're taking a trip tomorrow out to California, I'll measure up the curtains for the new place, things like that, and Lynnie can have some days on the beach and maybe try some surfing with those de Vesey boys. So look, why don't we take Gene with us, huh? . . . Sure, I've made reservations at The Vacationer in Santa Barbara . . . they're bound to have another room . . . "

I listened to her plans with disappointment. If I wanted to laze anywhere, it was right where I was, on the Midway Farm. By the peaceful pool in the quiet green garden, sleeping, drinking, and looking at Lynnie.

Eunice put down the receiver, and we had dinner, and late in the evening Dave rang through again.

"Gene?" he said, "Now listen, fella. Apart from curiosity, is there any good reason for finding those answers you talked about?"

"Forestalling repetition," I said promptly.

"No more stolen stallions and no more attacks on me?"

"That's right."

There was a pause.

"I'll buy the answers, then," he said, "if you can get them. And as for Allyx . . . if you think there's any chance of finding him alive and vigorous, then I guess I'm morally obliged to give you the go-ahead. I'd have to syndicate him all over again, of course. He'll be twelve now. That would give him only about six to eight more years of high potency . . . but his get from before his disappearance are winning all over Europe. Business-wise I'm not too happy about those three lost years. But blood-wise, it would be criminal not to try to get him back."

"All right," I said. "I'll see what I can do."

"What you spent on finding Chrysalis is less than his fee for covering a single mare. You've a free hand again for Allyx."

"Right," I said.

"Sim Keeble says you've got seven days' extension of leave. Something about it being due to you anyway, from a week you were entitled to at Christmas and didn't take."

"I'd forgotten about that."

"I guess I could fix it with him for more if the extra week isn't enough."

"If I haven't finished by then I'll have failed anyway, and might as well go home."

"Oh." He sounded disappointed. "Very well, we'll leave it like that for the present." He cleared his throat. "Eunice didn't seem to think you looked too well."

"The boy on the punt who knocked you out did the same thing for me."

"Gene!" His voice was shocked.

"Yeah. Don't tell my boss I'm that incompetent. Though come to think of it, he knows."

He laughed. "When you find that boy again give him a one-two from both of us."

"Sure," I said. But I'd been taught my job by cerebral people who didn't reckon a screener would ever have to fight for his life, and by the time I proved them wrong I was too old to become expert at boxing or judo, even if I'd liked the idea, which I didn't. I had learned instead to shoot straight, and the Luger had in the past three years extricated me unharmed from two sticky situations. But in a stand-up hand-to-hand affair with that young bull Matt Clive I would be a 500 to 1 loser, and "giving him a one-two from both of us" in any physical sense was a very dim possibility indeed.

"Keep in touch, fella," Dave said.

"Sure," I answered again, meaning it as little: and we rang off.

Curled opposite in a tomato armchair, Eunice said gloomily, "I gather we're stuck with that bloody Allyx."

"Only if we find him."

"Oh, you'll do that, blast you." Her bitterness was so marked that Lynnie stared at her. Too young to understand, I thought, that it wasn't me particularly that Eunice wanted to hurt, but life in general.

They went upstairs shortly afterward murmuring about California in the morning, and I switched off the light and sat in near darkness, finishing the fourth of Eunice's massive ideas on drink and working out the questions I would ask the next day. I could find Allyx on paper, if I was lucky: but he could hardly turn up loose after three years. Three weeks had been strictly the limit. The whole thing might have to be more orthodox, more public. And I wouldn't again, I decided mildly, put myself within accident reach of the murderous Clives.

After a while I deserted the last half of the drink and wandered upstairs to the spacious air-conditioned room Eunice had given me. With a tired hand I switched on the light inside the door, and yellow pools in frilly shades shone out on brown and gold and white furnishings.

One splash of jarring bright pink. Eunice herself, in a fluffy trimmed wrapper, was lying on my bed.

I walked slowly across the thick white carpet and sat beside her on the white dotted muslin coverlet.

"What do you want?" I said gently.

"What do you think?"

I shook my head.

"Does that mean no?" Her voice was abruptly matter-of-fact.

"I'm afraid it does," I said.

"You said you weren't queer."

"Well, I'm not." I smiled at her. "But I do have one unbreakable rule."

"And that is?"

"Not to sleep with the wives—or daughters—of the men I work for."

She sat bolt upright so that her face was close to mine. Her eyes had the usual contracted pupils of the quarter drunk.

"That includes Lynnie," she said.

"Yes. It does."

"Well, I'll be damned. You mean that night you spent in New York with her you didn't even try . . . "

"It wouldn't have been much good if I had," I said, half laughing.

"Don't you believe it. She never takes her eyes off you, and when you were away she talked about nothing else."

I stared at her in real surprise. "You must be wrong."

"I wasn't born yesterday," she said gloomily. "She has two photographs of you as well."

"What photographs?" I was staggered.

"Some her brother took. That day on the river."

"But she shouldn't . . . "

"Maybe she shouldn't," Eunice said dryly, "but she does." She swung her legs carelessly around to sit on the edge of the bed beside me and I saw that for someone bent on seduction she had come well wrapped up.

"You expected me to say no," I said.

She made a face. "I thought you might. But it was worth a try."

"Eunice, you're nuts," I said.

"I'm bored," she said explosively, and with an undoubted depth of unbearable truth.

"That puts me into the golf and bridge category."

She was still playing games.

"At least you're goddam human," she said, her mouth cracking into a smile. "More than you can say about most men."

"What do you like best about moving to California," I asked.

She stared. "Your mind's like a bloody grasshopper. What has that to do with sex?"

"You tell me and I'll tell you."

"For God's sake . . . " But she made some effort at concentrating, and in the end came up with the answer I had been most expecting.

"Fixing up the rooms, I guess."

"You did all these?" I waved my hand around, embracing the house.

"Yeah, I did. So what?"

"So why don't you start in business, doing it for other people?"

She half laughed, ridiculing the idea, and half clung to it; and I knew she'd thought of it in the past, because I hadn't surprised her.

"I'm no bloody genius."

"You have an eye for color. More than that: for mood. This is the most comforting house I've ever been in."

"Comforting?" she said, puzzled.

"Yeah. Laugh, clown, laugh. That sort of thing. You can fill other people even though you feel empty yourself."

Tears welled up in her gray-green eyes, and she shut the lids. Her voice remained normal.

"How do you know?"

"I know."

After a pause she said, "And I suppose what it has to do with sex is that interior decorating would be a suitable sublimation for a middle-aged woman whose physical attraction is fading faster than her appetite." The bitterness came from long acquaintance with the jargon and its point of view.

"No," I said mildly. "The opposite."

"Huh?" She opened her eyes. They were wet and shiny.

"Playing games is easier than working."

"Spell it out," she said. "You talk in goddam riddles."

"Sex . . . this sort of casual sex," I patted the bed where she'd lain, "can be a way of running away from real effort. A lover may be a sublimation of a deeper need. People who can't face the demands of one may opt for passing the time with the other."

"For Christ's sake, I don't understand a bloody word." She shut her eyes and lay flat back across the bed.

"Thousands of people never try anything serious because they're afraid of failing," I said.

She swallowed, and after a pause said, "And what if you do bloody fail? What then?"

I didn't answer her, and after a while she repeated the question insistently.

"Tell me what you do if you fail?"

"I haven't got that one licked myself yet."

"Oh." She laughed weakly. "Oh, God. The blind leading the blind. Just like the whole bloody human race."

"Yeah." I sighed and stood up. "We all stumble along in the dark, and that's a fact."

"I don't know if you'll believe it, but I've been utterly bloody faithful to Dave . . . except for this . . . "

"I'm sure of it," I said.

She got to her feet and stood swaying slightly.

"I guess I'm tight."

"Better than loose," I said, smiling.

"For God's sake, spare me goddam puns at one o'clock in the morning. I suppose if you're looking for that so-and-so Allyx there's no chance of your coming to California?"

"I wish there were."

"Goddam liar," she said vaguely. "Good night."

She made straight for the door and didn't look back.

I drove them to the airport in the morning. Eunice had lent me her car and the house for as long as I needed them, and had passed off her overnight visit with one sarcastic dig at breakfast. "Better undersexed than sorry."

"What?" said Lynnie.

"Eunice is offering a solution to the population explosion," I explained.

Lynnie giggled. Eunice showed me a double row of teeth and told me to pass the cream.

When I'd seen them off I followed a local road map and Eunice's inaccurate directions, and eventually arrived at the Perry Stud Farm, home of Jefferson L. Roots: chairman, among other things, of the Blood Horse

Breeders Association. A houseboy in a spotless white coat showed me through the house and onto the patio: a house made of large cool concrete boxes, with rough-case white walls and bare golden wood floors. The patio was shaded by a vine trailed across a trellis. There was a glass and metal table, and low comfortable lounging chairs around it. From one of these Jeff Roots extricated himself and held out a welcoming hand.

He was a thick man with a paunch which had defied health farms, and he worried about his weight. His manner had the gentle, deprecating ease of the really tough American; the power was inside, discernible but purring, like the engine in a Rolls. He was dressed in a tropical-weight city suit, and while I was there an efficient girl secretary came to remind him that time and his connection to Miami would wait for no man.

"A drink?" he suggested. "It's a hot day already. What would you like?"

"Lime juice?" I asked. "Or lemon."

I got lime, squeezed fresh onto crushed ice. My host drank sugar-free tonic water and made a face over it.

"Just the smell of french fries and I'm a size larger in shirts," he complained.

"Why worry?" I said.

"Ever heard of hypertension?"

"Thin people can have it too."

"Tell that to the birds . . . or rather, tell it to my wife. She starves me." He swirled his glass gloomily, ice and lemon rising perilously to the rim. "So, anyway, Mr. Hawkins, how can I help you today?"

He pushed a folded newspaper across the table and pointed at it with an appreciative smile.

"Chrysalis Cocooned," the headlines said. And underneath, in smaller letters, "High-price stallion loses liberty, corralled at Perry, reshipped to Midway. And are the mares there glad, or are they? Our tip is syndicators breathe again." There was a picture of Chrysalis in his paddock, some mention of Dave's leg, and a few snide remarks about the police and local horse folks who hadn't been able to spot a million dollars at ten paces.

"Where did you rustle him up from?" Roots asked. "Sam Hengelman wouldn't say. Most unlike him."

"Sam was an accessory to a conjuring trick. A little matter of substitution. We left a horse and took a horse. I guess he didn't want to talk himself into trouble."

"And naturally you paid him."

"Er, yes." I agreed. "So we did."

"But I gather from your call that it's not about Chrysalis that you want to see me now?"

"No. It's about Allyx."

"*Allyx?*"

"Yes, the other stallion which—"

"I know about all that," he interrupted. "They turned the whole state upside down looking for him and they found just as much trace as they did of Chrysalis."

"Do you by any chance remember, ten years ago, another horse called Showman?"

"Showman? Showman? He got loose from a groom who was supposed to be exercising him, or something like that, and was killed in the Appalachians."

"How certain was the identification?"

He put his tonic water down carefully on the table. "Are you suggesting he's still alive?"

"I just wondered," I said mildly. "From what I've been told, they found a dead horse two years after Showman vanished. But although he was in a high state of decomposition, he'd only been dead about three months. So it easily might *not* have been Showman, just somewhat like him in color and size."

"And if it wasn't?"

"We might just possibly turn him up with Allyx."

"Have you . . ." He cleared his throat. "Have you any idea where they . . . er . . . might be . . . turned up?"

"I'm afraid not. Not yet."

"They weren't . . . wherever you found Chrysalis?"

"No. That was only a shipping station, so to speak. Chrysalis was intended to go on somewhere else."

"And at that somewhere else, one might find . . .?"

"There's a good chance, I think."

"They might have been shipped abroad again. Down to Mexico or South America."

"It's possible, but I'm inclined against it, on the whole." Uncle Bark, whoever he was, lived somewhere in the States. Yola had not needed to call the overseas operator to get through to him on the telephone. She hadn't even made it person to person.

"The whole thing seems so extraordinary," Roots said, shaking his head. "Some nut going around stealing stallions whose value at once drops to zero, because he can't admit he's got them. Do you think some fanatic somewhere is conducting experiments. Trying to produce a super-horse? Or how about a criminal syndicate all getting their mares covered by bluest blood stallions at donkey prices? . . . No, that wouldn't work, they'd never be able to sell the foals for stud, they wouldn't be able to cash in on the bloodlines . . ."

"I think it's a good deal simpler than either of those," I said, smiling. "Much more down to earth."

"Then what?"

I told him.

He chewed it over and I drank my lime juice.

"Anyway," I said, "I thought I'd try along those lines, and see if it leads anywhere."

"It's fantastic," Roots said. "And I hope to God you're wrong."

I laughed. "Yes, I can see that."

"It'll take you months to plow through all that work yourself . . . and I don't suppose you have too close a knowledge of the thoroughbred scene over here . . . so why don't I get you some help?"

"I'd be very grateful."

There was an outside extension telephone close to his chair. He lifted the receiver and pressed buttons. I listened to him arranging with the publishers of a leading horse journal for me to have the run of their files and the temporary services of two long-memoried assistants.

"That's fixed, then," he said, standing up. "The office is on North Broadway, along in Lexington. I guess you'll let me know how you make out?"

"I certainly will."

"Dave and Eunice . . . they're great guys."

"They are."

"Give her my best," he said, looking at his watch.

"She's gone to California."

"The new place?"

I nodded.

"Crazy idea of Dave's, moving to the Coast. The center of the bloodstock industry is right here in Lexington, and this is the place to be."

I made the sort of noncritical, noncommittal noise in my throat necessary on such occasions, and Jeff Roots thrust out a rounded hand.

"I have this stockholders' meeting in Miami," he said apologetically, and walked with me through the house to where his secretary waited in a Cadillac parked beside Eunice's Toronado Oldsmobile.

At the newspaper offices, I found, anything Jeff Roots wanted done was done wholeheartedly, and on the double. My two temporary assistants proved to be an elderly man who spent most of his time compiling an annual stallion register, and a maiden lady in her fifties whose horse face and crisp masculine voice were easy to take, as she had an unexpectedly sweet smile and a phenomenal memory.

When I explained what I was looking for they both stared at me in dumb-struck silence.

"Isn't it possible?" I asked.

Mr. Harris and Miss Britt recovered themselves and said they guessed so.

"And while we're at it we might make a list of people whose name or nickname might be Bark. Or Bart, perhaps; though I think it's Bark."

Miss Britt promptly reeled off six names, all Barkleys, living in and around Lexington.

"Maybe that's not such a good idea," I sighed.

"No harm in it," Miss Britt said briskly. "We can make all the lists simultaneously."

She and Mr. Harris went into a huddle and from there to the reference room, and were shortly up to their elbows in papers and books. They told me to smoke and wait, which I did all day.

At five o'clock they came across with the results.

"This is the best we can do," Miss Britt said doubtfully. "There are well over three thousand stallions at stud in the States, you see. You asked us to sort out any whose fees had risen steadily over the past eight or nine years—there are two hundred and nine of them." She put a closely typed list in front of me.

"Next, you wanted the names of any stallions who had been conspicuously more successful at stud than one would have expected from their own breeding. There are two hundred and eighty-two of those." She gave me a second sheet.

"Next, you wanted to know if any of this year's two-year-olds had proved conspicuously better at racing than one would normally have expected from their breeding. There are twenty-nine of those." She added the third list.

"And, lastly, the people who could be called Bark . . . thirty-two of them. From the Bar K Ranch to Barry Kyle."

"You've done wonders," I said sincerely. "I suppose it's too much to hope that any one farm is concerned on all four lists?"

"Most of the stallions on the first list are the same as those on the second. That stands to reason. But none of the sires of the exceptional two-year-olds are on either of the first two lists. And none of the two-year-olds were bred by any of the Barks." Both of them looked downcast at such negative results after all their work.

"Never mind," I said. "We'll try it another way tomorrow."

Miss Britt snorted, which I interpreted as agreement. "Rome wasn't built in a day," she said, nodding. Mr. Harris seemed to doubt that this particular Rome could be built at all with the materials available, but he turned up uncomplaining at nine the following morning, and they both dived in again, on new permutations.

By noon the first two lists had been reduced to twenty. We all adjourned for a sandwich. At two o'clock the searching began again. At 3:10 Miss Britt gasped sharply and her eyes went wide. She scribbled quickly on a fresh piece of paper, considered the result with her head on one side, and then looked across to me.

"Well," she said. "Well . . ." The words wouldn't come.

"You've found them," I said.

She nodded, only half believing it.

"Cross-checking them all by where they raced, their years of purchase, their markings and their approximate ages, as you asked . . . we came up with twelve possibles which appeared on the first two lists. And one of the sires of the two-year-olds fits your requirements and comes from the same farm as one of the first twelve. Er . . . do you follow me?"

"On your heels," I said smiling.

Mr. Harris and I both joined her and looked over her shoulder at what she had written:

> Moviemaker, aged fourteen years; present stud fee $10,000.
> Centigrade, aged twelve years; this year's stud fee $1,500; fee next year $2,500.
> Both standing at Orpheus Farm, Los Caillos.
> The property of Culham James Offen.

Moviemaker and Centigrade: Showman and Allyx. As clear as a frosty sky.

Stallions were normally booked for thirty to forty mares each breeding season. Forty mares at $10,000 a throw meant $400,000 every year, give or take a live foal or two. Moviemaker had cost $150,000 at public auction ten years ago, according to Miss Britt's researches. Since then Offen had been paid somewhere near $2.5 million in stud fees.

Centigrade had been bought for $100,000 at a Keeneland sale. At

$2,500 a time he would earn that hundred thousand next year alone. And nothing was more likely than that he too would rise to a much higher fee.

"Culham James Offen is so well regarded," Miss Britt said in consternation. "I simply can't believe it. He's accepted as one of the top breeders."

"The only thing is, of course," said Mr. Harris regretfully, "that there's no connection with the name Bark."

Miss Britt looked at me and her smile shone out sweet and triumphant. "But there is, isn't there? Mr. Harris, you're no musician. Haven't you ever heard of 'Orpheus in the Underworld' . . . by Offenbach?"

12

WALT SAID, "For God's sake," four times and admitted Buttress Life might be willing to send him from coast to coast if Allyx was the pot of gold at the end of the rainbow.

"Los Caillos is a short distance northeast of Los Angeles," I said. "I thought of staying a bit farther north, on the coast."

"If you like."

"Come to the Vacationer, Grand Beach, Santa Barbara, then. I'll meet you there tomorrow."

He repeated the address. "Who's paying?" he said.

"Buttress Life and Dave Teller can fight it out between them. I'll put the motel on Teller's expenses. Can you wring the fare out of your office?"

"I guess so." His sigh came wearily over the wire. "My wife and kids aren't going to like it. I was fixing to take them on a picnic this Sunday."

"Postpone it a week," I suggested.

"It's been postponed twice already, on your account."

"Oh."

After a short pause he said, "Around six tomorrow, local time. That do?"

"That would do very well."

"See you," he said briefly, and put down his receiver with a crash. I returned the Teller instrument more kindly to its cradle and surveyed the green and tomato room.

Nothing to do.

Mixed a drink with precision, and drank it. Wandered down to the pool, thought about a swim in the dusk, and couldn't be bothered to undress. Went back to the house, and ate a dinner cooked and served by Eva, who chattered so long in her pleasure at having someone to speak to in her own language that I heartily regretted I'd ever used it. Wished desperately she would stop and go away, and when at last she did, that was no good either.

Tried to read and turned six pages without taking in a word. Wandered restlessly again into the black velvet-deep green garden and sat in one of the chairs by the pool, looking at darkness inside and out. Unreasonable,

I thought drearily, that I shouldn't have recovered normally from losing Caroline, that I didn't value the freedom other men envied, that I couldn't be content with all I had; cruel that depression was no respecter of status or achievement and struck so deep that no worldly success could alleviate it.

Great fame, universal honor, droves of personal friends had demonstrably failed to save a whole string of geniuses from its clutches, and every year it bagged its thousands from unimportant people like me who would never see their name in print or lights, and didn't necessarily want to. Probably depression was an illness as definite as jaundice, and one day they would inoculate babies against it. I supposed I could count myself lucky not to have had it in its acute form, where its gray-black octopus tentacles reached out and sucked into every corner of the spirit until quite quickly life became literally unbearable, and the high jump suddenly presented itself with blinding clarity as the only logical, the only possible relief.

I wouldn't come to that day if I could help it. I would *not*.

The Vacationer was right down on the beach, with the sound of the bright blue Pacific creeping in a murmur under the transistors, the air conditioning, the civilized chatter, the squalling of children, and the revving of cars. There were no ocean rooms left. Walt and I, next door to each other, overlooked the parking lot.

Eunice and Lynnie were out when I arrived and still out when Walt checked in at six, but they were back when I went down with him for a drink before dinner. I had left a note at the desk for Eunice, but I hadn't told Walt she would be there. He stopped dead in his tracks when he saw her sitting with Lynnie, and turned on me a narrow-eyed composite glance of dislike and anger. If I'd told him she was to be with us, he wouldn't have come: he knew that I knew it. He was entitled to his rage.

Eunice was, however, the wife of a very good client of his firm. He swallowed his feelings like a pill, and chased them down in silence with a double bourbon. Eunice and Lynnie were on frosted-looking daiquiris and happy with it. They both looked marvelous, with honey-brown skin and a languorous sun-filled way of moving. Eunice wore fluorescent green with bits of gold at anatomical points like ears, wrists and feet. Lynnie had acquired a local-grown hot pink-orange tunic, and the few straps of her sandals seemed to be made of polished semiprecious stones. Even Walt, after a while, couldn't take his eyes away from them for long.

We had dinner outside, under a trellis lit by hundreds of tiny multicolored lights, on a shallow terrace which led directly out onto the sand. Eunice's language was for once as soft as the sea breeze, and consequently as a social evening it developed into a reasonable success.

Over the coffee I asked Eunice with a casualness which drew a piercing glance from Walt, "Have you by any chance heard of a race horse breeder called Culham James Offen?"

"Heard of him?" she said. "Of course I have. Everyone has."

"I haven't," Walt said flatly. One couldn't expect complete capitulation. He was doing very well.

"I mean, everyone in the bloodstock world would have heard of him," Eunice explained without obvious patience. "He has that terrifically successful stallion Moviemaker. And Dave says one ought to think of sending mares to another one of his, Centigrade . . . the first crop of foals are winning two-year-old races this season all over the place. But quite apart from that," she smiled broadly, "I guess we'll be seeing a good deal of him from now on."

"Er . . . why?" I asked diffidently.

"Our new place is right next to his."

Walt's mouth fell open and I stopped stirring my coffee.

"What did you say?" I said, feeling my eyes go blank, as I knew they always did under shock.

"Our new place, where we're moving to, is right across the road from Offen. We can see his paddocks from our bedroom windows." I gaped in fascination at Eunice while she outlined in such blissful ignorance the reason for the attempted murder of her husband. He himself had told me that the executors of the late Davis L. Davis had accepted his tender for the farm only recently, during the week before our momentous trip on the river. So the something "goddam stupid" which had happened to Yola and Matt Clive's scheme was that they had discovered that of all the people on earth it was to be Dave Teller who was to be Offen's new close neighbor. They had discovered it *after* they'd hijacked the horse, or they wouldn't have gone ahead with the plan.

"Why are you laughing?" Eunice asked, frowning. "What's so funny?"

"It's not funny," I agreed, straightening my face. "Far from it. Do you know Culham James personally?"

"Not yet. Does it matter?" She still looked puzzled.

"It could be wiser not to make close friends with him in too much of a hurry."

"Why not?"

"Might prove a prickly flower." I had a mental vision of Dave looking out of his bedroom window day after day, looking over to the paddocks where Chrysalis and Allyx were let out to graze. He might never have recognized them. But also he might. Culham James simply couldn't take the risk. Yola and Matt had flown immediately to England to dispose of Dave a long way from the real scene of danger.

While Allyx remained at Orpheus Farm and Dave continued making active plans to move alongside, the explosive situation would still exist. Though Matt Clive might have given up temporarily, I fervently hoped that Radnor-Halley wouldn't let their vigilance slide a millimeter. A call to Keeble would be wise . . . even at California-London rates.

"I'm going for a walk on the shore," said Lynnie, kicking off the pebbly sandals. "Who's coming?"

I beat Walt to it by quicker reflexes, and collected a grim look from him as I left him alone with Eunice. Lynnie remarked on it, grinning, as we ambled silently away on the trickling sand.

"He's put off by the bloodies," I explained. "That's all."

"She says it less often over here," Lynnie commented. "And she doesn't drink, except one or two before lunch, until after we've changed in the evening. Why is that, do you think?"

"She's escaped from the Lexington cage."

"That heavenly house . . . a cage?"

"Uh-huh."

"The new one isn't half so beautiful," she protested.

"It will be when Eunice has finished. And then the walls will close in again."

"Another cage, do you mean?" She sounded uncertain.

"Another cage," I agreed.

"Life can't be just escaping from one cage and ending up in another," she said explosively, repudiating violently so bleak a vision.

"Everyone lives inside bars," I said. "The trick is not to want to get out."

"Stop it," she said in distress. "I don't want to hear that."

"They used to keep linnets as pets," I said. "But there aren't any linnets in cages any more. Budgerigars instead. You'll be all right, little linnet."

"I never know when you're being serious."

"Always."

"But half the time what you say is so—so crazy."

"Life is serious, life is crazy. Anything crazy is serious, and everything serious is crazy. . . . I'll race you along to the beach hut."

She beat me to it in her bare feet, and leaned against the rough wooden wall laughing and getting her breath back while I tipped half a ton of sand out of my shoes. We walked on a little farther, and then sat down in the warm night and looked out across the shadowy peaceful ocean. No land between us and Japan, half a world away.

"Did you come out here to be with us . . . or to find Allyx?" she said.

"Both."

She shook her head. "You brought Walt. That makes it to find Allyx."

"Walt would have chosen to stay somewhere else," I said, smiling. "So California for Allyx, Santa Barbara for you. Satisfied?"

She murmured something unintelligible, and we sat in silence while she scuffed sand into a heap with her toes.

"Will you find him, do you think?" she asked in the end.

"Allyx? We might do."

"When, roughly?"

"I don't know. Tomorrow, maybe."

"And then . . . you'll go home?"

"I guess."

"Back to an office . . ." She swept out an arm, embracing the wide sky. Back to an office, I thought coldly: and to the perpetual digging into people's privacy, to the occasional snaring of a bent applicant, to drizzle, to Putney, to the vacuum of the flat. To, in short, my normal life. The trick was not to want to slip through the bars.

"What are you going to do, now that you've left school?" I asked.

She sucked in a breath. "After this, all the old things seem horribly dreary."

"They'll soon give Dave a walking plaster."

"I *know,*" she wailed. "Don't think I don't know. I was supposed to be starting a secretarial course in September. I utterly don't want to, any more. Why can't everyone just live on the beach and be warm all the time?" She rocked with her arms laced round her bent-up knees.

"Not enough beach."

She giggled. "You are just about the least romantic man alive. Comes of being a civil servant, I suppose. Like Daddy."

In time we walked back along by the edge of the sea and paused when we came level with the motel. She put her hand on my arm and simply stood there waiting. I kissed her forehead, and then her nose, and finally her mouth. It was all very gentle, and utterly unnerving.

"This is no good," I said, taking my hands from her shoulders, "no good at all."

"I've been kissed before," she said anxiously. "I really have."

"That isn't what I meant," I said, half laughing. "You'd qualify for a diploma. No, it's just, little Lynnie, that we're a long way from home . . . and I never kiss brunettes more than once on a Friday." I turned away toward the motel and jerked my head for her to follow. The best resolutions in the world would come a cropper faced with something like Lynnie, and immediate flight was the only course. It didn't seem to be popular with Lynnie herself, but I couldn't help that. I walked her briskly up the beach and made a joke about what Walt would be saying to Eunice, and we arrived back in reasonable order to find that it was nothing: they were sitting across the table from each other in a miles-apart silence. Eunice gave us a long cool look and Walt one of disillusion, and Lynnie quite unnecessarily blushed, confirming their obvious suspicion. The harmless little walk hadn't been a good idea from any one of four points of view.

Walt and I drove quietly into Orpheus Farm the following morning. He did the talking: a thoroughly professional piece of work, insurance patter at the double. A survey for new fire regulations, he glibly explained, necessitated us seeing over the entire establishment.

We saw. Every stall in every barn, every hayloft, every straw bale, every inch. We saw Moviemaker. We saw Centigrade. We made a great many notes.

Culham James Offen himself escorted us around the coolest barn containing his four prize stallions. A great deal of self-satisfaction sat on his shoulders like an impervious duck's-back mantle. I considered this with uneasy suspicion.

Uncle Bark was not only a man in his fifties with white hair, but he had a gray station wagon in a third of his large garage. I saw Walt giving it a sidelong glance. Undoubtedly it was Uncle Bark who had delivered the Snail Express trailer to old Hagstrom's boy at Rock Springs; and very likely Uncle Bark who had followed Sam Hengelman's van along the turnpike. Impossible to prove, though, at this distance.

The color of his hair was premature. Very few wrinkles marked the smooth suntanned face, from which white eyebrows stood out like a bracket of snow, nearly meeting over the nose. His eyelashes also were white, but the albino nonpigmentation stopped short of the eyes: not pink, but a clear pale blue.

He carried his head stiffly on a thick muscular neck, and the large body beneath the airy white shirt looked solid more than soft. Not a man to ignore in any company. A physique which teemed naturally with success: and success had given him an arrogance of expression where a decent humility would have been more fitting.

The whole farm had the high gloss of money-no-object. Mathematically precise white-painted wood railings ringed the paddocks, and the approach to the Spanish-style house was landscaped with watered lawns and palms and an occasional bed of spiky red flowers with sharp purplish leaves. We didn't penetrate the house: Walt's fire insurance stretched only to the stabling.

After we'd seen the stallions Offen handed us over to his stud groom, a fair, surprisingly young man he called Kiddo, who had a drawling Western voice and an air of having been born without urgency. Every second word was "uh," and his walk was thirty-two frames a second; slow motion.

"Been here long?" I asked him, as he pointed out the spotless foaling stalls.

"Five or six months," he said, showing no resentment at a personal question: good-natured, unsuspicious, no sign of nerves.

"You must be good, to get a job like this so young," I congratulated him.

After a pause he said, "I got a feeling for horses, see? Mares, they foal down nearly always at night. Comes from having to give birth in the dark out in the wild, you understand?"

"Why in the dark?" asked Walt, puzzled.

Another pause. Not for a deliberate choice of what or what not to say, I realized, but just a moment of waiting while the instinctive knowledge coalesced into words.

"They drop 'em by day, some hungry hyena comes along and kills the foal in the first half hour. Foals, now, they're readier to run at birth than most other critturs, but you've got to give 'em a half hour to dry off."

"But they don't have to run, here," Walt protested.

"Nature don't know that," Kiddo pointed out reasonably. "Another thing, mares mostly drop their foals pretty quick. Don't take some of them no time at all. And then, see, I always know when a mare's ready, and most often I go out to the stall and make sure she's doing all right."

"How do you know?" I asked, fascinated.

A much longer pause. Then he said, "I don't know how I know. I got a feeling for it. I just wake up some nights and think that Rose is about ready, and I go on out to her, and maybe there she is, not needing a bit of help, or maybe with the cord round the foal's neck, strangling it. I bin with horses, see, all my life."

"Where were you before you came here?" I asked.

"Uh . . . all over. Had a job in Lexington a while back, but they said I didn't keep good time turning up at work." He grinned suddenly, a big mischievous lighting-up of the passive patient face. "Then . . . uh . . . I was with a feller in Maryland . . . he had a barn was falling down and honeysuckle breaking his fences and creeping into his windows, but he sure had some pretty mares and one of them was the dam of the horse who won the Preakness a year back. Though I don't go the races myself."

"Where after Maryland?" I asked.

"Uh . . . here. I seen this ad in the *Blood Horse,* and I wrote. It was a joke, mostly. I never expected to hear a word, knowing this was a big place and everything. But Mr. Offen, it seems he didn't want no great businessman, just someone with a feeling for the mares . . . and he's keeping me on, he says, though there was two before me he let go after they'd been here a month."

It didn't seem to worry him. He had the God-will-provide nature which doesn't understand anxiety and never stores up winter nuts. Not that he had any need to. His "feeling for mares" was in fact priceless: he would probably never cash in on it as he could, but he'd never want for a job.

Kiddo watched us go in the same calm friendliness with which he'd shown us around. Walt and I agreed on the way back to Santa Barbara that he was only potentially an opponent. Loyalty might be given to Offen if he demanded it, but at present Kiddo had no idea what was going on.

"Unless," Walt said thoughtfully, "he's a brilliant actor."

I shook my head. "He wasn't acting. None of the signs."

Walt looked at me curiously, taking his eyes too long off the road. "Can you always tell?"

I smiled. "That's one of those unanswerable questions. I've a feeling for it, like Kiddo with his mares. But if it lets me down sometimes, how am I to know?"

"You'd know soon enough when secrets started leaking to the other side," Walt pointed out. "Have you ever passed as clear anyone who turned out to be a spy?"

"Yes."

"How often?"

"Once."

"In your first year, I suppose," Walt said with mild sarcasm.

"In my second year. He was the first serious spy I had to deal with, and I didn't spot him. The counterespionage chaps turned him up six months later when he'd done a good deal of damage, and the press made the usual scathing remarks about the feebleness of our screening system."

"Which you took to heart," Walt said dryly.

"I guess so."

He drove a mile and then said, "And now you're so good at it that they beat you up. What do you think about things when that happens?"

"That there's a big fish coming down the pipeline and they want me out of the way."

"So you look all the harder." A statement, not a question.

"You might say so. Yes."

"They'll kill you one of these days."

I didn't answer. Walt flicked a glance sideways and sighed. "I suppose you don't care."

"There are a lot of others in the department."

Walt drove into Santa Barbara without another word, where we joined Eunice and Lynnie in the terrace restaurant for lunch. They had, they said, bought that morning the big bright dangling earrings which swung with every turn of their heads. Lynnie's were scarlet, Eunice's acid green; otherwise identical. Still friends, I thought in some relief. Still in harmony. Whether Eunice would do a small chore for me was, however, another matter.

We had clam chowder with shrimp to follow, and Lynnie said with all this seafood she'd be growing fins. During coffee, when she stood up restlessly and said she was going down to the sea, it was Walt, after a pause, who said he would go with her. She looked at me questioningly, worriedly, and then turned and walked quickly off with him, talking a good deal too brightly.

"Don't you hurt that child," Eunice said fiercely.

"I don't want to."

"You're too bloody attractive."

"Yeah. Charm the birds off the trees," I agreed sardonically. "Little wives spill their husbands' secrets into my bloody attractive ears."

She looked shocked. Quite a change, I thought, from dishing it out.

"You mean you . . . *use* it?"

"Like a can opener. And as a catalyst. Who doesn't? Salesmen, politicians, actors, women, all using it like mad."

"For God's sake . . ." Her voice was faint, but she was also laughing.

"But not on Lynnie," I added wryly.

"You didn't need to, I guess. Dragging Dave out of the Thames was a lot more effective."

I watched Lynnie and Walt's backs as they reached the tide line.

"So that's why . . .?" I said, almost to myself.

"Hero worship," Eunice said with barbs. "Does it give you a kick?"

"Like a mule's in the stomach."

She laughed. "It's not that you're so madly handsome in any obvious way."

"No," I agreed with truth, "I'm not."

She looked as if she was going to say more and then thought better of it. I jumped straight in while her mind was still half flirting, knowing, and despising the knowledge, that in that mood she was more likely to do what I asked.

"Has Lynnie still got those photographs of me?"

"Don't worry," she said sarcastically. "In a fire, she'd save them first."

"I'd like Culham James Offen to see them."

"You'd like *what?* What are you talking about?"

"About you and Lynnie driving over to pay a neighborly call on Culham James this afternoon. And easily, dearest Eunice, you could tell him about me pulling Dave out of the Thames, and Lynnie could show him my photograph. Especially the one of me sitting by a table outside a pub. That group of all of us."

She gaped and gasped, and then started thinking.

"You really can't be as pleased with yourself as all that . . . so, for God's sake, why?"

"An experiment."

"That's no answer."

"Earning my keep at the Vacationer."

A look of disgust turned down her mouth.

"Finding that bloody horse?"

"I'm afraid so."

"You don't mean . . . surely you can't mean that Offen has anything to do with it?"

"I'd like to make sure he hasn't."

"Oh, I see. Well, I guess that's not much to ask. Sure. I'll get Lynnie to come with me."

"And tell him I'm looking for Allyx."

She gave me a straight assessing stare, and said, "How about Chrysalis?"

"Whatever you like. Say that Dave employed me to get him back."

"I don't know why I'm doing it."

"More interesting than golf?" I suggested.

"Is it a game?" She was skeptical.

"Well, like hunting bears," I smiled.

"Oh, yes," She nodded sardonically. "A sport."

13

I PARKED a rented car in some scrub off the road leading to Orpheus Farm, and smoked a rare cigarette. The fierce afternoon sun roasted through the metal roof and a water mirage hung in a streak over the dry road. A day for lizards to look for shade. They'd run out of air-conditioned heaps at the car rental place: I'd had to take one of those old-fashioned jobs where you breathed fresh air by opening the window. The air in question was as fresh as last week's news and as hot as tomorrow's.

At five past four Eunice and Lynnie passed unseeingly across my bows, heading back to Santa Barbara. I finished the cigarette and stubbed it out carefully in the flaked chromium ashtray. I looked at my fingernails for ten minutes. No special inspiration. At half past four I started the car, pointed its nose toward Orpheus, and went to call on Uncle Bark.

This time I drove straight up to the house and rang the ornate bell. A houseboy came: all on the same scale as at Jeff Roots'. When he went to find Culham James I followed quietly on his heels, so my host, even if he had meant to, had no chance to say he was out. The houseboy opened the door onto a square comfortable office-sitting room and Culham James was revealed sitting at his desk with a green telephone receiver at his ear.

He gave the houseboy and me a murderous glare between us which changed to reasonable affability once he'd got control of it. "I'll call you later," he said to the telephone. "A Mr. Hawkins has this minute arrived . . . that's right . . . later then." He put down the receiver and raised his eyebrows.

"Did you miss something this morning?" he asked.

"No; should we have done?"

He shook his head in mild annoyance. "I am merely asking the purpose of this return visit."

"My colleague and I wanted answers to one or two extra questions about the precautions you take against fire, especially as regards those two exceptionally valuable stallions . . . er . . . Moviemaker and Centigrade."

Under his suntanned face, behind the white bracket of eyebrows, Culham James Offen was beginning to enjoy a huge joke. It fizzed like soda water in his pale-blue eyes and bubbled in his throat. He was even having difficulty preventing himself from sharing it: but after a struggle he had it nailed down under hatches, and calm with a touch of severity took over. We went solemnly through the farce of fire precautions, me leaning on his desk and checking off Walt's solid-sounding inventions one by one. They mostly had to deal with the amount of supervision in the stallions' barn at night. Whether there were any regular patrols, any dogs loose on watch, any photoelectric apparatus for detecting opacity, such as heavy smoke?

Offen cleared his throat and answered no to the lot.

"We have the extremely expensive and reliable sprinkler system which you saw this morning," he pointed out. "It is thoroughly tested every three months, as I told you earlier."

"Yes. Thank you, then. I guess that's all." I shut my notebook. "You've been most helpful, Mr. Offen."

"You're welcome," he said. The joke rumbled in his voice, but was colored now with unmistakable malice. High time to go, I thought: and went.

When I got back to the Vacationer some while later I found Eunice and Lynnie and Walt sitting in a glum row behind empty glasses. I flopped into a chair opposite them and said "Why the mass depression?"

"You're late," Walt said.

"I told you not to wait dinner." I caught a passing waiter on the wing and arranged refills all round.

"We were considering a search party," Eunice said.

I looked at all three of them more carefully. "You've been comparing notes," I said resignedly.

"I think it's terrible of you . . . *wicked,*" Lynnie burst out, "to have made me go and deliberately . . . *deliberately* . . . put you in such frightful danger."

"Lynnie, stop it. I wasn't in any danger. Here I am, aren't I?"

"But Walt said . . ."

"Walt needs his brains seen to."

Walt glared and compressed his mouth into a rigid line. "You didn't tell me you'd arranged for Offen to know you were the man who took Chrysalis. And you didn't tell me the Clives had tried to kill Mr. Teller."

"And you didn't tell *me,*" Eunice added, "that the couple in the background of the photograph Lynnie showed Culham Offen had tried to kill you too."

"Or you'd never have let Lynnie show it to him?"

"No," she said slowly.

"Just as well I didn't."

"And you deliberately misled me by saying you wanted to clear Offen. It wasn't true."

"Er . . . no. But I did want you to behave naturally with him. And, anyway, why all the fuss?"

"We thought . . ." Lynnie said in a subdued voice, "we almost thought . . . as you were gone so long . . . that you . . . that they . . ."

"They didn't," I pointed out obviously, smiling.

"But won't you please explain why?" Lynnie said. "*Why* did you want me to give you away like that?"

"Several reasons. One was to make Dave safer."

"I don't see how," Eunice objected.

"By letting Offen know, and through him the Clives, that we could prove the Clives were in England and beside the Thames on the day of Dave's accident. Murder by accident is only a good idea as long as there's no apparent motive and the murderers have no apparent connection with the victim. We've shown them that we know their motive and their connection, and they must now be aware that if Dave was killed they would be the first suspects. This makes it less likely they will try again."

"Crikey," Lynnie said. "Go on."

"When Walt and I went to Orpheus Farm this morning saying we were making a survey for new fire precautions, Offen wasn't worried. He didn't know me from Adam then, of course. It was before you showed him my photograph. But he showed no anxiety at all about two strangers turning up on a pretext that he didn't even bother to check. None of the edginess one might have expected if he'd just had one stolen horse pinched back from him, and was in possession of two others standing in his barn. I didn't like it. It didn't feel right."

"He hasn't got them," Eunice said with relief. "I was sure it couldn't possibly be right that Culham Offen would steal horses. I mean, he's *respected*."

Walt and I exchanged a glance of barely perceptible amusement. To be respected was the best cover in the world for fraud. Fraud, in fact, could rarely exist without it.

"So," I said, "I thought it would be helpful if he knew for certain that I was especially interested in Moviemaker and Centigrade, and that I wasn't in fire insurance, but was the man he had to thank for losing Chrysalis. When I went back, after you two had left, he still wasn't worried. On the contrary, he was enjoying the situation. It amused him enormously to think that I believed I was fooling him. I asked him a lot of questions about the security precautions surrounding Moviemaker and Centigrade, and he was still completely untroubled. So," I paused, "it's now quite clear that the two horses standing in his barn called Moviemaker and Centigrade are in actual fact exactly what he says: Moviemaker and Centigrade. He isn't worried about snoopers, he isn't worried about me making clumsy preparations to steal them. He must therefore be confident that any legal proceedings will prove the horses to be the ones he says they are. He'd ambush me if I tried to steal them, and have me in real deep trouble, which would be to him some small compensation for losing Chrysalis."

Walt nodded briefly.

Eunice said obstinately, "I think it only proves that you're barking up the wrong damn tree. He isn't worried simply because he isn't guilty of anything."

"You liked him?"

"Yes," she said. "He was bloody sweet."

Lynnie nodded. "I thought so too."

"What did he say when you showed him the photographs?"

"He just glanced at them at first," Lynnie said. "And then he took them over to the window. And then he asked me who had taken them, and where, and when. So I told him about the day on the river, and about you and Dave going under the weir . . ."

At the side of my vision Eunice gave me an I-told-you-so smile.

". . . and he said one or two nice things about you," Lynnie finished. "So I told him you came over here to look for Chrysalis, and somehow or other you found him."

"He asked where you found him." Eunice nodded. "But we didn't know. I said you were now trying to find Allyx, and it certainly didn't worry him. I'm sure you must be wrong."

I smiled at her. She didn't want the horse found, and as an ally she was as reliable as thin ice on a sunny day. I didn't intend to tell her anything in future which I wasn't prepared to have passed on to Offen. Like most law-abiding citizens, she had not grasped that a criminal mind didn't show, that an endearing social manner could coexist with fraud and murder. "Such a *nice* man," the neighbors say in bewilderment, when Mr. Smith's garden is found to be clogged with throttled ladies. "Always so pleasant."

Eunice, propelled by a strong semiconscious wish for him not to have Allyx, might tell Offen anything, simply because she couldn't visualize a "sweet" man being deadly. She might also tell him anything propelled by the same impulse which had made her point a gun at me.

"Let's have dinner," I suggested; and Eunice and Lynnie went away to freshen up.

Walt looked at me thoughtfully, then raised his eyebrows.

I nodded. "I put a bug on the underside of his desk, two feet from the telephone. I was late back because I was listening. He called Yola and told her about my visit but there wasn't much else. I left the set hidden, and came back here."

"Do you mean it, that those two horses really are Moviemaker and Centigrade?"

"Sure. He bought them, remember. Openly. At bloodstock sales. And obviously he's kept them. I suppose he never could be certain that some ex-owner would turn up for a visit. Those horses will have been tattooed inside their mouths with an identity number when they first began to race. They have to be, over here, don't they? It'll be quite easy to establish that they're the right two."

"You don't think Mrs. Teller's right—that he never had Showman and Allyx after all?"

"I'll play you his call to Yola sometime. He had the foresight to whisk those horses away from Orpheus when we got Chrysalis. He was more or less waiting for something like our visit this morning. No flies on Culham

James, I'm afraid. Er . . . Walt, did you give Eunice and Lynnie any details about our jaunt in the Tetons?''

He looked uncomfortable. ''I was annoyed with you.''

''What exactly did you tell them?''

''Not much. I was horrified at Lynnie's having shown Offen that picture of the Clives, and when Mrs. Teller said you'd planned it I said you must be mad, they'd tried to kill you once already.''

''And you told them how?''

He nodded, not meeting my eyes.

''Did you tell them about the bugs and the wireless set?''

''No.''

''It's important, Walt.''

He looked up. ''I didn't mention them.''

I relaxed. ''How about our mountain walk?''

''No details.''

''Place?''

''I'm pretty sure I mentioned the Tetons.''

Nothing there that would hurt.

''How much did you say about Showman and Allyx?''

''I told them that you'd worked out through the studbooks that Offen must have them.''

''Did you say the words 'Uncle Bark'?''

He shook his head. ''I'd forgotten about that.''

I sighed. ''Walt, Mrs. Teller doesn't want Allyx found any more than she wanted Chrysalis. Let's not entrust the state of the nation to the Indians.''

He flushed a little and compressed his mouth. Eunice and Lynnie came back shortly after, and though we all four had dinner together it proved a taciturn and not overfriendly affair.

Walt came up to my room for a conference after the coffee.

''How do we find them?'' he said, coming bluntly to the point and easing himself simultaneously into the only armchair.

''They've made us a gift of them, in one way,'' I said thoughtfully. ''We can send a bunch of lawyers in to query Moviemaker and Centigrade's identity, and get it established beyond doubt that the two Offen showed us are in fact those two horses. He'll be keen for them to do it: and once he's done it, he'll be stuck with them. We will meanwhile do another little vanishing trick with the other two and start our own identification parade on our own ground. Once they are established as Allyx and Showman, Offen cannot possibly claim them back.''

''Two objections,'' Walt said. ''We don't know where Allyx and Showman are. And if we find them, why not get lawyers into the act right away? Why go to all the danger and trouble of taking them?''

''Same as Chrysalis,'' I pointed out. ''The first sign of any real trouble, and they'd be shot. It's not illegal to kill a horse and whisk it smartly off to the dog food people. And vastly more difficult to identify a dead one. Impossible, I'd almost say, for the degree of certainty we need here.''

''Even if we take them, and establish their identity, and everything goes smoothly, Offen will still be raking in those colossal stud fees of half a million dollars a year, because we'd never be able to prove that for the past ten years Showman has been siring every foal that's down in the book as Moviemaker's."

I smiled. "We'll do something about that, once we've sorted out the rest."

"Which brings us back to square one," Walt said flatly. "Where the hell do we start?"

I perched on the window sill and looked down sideways into the brightly lit car park. Colored bulbs on the face of the motel raised rainbow shimmers on glossy hard tops and struck me as a deeply melancholy commentary on human achievement. Yet I wouldn't have wanted to live without cars or electricity . . . if I'd wanted to live. My room was only two floors up, with none above. Too near the ground. I'd known of a woman who'd jumped from five and bungled it. A gun was better.

"Well?" Walt said insistently.

"I'm sorry . . . ?" I said vaguely, turning my head back to him.

"Where do we look?"

"Oh . . . yes."

"On the ranch?"

"Very doubtful, don't you think? They must know that's the first place we'd think of."

"There's a lot of land there," he said. "And a lot of horses to lose them in."

I shook my head. "They'd have to keep them in a paddock close to the house. All the rest of the ranch is in the mountains, and they couldn't turn them loose for fear of their breaking a leg. We'd better check, though." I stared unseeingly at the carpet. "But I guess the horses are with Matt. Offen is at Orpheus Farm, and Yola is tied to the ranch seeing to about thirty guests, so where's Matt?"

"Where indeed," Walt said gloomily.

"He and Yola don't spend their winters on the ranch because the valley is blocked by snow. She told me that they go south. On one of those telephone calls she told Offen they couldn't keep Chrysalis at a place called Pitts, because it wasn't suitable. But that was when they didn't know we were after them . . . when it wasn't an emergency."

"So somewhere south of the Tetons we find this Pitts, and Matt and the horses will be waiting for us?"

"Yeah." I smiled briefly. "Sounds too easy."

"Easy!" Walt said.

"They must leave a forwarding address for mail," I pointed out. "They live a conventional law-abiding life with a long-standing business to give them obvious legal means of support. There must be dozens of people in Jackson who know their winter address."

"Our Buttress agent could get that, then. First thing in the morning."

"Fine."

Walt levered himself out of the armchair and hesitated.

"Come alone to my room," he said. "I've got a bottle."

I wasn't sure that I wanted to, but he smiled suddenly, wiping out all resentments, and one didn't kick that sort of olive branch in the teeth.

"Be glad to," I said.

The smile went deeper and lasted along the passage to his room, which was almost identical to mine. The window looked out on the same cars from a slightly different angle, and he had two armchairs instead of one. There was a bottle of Old Grand-dad on a round tray with glasses and a water jug, and on his bedside table stood a leather-framed photograph. I picked it up idly while he went to fetch ice from the machine along the passage. Walt with his family. A good-looking woman, a plain girl in her early teens, a thin boy of about ten: all four of them smiling cheerfully into the lens. He came back as I was putting them down.

"I'm sorry about the picnic," I said.

"Next week will do just as well," he said. "We've got the whole of the summer, I guess."

We sat in the armchairs, drinking slowly, I didn't like bourbon much; but that wasn't the point. He talked casually about the split-level ranch-type house they'd moved into the year before, and how his daughter got along just fine with the folks next door, and how they'd had trouble with the boy's health, he'd had rheumatic fever . . .

"How about your own future, with Buttress Life?" I asked.

"I've got about as high as I'll get," he said with surprising honesty. "There's only one more step up that I really want, and that's to chief investigator, claims division, and that'll come along next year when the present guy retires."

He poured more drinks, rubbed his thumb slowly over the round finger-tips, and said Amy and the kids were asking him for a pool in their back yard, and that Amy's mother was a problem since Amy's father died last fall, and that he hadn't caught a single ball game last season, he'd been that busy . . .

We sat for more than an hour without mentioning the horses once. He yawned finally and I uncurled myself from the soft chair, putting down the third-time empty glass. He said good night sleepily with easy friendliness and, for the first time since I'd known him, without tension. Back in my own room, undressing, I wondered how long it would last. Until I made the next unpopular suggestion, I supposed. I didn't know whether to envy him his enclosing domesticity or to feel stifled by it. I did know that I liked him both as a man and as a working companion, moods and all.

The Buttress Life agent in Jackson came through with the Clives' winter address within twenty minutes of Walt's telephone call: 40159 Pittsville Boulevard, Las Vegas, Nevada.

I remembered Yola's smile at the thought of winter. Las Vegas explained it. Yola liked to gamble.

"What now?" Walt said.

"I'll go on out there and take a look."

"Alone?" There was a certain amount of anxiety in his voice, which I interpreted as a desire not to be left in Santa Barbara with Eunice.

"We need you here," I said placatingly. "And don't tell her where I've gone."

He gave me a sharp glance. "I won't."

We drove in the rented car out to Orpheus Farm, where I showed him where I'd hidden the radio tape recorder between three rocks, with its aerial sticking up through the branches of a scrubby bush. The nearest neatly railed paddock was only feet away; the house, about four hundred yards. We picked up the radio and parked a short distance down the road.

"Supposing he sees us?" Walt said, watching me wind back the reel.

"He'll only think we're watching the farm routine, to know when to pinch Moviemaker. The radio will pick up the bug in his office from at least a quarter mile, but it gets fainter after that. It has to work on the air-vibration system. Not such good amplification as electricity. Do you ever use them?"

"Bugs?" He shook his head. "Not often. Cameras with telescopic lenses are better. Catch the claimants walking around on their paralyzed legs." Satisfaction echoed in his voice. Like me, a rogue hunter to the bone.

Smiling to myself, I switched on. Cutting in and out, Culham James's various conversations filled three quarters of an hour of tape time, but nothing he said was of any use to us. I rewound the reels again and we put the radio in among the rocks, Walt agreeing that he would come back after sunset and listen to the day's take.

He drove me then to the Los Angeles airport, where I hopped a plane to Las Vegas, arriving in midafternoon. The desert heat hit like a gust from an oven when the plane doors were opened, and from a nearby building the usual lighted numbers proclaimed to the populace that in the shade, if they could find any, it would be 108.

The air conditioning at the edge-of-town motel I booked into was turning itself inside out under the strain, and the Hertz man who presently took my money admitted that this was a little old heat wave, sure thing. Had to expect them in July. The inconspicuous Pontiac he rented me was this time, however, a cooled one. I drove around for a while to get my bearings, and then took a look at Pittsville Boulevard.

The high numbers ran two miles out of the town, expensive-looking homes along a paved road with the desert crowding in at their rear. The Clives' house was flanked by others on both sides: not near enough to touch, but too near for the invisible stabling of stallions. The place on Pitts wasn't suitable, as Yola had said.

It was low and white, with a flat roof and a frame of palms and orange trees. Blinds and screens blanked out the windows, and the grass on each side of the drive was a pale dry biscuit color, not green watered like its neighbors'. I stopped the car in the roadway opposite and looked it over. Not a leaf moved under the bleaching sun. Ten minutes ticked away. Nothing happened in the street. Inside the car, with the engine stopped, the temperature rose like Christmas prices. I started up again, sucked in the first cold blast from the air conditioner, and slid on along the way I was heading.

A mile past the Clives' house the paving ended, and the road ran out across the desert as a dusty streak of gravel. I turned the car and went back, thinking. The comparative dead-endedness of Pittsville Boulevard explained the almost total lack of traffic past the Clives', and also meant that I couldn't drive past there very often without becoming conspicuous to the neighbors. Keeping a check on an apparently empty house, however, wasn't going to get me much further.

About five houses along on the town side of the Clives' there was another with water-starved brownish grass. Taking a chance that these inhabitants too were away from home, I rolled the Pontiac purposefully into the palm-edged driveway and stopped outside the front door. Ready with some of Walt's insurance patter, I leaned on the bell and gave it a full twenty seconds. No one came. Everything was hot, quiet, and still.

Strolling, I walked down the drive and onto the road. Looking back one couldn't see the car for bushes. Satisfied I made the trip along to the Clives', trying to look as if walking were a normal occupation in a Nevada heat wave: and by the time I got there it was quite clear why it wasn't. The sweat burned dry on my skin before it had a chance to form into beads.

Reconnoitering the Clives' place took an hour. The house was shut up tight, obviously empty. The window screens were all securely fastened, and all the glass was covered on the inside with shades, so that one couldn't see in. The doors were securely fastened. The Clives had made casual breaking in by vagrants practically impossible.

With caution I eased round the acre of land behind the house. Palms and bushes screened a trefoil-shaped pool from behind overlooked too openly by the neighbors, but from several places it was possible to see the pools of the flanking houses some sixty yards away. Beside one of them, reminding me of Eunice, a woman in two scraps of yellow cloth lay motionless on a long chair, inviting heatstroke and adding to a depth of suntan which would have got her reclassified in South Africa. I moved even more quietly after I'd seen her, but she didn't stir.

The rear boundary of the Clives' land was marked by large stones painted white, with desert scrub on the far side and low-growing citrus bushes on the near. From their windows, brother and sister had a wide view of hills and wilderness; two miles down the road neon lights went twenty rounds with the midday sun, and the crash of fruit machines outdecibeled the traffic. I wondered idly how much of Uncle Bark's illicit proceeds found their way into Matt and Yola's pocket, and how much from there vanished into the greedy slot mouths in Vegas. The stud fees went around and around and only Buttress Life was the loser.

On the way back to the motel I stopped at every supermarket I came to, and bought two three-pound bags of flour from each.

From a hardware store I acquired a short ladder, white overalls, white-peaked cotton cap, brushes, and a half gallon can of bright yellow instant-drying paint.

14

WALT LISTENED to what I had to say in a silence which hummed down the telephone wires more eloquently than hysterics.

"You're crazy," he said at last, sounding as if he seriously meant it.

"Can you think of anything else?"

After a long pause he said grudgingly, "Nothing quicker."

"Right, then. I'll fix everything this end and give you a call in the morning. And let's hope it works."

"What if it doesn't?"

"Have to try something else."

Walt grunted gloomily and hung up.

I spent an hour at the airport, and then went back to the motel. The evening oozed away. I played some roulette without enthusiasm and lost backing black against a sequence of fourteen reds; and I ate a good steak listening to a girl singer whose voice was secondary to her frontage. After that I lay on my bed for a while and smoked, and kept the blues from crowding in too close by thinking exclusively of the job in hand.

At two I dressed in a dark-green cotton shirt and black jeans, went downstairs, stepped into the car, and drove along Pittsville Boulevard to 40159. The town itself was wide awake and rocking: the houses along Pitts were dark and silent. With dimmed lights I rolled quietly into the Clives' driveway and stacked the bags of flour close to the front door. Then, holding the car door but not shutting it, I eased the Pontiac back along the road and parked it in the driveway of the same empty house that I had used in the afternoon. Again, not wanting any neighbors to remember hearing a car door slam, I left it ajar and walked back to the Clives'.

The night was warm and gentle with a deep navy-blue sky and stars like fluorescent polka dots. Two miles away the blazing lights of Vegas raised a bell-shaped orange glow, but among the palms and orange trees the shadows were thick and black and comfortably concealing.

The Clives' was only the latest of a great many houses I had broken into. My short cuts to truth were scandalous by all public and private standards, and Keeble rarely asked how I got my information: and as I would have had the press, the police and public opinion all balefully against me if I'd ever been caught, Agag on eggs would have been clumsy in comparison. Law-abiding citizens never knew I'd been their guest. For the Clives, however, I had alternative plans.

Wearing surgeons' rubber gloves, and with my shoes stuck through my belt to the left of the Luger, I worked on the lock on the back door, and after not too bad a time, considering its complexity, the two sets of tumblers fell sweetly over, and the house was mine.

Inside, the air was stale and still, and dust sheets draped the furniture, looking like pale boulders in the dim light of my flashlight. The rear door opened into a spacious hall which led straight through to the front. I walked across, unbolted and unfastened the front door, brought in the bags of flour, and left the door ajar, as I'd left the one I'd come in by: the value of always being prepared for instant flight had been drummed into me by an ex-burglar who had once neglected it.

I went into the bedroom. Large separate single-bedded rooms again for Yola and Matt, and a guest bedroom, with a bathroom to each. I pulled all the covers off the furniture and flung onto the floor everything they had left in the chests and closets. Over the resulting mess in each room I shook six pounds of self-rising flour.

In the kitchen I emptied onto the floor a packet of soap flakes, a packet of rice, some cereal, and four pounds of brown sugar, which were all lying handy in the pantry. I unlocked the pantry window and unfastened its outer screen, leaving both open: and as an afterthought tumbled some canned fruit off the shelf beneath it, to show that the intruder had come in that way.

In the spacious living room I again removed all the covers, put every ornament and small loose object in a heap on the floor, and flung flour over them and around the whole place. A smaller cozier room, facing the road, contained a desk full of papers, two large bookshelves, and a well-filled sewing box. Together the jumbled contents made a splendid ankle-deep mess on the floor. Pounds of flour fell over everything like snow.

It was while I was tearing open the last bag, ready for a final scatter around the hall, that I heard the distant police siren. Frozen, I doubted for a second that it was for me: then considered that either a too-watchful neighbor had seen my flashlight in chinks through the blinds or else that the Clives' complicated locks weren't their only protection, and that they had a direct burglar alarm line to the police.

Without wasting much time I shut the front door and heard the lock engage. Emptied the last bag of flour over a plastic flower arrangement on a table in the hall. Flitted through the rear door and clicked it shut behind me. And thrust the flashlight into my pocket.

The siren wailed and stopped at the front of the house. Doors slammed, men shouted, boots ran. Someone with a megaphone urged me to come out with my hands on my head. The edges of the house were outlined by a spotlight shining on its front.

With bare seconds to spare before the first uniform appeared in silhouette around the corner I reached the nearest of the bushes flanking the trefoil pool and dived behind it. Being quiet enough was no problem, as the law was making an intimidating clatter all around the house, but staying invisible was more difficult. They brought another spotlight round to the rear and shone it full on the house. The shuttered windows stared blindly and unhelpfully back, reflecting the glare almost as far as my cover.

Lights appeared in neighboring houses, and heads stuck like black knobs out the windows. I eased gently away past a few more bushes and thought I was still a great deal too close to a spell in the zoo.

A shout from the side of the house indicated that they had found the open pantry window. Four troopers, I judged. All armed to the teeth. I grimaced in the darkness and moved another few yards with less caution. I wasn't going to give them any forefinger exercise if I could help it, but time was running out.

They were brave enough. One or more climbed in through the window and switched on the lights. I more rapidly crossed the last stretch of garden, stepped over the white-painted stones, and headed straight out into the desert.

Five steps convinced me I needed to put my shoes on. Ten steps had me certain that the only vegetation was prickly pear, and close-ranked at that. I should imagine I impaled myself on every one in the neighborhood.

Back at the Clives' they had temporarily stopped oohing and ahing over the mess, and were searching the grounds. Lights moved round the next-door houses as well. If they went five along and found the car, things would get very awkward indeed.

I had meant to be safely back in my motel long before I called the police early in the morning to say I was a civic-minded neighbor who had just seen a prowler coming out of the Clives' . . .

When they showed signs of shining the light out toward where I was stumbling along I lay down flat on the ground and listened to the thud of my heart. The spotlight beam flickered palely over the low scrubby bushes and outlined the flat spiky plates of the prickly pears, but in the shifting uneven shadows that they threw, I reckoned I must be just another clump. There was a good deal of shouted discussion about whether it was necessary to take a look-see in the desert, but to my relief no one came farther out than the boundary stones. Gradually, frustrated, the dazzle and commotion retreated and died away.

The lights inside the Clives' house went out. The police car drove off. The neighbors went back to bed. I got to my feet and brushed off the surplus of dry sandy earth. What with that and flour dust even the blindest cop would have little difficulty in buttoning me onto the crime.

With more care than on the outward trip I headed back toward the houses, but at an angle I hoped would bring me near the car. The sooner I beat it from that little neck of the woods, the better.

I stopped dead.

How might one catch a prowler? Just pretend to go away, and wait somewhere down the road, and when he thought everything was safe, he'd come carelessly along and fall into your waiting hands like a ripe plum.

I decided not to drive back toward Las Vegas from that quiet cul-de-sac. Just in case.

At the fifth house along everything was quiet. I cat-footed through the grounds, around the house, and took a distant look at the car. Still there. No trooper beside it. I stood in the shadows for longer than was probably necessary, then took a deep breath and risked it. I completed the steps to the car and peered in through the window. Empty. Made a quick cautious tour of the row of spiky low-growing palms hiding it from the road.

Nothing. No irate shouts. All quiet. Car undiscovered. Sighing with relief, the vision of the malicious Clives dancing at my trial fading a little, I pulled wide the already open door and folded like an understuffed rag doll into the driving seat. For five minutes I did nothing more energetic than to breathe freely, and enjoy it.

There remained, however, the problem of telephoning to Walt: and I chewed it over thoughtfully while absent-mindedly pulling prickly pear needles out of my legs.

I was a fair hand at wiretapping when I had the kit: but it was in Putney. No doubt there would be a telephone in the empty house alongside. But I wasn't sure that I wanted to risk this house too being directly connected to the police, if that was what had happened at the Clives'. On the other hand, I had been in the Clives' house twenty minutes before the police showed up. Yet they might be quicker on a second call.

After half an hour I pulled on the rubber gloves, climbed out of the car and picked the front door lock. It turned all right, but unfortunately the prudent householders had also used bolts. Always a tossup which door of the house people bolted. I walked round to the rear, and let myself in. There was a telephone on a table in the hall. I walked over to it, then turned, retraced my steps, left the door ajar, went round to the car, started up, and drove quietly away in the dead-end direction, not stopping until I was off the paved road onto the gravel, and round a couple of bends. I switched off the lights and smoked a cigarette.

Another half hour passed. No lights went on along the houses; no police sirens, no disturbances at all. I drove gently back, parked in the same spot as before, went round into the house, and called up Walt.

He wasn't amused at being woken at five A.M.

"A slight change of timing," I said apologetically. "The police have already seen the mess."

He drew in a sharp breath. "They didn't catch you!"

"No." No point in telling him how close it had been: he hadn't approved of my going in at all.

"I suppose you want me to come now, then?" he said with resignation.

"Yes, please. As soon as you can. Leave the car keys at the inquiry desk at Los Angeles airport, and I'll pick them up. The helicopter pilot I've engaged at Las Vegas is Michael King. He's expecting you. Just ask for him. The helicopter radio will pick up the frequency of the bug I've got with me, so you won't need to bring my recorder. Was there anything on the tape today?"

"Yesterday," Walt corrected. "Not much. I went over after dinner last night and ran it through. Offen had a friend over. There was two hours of just ordinary yapping. I didn't get back here to bed until one."

"When this is over you can sleep for a week."

"Yeah?" he said sarcastically. "Tell it to the Marines.'

He put down his receiver with less of a crash than usual. Smiling, I took out a five-dollar bill and left it stuck half under the telephone. Then I let myself out, relocked the door behind me, and went back to the car.

Three hours went by uneventfully. Night changed to day. The air temperature began its morning climb. A few energetic birds sang; and I smoked another cigarette.

Soon after eight a patrol car went up the road, siren fortissimo. Pittsville Boulevard woke up. I eased out of the car, walked carefully down toward the road, and tucked myself invisibly between a palm and a bush, from where I had a clear view of everyone driving up toward the Clives'.

From along the road I could hear several excited voices, most of them children's: and a small boy and a girl came past close to me doing an Indianapolis on their tricycles.

Several cars drove down from the houses, all with men alone, going in to Las Vegas. One woman followed. Three women came the other way, all looking eager. At 9:30 two men drove in from Vegas, one of them adjusting a large folding camera: the local press.

An hour later a quiet-engined helicopter drifted over and landed out of sight behind a fold of hill.

At 10:50 the hawk came to the lure.

A sky-blue convertible Ford, with the hood down. Matt, driving fast, hunched with anger. Youth, strength, and fury knotted into one callous, reckless personality. Even in a speeding car the impression came across with the solidity of a shock wave. Standing on his brakes flamboyantly late, he screeched down from sixty to nil outside his own house, scattering children like pigeons.

Satisfied, I got stiffly to my feet and went back up the drive to the car. There I removed from the trunk the white overalls, white cotton gloves and cap, and put them on, along with a new and darker pair of sunglasses. With a screwdriver from the tool kit I opened the tin of paint and gave the oily yellow contents an encouraging stir; cleaned and replaced the screwdriver, and rested the paint lid gently back on the tin. Then, picking it up by its handle with my right hand, and carrying brushes and ladder with my left, I strolled out onto the road, and along to the Clives'.

Matt's Ford stood at the door at a crooked angle to the patrol car. Many people were still standing around, staring and gossiping in the sun. I meandered slowly through them and took a closer look at the blue convertible, and then withdrew discreetly to the edge of the proceedings.

Taking the bug out of my pocket, I talked to Walt, hoping he could hear. He couldn't answer: it was strictly one way traffic on the midget transmitter.

"Do you read me, Walt? This is Gene. Our young friend came in his own car, not a rented one or a taxi. His name in on the registration. Pale-blue new Ford convertible, at present with the top down. Gray upholstery. Nevada plates, number 3711-42. I'll do the paint if I possibly can, though he may deal with it, of course; and I'll put this bug in the car. When he starts up, you'll hear him. Good luck. And for God's sake don't lose him."

Indirectly, vaguely, I again approached the car. No one took any notice. I was merely one of the time-passing onlookers, a workman who wasn't working. Several of the children and some of their mothers had seen the state of the well-floured rooms and thought it a dreadful shame. I leaned my ladder against the rear of the blue convertible, put the brushes and paint pot down casually on the flat surface of the trunk, and mopped not too imaginary sweat off my face and neck.

Some of the blinds in the Clives' house had been raised, so that in places one could see into the house. No one was looking out. I stretched a hand in over the side of the car with the bug in my palm, and felt its sucker cling snugly under the glove compartment.

Still no faces at the windows.

I said to the nearest little boy, "Someone told me the intruder got in through the pantry window, round that corner."

"No kidding!" he said, his eyes wide.

"Sure thing."

He told his mother. They went to look. Nearly everyone followed them, especially as someone nudged the press photographer, who said he would take a picture.

I took a last comprehensive look at the windows, turned to walk away, and with a quick backward flip of a gloved hand, tipped over the can of paint. The lid came off. The can rolled slowly across the flat top of the trunk and clanked heavily to the ground. The result was a bright broad spreading pool of yellow on blue, and a proper lake on the gravel.

I was out on the road when the first child saw it and ran after me.

"Your paint's tipped over, mister."

"Yeah, I know. Don't touch it. Don't let anyone touch it, huh? I'm just going to fetch the stuff to get it off."

He nodded importantly and ran back, and I made it safely along to the car, and drove away in peace toward Las Vegas, taking off the useful cap and gloves as I went. Back at the motel I showered, changed, packed, and paid my account; drove to the airport and returned the car to the Hertz agent; kept a very wary eye open in case Matt Clive had decided to travel by air; ate a much-needed sandwich, and caught the first plane out to Los Angeles.

When I collected the car keys at the inquiry desk, there was a note from Walt as well.

> You're one great crazy guy. And don't think I don't realize what you risked. If you're reading this, I guess you've made it, and aren't behind bars. My pal in the CIA told me you could be relied on to do mad things and, boy, was he right. What do you use for nerves? Count me strictly out next time.
>
> Walt.

Surprised, and not ungrateful that he should have bothered, I slipped his letter into my pocket and drove into the city to look for a good place for tape recorders. I managed in the end to rent for one week an elaborate recorder which would play at the ultraslow 15/16 of an inch per second, the speed of my own, and with it sitting on the passenger seat beside me, pointed my nose toward Orpheus Farm, Los Caillos. There I removed the full reel from the radio recorder and fixed it up with another: no one appeared to have disturbed it in its bush and boulder hiding place, and as far as I could tell, no one saw me come and go.

Lynnie and Eunice were just walking up from the beach when I got back to the Vacationer: but they both greeted me with ten degrees of frost and went straight on past, murmuring that they guessed they would see me at dinner.

Slightly puzzled, shrugging, I carried my bag and the recorder up to my room, rewound the tape I had collected, and started it to run through while I took off my city suit and turned the air conditioning to high.

Yola rang up, in great agitation. The houseboy answered, and went to tell Offen, who was still in bed. By great good fortune the houseboy neglected to go back to replace the downstairs receiver when Offen lifted the bedroom extension, and the bug in consequence had picked up the whole conversation.

"I've had a call from the cops in Vegas . . ."

"Don't shout, Yola. I'm not deaf."

She didn't listen. "Some vandals have wrecked the house at Pitts." She really minded: there was grief as well as anger in her voice.

"How do you mean, wrecked?"

"They say everything in the house has been thrown on the floor, and flour and sugar and stuff have been tipped over everything. They want to know what's been stolen, they want me or, better, Matt to go down there and deal with it . . . and I can't, Uncle Bark, I simply can't. We've got thirty-two people in, and I can't possibly get away. Matt will have to go."

"But Matt . . ."

"Sure," she wailed. "Do you think I don't *know?* But he'll have to. Those horses won't die if he leaves them for a few hours. It's much further for me, I'd be away at least two days. It's *hopeless*. Everything's gone wrong since we took that damn Chrysalis."

"And if you remember," Culham James said tartly, "that was your and Matt's idea. I always said it was too soon after the last one. You and Matt have been too greedy ever since you found out."

"Relatives ought to share their good luck, not keep it to themselves."

"So you're always saying."

Nothing like a little blackmail to cement a family together, I thought in amusement. Offen had been happy with his half million a year, it seemed; but Matt and Yola, stumbling on the honey pot, had been in a hurry for more. Impulsive, ingenious, greedy Clives; if they had only been content with a share from Showman and Allyx, Offen would never have been found out.

Yola glossed over the long-standing squabble and returned to the current disaster. "I didn't get Matt's number. What is it?"

"I haven't got it here, it's in my book downstairs . . ."

"Well, look, will you call him? Tell him to get right on over, the cops will be there waiting. Tell him to call me from there and tell me what gives. I can't bear it if those bastards have stolen my mink wrap . . . and there's all that money in the safe . . ."

"Better face up to it that it's gone," Offen said, with the tiniest trace of malice.

"They might not have had time," Yola said. "The alarms go off when anyone goes into the den, and there isn't supposed to be time for anyone to find the safe and open it before the cops get there. We paid enough for it . . ."

It had been their bad luck that by the merest chance I had left the den until last.

Yola disconnected, and after the twenty seconds gap on the tape, Uncle Bark called up Matt from the downstairs telephone. Matt's comments were mostly inaudible though detectably explosive. He agreed to go to the house, but nothing Offen said gave any clue as to where Matt was at that moment. It appeared only that he was somewhere within a reasonable radius of Las Vegas, as he was going to be able to drive there, see to things at the house, and get back in time to feed the horses in the evening: which narrowed it down to somewhere in an area of roughly 150,000 square miles. A pocket handkerchief.

A brief telephone conversation of no interest followed and then, presumably in the afternoon, Offen had switched on his television set to watch a racing program. As far as I could tell from spot checks, it had used up the whole of the rest of the four-hour playing time.

Sighing, I switched off, and went downstairs. Lynnie and Eunice, dressed in dazzling colors, were drinking daiquiris and watching the Pacific sunset. I got another cool welcome and monosyllabic replies to my inquiries about their day.

Finally Eunice said distantly, "Did you have a good time in San Francisco?"

I blinked. "Yes, thank you."

They relapsed into a longer silence, which was broken only by a waiter coming to tell me I was wanted on the telephone.

It was Walt.

"Where are you?" I said.

"Las Vegas airport."

"And how did it go?"

"You can relax," he said comfortably. "The horses are on a small farm in a valley in Arizona, out beyond Kingman. We landed there and I asked around some. Seems the couple who own the farm don't make much of a living, but last week they said a friend was giving them a trip to Miami, and a young fellow would be looking after the place while they were away."

"That's great," I said with emphasis.

"The paint made it easy. We heard him yelling blue murder when he saw it, but I guess it had dried on by then and he couldn't get it off, because it was way past midday, and I'd begun to worry that he'd gone already and we hadn't heard him or that they'd picked you up planting the bug. Anyway, we took off when his engine started, and the yellow splash was easy to see from a height, just as you said. He went right through Las Vegas and out on the Hoover Dam road and across into Arizona. I kept the binoculars on him and we never flew near enough for him to notice us, I'm certain of that. He went up a winding graded road into the hills southeast of Kingman, and that was it."

"You've done marvels."

"Oh, sure. It was simpler than we were prepared for, though. You could hear the bug pretty clearly through the helicopter's headsets as high as two thousand feet, and we could have followed him in the dark if we'd had to, especially as he had his radio on for most of the way. We could hear music and news broadcasts now and then.

"Are you coming back tonight?"

"Yeah, there's a plane a half hour from now. But it'll be better than midnight when I get in."

"I'll be awake," I said. "And just by the way, Walt, what did you tell Eunice and Lynnie I was doing in San Francisco?"

He cleared his throat. "I said you had some unfinished business there."

"What sort of business?"

"Uh . . . like . . . er . . . female."

"Thanks," I said sarcastically. "You're a right pal."

Something very like a laugh lingered in my ear as I disconnected.

15

LYNNIE AND Eunice talked brightly to each other over dinner and I sat making plans for the next day and didn't listen. Politely after coffee we parted for the night, and at eleven I drove out to Orpheus with a fresh reel for the receiver in the rocks, and brought back the one I had fitted earlier.

Walt came back into my room as I was running it through, and we both listened to Culham James Offen talking first to Matt and then to Yola.

Yola was a better bet from our point of view, because her angry feminine voice scattered higher sound waves out of the receiver, and one could imagine Uncle Bark holding it inches away out of deference to his eardrums.

He was doing his best to soothe her. "Matt says it could have been worse; some of these vandals have thrown molasses and preserves and even sewage around in people's houses . . ."

"He says the whole place is *covered* in flour . . . it'll take weeks to clean up."

"It'll vacuum quite easily, won't it? It's not sticky and it doesn't stain."

But she couldn't be consoled, not even when he reminded her that the money was safe and that her mink wrap hadn't been stolen.

"But Matt says," she wailed, "that it was *white*."

"Flour will shake out . . . and might even clean it."

"You don't understand."

"Sure I do, Yola," he said patiently. "You feel like it was you who was assaulted, not your house. You feel dirty and furious and you'd like to kick the bastards who did it. Sure, I know. We had thieves in here once, when your aunt Ellen was alive. They stole all her rings, and she said it was like being raped."

They talked about the break-in for a good while longer, and Walt raised an eyebrow and remarked that I seemed to have gotten reasonable revenge for that clap on the head.

We were both yawning by the time Offen was through for the evening. The last half hour consisted of his telling his houseboy his plans and requirements, and none of these betrayed any anxiety or uncertainty. Culham James was confident, and I was glad of it. Worried men patrol their defenses.

Walt went off to bed, and although I hadn't slept at all the previous night I woke again after only three hours. The colored lights on the outside of the motel threw prismatic reflections on the ceiling. I stared up at them, trying to make patterns and shapes, trying any silly ruse to stop my mind from nose-diving into the pit. The tug of the unfinished chase was very faint, and whether Allyx and Showman ever sired another foal seemed a matter of supreme unimportance. Fraud, theft, attempted murder . . . who cared?

I had left the Luger in its belt holster across the room on a chair. Neither the Clives nor Offen were likely to come creeping through the night to do me in, and my usual enemies were 6,000 miles to the east. The only danger lay in myself, the deadliest enemy of the lot. The theory that going to bed with the gun out of reach would lessen its magnetic temptation was proving a dreary flop.

One more day, I thought in the end. Anyone could manage just one more day. If one said that firmly enough every night, one might even finish the course.

Dawn crept up on the colored bulbs and washed them out. I took a shower and shaved, and admitted that I had seen healthier-looking men than the one in my reflection.

Walt came along to my room when I was midway through orange juice and coffee at 8:30. "What you need," he said, eying this, "is some good solid food."

"I don't feel hungry."

His eyes slid to my face and away. "Come on down and eat with me."

I shook my head. "I'll wait for you."

He wouldn't go alone. He ordered griddle cakes and eggs and coffee from room service, and we got straight down to business while he demolished them.

"It'll take two and a half days for Sam Hengelman to get to Kingman," I said.

He nodded with his mouth full.

"He was starting early this morning," I went on. "I called him last night, after you'd been through from Las Vegas. He's driving the van himself, and he's coming alone. That means his journey time will be longer, but it seemed better that way from the secrecy point of view."

"Did you tell him it was another snatch?" Walt said doubtfully.

I smiled. "I engaged him to come and collect a horse belonging to Dave Teller. He asked if we were likely to be collecting this one in a lonely place at night, and I said yes we probably would."

"And he didn't back out?"

"He merely remarked that he had no great objection to an easy buck if I would assure him he couldn't go to jail for it."

Walt wiped errant egg off his chin. "And could he?"

"I couldn't tell him it was impossible. Odds of a thousand to one, I said. He said a thousand bucks against one chance of going to jail wasn't enough."

Walt laughed. "So how much is he coming for?"

"Fifteen hundred, plus the normal renting fee, plus expenses."

"Not bad for one week's work." He paused, stirring sugar, then said tentatively, "What do you get out of this yourself?"

"Me?" I said in surprise. "I've no idea. Three weeks' heat wave instead of the English summer . . ."

"Didn't you negotiate a fee?"

"No."

"How come?"

"It didn't occur to me."

His face crinkled into a mixture of emotions with what appeared to be amazement and pity coming out on top.

"How about you?" I said.

"I'm not on vacation," he pointed out. "I get a pretty good salary, and also a cut of everything I save the company."

"So Chrysalis has been worth the extra work?"

"At a million and a half, are you kidding?" Walt looked at me earnestly. "Look, Gene, I'm going to give you one half of that cut—"

"No," I said interrupting. "I don't want it."

"You know darned well I wouldn't have found that horse, not in a million years. Nor got him back alive so quickly. And as for these other two . . ."

"You keep it for your kids," I said, "But thanks, anyway."

He would have gone on insisting, but I wouldn't listen, and after two attempts he gave it up. In the back of my mind, as I outlined what I suggested we should do next, there lingered a bitter suspicion that I hadn't accepted his gift because it would be a selfish waste if I didn't stick around to spend it. I had rejected any strings of conscience tying me to life. The death-seeking force was up to another of its tricks.

"A pincer movement, I think," I said. "Or, rather, a simultaneous attack on two fronts."

"Huh?"

"Keep Culham James Offen's attention riveted on the Moviemaker and Centigrade he has on his farm while we spirit away the others."

"Er, quite," Walt agreed.

"You can take Offen," I said.

"And you take the horses?"

I nodded. Walt considered what might happen if we exchanged roles, and didn't argue.

"What are the chances of finding out which company Matt insures the Las Vegas house with?"

Walt thought about it. "Our agent there might be able to. But why?"

"I . . . er . . . would rather take those horses when I know Matt is safely away."

Walt smiled.

"So," I went on, "it shouldn't be too difficult to get him to go back to the house on Pitts. Say, for instance, his insurance company required him to make an inspection of his security arrangements and sign some document or other, before they would renew full cover? We know from the telephone calls to Offen that Matt and Yola have a safe in the den with a lot of money in it. Matt won't want to be uninsured for more than a minute, after having one break-in already."

"We couldn't ask his company to do that." Walt paused and looked at me with suspicion.

"Quite right," I nodded. "You can. You know all the jargon. As soon as we hear from Sam Hengelman that he has reached the Arizona border, you can start the spiel on Matt."

"From here?"

"Yes. Ask him what time would be convenient for him, but try to maneuver him into coming late in the afternoon or early evening, say six or seven. Then it would be dark when he got home, and late, which should hamper him a bit when he finds the horses are gone . . . He might even stop off in Las Vegas for a couple of hours at the tables."

Walt said thoughtfully, "I suppose I'd better go to the house at Pittsville and meet him."

"No," I said abruptly.

He looked at me. "You'd thought of it?"

"You are not going anywhere near Matt Clive."

"And why not?"

"You want a split skull or something?"

"Like webbed feet." The smile hovered. "All the same, what is Matt going to do when he arrives at his house and no insurance man turns up? What would you do? Call the company, I guess. And then what? He discovers no one in the company knows anything about his having to come back to the house, and he starts thinking like crazy. And if I were him I'd call the local cops and get them whizzing out to the farm for a look-see. You didn't see the road there from Kingman. But I did. There are no turnings off it for the last ten miles to the farm. What if you met the cops head on, you and Sam Hengelman and two stolen horses?"

"He wouldn't risk calling in cops."

"He might reckon that if he was losing everything anyway, he'd make sure you went down as well. And I mean down."

Every instinct told me not to let Walt meet Matt Clive.

"Suppose he won't make a late appointment?" he said. "When, I grant, most of the company would have gone home and it would be more difficult to check. Suppose he insists on three in the afternoon, or even the next morning? Do you want to snatch those horses by day?"

"Not much. But it would take him at least two hours each way. Add an hour for waiting and checking. Even if he called the police, it wouldn't be for three hours after he left home. We'd have been gone with the horses for two of those."

Walt obstinately shook his head. "The limits are too narrow. A horse van won't be able to do better than thirty miles an hour on the farm road, if that much. You have to go into Kingman, which is in the opposite direction from Kentucky, and then round and across Arizona. There aren't too many roads in that state, it's mostly desert. The police could find you too easily."

"Down through Phoenix . . ."

"The road to Phoenix twists through mountains, with hairpin curves most of the way."

"I don't want you walking into an empty house with Matt Clive."

He looked at me without expression. "But you would go. If he didn't know you, I mean."

"That's different."

"How?" he said, half insulted, half challenging.

I looked at him sideways. "I bet I can run faster than you."

His forehead relaxed. "You're in pretty good shape, I'll give you that. All the same, I'm going to Las Vegas."

He'd maneuvered me into not being able to persuade him against it on the grounds of safety; and from all other points of view it was a good idea. Against my instinct I agreed in the end that he should go.

"I'll drift on out tomorrow and look at the farm beyond Kingman," I said. "I suppose you couldn't see whether there were any other horses there besides the two we're after?"

He looked startled. "You mean there might be another identification problem?"

"Perhaps. Though I'd say it's certain our two have Moviemaker and Centigrade's studbook numbers tattooed inside their mouths. They would have to, to satisfy visiting grooms, for instance, that their mares were being mated with the right stallion. But I've never seen them . . . Showman and Allyx. If there are other horses there, it'll simply mean going round peering into all their mouths until I find the right ones."

Walt raised his eyes to heaven. "You make everything sound so darned easy. Like it's only five miles to the top of Everest, and everyone can walk five miles, can't they?"

Smiling, I asked him for precise directions to the farm, and he told me.

"And now this end," I said. "How many strings can you pull with the Los Angeles fraud squad?"

"Not many," he said. "I don't know anyone out there."

"But with Buttress Life behind you?"

He sighed, "I suppose you want me to go and dip my toes in the water?"

"Jump right in," I agreed. "Talk your way to the top chap, and tell him Buttress Life suspect that Moviemaker and Centigrade are Showman and Allyx. Get everything nicely stirred up. Make Offen prove beyond any doubt that the two horses at Orpheus literally are Moviemaker and Centigrade."

He nodded. "O.K. I'll start this morning. Have to go a little carefully, though, or Offen will come up so fast with a libel suit that we'll wonder what hit us."

"You must be used to ducking."

"Yeah."

I gave him the page Miss Britt had written out for me in Lexington.

"Here are the figures. No one can question these, not even Offen. You might find them useful in getting the law moving."

He tucked the paper into his pocket and nodded, and shortly after, with the habitual martyred sigh, levered himself out of his chair and ambled on his way.

I sat and thought for a while but got nowhere new. There was going to be little else for me to do but wait and watch for the next few days while Sam Hengelman rolled his way 2,000 miles across the continent.

When I went down to lunch I found Eunice and Lynnie sitting in cool bright dresses under the dappled shade of the sea-facing terrace. Their hair was glossy and neat, their big earrings gently swinging, their legs smooth and tanned, the whites of their eyes a detergent white.

They didn't get the lingering scrutiny they deserved. With them, equally crisp, equally at ease, sat Culham James Offen, Uncle Bark.

All three seemed a trifle disconcerted when I folded myself gently onto the fourth chair round the low table on which stood their long frosted drinks.

Offen and I nodded to each other. There was still in his manner the superior, self-satisfied amusement he had treated me with at his house. Reassuring. Lynnie smiled, but with a quick sidelong glance at Eunice to make sure such treachery hadn't been noticed. Eunice had on an "I-am-your-employer's-wife" face, which didn't wipe from my mind, nor hers, I imagine, the memory of the fluffy pink wrapper.

"We thought you'd gone to L.A. with Walt," Lynnie said.

Eunice gave her a sharp glance which she didn't see. "We ran into Mr. Offen in the lobby here, wasn't that extraordinary?"

"Extraordinary," I agreed.

Offen's white eyebrows went up and down in an embarrassment he couldn't entirely smother.

"It sure has been a pleasure," he said, "to get to know you folks better." He spoke exclusively to Eunice, however.

She had warmed again to the charm he had switched on for her, and gave me the tag end of a scornful glance. How could I, she implied, imagine this nice influential citizen could be a crook?

"How are Matt and Yola these days?" I said conversationally.

Offen visibly jumped, and a blight fell on the party. "Such charming young people," I said benignly, and watched Eunice remembering what had happened to Dave, and also perhaps what Walt had told her about their attack on me. "Your nephew and niece, I believe?"

Offen's pale-blue eyes were the least impressive feature in his tanned face with its snow-white frame. I read in them a touch of wariness, and wondered whether in prodding Eunice to face reality I had disturbed his complacency too far.

"They would sure like to meet you again," he said slowly, and the heavy ill-feeling behind the words curdled finally for Eunice his milk-of-human-kindness image.

"Are you expecting them within the next few days?" I asked, dropping in the merest touch of anxiety.

He said he wasn't, and his inner amusement abruptly returned. I had succeeded in convincing him I would be trying to remove his horses from Orpheus pretty soon now; and shortly afterwards he got purposefully to his feet, bent a beaming smile on Eunice, a smaller one on Lynnie, and a smug one on me, and made an important exit through the motel.

After a long pause Eunice said flatly, "I guess I was wrong about that guy being sweet."

We ate an amicable lunch and spent the afternoon on the beach under a fringed umbrella, with the bright green-blue Pacific hissing gently on the sand. Out on the rollers the golden boys rode their surfboards, and flat by my side little Lynnie sighed to the bottom of her lungs with contentment.

"I wish this could go on forever," she said.

"So do I."

Eunice, on the other side of Lynnie, propped herself up on one elbow. "I'm going to take a dip," she said. "Coming?"

"In a minute," Lynnie said lazily, and Eunice went alone. We watched her tight, well-shaped figure walk unwaveringly down to the water, and Lynnie said what I was thinking. "She hardly drinks at all now."

"You're good for her."

"Oh, sure." She laughed gently, stretching like a cat. "Isn't this heat just gorgeous?"

"Mm."

"What are all those scars on you?"

"Lions and tigers and appendicitis."

She snorted. "Shall we go in and swim?"

"In a minute. What did you and Eunice and Offen say to each other before I arrived?"

"Oh . . . " She sounded bored. "He wanted to know what you were doing. Eunice told him you and Walt were cooking something up but she didn't know what. And . . . er . . . yes . . . he asked if Walt was really an insurance man, and Eunice said he was . . . and he asked other things about you, what your job was and so on, and why you were out here with us . . . "

"Did Eunice tell him I got her to show him that photograph on purpose? Did she tell him that I was certain the horses that he has at Orpheus Farm are Moviemaker and Centigrade?"

Lynnie shook her head.

"You're quite sure?"

"Yes, absolutely. Would it have been a nuisance if we had?"

"A fair way to being disastrous."

"Don't worry then. He was only here about a quarter of an hour before you came down, and all Eunice said was that you were er . . . er . . . well, her actual words were, some dim bloody little office worker on vacation." Lynnie laughed. "She said her husband had been grateful to you for saving his life and was paying your bill here, and that all you seemed to be interested in at present was a girl up in San Francisco."

I looked down to where Eunice's head bobbed in the surf and wondered whether she'd given him perfect answers from design or bitchiness.

"What's she like?" Lynnie said.

"Who?"

"The girl in San Francisco."

"You'd better ask Walt," I said, turning my head to look at her. "He invented her."

She gasped and laughed in one. "Oh, good! I mean . . . er . . . then what were you really doing?"

"Ah, well," I said, "now that's something I'd hate Eunice to have told Culham Offen."

She lay looking back at me steadily for several seconds. So much more assurance, I thought idly, than on that day on the river, when she had still been a child.

"Is that why you've told us practically nothing? Don't you trust her?"

"She's never wanted the horses back."

Lynnie blinked. "But she wouldn't . . . she wouldn't have ruined on purpose what you're trying to do. After all, you're doing it for her husband."

I smiled, and she sat up abruptly and put her arms round her knees.

"You make me feel so . . . *naïve*."

"You," I said, "are adorable."

"And now you're laughing at me."

I wanted impulsively to say that I loved her, but I wasn't sure that it was true. Maybe all I wanted was an antidote to depression. She was certainly the best I'd found.

"I'm going away again in the morning," I said.

"To San Francisco?"

"Somewhere like that."

"How long for?"

"Two nights."

"This is your last week," she said, looking out to sea.

The thought leapt involuntarily, *if only it were*. I shook my head abruptly, as if one could empty the brain by force, and climbed slowly onto my feet.

"There's today, anyway," I said smiling. "Let's go and get wet."

Walt came back at seven with dragging feet and a raging thirst.

"Those detectives from the D.A.'s office will scalp me if they find out we're only using them," he said gloomily, up in my room. "Two of them have agreed to go out to Orpheus Farm tomorrow, and I'm meeting them on the L.A. road to show them the way. Day after tomorrow, some guy from the bloodstock registry office is going out. I got the D.A.'s office to call him and fix it."

"Couldn't be better."

Walt recharged his batteries with Old Grand-dad and said, "So what's new with you?"

"Offen came here on a fact-finding mission."

"He did *what?*"

"Came looking for answers. Got some real beauties from Eunice, which won't help him any, and went away believing we'd be back on his doorstep pretty soon."

"I guess," Walt said, "that he wanted to know if we'd called it off and gone home, and whether it was safe to bring those horses back again. It's days since he saw any sign of us. Must have been like sitting on an H bomb with a tricky firing pin." He swallowed appreciatively and rolled his tongue over his gums. "He'll get all the action he wants tomorrow."

When he plodded tiredly off to shower before dinner, I telephoned to Jeff Roots.

"How was Miami?" I said.

"Hot and horrible, and I gained four pounds."

Commiserating, I thanked him for his help with the newspaper files and told him that owing to Miss Britt we had found the two stallions.

"I wish I didn't believe it. Are you certain?"

"Yes."

His sigh was heartfelt. "We'd better start proceedings . . . "

"I've . . . er . . . already started them. We may in a day or two have two horses on our hands which will need to be stabled somewhere eminently respectable while their identity is being investigated. Owing to the length of time they've been lost, it may take a couple of months to re-establish them. Where would you think it would be best to put them?"

After a pause he said, "I suppose you're asking me to have them here?"

"Not really," I explained. "Too much of a coincidence after Chrysalis, perhaps. I'd thought rather of a more official place . . . . I don't know what you have."

"I'll think of something." He coughed slightly. "There won't be anything illegal about their recovery?"

"No more than for Chrysalis."

"That's no answer."

"There shouldn't be any trouble with the police," I said.

"I guess that'll have to do." He sighed. "When do I expect them?"

"If all goes well, they should reach Lexington on Sunday."

"And if all doesn't go well?"

"You'll have no problem."

He laughed. "And you?"

"One more won't matter."

16

FOR MOST of thirty hours I sat in the mountainous Arizona desert and looked down at Matt Clive leading a boring life.

Like his sister, he was capable, quick, efficient. He watered the stock and mended a fence, swept out the house, and fed the hens; and spent a good deal of time in the largest barn on the place.

I had found myself a perch among the rocks on the east-facing side of the valley, half a mile off the dusty road to the farm. At nearly three thousand above sea level the heat was bearable, though the midday sun blazed down from nearly straight overhead, and eggs would have fried on the sidewalks if there had been any. Desert plants were designed to save themselves and no one else: at my back grew a large agave, its central stem rising six feet high with flat outspreading flowers turning from red to brilliant yellow. For leaves it had razor-sharp spikes springing outward from the ground in one large clump. Stiff; angular; not a vestige of shade. The spindly buckhorn and the flat devil's-fingers would have been pretty useless to a midget. I folded myself under the overhang of a jagged boulder and inched round with the meager shade patch until the sun cried quits behind the hill.

Showman and Allyx had to be in the big barn: though I saw no sign of them, nor of any other horses, on the first afternoon. By air to Las Vegas and rented car to Kingman had taken me all morning, and at the last fork on the way to the farm I'd had to decide whether to risk meeting Matt head on on the road or to walk ten miles instead. I'd risked it. Ten miles there was also ten miles back. The car had bumped protestingly off the road two miles short of his farm, and was now out of sight in a gully.

Binoculars brought every detail of the meager spread up clear and sharp. The small dilapidated house lay to the left, with the big barn on the right across a large dusty yard. Along most of a third side of the rough quadrangle stretched an uneven jumble of simple stone buildings, and behind those the rusting guts of two abandoned cars lay exposed to the sky.

Maintenance was at a minimum: no endemic prosperity here. The owners scratched for a living in a tiny valley among the Arizona hills, existing there only by courtesy of the quirk of rock formation which had brought underground water to the surface in a spring. The small river bed was easy to follow from where I sat. Grass and trees circled its origin, sparse paddocks stretched away to sagging fences on each side of its upper reaches, a corn patch grew beside it near the farm buildings, and lower down it ran off into the desert in a dry wide shallow sandy trough. Heavy rain would turn it every time into a raging torrent, as destructive as it was vital. High behind the house, dominating the whole place, a huge onion-shaped water storage tank sat squatly on top of a spindly-looking tower.

Mile after mile of plain dark poles stretched along the road to the farm, carrying an electric cable and a telephone wire, but civilization had fallen short of refuse collection. A sprawling dump at one side of the big barn seemed to consist of a brass bedstead, half a tractor, a bottomless tin bath, the bones of an old wagon, a tangled heap of unidentifiable rusting metal, and roughly fifty treadless tires of varying sizes. Filling every crevice among this lot were bottles and empty food cans with labels peeling and jagged lids mutely open like mouths. Over the top the air shimmered with reflected heat.

Matt had already spent at least a week in this ugly oasis. Walt shouldn't find it too hard to persuade him to make an evening visit to Las Vegas.

I watched until long after dark. Lights went on and off in the house, and Matt moved about, visible through the screens because he didn't draw any curtains. If, indeed, there were any.

Cautiously, at some time after one o'clock, when all the lights on my side of the house had been out for more than two hours, I picked my way down to the farm. The night was still warm, but as the only light came from the stars it was black dark on the ground, and with agave clumps in mind I reckoned my flashlight held lesser risk.

I reached the farmyard. Nothing stirred. Quietly, slowly, I made the crossing to the barn. Matt in the house slept on.

No padlocks: not even bolts. There weren't any. The wide door of the barn stood open; and with this invitation, I went in. Inside, the barn was divided into six stalls along one side, with feed bins and saddlery storage racks along the other. Here and everywhere else dilapidation and decay were winning hands down: everything my light flicked over looked in need of help.

Four of the stalls were empty, but in the two central ones, side by side, stood two horses. Gently, so as not to frighten them, I went over, talking soothingly in a murmur and shining the beam on the wall in front of their heads. Their eyes in the dim light rolled round inquiringly, but neither gave more than a single stamp of alarm.

The first one tried to back away when I shone the torch into his mouth: but an exceedingly strong-looking head collar and a remarkably new chain kept him from going more than a few feet. I ran my hand down his neck and talked to him, and in the end got my inspection done. The tattooed mark, as often, was none too clear: but discernibly it was 75207. The registration number of Moviemaker.

The tattoo on the second horse was more recent and also clearer: the registration number of Centigrade.

Satisfied, I gave them each a friendly slap, and with great care left the barn. Matt still slept. I hesitated, thinking that enough was enough, but in the end went down to the end of the farmyard to take a quick look through the other buildings. In one only, a deep narrow garage, was there anything of interest: a car.

It was not Matt's pale-blue convertible, but a tinny black sedan three or four years old. My flashlight picked out a piece of paper lying on the passenger seat, and I opened the door and took a look at it. A copy of a work sheet from a garage in Kingman. Customer's name: Clive. Work required: Remove yellow paint from Ford convertible. Further instructions: Complete as soon as possible.

I put the paper back on the seat and shone the light over the dashboard. A small metal plate screwed onto it bore the name of the garage in Kingman: Matt had rented this car while his own was being cleaned.

Outside, everything was still, and feeling like a shadow among shadows I went quietly out of the farmyard and along the dusty road toward Kingman. It seemed a lot farther than two miles to the flat stones I had left one on top of the other as a marker, and even after I had reached them it took me quite a while to find the hidden car and get it back on the road.

It was well after three when I called Walt. He sounded resigned, but he'd known it would be sometime in the night.

"Are they there?' he said.

"They are. They're quite unguarded, and there's only Matt on the place. How about things your end?"

"Oh." Amusement crept in. "Offen was full of offended dignity. Didn't know how anyone could suggest he was engaged in fraud; that sort of thing. It didn't impress the D.A.'s squad at all, because they get that sort of bluster every time. Made them all the keener, if anything. They had quite a long session with him, all fairly polite but definitely needling. Artists, they are. From our point of view Offen said nothing significant except for one little gem. The D.A.'s guys asked to see the stud groom. That's Kiddo, remember? The one who told us about the mares foaling at night?"

"I remember," I said.

"Well, it seems it's a slow time around studs just now, and Kiddo went off on a vacation the day after our first visit."

"He didn't say anything about that when we were there."

"He sure didn't. Offen says Kiddo will be back in three weeks. By then, I guess, he expects to have had Moviemaker and Centigrade identified as themselves, and then when the dust has settled he can bring Showman and Allyx quietly back, and it'll be safe for Kiddo to return. I guess Offen didn't know which way he'd jump, and booted him off out of trouble."

"I'm sure you're right," I said. "Anything interesting on the tape?"

"I've been listening to that damned machine until I'm bored to death with it,'' he said wearily. ''Today's run was mostly the D.A.'s men talking to Offen, so I heard all that twice over. He then called both Yola and Matt and told them about it, and he sounded pretty pleased with the way things were going. I'd say Matt was a mite annoyed at having to stay where he is: Offen was telling him not to be stupid, what was a week or two with so much at stake. Also Yola must be wanting Matt back, because Offen smoothed her down with the same spiel.'' Walt paused and cleared his throat. ''What would you say is the relationship between Matt and Yola?''

Smiling into the receiver I said, ''Such thoughts, Walt, from you!''

''It's possible . . . '' he said uncomfortably.

''It sure is. But there's nothing to indicate it except for their not being married.''

''Then you don't think . . . ?''

''I'd say they're certainly centered on each other, but how far it goes I couldn't guess. The only times I've seen them together they've had their hands full of punts and guns.''

''Yeah . . . . Well, maybe crime is how it takes them.''

I agreed that it probably was, and asked him if he'd got Matt set up for the insurance meeting.

''I sure have,'' he said, with satisfaction. ''I called him this afternoon. It must have been soon after he'd been talking to Offen, I guess, because he seemed to be glad enough to be given a reason for going to Las Vegas. I suggested six P.M. which sounded all right, but he himself asked if I could make it later.''

''He'll probably want to feed the horses about then, when the day gets cooler,'' I said. ''And those horses would come first.''

''Yeah. At three million for the two, they sure would. It beats me why he doesn't guard them every minute.''

''Against what?'' I said.

''You've got a point,'' he conceded. ''Only us. And we're obviously concentrating on the two at Orpheus. Right?''

''Right.''

''Anyway, Matt said could I make it later than six, and we agreed in the end on nine. That should mean he'll take that gander at the roulette tables on his way home, and maybe give us most of the night to get the horses clear.''

''Good,'' I said. ''That's fine. But, Walt . . . ''

''Yes?''

''Take care.''

''Go teach your grandmother,'' he said, and I smiled wryly and asked him if he'd heard from Sam Hengelman.

''Sure, he called this evening, like you asked. He'd reached Santa Rosa in New Mexico and he was going on to Albuquerque before stopping for the night. He said he'd be in Kingman by four or five tomorrow afternoon—today, I suppose, technically—and he'll meet you at the Mojave Motel. I told him the return trip wouldn't be starting before eight, so he's going to take a room there and catch a couple of hours' sleep.''

''Thanks, Walt, that's great,'' I said.

''We're all set, then?'' There was a hint of unease in his voice, and it raised prickles again in my early-warning mechanism.

"You don't have to go to Las Vegas," I said reasonably. "We've time enough without it."

"I'm going," he said. "And that's that."

"Well . . . all right. I think we could do with a checkpoint, though, in case anything goes wrong. Let's say you wait in the lobby of the Angel Inn from eight to eight-thirty tomorrow evening. That's where I stayed. It's right on the edge of Las Vegas, but it's an easy trip to Pittsville Boulevard. I'll call you there sometime during that half hour; and if I don't, you stay put, and don't go out to Matt's house."

"O.K.," he said, and although he tried there was distinct relief in his voice.

We disconnected, and I ate a sandwich and drank coffee at an all-night lunch counter at the bus station before returning to my rented car and pointing its nose again toward the farm and the hills. The two flat stones came up again in the headlights, and restowing the car in its former hiding place, I finished the journey on foot.

Back in the shelter of the same jagged rock I tried for a time to sleep. There was still an hour or more before dawn, and the sun wouldn't be too hot for a while after that, but in spite of knowing that I'd get no rest at all during the following night my brain stayed obstinately awake. I supposed an inability to sleep on open ground surrounded by cacti and within yelling distance of a man who'd kill me if he had a chance could hardly be classed as insomnia in the ordinary way; but I had no illusions. That was precisely what it was. The restless, racing thoughts, the electrical awareness, the feeling that everything in one's body was working full steam ahead and wouldn't slow down; I knew all the symptoms much too well. One could lie with eyes shut and relax every muscle until one couldn't tell where one's arms and legs were, and still sleep wouldn't come. Breathe deeply, count all the sheep of Canterbury, repeat once-learned verses; nothing worked.

The sun came up and shone in my eyes. Inching out of its revealing spotlight I retreated round the side of the rock and looked down to the farm through the binoculars. No movement. At five-thirty Matt was still in bed.

I put down the glasses and thought about a cigarette. There were only four left in the packet. Sighing, I reflected that I could easily have bought some in Kingman if I'd given it a thought. It was going to be a long day. All I'd brought with me besides the binoculars was a bottle of water, a pair of sunglasses, and the Luger in my belt.

At 7:30 Matt came out through the rickety screen door of the house, and stood in the yard stretching and looking around at the cloudless cobalt-blue sky. Then he went across to the barn and poked his head briefly inside.

Satisfied that the gold was still in the bank, he fetched buckets of water and joined it for long enough to muck out the stalls and see to the feed. After a time he came out with a barrowful of droppings and wheeled it away to empty on the far side of the barn, out of my sight.

The hens got their grits, and the calves in a near compound their ration of water, and Matt retired for his breakfast. The morning wore on. The temperature rose. Nothing else happened.

At noon I stood up for a while behind the rock to stretch my legs and restore some feeling to the bits that were numb from sitting. I drank some water and smoked a cigarette, and put on the sunglasses to circumvent a hovering glare headache: and having exhausted my repertoire except for a few shots from the Luger, folded myself back into the wedge of slowly moving shade, and took another look at the farm.

Status quo entirely unchanged. Maybe Matt was asleep, or telephoning, or watching television, or inventing systems for his trip to Las Vegas. He certainly was not doing much farming. Nor did he apparently propose to exercise the horses. They stayed in their stalls from dawn to dusk.

By two I knew intimately every spiny plant growing within a radius of ten feet of my rock, and found my eyes going far oftener to the broad sweep of desert on my left than to the dirty little farm below. The desert was clean in its way, and fierce, and starkly beautiful. All hills and endless sky. Parched sandy gray dust and scratchy cactus. Killing heat. A wild, uncompromising, lonely place.

When I first felt the urge just to get up and walk away into it I dragged my eyes dutifully back to the farm and smoked the second cigarette and thought firmly about Matt and the horses. That worked for a while, but the barren country pulled like a magnet.

I had only to walk out there, I thought, and keep on going until I was filled with its emptiness, and then sit down somewhere and put the barrel of the Luger against my head, and simply squeeze. So childishly easy; so appallingly tempting.

Walt, I thought desperately. I couldn't do it because of Walt and the unfinished business we were embarked on. The horses were there in front of me, and Walt and Sam Hengelman were on their way. It was impossible just to abandon them. I hit my hand against the rock and dragged my mind back to the farm and the night ahead. And when I'd gone through that piece by piece I concentrated one at a time on Yola and Offen, and Eunice and Dave Teller, and Keeble and Lynnie, trying to use them as pegs to keep me believing that what I did mattered to them. That anything I did mattered to anybody. That I cared whether anything I did mattered to anybody.

My hand had been bleeding. I hadn't even felt it. I looked dispassionately at the scraped skin, and loathed myself. I shut my eyes, and the desolation went so deep that for an unmeasurable age I felt dizzy with it, as if I were in some fearful pitch-black limbo, with no help, no hope, and no escape. Spinning slowly down an endless shaft in solitary despair. Lost.

The spinning stopped after a while. The internal darkness stayed.

I opened my eyes and looked down at the farm, only half seeing it, feeling myself trembling and knowing that there wasn't much further to go.

Matt came out of the house, walked across the yard, took a look into the barn, and retraced his steps. I watched him in a disoriented haze. Those horses in the barn, what did they matter? What did anything matter?

Who cared a sixpenny damn about bloodlines, it would all be the same in a hundred years.

Dave Teller cared.

Let him.

Dave Teller cared a $10,000 damn what happened to them.

Crystal clear, like distilled-water logic, it occurred to me that I could give us both what we wanted if I postponed my walk into the desert until later that night. I would pack the horses off with Hengelman and, instead of driving back to Kingman after him, I would set off on foot, and when it was nearly dawn, and everything looked gray and shadowy, and the step would be small . . . then . . .

Then.

Immediately after making this firm decision, which seemed to me extremely sensible, I felt a great invasion of peace. No more struggle, no more fuss. My body felt relaxed and full of well-being and my mind was calm. I couldn't think why such an obvious solution hadn't occurred to me before. All the sweat and sleeplessness had dissolved into a cool, inner, steady light.

This stage lasted until I remembered that I had once been determined not to reach it.

After that, creeping in little by little, came the racking conviction that I had merely surrendered, and was not only despicable but probably insane.

I sat for a while with my head in my hands, fearfully expecting that with the false peace broken up and gone, back would come the shattering vertigo.

It didn't. There was only so great a tiredness that what I'd called tiredness before was like a pinhead on a continent. The dreary fight was on again; but at least I'd survived the bloodiest battle yet. Touched bottom and come back. I felt as if I'd passed some obscure crisis, and that after this I really could climb right out if I went on trying.

A long way to go. But, then, I'd have all the time I needed.

17

I HAD cramps right down both legs. Matt came out of the house and I woke up to the fact that the shade patch had moved round while I hadn't. When he went into the barn I started to shift the necessary two yards and found my muscles in knots.

The shade wasn't much cooler, but much better cover. I sat in it waiting for Matt to come out of the barn and for my legs to unlock. What they needed was for me to get to my feet and stamp about: but if Matt caught sight of anyone moving so close to him the whole project would lie in ruins.

He fetched water for the horses, for the calves, and for the hens. I looked at my watch, and was horribly startled to see it was nearly six. It couldn't be, I thought; but it was. Four hours since I had last checked. Four hours. I shivered in the roasting air.

Matt brought the empty muck barrel around and into the barn, and came out with it filled. For the whole afternoon I'd fallen down on the surveillance, but looking back I was fairly sure nothing had changed at the farm. Certainly at this point things were as they had been: Matt had no helpers and no visitors, and when he left for Las Vegas the horses would be alone. For that piece of certainty I had been prepared to watch all day, and a poor job I'd made of it.

Matt shut the barn door and went into the house. Half an hour later he came out in a cream-colored jacket and dark trousers, a transformation from his habitual jeans and checked shirt. He opened the doors of the shed containing the car, went inside, started up, and drove out across the yard, round the bend onto the road, and away over the desert toward Kingman.

Satisfied, I finally got to my feet. The cramps had gone. I plodded tiredly off to the two-mile distant hidden car, and wished the night was over, not beginning. I hadn't enough energy to lick a stamp.

Matt's dust had settled when I followed him along the empty road, but when I got into Kingman he was still there. With shock I saw him standing outside a garage I was passing, and I pulled over to the curb fifty yards on and looked back. The black sedan he had rented and his own blue Ford were both standing there in the forecourt. An overalled girl attendant was filling the Ford's tank from the pump, and Matt was looking in snatches at his watch and exhibiting impatience: 7:20, and a hundred miles to Las Vegas. He would be a few minutes late for his appointment with Walt.

Slumping down in my seat I fixed the driving mirror so that I could watch him. He paid the girl for the gas and hopped into his car over the top, without opening the door. Then he pulled out onto the road, turned in my direction, and went past me with his foot impressively on the accelerator. I gently followed for a while at a respectable distance, content to keep him only just in sight, and turned back to the town once he was conclusively topping the speed limit on Route 93 to Las Vegas.

Outside the unprosperous-looking Mojave Motel Sam Hengelman's horse van took up a sixth of the parking space. Inside, they told me that he had arrived at 4:30 and was along in Room 6, sleeping. I left him to it, because we couldn't move anyway until I'd phoned Walt at eight, and went into the bus station for some coffee. It came in a plastic carton out of an automat, black but weak. I drank it without tasting and thought about some food, but I wasn't really hungry enough to bother, and I was too dirty and unshaven for anywhere good. Until after eight I sat on the bus station bench staring into space, and then used the bus station telephone to get through to Walt.

He came on the line with little delay.

"How's things?" he said.

"Matt left Kingman for Las Vegas at seven-thirty, so he will be a little late."

"Left Kingman?" Walt sounded surprised.

I explained about Matt changing cars.

"I suppose his Ford wasn't quite ready when he got there. Anyway, he's coming in that, not the rented one."

"Are you all right?" Walt said hesitantly.

"Of course."

"You don't sound it."

"Sam Hengelman's here," I said, ignoring him. "He's asleep along at the Mojave Motel. We'll start as soon as I get back there and wake him up."

"It's all safe at the farm?" He seemed anxious.

"Deserted," I assured him. "Has been all yesterday, all last night, and all today. No one around but Matt. Stop worrying. You just see Matt and put on your act, and then head straight back to Santa Barbara. As soon as Sam's clear of the area I'll follow you. See you for breakfast about twelve hours from now."

"Right," he said. "Well, keep your nose clean."

"You too."

"Sure thing. It's not me that's nuts."

The line clicked clear before I found an answer, and it left me with a vague feeling that there was more I should have said, though I didn't know what.

I knocked on Sam's door at the motel, and he came sleepily stretching to switch on the light and let me in.

"With you in a minute," he said, reaching for his shoes and looking round for his tie.

"Sam, you don't have to come."

"Eh?"

"Go back to sleep. I'll go and fetch the horses. That way you won't be so involved."

He sat on the edge of the bed looking down at the floor. "I'm still driving them to Lexington?"

"Unless you want out. Leave the van and fly home."

"Nope." He shook his head. "A bargain's a bargain. And I may as well come all the way. That van's none too easy in reverse . . . don't know that you could handle it."

I half smiled and didn't argue. I'd wanted him with me, but only willingly, and I'd got that. He knotted his tie and brushed his hair and then took a sidelong glance at my own appearance, which fell a ton short of his. He was a fleshy man of about fifty, bald, pale skinned, and unexcitable. His nerves, I thought, were going to be at least equal to the evening's requirements.

"Let's go, then," he said cheerfully. "I paid in advance."

I followed him across to the van and climbed into the cab. Sam started the engine, told me he'd filled up with gas when he'd first reached Kingman, and rolled out southeast on the road to the farm. His broad face looked perfectly calm in the glow from the dashboard, and he handled his six-stall horsebox like a kiddycar. We went eight miles in silence, and then all he said was "I'd sure hate to live this far from town, with nowhere to get a beer."

We passed the third of the three side roads and started on the last ten uninhabited miles to the farm. Three miles farther Sam gave an alarmed exclamation and braked from his cautious thirty to a full stop. "What is it?" I asked.

"That gauge." He pointed, and I looked. The needle on the temperature gauge was quivering on red.

"Have to look-see," he grunted, and switched off the engine. My thoughts as he disappeared out of the cab were one enormous curse. Of all hopeless, dangerous places for his van to break down.

He came back and opened the door on my side. I jumped down beside him and he took me round to show me the exhaust.

"Look," he said unnecessarily. "Water."

Several drops slid out, glistening in the beam of his flashlight.

"Gasket," he said, putting into one word the enormity of the disaster, and what he thought of fate for trapping us in it.

"No water in the radiator," I said.

"Right."

"And if we go on, the engine will seize up."

"Right again."

"I suppose you don't carry any extra water in the van?"

"We sure do," he said. "Never travel without it."

"Can't we pour some in the radiator?"

"Yeah," he said. "We can. There's two gallons. We can pour in a quart, and go three miles maybe before it's all leaked out, and then another quart, another three miles. Four quarts, twelve miles. And that's it."

Thirteen miles out from Kingman. We could just about get back. Seven to the farm. We could refill the radiator at the farm, but Sam couldn't set out on his 3000-mile journey with a stolen cargo in a van emptying like a dry dock.

"There's an extra gasket, of course," he said.

"A spare one?"

"Sure. Always carry a full set of spares. Never know where you're going to need them. Universal joints, big ends, carburetors—I carry them all. Anyone with any sense does that."

"Well," I said in relief, "how long will it take you to fit the spare?"

He laid the engine bare and considered it.

"Cylinder head gasket. Say three hours."

"*Three hours!*"

"Won't take much less," he said. "What do you want to do?"

I looked at my watch. 8:50. Three hours made 11:50; and if we then went on to the farm and picked up the horses we couldn't be back through Kingman until 1:15.

Matt would reach Pittsville Boulevard by 9:30, and finish his insurance business long before ten. If he drove straight home again he would be on the farm road at midnight. If Sam changed the gasket, so would we.

If Matt stopped to play the tables, he would be at least an hour later. His clothes had suggested he would stop. But whether for one hour or six, there was no way of telling.

"Change the gasket," I said abruptly. "Then we'll see."

Sam nodded philosophically. It was what he would have done in any case if the van had broken down anywhere else, and without more ado he sorted out what he wanted and started unscrewing.

"Can I help?" I said.

He shook his head and clipped his flashlight onto a convenient spar to give a steady working light. There seemed to be little haste in his manner, but also no hesitation and a good deal of expertise. The heap of unplugged parts grew steadily on a square of canvas at his feet.

I walked away a few steps and felt for the cigarettes. Two left. I'd still forgotten to buy more. The smoke didn't help much toward making the next decision: to go on or to go back.

I'd already gambled on Matt's staying to play. If it had been Yola, I would have felt surer that it would be for most of the night: but her brother might not have the fever, might only want a short break in his boring stint with the horses. How short? How long?

The decision I came to, if you could call it that, was to wait and see at what time Sam restarted the engine.

The night, outside the bright pool by the van, was as dark as the one before. The stars glittered remotely, and the immensity of the American continent marked their indifference to the human race. Against such size, what did one man matter? A walk into the desert . . .

Carefully I pinched out the end of my cigarette and put the stub in my pocket. A good criminal, I thought wryly: I'd always been that. I had a job to do, and even when I'd finished it I was going for no walks into the desert. I was going back to Santa Barbara, to have breakfast with Walt and Eunice and Lynnie. The prospect at that moment seemed totally unreal, so far were the Arizona hills from the lush coast, so far had I been into the wasteland inside me.

I went back to Sam and asked how it was going. He had the cylinder head off and was removing the cracked gasket.

"So-so," he said calmly, "I'm breaking the record."

I did my best at a smile. He grunted, and said he could do with a cup of coffee, and I said so could I. We hadn't brought any.

He worked on. The air was still warmer than an English summer and he wiped sweat off his bald forehead with the back of a greasy hand. The light shone on his thick stubby fingers, and the click of his wrench echoed across the empty land. The hands on my watch went round in slow fractions. The gasket was wasting the night. And where was Matt?

After two hours Sam's spanner slipped on a nut and he cursed. In spite of his calm, the tension wasn't far from the surface. He stopped what he was doing, stretched upright, took three deep breaths and a look at the night sky, and waited for me to say something.

"You're doing fine," I said.

He sniffed, "What'll happen if they catch us here?"

"We won't get the horses."

He grimaced at my nonanswer and went back to his task. "What have you been doing all day?"

"Nothing. Sitting still."

"You look half dead," he commented. "Pass me those two washers, will you?"

I gave him the washers. "How much longer?"

"Can't say."

I stifled the urge to tell him to hurry. He was going as fast as he could. But time was ticking away, and the postponed decision had got to be made. Turning my back on the tugging desert I climbed up to sit in the cab.

11:20. Matt could be a bare quarter of an hour out from Kingman. Or glued to the green baize and the tricky numbers in Las Vegas.

Which?

For a long half hour I looked out the back windows while no helpful telepathic messages flowed through them. A straightforward gamble, I thought. Just decide if the winnings were worth the risk.

An easier decision if I'd come alone: but if I'd come alone I couldn't have mended the gasket.

At 11:40 Sam said gloomily that he was having to fix the water pump as well. It was sticking.

"How long?"

"Another twenty minutes."

We stared at each other in dismay.

"Go on then," I said in the end. There was nothing else to do.

I left the cab and walked restlessly a short way back along the road, fearing every second to see Matt's headlights and wondering how best to deal with him if we had to. I was all for stealing from him what wasn't his, but not for damaging his skin. He, however, would have no such inhibitions. There would certainly be blood. Not fair to make it Sam's.

At two minutes past midnight he called out that he had finished, and I walked quickly back to join him. He was pouring water into the radiator, and screwed on the cap as I came up.

"It should be O.K. now," he said. His hands were covered in grease and his big body hung tiredly from the shoulders. "Which way do we go?"

"On."

He nodded with a wide slicing grin.

"I figured you'd say that. Well, I guess that's O.K. by me."

He swung up into the cab and I climbed in beside him. The engine started sweetly at first try, and switching on his headlight, he released the brake and eased away along the road.

"If anyone catches us here from now on," I said "duck."

"Yeah?"

"Yeah."

"Tell you something," he said comfortably. "I swing a mean left hook."

"The chap we'd be taking on goes for the head. But with a club of some sort in his fist."

"Nice guys you play with," he said. "I'll remember that."

We covered the remaining distance at a good speed and in silence. The horsebox crept round the last corner and its headlights flickered over the farm ahead. I put my hand on Sam's arm, and he braked to a halt a short way from the yard.

"Switch off, would you? Lights too," I said, and jumped quickly down from the cab to wait a few precious seconds until my eyes and ears got used to silence and dark.

No lights in the house. No sound anywhere except the ultrafaint ringing vibration of limitless air. The calves and hens were asleep. The horses were quiet. I banged on the cab door and Sam switched his headlights on again before climbing down to join me. The bright shafts lit up the back of the house and wouldn't shine straight into the horses' eyes when I led them from the barn. Over on the shadowy side of the yard the open doors of the shed where Matt had kept his car yawned in a deep black square. The jumbled rubbish dump just in front of us threw surrealist shadows across the dusty ground, and its smell of decay brushed past our noses.

Sam swept it all with a practiced glance. "Not much of a place." His voice was as low as a whisper.

"No. . . . If you'll unclip the ramp, I'll go fetch the horses. One at a time, I think."

"O.K." He was breathing faster and his big hands were clenched. Not used to it, after all.

I hurried down toward the barn. It wasn't far; about forty yards. Now that we were totally committed my mind raced with urgency to be done, to be away, to be safely through Kingman before Matt came back. He could have been on the road behind us, be rushing at this moment across the desert to the farm. . . .

What happened next happened very fast, in one terrifying cataclysmic blur.

There was an urgent shout behind me.

"Gene!"

I turned, whirling. There were two sets of headlights where there should have been one.

Matt.

The voice again, yelling. "Gene! Look out." And a figure running down the yard toward me.

Then there was a roar behind me and I turned again and was met full in the eyes by the blinding glare of two more headlights, much closer. Much closer.

Moving.

I was dazzled and off balance and I'd never have got clear. The running figure threw itself at me in a football tackle with outstretched arms and knocked me over out of the way, and the roaring car crashed solidly into the flying body and left it crumpled and smashed and lying on top of my legs.

The car which had hit him turned in a wide sweep at the end of the yard and started back. The headlights lined themselves up like twin suns on their target and with a fraction of my mind I thought it ironic that now, when I'd decided not to, I was going to die.

Half sitting, half kneeling, I jerked out the Luger and pumped all of its eight bullets toward the windshield. I couldn't see to aim straight . . . my eyes were hurting from the glare . . . Not that bullets would do any good . . . the angle was wrong . . . they'd miss the driver. . . . By the time I fired the last one the left headlight was six feet away. I uselessly set my teeth against the mangling, tearing, pulping collision . . . and in the last tenth of a second the straight line wavered . . . the smooth side of the car hit the back of my shoulder, the front wheel ran over a fold of my shirt, and the rear wheel gave me a clear inch.

Almost before I realized it had missed me, the car crashed head on into one of the buildings at my back with a jolting screech of wood and metal.

The bodywork crumpled and cracked. The stabbing lights went black. The engine stopped. Air hissed fiercely out of a punctured tire.

Gasping, dreading what I would find, I leaned over the heavy figure lying on my legs. There were more running footsteps in the yard, and I looked up hopelessly, unable to do any more. I'd used all the bullets . . . none left.

"You're alive!" The voice came from the level of my ear, the man kneeling. Sam Hengelman. I looked at him in a daze.

"I thought . . ." I said, with no breath, "this was you."

He shook his head. "No . . ."

He helped me raise and turn the man who'd saved me; and with sickness and unbearable regret I saw his face.

It was Walt.

We laid him on his back, in the dust.

"Look in the car," I said.

Sam lumbered silently to his feet and went away. I heard his footsteps stop and then start back.

Walt opened his eyes. I leaned over him, lifting his hand, feeling with surging hope for his pulse.

"Gene?" his voice mumbled.

"Yes."

"He didn't come."

"Didn't . . .?"

"Came to help you . . ."

"Yes," I said. "Thanks, Walt."

His eyes slid aimlessly away from my face.

"Christ," he said distinctly, "this is it. This is . . . really . . . it."

"Walt . . ." His hand was warm in mine, but it didn't move.

"Sod it," he said. "I wanted . . . I wanted . . ."

His voice stopped. There was no pulse. No heartbeat. Nothing. Nothing at all.

I put down gently on the ground the warm hand with the rounded fingertips, and stretched out my own, and shut his eyes. It should have been me lying there, not Walt. I shook with sudden impotent fury that it wasn't me, that Walt had taken what I'd wanted, stolen my death. . . . It would have mattered so little if it had been me. It wouldn't have mattered at all.

Walt . . . Walt . . .

Sam Hengelman said, "Is he dead?"

I nodded without looking up.

"There's a young guy in the car," he said. "He's dead too."

I got slowly, achingly, to my feet and went to look. The car was the blue Ford convertible and the young guy was Matt.

Without caring, automatically, I took in that the car had smashed the right-hand door of the garage shed and plowed into the wall behind it. Most of the windshield was scattered in splintered fragments all over the inside of the car, but in one corner, where some still clung to the frame, there was a fingersized hole.

Matt was lying over the steering wheel, his arms dangling, his eyes open. The skull above the left eyebrow was pierced and crumpled inward, and there was blood and hair on the chromium upright which had held the windshield. I didn't touch him. After a while I went back to Walt.

"What do we do?" Sam Hengelman said.

"Give me a moment . . ."

He waited without speaking until eventually I looked up and down the yard. Two sets of headlights still blazed at the way in.

"That's Walt's car up there?"

"Yeah. He drove up with the devil on his tail and jumped out and ran down after you . . ."

I turned the other way and looked at the dark garage.

"The young guy must have been in there all the time, waiting for us," Sam said. "He came roaring out and drove straight at you. I couldn't have stopped him . . . too far away. Walt was halfway down the yard . . ."

I nodded. Matt had been there all the time. Not in Las Vegas. Not on the road. Lying in ambush, waiting.

He hadn't passed us on the road, and there was no other way to the farm. He must have gone back ahead of us. Turned round on the road to Las Vegas and driven back through Kingman while I was sitting in the bus station waiting to telephone to Walt.

But why? *Why* should he have gone back? He hadn't seen me following him. I'd been much too far behind, and in any case I'd left him once he was safely on the highway.

It didn't matter why. It only mattered that he had. Sam Hengelman looked down at Walt and summed up the mess we were entangled in.

"Well, what the heck do we do now?"

I took a deep breath.

"Will you fetch that flashlight of yours?" I asked, and he nodded and brought it from his van. I went with it over to the Ford, and took a longer, closer look. There wasn't much to see that I hadn't seen before, except for a bottle of bourbon that had been smashed in the impact. The neck and jagged top half lay on the floor to Matt's right, along with several smaller pieces and an uneven damp patch.

I walked into the garage and looked at the Ford from the front. It wouldn't be driving anywhere any more.

The big torch lit up clearly the interior of the deep shadowy garage. Quite empty now, except for a scatter of cigarette stubs against the left-hand wall. Matt had been smoking and drinking while he waited. And he'd waited a very long time.

The bullet hole faced me in the windshield and left me with the worst question unanswered.

I'd have to know.

I stood beside Matt and went over every inch of his body down to the waist. He'd taken off the cream-colored jacket and was wearing the checked shirt he'd worked in. There were no holes in it: no punctures underneath. His head was heavy. I laid it gently on the steering wheel and stepped away.

None of the bullets had hit him. They'd only smashed the windshield and blinded him, and he'd slewed a foot off course and run into the wall instead of me, and his head had gone forward hard against the slim metal post.

Slowly I returned to where Sam Hengelman stood beside Walt. He drooped with the utmost dejection and looked at me without hope.

"Did you unclip the ramp?" I asked abruptly.

He shook his head. "Didn't have time."

"Go and do it now. We're taking the horses."

He was aghast. "We can't!"

"We've got to. For Walt's sake, and your sake, and Dave Teller's sake. And mine. What do you propose? That we call the police and explain what we were all doing here?"

"We'll have to," he said despairingly.

"No. Definitely not. Go and let down the ramp."

He hesitated unbelievingly for a few seconds, and then went and did as I asked. The horses stood peacefully in the barn, apparently undisturbed by the racket, the shots and the crash. I untied the nearest, Showman, and led him quietly up the yard and into the van.

Sam watched me in silence while I tied him into one of the stalls.

"We'll never get away with it."

"Yes, we will," I said. "As long as you take these horses safely back to Lexington and never tell anyone, anyone at all, what happened here tonight. Blot it out of your mind. I'll let you know, when you get back, that you've nothing to worry about. And as long as you tell no one, you won't have."

The broad fleshy face was set in lines of anxiety.

"You've collected two horses," I said matter-of-factly. "An everyday job, collecting two horses. Forget the rest."

I returned to the barn, fetched Allyx, and loaded him up. Sam still hadn't moved.

"Look," I said, "I've . . . arranged . . . things before. There's a rule where I come from—you take a risk, you get into a mess, you get out." He blinked. "Walt threw himself in the way of that car," I said. "Matt didn't intend to kill *him*. . . . You didn't see a murder. Matt drove straight into the wall himself . . . and that too was an accident. Only two automobile accidents. You must have seen dozens. Forget it." He didn't answer, and I added brusquely, "The water can's empty. You can fill it over there."

With something like a shudder he picked up the container and went where I pointed. Sighing, I checked that he had brought three days' fodder for the stallions, which he had, and with his help, on his return, shut the precious cargo up snugly for their long haul.

"You don't happen to have any gloves around?" I asked.

"Only an old cotton pair in the tool kit."

He rooted about and finally produced them, two filthy objects covered with oil and grease which would leave marks on everything they touched, as talebearing as fingerprints. I turned them inside out and found they were thick enough to be clean on the inside. Sam watched wordlessly while I put them on, clean side out.

"O.K.," I said. "Will you turn the van, ready to go?"

He did it cautiously as far away from Walt as he could; and when he'd finished I stepped with equal care into the car Walt had come in, touching it as little and as lightly as possible, and drove it down into the yard, stopping a little short of the screen door to the house. There I switched off the engine and lights, put on the brake, and walked back to talk to Sam where he sat in his cab.

"I've three jobs to do," I said. "I'll be back as quick as I can. Why don't you just shut your eyes for a couple of minutes and catch a nap."

"You're kidding."

I concocted a replica of a smile, and a fraction of the tension in his face unwound.

"I won't be long," I said, and he nodded, swallowing.

With his flashlight I surveyed the yard. The Luger was an automatic pistol, which meant it threw out the cartridge after each shot. No one would find the spent bullets, but eight shiny metal shells scattered near Walt's body were something else. Seven of them winked in the light as I inched the light carefully around, and I collected them into my pocket. The eighth remained obstinately invisible.

The ejection slot had been on the side of the gun away from Walt, but the cases sometimes shot out straight upward instead of sideways, and I began to wonder if the eighth could possibly have traveled far enough over to be underneath him. I didn't want to disturb him: but I had to find the little brass thimble.

Then, when I'd decided I had no choice, I saw it. Bent and dusty, partly flattened, no longer shining. I picked it up from the spot where I had been half lying in the path of Matt's car. He had run over it.

After that I attended to the ground itself. Tire marks didn't show on the rough dusty surface, but the hoofprints did to some extent. I fetched a broom of twigs from the barn and swept them out.

The garage was next. I punched through into the car the remaining corner of the windshield with its significant bullet hole, and I picked up every one of the cigarette stubs which told where and how long Matt had waited. They went into a trash can standing a few yards away from the house door.

Matt hadn't locked the house when he went out. I went in to look for one essential piece of information; the address of the place, and the name of its owner. The flashlight swept over the threadbare covers and elderly furniture, and in one drawer of a large dresser I found what the farmer used for an office. The jumble of bills and letters gave me what I wanted. Wilbur Bellman, Far Valley Farm, Kingman. On the scratch pad beside the telephone Matt had written a bonus. In heavy black ballpoint were the simple words: "Insurance. 9 p.m."

Before leaving I gave the big dilapidated living room a final circuit and the beam flickered over a photograph in a cardboard folder standing on a shelf. Something about the face in it struck me as familiar, and I swung the light back for a second and closer look.

The patient passive face of Kiddo smiled out, as untroubled as it had been when he told Walt and me about Offen's mares. Loopy unformed writing straggled over the lower half of the picture. "To Ma and Pa, from your loving son."

If Offen had sent his stud groom to Miami to join his parents, Kiddo's loyalty to his employer was a certainty. I almost admired Offen's technique in furnishing himself in one throw with an obscure hideout for the horses and a nontalking employee.

After the house there remained only Walt. Nothing to do but to say good-by.

I went down on my knees beside him in the dust, but the silent form was already subtly not Walt. Death showed. I took off one glove and touched his hand: still warm in the warm air, but without the firmness of life.

There was no point in saying to him what I felt. If his spirit was still hovering somewhere around, he would know.

I left him lying there in the dark, and went back to Sam.

He took one slow look at my face and said in an appalled voice, "You're not leaving him there?"

I nodded, and climbed up beside him.

"But you *can't . . .*"

I simply nodded again, and gestured to him to start up and drive away. He did it with a viciousness that must have rocked the stallions on their feet, and we went back to Kingman without speaking. His revulsion at what I had done reached me in almost tangible waves.

I didn't care. I felt only one grim engulfing ache for the man I'd left behind.

18

LYNNIE PUT her brown hand tentatively on mine and said, "Gene, what's the matter?"

"Nothing," I said.

"You look worse than you did when you came back with Chrysalis. Much worse."

"The food doesn't agree with me."

She snorted and took her hand away. We were sitting on the sea terrace, waiting for Eunice to come down for dinner, with the sun galloping the last lap to dusk and the daiquiris tinkling with civilized ice.

"Is Walt back yet?" Lynnie said.

"No."

"He's a funny man, isn't he?" she said. "All moods and glum looks, and then suddenly he smiles, and you realize how nice he is. I like him."

After a pause I said, "So do I."

"How was San Francisco?" she asked.

"Foggy."

"What's the matter?"

"Nothing."

She sighed and shook her head.

Eunice arrived in a cloud of yellow chiffon and clanked her gold bracelet as she stretched for her drink. She was cheerful and glowing; almost too much to bear.

"Well, you son of a bitch, when did you crawl in?"

"This afternoon," I said.

"So what's new?"

"I've given up trying to find the horses."

Eunice sat up straight with a jerk. "For crying out loud!"

"I'll be starting home soon. Tomorrow evening, I expect."

"Oh, no," Lynnie said.

"Oh, yes, I'm afraid so. The holidays are over."

"You don't look as if they've done you much good," Eunice observed. "So now how do you deal with it?"

"With what?"

"With flopping. With not making out."

I said wryly, "Look it smack in the eye and dare it to bite you."

"It probably will," said Eunice sardonically. "It'll chew me to bloody bits." She drank the second quarter of her drink and looked me thoughtfully over. "Come to think of it, it seems to have done that to you already."

"Maybe I'll take up golf."

She laughed, more internally relaxed than I'd ever seen her. "Games," she said, "are a bore."

When they went in to eat I couldn't face it, and drove off instead to fetch the tape recorder from the rocks at Orpheus Farm. The short journey seemed tiresomely long. It had been nearly 450 miles back to Santa Barbara from Kingman, and neither bath, shave, nor two hours flat on the bed seemed to have had any effect.

Back in my room at the Vacationer I listened to the whole of the tape's four-hour playing time. The first conversations, two or three business calls, were from the previous morning, after Walt had put in a new reel. Then there was almost an hour and a half of an interview between Offen and a man from the bloodstock registry office. They had already been out to see the horses, and Offen was piling proof on proof that the horses in his barn were veritably Moviemaker and Centigrade. A groom who had cared for Centigrade during his racing days was asked in to sign a statement he'd made that he recognized the horse and would if necessary swear to its identity in any inquiry.

The bloodstock man apologized constantly that anyone should have doubted Offen. Offen enjoyed the scene, the joke rumbling like an undertone. After they'd gone he laughed aloud. I hoped he'd enjoyed it. He wouldn't be laughing much for a long time to come.

Next on the tape was a piece of Offen giving his houseman instructions for replenishing the drink stocks, then an hour's television program. And after that Matt telephoned.

I couldn't hear his voice at all, only Offen's replies: but they were enough.

"Hello—Matt."

"Slow down, I'm not taking this in. Where did you say you were?"

"What are you doing on the road to Las Vegas?"

"Well, I can see the house must be insured."

"You found *what* under the glove compartment?"

"How do you know it's a homer?"

"All these minute transmitters are a mystery to me."

"Who could have put it there?"

"I don't follow you. What was that about yellow paint?"

"But the police said it was vandals!"

"All right, Matt, don't shout. I'm doing my best. Now, let's get this clear. You were fumbling for a pack of cigarettes and you dislodged this . . . thing. Bug, whatever you said. And you're worried now that Hawkins and Prensela put it in your car, and that they used that and the yellow paint to follow you, so that they know where you've been staying, or maybe. Is that right?"

"Matt, I think you're blowing this thing up too big."

"But did you actually *see* a plane following you?"

"Well, yes, sure, if you think you should go back, go back. The horses are far more important than the insurance on the house. But I think you're wrong. Hawkins and Prensela have been concentrating on Moviemaker and Centigrade here, they've stirred up the D.A.'s office from L.A. and the bloodstock registry, and it's been a three-ringed circus here for the last couple of days. They wouldn't have been trying to find any horses anywhere else, because they're sure they're here in the barn."

"Well, I don't *know* who could have planted the bug."

"Yeah. All right. Go on back, then."

"Call me in the morning."

"Good night, Matt."

The receiver went down, and for a few seconds there were the indistinct noises of Offen going over the conversation again in his mind, punctuating it with "umphs" and small doubtful grunts.

I switched the tape off temporarily and thought bitterly about Matt finding the bug. I hadn't had a chance to remove it: on my first night visit to the farm the car in the garage had been the one he'd rented while his own was being cleaned of paint. But neither had I looked upon it as a very great hazard, because the little capsules were light and clung tightly. It had been long odds against him groping for cigarettes while driving in the dark, and dislodging it. I hadn't taken it into account.

Some time on his way back to the farm it must have struck him that the insurance appointment might be phony; that if we had tricked him into going to Las Vegas once already, we might be tricking him again. If we'd got him out of the way, it could only be to take the horses. So he'd wait; in the dark, ready to spring.

He must have begun to think, when he'd sat out the three hours it took to mend the gasket, that Uncle Bark was right and he was wrong: but all the same he'd gone on waiting. And, in the end, we had come.

I switched the tape on again for the rest. The whole night had been telescoped into the few seconds' silence, because when Offen made his next call it was clearly morning.

"Yola, is that you?"

A faint clacking reached the bug. Yola's higher-pitched voice disturbed more air.

"Have you heard from Matt?"

"______."

"No, he said he'd call me this morning, and he hasn't. I can't get any answer from the farm."

"______."

"I'd forgotten the hens and the calves."

"______."

"Well, not really. He called me last night because he had some crazy idea Hawkins had traced the horses . . ."

A loud squawk from Yola.

"Something about a listening bug and yellow paint."

Yola talked for some time and when Offen answered he sounded anxious.

"Yeah, I know he found the first one when we thought that was impossible . . . Do you really think Matt may be right?"

"______."

"Yola, that's right out. Why don't you go yourself?"

"______."

"Close the ranch then. Send them all home."

"______."

"Look, if you're right, if Matt's right . . . Say when he went back last night the D.A.'s men were sitting there waiting for him? Say they're sitting there right now, waiting for me to turn up and see why Matt doesn't answer his calls? No, Yola, I'm not walking into that farm and find I have to answer questions like what I am doing there, and what are those two horses in the barn, with Moneymaker and Centigrade's registrations tatooed inside their lips? I'm not going."

"______."

"Matt may be off on some plan of his own."

"______."

"No. I'll give him today. If I haven't heard from him by morning I'll . . . well, I'll think of something."

Yola's final remark was loud, and I heard it clearly. Full of anxiety, full of anguish.

"If anything's happened to Matt . . ."

The end of the tape ran off the reel, and I switched off the recorder. For Yola, as for Walt's wife, life would never be the same again.

I went to bed and lay awake, feeling feverish from lack of sleep. Relaxed every limb, but my mind would have none of it. It was filled too full, as it had been all day, of a picture of Walt still lying on his back in the farmyard. The sun had risen and blazed on him, and set again. He would have no shelter until tomorrow. I couldn't sleep until he had. I tried to, but I couldn't.

On my way back to Santa Barbara I'd stopped for coffee and a handful of change, and I'd telephoned to Paul M. Zeissen in the Buttress Life office on Thirty-third Street. It had been nearly 6 P.M. New York time. Zeissen was preparing to go home for the weekend. I was a little worried,

I told him, about Walt. He had gone to do some life insurance business on a farm in Arizona, and I hadn't heard from him since. Zeissen and I talked it over for a few minutes in unurgent civilized tones, and arranged finally that if I hadn't heard from Walt by morning, Buttress Life would ring the Arizona State Police in Kingman, and ask them as a favor to go out to the farm, just to check.

In the morning I would ring Zeissen at his home. By noon, perhaps, the Kingman police would reach the farm. They would read the story: insurance salesman arrives for appointment, gets out of car. Matt Clive, hurrying back to meet him, swings into the yard, sees a dark figure too late, hits him, runs straight on into wall because judgment suspended by horror at collision. Matt, with whiskey inside him and a bottle in the car. Inside the house, the 9 P.M. insurance appointment written in Matt's hand. And nothing else. No horses. No suggestion of visitors. No sign that it could have been anything but a tragically unlucky accident.

Matt had been good at accidents.

So was I.

I lay on my stomach on the beach all morning while Lynnie sat beside me and trickled sand through her fingers. Eunice had gone to Santa Monica, down the coast.

"Are you really going home this evening?" Lynnie said.

"First hop, yes."

"Would you mind . . . if I came with you?"

I stirred in surprise.

"I thought you wanted to stay here forever."

"Mm. But that was with you . . . and Eunice. Now you're going . . . and Eunice hasn't been here much this week, you know. I've spent ages all on my own, and there isn't that much to do on a beach, when you do it every day."

"Where has Eunice been?"

"Santa Monica, like now. There's some place there she spends all her time in, where they import vases and bits of sculpture and expensive light fittings, and things like that. She took me there the day before yesterday . . . I must say it's pretty gorgeous. Marvelous fabrics, too."

"She might feel hurt if you just pack up and leave her."

"Well, no. I mentioned it to her before she went this morning, and honestly I think if anything she was relieved. She just said if I really wanted to go, O.K., and she would probably be moving down to Santa Monica in a day or two anyway."

"If you really want to, then. I'm catching the night flight to Washington . . . I've a visit to make in Lexington tomorrow morning. After that, back to New York, and home."

"You don't mind if I tag along?" She sounded a bit uncertain.

"Come to think of it," I said, "you can wake me at the stops."

We had a sandwich for lunch which I couldn't eat, and at two the girl from the reception desk came to say I was wanted on the telephone. Paul M. Zeissen told me in a suitably hushed voice that the Arizona police had been most cooperative and had gone to Bellman's farm as asked, and had found Walt dead. I made shocked noises. Zeissen said would I pack Walt's things and send them back? I said I would.

"I suppose," he suggested diffidently, "that you and he had not completed your other business?"

"The horses?"

"One horse. Allyx," he said reprovingly. "Showman was insured with another company."

"Oh . . . yes. Allyx should be in circulation, safe and authenticated, within a month or so. I expect the Blood Horse Breeders Association will be getting in touch with you. Walt worked very hard at this, and it was entirely owing to his efforts that Buttress Life will be recovering most of the million and a half it paid out."

"Where did he find the horse?"

"I can't tell you. Does it matter?"

"No . . ." he said thoughtfully. "Goods back, no questions asked . . . we work on that principle, the same as any other company."

"Right then," I said. "And you'll of course pay his commission to his widow?"

"Uh . . . of course. And naturally Walt had insured his life with us . . . Mrs. Prensela will be well provided for, I feel sure."

Provided for. Money. But no Walt. No picnic.

I said good-by to Zeissen and went slowly back to Lynnie. When I told her Walt was dead, she cried for him.

Upstairs, when I packed his clothes, I lingered a good while over the framed photograph of him with Amy and the kids, and in the end put it in my suitcase, not his. It could hardly be the only photograph his wife would have of him, and I didn't think she'd worry much if it didn't return with his baggage.

Eunice came back tired and abstracted from Santa Monica, and after absorbing the shock of Walt's death was unaffected when Lynnie told her over early dinner that she was going home with me.

"Much better to travel with a man to look after you, honey," she agreed absent-mindedly: and then, giving me a more characteristic sharp glance, added, "Don't let him get up to any tricks."

Lynnie sighed. "He wouldn't."

"Huh," she said, but without conviction, and then asked me, "Will you be seeing Dave when you get back?"

I nodded. "Very soon after."

"Tell him then, will you, that I've found a darling little business in Santa Monica. They're looking for a partner with some capital, to open another branch, and if the accounts are right I'd like to do it. I'll write him, of course, but you could explain. . . . I guess you could explain better than anyone."

"I'll explain."

She said she was too tired to come all the way back to Los Angeles to see us off, and we said good-by to her in the lobby, where she kissed

Lynnie and then me on the cheek with a quite surprising strength of feeling.

Lynnie said, as we drove away, "I'll miss her. Isn't that extraordinary. I'll really miss her."

"You'll come back."

"It won't be the same."

I returned the rented car to the Hertz agent at the airport, we caught the plane to Washington, and I made up on parts of the way for the three nights without sleep. Lynnie said at Lexington that she could quite see why I needed someone to wake me at the stops.

We went in a taxi to Jeff Roots's house and his teen-age daughters took Lynnie off for a swim in the pool while I sat with him under his vine-covered trellis and thought how cool and substantial he looked in his bright open-necked Sunday shirt.

"Sam Hengelman should reach Lexington sometime this afternoon or early evening." I said. "He'll call you to know where to take the horses."

"That's all fixed," Roots nodded.

"Would you give him a message from me?"

"Sure."

"Just tell him everything's O.K.; that I said so."

"Sure. You are, aren't you, one hundred percent certain that these two definitely are Showman and Allyx?"

"One hundred percent. There isn't the slightest doubt."

He sighed. "I'll get the identification started. Though who is to know Showman after ten years? A bay with no markings . . . and only a four-year-old when he came from England." He paused, then said, "Have you any suggestions as to how we can start prosecuting Offen for fraud and theft?"

I shook my head. "I'm not a policeman. Not interested in punishment, only prevention." I smiled briefly. "I came to get the horses back. Nothing else. Well, they're back. I've done what I was engaged for, and that's as far as I go."

He eyed me assessingly. "Do you want Offen to go on collecting huge stud fees, then?"

"He won't," I said. "Not if someone starts a quick rumor immediately that both Moviemaker and Centigrade have been suffering from an obscure virus which will certainly have affected their virility. Owners of mares can be quietly advised to insist they don't pay any stud fees until the foals have shown their quality. After that . . . Well, Offen does legally own Moviemaker and Centigrade, and he's entitled to the fees they earn on their own merits."

"You're extraordinary," he said. "Don't you want to see Offen behind bars?"

"Not passionately," I said. Offen had enjoyed his prestige almost more than his income. He would be losing both. And Yola . . . She was going to have to work hard without Matt, and probably without the expensive house on Pitts. Bars seemed superfluous.

He shook his head, giving me up as a bad job. "We'll have to prosecute, I'm sure of it. I'll have to get lawyers to see about it."

He called the houseman to bring out drinks, and merely sighed when I said I'd as soon share his sugar-free tonic.

We sipped the well-iced innocuous stuff and he said again that Offen would have to be prosecuted, if only to provide a reason for Allyx and Showman having disappeared for so long a time and to account for the tattoo marks inside their mouths.

"I can see you would think that," I said. "I also think you'll have a terrible job proving that any of the mares booked to Moviemaker and Centigrade were actually covered by Showman or Allyx. I didn't find Showman and Allyx on Offen's farm. I doubt if anyone would testify that they were ever there. Certainly Offen would deny it, and go on denying it to the bitter end. It's his only hope." I paused. "I did manage to get some tape recordings, but unfortunately, even if they could be used as evidence, they are inconclusive. Offen never mentioned Showman or Allyx by name."

Roots stared gloomily into space.

"This makes it difficult," he said. "What you are in fact saying is that we know Offen switched the stallions, because of the tattoo marks, but no one will be able to prove it?"

I looked down to where Lynnie was jumping into the pool in a big-splash contest with Roots's daughters. Her lighthearted laughter floated up, carefree and very young.

"I wouldn't try," I said. "Rightly or wrongly I decided to repossess the stolen goods by stealing them back. First, so that Offen would have no chance of destroying them. Second, so that there shouldn't be years of delay while lawyers argued the case, years of the stallions standing idle, with their value diminishing day by day and their bloodlines wasting. Third, and most important, that there should be no chance of Offen getting them back once the dust had settled. Because if he had any sense he would swear, and provide witnesses to swear, that the horses in dispute were two unraced half-bred animals of no account, and he'd explain the tattoos on their lips by saying he'd used them to try out some new type of ink. What more likely, he would say, than that he should repeat the numbers of his two best horses? He could make it sound a lot more reasonable than that he should have stolen two world-famous stallions and conducted a large-scale fraud. He has great personal charm."

Roots nodded. "I've met him."

"Showman and Allyx were being looked after by Offen's nephew," I said. "Offen can say he'd lent him two old nags to hack around on, and he can't imagine why anyone would want to steal them."

"He could put up an excellent defense, I see that," he admitted.

"His present stud groom is innocent," I added. "And would convince anyone of it. If you leave things as they are, Offen won't get Allyx and Showman back. If you prosecute him, he may."

He looked shattered, staring into his glass but seeing with experienced eyes every side of the sticky problem.

"We could try blood tests," he said at last.

"Blood tests?"

"For paternity," he nodded. "If there is any doubt about which horse has sired a certain foal, we take blood tests. If one disputed sire's blood is of a similar group to the foal's, and the other disputed sire's is different, we conclude that the foal was sired by the similar sire."

"And like in human beings," I asked, "you can tell which horse could *not* have sired which foal, but you couldn't say which, of a similar blood group, actually did?"

"That's right."

We thought it over. Then he said cheerfully. "If we can prove that none of the so-called Moviemaker foals could in fact have been sired by Moviemaker, but could all have been sired by Showman, we'll have Offen sewed up tight."

"Couldn't he possibly have made sure, before he ever bought Moviemaker, that his and Showman's blood groups were similar? I mean, if he's a breeder, he'd know about blood tests."

Roots's gloom returned. "I suppose it's possible. And possible that Centigrade and Allyx are similar too." He looked up suddenly and caught me smiling. "It's all right for you to think it's funny," he said wryly, matching my expression. 'You don't have to sort out the mess. What in God's name are we going to do about the Studbook? Moviemaker's—that is, Showman's—get are already siring foals, in some cases. The mix-up is in the second generation. How are we ever going to put it straight?"

"Even if," I pointed out, trying hard to keep the humor out of my voice and face, "even if you prove Moviemaker couldn't have sired the foals he's supposed to have done, you can't prove Showman *did*."

He gave me a comically pained look. "What other sire could have got such brilliant stock?" He shook his head. "We'll pin it on Offen in the end, even if we have to wait until after Showman and Allyx have been resyndicated and their first official crops have won as much stake money as all the others. Offen wouldn't be able to say then that they were two half-bred nags he'd given his nephew to hack around on. We'll get him in the end."

"The racing scandal of the year," I said, smiling.

"Of the year? Are you kidding? Of the century."

Lynnie and I flew from Kennedy that night on a Super VC 10, with dinner over Canada at midnight and breakfast over Ireland three hours later. I spent the interval looking at her while she slept beside me in her sloped-back chair. Her skin was close-textured like a baby's and her face was that of a child. The woman inside was still a bud, with a long way to grow.

Keeble met us at Heathrow, and as usual it was raining. Lynnie kissed him affectionately. He went so far as to shake my hand. There was a patch of stubble on his left cheek, and the eyes blinked quickly behind the mild glasses. Santa Barbara was 6,000 miles away. We were home.

Keeble suggested a cup of coffee before we left the airport and asked his daughter how she'd enjoyed herself. She told him nonstop for twenty minutes, her suntan glowing in the gray summer morning and her brown eyes alight.

He looked finally from her to me, and his face subtly contracted.

"And what have you been doing?" he said.

Lynnie answered when I didn't. "He's been with us on the beach a good deal of the time," she said doubtfully.

Keeble stroked her arm. "Did you find the horses?" he asked.

I nodded.

"All three?"

"With help."

"I told Dave I'd drop you off at the hospital when we leave here," he said. "He's still strung up, but he hopes to be out next week."

"I've a lot to tell him, and there's a lot he'll have to decide." The worst being, I thought, whether to carry on with his move alongside Orpheus Farm, or to disappoint Eunice in her new-found business. Nothing was ever simple. Nothing was easy.

"You don't look well," Keeble said abruptly.

"I'll live," I said, and his eyes flickered with a mixture of surprise and speculation. I smiled lopsidedly and said it again, "I'll live."

We stood up to go. Instead of shaking hands Lynnie suddenly put her arms round my waist and her head on my chest.

"I don't want to say good-by," she said indistinctly. "I want to see you again."

"Well," I said reasonably, "you will."

"I mean . . . often."

I met Keeble's eyes over her head. He was watching her gravely, but without disquiet.

"She's too young," I said to him, and he knew exactly what I meant. Not that I was too old for her, but that she was too young for me. Too young in experience, understanding, and wickedness.

"I'll get older," she said. "Will twenty-one do?"

Her father laughed, but she gripped my arm. "Will it?"

"Yes," I said recklessly, and found one second later that I really meant it.

"She'll change her mind," Keeble said with casual certainty.

I said, "Of course," to him, but Lynnie looked up into my eyes and shook her head.

It was late afternoon when I got back to the flat. The tidy, dull, unwelcoming rooms hadn't changed a bit. When I looked at the kitchen I remembered Lynnie making burned scrambled eggs, and I felt a fierce disturbing wish that she would soon make some more.

I unpacked. The evening stretched grayly ahead.

I sat and stared vacantly at the bare walls.

If was a grinding word, I thought. If Sam Hengelman had taken longer to mend that gasket, Walt would have found us on the road and would have stopped us from going to the farm. If Sam had mended it faster, we'd have reached the farm well before Walt, and Matt would have killed me, as he'd meant.

If I hadn't decided to recover the horses by stealing them, Walt would be alive. They might collectively be worth nearly $5 million, but they weren't worth Walt's life.

I wished I'd never started.

The gray day turned to gray dusk. I got up and switched on the light, and fetched two objects to put on the low table beside my chair.

The Luger, and the photograph of Walt with his wife and kids.

The trouble with being given a gift you don't really want is that you feel so mean if you throw it away. Especially if it cost more than the giver could afford.

I won't throw away Walt's gift. Even if Lynnie changes her mind, I'll survive.

Tired beyond feeling, I went to bed at ten. I put the Luger under the pillow, and hung the photograph on the wall.

And slept.

RAT RACE

1

I PICKED four of them up at White Waltham in the new Cherokee Six 300 that never got a chance to grow old. The pale blue upholstery still had a new leather smell and there wasn't a scratch on the glossy white fuselage. A nice little airplane, while it lasted.

They had ordered me for noon but they were already in the bar when I landed at eleven-forty. Three double whiskies and a lemonade.

Identification was easy: several chairs around a small table were draped with four lightweight raincoats, three binocular cases, two copies of *Sporting Life* and one lightweight racing saddle. The four passengers were standing nearby in the sort of spread-about group indicative of people thrown together by business rather than natural friendship. They were not talking to each other, though it looked as though they had been. One, a large man, had a face full of anger. The smallest, evidently a jockey, was flushed and rigid. Two others, an elderly man and a middle-aged woman, were steadfastly staring at nothing in particular in the way that meant a lot of furious activity was going on inside their heads.

I walked toward them across the large lounge-reception room and spoke to an indeterminate spot in midair.

"Major Tyderman?"

The elderly man who said "Yes?" had been made a major a good long time ago. Nearer seventy than sixty; but still with a tough little body, wiry little mustache, sharp little eyes. He had thin salt-and-pepper hair brushed sideways across a balding crown and he carried his head stiffly, with his chin tucked back into his neck. Tense: very tense. And wary, looking at the world with suspicion.

He wore a lightweight speckled fawn suit vaguely reminiscent in cut of his military origins, and unlike the others, had not parked his binoculars but wore them with the strap diagonally across his chest and the case facing forward on his stomach, like a sporran. Club badges of metal and colored cardboard hung in thick clusters at each side.

"Your airplane is here, Major," I said. "I'm Matt Shore. . . . I'm flying you."

He glanced over my shoulder, looking for someone else.

"Where's Larry?" he asked abruptly.

"He left," I said. "He got a job in Turkey."

The Major's gaze came back from the search with a click. "You're new," he said accusingly.

"Yes," I agreed.

"I hope you know the way."

He meant it seriously. I said politely, "I'll do my best."

The second of the passengers, the woman on the Major's left, said flatly, "The last time I flew to the races, the pilot got lost."

I looked at her, giving her my best approximation to a confidence-boosting smile. "The weather's good enough today not to have any fear of it."

It wasn't true. There were cu-nims forecast for the June afternoon. And anyone can get lost anytime if enough goes wrong. The woman on the left of Major Tyderman gave me a disillusioned stare and I stopped wasting my confidence builder. She didn't need it. She had all the confidence in the world. She was fifty and fragile-looking, with graying hair cut in a straight-across fringe and a jaw-length bob. There were two mild brown eyes under heavy dark eyebrows and a mouth that looked gentle; yet she held herself and behaved with the easy authority of a much higher command than the Major's. She was the only one of the group not outwardly ruffled.

The Major had been looking at his watch. "You're early," he said. "We've got time for the other half." He turned to the barman and ordered refills, and as an afterthought said to me, "Something for you?"

I shook my head. "No, thank you."

The woman said indifferently, "No alcohol for eight hours before a flight. Isn't that the rule?"

"More or less," I agreed.

The third passenger, the large angry-looking man, morosely watched the barman push the measure up twice on the Johnnie Walker. "Eight hours. Good God," he said. He looked as if eight hours seldom passed for him without topping up. The bulbous nose, the purple thread veins on his cheeks, the swelling paunch—they had all cost a lot in excise duty.

The atmosphere I had walked into slowly subsided. The jockey sipped his low-calorie lemonade, and the bright pink flush faded from his cheekbones and came out in fainter mottles on his neck. He seemed about twenty-one or two, reddish-haired, with a naturally small frame and a moist-looking skin. Few weight problems, I thought. No dehydration. Fortunate for him.

The Major and his large friend drank rapidly, muttered unintelligibly, and removed themselves to the Gents. The woman eyed the jockey and said in a voice which sounded more friendly than her comment, "Are you out of your mind, Kenny Bayst? If you go on antagonizing Major Tyderman, you'll be looking for another job."

The jockey flicked his eyes to me and away again, compressing his rosebud mouth. He put the half-finished lemonade on the table and picked up one of the raincoats and the racing saddle.

"Which plane?" he said to me. "I'll stow my gear."

He had a strong Australian accent with a resentful bite to it. The woman watched him with what would have passed for a smile but for the frost in her eyes.

"The baggage door is locked," I said. "I'll come over with you." To the woman I said, "Can I carry your coat?"

"Thank you." She indicated the coat which was obviously hers, a shiny rust-colored affair with copper buttons. I picked it up, and also the businesslike binoculars lying on top, and followed the jockey out of the door.

After ten fuming paces, he said explosively, "It's too damn easy to blame the man on top."

"They always blame the pilot," I said mildly. "Fact of life."

"Huh?" he said. "Oh, yeah. Too right. They do."

We reached the end of the path and started across the grass. He was still oozing grudge. I wasn't much interested.

"For the record," I said, "what are the names of my other passengers? Besides the Major, that is."

He turned his head in surprise. "Don't you know her? Our Annie Villars? Looks like someone's cozy old granny and has a tongue that would flay a kangaroo. Everyone knows our little Annie." His tone was sour and disillusioned.

"I don't know much about racing," I said.

"Oh? Well, she's a trainer, then. A damned good trainer, I'll say that for her. I wouldn't stay with her else. Not with that tongue of hers. I'll tell you, sport, she can roust her stable lads out on the gallops in words a sergeant major never thought of. But sweet as milk with the owners. Has them eating out of her little hand."

"The horses, too?"

"Uh? Oh, yeah. The horses love her. She can ride like a jock, too, when she's a mind to. Not that she does it much now. She must be getting on a bit. Still, she knows what she's at, true enough. She knows what a horse can do and what it can't, and that's most of the battle in this game."

His voice held resentment and admiration in roughly equal amounts.

I said, "What is the name of the other man? The big one."

This time it was pure resentment: no admiration. He spat the name out syllable by deliberate syllable, curling his lips away from his teeth.

"Mr. Eric Goldenberg."

Having got rid of the name, he shut his mouth tight and was clearly taking his employer's remarks to heart. We reached the aircraft and stowed the coats and his saddle in the baggage space behind the rear seats.

"We're going to Newbury first, aren't we?" he asked. "To pick up Colin Ross?"

"Yes."

He gave me a sardonic look. "Well, you *must* have heard of Colin Ross."

"I guess," I said, "that I have."

It would have been difficult not to, since the champion jockey was twice as popular as the Prime Minister and earned six times as much. His face appeared on half the billboards in Britain encouraging the populace to drink more milk, and his sharp wits convulsed the headlines at least once a month. There was even a picture strip about him in a children's comic. Everyone, but everyone, had heard of Colin Ross.

Kenny Bayst climbed in through the rear-end door and sat in one of the two rear seats. I took a quick look round the outside of the aircraft, even though I'd done a thorough preflight check on it not an hour before, when I left base. It was my first week, my fourth day, my third flight for Derrydowns Sky Taxis, and after the way fate had clobbered me in the past, I was taking no chances.

There were no nuts loose, no rivets missing on the sharp-nosed little six-seater. There were eight quarts of oil where there should have been eight quarts of oil, there were no dead birds clogging up the air intakes to the engine, there were no punctures in the tires, no cracks in the green or red glass over navigation lights, no chips in the propeller blades, no loose radio aerials. The pale blue cowling over the engine was securely clipped down, and the matching pale blue cowling over the struts and wheels of the fixed undercarriage were as solid as rocks.

By the time I'd finished, the other three passengers were coming across the grass. Goldenberg was doing the talking with steam still coming out of his ears, while the Major nodded agreement in unhappy little jerks and Annie Villars looked as if she wasn't listening. When they arrived within earshot, Goldenberg was saying ". . . can't lay the horse unless we're sure he'll pull it—" But he stopped short when the Major gestured sharply in my direction. He need hardly have bothered. I had no curiosity about their affairs.

On the principle that in a light aircraft it is better to have the center of gravity as far forward as possible, I asked Goldenberg to sit in front in the right-hand seat beside me, and put the Major and Annie Villars in the center two seats, and left Kenny in one of the last two, with the empty one ready for Colin Ross. The four rear seats were reached by the port-side door, but Goldenberg had to climb in by stepping up on the low wing on the starboard side and lowering himself into his seat through the forward door. He waited while I got in before him and moved over to my side, then squeezed his bulk in through the door and settled heavily into his seat.

They were all old hands at air taxis: they had their safety belts fastened before I did mine, and when I looked round to check that they were ready to go, the Major was already deep in *Sporting Life*. Kenny Bayst was cleaning his nails with fierce little jabs, relieving his frustration by hurting himself.

I got clearance from the tower and lifted the little airplane away for the twenty-mile hop across Berkshire. Taxi flying was a lot different from the airlines, and finding racecourses looked more difficult to me than being radar-vectored into Heathrow. I'd never before flown a racecourse trip, and I'd asked my predecessor Larry about it that morning when he'd come into the office to collect his cards.

"Newbury's a cinch," he said offhandedly. "Just point its nose at that vast runway the Yanks built at Greenham Common. You can practically see it from Scotland. The racecourse is just north of it, and the landing strip is parallel with the white rails of the finishing straight. You can't miss it. Good long strip. No problems. As for Haydock, it's just where the M6 motorway crosses the East Lancs road. Piece of cake."

He took himself off to Turkey, stopping on one foot at the doorway for some parting advice. "You'll have to practice short landings before you go to Bath; and avoid Yarmouth in a heat wave. It's all yours now, mate, and the best of British Luck."

It was true that you could see Greenham Common from a long way off, but on a fine day it would anyway have been difficult to lose the way from White Waltham to Newbury: the main railway line to Exeter ran more or less straight from one to the other. My passengers had all flown into Newbury before, and the Major helpfully told me to look out for the electric cables strung across the approach. We landed respectably on the newly mown grass and taxied along the strip toward the grandstand end, braking to a stop just before the boundary fence.

Colin Ross wasn't there.

I shut down the engine, and in the sudden silence Annie Villars remarked, "He's bound to be late. He said he was riding work for Bob Smith, and Bob's never on time getting his horses out."

The other three nodded vaguely, but they were still not on ordinarily chatty terms with one another, and after about five minutes of heavy silence I asked Goldenberg to let me out to stretch my legs. He grunted and mumbled at having to climb out onto the wing to let me past him, and I gathered I was breaking Derrydowns' Number 1 rule: never annoy the customers; you're going to need them again.

Once I was out of their company, however, they did start talking. I walked round to the front of the aircraft and leaned against the leading edge of the wing, and looked up at the scattered clouds in the blue-gray sky and thought unprofitably about this and that. Behind me their voices rose acrimoniously, and when they opened the door wide to get some air, scraps of what they were saying floated across.

". . . simply asking for a dope test." Annie Villars.

". . . if you can't ride a losing race better than last time . . . find someone else." Goldenberg.

". . . very difficult position . . ." Major Tyderman.

A short sharp snap from Kenny, and Annie Villars' exasperated exclamation. "Bayst!"

". . . not paying you more than last time." The Major, very emphatically.

Indistinct protest from Kenny, and a violently clear reaction from Goldenberg: "Bugger your license."

Kenny, my lad, I thought remotely, if you don't watch out you'll end up like me, still with a license but with not much else.

A Ford-of-all-work rolled down the road past the grandstands, came through the gate in the boundary fence, and bounced over the turf toward the aircraft. It stopped about twenty feet away, and two men climbed out. The larger, who had been driving, went round to the back and pulled out a brown canvas-and-leather overnight grip. The smaller one walked on over the grass. I took my weight off the wing and stood up. He stopped a few paces away, waiting for the larger man to catch up. He was dressed in faded blue jeans and a whitish cotton sweat shirt with navy-blue edgings. Black canvas shoes on his narrow feet. He had nondescript brownish hair over an exceptionally broad forehead, a short straight nose, and a delicate feminine-looking chin. All his bones were fine and his waist and hips would have been the despair of Victorian maidens. Yet there was something unmistakably masculine about him: and more than that, he was mature. He looked at me with the small still smile behind the eyes which is the hallmark of those who know what life is really about. His soul was old. He was twenty-six.

"Good morning," I said.

He held out his hand, and I shook it. His clasp was cool, firm, and brief.

"No Larry?" he inquired.

"He's left. I'm Matt Shore."

"Fine," he said noncommittally. He didn't introduce himself. He knew there was no need. I wondered what it was like to be in that position. It hadn't affected Colin Ross. He had none of the "I am" aura which often clings around the notably successful, and from the extreme understatement of his clothes I gathered that he avoided it consciously.

"We're late, I'm afraid," he said. "Have to bend the throttle."

"Do my best. . . ."

The larger man arrived with the grip, and I stowed it in the forward luggage locker between the engine wall and the forward bulkhead of the cabin. By the time the baggage door was securely fastened, Colin Ross had found his empty seat and strapped himself into it. Goldenberg, with heavy grunts, moved out again so that I could get back to my left-hand place. The larger man, who was apparently the dilatory trainer Bob Smith, said his hellos and goodbyes to the passengers, and stood watching afterward while I started the engine and taxied back to the other end of the strip to turn into wind for takeoff.

The flight north was uneventful: I went up the easy way under the Amber 1 airway, navigating on the radio beacons at Daventry, Lichfield, and Oldham. Manchester control routed us right round the north of their zone, so that I had to drop down southward toward Haydock racecourse, and there it was, just as Larry had said, near the interchange of the two giant roads. We touched down on the grass strip indicated in the center of the course, and I taxied on and parked where the Major told me to, near the rails of the track itself, a mere hundred yards from the grandstand.

The passengers disembarked themselves and their belongings and Colin Ross looked at his watch. A faint smile hovered and was gone. He made no comment. He said merely, "Are you coming in to the races?"

I shook my head. "Think I'll stay over here."

"I'll arrange with the man on the gate to let you into the paddock, if you change your mind."

"Thanks," I said in surprise. "Thanks very much."

He nodded briefly and set off without waiting for the others, ducking under the white-painted rails and trudging across the track.

"Pilots' perks," Kenny said, taking his raincoat from my hand and putting his arm forward for the saddle. "You want to take advantage."

"Maybe I will," I said, but I didn't mean to. Horse racing began and ended with the Derby as far as I was concerned, and also I was a non-gambler by nature.

Annie Villars said in her deceptively gentle voice, "You do understand that we're all going on to Newmarket after the races, and not back to Newbury?"

"Yes," I assured her. "That's what I was told."

"Good."

"If we don't go to jail," Kenny said under his breath. Goldenberg looked at me sharply to see if I'd heard that, and I gave no sign of it. Whatever they were about, it was as little my concern as who killed Cock Robin.

Major Tyderman pushed at his mustache with a hand rigid with nervous energy and said, "Last race at four-thirty. Need a drink after that. Ready to start back at, say, five-fifteen. That all right with you?"

"Perfectly, Major." I nodded.

"Right," he said. "Good." His gaze was flicking from one to another of his traveling companions, assessing and suspicious. His eyes narrowed fiercely at Kenny Bayst, opened and narrowed again rapidly on Goldenberg, relaxed on Annie Villars, and went cold on the vanishing back of Colin Ross. The thoughts behind the outward physical reactions were unguessable, and when he finally looked back at me he didn't really see me; he was busy with the activity inside his head.

"Five-fifteen," he repeated vaguely. "Good."

Kenny said to me, "Don't waste your money in the three-thirty, sport," and Goldenberg raised his fist, his face going purple with anger, and nearly hit him.

Annie Villars' voice rapped into him, the steel sticking through the cream with a vengeance, the top-brass quality transcendent and withering. "Control yourself, you stupid man."

Goldenberg's mouth literally dropped open, to reveal a bottom row of unappetizing brown-stained teeth. His raised fist lowered slowly, and he looked altogether foolish.

"As for you," she said to Kenny, "I told you to keep your tongue still, and that was your last chance."

"Are you sacking me?" he asked.

"I'll decide that at the end of the afternoon."

Kenny showed no anxiety about keeping his job, and I realized that in fact what he had been doing was trying to provoke them into getting rid of him. He'd got himself into nutcrackers and while they squeezed he couldn't get out.

I became mildly curious to see what would happen in the three-thirty. It would help to pass the afternoon.

They straggled off toward the stands, Kenny in front, the Major and Goldenberg together, with Annie Villars several paces behind. The Major kept stopping and looking back and waiting for her, but each time just as she reached him he turned and went off again in front, so that as a piece of courtesy the whole thing was wasted. He reminded me vividly of an aunt who had taken me for childhood walks in just that way. I remembered quite clearly that it had been infuriating.

I sighed, shut the baggage doors, and tidied up the airplane. Annie Villars had been smoking thin brown cigars. Goldenberg had been eating indigestion tablets, each from a square wrapper. The Major had left his *Sporting Life* in a tumbled heap on the floor.

While I was fiddling around with the debris, two more airplanes flew in, a four-seat high-winged Cessna and a six-seat twin-engined Aztec.

I watched their touchdowns with an uncritical eye, though I wouldn't have given the Aztec pilot a gold medal for his double bounce. Several small men disgorged themselves and made a dart like a flock of starlings across the track toward the paddock. They were followed by three or four larger and slower-moving people, slung around with binoculars and what I later learned to be bags for carrying sets of racing colors. Finally out of each aircraft popped the most leisurely of all the inmates, a man dressed very much as I was, in dark trousers, white shirt, neat dark tie.

They strolled toward each other and lit cigarettes. After a while, not wanting to seem unsociable, I wandered across to join them. They turned and watched me come, but with no welcome in unsmiling faces. "Hello," I said moderately. "Nice day."

"Perhaps," said one.

"You think so?" said the other.

They offered me fish-eyed stares but no cigarette. I had grown hardened to that sort of thing. I turned half away from them to read the names of the firms they flew for, which were painted on the tails of their aircraft. It was the same name on both. Polyplane Services.

How dreary of them, I thought, to be so antagonistic. I gave them the benefit of a very small doubt and made one more approach.

"Have you come far?"

They didn't answer. Just gave me the stares, like two cod.

I laughed at them as if I thought their behavior pathetic, which in fact I did, and turned on my heel to go back to my own territory. When I'd gone several steps, one of them called after me, "Where's Larry Gedge?" He didn't sound as if he liked Larry any better than me.

I decided not to hear: if they really wanted to know, they could come and ask nicely. It was their turn to cross the grass.

They didn't bother. I wasn't particularly sorry. I had long ago learned that pilots were not all one great happy brotherhood. Pilots could be as bloody-minded to each other as any group on earth.

I climbed back into my seat in the Cherokee and sorted out my maps and flight plans for the return journey. I had four hours to do it in and it took me ten minutes. After that, I debated whether to go over to the stands and find some lunch, and decided I wasn't hungry. After that, I yawned. It was a habit.

I had been depressed for so long that it had become a permanent state of mind. Expectations might lift the edge of the cloud every time one took a new job, but life never turned out to be as good as the hopes. This was my sixth job since I'd gone to learn flying with stars in my eyes, my fourth since the stars had faded for good. I had thought that taxi flying might be interesting, and after crop spraying, which I'd been doing last, anything would be; and perhaps it would indeed be interesting, but if I'd thought it might be free of gripe and bad temper I'd been kidding myself. For here it all was, as usual. Squabbling passengers and belligerent competitors and no discernible joy anywhere.

There was a small buffet on the side of the fuselage and the jar and sound of someone stepping up onto the wing. The slightly open door was pushed wide with a crash, and into its space appeared a girl, bending at the waist and knees and neck so that she could look inside and across at me.

She was slim and dark-haired and she was wearing large square sunglasses. Also she had on a blue linen dress and long white boots. She looked great. The afternoon instantly improved.

"You lousy bloody skunk," she said.

It really was one of those days.

2

"WOW," SHE said. "Wrong man." She took off the sunglasses and folded them away in the white handbag which hung from her shoulder by a thick red, white, and blue cord.

"Think nothing of it."

"Where's Larry?"

"Gone to Turkey."

"Gone?" she said blankly. "Do you mean literally gone already, or planning to go, or what?"

I looked at my watch. "Took off from Heathrow twenty minutes ago, I believe."

"Damn," she said forcefully. "Bloody damn."

She straightened up so that all I could see of her was from the waist down. A pleasant enough view for any poor aviator. The legs looked about twenty-three years old and there was nothing wrong with them.

She bent down again. Nothing wrong with the rest of her, either.

"When will he be back?"

"He had a three-year contract."

"Oh, *hell*." She stared at me in dismay for a few seconds, then said, "Can I come in there and talk to you for a minute?"

"Sure," I said, and moved my maps and stuff off Goldenberg's seat. She stepped down into the cockpit and slid expertly into place. By no means her first entrance into a light aircraft. I wondered about Larry. Lucky Larry.

"I suppose he didn't give you . . . a parcel . . . or anything . . . to give me, did he?" she said gloomily.

"Nothing, I'm afraid."

"He's an absolute beast, then. . . . Er, is he a friend of yours?"

"I've met him twice, that's all."

"He's pinched my hundred quid," she said bitterly.

"He's pinched? . . ."

"He bloody has. Not to mention my handbag and keys and everything." She stopped and compressed her mouth in anger. Then she added, "I left my handbag in this airplane three weeks ago, when we flew to Doncaster. And Larry has been saying ever since that he'll bring it on the next trip to the races and give it to Colin to give to me, and for three solid weeks he's kept on forgetting it. I suppose he knew he was going to Turkey, and he thought if he could put it off long enough he would never have to give my bag back."

"Colin . . . Colin Ross?" I asked.

She nodded abstractedly.

"Is he your husband?"

She looked startled, then laughed. "Good Lord, no. He's my brother. I saw him just now in the paddock and I said, 'Has he brought my handbag?' and he shook his head and started to say something, but I belted off over here in a fury without stopping to listen, and I suppose he was going to tell me it wasn't Larry who had come in the plane. . . . Oh, damn it, I *hate* being robbed. Colin would have lent him a hundred quid if he was that desperate. He didn't have to pinch it."

"It was a lot of money to have in a handbag," I suggested.

"Colin had just given it to me, you see. In the plane. Some owner had handed him a terrific present in readies, and he gave me a hundred of it to pay a bill with, which was really sweet of him, and I can hardly expect him to give me another hundred just because I was silly enough to leave the first one lying about. . . ." Her voice trailed off in depression. "The bill," she added wryly, "is for flying lessons."

I looked at her with interest. "How far have you got?"

"Oh, I've got my license," she said. "These were instrument-flying lessons. And radio navigation, and all that jazz. I've done about ninety-five hours, altogether. Spread over about four years, though, sad to say."

That put her in the experienced-beginner class and the dangerous time bracket. After eighty hours' flying, pilots are inclined to think they know enough. After a hundred hours, they are sure they don't. Between the two, the accident rate is at its peak.

She asked me several questions about the airplane, and I answered them. Then she said, "Well, there's no point in sitting here all afternoon," and began to lever herself out onto the wing. "Aren't you coming over to the races?"

"No." I shook my head.

"Oh, come on," she said. "Do."

The sun was shining and she was very pretty. I smiled and said "O.K.," and followed her out onto the grass. It is profitless now to speculate on the different course things would have taken if I'd stayed where I was.

I collected my jacket from the rear baggage compartment and locked all the doors and set off with her across the track. The man on the gate duly let me into the paddock, and Colin Ross's sister showed no sign of abandoning me once we were inside. Instead she diagnosed my almost total ignorance and seemed to be pleased to be able to start dispelling it.

"You see that brown horse over there," she said, steering me toward the parade-ring rails, "That one walking round the far end, Number Sixteen, that's Colin's mount in this race. It's come out a bit light but it looks well in its coat."

"It does?"

She looked at me in amusement. "Definitely."

"Shall I back it, then?"

"It's all a joke to you."

"No," I protested.

"Oh, yes, indeed." She nodded. "You're looking at this race meeting in the way I'd look at a lot of spiritualists. Disbelieving and a bit superior."

"Ouch."

"But what you're actually seeing is a large export industry in the process of marketing its wares."

"I'll remember that."

"And if the industry takes place out-of-doors on a nice fine sunny day with everyone enjoying themselves—well, so much the better."

"Put that way," I said, "it's a lot more jolly than a car factory."

"You will get involved," she said with certainty.

"No." I was equally definite.

She shook her head. "You will, you know, if you do much racecourse taxi work. It'll bust through that cool shell of yours and make you feel something, for a change."

I blinked. "Do you always talk like that to total strangers?"

"No," she said slowly, "I don't."

The bright little jockeys flooded into the parade ring and scattered to small earnest owner-trainer groups where there were a lot of serious conversations and much nodding of heads. On the instructions of Colin Ross's sister, I tried moderately hard to take it all seriously. Not with much success.

Colin Ross's sister . . .

"Do you have a name?" I asked.

"Often."

"Thanks."

She laughed. "It's Nancy. What's yours?"

"Matt Shore."

"Hmm. A flat mat name. Very suitable."

The jockeys were thrown up like confetti and landed in their saddles, and their spindly shining long-legged transporation skitttered its way out onto the track. Two-year-olds, Nancy said.

She walked me back toward the stands and proposed to smuggle me into the "Owners and Trainers." The large official at the bottom of the flight of steps beamed at her until his eyes disappeared, and he failed to inspect me for the right bit of cardboard.

It seemed that nearly everyone on the small rooftop stand knew Nancy, and obvious that they agreed with the beaming official's assessment. She introduced me to several people whose interest collapsed like a soufflé in a draft when they found I didn't understand their opening bids.

"He's a pilot," Nancy explained apologetically. "He flew Colin here today."

"Ah," they said. "Ah."

Two of my other passengers were there. Annie Villars was watching the horses canter past with an intent eye and a pursed mouth: the field-marshal element was showing strongly, the feminine camouflage in abeyance. Major Tyderman, planted firmly with his legs apart and his chin tucked well back into his neck, was scribbling notes into his race card. When he looked up, he saw us and made his way purposefully across.

"I say," he said to me, having forgotten my name. "Did I leave my *Sporting Life* over in the plane, do you know?"

"Yes, you did, Major."

"Blast," he said. "I made some notes on it. . . . Must get it, you know. Have to go across after this race."

"Would you like me to fetch it?" I asked.

"Well, that's very good of you, my dear chap. But—no—couldn't ask it. Walk will do me good."

"The aircraft's locked, Major," I said. "You'll need the keys." I took them out of my pocket and gave them to him.

"Right." He nodded stiffly. "Good."

The race started away off down the track and was all over long before I sorted out the colors of Colin Ross. In the event, it wasn't difficult. He had won.

"How's Midge?" Annie Villars said to Nancy, restoring her giant race glasses to their case.

"Oh, much better, thank you. Getting on splendidly."

"I'm so glad. She's had a bad time, poor girl."

Nancy nodded and smiled, and everyone trooped down the stairs to the ground.

"Well, now," Nancy said. "How about some coffee? And something to munch, perhaps?"

"You must have others you'd prefer to be with. . . . I won't get into trouble, you know, on my own."

Her lips twitched. "Today I need a bodyguard. I elected you for the job. Desert me if you like, but if you want to please, stick."

"Not difficult," I said.

"Great. Coffee, then."

It was iced coffee, rather good. Halfway through the turkey sandwiches, the reason Nancy wanted me with her drifted up to the small table where we sat and slobbered all over her. She fended off what looked to me like a random assembly of long hair, beard, beads, fringes, and a garment like a tablecloth with a hole in it, and yelled to me through the undergrowth, "Buddy, your job starts right now."

I stood up, reached out two hands, caught hold of an assortment of wool and hair, and pulled firmly backward. The result resolved itself into a surprised youngish man sitting down much more suddenly than he'd intended.

"Nancy," he said in an aggrieved voice.

"This is Chanter," she said to me. "He's never grown out of the hippie thing, as you can see."

"I'm an artist," he said. He had an embroidered band across his forehead and round his head: like the horses' bridles, I thought fleetingly. All the hair was clean, and there were shaven parts on his jaw just to prove that it wasn't from pure laziness that he let everything grow. On closer inspection, I was sure that it was indeed a dark green chenille tablecloth, with a central hole for his head. Underneath that he wore low-slung buckskin trousers fringed from hip to ankle, and a creepy crêpy dim mauve shirt curved to fit his concave stomach. Various necklaces and pendants on silver chains hung round his neck. Under all the splendor he had dirty bare feet.

"I went to art school with him," Nancy said resignedly. "That was in London. Now he's at Liverpool, just down the road. Any time I come racing up here, he turns up, too."

"Uh," Chanter said profoundly.

"Do you get grants forever?" I asked: not sneeringly; I simply wanted to know.

He was not offended. "Look, man, like, up here I'm the fuzz."

I nearly laughed. Nancy said, "You know what he means, then?"

"He teaches," I said.

"Yeah, man, that's what I said." He took one of the turkey sandwiches. His fingers were greenish with black streaks. Paint.

"You keep your impure thoughts off this little bird," he said to me, spitting out bits of bread. "She's strictly my territory. But strictly, man."

"Zat so?"

"Zat definitely—but definitely—is so, man."

"How come?"

He gave me a look which was as offbeat as his appearance.

"I've still got the salt to put on this little bird's tail," he said. "Shan't be satisfied till it's there. . . ."

Nancy was looking at him with an expression which meant that she didn't know whether to laugh at him or be afraid of him. She couldn't decide whether he was Chanter the amorous buffoon or Chanter the frustrated sex maniac. Nor could I. I understood her needing help when he was around.

"He only wants me because I won't," she said.

"The challenge bit." I nodded. "Affront to male pride, and all that."

"Practically every other girl has," she said.

"That makes it worse."

Chanter looked at me broodingly. "You're a drag, man. I mean, cubic."

"To each his scene," I said ironically.

He took the last of the sandwiches, turned his back studiously toward me, and said to Nancy, "Let's you and me lose this dross, huh?"

"Let's you and me do nothing of the sort, Chanter. If you want to tag along, Matt comes in the deal."

He scowled at the floor and then suddenly stood up so that all the fringes and beads danced and jingled.

"Come on, then. Let's get a look at the horses. Life's a-wasting."

"He really can draw," Nancy said as we followed the tablecloth out into the sunshine.

"I wouldn't doubt it. I'll bet half of what he does is caricature, though, with a strong element of cruelty."

"How d'you know?" she said, startled.

"He just seems like that."

He padded along beside us in his bare feet and was a sufficiently unusual sight on a racecourse to attract a barrage of stares, ranging from amusement to apoplexy. He didn't seem to notice. Nancy looked as if she were long used to it.

We came to a rest against the parade-ring rails, where Chanter rested his elbows and exercised his voice.

"Horses," he said. "I'm not for the Stubbs and Munnings thing. When I see a racehorse, I see a machine, and that's what I paint, a horse-shaped machine with pistons thumping away and muscle fibers like connecting rods and a crack in the crankcase with the oil dripping away drop by drop into the body cavity—" He broke off abruptly, but with the same breath finished, "How's your sister?"

"She's much better," Nancy said, not seeming to see any great change of subject. "She's really quite well now."

"Good," he said, and went straight on with his lecture. "And then I draw some distant bulging stands with hats flying off and everyone cheering, and all the time the machine is bursting its gut. . . . I see components, I see what's happening to the bits . . . the stresses. . . . I see colors in components, too. . . . Nothing on earth is a whole . . . nothing is ever what it seems . . . everything is components." He stopped abruptly, thinking about what he'd said.

After a suitably appreciative pause, I asked, "Do you ever sell your paintings?"

"Sell them?" He gave me a scornful, superior stare. "No, I don't. Money is disgusting."

"It's more disgusting when you haven't got it," Nancy said.

"You're a renegade, girl," he said fiercely.

"Love on a crust," she said, "is fine when you're twenty, but pretty squalid when you're sixty."

"I don't intend to be sixty. Sixty is strictly for grandfathers. Not my scene at all."

We turned away from the rails and came face to face with Major Tyderman, who was carrying his *Sporting Life* and holding out the aircraft's keys. His gaze swept over Chanter and he controlled himself admirably. Not a twitch.

He handed me the keys, nodded, glanced once more at Chanter, and retreated in good order.

Even for Nancy's sake, the official wouldn't let Chanter up the steps to the "Owners and Trainers." We watched at grass level with Chanter muttering "stinking bourgeois" at regular intervals.

Colin Ross finished second. The crowd booed and tore up a lot of tickets. Nancy looked as though she were long used to that, too.

Between the next two races, we sat on the grass while Chanter gave us the uninterrupted benefit of his views on the evils of money, racism, war, religion, and marriage. It was regulation stuff, nothing new. I didn't say I thought so. During the discourse, he twice without warning stretched over and put his hand on Nancy's breast. Each time, without surprise, she picked if off again by the wrist and threw it back at him. Neither of them seemed to think it needed comment.

After the next race (Colin was third), Chanter remarked that his throat was dry, and Nancy and I obediently followed him off to the Tattersall's bar for lubrication. Coca-Colas for three, splashed out of the bottles by an overworked barmaid. Chanter busily juggled the three glasses so that it was I who paid, which figured.

The bar was only half full but a great deal of space and attention was being taken up by one man, a large tough-looking individual with a penetrating Australian accent. He had an obviously new white plaster cast on his leg and a pair of crutches which he hadn't mastered. His loud laugh rose above the general buzz as he constantly apologized for knocking into people.

"Haven't got the hang of these props yet. . . ."

Chanter regarded him, as he did most things, with some disfavor.

The large Australian went on explaining his state to two receptive acquaintances.

"Mind you, can't say I'm sorry I broke my ankle. Best investment I ever made." The laugh rang out infectiously and most people in the bar began to grin. Not Chanter, of course.

"See, I only paid my premium the week before, and then I fell down these steps and I got a thousand quid for it. Now that ain't whistling, that ain't, eh? A thousand bleeding quid for falling down a flight of steps." He laughed again hugely, enjoying the joke. "Come on, mates," he said, "drink up, and let's go and invest some of this manna from heaven on my good friend Kenny Bayst."

I jumped a fraction and looked at my watch. Coming up to three-thirty. Kenny Bayst clearly hadn't told his good friend not to speculate. Absolutely none of my business. Telling him myself would be the worst favor I could do for Kenny Bayst.

The large Australian swung himself out of the bar, followed by the two mates. Chanter's curiosity overcame his disinclination to show himself at a loss.

"Who," he said crossly, "is going to give that schmo a thousand quid for breaking his ankle?"

Nancy smiled. "It's a new insurance fund, specially for people who go racing. Accident insurance. I don't really know. I've heard one or two people mention it lately."

"Insurance is immoral," Chanter said dogmatically, sliding round behind her and laying his hand flat on her stomach. Nancy picked it off and stepped away. As a bodyguard, I didn't seem to be doing much good.

Nancy said she particularly wanted to see this race properly, and left Chanter looking moody at the bottom of the staircase. Without asking her, I followed her up the steps: a period alone with Chanter held no attractions.

Kenny Bayst, according to my slantwise look at Nancy's race card, was riding a horse called Rudiments: Number 7, owned by the Duke of Wessex, trained by Miss Villars, carrying olive green with silver crossbelts and cap. I watched the horse canter down past the stands on the olive-green grass and reflected that the Duke of Wessex had chosen colors which were as easy to distinguish as coal on a black night.

I said to Nancy, "What did Rudiments do in his last race?"

"Hmm?" she said absent-mindedly, all her attention on the rose-pink-and-white shape of her brother. "Did you say Rudiments?"

"That's right. I brought Kenny Bayst and Annie Villars here, as well."

"Oh. I see." She looked down at her race card. "Last time out . . . it won. Time before that, it won. Time before that, it came fourth."

"It's good, then?"

"Fairly, I suppose." She wrinkled her nose at me. "I told you you'd get involved."

I shook my head. "Just curious."

"Same thing."

"Is it favorite?"

"No, Colin is. But—you can see over there, on that big board, see?—Rudiments is second favorite on the Tote at about three to one."

"Well," I said, "what does it mean, to lay a horse?"

"It means to stand a bet. It's what bookmakers do. What the Tote does, really, come to that."

"Can people do it who aren't bookmakers?"

"Oh, sure. They do. Say the bookmakers are offering three to one, and you yourself don't think the horse will win, you could say to your friends, I'll lay you four to one; so they'd bet with you because you were offering more. Also, no betting tax. Private wager, you see."

"And if the horse wins, you pay out?"

"You sure do."

"I see," I said. And I did. Eric Goldenberg had laid Rudiments the last time it had run because Kenny Bayst had agreed to lose, and then he'd gone and won. Their tempers were still on the dicky side as a result; and they had been arguing today about whether or not to try again.

"Colin thinks he'll win this," Nancy said. "I do hope so."

Bonanza for Bayst, I thought.

It was a seven-furlong race, it seemed. The horses accelerated from standing to 30 m.p.h. in times which would have left a Porsche gasping. When they swung away round the far bend, Rudiments was as far as I was concerned invisible, and until the last hundred yards I didn't see him once. Then all of a sudden there he was, boxed in in a bunch on the rails and unable to get past Colin Ross directly in front.

Kenny didn't find his opening. He finished the race in third place, still pinned in by Colin in front and a dappled gray alongside. I couldn't begin to tell whether or not he had done it on purpose.

"Wasn't that *great?*" Nancy exclaimed to the world in general, and a woman on the far side of her agreed that it was, and asked after the health or her sister Midge.

"Oh, she's fine, thanks," Nancy said. She turned to me, and there was less joy in her eyes than in her voice. "Come over here," she said. "You can see them unsaddling the winner."

The "Owners and Trainers" turned out to be on the roof of the weighing room. We leaned over the rails at the front and watched Colin and Kenny unbuckle the saddle girths, loop the saddles over their arms, pat their steaming horses, and disappear into the weighing room. The group in the winner's enclosure were busy slapping backs and unburdening to the press. The group in the third enclosure wore small tight smiles and faraway eyes. I still couldn't tell if they were ecstatic and hiding it, or livid and ditto.

The horses were led away and the groups dispersed. In their place appeared Chanter, staring up and waving his arm.

"Come on down!" he shouted.

"No inhibitions, that's his trouble," Nancy said. "If we don't go down, he'll just go on shouting."

He did. An official strode up manfully to ask him to belt up and buzz off, but it was like ripples trying to push over Bass Rock.

"Come on down, Nancy!" Fortissimo.

She pushed herself away from the rails and took enough steps to be out of his sight.

"Stay with me," she said. It was more than half a question.

"If you want it."

"You've seen what he's like. And he's been mild today. Mild. Thanks to you."

"I've done absolutely nothing."

"You're here."

"Why do you come to Haydock, if he always bothers you too much?"

"Because I'm bloody well not letting him frighten me away."

"He loves you," I said.

"No. Can't you tell the difference, for God's sake?"

"Yes," I said.

She looked startled, then shook her head. "He loves Chanter, full stop."

She took three more steps toward the stairs, then stopped again.

"Why is it that I talk to you as if I'd known you for years?"

To a certain extent I knew, but I smiled and shook my head. No one cares to say straight out that it's because one is as negative as wallpaper.

Chanter's plaintive voice floated up the steps. "Nancy, come on down. . . ."

She took another step, and then stopped again. "Will you do me another favor? I'm staying up here a few more days with an aunt, but I bought a present for Midge this morning and I've given it to Colin to take home. But he's got a memory like a string vest for everything except horses, so would you check with him that he hasn't left it in the changing room, before you take off?"

"Sure," I said. "Your sister . . . I gather she's been ill."

She looked away up the sun-filled sky and down again and straight at me, and in a shattering moment of awareness I saw the pain and the cracks behind the bright public façade.

"Has been. Will be," she said. "She's got leukemia."

After a pause, she swallowed and added the unbearable bit.

"She's my identical twin."

3

AFTER THE fifth race, Chanter gloomily announced that about fifty plastic students were waiting for him to pat their egos and that although he despised the system he was likely to find eating a problem if he actually got the sack. His farewell to Nancy consisted in wiping his hands all over her, front and back, and giving her an openmouthed kiss which, owing to her split-second evasive action, landed on her ear.

He glared at me as if it were my fault. Nancy not relenting, he scowled at her and muttered something about salt, then twirled around on his bare heel, so that the tablecloth and all the hair and fringes and beads swung out with centrifugal force, and strode away at high speed toward the exit.

"The soles of his feet are like leather," she said. "Disgusting." But from the hint of indulgence in her face I gathered that Chanter's cause wasn't entirely lost.

She said she was thirsty again and could do with a Coke, and since she seemed to want me still to tag along, I tagged. This time, without Chanter, we went to the members' bar in the Club enclosure, the small downstairs one that was open to the main entrance hall.

The man in the plaster cast was there again. Different audience. Same story. His big cheerful booming voice filled the little bar and echoed round the whole hall outside.

"You can't hear yourself think," Nancy said.

In a huddle in a far corner were Major Tyderman and Eric Goldenberg, sitting at a small table with what looked like treble whiskies in front of them. Their heads were bent toward each other, close, almost touching, so that they could each hear what the other was saying amid the din, yet not be overheard. Relations between them didn't seem to be at their most cordial. There was a great deal of rigidity in their downbent faces, and no friendliness in the small flicking glances they occasionally gave each other.

"The *Sporting Life* man," Nancy said, following my gaze.

"Yes. The big one is a passenger, too."

"They don't look madly happy."

"They weren't madly happy coming up here, either."

"Owners of chronic losers?"

"No—well, I don't think so. They came up because of that horse, Rudiments, which Kenny Bayst rode for Annie Villars, but they aren't down in the race card as its owners."

She flicked back through her card. "Rudiments. Duke of Wessex. Well, neither of those two is him, poor old booby."

"Who, the Duke?"

"Yes," she said. "Actually, I suppose he isn't all that old, but he's dreadfully dim. Big important-looking man with a big important-looking rank, and as sweet as they come, really, but there's nothing but cotton wool upstairs."

"You know him well?"

"I've met him often."

"Subtle difference."

"Yes."

The two men scraped back their chairs and began to make their way out of the bar. The man in the plaster cast caught sight of them and his big smile grew even bigger.

"Say, if it isn't Eric—Eric Goldenberg, of all people. Come over here, me old sport, come and have a drink."

Goldenberg looked less than enthusiastic at the invitation, and the Major sidled away quickly to avoid being included, giving the Australian a glance full of the dislike of the military for the flamboyant.

The man in the cast put one arm clumsily round Goldenberg's shoulder, the crutch swinging out widely and knocking against Nancy.

"Say," he said. "Sorry, lady. I haven't got the hang of these things yet."

"That's all right," she said, and Goldenberg said something to him that I couldn't hear, and before we knew where we were we had been encompassed into the Australian's circle and he was busy ordering drinks all round.

Close to, he was a strange-looking man because his face and hair were almost colorless. The skin was whitish, the scalp, half bald, was fringed by silky hair that had been fair and was turning white, the eyelashes and eyebrows made no contrast, and the lips of the smiling mouth were creamy pale. He looked like a man made up to take the part of a large cheerful ghost. His name, it appeared, was Acey Jones.

"Aw, come on," he said to me in disgust. "Coke is for milksops, not men." Even his eyes were pale: a light indeterminate bluey gray.

"Just lay off him, Ace," Goldenberg said. "He's flying me home. A drunken pilot I can do without."

"A pilot, eh?" The big voice broadcast the information to about fifty people who weren't in the least interested. "One of the flyboys? Most pilots I know are a bunch of proper tearaways. Live hard, love hard, drink hard. Real characters, those guys." He said it with an expansive smile which hid the implied slight. "C'mon now, sport, live dangerously. Don't disillusion all these people."

"Beer, then, please," I said.

Nancy was equally scornful, but for opposite reasons. "Why did you climb down?"

"Antagonizing people when you don't have to is like casting your garbage on the waters. One day it may come floating back, smelling worse."

She laughed. "Chanter would say that was immoral. Stands must be made on principles."

"I won't drink more than half of the beer. Will that do?"

"You're impossible."

Acey Jones handed me the glass and watched me take a mouthful, and went on a bit about hell-raising and beating up the skies and generally living the life of a high-powered gypsy. He made it sound very attractive, and his audience smiled and nodded their heads and none of them seemed to know that the picture was fifty years out of date, and that the best thing a pilot can be is careful: sober, meticulous, receptive, and careful. There are old pilots and foolish pilots, but no old foolish pilots. Me, I was old, young, wise, foolish, thirty-four. Also depressed, divorced, and broke.

After aviation, Acey Jones switched back to insurance and told Goldenberg and Nancy and me and the fifty other people about getting a thousand pounds for breaking his ankle, and we had to listen to it all again, reacting with the best we could do in surprised appreciation.

"No, look—no kidding, sport," he said to Goldenberg, with his first sign of seriousness. "You want to get yourself signed up with this outfit. Best fiver I've ever spent . . . ."

Several of the fifty onlookers edged nearer to listen, and Nancy and I filtered toward the outside of the group. I put down the tasted beer on an inconspicuous table out in the hall while Nancy dispatched the bottom half of her Coke, and from there we drifted out into the air.

The sun was still shining, but the small round white clouds were expanding into bigger round clouds with dark gray centers. I looked at my watch. Four-twenty. Still nearly an hour until the time the Major wanted to leave. The longer we stayed, the bumpier the ride was likely to be, because the afternoon forecast for scattered thunderstorms looked accurate.

"Cu-nims forming," Nancy said, watching them. "Nasty."

We went and watched her brother get up on his mount for the last race, and then we went up on the "Owners and Trainers" and watched him win it, and that was about that. She said goodbye to me near the bottom of the steps, outside the weighing room.

"Thanks for the escort duty. . . ."

"Enjoyed it. . . ."

She had smooth gilded skin and grayish-brown eyes. Straight dark eyebrows. Not much lipstick. No scent. Very much the opposite of my blond, painted, and departed wife.

"I expect," she said, "that we'll meet again, because I sometimes fly with Colin if there's a spare seat."

"Do you ever take him yourself?"

"Good Lord, no." She laughed. "He wouldn't trust me to get him there on time. And anyway there are too many days when the weather is beyond what I can do. Maybe one day, though. . . ."

She held out her hand and I shook it. A grip very like her brother's, and just as brief.

"See you, then," she said.

"I hope so."

She nodded with a faint smile and went away. I watched her neat blue-and-white back view and stifled a sudden unexpected inclination to run after her and give her a Chanter-type farewell.

When I walked across the track toward the airplane, I met Kenny Bayst coming back from it with his raincoat over his arm. His skin was blotched pink again with fury, clashing with his carroty hair.

"I'm not coming back with you," he said tightly. "You tell Miss Annie effing Villars that I'm not coming back with you. There's no bloody pleasing her. Last time I nearly got the push for winning, and this time I nearly got the push for not winning. You'd think that both times I'd had the slightest choice in the matter. I'll tell you straight, sport, I'm not coming back in your bloody little airplane having them gripe, gripe, gripe at me all the way back."

"All right," I said. I didn't blame him.

"I've just been over to fetch my raincoat. I'll go home by train—or get a lift."

"Raincoat . . . but the aircraft is locked."

"No, it isn't. I just got my raincoat out of the back. Now, you tell them I've had enough, right?"

I nodded, and while he hurried off I walked on toward the airplane, a bit annoyed. Major Tyderman should have locked up again after he had fetched his *Sporting Life*, but apparently he hadn't.

Both the doors on the port side were unlocked, the passenger door and the baggage locker. I wasn't too pleased, because Derrydowns had told me explicitly never to leave the aircraft open, as they'd had damage done by small boys on several occasions: but all looked well and there were no signs of sticky fingers.

I did the external checks again and glanced over the flight plan for the return. If we had to avoid too many thunderclouds, it might take a little longer to reach Newmarket, but unless there was one settled and active over the landing field there should be no problem.

The passengers of the two Polyplane aircraft assembled by ones and twos, shoveled themselves inside, shut the doors, and were trundled down to the far end of the course. One after the other, the two airplanes raced back over the grass and lifted away, wheeling like black darts against the blue, gray, and white patchwork of the sky.

Annie Villars came first of my lot. Alone, composed, polite; giving nothing away. She handed me her coat and binoculars and I stored them for her. She thanked me. The deceptive mild brown eyes held a certain blankness, and every few seconds a spasmodic tightening belied the gentle set of her mouth. A formidable lady, I thought. What was more, she herself knew it. She was so conscious of the strength and range of her power that she deliberately manufactured the disarming exterior in order not exactly to hide it, but to make it palatable. Made a nice change, I thought ironically, from all those who put up a big tough front to disguise their inner lack.

"Kenny Bayst asked me to tell you that he has got a lift home to Newmarket and won't be coming back by air," I said.

A tiny flash of fire in the brown eyes. The gentle voice, completely controlled, said, "I'm not surprised." She climbed into the airplane and strapped herself into her seat and sat there in silence, looking out over the emptying racecourse with eyes that weren't concentrating on the grass and the trees.

Tyderman and Goldenberg returned together, still deep in discussion. The Major's side mostly consisted of decisive nods, but words were pouring out of Goldenberg. Also he was past worrying about what I overheard.

"I would be surprised if the little shit hasn't been double-crossing us all the time and collecting from some bookmaker or other even more than he got from us. Making fools of us, that's what he's been doing. I'll murder the little sod. I told him so, too."

"What did he say?" the Major asked.

"Said I wouldn't get the chance. Cocky little bastard."

They thrust their gear angrily into the baggage compartment and stood talking by the rear door in voices rumbling like the distant thunder.

Colin Ross came last, slight and inconspicuous, still wearing the faded jeans and the now crumpled sweat shirt.

I went a few steps to meet him. "Your sister Nancy asked me to check with you whether you had remembered to bring the present for Midge."

"Oh, damn. . . ." More than irritation in his voice, there was weariness. He had ridden six hard races, won three of them. He looked as if a toddler could knock him down.

"I'll get it for you, if you like."

"Would you?" He hesitated, then with a tired flap of his wrist said, "Well, I'd be grateful. Go into the weighing room and ask for my valet, Ginger Mundy. The parcel's on the shelf over my peg. He'll get it for you."

I nodded and went back across the track. The parcel, easily found, proved to be a little smaller than a shoe box and was wrapped in pink-and-gold paper with a pink ribbon bow. I took it over to the airplane, and Colin put it on Kenny Bayst's empty seat.

The Major had already strapped himself in and was drumming with his fingers on his binocular case, which was as usual slung around him. His body was still stiff with tension. I wondered if he ever relaxed.

Goldenberg waited without a smile while I clambered across into my seat, then followed me in and clipped shut the door in gloomy silence. I sighed, started the engine, and taxied down to the far end of the course. Ready for takeoff, I turned round to my passengers and tried a bright smile.

"All set?"

I got three grudging nods for my pains. Colin Ross was asleep. I took the hilarious party off the ground without enthusiasm, skirted the Manchester zone, and pointed the nose in the general direction of Newmarket. Once up in the sky, it was all too clear that the air had become highly unstable. At lower levels, rising pockets of heat from the built-up areas bumped the airplane about like a puppet, and to enormous heights great heaps of cumulo-nimbus cloud were boiling up all round the horizon.

Airsick-making weather. I looked round to see if an issue of waterproof bags was going to be required. Needn't have bothered. Colin was still asleep, and the other three had too much on their minds to worry about a few lurches. I told Annie Villars where the bags were to be found if wanted, and she seemed to think I had insulted her.

Although by four thousand feet the worst of the bumps were below us, the flight was a bit like a bending race as I tracked left and right to avoid the dark towering cloud masses. Mostly we stayed in the sunshine: occasionally raced through the small veiling clouds which were dotted among the big ones. I wanted to avoid even the medium-sized harmless ones, as these sometimes hid a dangerous whopper just behind, and at 150 m.p.h. there was little chance to dodge. Inside every well-grown cumulo-nimbus, there were vertical rushing air currents which could lift and drop even an airliner like a yo-yo. Also one could meet hailstones and freezing rain. Nobody's idea of a jolly playground. So it was a good idea to avoid the black churning brutes, but it was a rougher ride than one should aim for with passengers.

Everyone knows the horrible skin-prickling heart-thudding feeling when the normal suddenly goes wrong. Fear, it's called. The best place to feel it is not with a jerk at four thousand feet in a battlefield of cu-nims.

I was used to far worse weather; to bad, beastly, even lethal weather. It wasn't the state of the sky which distracted me, which set the fierce little adrenalin-packed alarm bell ringing like crazy.

There was something wrong with the airplane.

Nothing much. I couldn't even tell what it was. But something. Something . . .

My instinct for safety was highly developed. Overdeveloped, many had said when it had got me into trouble. Bloody coward was how they'd put it.

You couldn't ignore it, though. When the instinct switched to danger, you couldn't risk ignoring it, not with passengers on board. What you could do when you were alone was a different matter, but civil commercial pilots seldom got a chance to fly alone.

Nothing wrong with the instruments. Nothing wrong with the engine.

Something wrong with the flying controls.

When I swerved gently to avoid yet another lurking cu-nim, the nose of the aircraft dropped and I had a shade of difficulty pulling it up again. Once level, nothing seemed wrong. All the gauges seemed right. Only the instinct remained. Instinct and the memory of a slightly sluggish response.

The next time I made a turn, the same thing happened. The nose wanted to drop, and it needed more pressure than it should have done to hold it level. At the third turn, it was worse.

I looked down at the map on my knees. We were twenty minutes out of Haydock . . . south of Matlock . . . approaching Nottingham. Another eighty nautical miles to Newmarket.

It was the hinged part of the tail plane which raised or lowered the aircraft's nose. The elevators, they were called. They were linked by wires to the control column in such a way that when you pushed the control column forward the tail went up and tipped the nose down. And vice versa.

The wires ran through rings and over pulleys, between the cabin floor and the outer skin of the fuselage. There wasn't supposed to be any friction.

Friction was what I could feel.

I thought perhaps one of the wires had somehow come off one of the pulleys during the bumpy ride. I'd never heard of it happening before, but that didn't mean it couldn't. Or perhaps a whole pulley had come adrift, or had broken in half. . . . If something was rolling around loose, it could affect the controls fairly seriously.

I turned to the cheerful company.

"I'm very sorry, but there will be a short delay on the journey. We're going to land for a while at the East Midlands Airport, near Nottingham, while I get a quick precautionary check done on the aircraft."

I met opposition.

Goldenberg said belligerently, "I can't see anything wrong." His eyes swept over the gauges, noticing all the needles pointing to the green safety segments on all the engine instruments. "It all looks the same as it always does."

"Are you sure it's necessary?" Annie Villars said. "I particularly want to get back to see my horses at evening stables."

The Major said "Damn it all!" fiercely and frowned heavily and looked more tense than ever.

They woke up Colin Ross.

"The pilot wants to land here and make what he calls a precautionary check. We want to go straight on. We don't want to waste time. There isn't anything wrong with the plane, as far as we can see. . . . "

Colin Ross's voice came across, clear and decisive. "If he says we're going down, we're going down. He's the boss."

I looked round at them. Except for Colin, they were all more moody and gloomy than ever. Colin unexpectedly gave me a flicker of a wink. I grinned as much to myself as to him, called up East Midlands on the radio, announced our intention to land, and asked them to arrange for a mechanic to be available for a check.

On the way down, I regretted it. The friction seemed no worse: if anything, it was better. Even in the turbulent air near the ground, I had no great trouble in moving the elevators. I'd made a fool of myself and the passengers would be furious and Derrydowns would be scathing about the unnecessary expense, and at any time at all I would be looking for my seventh job.

It was a normal landing. I parked where directed on the apron and suggested everyone get out and go into the airport for a drink, as the check would take half an hour, and maybe more.

They were by then increasingly annoyed. Up in the air, they must have had a lingering doubt that I was right about landing. Safe on the ground, they were becoming sure it was unnecessary.

I walked some of the way across the tarmac with them toward the airport passenger doors, then peeled off to go to the control office for the routine report after landing, and to ask for the mechanic to come for a look-see as soon as possible. I would fetch them from the bar, I said, once the check was done.

"Hurry it up," Goldenberg said rudely.

"Most annoying. Most annoying indeed." The Major.

"I was away last night. . . . Particularly wanted to get back early this evening. Might as well go by road, no point in paying for speed if you don't get it." Annie Villars' irritation overcoming the velvet glove.

Colin Ross said, "If your horse coughs, don't race it."

The others looked at him sharply. I said "Thanks" gratefully, and bore off at a tangent to the left. I saw them out of the side of my vision, looking briefly back toward the aircraft and then walking unenthusiastically toward the big glass doors.

There was a crack behind me like a snapping branch, and a monstrous boom, and a roaring gust of air.

I'd heard that sequence before. I spun round, appalled.

Where there had stood a smart little blue-and-white Cherokee there was an exploding ball of fire.

4

THE BOMB had taken a fraction of a second to detonate. The public impact lasted three days. The investigations dragged on for weeks.

Predictably, the dailies went to town on "COLIN ROSS ESCAPES DEATH BY ONE MINUTE" and "CHAMPION JOCKEY WINS RACE AGAINST TIME." Annie Villars, looking particularly sweet and frail, said in a television news interview that we had all been fantastically lucky. Major Tyderman was quoted as saying, "Fortunately there was something wrong with the plane, and we landed for a check. Otherwise . . . " And Colin Ross had apparently finished his sentence for him: "Otherwise we would all have been raining down on Nottingham in little bits."

That was after they had recovered, of course. When I reached them at a run near the airport doors, their eyes were stretched wide and their faces were stiff with shock. Annie Villars' mouth had dropped open and she was shaking from head to foot. I put my hand on her arm. She looked at me blankly and then made a small mewing sound and crumpled against me in a thoroughly un-Napoleonic faint. I caught her on the way down and lifted her up in my arms to save her falling on the shower-soaked tarmac. She weighed even less than she looked.

"God," said Goldenberg automatically. "God." His mind and tongue seemed to be stuck on the single word.

The Major's mouth was trembling and he was losing the battle to keep it still with his teeth. Sweat stood out in fine drops on his forehead and he was breathing in short shocked gasps.

Holding Annie Villars, I stood beside them and watched the death throes of the airplane. The first explosion had blown it apart, and almost immediately the fuel tanks had ignited and finished the job. The wreckage lay strewn in burning twisted pieces over a radius of wet tarmac, the parts looking too small ever to have formed the whole. Rivers of burning petrol ran among them, and great curling orange-and-yellow flames roared round the largest piece, which looked like the front part of the cabin.

My seat. My hot, hot seat.

Trouble followed me around like the rats of Hamelin.

Colin Ross looked as shocked as the others, but his nerves were of sterner stuff. "Was that . . . a bomb?"

"Nothing but," I said flippantly.

He looked at me sharply. "It's not funny."

"It's not tragic, either," I said. "We're still here."

A lot of the stiffness left his face and body. The beginnings of a smile appeared. "So we are," he said.

Someone in the control tower had pressed the panic button. Fire engines screamed up, and foam poured out of the giant hoses onto the pathetic scraps. The equipment was designed to deal with jumbos. It took about ten seconds to reduce the Cherokee-sized flames to black memories.

Three or four airport cars buzzed around like gnats, and one filled with agitated officials dashed in our direction.

"Are you the people who came in that aircraft?"

The first of the questions. By no means the last. I knew what I was in for. I had been taken apart before.

"Which is the pilot? Will you come with us, then, and your passengers can go to the manager's office. . . . Is the lady injured?"

"Fainted," I said.

"Oh . . . " He hesitated. "Can someone else take her?" He looked at the others. Goldenberg, large and flabby; the Major, elderly; Colin, frail. His eyes passed over Colin and then went back, widening, the incredulity fighting against recognition.

"Excuse me . . . are you?"

"Ross," said Colin flatly. "Yes."

They rolled out the red carpet, after that. They produced smelling salts and a ground hostess for Annie Villars, stiff brandies for the Major and Goldenberg, autograph books for Colin Ross. The manager himself took charge of them. And someone excitedly rang up the national press.

The Board of Trade investigators were friendly and polite. As usual. And persistent, scrupulous, and ruthless. As usual.

"Why did you land at East Midlands?"

Friction.

"Had you any idea there was a bomb on board?"

No.

"Had you made a thorough preflight investigation?"

Yes.

"And no bomb?"

No.

Did I know that I was nevertheless responsible for the safety of the aircraft and could technically be held responsible for having initiated a flight with a bomb on board?

Yes.

We looked at each other. It was an odd rule. Very few people who took off with a bomb on board lived to be held responsible. The Board of Trade smiled, to show they knew it was silly to think anyone would take off with a bomb, knowing it was there.

"Did you lock the aircraft whenever you left it?"

I did.

"And did it remain locked?"

The knife was in. I told them about the Major. They already knew.

"He says he is sure that he relocked the doors," they said. "But even so wasn't it your responsibility to look after the safety of the aircraft, not his?"

Quite so.

"Wouldn't it have been prudent of you to accompany him to fetch the paper?"

No comment.

"The safety of the aircraft is the responsibility of the captain."

Whichever way you turned, it came back to that.

This was my second interview with the Board of Trade. The first, the day after the explosion, had been friendly and sympathetic, a fact-finding mission during which the word "responsibility" had not cropped up once. It had hovered delicately in the wings. Inevitably it would be brought on later and pinned to someone's chest.

"During the past three days, we have interviewed all your passengers, and none of them has any idea who would have wanted to kill them, or why. We now feel we must go more carefully into the matter of opportunity, so we do hope you won't mind answering what may be a lot of questions. Then we can piece together a statement for you, and we would be glad if you would sign it. . . ."

"Do all I can," I said. Dig my own grave. Again.

"They all agreed that the bomb must have been in the gift-wrapped parcel which you yourself carried on board."

Nice.

"And that the intended victim was Colin Ross."

I sucked my teeth.

"You don't think so?"

"I honestly have no idea who it was intended for," I said. "But I don't think the bomb was in the parcel."

"Why not?"

"His sister bought it, that morning."

"We know." He was a tall man, with inward-looking eyes, as if they were consulting a computer in his head, feeding in every answer he was given, and waiting for the circuits to click out a conclusion. There was no aggression anywhere in his manner, no vengeance in his motivation. A fact finder, a cause seeker: like a truffle hound. He knew the scent of truth. Nothing would entice him away.

"And it sat on a shelf in the changing room all afternoon," I said. "And no one is allowed into the changing room except jockeys and valets."

"We understand that that is so." He smiled. "Could the parcel have been the bomb? Weightwise?"

"I suppose so."

"Miss Nancy Ross says it contained a large fancy bottle of bath oil."

"No pieces in the wreckage?" I asked.

"Not a thing." The tall man's nose wrinkled. "I've seldom seen a more thorough disintegration."

We were sitting in what was called the crew room in the Derrydown office on the old R.A.F. airfield near Buckingham. Such money as Derrydowns spent on appearances began in the manager's office and ended in the passengers' waiting lounge across the hall. The crew room looked as if the paint and the walls were coming up to their silver wedding. The linoleum had long passed the age of consent. Three of the four cheap armchairs looked as if they had still to reach puberty, but the springs in the fourth were so badly broken that it was more comfortable to sit on the floor.

Much of the wall space was taken up by maps and weather charts and various "Notices to Airmen," several of them out of date. There was a duty roster upon which my name appeared with the utmost regularity, and a notice typed in red capitals to the effect that anyone who failed to take the aircraft's documents with him on a charter flight would get the sack. I had duly taken all the Cherokee's records and maintenance certificates with me, as the Air Navigation Order insisted. Now they were burned to a crisp. I hoped someone somewhere saw some sense in it.

The tall man looked carefully round the dingy room. The other—shorter, broader, silent—sat with his green bitten HB poised over his spiral-bound notebook.

"Mr. Shore, I undertand you hold an airline transport pilot's license. And a flight navigator's certificate."

He had been looking me up. I knew he would have.

I said flatly, "Yes."

"This taxi work is hardly—well, what you were intended for."

I shrugged.

"The highest possible qualifications. . . ." He shook his head. "You were trained by B.O.A.C. and flew for them for nine years. First officer. In line for captain. And then you left."

"Yes." And they never took you back. Policy decision.

Never.

He delicately consulted his notes. "And then you flew as captain for a private British airline until it went into liquidation? And after that for a South American airline, who, I believe, dismissed you. And then all last year a spot of gunrunning, and this spring some crop spraying. And now this."

They never let go. I wondered who had compiled the list.

"It wasn't guns. Food and medical supplies in, refugees and wounded out."

He smiled faintly. "To some remote African airstrip on dark nights? Being shot at?"

I looked at him.

He spread out his hands. "Yes, I know. All legal and respectable, and not our business, of course." He cleared his throat. "Weren't you the—er—the subject—of an investigation about four years ago? While you were flying for British Interport?"

I took in a slow breath. "Yes."

"Mmm." He looked up, down, and sideways. "I've read an outline of that case. They didn't suspend your license."

"No."

"Though, on the face of it, one might have expected them to."

I didn't answer.

"Did Interport pay the fine for you?"

"No."

"But they kept you on as captain. You were convicted of gross negligence, but they kept you on." It was halfway between a statement and a question.

"That's right," I said.

If he wanted all the details, he could read the full report. He knew it and I knew it. He wasn't going to get me to tell him.

He said, "Yes. . . . Well. Who put this bomb in the Cherokee? When and how?"

"I wish I knew."

His manner hadn't changed. His voice was still friendly. We both ignored his tentative shot at piling on the pressure.

"You stopped at White Waltham and Newbury. . . ."

"I didn't lock up at White Waltham. I parked on the grass outside the reception lounge. I could see the airplane most of the time, and it was only on the ground for half an hour. I got there early. . . . I can't see that anyone had a chance, or could rely on having a chance, to put a bomb on board at White Waltham."

"Newbury?"

"They all stayed in their seats except me. Colin Ross came. . . . We put his overnight bag in the front baggage locker. . . ."

The tall man shook his head. "The explosion was further back. Behind the captain's seat, at the very least. The blast evidence makes it certain. Some of the metal parts of the captain's seat were embedded in the instrument panel."

"One minute," I said reflectively. "Very nasty."

"Yes. . . . Who had an opportunity at Haydock?"

I sighed inwardly. "I suppose anyone, from the time I gave the keys to Major Tyderman until I went back to the aircraft."

"How long was that?"

I'd worked it out. "Getting on for three hours. But . . ."

"But what?"

"No one could have counted on the aircraft being left unlocked."

"Trying to wriggle out?"

"Do you think so?"

He dodged an answer, said: "I'll give it to you that no one could have known whether it would be locked or unlocked. You just made it easy."

"All right," I said. "If you'll also bear in mind that pickers and stealers unlock cars every day of the week, and that aircraft keys are the same type. Anyone who could manufacture and plant a bomb could open a little old lock."

"Possibly," he said, and repeated, "But you made it easy."

Damn Major Tyderman, I thought bleakly. Stupid, careless old fool. I stifled the thought that I probably would have gone across with him, or insisted on fetching his newpaper for him, if I hadn't been unwilling to walk away and leave Nancy.

"Who could have had access . . . leaving aside the matter of locks?"

I shrugged one shoulder. "All the world. They had only to walk across the track."

"The aircraft was parked opposite the stands, I believe, in full view of the crowds."

"Yes. About a hundred yards, in fact, from the stands. Not close enough for anyone to see exactly what someone was doing, if he seemed to be walking round peering in through the windows. People do that, you know, pretty often."

"You didn't notice anyone yourself?"

I shook my head. "I looked across several times during the afternoon. Just a casual glance, though. I wasn't thinking about trouble."

"Hmm." He reflected for a few seconds. Then he said, "Two of the Polyplanes were there as well, I believe."

"Yes."

"I think I'd better talk to the pilots, to see if they noticed anything."

I didn't comment. His eyes suddenly focused on mine, sharp and black. "Were they friendly?"

"The pilots? Not particularly."

"How's the feud?"

"What feud?"

He stared at me assessingly. "You're not that dumb. No one could work for Derrydowns and not know that they and Polyplanes are permanently engaged in scratching each other's eyes out."

I sighed. "I don't give a damn."

"You will when they start reporting you."

"Reporting me? For what? What do you mean?"

He smiled thinly. "If you infringe the rules by as much as one foot, Polyplanes will be on to us before your wheels have stopped rolling. They're doing their best to put Derrydowns out of business. Most of it we shrug off as simply spite. But if they catch you breaking the regulations, and can produce witnesses, we'd have to take action."

"Charming."

He nodded. "Aviation will never need a special police force to detect crime. Everyone is so busy informing on everyone else. Makes us laugh, sometimes."

"Or cry," I said.

"That, too." He nodded wryly. "There are no permanent friendships in aviation. The people you think are your friends are the first to deny they associate with you at the faintest hint of trouble. The cock crows until it's hoarse, in aviation." The bitterness in his voice was unmistakable. But impersonal, also.

"You don't approve."

"No. It makes our job easier, of course. But I like less and less the sight of people scrambling to save themselves at any cost to others. It diminishes them. They are small."

"You can't always blame them for not always wanting to be involved. Aviation law cases are so fierce, so unforgiving. . . ."

"Did your friends at Interport rally round and cheer you up?"

I thought back to those weeks of loneliness. "They waited to see."

He nodded. "Didn't want to be contaminated."

"It's a long time ago," I said.

"You never forget rejection," he said. "It's a trauma."

"Interport didn't reject me. They kept me on for another year, until they went bust. And," I added, "I didn't have anything to do with *that*."

He gently laughed. "Oh, I know. My masters the Government put on one of its great big squeezes, and by one means or another forced them out of business."

I didn't pursue it. The history of aviation was littered with the bodies of murdered air firms. Insolvency sat like a vulture in every board room in the industry and constantly pecked away at the bodies before they were dead. British Eagle, Handley Page, Beagle—the list of corpses was endless. Interport had been one of the largest, and Derrydowns, still struggling, one of the smallest, but their problems were identical. Huge inexorable costs. Fickle variable income. Write the sum in red.

I said, "There is one other place, of course, where the bomb could have been put on board." I stopped.

"Spell it out, then."

"Here."

The tall investigator and his silent friend with the pencil went down to the hangar to interview old Joe.

Harley called me into his office.

"Have they finished?"

"They've gone to ask Joe if he put the bomb in the Cherokee."

Harley was irritated, which was with him a common state of mind. "Ridiculous."

"Or if Larry did."

"*Larry* . . ."

"He left for Turkey that afternoon," I pointed out. "Would he have planted a legacy?"

"No." Short, snappy, and vehement.

"Why did he leave?"

"He wanted to." He gave me a sharp glance bordering on dislike. "You sound like the Board of Trade."

"Sorry," I said in conciliation. "Must be catching."

Harley's office dated back to a more prosperous past. There was a carpet of sorts on the floor and the walls had been painted within living memory, and his good-quality desk had mellowed instead of chipping. Limp blue curtains framed the big window looking out over the airfield and several good photographs of airplanes had been framed and hung. Customers, when they visited him, were allowed the nearly new lightweight armchair; crew sat on the wooden upright.

Harley himself was proprietor, manager, chief flying instructor, booking clerk, and window cleaner. His staff consisted of one qualified mechanic past retiring age, one part-time boy helper, one full-time taxi pilot (me), and one part-time pilot who switched from taxiing to teaching, whichever was required, and on alternate days taught a flying club twenty miles to the north.

Derrydowns' other assets had been, before the Cherokee blew up, three useful aircraft and one bright girl.

The remaining two aircraft were a small single-engine trainer and a twin-engine eight-year-old Aztec, equipped with every possible flying aid, for which Harley was paying through the nose on a five-year lease.

The girl, Honey, his brother's daughter, worked for love and peanuts and was the keystone which held up the arch. I knew her voice better than her face, as she sat up in the control tower all day directing such air traffic as came along. Betweentimes she typed all the letters, kept the records, did the accounts, answered the telephone if her uncle didn't, and collected landing fees from visiting pilots. She was reputed to be suffering from a broken heart about Larry and consequently came down from her crow's nest as seldom as possible.

"She's made puffballs out of her eyes, crying for that louse" was how my part-time colleague put it. "But you wait just a week or two. She'll lie down for you instead. Never refused a good pilot yet, our Honey hasn't."

"How about you?" I asked, amused.

"Me? She'd squeezed me like a lemon long before that God-damned Larry ever turned up."

Harley said crossly, "We've lost two charters since the bomb. They say the Aztec's too expensive; they would rather go by road." He ran his hand over his head. "There's another Cherokee Six up at Liverpool that's available to lease. I've just been talking to them on the phone. It sounds all right. They're bringing it across here tomorrow afternoon, so you can take it up when you get back from Newmarket and see what you think."

"How about the insurance on the old one?" I asked idly. "It would be cheaper in the long run to buy rather than lease."

"It was on hire-purchase," he said gloomily. "We'll be lucky if we get a penny. And it's not really your business."

Harley was slightly plump and slightly bald and just not quite forceful enough to lift Derrydowns up by its bootstraps. His manner to me was more bossy than friendly, a reaction I understood well enough.

"The last person on earth to put a bomb on any aircraft would be Joe," he said explosively. "He looks after them like a mother. He *polishes* them."

It was true. The Derrydowns aircraft sparkled outside and were shampooed inside. The engines ran like silk. The general slightly misleading air of prosperity which clung around the public face of the firm was mostly Joe's work.

The Board of Trade came back from the hangar looking vaguely sheepish. The rough side of Joe's tongue, I guessed. At sixty-nine and with savings in the bank, he was apt to lay down his own laws. He had taken exception to my theory that a pulley on the elevator wires had come adrift. No such thing was possible in one of his aircraft, he had told me stiffly, and I could take my four gold rings away and I knew what I could do with them. As I hadn't worn my captain's jacket for nearly two years, I told him the moths had beaten me to it, and although it was a feeble joke he gave me a less sour look and told me it couldn't have been a broken pulley, he was sure it couldn't, and if it was, it was the manufacturer's fault, not his.

"It saved Colin Ross's life," I pointed out. "You should be claiming a medal for it." Which opened his mouth and shut him up.

The Board of Trade trooped into Harley's office. The tall man sat in the armchair and Green Pencil on the hard one. Harley behind his desk. I leaned against the wall, on my feet.

"Well, now," said the tall man. "It seems as if everyone on this airfield had a chance to tamper with the Cherokee. Everyone in the company, and any customers who happened to be here that morning, and any member of the public wandering around for a look-see. We've assumed the bomb was aimed at Colin Ross, but we don't really know that. If it was, someone had a pretty accurate idea of when he would be in the aircraft."

"Last race four-thirty. He was riding in it," Harley said. "Doesn't take too much figuring to assume that at five-forty he'd be in the air."

"Five-forty-seven," said the tall man. "Actually."

"Any time about then," said Harley irritably.

"I wonder what the bomb was *in*," said the tall man reflectively. "Did you look inside the first-aid tin?"

"No," I said, startled. "I just checked that it was there. I've never looked inside it. Or inside the fire extinguishers, or under the seats or inside the life-jacket covers. . . ."

The tall man nodded. "It could have been in any of those places. Or it could, after all, have been in that fancy parcel."

"Ticking away," said Harley.

I peeled myself slowly off the wall. "Suppose," I said hesitantly, "suppose it wasn't in any of those places. Suppose it was deeper, out of sight. Somewhere between the cabin wall and the outside skin—like a limpet mine, for instance. Suppose that that bumpy ride—and all those turns I did to avoid the cu-nims—dislodged it, so that it was getting jammed in the elevator wires. . . . Suppose that was what I could feel—and why I decided to land—and that what saved us was the bomb itself."

5

THE NEXT day, I took five jockeys and trainers from Newmarket to Newcastle races and back in the Aztec, and listened to them grousing over the extra expense, and in the evening I tried out the replacement Cherokee, which flew permanently left wing down on the autopilot, had an unserviceable fuel-flow meter, and had an overload somewhere on the electrical circuit.

"It isn't very good," I told Harley. "It's old and noisy and it probably drinks fuel and I shouldn't think the battery's charging properly."

He interrupted me. "It flies. And it's cheap. And Joe will fix it. I'm taking it."

"Also it's orange and white, just like the Polyplanes."

He gave me an irritable glare. "I'm not blind. I know it is. And it's not surprising, considering it used to belong to them."

He waited for me to protest so that he could slap me down, so I didn't. I shrugged instead. If he wanted to admit to his bitterest rivals that his standards were down to one of their third-hand clapped-out old buggies, that was his business.

He signed the lease on the spot and gave it to the pilot who had brought the airplane to take back with him on the train, and the pilot smiled a pitying smile and went off shaking his head.

The orange-and-white Cherokee went down to the hangar for Joe to wave his wand over, and I walked round the perimeter track to home sweet home.

One caravan, pilots', for the use of. Larry had lived in it before me, and others before him: Harley's taxi pilots stayed, on average, eight months, and most of them settled for the caravan because it was easiest. It stood on a dusty square of concrete which had once been the floor of an R.A.F.

hut, and it was connected to the electricity, water, and drainage mains which had served the long-departed airmen.

As caravans go, it must once have held up its head, but generations of beer-drinking bachelors had left tiny teeth marks of bottle caps along the edges of all the fitments, and circular greasy head marks on the wall above every seat. Airport dirt had clogged the brown haircord upholstery into a grayish cake, relieved here and there by darker irregular stains. Shabby pin-ups of superhuman mammalian development were stuck to the walls with tape, and a scatter of torn-off patches of paint showed where dozens of others had been stuck before. Tired green curtains had opened and shut on a thousand hangovers. The flyblown mirror had stared back at a lot of disillusion, and the bedsprings sagged from the weight of a bored succession of pilots with nothing to do except Honey.

I had forgotten to get anything to eat. There was half a packet of cornflakes in the kitchen and a jar of instant coffee. Neither was much use, as yesterday's half pint of milk had gone sour in the heat. I damned it all and slouched on the two-seat approximation to a sofa, and resignedly dragged out of my pocket the two letters which had lain unopened there since that morning.

One was from a television rental firm who said they confirmed that they were transferring the rental from Larry's name to mine, as requested, and could I now be so good as to pay immediately the six weeks for which he was in arrears. The other from Susan, said briefly that I was late with the alimony yet again.

I put down both the letters and stared unseeingly through the opposite window toward the darkening summer sky. All the empty airfield stretched away into the dusk, calm, quiet, undemanding, and shadowy—everything I needed for a few repairs to the spirit. The only trouble was the process was taking longer than I'd expected. I wondered sometimes whether I'd ever get back to where I'd once been. Maybe if you'd hashed up your life as thoroughly as I had, there was never any going back. Maybe one day soon I'd stop wanting to. Maybe one day I would accept the unsatisfactory present not as a healing period but as all there was ever going to be. That would be a pity, I thought. A pity to let the void take over for always.

I had three pounds in my pocket and sixteen in the bank, but I had finally paid all my debts. The crippling fine, the divorce, and the mountainous bills Susan had run up everywhere in a cold orgy of hatred toward me in the last weeks we were together—everything had been settled. The house had always been in her name because of the nature of my job, and she had clung to that like a leech. She was still living in it, triumphant, collecting a quarter of everything I earned and writing sharp little letters if I didn't pay on the nail.

I didn't understand how love could curdle so abysmally: looking back, I still couldn't understand. We had screamed at each other: hit each other, intending to hurt. Yet when we married, at nineteen, we'd been entwined in tenderness, inseparable and sunny. When it started to go wrong, she said it was because I was away so much, long ten-day tours to the West Indies all the time, and all she had was her job as a doctor's secretary and the dull endless housework. In an uprush of affection and concern for her, I resigned from B.O.A.C. and joined Interport instead, where I flew short-haul trips, and spent most of my nights at home. The pay was a shade less good, the prospects a lot less good, but for about three months we were happier. After that, there was a long period in which we both tried to make the best of it, and a last six months in which we had torn each other's nerves and emotions to shreds.

Since then, I had tried more or less deliberately not to feel anything for anybody. Not to get involved. To be private, and apart, and cold. An ice pack after the tempest.

I hadn't done anything to improve the caravan, to stamp anything of myself upon it. I didn't suppose I would, because I didn't feel the need. I didn't want to get involved, not even with a caravan.

And certainly not with Tyderman, Goldenberg, Annie Villars, and Colin Ross.

All of them except Goldenberg were on my next racing trip.

I had spent two more days in the Aztec, chauffeuring some business executives on their regular monthly visit to subsidiary factories in Germany and Luxembourg, but by Saturday Joe had tarted up the replacement Cherokee, so I set off in that. The fuel-flow meter still resolutely pointed to naught, which was slightly optimistic, but the electrical fault had been cured: no overload now on the generator. And if it still flew one wing low, at least the wing in question sparkled with a new shine. The cabin smelt of soap and air freshener, and all the ashtrays were empty.

The passengers were to be collected that day at Cambridge, and although I flew into the airport half an hour early, the Major was already there, waiting on a seat in a corner of the entrance hall.

I saw him before he saw me, and as I walked toward him he took the binoculars out of their case and put them on the low table beside him. The binoculars were smaller than the case suggested. In went his hand again and out came a silver-and-pigskin flask. The Major took a six-second swig and, with a visible sigh, screwed the cap back into place.

I slowed down and let him get the binoculars back on top of his courage before I came to a halt beside him and said good morning.

"Oh. . . . Good morning," he said stiffly. He stood up, fastening the buckle of the case and giving it a pat as it swung into its usual facing-forward position on his stomach. "All set?"

"The others are not here yet. It's still early."

"Ah. No. Of course." He wiped his mustache carefully with his hand and tucked his chin back into his neck. "No bombs today, I hope?"

He wasn't altogether meaning to joke.

"No bombs," I assured him.

He nodded, not meeting my eyes. "Very upsetting, last Friday. Very upsetting, you know." He paused. "Nearly didn't come today, when I heard that Colin—er—" He stopped.

"I'll stay in the airplane all afternoon," I promised him.

The Major nodded again, sharply. "Had a Board of Trade fellow come to see me. Did you know that?"

"They told me so."

"Been to see you, too, I suppose."

"Yes."

"They get about a bit."

"They're very thorough. They'll go a hundred miles to get a single answer to a simple question."

He looked at me sharply. "Speaking from bitter experience?"

I hadn't known there was any feeling in my voice. I said, "I've been told they do."

He grunted. "Can't think why they don't leave it to the police."

No such luck, I thought. There was no police force in the world as tenacious as the British Board of Trade.

Annie Villars and Colin Ross arrived together, deep in a persuasive argument that was getting nowhere.

"Just say you'll ride my horses whenever you can."

". . . too many commitments."

"I'm not asking a great deal."

"There are reasons, Annie. Sorry, but no." He said it with an air of finality, and she looked startled and upset.

"Good morning," she said to me abstractedly. "Morning, Rupert."

"Morning, Annie," said the Major.

Colin Ross had achieved narrow pale-gray trousers and a blue open-necked shirt.

"Morning, Matt," he said.

The Major took a step forward, bristling like a terrier. "Did I hear you turning down Annie's proposition?"

"Yes, Major."

"Why?" he asked in an aggrieved tone. "Our money is as good as anyone else's, and her horses are always fit."

"I'm sorry, Major, but no. Just let's leave it at that."

The Major looked affronted and took Annie Villars off to see if the bar was open. Colin sighed and sprawled in a wooden armchair.

"God save me," he said, "from crooks."

I sat down, too. "She doesn't seem crooked to me."

"Who, Annie? She isn't really. Just not one-hundred-per-cent permanently scrupulous. No, it's that crummy slob Goldenberg that I don't like. She does what he says, a lot too much. I'm not taking indirect riding orders from him."

"Like Kenny Bayst?" I suggested.

He looked at me sideways. "The word gets around, I see. Kenny reckons he's well out of it. Well, I'm not stepping in." He paused reflectively. "The Board of Trade investigator who came to see me asked if I thought there was any significance in Bayst having cried off the return trip the other day."

"What did you say?"

"I said I didn't. Did you?"

"I confess I wondered, because he did go across to the airplane after the races, and he certainly felt murderous, but. . ."

"But," he agreed. "Would Kenny Bayst be cold-blooded enough to kill you and me as well?" He shook his head. "Not Kenny, I wouldn't have thought."

"And besides that," I said, nodding, "he only came to the steaming boil after he lost the three-thirty, and just how would he rustle up a bomb at Haydock in a little over one hour?"

"He would have to have arranged it in advance."

"That would mean that he knew he would lose the race. . . ."

"It's been done," said Colin dryly.

There was a pause. Then I said, "Anyway, I think we had it with us all the time. Right from before I left base."

He swiveled his head and considered it. "In that case . . . Larry?"

"Would he?"

"God knows. Sneaky fellow. Pinched Nancy's hundred quid. But a bomb . . . And what was the point?"

I shook my head.

Colin said, "Bombs are usually either political or someone's next of kin wanting to collect the insurance."

"Fanatics or family . . . " I stifled the beginnings of a yawn.

"You don't really care, do you?" he said.

"Not that much."

"It doesn't disturb you enough to wonder whether the bomb merchant will try again?"

"About as much as it's disturbing you."

He grinned. "Yes . . . well. It would be handy to know for sure whose name was on that one. One would look so damn silly taking fiddly precautions if it was the Major who finally got clobbered. Or you."

"Me?" I said in astonishment.

"Why not?"

I shook my head. "I don't stand in anyone's way to anything."

"Someone may think you do."

"Then they're nuts."

"It takes a nut—a regular psycho—to put a bomb in an airplane."

Tyderman and Annie Villars came back from the direction of the bar with two more people, a man and a woman.

"Oh, Christ," Colin said under his breath. "Here comes my own personal Chanter." He looked at me accusingly. "You didn't tell me who the other passengers were."

"I don't know them. Who are they? I don't do the bookings."

We stood up. The woman, who was in her thirties but dressed like a teen-ager, made a straight line for Colin and kissed him exuberantly on the cheek.

"Colin, darling, there was a spare seat and Annie said I could come. Wasn't that absolutely super of her?"

Colin glared at Annie, who pretended not to notice.

The girl-woman had a strong upper-class accent, white knee socks, a camel-colored high-waisted dress, several jingling gold barcelets, streaky long fair brown hair, a knock-you-down exotic scent, and an air of expecting everyone to curl up and die for her.

She latched her arm through Colin's so that he couldn't disentangle without giving offense, and said with a somehow unattractive gaiety, "Come along, everyone, let's take the plunge. Isn't it all just too unnerving, flying around with Colin these days?"

"You don't actually have to come," Colin said without quite disguising his wishes.

She seemed oblivious. "Darling," she said, "too riveting. Nothing would stop me."

She moved off toward the door, followed by the Major and Annie and the new man together, and finally by me. The new man was large and had the same air as the woman of expecting people to jump to it and smooth his path. The Major and Annie Villars were busy smoothing it, their ears bent deferentially to catch any falling crumbs of wisdom, their heads nodding in agreement over every opinion.

The two just-teen-age girls I had stationed beside the locked aircraft were still on duty, retained more by the promise of Colin's autographs than by my money. They got both, and were delighted. No one, they anxiously insisted, had even come close enough to ask what they were doing. No one could possibly have put a piece of chewing gum onto the airplane, let alone a bomb.

Colin, signing away, gave me a sidelong look of amusement and appreciation, and said safety came cheap at the price. He was less amused to find that the affectionate lady had stationed herself in one of the rear seats and was beckoning him to come and sit beside her.

"Who is she?" I asked.

"Fenella Payne-Percival. Fenella pain-in-the-neck."

I laughed. "And the man?"

"Duke of Wessex. Annie's got a horse running for him today."

"Not Rudiments again?"

He looked up in surprise from the second autograph book.

"Yes. That's right. Bit soon, I would have thought."

He finished the book and gave it back. "Kenny Bayst isn't riding it." His voice was dry.

"You don't say."

The passengers had sorted themselves out so that Annie and the Duke sat in the center seats, with the Major waiting beside the first two for me to get in before him. As I stepped up onto the wing he nodded his stiff little nod and pushed at his mustache. Less tense, slightly less rigid than last time. The owner was along instead of Goldenberg and Kenny wasn't there to stir things up. No coup today, I thought. No coup to go wrong.

The flight up was easy and uneventful, homing to the radio beacon on the coast at Ottringham and tracking away from it on a radial to Redcar. We landed without fuss on the racecourse, and the passengers yawned and unbuckled themselves.

"I wish every racecourse had a landing strip," Colin said with a sigh. "It makes the whole day so much easier. I hate all those dashes from airport to course by taxi."

The racecourses which catered to airplanes were in a minority, which seemed a shame considering there was room on most, if anyone cared enough. Harley constantly raved in frustration at having to land ten or fifteen miles away and fix up transportation for the passengers. All the conveniently placed R.A.F. airfields with superb runways that either refused to let private aircraft land at all or shut their doors firmly at 5 P.M. weekdays and all day on Saturdays had him on the verge of tears. As also did the airfields whose owners said they wouldn't take the responsibility of having an aircraft land there or take off if they didn't have a fire engine standing by, even though Harley's own insurance didn't require it.

"The English are as air-minded as earthworms," Harley said.

On the other hand, Honey had tacked a list to the office wall which started in big red letters "God Bless . . . " and continued with all the friendly and accommodating places like Kempton Park, which let you land up the five-furlong straight (except during five-furlong races), and R.A.F. stations like Wroughton and Leeming and Pershore, which really tried for you, and the airfields that could let you land when they were officially shut, and all the privately owned strips whose owners generously agreed to your using them any time you liked.

Harley's view of heaven was an open public landing field outside every town and a wind sock and a flat four furlongs on every racecourse. It wasn't much to ask, he said plaintively. Not in view of the dozens of enormous airfields which had been built during World War II and were now disused and wasted.

He could dream, I thought. There was never any money for such schemes, except in wars.

The passengers stretched themselves onto the grass. Fenella Payne-Percival made little up and down jumps of excitement like a small girl, the Major patted his binocular case reassuringly, Annie Villars efficiently picked up her own belongings and directed a look of melting feminine helplessness toward the Duke, Colin looked at his watch and smiled, and the Duke himself glanced interestedly around and said, "Nice day, what?"

A big man, he had a fine-looking head with thick graying hair, eyebrows beginning to sprout, and a strong square jaw, but there wasn't enough living stamped on his face for a man in his fifties, and I remembered what Nancy had said of him: sweet as they come, but nothing but cotton wool upstairs.

Colin said to me, "Are you coming into the paddock?"

I shook my head. "Better stay with the airplane this time."

The Duke said, "Won't you need some lunch, my dear chap?"

"It's kind of you, sir, but I often don't have any."

"Really?" He smiled. "Must have my lunch."

Annie Villars said, "We'll leave soon after the last. About a quarter to five."

"Right," I agreed.

"Doesn't give us time for a drink, Annie," complained the Duke.

She swallowed her irritation. "Any time after that, then."

"I'll be here," I said.

"Oh, do come on," said Fenella impatiently. "The pilot can look after himself, can't he? Let's get going, do. Come on, Colin, darling." She twined her arm in his again and he all but squirmed. They moved away toward the paddock obediently, with only Colin looking back. I laughed at the desperation on his face, and he stuck out his tongue.

There were three other aircraft parked in a row. One private, one from a Scottish taxi firm, and one Polyplane. All the pilots seemed to have gone in to the races, but when I climbed out halfway through the afternoon to stretch my legs, I found the Polyplane pilot standing ten yards away, staring at the Cherokee with narrowed eyes and smoking a cigarette.

He was one of the two who had been at Haydock. He seemed surprised that I was there.

"Hello," I said equably. Always a sucker.

He gave me the old hard stare. "Taking no chances today, I see."

I ignored the sneer in his voice. "That's right."

"We got rid of that aircraft," he said sarcastically, nodding toward it, "because we'd flown the guts out of it. It's only suitable now for minor operators like you."

"It shows signs of the way you flew it," I agreed politely: and that deadly insult did nothing toward cooling the feud.

He compressed his lips and flicked the end of his cigarette away into the grass. A thin trickle of blue smoke arose from among the tangled green blades. I watched it without comment. He knew as well as I did that smoking near parked aircraft was incredibly foolish, and on all airfields forbidden.

He said, "I'm surprised you take the risk of flying Colin Ross. If your firm are proved to be responsible for his death, you'll be out of business."

"He's not dead yet."

"If I were him, I wouldn't risk flying any more with Derrydowns."

"Did he, by any chance," I asked, "once fly with Polyplanes? Is all this sourness due to his having transferred to Derrydowns instead?"

He gave me a bitter stare. "No," he said.

I didn't believe him. He saw that I didn't. He turned on his heel and walked away.

Rudiments won the big race. The dim green colors streaked up the center of the track at the last possible moment and pushed Colin on the favorite into second place. I could hear the boos all the way from the stands.

An hour until the end of racing. I yawned, leaned back in my seat, and went to sleep.

A young voice saying "Excuse me" several times woke me up. I opened my eyes. He was about ten, slightly shy, ultra-well bred. Squatting down on the wing, he spoke through the open door.

"I say, I'm sorry to wake you, but my uncle wanted me to come over and fetch you. He said you hadn't had anything to eat all day. He thinks you ought to. And besides he's had a winner and he wants you to drink his health."

"Your uncle is remarkably kind," I said, "but I can't leave the airplane."

"Well, actually, he thought of that. I've brought my father's chauffeur over with me, and he is going to sit here for you until you come back." He smiled with genuine satisfaction at these arrangements.

I looked past him out of the door, and there, sure enough, was the chauffeur, all togged up in dark green with a shining peak to his cap.

"O.K.," I said. "I'll get my jacket."

He walked with me along to the paddock, through the gate, and across to the members' bar.

"Awfully nice chap, my uncle," he said.

"Unusually thoughtful," I agreed.

"Soft, my mother says," he said dispassionately. "He's her brother. They don't get along very well."

"What a pity."

"Oh, I don't know. If they were frightfully chummy, she would always be wanting to come with me when I go to stay with him. As it is, I go on my own, and we have some fantastic times, him and me. That's how I know how super he is." He paused. "Lots of people think he's terribly thick, I don't know why." There was a shade of anxiety in his young voice. "He's really awfully kind."

I reassured him. "I only met him this morning, but I think he's very nice."

His brow cleared. "You do? Oh, good."

The Duke was knee deep in cronies, all armed with glasses of champagne. His nephew disappeared from my side, dived through the throng, and reappeared tugging at his uncle's arm.

"What?" The kind brown eyes looked round; saw me. "Oh, yes." He bent down to talk, and presently the boy came back.

"Champagne or coffee?"

"Coffee, please."

"I'll get it for you."

"I'll get it," I suggested.

"No. Let me. Do let me. Uncle gave me the money." He marched off to the far end of the counter and ordered a cup of coffee and two rounds of smoked-salmon sandwiches, and paid for them with a well-crushed pound note.

"There," he said triumphantly. "How's that?"

"Fine," I said. "Terrific. Have a sandwich."

"All right."

We munched companionably.

"I say," he said. "Look at that man over there, he looks like a ghost."

I turned my head. Big blond man with very pale skin. Pair of clumsy crutches. Large plaster cast. Acey Jones.

Not so noisy today. Drinking beer very quietly in a far corner with a nondescript friend.

"He fell down some steps and broke his ankle and collected a thousand pounds from an insurance policy," I said.

"Golly," said the boy. "Almost worth it."

"He thinks so, too."

"Uncle has something to do with insurance. Don't know what, though."

"An underwriter?" I suggested.

"What's that?"

"Someone who invests money in insurance companies, in a special sort of way."

"He talks about Lloyd's, sometimes. Is it something to do with Lloyd's?"

"That's right."

He nodded and looked wistfully at the sandwiches.

"Have another," I suggested.

"They're yours, really."

"Go on. I'd like you to."

He gave me a quick bright glance and bit into Number 2.

"My name's Matthew," he said.

I laughed. "So is mine."

"Is it really? Do you really mean it?"

"Yes."

"Wow."

There was a step behind me and the deep Eton-sounding voice said, "Is Matthew looking after you all right?"

"Great, sir, thank you," I said.

"His name is Matthew, too," said the boy.

The Duke looked from one of us to the other. "A couple of Matts, eh? Don't let too many people wipe their feet on you."

Matthew thought it a great joke, but the touch of sadness in the voice was revealing. He was dimly aware that, despite his ancestry and position, one or two sharper types had wiped their feet on *him*.

I began to like the Duke.

"Well done with Rudiments, sir," I said.

His face lit up. "Splendid, wasn't it? Absolutely splendid. Nothing on earth gives me more pleasure than seeing my horses win."

I went back to the Cherokee just before the last race and found the chauffeur safe and sound and reading *Doctor Zhivago*. He stretched, reported nothing doing, and ambled off.

All the same, I checked the aircraft inch by inch inside and even unscrewed the panel to the aft baggage compartment, so that I could see into the rear part of the fuselage, right back to the tail. Nothing there that shouldn't be. I screwed the panel on again.

Outside the aircraft, I started in the same way. Started only: because when I was examining every hinge in the tail plane, I heard a shout from the next aircraft.

I looked round curiously but without much haste.

Against that side of the Polyplane which faced away from the stands, two large men were laying into Kenny Bayst.

6

THE PILOT of the Polyplane was standing aside and watching. I reached him in six strides.

"For God's sake," I said, "come and help him."

He gave me a cold stolid stare. "I've got my medical tomorrow. Do it yourself."

In three more steps, I caught one of the men by the fist as he lifted it high to smash into the crumpling Kenny, bent his arm savagely backward, and kicked him hard in the left hamstring. He fell over on his back with a shout of mixed anger, surprise, and pain, closely echoed in both emotion and volume by his colleague, who received the toe of my shoe very solidly at the base of his spine.

Bashing people was their sort of business, not mine, and Kenny hadn't enough strength left to stand up, let alone fight back, so that I got knocked about a bit here and there. But I imagined that they hadn't expected any serious opposition, and it must have been clear to them from the beginning that I didn't play their rules.

They had big fists all threateningly bunched and the hard round sort of toecaps which cowards hide behind. I kicked their knees with vigor, stuck my fingers out straight and hard toward their eyes, and chopped the sides of my palms at their throats.

I'd had enough of it before they had. Still, I outlasted them for determination, because I really did not want to fall down and have their boots bust my kidneys. They got tired in the end and limped away quite suddenly, as if called off by a whistle. They took with them some damaged knee cartilage, aching larynxes and one badly scratched eye; and they left behind a ringing head and a set of sore ribs.

I leaned against the airplane, getting my breath back and looking down at Kenny where he sat on the grass. There was a good deal of blood on his face. His nose was bleeding, and he had tried to wipe it with the back of his hand.

I bent down presently and helped him up. He came to his feet without any of the terrible slowness of the severely injured and there was nothing wrong with his voice.

"Thanks, sport." He squinted at me. "Those sods said they were going to fix me so my riding days were over. . . . God . . . I feel crook. . . . Here, have you got any whisky? Aah . . . Jesus . . ." He bent double and vomited rackingly onto the turf.

Straightening up afterward, he dragged a large handkerchief out of his pocket and wiped his mouth, looking in dismay at the resulting red stains.

"I'm bleeding. . . ."

"It's your nose, that's all."

"Oh . . ." He coughed weakly. "Look, sport, thanks. I guess thanks isn't enough. . . ." His gaze sharpened on the Polyplane pilot still standing aloof a little way off. "That bastard didn't lift a finger. . . . They'd have crippled me and he wouldn't come. . . . I shouted."

"He's got his medical tomorrow," I said.

"Sod his bloody medical."

"If you don't pass your medical every six months, you get grounded. If you get grounded for long in the taxi business, you lose either your whole job or at least half your income. . . ."

"Yeah," he said. "And your own medical, when does that come up?"

"Not for two months."

He laughed a hollow, sick-sounding laugh. Swallowed. Swayed. Looked suddenly very small and vulnerable.

"You'd better go over and see the doctor," I suggested.

"Maybe . . . but I've got the ride on Volume Ten on Monday. . . . Big race . . . opportunity if I do well of a better job than I've had with Annie Villars. . . . Don't want to miss it. . . ." He smiled twistedly. "Doesn't do jockeys any good to be grounded either, sport."

"You're not in very good shape."

"I'll be all right. Nothing broken . . . except maybe my nose. That won't matter; done it before." He coughed again. "Hot bath. Spell in the sauna. Good as new by Monday. Thanks to you."

"How about telling the police?"

"Yeah. Great idea." He was sarcastic. "Just imagine their sort of questions. 'Why was anyone trying to cripple you, Mr. Bayst?' 'Well, Officer, I'd promised to fiddle their races, see, and this sod Goldenberg—I beg his pardon, gentlemen, Mr. Eric Goldenberg—sicks these two heavies onto me to get his own back for all the lolly he had to cough up when I won. . . .' 'And why did you promise to fiddle the race, Mr. Bayst?' 'Well, Officer, I done it before, you see, and made a handy bit on the side. . . .' " He gave me a flickering glance and decided he'd said enough. "Guess I'll see how it looks tomorrow. If I'm in shape to ride Monday, I'll just forget it happened."

"Suppose they try again?"

"No." He shook his head a fraction. "They don't do it twice."

He picked himself off the side of the fuselage and, looking at his reflection in the Polyplane's window, licked his handkerchief and wiped most of the blood off his face.

The nose had stopped bleeding. He felt it gingerly between thumb and forefinger.

"It isn't moving. Can't feel it grate. It did when I broke it."

Without the blood, he looked pale under the red hair but not leaden. "Guess I'll be all right. Think I'll get into the plane and sit down, though. . . . Came in it, see. . . ."

I helped him in. He sagged down weakly in his seat, and didn't look like someone who would be fit to ride a race horse in forty-six hours.

"Hey," he said, "I never asked you. . . . Are you O.K. yourself?"

"Yes. . . . Look, I'll get your pilot to fetch you some whisky."

His reaction showed how unsettled he still felt. "That would be . . . fair dinkum. He won't go, though."

"He will," I said.

He did. British aviation was a small world. Everyone knew someone who knew someone else. News of certain sorts traveled slowly but surely outward and tended to follow one around. He got the message. He also agreed to buy the whisky himself.

By the time he came back, bearing a full quarter bottle and a scowl, the last race was over and the passengers for all the airplanes were turning up in little groups. Kenny began to look less shaky, and when two other jockeys arrived with exclamations and consolations, I went back to the Cherokee.

Annie Villars was waiting, not noticeably elated by her win with Rudiments.

"I thought you said you were going to stay with the plane," she said. Ice crackled in her voice.

"Didn't take my eyes off it."

She snorted. I did a quick double check inside, just to be sure, but no one had stored anything aboard since my last search. The external check I did more slowly and thoroughly. Still nothing.

The thumping I'd collected started to catch up. The ringing noise in my head was settling into a heavy ache. Various soggy areas on my upper arms were beginning to stiffen. My solar plexus and adjacent areas felt like Henry Cooper's opponent's on the morning after.

"Did you know," I said to Annie Villars conversationally, "that two men just had a go at beating up Kenny Bayst?"

If she felt any compassion, she controlled it admirably. "Is he badly hurt?"

"An uncomfortable night should see him through."

"Well, then . . . I dare say he deserved it."

"What for?"

She gave me a direct stare. "You aren't deaf."

I shrugged. "Kenny thinks Mr. Goldenberg arranged it."

She hadn't known it was going to happen. Didn't know whether Goldenberg was responsible or not. I saw her hesitating, summing the information up.

In the end, she said vaguely, "Kenny never could keep his tongue still," and a minute later, under her breath, "Stupid thing to do. Stupid man."

Major Tyderman, the Duke of Wessex, and Fenella Payne-in-the-neck arrived together, the Duke still talking happily about his winner.

"Where's Colin?" asked Fenella. "Isn't he here, after all? What a frantic nuisance. I asked for him at the weighing room and that man—who did he say he was? His valet—oh, yes, of course. . . . His valet said that he had already gone to the plane." She pouted, thrusting out her lower lip. There was champagne in her eyes and petulance in her voice. The gold bracelets jingled. The heavy scent didn't seem to have abated during the afternoon. I thought Colin had dodged very neatly. The Major had also been included in the celebrations. He looked slightly fuzzy round the eyes and a lot less rigid everywhere else. The hand that pushed at the wiry mustache looked almost gentle. The chin was still tucked well back into the neck, but there was nothing aggressive any more: it seemed suddenly only the mannerism of one who used suspiciousness instead of understanding to give himself a reputation for shrewdness.

The Duke asked the Major if he minded changing places on the way home so that he, the Duke, could sit in front. "I like to see the dials go round," he explained.

The Major, full of ducal champagne, gracefully agreed. He and Fenella climbed aboard and I waited outside with the Duke.

"Is there anything the matter, my dear chap?" he said.

"No, sir."

He studied me slowly. "There is, you know."

I put my fingers on my forehead and felt the sweat. "It's a hot day," I said.

Colin came eventually. He, too, was sweating: his crumpled open shirt had great dark patches under the arms. He had ridden five races. He looked thin and exhausted.

"Are you all right?" he said abruptly.

"I *knew,*" said the Duke.

"Yes, thank you."

Colin looked back to where the Polyplane still waited on the ground.

"Is Kenny bad?"

"A bit sore. He didn't want anyone to know."

"One of the jockeys with him on the trip came back over and told us. Kenny said you saved him from a fate worse than death, or words to that effect."

"What?" said the Duke.

Colin explained. They looked at me anxiously.

"I'm fit to fly, if that's what's worrying you."

Colin made a face. "Yeah, boy, it sure is." He grinned, took a deep breath, and dived into the back with the tentacled Fenella. The Duke folded himself after me into the front seat and we set off.

There was thick cloud over the Humber at Ottringham and all the way south to Cambridge. As he could see just about as far forward as the propeller, the Duke asked me what guarantee there was that we wouldn't collide with another aircraft.

There wasn't any guarantee. Just probability.

"The sky is huge," I said. "And there are strict rules for flying in clouds. Collisions practically never happen."

His hands visibly relaxed. He shifted into a more comfortable position. "How do you know where we are?" he asked.

"Radio," I said. "Radio beams from transmitters on the ground. As long as that needle on the dial points centrally downward, we are going straight to Ottringham, where the signal is coming from."

"Fascinating," he said.

The replacement Cherokee had none of the sophistication of the one which had been blown up. That had had an instrument which locked the steering onto the radio beam and took the aircraft automatically to the transmitter. After the attentions of Kenny Bayst's assailants, I regretted not having it around.

"How will we know when we get to Cambridge?" asked the Duke.

"The needle on that other dial down there will swing from pointing straight up and point straight down. That will mean we have passed over the top of the transmitter at Cambridge."

"Wonderful what they think of," said the Duke.

The needles came up trumps. We let down through the cloud over Cambridge into an overcast angry-looking afternoon and landed on the shower-soaked tarmac. I taxied them over close to the buildings, shut down the engine, and took off my headset, which felt a ton heavier than usual.

"Wouldn't have missed it," said the Duke. "Always motored everywhere before, you know." He unfastened his safety belt. "Annie persuaded me to try flying. Just once, she said. But I'll be coming with you again, my dear chap."

"That's great, sir."

He looked at me closely, kindly. "You want to go straight to bed when you get home, Matthew. Get your wife to tuck you up nice and warm, eh?"

"Yes," I said.

"Good, good." He nodded his fine head and began to heave himself cumbersomely out of the door and onto the wing. "You made a great hit with my nephew, my dear chap. And I respect Matt's opinion. He can spot good'uns and bad'uns a mile off."

"He's a nice boy," I said.

The Duke smiled happily. "He's my heir."

He stepped down from the wing and went round to help Annie Villars put on her coat. No doubt I should have been doing it. I sat with my belt still fastened, feeling too rough to be bothered to move. I didn't relish the thought of the final hop back to Buckingham, up into the clouds again and with no easy well-placed transmitter to help me down at the other end. I'd have to go round the Luton complex. . . . Could probably get a steer home from there, from the twenty-four-hour radar at Bedford. . . .

I ached. I thought of the caravan. Cold little harbor.

The passengers collected their gear, shut the rear door, waved, and walked off toward the buildings. I looked at the map, picked out a heading, planned the return journey in terms of time and the cross references I'd need to tell me when I'd got to Buckingham, if the radar should be out of service. After that, I sat and stared at the flight plan and told myself to get on with it. After that, I rested my head on my hand and shut my eyes.

Ridiculous wasting time, I thought. Cambridge Airport charged extra for every minute they stayed open after five o'clock, and the passengers were already committed to paying for a couple of hours. Every moment I lingered cost them a little more.

There was a tap on the window beside me. I raised my head more quickly than proved wise. Colin Ross was standing there, watching me with a gleam of humor. I twisted the catch and opened the window flap on its hinge.

"Fit to fly, didn't you say?" he said.

"That was two hours ago."

"Ah, yes. Makes a difference." He smiled faintly. "I just wondered, if you don't feel like going on, whether you'd care to let me take you home for the night? Then you can finish the trip tomorrow. It might be a fine day tomorrow."

He had flown a great deal and understood the difficulties. All the same, I was surprised he had troubled to come back.

"It might," I agreed. "But I could stay in Cambridge. . . ."

"Get out of there and fix the hangarage," he said calmly.

"I'll have to check with Derrydowns. . . ."

"Check, then."

I climbed too slowly out of the airplane and struggled into my jacket. We walked together across into the building.

"Call your wife, too," he said.

"Haven't got one."

"Oh." he looked at me with speculative curiosity.

"No," I said. "Not that. Married twelve years, divorced three."

Humor crinkled the skin round his eyes. "Better than me," he said. "Married two years, divorced four."

Harley answered at the first ring.

"Where are you? Cambridge? . . . No, come back now. If you stay at Cambridge, we'll have to pay the hangarage." I hadn't told him about the fight, about the way I felt.

"I'll pay it," I said. "You can deduct it from my salary. Colin Ross has asked me to stay with him." That would clinch it. Harley saw the importance of pleasing, and Colin Ross was his best customer.

"Oh . . . that's different. All right, then. Come back in the morning."

I went into the control office and arranged for the aircraft to be stowed under cover for the night, one last overtime job for the staff before they all went home. After that, I sank into the Ross Aston Martin and let the world take care of itself.

He lived in an ordinary-looking brick-built bungalow on the outskirts of Newmarket. Inside, it was colorful and warm, with a large sitting room stocked with deep luxurious velvet-upholstered armchairs.

"Sit down," he said.

I did. Put my head back. Shut my eyes.

"Whisky or brandy?" he asked.

"Whichever you like."

I heard him pouring. It sounded like a tumblerful.

"Here," he said.

I opened my eyes and gratefully took the glass. It was brandy-and-water. It did a grand job.

There were sounds of pans from the kitchen and a warm smell of roasting chicken. Colin's nose twitched.

"Dinner will be ready soon. . . . I'll go and tell the cooks there will be one extra."

He went out of the room and came back almost immediately with his two cooks.

I stood up slowly. I hadn't given it a thought, was quite unprepared.

They looked at first sight like two halves of one whole: Nancy and Midge. Same dark hair, tied high on the crown with black velvet bows. Same dark eyes, straight eyebrows, spontaneous smiles.

"The birdman himself," Nancy said. "Colin, how did you snare him?"

"Potted a sitting duck. . . ."

"This is Midge," she said. "Midge . . . Matt."

"Hi," she said. "The bomb man, aren't you?"

When you looked closer, you could see. She was thinner than Nancy, and much paler, and she seemed fragile where Nancy was strong: but without the mirror comparison with her sister there was no impression of her being ill.

"First and last bomb, I hope," I said.

She shivered. "A lot too ruddy close."

Colin poured each of them a Dubonnet and took whisky for himself. "Bombs, battles—some introduction you've had to racing."

"An eventful change from crop spraying," I said.

"Is that a dull job?" Midge asked, surprised.

"Dull and dangerous. You get bored to death trudging up and down some vast field for six hours a day. It's all low flying, you see, so you have to be wide awake, and after a while you start yawning. One day maybe you get careless and touch the ground with your wing in a turn, and you write off an expensive machine, which is apt to be unpopular with the boss."

Nancy laughed. "Is that what you did?"

"No. . . . I went to sleep for a second in the air one day and woke up twenty feet from a pylon. Missed it by millimeters. So I quit while everything was still in one piece."

"Never mind," Midge said. "The next plane you touched disintegrated beautifully."

They laughed together, a united family, close.

Colin told them about Kenny Bayst's fracas and they exclaimed sympathetically, which made me feel a humbug: Colin habitually drove himself to exhaustion and Midge was irretrievably afflicted, and all I had were a few minor bruises.

Dinner consisted simply of the hot roast chicken and a tossed green salad, with thick wedges of cheese afterward. We ate in the kitchen with our elbows on the scarlet table, and chewed the chicken bones. I hadn't passed a more basically satisfying evening for many a long weary year.

"What are you thinking?" Nancy demanded. "At this moment?"

"Making a note to fall frequently sick at Cambridge."

"Well," said Midge. "Don't bother. Just come any time." She looked inquiringly at her sister and brother, and they nodded. "Just come," she repeated. "Whenever it's handy."

The old inner warning raised its urgent head: don't get involved, don't feel anything, don't risk it.

Don't get involved.

I said, "Nothing I'd like better," and didn't know whether I meant it or not.

The two girls stacked the plates in a dishwasher and made coffee. Nancy poured cream carefully across the top of her cup.

"Do you think that bomb was really intended for Colin?" she asked suddenly.

I shrugged. "I don't know. It could just as well have been intended for Major Tyderman or Annie Villars or Goldenberg, or even Kenny Bayst, really, because it must have been on board before he decided not to come. Or it might have been intended for putting the firm out of action—for Derrydowns itself, if you see what I mean, because if Colin had been killed, Derrydowns would probably have gone bust."

"I can't see why anyone would want to kill Colin," Midge said. "Sure, people are jealous of him, but jealousy is one thing and killing five people is another. . . ."

"Everyone seems to be taking it so calmly," Nancy suddenly exploded. "Here is this bloody bomb merchant running around loose with no one knowing just what he'll do next, and no one seems to be trying to find out and lock him up."

"I don't see how they can find him," Colin said. "And anyway I don't suppose he will risk trying it again."

"Oh, you—you—*ostrich,*" she said bitterly. "Doesn't it occur to you that you don't just lightly put a bomb in an airplane? Whoever did it must have had an overwhelming reason, however mad it was, and since the whole thing went wrong they still have the same motive rotting away inside them, and what do you think Midge and I will do if next time you get blown to bits?"

I saw Midge looking at her with compassion and understood the extent of Nancy's fear. One day she was certainly going to lose her sister. She couldn't face losing her brother as well.

"It won't happen," he said calmly.

They looked at him, and at me. There was a long, long pause. Then Midge picked up the wishbone of the chicken and held it out for me to pull. It snapped with the bigger side in her fist.

"I wish," she said seriously, "that Colin would stop cutting his toenails in the bath."

7

I SLEPT on a divan bed in Colin's study, a small room crammed with racing trophies, filing cabinets, and form books. Every wall was lined with rows of framed photographs of horses passing winning posts and owners proudly leading them in. Their hoofs thudded through my head most of the night, but all was peace by morning.

Colin brought me a cup of tea, yawning in his dark woolly bathrobe. He put the cup down on the small table beside the divan and pulled back the curtains.

"It's drizzling cats and dogs," he announced. "There's no chance of you flying this morning, so you may as well relax and go back to sleep."

I looked out at the misty rain. Didn't mind a bit.

"It's my day off," I said.

"Couldn't be better."

He perched his bottom on the edge of the desk.

"Are you O.K. this morning?"

"Fine," I said. "That hot bath loosened things a lot."

"Every time you moved yesterday evening, you could see it hurt."

I made a face. "Sorry."

"Don't be. In this house, you say ouch."

"So I've noticed," I said dryly.

He grinned. "Everyone lives on a precipice. All the time. And Midge keeps telling me and Nancy that if we're not careful she'll outlive us both."

"She's marvelous."

"Yes, she is." He looked out of the window. "It was a terrible shock at first. Terrible. But now . . . I don't know . . . we seem to have accepted it. All of us. Even her."

I said hesitantly, "How long? . . ."

"How long will she live? No one knows. It varies so much, apparently. She's had it, they think, for about three years now. It seems a lot of people have it for about a year before it becomes noticeable enough to be diagnosed, so no one knows when it started with Midge. Some people die within days of getting it. Some have lived for twenty years. Nowadays, with all the modern treatments, they say the average after diagnosis is from two to six years, but it will possibly be ten. We've had two. . . . We just believe it will be ten . . . and that makes it much easier. . . ."

"She doesn't look especially ill."

"Not at the moment. She had pneumonia a short while ago, and the odd thing about that is that it reverses leukemia for a while. Any fever does it, apparently. Actually makes her better. So do doses of radiation on her arms and legs, and other bones and organs. She's had several relapses and several good long spells of being well. It just goes on like that. . . . But her blood is different, and her bones are changing inside all the time—I've seen pictures of what is happening—and one day . . . Well, one day she'll have a sort of extreme relapse, and she won't recover."

"Poor Midge. . . ."

"Poor all of us."

"What about . . . Nancy? Being her twin . . ."

"Do identical bodies get identical blood diseases, do you mean?" He looked at me across the room, his eyes in shadow. "There's that, too. They say the chances are infinitesimal. They say there are only eighteen known cases of leukemia occurring twice in the same family unit. You can't catch it, and you can't inherit it. A girl with leukemia can have a baby, and the baby won't have leukemia. You can transfuse blood from someone with leukemia into someone without it, and he won't catch it. They say there's no reason why Nancy should develop it any more than me or you or the postman. But they don't *know*. The books don't record any cases of an identical twin having it, or what became of the other one." He paused. Swallowed. "I think we are all more afraid of Nancy getting it, too, than of anything on earth."

I stayed until the sky cleared up at five o'clock. Colin spent most of the day working out which races he wanted to ride in during the coming week and answering telephone calls from owners and trainers anxious to engage him. Principally he rode for a stable half a mile down the road, he said, but the terms of his retainer there gave him a good deal of choice.

He worked at a large chart with seven columns, one for each day of the week. Under each day he listed the various meetings, and under each meeting he listed the names, prizes, and distances of the races. Toward the end of the afternoon, there was a horse's name against a fair proportion of races, especially, I noticed, those with the highest rewards.

He grinned at my interest. "A business is a business," he said.

"So I see. A study in time and motion."

On three of the days, he proposed to ride at two meetings.

"Can you get me from Brighton to Windsor fast enough for two races an hour and a half apart? Three-o'clock race at Brighton. Four-thirty Windsor. And on Saturday three-o'clock race at Bath, four-thirty at Brighton?"

"With fast cars both ends, don't see why not."

"Good." He crossed out a couple of question marks and wrote ticks instead. "And next Sunday can you take me to France?"

"If Harley says so."

"Harley will say so," he said with certainty.

"Don't you ever take a day off?"

He raised his eyebrows in surprise. "Today," he said, "is off. Hadn't you noticed?"

"Er . . . yes."

"The horse I was gong over to ride today went lame on Thursday. Otherwise I was going to Paris. B.E.A., though, for once."

Nancy said with mock resignation, "The dynamo whirs nonstop from March to November in England and Europe, and then goes whizzing off to Japan and so on, and around about February there might be a day or two when we can all flop back in armchairs and put our feet up."

Midge said, "We put them up in the Bahamas last time. It was gorgeous. All that hot sun . . ."

The others laughed. "It rained the whole of the first week."

The girls cooked steaks for lunch. "In your honor," Midge said to me. "You're too thin."

I was fatter than any of them; which wasn't saying much.

Midge cleared the things away afterward and Nancy covered the kitchen table with maps and charts.

"I really am flying Colin to the races one day soon, and I wondered if you'd help. . . ."

"Of course."

She bent over the table, the long dark hair swinging down over her neck. Don't get involved, I said to myself. Just don't.

"Next week, to Haydock. If the weather's good enough."

"She's doing you out of a job," Midge observed, wiping glasses.

"Wait till it thunders."

"Beast," Nancy said.

She had drawn a line on the map. She wanted me to tell her how to proceed in the Manchester control zone, and what to do if they gave her instructions she didn't understand.

"Ask them to repeat them. If you still don't understand, ask them to clarify."

"They'll think I'm stupid," she protested.

"Better that than barging on regardless and crashing into an airliner."

"O.K." She sighed. "Point taken."

"Colin deserves a medal," Midge said.

"Just shut up," Nancy said. "You're all bloody rude."

When the drizzle stopped, they all three took me back to Cambridge, squashing into the Aston Martin. Midge drove, obviously enjoying it. Nancy sat half on Colin and half on me, and I sat half on the door handle.

They stood in a row, and waved when I took off. I rolled the wings in salute and set course for Buckingham, and tried to ignore the regret I felt to be leaving.

Honey was up in the control tower at Derrydowns, Sunday or no Sunday, and Harley was aloft in the trainer giving someone a lesson. When he heard me on the radio, he said snappily, "And about time, too," and I remembered the dimensions of my bank balance and didn't snap back. Chanter, I thought wryly, would have plain despised me.

I left the Cherokee Six in the hangar and walked round to the caravan. It seemed emptier, more sordid, more dilapidated than before. The windows all needed cleaning. The bed wasn't made. Yesterday's milk had gone sour again, and there was still no food.

I sat for a while watching the evening sun struggle through the breaking clouds, watching Harley's pupil stagger through some ropy landings, wondering how long it would be before Derrydowns went broke, and wondering if I could save enough before that happened to buy a car. Harley was paying me forty-five pounds a week, which was more than he could afford and less than I was worth. Of that, Susan, taxes, and insurance would be taking exactly half, and with Harley deducting four more for my rent it wasn't going to be easy.

Impatiently I got up and cleaned all the windows, which improved my view of the airfield but not of the future.

When the light began to fade, I had a visitor. A ripe shapely girl in a minimum of green cotton dress. Long fair hair. Long legs. Large mouth. Slightly protruding teeth. She walked with a man-eating sway and spoke with the faintest of lisps.

Honey Harley had come down from her tower.

She knocked on her way in. All the same if I'd been naked. As it was, I had my shirt off from the window cleaning, and for Honey, it seemed, that was invitation enough. She came over holding out a paper in one hand and putting the other lightly on my shoulder. She let it slide down against my skin to halfway down my back and then brought it up again to the top.

"Uncle and I were making out the list for next week. We wondered if you fixed anything up with Colin Ross."

I moved gently away, picked up a nylon sweater, and put it on.

"Yes. . . . He wants us Tuesday, Friday, Saturday, and Sunday."

"Great."

She followed me across the small space. One step further backward and I'd be in my bedroom. Internally I tried to stifle a laugh. I stepped casually round her, back toward the door. Her face showed nothing but businesslike calm.

"Look," she said, "Monday, that's tomorrow, then, you collect a businessman at Coventry, take him to Rotterdam, wait for him, and bring him back. That's in the Aztec. Tuesday, Colin Ross. Wednesday, nothing yet. Thursday, probably a trainer in Lambourn wanting to look at a horse for sale in Yorkshire—he'll let us know—and then Colin Ross again all the end of the week."

"O.K."

"And the Board of Trade want to come out and see you again. I told them early Tuesday or Wednesday."

"All right." As usual, the automatic sinking of the heart even at the words "Board of Trade": though this time, surely, surely, my responsibility was a technicality. This time, surely, I couldn't get ground to bits.

Honey sat down on the two-seat sofa and crossed her legs. She smiled.

"We haven't seen much of each other yet, have we?"

"No," I said.

"Can I have a cigarette?"

"I'm sorry. . . . I don't smoke. . . . I haven't any."

"Oh. Well, give me a drink, then."

"Look, I really am sorry. . . . All I can offer you is black coffee . . . or water."

"Surely you've got some beer?"

"Afraid not."

She stared at me. Then she stood up, went into the tiny kitchen, and opened all the cupboards. I thought it was because she thought I was lying, but I'd done her an injustice. Sex-minded she might be, but no fool.

"You've no car, have you? And the shops and the pub are nearly two miles away." She came back frowning, and sat down again. "Why didn't you ask someone to give you a lift?"

"Didn't want to be a bother."

She considered it. "You've been here three weeks and you don't get paid until the end of the month. So . . . have you any money?"

"Enough not to starve," I said. "But thanks all the same."

I'd sent ten pounds to Susan and told her she'd have to wait for the rest until I got my check. She'd written back short and to the point. Two months, by then, don't forget. As if I could. I now had under four pounds left in the world and too much pride.

"Uncle would give you an advance."

"I wouldn't like to ask him."

A small smile lifted the corners of her mouth. "No, I can see that, as he's so intent on slapping you down."

"Is he?"

"Don't pretend to be surprised. You know he is. You give him a frightful inferiority complex and he's getting back at you for it."

"It's silly."

"Oh, sure. But you are the two things he longs to be and isn't, a top-class pilot and an attractive man. He needs you badly for the business, but he doesn't have to like it. And don't tell me you didn't know all this, because it's been obvious all along that you understand; otherwise you would have lost your temper with him every day at the treatment he's been handing out."

"You see a lot from your tower," I said, smiling.

"Sure. And I'm very fond of my uncle. And I love this little business, and I'd do anything to keep us afloat." She said it with intense feeling. I wondered whether "anything" meant sleeping with the pilots, or whether that came under the heading of pleasure, not profit. I didn't intend to find out. Not getting involved included Honey, in the biggest possible way.

I said, "It must have been a blow to the business, losing that new Cherokee."

She pursed her mouth and put her head on one side. "Not altogether. In fact, absolutely the reverse. We had too much capital tied up in it. We had to put down a lump sum to start with, and the H.P. installments were pretty steep. . . . I should think when everything's settled, and we get the insurance, we will have about five thousand pounds back, and with that much to shore us up we can keep going until times get better."

"If the aircraft hadn't blown up, would you have been able to keep up with the H.P.?"

She stood up abruptly, seeming to think that she had already said too much. "Let's just leave it that things are all right as they are."

The daylight was fading fast. She came and stood close beside me, not quite touching.

"You don't smoke, you don't eat, you don't drink," she said softly. "What else don't you do?"

"That, too."

"Not ever?"

"Not now. Not here."

"I'd give you a good time."

"Honey . . . I just . . . don't want to."

She wasn't angry. Not even hurt. "You're cold," she said judiciously. "An iceberg."

"Perhaps."

"You'll thaw," she said. "One of these days."

The Board of Trade had sent the same two men, the tall one and the silent one, complete with notebook and bitten green pencil. As before, I sat with them in the crew room and offered them coffee from the slot machine in the passengers' lounge. They accepted, and I went and fetched three plastic cupfuls. The staff, as well as the customers, had to buy their coffee or whatever from the machine. Honey kept it well stocked. It made a profit.

Outside on the airfield my part-time colleague, Ron, was showing a new pupil how to do the external checks. They crept round the trainer inch by inch. Ron talked briskly. The pupil, a middle-aged man, nodded as if he understood.

The tall man was saying in effect that they had got nowhere with the bomb.

"The police have been happy to leave the investigation with us, but frankly in these cases it is almost impossible to find the identity of the perpetrator. Of course, if someone on board is a major political figure, or a controversial agitator . . . Or if there is a great sum of personal insurance involved . . . But in this case there is nothing like that."

"Isn't Colin Ross insured?" I asked.

"Yes, but he has no new policy, or anything exceptional. And the beneficiaries are his twin sisters. I cannot believe . . ."

"Impossible," I said with conviction.

"Quite so."

"How about the others?"

He shook his head. "They all said, in fact, that they ought to be better insured than they were." He coughed discreetly. "There is, of course, the matter of yourself."

"What d'you mean?"

His sharp eyes stared at me unblinkingly.

"Several years ago, you took out a policy for the absolute benefit of your wife. Although she is now your ex-wife, she would still be the beneficiary. You can't change that sort of policy."

"Who told you all this?"

"She did," he said. "We went to see her in the course of our inquiries." He paused. "She didn't speak kindly of you."

I compressed my mouth. "No. I can imagine. Still, I'm worth more to her alive than dead. She'll want me to live as long as possible."

"And if she wanted to get married again? Your alimony payments would stop then, and a lump sum from insurance might be welcome."

I shook my head. "She might have killed me in a fury three years ago, but not now, cold-bloodedly, with other people involved. It isn't in her nature. And besides she doesn't know anything about bombs and she had no opportunity. . . . You'll have to cross out that theory, too."

"She has been going out occasionally with an executive from a firm specializing in demolitions."

He kept his voice dead even, but he had clearly expected more reaction than he got. I wasn't horrified or even much taken aback.

"She wouldn't do it. Or put anyone else up to doing it. Ordinarily, she was too—too kindhearted. Too sensible, anyway. She used to be so angry whenever innocent passengers were blown up. . . . She would never do it herself. Never."

He watched me for a while in the special Board of Trade brand of unnerving silence. I didn't see what I could add. Didn't know what he was after.

Outside on the airfield, the trainer started up and taxied away. The engine noise faded. It was very quiet. I sat. I waited.

Finally he stirred. "All in all, for all our trouble, we have come up with only one probability. And even that gets us no nearer knowing who the bomb was intended for, or who put it on board."

He put his hand in his inner pocket and brought out a stiff brown envelope. Out of that he shook onto the crew-room table a twisted piece of metal. I picked it up and looked at it. Beyond the impression that it had once been round and flat, like a button, it meant nothing.

"What is it?"

"The remains," he said, "of an amplifier."

I looked up, puzzled. "Out of the radio?"

"We don't think so." He chewed his lip. "We think it was in the bomb. We found it embedded in what had been the tail plane."

"Do you mean . . . it wasn't a time bomb after all?"

"Well . . . probably not. It looks as if it was exploded by a radio transmission. Which puts, do you see, a different slant on things."

"What difference? I don't know much about bombs. How does a radio bomb differ from a time bomb?"

"They can differ a lot, though in many the actual explosive is the same. In those cases, it's just the trigger mechanism that's different." He paused. "Well, say you have a quantity of plastic explosive. Unfortunately that's all too easy to get hold of nowadays. In fact, if you happen to be in Greece, you can go into any hardware shop and buy it over the counter. On its own, it won't explode. It needs a detonator. Gunpowder, old-fashioned gunpowder, is the best. You also need something to ignite the gunpowder before it will detonate the plastic. Are you with me?"

"Faint but pursuing," I said.

"Right. The easiest way to ignite gunpowder—from a distance, that is—is to pack it round a thin filament of fuse wire. Then you pass an electric current through the filament. It becomes red hot, ignites the gunpowder—"

"And, boom, you have no Cherokee Six."

"Er, yes. Now, in this type of bomb you have a battery, a high-voltage battery about the size of a sixpence, to provide the electric current. The filament will heat up if you bend it round and fasten one end to one terminal of the battery, and the other to the other."

"Clear," I said. "And the bomb goes off immediately."

He raised his eyes to heaven. "Why did I ever start this? Yes, it would go off immediately. So it is necessary to have a mechanism that will complete the circuit after the manufacturer is safely out of the way."

"By a spring?" I suggested.

"Yes. You hold the circuit open by a hairspring on a catch. When the catch is removed, the spring snaps the circuit shut, and that's that. Right? Now, the catch can be released by a time mechanism like an ordinary alarm clock. Or it can be released by a radio signal from a distance, via a receiver, an amplifier, and a solenoid, like mechanisms in a space craft."

"What is a solenoid, exactly?"

"A sort of electric magnet, a coil with a rod in the center. The rod moves up and down inside the coil when a pulse is passed through the coil. Say the top of the rod is sticking up out of the coil to form the catch on the spring, when the rod moves down into the coil the spring is released."

I considered it. "What is there to stop someone detonating the bomb by accident, by unknowingly transmitting on the right frequency? The air is packed with radio waves—surely radio bombs are impossibly risky?"

He cleared his throat. "It is possible to make a combination-type release mechanism. One could make a bomb in which, say, three radio signals had to be completed. For such a release mechanism, you would need three separate sets of receivers, amplifiers, and solenoids to complete the circuit. . . . We were exceptionally fortunate to find this amplifier. We doubt if it was the only one. . . ."

"It sounds much more complicated than the alarm clock."

"Oh, yes, it is. But also more flexible. You are not committed to a time in advance to set it off."

"So no one had to know what time we would be leaving Haydock. They would just have to see us go."

"Yes. . . . Or be told you had gone."

I thought a bit. "It does put a different slant, doesn't it?"

"I'd appreciate your thinking."

"You must be thinking the same," I said. "If the bomb could be set off at any hour, any day—any week, even—it could have been put in the aircraft at any time after the last maintenance check."

He smiled thinly. "And that would let you halfway off the hook?"

"Halfway," I agreed.

"But only half."

"Yes."

He sighed. "I've sprung this on you. I'd like you to think it over, from every angle. Seriously. Then tell me if anything occurs to you. If you care at all to find out what happened, that is, and maybe prevent it from happening again."

"You think I don't care?"

"I got that impression."

"I would care now," I said slowly, "if Colin Ross were blown up."

He smiled. "You are less on your guard today."

"You aren't sniping at me from behind the bushes."

"No. . . ." He was surprised. "You're very observant, aren't you?"

"More a matter of atmosphere."

He hesitated. "I have now read the whole of the transcript of your trial."

"Oh." I could feel my face go bleak. He watched me.

"Did you know," he said, "that someone has added to the bottom of it in pencil a highly libelous statement?"

"No," I said. Waited for it.

"It says that the Chairman of Interport is of the undoubtedly correct opinion that the first officer lied on oath throughout, and that it was because of the first officer's own gross negligence, not that of Captain Shore, that the airliner strayed so dangerously off course."

Surprised, shaken, I looked away from him, out of the window, feeling absurdly vindicated and released. If that postscript was there for anyone who read the transcript to see, then maybe my name hadn't quite so much mud on it as I'd thought. Not where it mattered, anyway.

I said without heat, "The captain is always responsible. Whoever does what."

"Yes."

A silence lengthened. I brought my thoughts back from four years ago and my gaze from the empty airfield.

"Thank you," I said.

He smiled very slightly. "I wondered why you hadn't lost your license—or your job. It didn't make sense to me that you hadn't. That's why I read the transcript, to see if there was any reason."

"You're very thorough."

"I like to be."

"Interport knew one of us was lying—we both said the other had put the ship in danger—but I was the captain. It inevitably came back to me. It was, in fact, my fault."

"He willfully disobeyed your instructions. . . ."

"And I didn't find out until it was nearly too late."

"Quite . . . but he needn't have lied about it."

"He was frightened." I sighed. "Of what would happen to his career."

He let half a minute slip by without comment. Then he cleared his throat and said, "I suppose you wouldn't like to tell me why you left the South American people?"

I admired his delicate approach. "Gap in the dossier?" I suggested.

His mouth twitched. "Well, yes." A pause. "You are of course not obliged. . . ."

"No," I said. "Still . . ." Something for something. "I refused to take off one day because I didn't think it was safe. They got another pilot who said it was. So he took off, and nothing happened. And they sacked me. That's all."

"But," he said blankly, "it's a captain's absolute right not to take off if he thinks it's unsafe."

"There's no B.A.L.P.A. to uphold your rights there, you know. They said they couldn't afford to lose custom to other airlines because their captains were cowards. Or words to that effect."

"Good gracious."

I smiled. "Probably the Interport business accounted for my refusal to take risks."

"But then you went to Africa and took them," he protested.

"Well . . . I needed money badly, and the pay was fantastic. And you don't have the same moral obligation to food and medical supplies as to airline passengers."

"But the refugees and wounded, coming out?"

"Always easier flying out than in. No difficulties finding the home base, not like groping for some jungle clearing on a black night."

He shook his head wonderingly, giving me up as a bad job.

"What brought you back here to something as dull as crop spraying?"

I laughed. Never thought I could laugh in front of the Board of Trade. "The particular war I was flying in ended. I was offered another one a bit further south, but I suppose I'd had enough of it. Also I was nearly solvent again. So I came back here, and crop spraying was the first thing handy."

"What you might call a checkered career," he commented.

"Mild compared with some."

"Ah, yes. That's true." He stood up and threw his empty coffee beaker into the biscuit tin which served as a waste-paper basket. "Right, then. . . . You'll give a bit of thought to this bomb business?"

"Yes."

"We'll be in touch with you again." He fished in an inner pocket and produced a card. "If you should want me, though, you can find me at this number."

"O.K."

He made a wry face. "I know how you must feel about us."

"Never mind," I said. "Never mind."

8

FOR MOST of that week, I flew where I was told to, and thought about radio bombs, and sat on my own in the caravan in the evenings.

Honey didn't come back, but on the day after her visit I had returned from Rotterdam to find a large bag of groceries on the table: eggs, butter, bread, tomatoes, sugar, cheese, powdered milk, tins of soup. Also a pack of six half pints of beer. Also a note from Honey: "Pay me next week."

Not a bad guy, Honey Harley. I took up eating again. Old habits die hard.

Tuesday I took Colin and four assorted others to Wolverhampton races; Wednesday, after the Board of Trade departed, I took a politician to Cardiff to a union strike meeting; and Thursday I took the race-horse trainer to various places in Yorkshire and Northumberland to look at some horses to see if he wanted to buy any.

Thursday evening I made myself a cheese-and-tomato sandwich and a cup of coffee, and ate them looking at the pin-ups, which were curling a bit round the edges. After I'd finished the sandwich, I unstuck the tape and took all the bosomy ladies down. The thrusting pairs of heavily ringed nipples regarded me sorrowfully, like spaniels' eyes. Smiling, I folded them decently over and dropped them in the rubbish bin. The caravan looked just as dingy, however, without them.

Friday morning, when I was in Harley's office filing flight records, Colin rang Harley and said he wanted me to stay overnight at Cambridge, ready again for Saturday.

Harley agreed. "I'll charge Matt's hotel bill to your account."

Colin said, "Fine. But he can stay with me again if he likes."

Harley relayed the message. Did I like? I liked.

Harley put down the receiver. "Trying to save money," he said disparagingly, "having you to stay." He brightened: "I'll charge him the hangarage, though."

I took the Cherokee over to Cambridge and fixed for them to give it shelter that night. When Colin came, he was with four other jockeys: three I didn't know, and Kenny Bayst. Kenny said how was I. I was fine, how was he? Good as new, been riding since Newbury, he said.

Between them they had worked out the day's shuttle. All to Brighton, Colin to White Waltham for Windsor, airplane to return to Brighton, pick up the others, return to White Waltham for Colin, return to Cambridge.

"Is that all right?" Colin asked.

"Sure. Anything you say."

He laughed. "The fusses we used to have when we used to ask this sort of thing. . . ."

"Don't see why," I said.

"Larry was a lazy sod. . . ."

They loaded themselves on board and we tracked down east of the London control zone and over the top of Gatwick to Shoreham Airport for Brighton. When we landed, Colin looked at his watch and Kenny nodded and said, "Yeah, he's always faster than Larry. I've noticed it, too."

"Harley will give him the sack," Colin said dryly, unfastening his seat belt.

"He won't, will he?" Kenny sounded faintly anxious. Quicker journeys meant smaller bills.

"It depends on how many customers he pinches from Polyplanes through being fast." Colin grinned at me. "Am I right?"

"You could be," I said.

They went off laughing about it to the waiting taxi. A couple of hours later, Colin came back at a run in his breeches and colors and I whisked him over to White Waltham. He had won, it appeared, at Brighton. A close finish. He was still short of breath. A fast car drove right up to the aircraft as soon as I stopped and had him off down the road to Windsor in a cloud of dust. I went more leisurely back to Shoreham and collected the others at the end of their program. It was a hot sunny day, blue and hazy. They came back sweating.

Kenny had ridden a winner and had brought me a bottle of whisky as a present. I said he didn't need to give me a present.

"Look, sport, if it weren't for you, I wouldn't be riding any more bleeding winners. So take it."

"All right," I said. "Thanks."

"Thanks yourself."

They were tired and expansive. I landed at White Waltham before Colin arrived back from Windsor, and the other four yawned and gossiped, opening all the doors and fanning themselves.

". . . gave him a breather coming up the hill."

"That was no breather. That was the soft bugger dropping his bit. Had to give him a sharp reminder to get him going again."

"Can't stand that fellow Fossel. . . ."

"Why do you ride for him, then?"

"Got no choice, have I? Small matter of a retainer . . ."

". . . What chance you got on Candlestick?"

"Wouldn't finish in the first three if it started now. . . ."

"Hey," said Kenny Bayst, leaning forward and tapping me on the shoulder. "Got something that might interest you, sport." He pulled a sheet of paper out of his trouser pocket. "How about this, then?"

I took the paper and looked at it. It was a leaflet, high-quality printing on good glossy paper. An invitation to all racegoers to join the Racegoers' Accident Fund.

"I'm not a racegoer," I said.

"No, read it. Go on," he urged. "It came in the post this morning. I thought you'd be interested, so I brought it."

I read down the page: "Up to one thousand pounds for serious personal injury, five thousand pounds for accidental death. Premium five pounds. Double the premium, double the insurance. The insurance everyone can afford. Stable lads, buy security for your missus. Jockeys: out of work but in the money. Race crowds, protect yourself against road accidents on the way home. Trainers who fly to meetings, protect yourself against bombs!"

"Damn it," I said.

Kenny laughed. "I thought you'd like it."

I handed the leaflet back, smiling. "Yeah. The so-and-sos."

"Might not be a bad idea, at that."

Colin's hired car drove up and decanted the usual spent force. He climbed wearily into his seat, clipped shut his belt, and said "Wake me at Cambridge."

"How did it go?" Kenny asked.

"Got that sod Export home by a whisker. . . . But, as for Uptight," he said, yawning, "they might as well send him to the knackers. Got the slows right and proper, that one has."

We woke him at Cambridge. It was a case of waking most of them, in point of fact. They stretched their way onto the tarmac, shirt necks open, ties hanging loose, jackets on their arms. Colin had no jacket, no tie: for him, the customary jeans, the rumpled sweat shirt, the air of being nobody, of being one in a crowd, instead of a crowd in one.

Nancy and Midge had come in the Aston Martin to pick us up.

"We brought a picnic," Nancy said, "as it's such a super evening. We're going to that place by the river."

They had also brought swimming trunks for Colin and a pair of his for me. Nancy swam with us, but Midge said it was too cold. She sat on the bank wearing four watches on her left arm and stretching her long bare legs in the sun.

It was cool and quiet and peaceful in the river after the hot sticky day. The noise of engine throb inside my head calmed to silence. I watched a moorhen gliding along by the reeds, twisting her neck cautiously to fasten me with a shiny eye, peering suspiciously at Colin and Nancy floating a way ahead. I pushed a ripple toward her with my arm. She rode on it like a cork. Simple being a moorhen, I thought. But it wasn't really. All of nature had its pecking order. Everywhere, someone was the pecked.

Nancy and Colin swam back. Friendly eyes, smiling faces. Don't get involved, I thought. Not with anyone. Not yet.

The girls had brought cold chicken and long crisp Cos lettuce leaves with a tangy sauce to dip them in. We ate while the sun went down, and drank a cold bottle of Chablis, sitting on a large blue rug by the river.

When she had finished, Midge lay back on the rug and shielded her eyes from the last slanting rays.

"I wish this could go on forever," she said casually. "The summer, I mean. Warm evenings. We get so few of them."

"We could go and live in the South of France, if you like," Nancy said.

"Don't be silly. . . . Who would look after Colin?"

They smiled, all three of them. The unspoken things were all there. Tragic. Unimportant.

The slow dusk drained all colors into shades of gray. We lazed there, relaxing, chewing stalks of grass, watching the insects flick the surface of the water, talking a little in soft summer-evening murmuring voices.

"We both lost half a stone in Japan, that year we went with Colin. . . ."

"That was the food more than the heat."

"I never did get to like the food. . . ."

"Have you ever been to Japan, Matt?"

"Used to fly there for B.O.A.C."

"B.O.A.C?" Colin was surprised. "Why ever did you leave?"

"Left to please my wife. Long time ago now, though."

"Explains how you fly."

"Oh, sure. . . ."

"I like America better," Midge said. "Do you remember Mr. Kroop, in Laurel, where you got those riding boots made in a day?"

"Mmm. . . ."

"And we kept driving round that shopping center there, and getting lost in the one-way streets. . . ."

"Super, that week was. . . ."

"Wish we could go again. . . ."

There was a long regretful silence. Nancy sat up with a jerk and slapped her leg.

"Bloody mosquitoes."

Colin scratched lazily and nodded. "Time to go home."

We wedged back into the Aston Martin. Colin drove. The twins sat on my legs, leaned on my chest, and twined their arms behind my neck for balance. Not bad, not bad at all. They laughed at my expression.

"Too much of a good thing," Nancy said.

When we went to bed, they both kissed me good night, with identical soft lips, on the cheek.

Breakfast was brisk, businesslike, and accompanied throughout by telephone calls. Annie Villars rang to ask if there was still a spare seat on the Cherokee.

"Who for?" Colin asked cautiously. He made a face at us. "Bloody Fenella," he whispered over the mouthpiece. "No, Annie, I'm terribly sorry. I've promised Nancy. . . ."

"You have?" Nancy said. "First I've heard of it."

He put the receiver down. "I rescue you from Chanter, now it's your turn."

"Rescue my foot. You're in and out of the weighing room all day. Fat lot of good that is."

"Do you want to come?"

"Take Midge," she said. "It's her turn."

"No, you go," Midge said. "Honestly, I find it tiring. Especially as it's one of those rush-from-course-to-course days. I'll go along to the meeting here next week. That will do me fine."

"Will you be all right?"

"Naturally I will. I'll lie in the sun in the garden and think of you all exhausting yourselves racing round in circles."

When it turned out that there were two other empty seats as well, in spite of Nancy being there, Annie Villars gave Colin a reproachful look of carefully repressed annoyance and said it would have been useful to have had Fenella along to share the cost. Why else did Colin think she had suggested it?

"I must have miscounted," said Colin happily. "Too late to get her now."

We flew to Bath without incident, Nancy sitting in the right-hand seat beside me and acting as co-pilot. It was clear that she intensely enjoyed it, and there was no pain in it for me either. I could see what Larry had meant about practicing short landings, as the Bath runways were incredibly short, but we got down in fair order and parked alongside the opposition's Cessna.

Colin said, "Lock the airplane and come into the races. You can't forever stand on guard."

The Polyplane pilot was nowhere to be seen. I hoped for the best, locked up, and walked with the others in to the racecourse next door.

The first person we saw was Acey Jones, balancing on his crutches with the sun making his pale head look fairer than ever.

"Oh, yes. Colin," Nancy said. "Do you want me to send a fiver to the accident-insurance people? You remember, the leaflet that came yesterday? That man reminded me. . . . He got a thousand pounds from the fund from cracking his ankle. I heard him saying so, at Haydock."

"If you like," he agreed. "A fiver won't break the bank. May as well."

"Bobbie Wessex is sponsoring it," Annie commented.

"Yes." Nancy nodded. "It was on the leaflet."

"Did you see the bit about the bombs?" I asked.

Annie and Nancy both laughed. "Someone in insurance has got a sense of humor, after all."

Annie hustled off to the weighing room to see to her runner in the first race, and Colin followed her to change.

"Lemonade?" I suggested to Nancy.

"Pints of it. Whew, it's hot."

We drank it in a patch of shade, out on the grass. Ten yards away, loud and clear, Eric Goldenberg was conducting a row with Kenny Bayst.

". . . And don't you think, sport, that you can set your gorillas on me and expect me to do your favors afterward, because if you think that, you've got another think coming."

"What gorillas?" Goldenberg demanded, not very convincingly.

"Oh, come off it. Set them to cripple me. At Redcar."

"Must have been those bookmakers you swindled while you were busy double-crossing us."

"I never double-crossed you."

"Don't give me that crap," Goldenberg said heavily. "You know bloody well you did. You twisty little bastard."

"If you think that, why the frigging hell are you asking me to set up another touch for you now?"

"Bygones are bygones."

"Bygones bloody aren't." Kenny spat on the ground at Goldenberg's feet and removed himself to the weighing room. Goldenberg watched him go with narrowed eyes and a venomous twist to his mouth. The next time I saw him, he was holding a well-filled glass and adding substantially to his paunch, while muttering belligerently to a pasty slob who housed all his brains in his biceps. The slob wasn't one of the two who had lammed into Kenny at Redcar. I wondered if Goldenberg intended mustering reinforcements.

"What do you think of Kenny Bayst?" I asked Nancy.

"The big little Mister I-Am from Down Under," she said. "He's better than he used to be, though. He came over here thinking everyone owed him a living, as he'd had a great big successful apprenticeship back home."

"Would he lose to order?"

"I expect so."

"Would he agree to lose to order, take the money, back himself, and try to win?"

She grinned. "You're learning fast."

We watched Colin win the first race. Annie Villars' horse finished third from last. She stood glumly looking at its heaving sides while Kenny's successor made the best of explaining away his own poor showing.

"Annie should have kept Kenny Bayst," Nancy said.

"He wanted out."

"Like Colin doesn't want in." She nodded. "Annie's being a bit of a fool this season."

Before the third race, we went back to the airplane. The Polyplane pilot was standing beside it, peering in through the windows. He was not the standoff merchant from Redcar, but his colleague from Haydock.

"Good afternoon," Nancy said.

"Good afternoon, Miss Ross." He was polite in the way that is more insolent than rudeness. Not the best method, I would have thought, of seducing Colin's custom back from Derrydowns. He walked away, back to his Cessna, and I went over the Cherokee inch by inch looking for anything wrong. As far as I could see, there was nothing. Nancy and I climbed aboard, and I started the engine to warm it up ready to take off.

Colin and Annie arrived in a hurry and loaded themselves in, and we whisked off across southern England to Shoreham. Colin and Annie again jumped into a waiting taxi and vanished. Nancy stayed with me and the Cherokee, and we sat on the warm grass and watched little airplanes landing and taking off, and talked now and then without pressure about flying, racing, life in general.

Toward the end of the afternoon, she asked, "Will you go on being a taxi pilot all your life?"

"I don't know. I don't look far ahead any more."

"Nor do I," she said.

"No."

"We've been happy, these last few weeks, with Midge being so much better. I wish it would last."

"You'll remember it."

"That's not the same."

"It's only special because of what's coming," I said.

There was a long pause while she thought about it. At length, she asked disbelievingly, "Do you mean that it is because Midge is dying that we are so happy now?"

"Something like that."

She turned her head; considered me. "Tell me something else. I need something else."

"Comfort?"

"If you like."

I said, "You've all three been through the classic progression these last two years. All together, not just Midge herself. Shock, disbelief, anger, and in the end acceptance." I paused. "You've come through the dark tunnel. You're out in the sun the other end. You've done most of your grieving already. You are a most extraordinarily strong family. You'll remember this summer because it will be something worth remembering."

"Matt. . . ."

There were tears in her eyes. I watched the bright little dragonfly airplanes dart and go. They could heal me, the Ross family, I thought. Their strength could heal me. If it would take nothing away from them. If I could be sure.

"What was Colin's wife like?" I asked after a while.

"Oh. . . ." She gave a laugh which was half a sniff. "A bit too much like Fenella. He was much younger then. He didn't know how to duck. She was thirty-three and bossy and rich, and he was twenty and madly impressed by her. To be honest, Midge and I thought she was fabulous, too. We were seventeen and still wet behind the ears. She thought it would be marvelous being married to a genius, all accolades and champagne and glamour. She didn't like it when it turned out to be mostly hard work and starvation and exhaustion. . . . So she left him for a young actor who'd just had rave notices for his first film, and it took Colin months to get back to being himself from the wreck she'd made of him."

"Poor Colin." Or lucky Colin. Strong Colin. Months . . . it was taking me years.

"Yeah." She grinned. "He got over it. He's got some bird now in London. He slides down to see her every so often when he thinks Midge and I aren't noticing."

"I must get me a bird," I said idly. "One of these days."

"You haven't got one?"

I shook my head. I looked at her. Straight eyebrows, straight eyes, sensible mouth. She looked back. I wanted to kiss her. I didn't think she would be angry.

"No," I said absent-mindedly. "No bird."

Take nothing away from them. Nothing from Midge.

"I'll wait a while longer," I said.

Several days—several flights—later, I telephoned the Board of Trade. Diffidently. Sneering at myself for trying to do their job for them, for thinking I might have thought of something they hadn't worked out for themselves. But then I'd been on the flight with the bomb, and they hadn't. I'd seen things, heard things, felt things that they hadn't.

Partly for my own sake, but mainly because of what Nancy had said about the bomb merchant still running around loose with his motives still rotting away inside him, I had finally found myself discarding the thought that it was none of my business, that someone else could sort it all out, and coming round to the view that if I could in fact come up with anything it might be a profitable idea.

To which end I wasted a lot of brain time chasing down labyrinths of speculation, and fetched up against a series of reasons why not.

There was Larry, for instance. Well, what about Larry? Larry had had every chance to put the bomb on board, right up to two hours before I set off to collect the passengers from White Waltham. But however strong a motive he had to kill Colin or ruin Derrydowns—and none had so far appeared bar a few trivial frauds—if it was true it was a radio and not a time bomb, he couldn't have set it off, because when it exploded he was in Turkey. If it had been Larry, a time bomb would have been the only simple and practical way.

Then, Susan. . . . Ridiculous as I thought it, I went over again what the Board of Trade man had said: she was going out occasionally with a demolitions expert. Well, good luck to her. The sooner she got married again, the better off I'd be. Only trouble was, the aversion therapy of that last destructive six months seemed to have been just as successful with her as it had been with me.

I couldn't believe that any executive type in his right mind would bump off his occasional girl friend's ex-husband for the sake of about six thousand pounds of insurance, especially as the longer I lived, the greater would be the sum she eventually collected. I had three years ago stopped paying any more premiums, but the value of the payoff automatically went on increasing.

Apart from knowing her incapable of the cold-blooded murder of innocent people, I respected her mercenary instincts. The longer I lived, the better off she would be on all counts. It was as simple as that.

Honey Harley . . . had said she would do "anything" to keep Derrydowns in business, and the blowing up of the Cherokee had eased the financial situation. One couldn't sell things which were being bought on the hire-purchase, and if one couldn't keep up the installments the aircraft technically belonged to the H.P. company, who might sell it at a figure which did little more than cover themselves, leaving a molehill for Derrydowns to salvage. Insurance, on the other hand, had done them proud: paid off the H.P. and left them with capital in hand.

Yet killing Colin Ross would have ruined Derrydowns completely. Honey Harley would never have killed any of the customers, let alone Colin Ross. And the same applied to Harley himself, all along the line.

The Polyplane people, then? Always around, always belligerent, trying their damnedest to put Derrydowns out of business and win back Colin Ross. Well . . . the bomb would have achieved the first object but have put the absolute dampers on the second. I couldn't see even the craziest Polyplane pilot killing the golden goose.

Kenny Bayst . . . livid with Eric Goldenberg, Major Tyderman, and Annie Villars. But, as I'd said to Colin, where would he have got a bomb from in the time, and would he have killed Colin and me, too? It didn't seem possible, any of it. No to Kenny Bayst.

Who, then?

Who?

Since I couldn't come up with anyone else, I went back over the possibilities all over again. Larry, Susan, the Harleys, Polyplanes, Kenny Bayst. Looked at them up, down, and sideways. Got nowhere. Made some coffee, went to bed, went to sleep.

Woke up at four in the morning with the moon shining on my face. And one fact hitting me with a bang. Look at things laterally. Start from the bottom.

I started from the bottom. When I did that, the answer rose up and stared me in the face. I couldn't believe it. It was too darned simple.

In the morning, I made a lengthy telephone call to a long-lost cousin, and two hours later got one back. And it was then, expecting a flat rebuff, that I rang up the Board of Trade.

The tall polite man wasn't in. He would, they said, call back later.

When he did, Harley was airborne with a pupil and Honey answered in the tower. She buzzed through to the crew room, where I was writing up records.

"The Board of Trade want you. What have you been up to?"

"It's only that old bomb," I said soothingly.

"Huh."

When the tall man came on the line, she was still listening on the tower extension.

"Honey," I said. "Quit."

"I beg your pardon," said the Board of Trade.

Honey giggled, but she put her receiver down. I heard the click.

"Captain Shore?" the voice said reprovingly.

"Er, yes."

"You wanted me?"

"You said . . . if I thought of any angle on the bomb."

"Indeed, yes." A shade of warmth.

"I've been thinking," I said, "about the transmitter which was needed to set it off."

"Yes?"

"How big would the bomb have been?" I asked. "All that plastic explosive and gunpowder and wires and solenoids?"

"I should think quite small. . . . You would probably pack a bomb like that into a flat tin about seven inches by four by two inches deep. Possibly even smaller. The tighter they are packed, the more fiercely they explode."

"And how big would the transmitter have to be to send perhaps three different signals?"

"Nowadays, not very big. If size were important . . . a pack of cards, perhaps. But in this case I would have thought . . . larger. The transmissions must have had to carry a fairly long way . . . and to double the range of a signal you have to quadruple the power of the transmitter, as no doubt you know."

"Yes. . . . I apologize for going through all this the long way, but I wanted to be sure. Because although I don't know *why,* I've a good idea of *when* and *who*."

"What did you say?" His voice sounded strangled.

"I said—"

"Yes, yes," he interrupted. "I heard. When—when, then?"

"It was put on board at White Waltham. Taken off at Haydock. And put back on again at Haydock."

"What do you mean?"

"It came with one of the passengers."

"Which one?"

"By the way," I said. "How much would such a bomb cost?"

"Oh—about eighty pounds or so," he said impatiently. "Who?"

"And would it take a considerable expert to make one?"

"Someone used to handling explosives and with a working knowledge of radio."

"I thought so."

"Look," he said, "look, will you please stop playing cat-and-mouse. I dare say it amuses you to tease the Board of Trade. . . . I don't say I absolutely blame you, but will you please plainly tell me which of the passengers had a bomb with him?"

"Major Tyderman," I said.

"Major . . ." He took an audible breath. "Are you meaning to say now that it wasn't the bomb rolling around on the elevator wires that caused the friction which persuaded you to land? . . . That Major Tyderman was carrying it around unknown to himself all the afternoon? Or what?"

"No," I said. "And no."

"For God's sake. . . ." He was exasperated. "I suppose you couldn't simplify the whole thing by telling me exactly who planted the bomb on Major Tyderman? Who intended to blow him up?"

"If you like."

He took a shaking grip. I smiled at the crew-room wall.

"Well, who?"

"Major Tyderman," I said. "Himself."

Silence. Then a protest.

"Do you mean suicide? It can't have been. The bomb went off when the airplane was on the ground. . . ."

"Precisely," I said.

"What?"

"If a bomb goes off in an airplane, everyone automatically thinks that it was intended to blow up in the air and kill all the people on board."

"Yes, of course."

"Suppose the real intended victim was the airplane itself, not the people?"

"But why?"

"I told you, I don't know why."

"All right," he said. "All right." He took a deep breath. "Let's start from the beginning. You are saying that Major Tyderman, intending to blow up the airplane for reasons unknown, took a bomb with him to the races."

"Yes."

"What makes you think so?"

"Looking back. . . . He was rigidly tense all day, and he wouldn't be parted from his binocular case, which was large enough to contain a bomb of the size you described."

"That's absurdly circumstantial," he protested.

"Sure," I agreed. "Then, it was the Major who borrowed the keys from me to go over to the aircraft to fetch the *Sporting Life* which he had left there. He wouldn't let me go, though I offered. He came back and gave me the keys. Of course, he hadn't locked up. He wanted to create a little confusion. While he was over there, he unscrewed the back panel of the luggage bay and put the bomb behind it, against the fuselage. Limpet gadget, I expect, as I said before, which came unstuck on the bumpy flight."

"He couldn't have foreseen you'd land at East Midlands. . . ."

"It didn't matter where we landed. As soon as everyone was clear of the aircraft, he was ready to blow it up."

"That's sheer guesswork."

"He did it in front of my eyes, at East Midlands. I saw him look round, to check there was no one near it. Then he was fiddling with his binocular case—sending the signals. They could have been either very low or super-high frequencies. They didn't have very far to go. But, more important, the transmitter would have been very low-powered . . . and very small."

"But—by all accounts—and yours, too—he was severely shocked after the explosion."

"Shocked by the sight of the disintegration he had been sitting on all day. And acting a bit, too."

He thought it over at length. Then he said, "Wouldn't someone have noticed that the Major wasn't using binoculars although he was carrying the case?"

"He could say he'd just dropped them and they were broken . . . and anyway he carries a flask in that case normally as well as the race glasses. . . . Lots of people must have seen him taking a swig, as I have. They wouldn't think it odd. They might think he'd brought the flask but forgotten the glasses."

I could imagine him shaking his head. "It's a fantastic theory altogether. And not a shred of evidence. Just a guess." He paused. "I'm sorry, Mr. Shore, I'm certain you've done your best, but . . ."

I noticed he'd demoted me from captain. I smiled thinly.

"There's one other tiny thing," I said gently.

"Yes?" He was slightly, very slightly apprehensive, as if expecting yet more fantasy.

"I got in touch with a cousin in the army, and he looked up some old records for me. In World War II, Major Tyderman was in the Royal Engineers, in charge of a unit which spent nearly all of its time in England."

"I don't see—"

"They were dealing," I said, "with unexploded bombs."

9

It was the next day that Nancy flew Colin to Haydock. They went in the four-seat 140-horsepower small-version Cherokee, which she normally hired from her flying club for lessons and practice, and they set off from Cambridge shortly before I left there myself with a full load in the replacement Six. I had been through her flight plan with her and helped her all I could with the many technicalities and regulations she would meet in the complex Manchester control zone. The weather forecast was for clear skies until evening; there would be radar to help her if she got lost; and I would be listening to her nearly all the time on the radio as I followed her up.

Colin grinned at me. "Harley would be horrified at the care you're taking to look after her. 'Let them frighten themselves silly,' he'd say. 'Then he'll fly with us all the time, with none of this do-it-yourself nonsense.' "

"Yeah," I said. "And Harley wants you safe, too, don't forget."

"Did he tell you to help us?"

"Not actually, no."

"Thought not."

Harley had said crossly, "I don't want them making a habit of it. Persuade Colin Ross she isn't experienced enough."

Colin didn't need persuading: he knew. He also wanted to please Nancy. She set off with shining eyes, like a child being given a treat.

The Derrydowns Six had been hired by an unclued-up trainer who had separately agreed to share the trip with both Annie Villars and Kenny Bayst. Even diluted by the hiring trainer, the large loud-voiced owner of the horse he was running, and the jockey who was to ride it, the atmosphere at loading time was poisonous.

Jarvis Kitch, the hiring trainer, who could have helped, retreated into a huff.

"How was I to know," he complained to me in aggrieved anger, "that they loathe each other's guts?"

"You couldn't," I said soothingly.

"They just rang up and asked if there was a spare seat. Annie yesterday, Bayst the day before. I said there was. How was I to know?"

"You couldn't."

The loud-voiced owner, who was evidently footing the bill, asked testily what the hell it mattered, they would be contributing their share of the cost. He had a North Country accent and a bullying manner, and he was the sort of man who considered that when he bought a man's services he bought his soul. Kitch subsided hastily: the small attendant jockey remained cowed and silent throughout. The owner, whose name I later discovered from the race card was Ambrose, then told me to get a move on as he hadn't hired me to stand around all day on the ground at Cambridge.

Annie Villars suggested in embarrassment that the captain of an aircraft was like the captain of a ship.

"Nonsense," he said. "In a two-bit little outfit like this, he's only a chauffeur. Taking me from place to place, isn't he? For hire?" He nodded. "Chauffeur." His voice left no one in any doubt about his opinion on the proper place of chauffeurs.

I sighed, climbed aboard, strapped myself in. Easy to ignore him, as it was far from the first time in my life I'd met that attitude. All the same, hardly one of the jolliest of trips.

The Cherokee Six cruised at fifty miles an hour faster than the 140, so that I passed Nancy somewhere on the way up. I could hear her calling the various flight-information regions on the radio, as she could hear me. It was companionable, in an odd sort of way. And she was doing all right.

I landed at Haydock a few minutes before her, and unloaded the passengers in time to watch her come in. She put on a show to impress the audience, touching down like a feather on the grass. I grinned to myself. Not bad for a ninety-five-hour amateur. It hadn't been the easiest of trips, either. There would be no holding her after this.

She rolled to a stop a little way along the rails from me, and I finished locking the Six and walked over to tell her she would smash the undercarriage next time she thumped an airplane down like that.

She made a face at me, excited and pleased. "It was super. Great. The Liverpool radar people were awfully kind. They told me exactly which headings to fly round the control zone, and then told me they would put me smack overhead the racecourse, and they did."

Colin was proud of her and teased her affectionately. "Sure, we've got here, but we've got to go home yet."

"Going home's always easier," she said confidently. "And there are none of those difficult control-zone rules round Cambridge."

We walked together across the track to the paddock, ducking under the rails. Nancy talked the whole way, as high as if she'd taken Benzedrine. Colin grinned at me. I grinned back. Nothing as intoxicating as a considerable achievement.

We left him at the weighing room and went off to have some coffee.

"Do you know it's only four weeks since we were at Haydock before?" she said. "Since the bomb. Only four weeks. I seem to have known you half my life."

"I hope you'll know me for the other half," I said.

"What did you say?"

"Nothing. . . . Turkey sandwiches all right?"

"Mmm, lovely." She looked at me, unsure. "What did you mean?"

"Just one of those pointless things people say."

"Oh."

She bit into the soft thick sandwich. She had good straight teeth. I was being a fool, I thought. A fool to get involved, a fool to grow fond of her. I had nothing but a lot of ruins to offer anyone, and she had the whole world to choose from, the sister of Colin Ross. If I was an iceberg, as Honey said, I'd better stay an iceberg. When ice melted, it made a mess.

"You've clammed up," she said, observing me.

"I haven't."

"Oh, yes, you have. You do, sometimes. You look relaxed and peaceful, and then something inside goes snap shut and you retreat out into the stratosphere. Somewhere very cold." She shivered. "Freezing."

I drank my coffee and let the stratosphere do its stuff. The melting edges safely refroze.

"Will Chanter be here today?" I asked.

"God knows." She shrugged. "Do you want him to be?"

"No." It sounded more vehement than I meant.

"That's something, anyhow," she said under her breath.

I let it go. She couldn't mean what it sounded like. We finished the sandwiches and went out to watch Colin ride, and after that, while we were leaning against the parade-ring rails, Chanter appeared out of nowhere and smothered Nancy in hair and fringes and swirling fabric, as closely as if he were putting out a fire with a carpet.

She pushed him away. "For God's sake . . ."

He was unabashed. "Aw, Nancy. C'mon now. You and me, we'd have everything going for us if you'd just loosen up."

"You're a bad trip, Chanter, as far as I'm concerned."

"You've never been on any real trip, chick, that's your problem."

"And I'm not going," she said firmly.

"A little acid lets you into the guts of things."

"Components," I said. "As you said before. You see things in fragments."

"Huh?" Chanter focused on me. "Nancy, you still got this creep in tow? You must be joking."

"He sees things whole," she said. "No props needed."

"Acid isn't a prop, it's a doorway," he declaimed.

"Shut the door," she said. "I'm not going through."

Chanter scowled at me. The green chenille tablecloth had been exchanged for a weird shapeless tunic made of irregular-shaped pieces of fabrics, fur, leather, and metal, all stapled together instead of sewn.

"This is your doing, man, you're bad news."

"It's not his doing," Nancy said. "The drug scene is a drag. It always was. Maybe at art school I thought getting woozy on pot was a gas, but not any more. I've grown up, Chanter. I've told you before, I've grown up."

"He's brainwashed you."

She shook her head. I knew she was thinking of Midge. Face something big enough and you always grow up.

"Don't you have any classes today?" she asked.

He scowled more fiercely. "The sods are out on strike."

She laughed. "Do you mean the students?"

"Yeah. Demanding the sack for the deputy Head for keeping a record of what demos they go to."

I asked ironically, "Which side are you on?"

He peered at me. "You bug me, man, you do really."

For all that, he stayed with us all afternoon, muttering, scowling, plonking his hands on Nancy whenever he got the chance. Nancy bore his company as if she didn't altogether dislike it. As for me, I could have done without it. Easily.

Colin won two races, including the day's biggest. Annie Villars' horse came second, Kenny Bayst won a race on an objection. The loud-voiced Ambrose's horse finished fast but fourth, which didn't bode well for sweetness and light on the way home.

The way home was beginning to give me faint twinges of speculation. The weak warm front which had been forecast for late evening looked as if it were arriving well before schedule. From the southwest, the upper winds were drawing a strip of cloud over the sky like a sheet over a bed.

Nancy looked up when the sun went in.

"Golly, where did all that cloud come from?"

"It's the warm front."

"Damn. . . . Do you think it will have got to Cambridge?"

"I'll find out for you, if you like."

I telephoned to Cambridge and asked them for their actual and forecast weather. Nancy stood beside me inside the telephone box, and Chanter fumed suspiciously outside. I had to ask Cambridge to repeat what they'd said. Nancy smelled faintly of a fresh flowering scent. "Did you say two thousand feet?" Yes, said Cambridge with exaggerated patience, we've told you twice already.

I put down the receiver. "The front isn't expected there for three or four hours, and the forecast cloud base even then is as high as two thousand feet, so you should be all right."

"Anyway," she said, "I've done dozens of practice letdowns with

Cambridge. Even if it should be cloudy by the time we get back, I'm sure I could do it in earnest."

"Have you ever done it without an instructor?"

She nodded. "Several times. On fine days, of course."

I pondered. "You aren't legally qualified yet to carry passengers in clouds."

"Don't look so fraught. I won't have to. They said it was clear there now, didn't they? And if the base is two thousand feet when I get there, I can keep below that easily."

"Yes, I suppose you can."

"And I've got to get back, haven't I?" she said reasonably.

"Mmm. . . ."

Chanter pulled open the telephone-box door. "You taking a lease on that space, man?" he inquired. He put his arm forward over Nancy's chest a millimeter south of her breasts and scooped her out. She half disappeared into the enveloping fuzz and emerged blushing.

"Chanter, for God's sake, we're at the races!"

"Transfer to my pad, then."

"No, thank you."

"Women," he said in disgust. "Goddamn women. Don't know what's good for them."

"How's that for a right-wing reactionary statement?" I inquired of the air in general.

"You cool it, man. Just cool it."

Nancy smoothed herself down and said, "Both of you cool it. I'm going back to the airplane now to get set for going home, and you're not coming with me, Chanter. I can't concentrate with you crawling all over me."

He stayed behind with bad grace, complaining bitterly when she took me with her.

"He's impossible," she said as we walked across the track. But she was smiling.

Spreading the map out on the wing, I went through the flight plan with her, step by step, as that was what she wanted. She was going back as we'd come, via the radio beacon at Lichfield: not a straight line but the easiest way to navigate. As she had said, it was a simpler business going home. I worked out the times between points for her and filled them in on her planning sheet.

"You are five times as quick at it as I am." She sighed.

"I've had a spot more practice."

I folded the map and clipped the completed plan onto it. "See you at Cambridge," I said. "With a bit of luck."

"Meany."

"Nancy. . . ."

"Yes?"

I didn't exactly know what I wanted to say. She waited. After a while, I said earnestly, "Take care."

She half smiled. "I will, you know."

Colin came across the track, dragging his feet. "God, I'm tired," he said. "How's my pilot?"

"Ready, willing, and, if it's your lucky day, able."

I did the external checks for her while they climbed aboard. No bombs to be seen. Didn't expect any. She started the engine after I'd given her the all clear, and they both waved as she taxied off. She turned into wind at the far end of the field, accelerated quickly, and lifted off into the pale gray sky. The clouds were a shade lower than they had been. Nothing to worry about. Not if it was clear at Cambridge. I strolled across to the Derrydowns Six. Annie Villars and Kenny Bayst were both there already, studiously looking in opposite directions. I unlocked the doors, and Annie embarked without a word. Kenny gave her a sour look and stayed outside on the ground. I congratulated him on his winner. It all helped, he said.

Ambrose's trainer and jockey trickled back looking pensive, and finally Ambrose came himself, reddish in the face and breathing out beer fumes in a sickly cloud. As soon as he reached the aircraft, he leaned toward me and gave me the full benefit.

"I've left me hat in the cloakroom," he said. "Hop over and fetch it for me."

Kenny and the other two were all of a sudden very busy piling themselves aboard and pretending they hadn't heard. Short of saying "Fetch it yourself" and losing Harley a customer, I was stuck with it. I trudged back across the track, through the paddock, into the members' Gents, and collected the hat off the peg it was hanging on. Its band was so greasy that I wondered how Ambrose had the nerve to let anyone see it.

Turned, made for the door. Felt my arm clutched in a fiercely urgent grip.

I swung round. The hands holding on to my arm like steel grabs belonged to Major Tyderman.

"Major," I exclaimed in surprise. I hadn't seen him there all through the afternoon.

"Shore!" He was far more surprised to see me. And more than surprised. Horrified. The color was draining out of his face while I watched.

"Shore. . . . What are you doing here? Did you come back?"

Puzzled, I said, "I came over for Mr. Ambrose's hat."

"But—you flew—you took off with Colin and Nancy Ross."

I shook my head. "No, I didn't. Nancy was flying."

"But—you came with them." He sounded agonized.

"I didn't. I flew the Six here with five passengers." The extreme state of his shock got through to me like a tidal wave. He was clinging on to my arm now more for support than to attract my attention.

"Major," I said, the terrible, terrifying suspicion shaking in my voice, "you haven't put another bomb on that aircraft? Not—oh, God—another bomb?"

"I—I—" His voice strangled in his throat.

"Major." I disengaged my arm and seized both of his. Ambrose's hat fell and rolled unnoticed on the dirty floor. "Major." I squeezed him viciously. *"Not another bomb?"*

"No—but—"

"But *what?*"

"I thought—you were flying them—I thought you were with them—You would be able to cope. . . ."

"Major." I shook him, gripping as if I'd pull his arms in two. "What have you done to that airplane?"

"I saw you—come with them, when they came. And go back—and look at the map—and do the checks. . . . I was sure—it was you that was flying—and you—you—could deal with— But Nancy Ross. . . . Oh, my God. . . ."

I let go one of his arms and slapped him hard in the face.

"What have you done to that airplane?"

"You can't—do anything. . . ."

"I'll get her back. Get her down on the ground at once."

He shook his head. "You won't—be able to. . . . She'll have no radio. . . . I put . . ." He swallowed and put his hand to his face where I'd hit him. "I put—a plaster—nitric acid—on the lead—to the master switch. . . ."

I let go of his other arm and simply looked at him, feeling the coldness sink in. Then I blindly picked up Ambrose's hat and ran out of the door. Ran. Ran across the paddock, across the track, down to the aircraft. I didn't stop to slap out of the Major what he'd done it for. Didn't think of it. Thought only of Nancy Ross with her limited experience having to deal with a total electrical failure.

She could do it, of course. The engine wouldn't stop. Several of the instruments would go on working. The altimeter, the air-speed indicator, the compass—none of those essentials would be affected. They worked on magnetism, air pressure, and engine-driven gyroscopes, not electricity.

All the engine instruments would read zero, and the fuel gauge would register empty. She wouldn't know how much fuel she had left. But she did know, I thought, that she had enough for at least two hours' flying.

The worst thing was the radio. She would have no communication with the ground, nor could she receive any signals from the navigation beacons. Well . . . dozens of people flew without radio, without even having it installed at all. If she was worried about getting lost, she could land at the first suitable airfield.

It might not have happened yet, I thought. Her radio might still be working. The nitric acid might not yet have eaten through the main electrical cable.

While I was on the ground, I was too low down for them to hear me, but if I got up in the air fast enough, I could tell the Manchester control people the situation, get them to relay the facts to her, tell her to land at an airfield as soon as she could. . . . A fairly simple matter to repair the cable, once she was safe on the ground.

I gave Ambrose his hat. He was still outside on the grass, waiting for me to climb through to the left-hand seat. I shifted myself across onto it with no seconds wasted, and he hauled himself up after me. By the time he'd strapped himself in, I had the engine running, my headset in place, and the radios warming up.

"What's the rush?" Ambrose inquired as we taxied at just under takeoff speed down to the far end.

"Have to send a radio message to Colin Ross, who's in the air ahead of us."

"Oh." He nodded heavily. He knew the Rosses had come up when we had, knew that Nancy was flying. "All right, then."

I thought fleetingly that if he thought I couldn't even hurry without getting his permission first, he was in for a moderate shock. I wasn't taking him back to Cambridge until I was certain Nancy and Colin were safe.

As there was only one headset on board, Ambrose couldn't hear any incoming transmissions, and with the microphone close against my lips I doubted if he could hear over the engine noise anything I sent outward. I thought I would delay as long as possible inviting his objections.

Two hundred feet off the ground, I raised the Air Traffic Controller at Liverpool. Explained that Nancy's radio might be faulty; asked if he had heard her.

Yes, he had. He'd given her radar clearance out of the control zone, and handed her on to Preston Information. Since I had to stay on his frequency until I was out of the zone myself, I asked him to find out from Preston if they still had contact with her.

"Stand by," he said.

After a long two minutes, he came back. "They did have," he said briefly. "They lost her in the middle of one of her transmissions. They can't raise her now."

Sod the Major, I thought violently. Stupid, dangerous little man.

I kept my voice casual. "Did they have her position?"

"Stand by." A pause. He came back. "She was on track to Lichfield, E.T.A. Lichfield five three, flying visual on top at flight level four five."

"On top?" I repeated with apprehension.

"Affirmative."

We had been climbing steadily ourselves. We went into thin cloud at two thousand feet and came through it into the sunshine at four thousand. Everywhere below us in all directions spread the cotton-wool blanket, hiding the earth beneath. She would have had to climb to that height as well, because the Pennines to the east of Manchester rose to nearly three thousand feet and the high ridges would have been sticking up into the clouds. With no room for her between the clouds and the hills, she would have either had to go back or go up. She wouldn't see any harm in going up. With radio navigation and a good forecast for Cambridge, it was merely the sensible thing to do.

"Her destination is Cambridge," I said. "Can you check the weather there?"

"Stand by." A much longer pause. Then his voice, dead level, spelling it out. "Cambridge actual weather, cloud has spread in fast from the southwest, now eight-eighths cover, base twelve hundred feet, tops three thousand five hundred."

I didn't acknowledge him at once: was digesting the appalling implications.

"Confirm weather copied," he said baldly.

"Weather copied."

"Latest meteorological reports indicate total cloud cover over the entire area south of the Tees." He knew exactly what he was saying. The laconic non-panic voice was deliberately unexcited. Nancy was flying above the cloud layer with no means of telling where she was. She couldn't see the ground and couldn't ask anyone for directions. Eventually she would have to come down, because she would run out of fuel. With the gauge out of action, she couldn't tell exactly how long she could stay airborne, and it was essential for her to go down through the clouds while the engine was still running, so that she could find somewhere to land once she was underneath. But if she went down too soon or in the wrong place, she could all too easily fly into a cloud-covered hill. Even for a highly experienced pilot, it was a sticky situation.

I said, with the same studied artificial calm, "Can the R.A.F. radar stations find her and trace her where she goes? I know her flight plan. . . . I made it out for her. She is likely to stick to it, as she thinks it is still clear at Cambridge. I could follow . . . and find her."

"Stand by." Again the pause for consultations. "Change frequency to Birmingham radar on one two three three."

"Roger," I said. "And thanks very much."

"Good luck," he said. "You'll need it."

10

HE HAD explained the situation to Birmingham. I gave the radar controller Nancy's planned track and air speed and estimated time for Lichfield, and after a few moments he came back and said there were at least ten aircraft on his screen which were possibles, but he had no way of telling who they were. "I'll consult with the R.A.F. Wymeswold. . . . They may not be as busy as we are. They can concentrate on it more."

"Tell them that at about five three she will change her heading to one two five."

"Roger," he said. "Stand by."

He came back. "R.A.F. Wymeswold say they will watch for her."

"Great," I said.

After a few moments, he said in an incredulous voice, "We have a report that Colin Ross is aboard the non-radio aircraft. Can you confirm?"

"Affirmative" I said. "The pilot is his sister."

"Good God," he said. "Then we'd better find her."

I had got them to route me straight through the control zone instead of round it, and was making for Northwich, and then the Lichfield beacon. We had taken off, I calculated, a good thirty minutes behind her, and in spite of the short cut and the Six's superior speed, it would be barely possible to overtake her before Cambridge. I looked at my watch for about the twentieth time. Five-fifty. At five-fifty-three, she would be turning over Lichfield . . . except that she wouldn't know she was at Lichfield. If she turned as scheduled, it would be on her part simply blind faith.

Birmingham radar called me up. "Cambridge report a steady deterioration in the weather. The cloud base is now eight hundred feet."

"Roger," I said flatly.

After another five minutes, during which five-fifty-three came and went in silence, he said, "Wymeswold report that an aircraft on their screen has turned from one six zero onto one two five, but it is five miles northeast of Lichfield. The aircraft is unidentified. They will maintain surveillance."

"Roger," I said.

She could be drifting northeast, I thought, because the wind from the southwest was stronger than it had been on the northward journey, and I hadn't made enough allowance for it on the flight plan. I pressed the transmit button and informed the radarman.

"I'll tell them," he said.

We flew on. I looked round at the passengers. They looked variously bored, thoughtful, and tired. Probably none of them would notice when we left our direct course to go and look for Nancy: but they'd certainly notice if or when we found her.

"Wymeswold report the aircraft they were watching has turned north onto zero one zero."

"Oh, no," I said.

"Stand by. . . ."

Too easy, I thought despairingly. It had been too easy. The aircraft which had turned onto the right heading at the right time at roughly the right place hadn't been the right aircraft after all. I took three deep deliberate breaths. Concentrated on the fact that wherever she was she was in no immediate danger. She could stay up for more than another hour and a half.

I had over an hour in which to find her. In roughly three thousand square miles of sky as featureless as the desert. Piece of cake.

"Wymeswold report that the first aircraft has apparently landed at East Midlands, but that they have another possibility ten miles east of Lichfield, present heading one two zero. They have no height information."

"Roger," I said again. No height information meant that the blip on their screen could be flying at anything up to thirty thousand feet or more, not four thousand five hundred.

"Stand by."

I stood by. Mentally bit my nails. Slid a sidelong glance at Ambrose and went unhurriedly about checking our own height, speed, direction. Lichfield dead ahead, eleven minutes away. Forty minutes to Cambridge. Too long. Have to go faster. Pushed the throttle open another notch and came up against the stops. Full power. Nothing more to be done.

"Possible aircraft now tracking steady one zero five. Present track if maintained will take it thirty miles north of Cambridge at estimated time two zero."

"Roger." I looked at my watch. Did a brief sum. Pressed the transmit button. "That's the wrong aircraft. It's traveling too fast. At ninety knots, she couldn't reach the Cambridge area before three five or four zero."

"Understood." A short silence. "Retune now to R.A.F. Cottesmore, Northern Radar, one four two decimal two nine. I'm handing you on to them."

I thanked him. Retuned. Cottesmore said they were in the picture, and looking. They had seven unidentified aircraft traveling from west to east to the south of them, all at heights unknown.

Seven. She could be any one of them. She could have gone completely haywire and turned round and headed back to Manchester. I felt my skin prickle. Surely she would have enough sense not to fly straight into a control zone without radio. And anyway she still believed it was clear at Cambridge. . . .

I reached the Lichfield beacon. Turned onto course for Cambridge. Informed Cottesmore radar that I had done so. They didn't have me on their screen yet, they said: I was still too far away.

I tracked doggedly on toward Cambridge over the cotton-wool wastes. The sun shone hotly into the cabin, and all the passengers except Ambrose went to sleep.

"One unidentified aircraft has landed at Leicester," Cottesmore radar said. "Another appears to be heading directly for Peterborough."

"That leaves five?" I asked.

"Six. . . . There's another now further to the west."

"It may be me."

"Turn left thirty degrees for identification."

I turned, flew on the new heading.

"Identified," he said. "Return to former heading."

I turned back on track, stifling the raw anxiety which mounted with every minute. They must find her, I thought. They *must*.

Cottesmore said, "One aircraft which passed close to the south of us five minutes ago has now turned north."

Not her.

"The same aircraft has now flown in a complete circle and resumed a track on one one zero."

It might be. If she had spotted a thin patch. Had gone to see if she could see the ground and get down safely to below the cloud. Had found she couldn't; had gone on again in what she thought was the direction of Cambridge.

"That might be her," I said. Or someone else in the same difficulties. Or someone simply practicing turns. Or anything.

"That particular aircraft has now turned due south . . . slightly west . . . now round again to southeast . . . back on one one zero."

"Could be looking for thin patches in the cloud," I said.

"Could be. Stand by." A pause. Then his voice, remote and careful. "Cloud base in this area is down to six hundred feet. Eight-eights cover. No clear patches."

Oh, Nancy. . . .

"I'm going to look for that one," I said. 'Can you give me a steer to close on its present track?"

"Will do," he said. "Turn left onto zero nine five. You are thirty-two miles to the west. I estimate your ground speed at one fifty knots. The aircraft in question is traveling at about ninety-five knots."

In the twelve minutes it would take me to reach the other aircraft's present position, it would have shifted twenty further on. Catching up would take twenty-five to thirty minutes.

"The aircraft in question is circling again . . . now tracking one one zero. . . ."

The more it circled, the sooner I'd catch it. But if it wasn't Nancy after all . . . I thrust the thought violently out of my mind. If it wasn't Nancy, we might never find her.

Ambrose touched my arm, and I had been concentrating so hard that I jumped.

"We're off course," he said dogmatically. He tapped the compass. "We're going due east. We'd better not be lost."

"We're under radar control," I said matter-of-factly.

"Oh. . . ." He was uncertain. "I see."

I would have to tell him, I thought. Couldn't put if off any longer. I explained the situation as briefly as I could, leaving out Major Tyderman's part in it and shouting to make myself heard over the noise of the engine.

He was incredulous. "Do you mean we're chasing all over the sky looking for Colin Ross?"

"Directed by radar," I said briefly.

"And who," he asked belligerently, "is going to pay for this? I am certainly not. In fact, you have been totally irresponsible in changing course without asking my permission first."

Cottesmore reported, "The aircraft is now overhead Stamford, and circling again."

"Roger," I said. And for God's sake, Nancy, I thought, don't try going down through the cloud just there. There were some hills round about a radio mast five hundred feet high.

"Steer one zero zero to close."

"One zero zero."

"Aircraft has resumed its former heading."

I took a considerable breath of relief.

"Did you hear what I said?" Ambrose demanded angrily.

'We have a duty to go to the help of an aircraft in trouble," I said.

"Not at my expense, we don't."

"You will be charged." I said patiently, "only the normal amount for the trip."

"That's not the point. You should have asked my permission. I am seriously displeased. I will complain to Harley. We should not have left our course. Someone else should have gone to help Colin Ross. Why should we be inconvenienced?"

"I am sure he will be pleased to hear your views," I said politely. "And no doubt he will pay any expenses incurred in his rescue."

He glared at me speechlessly, swept by fury.

Annie Villars leaned forward and tapped me on the shoulder.

"Did I hear you say that Colin Ross is lost? Up here, do you mean? On top of the clouds?"

I glanced round. They were all awake, all looking concerned.

"Yes," I said briefly. "With no radio. The radar people think they may have found him. We're going over to see . . . and to help."

"Anything we can do. . . ." Annie said. "Of course, call on us."

I smiled at her over my shoulder. Ambrose turned round to her and started to complain. She shut him up smartly. "Do you seriously propose we make no attempt to help? You must be out of your mind. It is our clear and absolute duty to do whatever we can. And a captain doesn't have to consult his passengers before he goes to help another ship in distress."

He said something about expense. Annie said crisply, "If you are too mean to pay a few extra pounds as your share of perhaps saving the life of Colin Ross, I shall be pleased to contribute the whole amount myself."

"Atta girl," Kenny Bayst said loudly. Annie Villars looked startled, but not displeased. Ambrose swiveled to face forward. He had turned a dark purplish red. I hoped it was shame and embarrassment, not an incipient thrombosis.

"The aircraft is circling again," Cottesmore reported. "Its position now is just south of Peterborough. . . . Remain on your present heading. . . . I am handing you on now to Wytton. . . . No need for you to explain to them . . . they know the situation."

"Thank you very much," I said.

"Good luck. . . ."

Wytton, the next in the chain, the R.A.F. master station northeast of Cambridge, was crisp, cool, efficient.

"Cloud base at Cambridge six hundred feet, no further deterioration in past half hour. Visibility three kilometers in light rain. Surface wind two four zero, ten knots."

"Weather copied," I said automatically. I was looking at the map. Another radio mast, this one seven hundred feet high, south of Peterborough. Go on, Nancy, I thought, go on further east. Don't try there. Not there . . .

Wytton said, "Aircraft now back on one one zero."

I rubbed a hand round the back of my neck. I could feel the sweat.

"Steer zero nine five. You are now ten miles west of the aircraft."

"I'm climbing to flight level eight zero. To see better."

"Cleared to eight zero."

The altimeter hands crept round to eight thousand feet. The blanket of white fleece spread out unbroken in all directions to the horizon, soft and pretty in the sun. The passengers murmured, perhaps realizing for the first time the extent of Nancy's predicament. Mile after mile after mile of emptiness, and absolutely no way of telling where she was.

"Aircraft's circling again. . . . Maintain zero nine five. You are now seven miles to the west."

I said over my shoulder to Annie Villars, "We'll see them soon. . . . Would you take this notebook"—I handed her the spiral-bound reporters' notebook I used for jotting during flights—"and make some letters out of the pages? As big as you can. We will need, you see, to hold them up in the window, so that Nancy and Colin can read what we want them to do."

And let it be them, I thought coldly. Just let it be them, and not some other poor lost souls. Because we'd have to stay to help. We couldn't leave them to struggle, and look somewhere else for the ones we wanted. . . .

Annie Villars fumbled in her handbag and produced a small pair of scissors.

"Which letters?" she said economically. "You say, and I'll write them down, and then make them."

"Right. . . . F O L W B A S E. That will do to start with."

I twisted my head and saw her start snipping. She was making the letters full-page size and as bold as possible. Satisfied, I looked forward again, scanning the sunny waste, searching for a small black cigarette shape moving ahead.

"Turn onto one zero five," Wytton said. "The aircraft is now in your one-o'clock position five miles ahead."

I looked down over to the right of the aircraft's nose. Ambrose reluctantly looked out of the window in sulky silence.

"*There,*" Kenny Bayst said. "Over there, down there." I looked where he was pointing . . . and there it was, slightly more over to our right, beginning another circling sweep over a darker patch of cloud which might have been a hole, but wasn't.

"Contact," I said to Wytton. "Closing in now."

"Your intentions?" he asked unemotionally.

"Lead them up to The Wash, descend over the sea, follow the river and railway from King's Lynn to Cambridge."

"Roger. We'll advise Marham. They'll give you radar coverage over the sea."

I put the nose down, built up the speed, and overhauled the other aircraft like an E-type catching a bicycle. The nearer we got, the more I hoped. . . . It was a low-winged airplane . . . a Cherokee . . . white with red markings . . . and finally the registration number . . . and someone frantically waving a map at us from the window.

The relief was overpowering.

"It's them," Annie said, and I could only nod and swallow.

I throttled back and slowed the Six until it was down to Nancy's cruising speed, then circled until I came up on her left-hand side, and about fifty yards away. She had never done any formation flying. Fifty yards was the closest it was safe to go to her, and even fifty yards was risking it a bit. I kept my hand on the throttle, my eyes on her, and an extra pair of eyes I didn't know I had fixed on the heading.

To Annie Villars I said, "Hold up the letters for 'follow.' Slowly. One by one."

"Right." She held them flat against the window beside her. We could see Colin's head leaning back behind Nancy's. When Annie finished the word, we saw him wave his hand, and after that Nancy waved her map against her window, which showed up better.

"Wytton," I reported. "It is the right aircraft. They are following us to The Wash. Can you give me a steer to King's Lynn?"

"Delighted," he said. "Steer zero four zero, and call Marham on this frequency."

"Thanks a lot," I said with feeling.

"You're very welcome."

Good guys, I thought. Very good guys, sitting in their darkened rooms wearing headsets and staring at their little dark circular screens, watching the multitude of yellow-orange dots which were aircraft swimming slowly across like tadpoles. They'd done a terrific job finding the Rosses. Terrific.

"Can you make a figure 4?" I asked Annie Villars.

"Certainly." The scissors began to snip.

"When you have, would you hold up the 0, then the 4, then the 0 again?"

"With pleasure."

She held up the figures. Nancy waved the map. We set off northeastward to the sea, Nancy staying behind us to the right, with me flying looking over my shoulder to keep a steady distance between us. I judged it would take thirteen minutes at her speed to reach the sea, five to ten to let down, and twenty or so more to return underneath the cloud base to Cambridge. Her fuel by the time she got there would be low, but there was less risk of her running dry than of hitting a hill or trees or a building by going down over the land. Letting down over the sea was in these circumstances the best procedure whenever possible.

"We're going to need some more letters," I told Annie.

"Which?"

"Umm. . . . R, I, V, and N, D, C, and a T, and a 9."

"Right."

Out of the corner of my eye I could see Annie Villars snipping and Kenny Bayst, sitting behind her, sorting out the letters she had already made so that she could easily pick them out when they were needed. There was, I thought with a small internal smile, a truce in operation in that area.

Marham radar reported, "You have four miles to run to the coast."

"Hope the tide's in," I said facetiously.

"Affirmative," he said with deadpan humor. "High water eighteen forty hours B.S.T."

"And . . . er . . . the cloud base?"

"Stand by." Down in his dark room, he couldn't see the sky. He had to ask the tower dwellers above.

"Cloud base between six and seven hundred feet above sea level over the entire area from The Wash to Cambridge. Visibility two kilometers in drizzle."

"Nice," I said with irony.

"Very."

"Could I have the regional pressure settings?"

"Nine nine eight millibars."

"Nine nine eight," I repeated, and took my hand off the throttle long enough to set that figure on the altimeter subscale. To Annie Villars I said, "Can you make an 8, as well?"

"I expect so."

"Crossing the coast," Marham said.

"Right. . . . Miss Villars will you hold up S E A?"

She nodded and did so. Nancy waved the map.

"Now hold up S E T, then 9 9 8, then M B S."

"S . . . E . . . T," she repeated, holding them against the window. "Nine . . . nine . . . eight." she paused. "There's no M cut out."

"W upside down," Kenny Bayst said, and gave it to her.

"Oh, yes. M . . . B . . . S. What does MBS mean?"

"Millibars," I said.

Nancy waved the map, but I said to Annie, "Hold up the nine nine eight again, it's very important."

She held them up. We could see Nancy's head nodding as she waved back vigorously.

"Why is it so important?" Annie said.

"Unless you set the altimeter to the right pressure on the subscale, it doesn't tell you how high you are above the sea."

"Oh."

"Now would you hold up B A S E, then 6 0 0, then F T."

"Right. . . . Base . . . six hundred . . . feet."

There was a distinct pause before Nancy waved, and then it was a small, halfhearted one. She must have been horrified to find that the clouds were so low: she must have been thanking her stars that she hadn't tried to go down through them. Highly frightening piece of information, that six hundred feet.

"Now," I said to Annie, "hold up 'Follow river and rail one nine zero to Cambridge.' "

"Follow . . . river . . . and . . . rail . . . one . . . nine . . . zero . . . to . . . Cambridge. . . . No G. . . . Never mind, C will do, then E." She spelt it out slowly. Nancy waved.

"And just one more . . . 4 0, then N, then M."

"Forty nautical miles," she said triumphantly. She held them up and Nancy waved.

"Now hold up 'follow' again."

"Right."

I consulted Marham, took Nancy out to sea a little further, and led her round in a circle until we were both heading just west of south on one nine zero, and in a straight line to the railway and river from King's Lynn to Cambridge.

"Hold up D O W N," I said.

She did it without speaking. Nancy gave a little wave. I put the nose of the six down toward the clouds and accelerated to a hundred and forty knots so that there would be no possibility of her crashing into the back of us. The white fleecy layer came up to meet us, embraced us in sunlit feathery wisps, closed lightly around us, became denser, darker, an anthracite fog pressing on the windows. The altimeter unwound, the clock needles going backward through 3,000 feet, 2,000 feet, 1,000 feet, still no break at 800 feet, 700 . . . and there, there at last the mist receded a little and became drizzly haze, and underneath us, pretty close underneath, were the restless rain-swept dark greeny-gray waves.

The passengers were all silent. I glanced round at them. They were all looking down at the sea in varying states of awe. I wondered if any of them knew I had just broken two laws and would undoubtedly be prosecuted again by the Board of Trade. I wondered if I would ever, ever learn to keep myself out of trouble.

We crossed the coast over King's Lynn and flew down the river to Ely and Cambridge, just brushing through the misty cloud base at seven hundred feet. The forward visibility was bad, and I judged it silly to go back and wait for Nancy, because we might collide before we saw each other. I completed the journey as briefly as possible, and we landed on the wet tarmac and taxied round toward the airport buildings. When I stopped the engine, everyone, as if moved by one mind, climbed out and looked upward; even Ambrose.

The drizzle was light now, like fine mist. We stood quietly in it, getting damp, listening for the sound of an engine, watching for the shadow against the sky. Minutes ticked past. Annie Villars looked at me anxiously. I shook my head, not knowing exactly what I meant.

She couldn't have gone down too far . . . hit the sea . . . got disorientated in the cloud . . . lost when she came out of it . . . still in danger.

The drizzle fell. My heart also.

But she hadn't made any mistakes.

The engine noise crept in as a hum, then a buzz, then a definite rhythm. The little red-and-white airplane appeared suddenly against the right-hand sky, and she was circling safely round the outskirts of the field and coming sedately down to land.

"Oh. . . ." Annie Villars said, and wiped two surprising tears of relief out of her eyes.

Ambrose said sulkily, "That's all right, then. Now I hope we can get off home," and stomped heavily off toward the buildings.

Nancy taxied round and stopped her Cherokee a short distance away. Colin climbed out on the wing, grinned hugely in our direction, and waved.

"He's got no bloody nerves," Kenny said. "Not a bleeding nerve in his whole body."

Nancy came out after him, jumping down onto the tarmac and staggering a bit as she landed on her wobbly knees. I began to walk toward them. She started slowly to meet me, and then faster, and then ran, with her hair swinging out and her arms stretched wide. I grabbed her round the waist and swung her up and round in the air, and when I put her down she wrapped her arms behind my neck and kissed me.

"Matt. . . ." She was half laughing, half crying, her eyes shining, her cheeks a burning red, the sudden release of tension making her tremble down to her fingertips.

Colin reached us and gave me a pat on the shoulder.

"Thanks, chum."

"Thank the R.A.F. They found you on their radar."

"But how did you know? . . ."

"Long story," I said. Nancy was still holding on to me as if she would fall down if she let go. I made the most of it by kissing her again, on my own account.

She laughed shakily and untwined her arms. "When you came—I can't tell you—it was such a relief. . . ."

Annie Villars came up and touched her arm and she turned to her with the same hectic overexcitement.

"Oh . . . *Annie*."

"Yes, dear," she said calmly. "What you need now is a strong brandy."

"I ought to see to . . ." She looked vaguely in my direction, and back to her Cherokee.

"Colin and Matt will see to everything."

"All right, then. . . ." She let herself be taken off by Annie Villars, who had recovered her poise and assumed total command as a good general should. Kenny and the other jockey and trainer meekly followed.

"Now," said Colin. "How on earth did you know we needed you?"

"I'll show you," I said abruptly. "Come and look." I walked him back to the little Cherokee, climbed up onto the wing, and lay down on my back across the two front seats, looking up under the control panel.

"What on earth? . . ."

The device was there. I showed it to him. Very neat, very small. A little polyethylene-wrapped packet swinging free on a rubber band which was itself attached to the cable leading to the master switch. Nearer the switch, one wire of the two-wire cable had been bared: the two severed ends of copper showed readily against the black plastic casing.

I left everything where it was and eased myself out onto the wing.

"What is it? What does it mean?"

"Your electric system was sabotaged."

"For God's sake . . . why?"

"I don't know." I sighed. "I only know who did it. The same person who planted the bomb a month ago. Major Rupert Tyderman."

He stared at me blankly. "It doesn't make sense."

"Not much. No."

I told him how the Major had set off the bomb while we were safely on the ground, and that today he had thought I was flying Nancy's Cherokee and could get myself out of trouble.

"But that's— That means—"

"Yes," I said.

"He's trying to make it look as though someone's trying to kill me."

I nodded. "While making damn sure you survive."

11

THE BOARD of Trade came down like the hounds of hell, and it wasn't the tall reasonable man I faced this time in the crew room but a short hard-packed individual with an obstinate jaw and unhumorous eyes. He refused to sit down: preferred to stand. He had brought no silent note taker along. He was strictly a one-man band. And hot on percussion.

"I must bring to your attention the Air Navigation Order 1966." His voice was staccato and uncompromising, the traditional politeness of his department reduced to the thinnest of veneers.

I indicated that I was reasonably familiar with the order in question. As it ruled every cranny of a professional pilot's life, this was hardly surprising.

"We have been informed that on Friday last you contravened Article Twenty-five, Paragraph Four, Subsection A, and Regulation Eight, Paragraph Two."

I waited for him to finish. Then I said, "Who informed you?"

He looked at me sharply. "That is beside the point."

"Could it have been Polyplanes?"

His eyelids flickered in spite of himself. "If we receive a complaint which can be substantiated, we are bound to investigate."

The complaint could be substantiated, all right. Saturday's newspapers were still strewn around the crew room this Monday morning, all full of the latest attempt on Colin Ross's life. Front-page stuff. Also minute details from all my passengers about how we had led him out to sea and brought him home under the 700-foot cloud base.

Only trouble was it was illegal in a single-engine airplane like the Six to take paying customers out over the sea as low as I had, and to land them at an airport where the cloud base was lower than one thousand feet.

"You admit that you contravened Article—"

I interrupted him. "Yes."

He opened his mouth and shut it again. "Er, I see." He cleared his throat. "You will receive a summons in due course."

"Yes," I said again.

"Not your first, I believe." An observation, not a sneer.

"No," I said unemotionally.

A short silence. Then I said, "How did that gadget work? The nitric-acid package on the rubber band."

"That is not your concern."

I shrugged. "I can ask any schoolboy who does chemistry."

He hesitated. He was not of the stuff to give anything away. He would never, as the tall man had, say or imply that there could be any fault in his Government or the Board. But, having searched his conscience and no doubt his standing orders, he felt able after all to come across.

"The package contained fluffy fiberglass soaked in a weak solution of nitric acid. A section of wire in the cable to the master switch had been bared, and the fiberglass wrapped around it. The nitric acid slowly dissolved the copper wire, taking, at that concentration, probably about an hour and a half to complete the process." He stopped, considering.

"And the rubber band?" I prompted.

"Yes. . . . Well, nitric acid, like water, conducts electricity, so that while the fiberglass was still in position the electrical circuit would be maintained, even though the wire itself had been completely dissolved. To break the circuit, the fiberglass package had to be removed. This was done by fastening it under tension via the rubber band to a point further up the cable. When the nitric acid dissolved right through the wire and the two ends parted, there was nothing to stop the rubber band contracting and pulling the fiberglass package away. Er . . . do I make myself clear?"

"Indeed," I agreed, "you do."

He seemed to give himself a little mental and physical shake, and turned with sudden energy toward the door.

"Right," he said briskly. "Then I need a word with Mr. Harley."

"Did you get a word with Major Tyderman?" I asked.

After the merest hiatus, he said again, "That is not your concern."

"Perhaps you have seen him already?"

Silence.

"Perhaps, though, he is away from home?"

More silence. Then he turned to me in stiff exasperation. "It is not your business to question me like this. I cannot answer you any more. It is I who am here to inquire into you, not the other way round." He shut his mouth with a snap and gave me a hard stare. "And they even warned me," he muttered.

"I hope you find the Major," I said politely, "before he plants any more little devices in inconvenient places."

He snorted, and strode before me as we left the crew room and went along to Harley's office. Harley knew what he was there for and had been predictably furious with me ever since Friday.

"Mr. Shore admits the contraventions," the Board of Trade said.

"He'd be hard pushed not to," Harley said angrily, "considering every R.A.F. base across the country told him about the low cloud base at Cambridge."

"In point of fact," agreed the Board of Trade, "he should have returned immediately to Manchester, which was then still within the legal limit, and waited there until conditions improved, instead of flying all the way to East Anglia and leaving himself with too small a fuel margin to go on to any cloud-free airport. The proper course was certainly to turn back right at the beginning."

"And to hell with Colin Ross," I said conversationally.

Their mouths tightened in chorus. There was nothing more to be said. If you jumped red traffic lights and broke the speed limit rushing someone to hospital to save his life, you could still be prosecuted for the offenses. Same thing exactly. Same impasse. Humanity versus law, an age-old quandary. Make your choice and lie on it.

"I'm not accepting any responsibility for what you did," Harley said heavily. "I will state categorically, and in court if I have to, that you were acting in direct opposition to Derrydowns' instructions, and that Derrydowns disassociates itself entirely from your actions."

I thought of asking him if he'd like a basin for the ritual washing of hands. I also thought that on the whole I'd better not.

He went on, "And of course if there is any fine involved you will pay it yourself."

Always my bad luck, I reflected, to cop it when the firm was too nearly bankrupt to be generous. I said merely, "Is that all, then? We have a charter, if you remember. . . ."

They waved me away in disgust, and I collected my gear and flew off in the Aztec to take a clutch of businessmen from Elstree to The Hague.

By the time, the previous Friday, that Colin and I had locked Nancy's Cherokee and insured that no one would touch it, the first cohorts of the local press had come galloping up with ash on their shirt fronts, and the Board of Trade, who neither slumbered nor slept, were breathing heavily down the S.T.D.

Aircraft radios are about as private as Times Square: it appeared that dozens of ground-based but air-minded Midlands enthusiasts had been listening in to my conversation with Birmingham radar and had jammed the switchboard at Cambridge ringing up to find out if Colin Ross was safe. Undaunted, they had conveyed to Fleet Street the possibility of his loss. His arrival in one piece was announced on a television news broadcast forty minutes after we landed. The great British media had pulled out every finger they possessed. Nancy and Annie Villars had answered questions until their throats were sore, and had finally taken refuge in the Ladies' Cloaks. Colin was used to dealing with the press, but by the time he extricated himself from their ever-increasing news-hungry numbers he, too, was pale blue from tiredness.

"Come on," he said to me. "Let's get Nancy out and go home."

"I'll have to ring Harley. . . ."

Harley already knew and was exploding like a firecracker. Someone from Polyplanes, it appeared, had telephoned at once to inform him with acid sweetness that his so highly qualified chief pilot had broken every law in sight and put Derrydowns thoroughly in the cart. The fact that his best customer was still alive to pay another day didn't seem to have got through to Harley at all. Polyplanes had made him smart, and it was all my fault.

I stayed in Cambridge by promising to foot the bill for hangarage again, and went home with Nancy and Colin.

Home.

A dangerous, evocative word. And the trouble was it *felt* like home. Only the third time I'd been there, and it was already familiar, cozy, undemanding, easy. . . . It was no good feeling I belonged there, because I didn't.

Saturday morning I spent talking to the police face-to-face in Cambridge and the Board of Trade in London on the telephone. Both forces cautiously murmured that they might perhaps ask Major Rupert Tyderman to help them with their inquiries. Saturday afternoon I flew Colin back to Haydock without incident; Saturday night I again stayed contentedly at Newmarket; Sunday I took him to Buckingham, changed over to the Aztec, and flew him to Ostend. Managed to avoid Harley altogether until I got back Sunday evening, when he lay in wait for me as I taxied down to the hangar and bitched on for over half an hour about sticking to the letter of the law. The gist of his argument was that, left to herself, Nancy would have come down safely somewhere over the flat land of East Anglia. Bound to have done. She wouldn't have hit any of the radio masts or power-station chimneys which scattered the area and which had stuck up into the clouds like needles. They were all marked there, disturbing her, on the map. She had known that if she had to go down at random she had an average chance of hitting one. The television mast at Mendlesham stretched upward for more than a thousand feet. . . . But, said Harley, she would have missed the lot. Certain to have done.

"What would you have felt like in her position?" I asked.

He didn't answer. He knew well enough. As pilot, as businessman, he was a bloody fool.

On Tuesday morning, he told me that Colin had telephoned to cancel his trip to Folkestone that day, but that I would still be going in the Six, taking an owner and his friends there from Nottingham.

I imagined that Colin had changed his intention to ride at Folkestone and gone to Pontefract instead, but it wasn't so. He had, I found, flown to Folkestone. And he had gone in a Polyplane.

I didn't know he was there until after the races, when he came back to the airport in a taxi. He climbed out of it in his usual wilted state, surveyed the row of parked aircraft, and walked straight past me toward the Polyplane.

"Colin," I said.

He stopped, turned his head, gave me a straight stare. Nothing friendly in it, nothing at all.

"What's the matter?" I said, puzzled. "What's happened?"

He looked away from me, along to the Polyplane. I followed his glance. The pilot was standing there smirking. He was the one who had refused to help Kenny Bayst, and he had been smirking vigorously all afternoon.

"Did you come with him?" I asked.

"Yes, I did." His voice was cold. His eyes also.

I said in surprise, "I don't get it. . . ."

Colin's face turned from cold to scorching. "You—you—I don't think I can bear to talk to you."

A feeling of unreality clogged my tongue. I simply looked at him in bewilderment.

"You've properly bust us up. . . . Oh, I dare say you didn't mean to . . . but Nancy has lit off out of the house and I left Midge at home crying. . . ."

I was appalled. "But why? On Sunday morning when we left, everything was fine. . . ."

"Yesterday," he said flatly. "Nancy found out yesterday, when she went to the airfield for a practice session. It absolutely threw her. She came home in a dreadful mood and raged round the house, practically throwing things, and this morning she packed a suitcase and walked out. . . . Neither Midge nor I could stop her and Midge is frantically distressed—" He stopped, clenched his jaw, and said with shut teeth, "Why the hell didn't you have the guts to tell her yourself?"

"Tell her what?"

"*What?*" He thrust his hand into the pocket of his faded jeans and brought out a folded wad of newspaper. "This."

I took it from him. Unfolded it. Felt the woodenness take over in my face; knew that it showed.

He had handed me the most biting, the most damaging of the tabloid accounts of my trial and conviction for negligently putting the lives of eighty-seven people in jeopardy. A one-day wonder to the general public; long forgotten. But always lying there in the files, if anyone wanted to dig it up.

"That wasn't all," Colin said. "He told her also that you'd been sacked from another airline for cowardice."

"Who told her?" I said dully. I held out the cutting. He took it back.

"Does it matter?"

"Yes, it does."

"He had no axe to grind. That's what convinced her."

"No axe . . . Did he say that?"

"I believe so. What does it matter?"

"Was it a Polyplane pilot who told her? The one, for instance, who is flying you today?" Getting his own back, I thought, for the way I'd threatened him at Redcar.

Colin's mouth opened.

"No axe to grind," I said bitterly. "That's a laugh. They've been trying to pry you loose from Derrydowns all summer, and now it looks as if they've done it."

I turned away from him, my throat physically closing. I didn't think I could speak. I expected him to walk on, to walk away, to take himself to Polyplanes and my future to the trash can.

Instead of that, he followed me and touched my arm.

"Matt. . . ."

I shook him off. "You tell your precious sister," I said thickly, "that because of the rules I broke leading her back to Cambridge last Friday I am going to find myself in court again, and convicted and fined and in debt again . . . and this time I did it with my eyes open . . . not like that"—I pointed to the newspaper clipping with a hand that trembled visibly—"when I had to take the rap for something that was mostly not my fault."

"Matt!" He was himself appalled.

"And as for the cowardice bit, she's got her facts wrong. . . . Oh, I've no doubt it sounded convincing and dreadful—Polyplanes had a lot to gain by upsetting her to the utmost—but I don't see—I don't see why she was more upset than just to persuade you not to fly with me."

"Why didn't you tell her yourself?"

I shook my head. "I probably might have done, one day. I didn't think it was important."

"Not important!" He was fierce with irritation. "She seems to have been building up some sort of hero image of you, and then she discovered you had clay feet in all directions. . . . Of course you should have told her, as you were going to marry her. That was obviously what upset her most."

I was speechless. My jaw literally dropped. Finally I said foolishly, "Did you say *marry?* . . ."

"Well, yes, of course," he said impatiently, and then seemed struck by my state of shock. "You were going to marry her, weren't you?"

"We've never—even talked about it."

"But you must have," he insisted. "I overheard her and Midge discussing it on Sunday evening, after I got back from Ostend. 'When you are married to Matt,' Midge said. I heard her distinctly. They were in the kitchen, washing up. They were deciding you would come and live with us in the bungalow. . . . They were sharing out the bedrooms. . . ." His voice tailed off weakly. "It isn't—it isn't true?"

I silently shook my head.

He looked at me in bewilderment. "Girls," he said. "Girls."

"I can't marry her," I said numbly. "I've hardly enough for a license."

"That doesn't matter."

"It does to me."

"It wouldn't to Nancy," he said. He did a sort of double take. "Do you mean—she wasn't so far out—after all?"

"I suppose . . . not so far."

He looked down at the cutting in his hand, and suddenly screwed it up. "It looked so bad," he said with a tinge of apology.

"It was bad," I said.

He looked at my face. "Yes. I see it was."

A taxi drew up with a jerk and out piled my passengers, all gay and flushed with a winner and carrying a bottle of champagne.

"I'll explain to her," Colin said. "I'll get her back. . . ." His expression was suddenly horrified. Shattered.

"Where has she gone?" I asked.

He screwed up his eyes as if in pain.

"She said"—he swallowed—"she went—to Chanter."

I sat all evening in the caravan wanting to smash something. Smash the galley. Smash the windows. Smash the walls.

Might have felt better if I had.

Chanter. . . .

Couldn't eat, couldn't think, couldn't sleep.

Never had listened to my own advice: don't get involved. Should have stuck to it, stayed frozen. Icy. Safe.

Tried to get back to the arctic and not feel anything, but it was too late. Feeling had come back with a vengeance and of an intensity I could have done without.

I hadn't known I loved her. Knew I liked her, felt easy with her, wanted to be with her often and for a long time to come. I'd thought I could stop at friendship, and didn't realize how far, how deep I had already gone.

Oh, Nancy. . . .

I went to sleep in the end by drinking half of the bottle of whisky Kenny Bayst had given me, but it didn't do much good. I woke up at six in the morning to the same dreary torment and with a headache on top.

There were no flights that day to take my mind off it.

Nancy and Chanter. . . .

At some point in the morning, I telephoned from the coin box in the customers' lounge to the art school in Liverpool, to ask for Chanter's home address. A crisp secretarial female voice answered: very sorry, absolutely not their policy to divulge the private addresses of their staff. If I could write, they would forward the letter.

"Could I speak to him, then, do you think?" I asked; though what good that would do, heaven alone knew.

"I'm afraid not, because he isn't here. The school is temporarily closed, and we are not sure when it will reopen."

"The students," I remembered, "are on strike?"

"That—er—is so," she agreed.

"Can't you possibly tell me how I could get in touch with Chanter?"

"Oh, dear. . . . You are the second person pressing me for help . . . but honestly, to tell you the truth, we don't know where he lives. . . . He moves frequently and seldom bothers to keep us up to date." Secretarial disapproval and despair in the tidy voice. "As I told Mr. Ross, with all the best will in the world, I simply have no idea where you could find him."

I sat in the crew room while the afternoon dragged by. Finished writing up all records by two-thirty, read through some newly arrived information circulars, calculated I had only three weeks and four days to run before my next medical, worked out that if I bought four cups of coffee every day from Honey's machine I was drinking away one-fifteenth of my total week's spending money, decided to make it water more often, looked up when Harely came stalking in, received a lecture on loyalty (mine to him), heard that I was on the next day to take a Wiltshire trainer to Newmarket races, and that if I gave Polyplanes any more grounds for reporting me or the firm to the Board of Trade, I could collect my cards.

"Do my best not to," I murmured. Didn't please him.

Looked at the door swinging shut behind his back.

Looked at the clock. Three-twenty-two.

Chanter and Nancy.

Back in the caravan, the same as the evening before. Tried turning on the television. Some comedy about American suburban life punctuated by canned laughter. Stood five minutes of it, and found the silence afterward almost as bad.

Walked halfway round the airfield, cut down to the village, drank half a pint in the pub, walked back. Total, four miles. When I stepped into the caravan, it was still only nine o'clock.

Honey Harley was waiting for me, draped over the sofa with maximum exposure of leg. Pink checked cotton sundress, very low cut.

"Hi," she said with self-possession. "Where've you been?"

"For a walk."

She looked at me quizically. "Got the Board of Trade on your mind?"

I nodded. That, and other things.

"I shouldn't worry too much. Whatever the law says or does, you couldn't have just left the Rosses to flounder."

"Your uncle doesn't agree."

"Uncle," she said dispassionately, "is a nit. And anyway play your cards right, and even if you do get a fine, Colin Ross will pay it. All you'd have to do would be to ask."

I shook my head.

"You're daft," she said. "Plain daft."

"You may be right."

She sighed, stirred, stood up. The curvy body rippled in all the right places. I thought of Nancy: much flatter, much thinner, less obviously sexed, and infinitely more desirable. I turned abruptly away from Honey.

Like hitting a raw nerve, the thought of Chanter, with his hair and his fringes . . . and his hands.

"O.K., iceberg," she said mistakenly, "relax. Your virtue is quite safe. I only came down, to start with, to tell you there was a phone call for you, and would you please ring back."

"Who?" I tried hard to keep it casual.

"Colin Ross," Honey said matter-of-factly. "He wants you to call sometime this evening, if you can. I said if it was about a flight I could deal with it, but apparently it's something personal." She finished the sentence halfway between an accusation and a question and left me ample time to explain.

I didn't. I said, "I'll go up now, then, and use the telephone in the lounge."

She shrugged. "All right."

She walked up with me, but didn't quite have the nerve to hover close enough to listen. I shut the lounge door in front of her resigned and rueful face.

Got the number.

"Colin? Matt."

"Oh, good," he said. "Look. Nancy rang up today while Midge and I were at the races. . . . I took Midge along on the Heath because she was so miserable at home, and now of course she's even more miserable that she missed Nancy. . . . Anyway, our cleaning woman answered the telephone, and Nancy left a message."

"Is she—I mean, is she all right?"

"Do you mean, is she with Chanter?" His voice was strained. "She told our cleaner she had met an old art-school friend in Liverpool and was spending a few days camping with her near Warwick."

"*Her?*" I exclaimed.

"Well, I don't know. I asked our Mrs. Williams, and she then said she *thought* Nancy said 'her,' but of course she would think that, wouldn't she?"

"I'm afraid she would."

"But anyway Nancy had been much more insistent that Mrs. Williams tell me something else. . . . It seems she has seen Major Tyderman."

"She didn't!"

"Yeah. . . . She said she saw Major Tyderman in the passenger seat of a car on the Stratford road out of Warwick. Apparently there were some roadworks, and the car stopped for a moment just near her."

"He could have been going anywhere . . . from anywhere."

"Yes," he agreed in depression. "I rang the police in Cambridge to tell them, but Nancy had already been through to them when she called home. All she could remember about the driver was that he wore glasses. She thought he might have had dark hair and perhaps a mustache. She only glanced at him for a second because she was concentrating on Tyderman. Also she hadn't taken the number, and she's hopeless on the make of cars, so altogether it wasn't a great deal of help."

"No. . . ."

"Anyway, she told Mrs. Williams she would be coming home on Saturday. She said if I would drive to Warwick races instead of flying, she would come home with me in the car.''

''Well . . . thank God for that.''

''If for nothing else,'' he said aridly.

12

I FLEW the customers from Wiltshire to Newmarket and parked the Six as far as possible from the Polyplane. When the passengers had departed standward, I got out of the fuggy cabin and into the free air, lay propped on one elbow on the grass, loosened my tie, opened the neck of my shirt. Scorching-hot day, a sigh of wind over the Heath, a couple of small cumulus clouds defying evaporation, blue sky over the blue planet.

A suitable day for camping.

Wrenched my thoughts away from the profitless grind: Nancy despised me, despised herself, had chosen Chanter as a refuge, as a steadfast known quantity, had run away from the near-stranger who had not been what he seemed, and gone to where she knew she was wanted. Blind, instinctive, impulsive flight. Reckless, understandable, forgivable flight. . . .

I could take Chanter, I thought mordantly. I could probably take the thought and memory of Chanter, if only she would settle for me in the end.

It was odd that you had to lose something you didn't even know you had before you began to want it more than anything on earth.

Down at the other end of the row of aircraft, the Polyplane pilot was strolling about, smoking again. One of these fine days he would blow himself up. There was no smile in place that afternoon: even from a hundred yards one could detect the gloom in the heavy frowns he occasionally got rid of in my direction.

Colin had booked with Harley for the week ahead. Polyplanes must have been wondering what else they would have to do to get him back.

They played rough, no doubt of that. Informing on Derrydowns to the Board of Trade, discrediting their pilot, spreading smears that they weren't safe. But would they blow up a Derrydowns aircraft? Would they go as far as that?

They would surely have had to feel certain they would gain from it before they risked it. But in fact they hadn't gained. No one had demonstrably been frightened away from using Derrydowns, particularly not Colin Ross. If the bomb had been meant to look like an attack on Colin's life, why should Colin think he would be any safer in a Polyplane?

If they had blown up the aircraft with passengers aboard, *that* would have ruined Derrydowns. But even if they had been prepared to go that far, they wouldn't have chosen a flight with Colin Ross on it.

And why Major Tyderman, when their own pilots could get near the Derrydowns aircraft without much comment? That was easier . . . they needed a bomb expert. Someone completely unsuspectible. Someone even their pilots didn't know. Because if the boss of Polyplanes had taken the dark step into crime, he wouldn't want chatty employees like pilots spilling it into every aviation bar from Prestwick to Lydd.

The second airplane, though, that Tyderman had sabotaged, hadn't been one of Derrydowns' at all. On the other hand, he had thought it was.

I stood up, stretched, watched the straining horses scud through the first race, saw in the distance a girl with dark hair and a blue dress, and thought for one surging moment it was Nancy. It wasn't Nancy. It wasn't even Midge. Nancy was in Warwickshire, living in a tent.

I thrust my balled fists into my pockets. Not the slightest use thinking about it. Concentrate on something else. Start from the bottom again, as before. Look at everything the wrong way up.

No easy revelation this time. Just the merest flicker of speculation.

Harley? . . .

He had recovered ill-invested capital on the first occasion. He had known Colin would not rely often on his sister's skill after the second. But would Harley go so far? . . . And Harley had known I wasn't flying Colin, though Tyderman had thought I was.

Rats on treadwheels, I thought, go round and round in small circles and get nowhere, just like me.

I sighed. It wasn't much use trying to work it all out when I obviously lacked about fifty pieces of vital information. Decision: did I or did I not start actively looking for some of the pieces? If I didn't, a successor to Major Tyderman might soon be around playing another lot of chemical tricks on airplanes, and if I did, I could well be heading myself for yet more trouble.

I tossed an imaginary coin. Heads you do, tails you don't. In mid-toss I thought of Nancy. All roads led back to Nancy. If I just let everything slide and lay both physically and metaphorically on my back on the grass in the sun, I'd have nothing to think about except what I hated to think about. Very poor prospect. Almost anything else was better.

Took the plunge, and made a start with Annie Villars.

She was standing in the paddock in a sleeveless dark red dress, her graying short hair curling neatly under a black straw hat chosen more for generalship than femininity. From ten paces, the authority was clearly uppermost: from three, one could hear the incongruously gentle voice, see the nonaggression in the consciously curved lips, realize that the velvet glove was being given a quilted lining.

She was talking to the Duke of Wessex. She was saying, "Then if you agree, Bobbie, we'll ask Kenny Bayst to ride it. This new boy had no judgment of pace, and, for all his faults, Kenny does know how to time a race."

The Duke nodded his distinguished head and smiled at her benevolently. They caught sight of me hovering near them and both turned toward me with friendly expressions, one deceptively and one authentically vacant.

"Matt," said the Duke, smiling. "My dear chap. Isn't it a splendid day?"

"Beautiful, sir," I agreed. As long as one could obliterate Warwickshire.

"My nephew Matthew," he said. "Do you remember him?"

"Of course I do, sir."

"Well—it's his birthday soon, and he wants—he was wondering if for a birthday present I would give him a flight in an airplane. With you, he said. Especially with you."

I smiled. "I'd like to do that very much."

"Good, good. Then—er—how do you suggest we fix it?"

"I'll arrange it with Mr. Harley."

"Yes. Good. Soon, then. He's coming down to stay with me tomorrow, as it's the end of term and his mother is off somewhere in Greece. So next week, perhaps?"

"I'm sure that will be all right."

He beamed happily. "Perhaps I'll come along, too."

Annie Villars said patiently, "Bobbie, we ought to go and see about saddling your horse."

He looked at his watch. "By Jove, yes. Amazing where the afternoon goes to. Come along, then." He gave me another large smile, transferred it intact to Annie, and obediently moved off after her as she started purposefully toward the saddling boxes.

I bought a race card. The Duke's horse was a two-year-old maiden called Thundersticks. I watched the Duke and Annie watch Thundersticks walk round the paddock, one with innocent beaming pride, the other with judicious noncommitment. The pace-lacking boy rode a bad race, even to my unpracticed eye: too far out in front over the first furlong, too far out the back over the last. Just as well the Duke's colors were inconspicuous, I thought. He took his disappointment with charming grace, reassuring Annie that the colt would do better next time. Sure to. Early days yet. She smiled back at him in soft agreement, and bestowed on the jockey a look which would have bored a hole through steel plating.

After they had discussed the sweating colt's performance yard by yard, and patted him and packed him off with his lad toward the stables, the Duke took Annie away to the bar for a drink. After that, she had another loser for another owner, and another thoughtful detour for refreshment, so that I didn't manage to catch her on her own until between the last two races.

She listened without comment to me explaining that I thought it might be possible to do something positive about solving the Great Bomb Mystery, if she would help.

"I thought it was solved already."

"Not really. No one knows why."

"No. Well, I don't see how I can help."

"Would you mind telling me how well Major Tyderman and Mr. Goldenberg know each other, and how they come to have any say in how Rudiments should run in its various races?"

She said mildly, "It's none of your business."

I knew what the mildness concealed. "I know that."

"And you are impertinent."

"Yes."

She regarded me straightly, and the softness gradually faded out of her features to leave taut skin over the cheekbones and a stern set to the mouth.

"I am fond of Midge and Nancy Ross," she said. "I don't see how anything I can tell you will help, but I certainly want no harm to come to those two girls. That last escapade was just a shade too dangerous, wasn't it? And if Rupert Tyderman could do that . . ." She paused, thinking deeply. "I will be obliged if you will keep anything I may tell you to yourself."

"I will."

"Very well. . . . I've known Rupert for a very long time. More or less from my childhood. He is about fifteen years older. . . . When I was a young girl, I thought he was a splendid person, and I didn't understand why people hesitated when they talked about him." She sighed. "I found out, of course, when I was older. He had been wild, as a youth. A vandal when vandalism wasn't as common as it is now. When he was in his twenties, he borrowed money from all his relations and friends for various grand schemes, and never paid them back. His family bought him out of one mess where he had sold a picture entrusted to him for safekeeping and spent the proceeds. . . . Oh, lots of things like that. Then the war came and he volunteered immediately, and I believe all during the war he did very well. He was in the Royal Engineers, I think . . . but afterward, after the war ended, he was quietly allowed to resign his commission for cashing dud checks with his fellow officers."

She shook her head impatiently. "He has always been a fool to himself. . . . Since the war, he has lived on some money his grandfather left in trust, and on what he could cadge from any friends he had left."

"You included?" I suggested.

She nodded. "Oh, yes. He's always very persuasive. It's always for something extremely plausible, but all the deals fall through. . . ." She looked away across the Heath, considering. "And then this year, back in February or March, I think, he turned up one day and said he wouldn't need to borrow any more from me, he'd got a good thing going which would make him rich."

"What was it?"

"He wouldn't say. Just told me not to worry, it was all legal. He had gone into partnership with someone with a cast-iron idea for making a fortune. Well, I'd heard that sort of thing from him so often before. The only difference was that this time he didn't want money. . . ."

"He wanted something else?"

"Yes." She frowned. "He wanted me to introduce him to Bobbie Wessex. He said—just casually—how much he'd like to meet him, and I suppose I was so relieved not to find him cadging five hundred or so that I instantly agreed. It was very silly of me, but it didn't seem important. . . ."

"What happened then?"

She shrugged. "They were both at the Doncaster meeting at the opening of the flat season, so I introduced them. Nothing to it. Just a casual racecourse introduction. And then"—she looked annoyed—"the next time Rupert turned up with that man Goldenberg, saying Bobbie Wessex had given him permission to decide how Rudiments should be run in all his races. I said he certainly wasn't going to do that, and telephoned to Bobbie. But," she said, sighing, "Rupert had indeed talked him into giving him carte blanche with Rudiments. Rupert is an expert persuader, and Bobbie—well, poor Bobbie is easily open to suggestion. Anyone with half an eye could see that Goldenberg was as straight as a corkscrew, but Rupert said he was essential, as someone had got to put the bets on and he, Rupert, couldn't, as no bookmaker would accept his credit and you had to have hard cash for the Tote."

"And then the scheme went wrong," I said.

"The first time Rudiments won, they'd both collected a lot of money. I had told them the horse would win. Must win. It started at a hundred to six, first time out, and they were both as high as kites afterward."

"And next time Kenny Bayst won again, when he wasn't supposed to, when they had laid it?"

She looked startled. "So you did understand what they were saying."

"Eventually."

"Just like Rupert to let it out. No sense of discretion."

I sighed. "Well, thank you very much for being so frank. Even if I still can't see what connection Rudiments has with Major Tyderman blowing up one aircraft and crippling another."

She twisted her mouth. "I told you," she said, "right at the beginning that nothing I told you would be of any help."

Colin stopped beside me in pink-and-green silks on his way from the weighing room to the paddock for the last race. He gave me a concentrated inquiring look which softened into something like compassion.

"The waiting's doing you no good," he said.

"Has she telephoned again?"

He shook his head. "Midge won't leave the house, in case she does."

"I'll be at Warwick races on Saturday—flying some people up from Kent. . . . Will you ask her—just to talk to me?"

"I'll wring her stupid little neck," he said.

I flew the customers back to Wiltshire and the Six back to Buckingham. Harley, waiting around with bitter eyes, told me the Board of Trade had let him know they were definitely proceeding against me.

"I expected they would."

"But that's not what I wanted to speak to you about. Come into the office." He was unfriendly, as usual. Snappy. He picked up a sheet of paper from his desk and waved it at me.

"Look at these times. I've been going through the bills Honey has sent out since you've been here. All the times are shorter. We've had to charge less. . . . We're not making enough profit. It's got to stop. D'you understand? Got to stop."

"Very well."

He looked nonplused: hadn't expected such an easy victory.

"And I'm taking on another pilot."

"Am I out, then?" I found I scarcely cared.

He was surprised. "No. Of course not. We simply seem to be getting too much taxi work just lately for you to handle on your own, even with Don's help."

"Maybe we're getting more work because we're doing the trips faster and charging less," I suggested.

He was affronted. "Don't be ridiculous."

Another long evening in the caravan, aching and empty.

Nowhere to go, no way of going, and nothing to spend when I got there. That didn't matter, because wherever I went, whatever I spent, the inescapable thoughts lay in wait. Might as well suffer them alone and cheaply as anywhere else.

For something to do, I cleaned the caravan from end to end. When it was finished, it looked better, but I, on the whole, felt worse. Scrambled myself two eggs, ate them unenthusiastically on toast. Drank a dingy cup of dried coffee, dried milk.

Switched on the television. Old movie, *circa* 1950, pirates, cutlasses, heaving bosoms. Switched off.

Sat and watched night arrive on the airfield. Tried to concentrate on what Annie Villars had told me, so as not to think of night arriving over the fields and tents of Warwickshire. For a long time, had no success at all.

Look at everything upside down. Take absolutely nothing for granted.

The middle of the night produced out of a shallow restless sleep a singularly wild idea. Most sleep-spawned revelations from the subconscious wither and die of ridicule in the dawn, but this time it was different. At five, six, seven o'clock, it still looked possible. I traipsed in my mind through everything I had seen and heard since the day of the bomb, and added a satisfactory answer to *why* to the answer to *who* and *when*.

That Friday, I had to set off early in the Aztec to Germany with some television cameramen from Denham, wait while they took their shots, and bring them home again. In spite of breaking Harley's ruling about speed into pin-sized fragments, it was seven-thirty before I climbed stiffly out of the cockpit and helped Joe push the sturdy twin into the hangar.

"Need it for Sunday, don't you?" he asked.

"That's right. Colin Ross to France." I stretched and yawned, and picked up my heavy flight bag with all its charts and documents.

"We're working you hard."

"What I'm here for."

He put his hands in his overall pockets. "You're light on those airplanes, I'll give you that. Larry, now—Larry was heavy-handed. Always needing things repaired, we were, before you came."

I gave him a sketch of an appreciative smile and walked up to fill in the records in the office. Harley and Don were both still flying, Harley giving a lesson, and Don a sightseeing trip in the Six, and Honey was still traffic-copping up in the tower. I climbed up there to see her and ask her a considerable favor.

"Borrow my Mini?" she repeated in surprise. "Do you mean now, this minute?"

I nodded. "For the evening."

"I suppose I could get Uncle to take me home," she reflected. "If you'll fetch me in the morning?"

"Certainly."

"Well . . . all right. I don't really need it this evening. Just fill it up with petrol before you hand it back."

"O.K. And thanks a lot."

She gave me a frankly vulgar grin. "Minis are too small for what you want."

I managed to grin back. "Yeah. . . ."

Given the wheels, make the appointment. A pleasant male voice answered the telephone, polite and quiet.

"The Duke of Wessex? Yes, this is his house. Who is speaking, please?"

"Matthew Shore."

"One moment, sir."

The one moment stretched to four minutes, and I fed a week's beer money into the greedy box. At last the receiver at the other end was picked up and, with slightly heavy breathing, the Duke's unmistakable voice said, "Matt? My dear chap, what can I do for you?"

"If you are not busy this evening, sir, could I call in to see you for a few minutes?"

"This evening? Busy? Hmm. . . . Is it about young Matthew's flight?"

"No, sir, something different. I won't take up much of your time."

"Come by all means, my dear chap, if you want to. After dinner, perhaps? Nine o'clock, say?"

"Nine o'clock," I confirmed. "I'll be there."

The Duke lived near Royston, west of Cambridge. Honey's Mini ate up the miles like Billy Bunter, so that it was nine o'clock exactly when I stopped at a local garage to ask for directions to the Duke's house. On Honey's radio, someone was reading the news. I listened idly at first while the attendant finished filling up the car in front, and then with sharp and sickened attention. "Race-horse trainer Jarvis Kitch and owner Dobson Ambrose, whose filly Scotchbright won the Oaks last month, were killed today in a multiple traffic accident just outside Newmarket. The Australian jockey Kenny Bayst, who was in the car with them, was taken to hospital with multiple injuries. His condition tonight is said to be fair. Three stable lads, trapped when a lorry crushed their car, also died in the crash."

Mechanically I asked for, got, and followed, the directions to the Duke's house. I was thinking about poor large aggressive Ambrose and his cowed trainer Kitch, hoping that Kenny wasn't too badly hurt to race again, and trying to foresee the ramifications.

There was nothing else on the news except the weather forecast: heat wave indefinitely continuing.

No mention of Rupert Tyderman. But Tyderman, that day, *had* been seen by the police.

13

THE DUKE'S manservant was as pleasant as his voice: a short, assured, slightly popeyed man in his late forties with a good deal of the Duke's natural benevolence in his manner. The house he presided over opened to the public, a notice read, every day between 1st March and 30th November. The Duke, I discovered, lived privately in the upper third of the southwest wing.

"The Duke is expecting you, sir. Will you come this way?"

I followed. The distance I followed accounted for the length of time I had waited for the Duke to come to the telephone and also his breathlessness when he got there. We went up three floors, along a two-furlong straight, and up again, to the attics. The attics in eighteenth-century stately homes were a long way from the front hall.

The manservant opened a white-painted door and gravely showed me in.

"Mr. Shore, Your Grace."

"Come in, come in, my dear chap," said the Duke.

I went in, and smiled with instant, spontaneous delight. The square low-ceilinged room contained a vast toy electric-train set laid out on an irregular ring of wide green-covered trestle tables. A terminus, sidings, two small towns, a branch line, tunnels, gradients, viaducts—the Duke had the lot. In the center of the ring, he and his nephew Matthew stood behind a large control table pressing the switches which sent about six different trains clanking on different courses round the complex.

The Duke nudged his nephew. "There you are, what did we say? He likes it."

Young Matthew gave me a fleeting glance and went back to some complicated points-changing. "He was bound to. He's got the right sort of face."

The Duke said, "You can crawl in here best under that table with the signal box and level crossing." He pointed, so I went down on hands and knees and made the indicated journey. Stood up in the center. Looked around at the rows of lines and remembered the hopeless passion I'd felt in toyshops as a child: my father had been an underpaid schoolmaster who had spent his money on books.

The two enthusiasts showed me where the lines crossed and how the trains could be switched without crashing. Their voices were filled with contentment, their eyes shining, their faces intent.

"Built this lot up gradually, of course," the Duke said. "Started when I was a boy. Then for years I never came up here. Not until young Matthew got old enough. Now, as I expect you can see, we have great times."

"We're thinking of running a branch line right through that wall over there into the next attic," Matthew said. "There isn't much more room in here."

The Duke nodded. "Next week, perhaps. For your birthday."

Young Matthew gave him a huge grin and deftly let a Pullman cross three seconds in front of a chugging goods. "It's getting dark," he observed. "Lighting-up time."

"So it is," agreed the Duke.

Matthew with a flourish pressed a switch, and they both watched my face. All round the track, and on all the stations and signal boxes and in the signals themselves, tiny electric lights suddenly shone out. The effect, to my eyes, was enchanting.

"There you are," said the Duke. "He likes it."

"Bound to," young Matthew said.

They played with the trains for another whole hour, because they had worked out a timetable and they wanted to see if they could keep to it before they pinned it up on the notice board in the terminal. The Duke apologized, not very apologetically, for keeping me waiting, but it was, he explained, Matthew's first evening out of school, and they had been waiting all through the term for this occasion.

At twenty to eleven, the last shuttle service stopped at the buffers in the terminal and Matthew yawned. With the satisfaction of a job well done, the two railwaymen unfolded several large dust sheets and laid them carefully over the silent tracks, and then we all three crawled back under the table which held the level crossing.

The Duke led the way down the first flight and along the two furlongs, and we were then, it appeared, in his living quarters.

"You'd better cut along to bed now, Matthew," he said to his nephew. "See you in the morning. Eight o'clock sharp, out in the stables."

"Sure thing," Matthew said. "And after that the races." He sighed with utter content. "Better than school," he said.

The Duke showed me into a smallish white-painted sitting room furnished with Persian rugs, leather armchairs, and endless sporting prints.

"A drink?" he suggested, indicating a tray.

I looked at the bottles. "Whisky, please."

He nodded, poured two, added water, gave me the glass, and waved me to an armchair.

"Now, my dear chap? . . ."

It suddenly seemed difficult, what I had come to ask him, and what to explain. He was so transparently honest, so incapable of double-dealing: I wondered if he could comprehend villainy at all.

"I was talking to Annie Villars about your horse Rudiments," I said.

A slight frown lowered his eyebrows. "She was annoyed with me for letting her friend Rupert Tyderman advise me. . . . I do so dislike upsetting Annie, but I'd promised. . . . Anyway, she has sorted it all out splendidly, I believe, and now that her friend has turned out to be so extraordinary—with that bomb, I mean—I don't expect he will want to advise me about Rudiments any more."

"Did he, sir, introduce to you any friend of his?"

"Do you mean Eric Goldenberg? Yes, he did. Can't say I really liked the fellow, though. Didn't trust him, you know. Young Matthew didn't like him, either."

"Did Goldenberg ever talk to you about insurance?"

"Insurance?" he repeated. "No, I can't remember especially that he did."

I frowned. It had to be insurance.

It had to be.

"It was his other friend," said the Duke, "who arranged the insurance."

I stared at him. "Which other friend?"

"Charles Carthy-Todd."

I blinked. "Who?"

"Charles Carthy-Todd," he repeated patiently. "He was an acquaintance of Rupert Tyderman's. Tyderman introduced us one day. At Newmarket races, I think it was. Anyway, it was Charles who suggested the insurance. Very good scheme, I thought it was. Sound. Very much needed. An absolute boon to a great many people."

"The Racegoers' Accident Fund," I said. "Of which you are patron."

"That's right," He smiled. "So many people have complimented me on giving it my name. A splendid undertaking altogether."

"Could you tell me a little more about how it was set up?"

"Are you interested in insurance, my dear chap? I could get you an introduction at Lloyd's . . . but . . ."

I smiled. To become an underwriter at Lloyd's, one had to think of a stake of a hundred thousand pounds as loose change. The Duke, in his quiet good-natured way, was a very rich man indeed.

"No, sir. It's just the Accident Fund I'm interested in. How it was set up, and how it is run."

"Charles sees to it all, my dear chap. I can't seem to get the hang of these things at all, you know. Technicalities, and all that. Much prefer horses, don't you see?"

"Yes, sir, I do see. Could you perhaps, then, tell me about Mr. Carthy-Todd? What he's like, and so on."

"He's about your height but much heavier and he has dark hair and wears spectacles. I think he has a mustache. . . . Yes, that's right, a mustache."

I was jolted. The Duke's description of Charles Carthy-Todd fitted almost exactly the impression Nancy had had of Tyderman's companion. Dozens of men around, though, with dark hair, mustaches, glasses. . . .

"I really meant, sir, his—er—character."

"My dear chap. Sound. Very sound. A thoroughly good fellow. An expert in insurance, spent years with a big firm in the City."

"And—his background?" I suggested.

"Went to Rugby. Then straight into an office. Good family, of course."

"You've met them?"

He looked surprised at the question. "Not actually, no. Business connection, that's what I have with Charles. His family came from Herefordshire, I think. There are photographs in our office. . . . Land, horses, dogs, wife and children—that sort of thing. Why do you ask?"

I hesitated. "Did he come to you with the accident scheme complete?"

He shook his fine head. "No, no, my dear chap. It arose out of conversation. We were saying how sad it was for the family of that small steeplechase trainer who was drowned on holiday and what a pity it was that there wasn't some scheme which covered everyone engaged in racing, not just the jockeys. Then of course when we really went into it, we broadened it to include the racing public as well. Charles explained that the more premiums we collected the more we could pay out in compensation."

"I see."

"We have done a great deal of good already." He smiled happily. "Charles was telling me the other day that we have settled three claims for injuries so far, and that those clients are so pleased that they are telling everyone else to join in."

I nodded. "I've met one of them. He'd broken his ankle and received a thousand pounds."

He beamed. "There you are, then."

"When did the scheme actually start?"

"Let me see. In May, I should think. Toward the end of May. About two months ago. It took a little while to organize, of course, after we'd decided to go ahead."

"Charles did the organizing?"

"My dear chap, of course."

"Did you take advice from any of your friends at Lloyd's?"

"No need, you know. Charles is an expert himself. He drew up all the papers. I just signed them."

"But you read them first?"

"Oh, yes," he said reassuringly, then smiled like a child. "Didn't understand them much, of course."

"And you yourself guaranteed the money?" Since the collapse of cut-price car-insurance firms, I'd read somewhere, privately run insurance schemes had to show a minimum backing of fifty thousand pounds before the Board of Trade would give them permission to exist.

"That's right."

"Fifty thousand pounds?"

"We thought a hundred thousand might be better. Gives the scheme better standing, more weight, don't you see?"

"Charles said so?"

"He knows about such things."

"Yes."

"But of course I'll never have to find that money. It's ony a guarantee of good faith, and to comply with the law. The premiums will cover the compensation and Charles's salary and all the costs. Charles worked it all out. And I told him right at the beginning that I didn't want any profit out of it just for lending it my name. I really don't need any profit. I told him just to add my share into the paying-out fund, and he thought that was a most sensible suggestion. Our whole purpose, you see, is to do good."

"You're a singularly kind, thoughtful, and generous man, sir," I said.

It made him uncomfortable. "My dear chap . . ."

"And after tonight's news, I think several widows in Newmarket will bless you."

"What news?"

I told him about the accident in which Kitch and Ambrose and the three stable lads had died. He was horrified.

"Oh, the poor fellows. The poor fellows. One can only hope that you are right, and that they had joined our scheme."

"Will the premiums you have already collected be enough to cover many large claims all at once?"

He wasn't troubled. "I expect so. Charles will have seen to all that. But even if they don't, I will make up the difference. No one will suffer. That's what guaranteeing means, do you see?"

"Yes, sir."

"Kitch and Ambrose," he said. "The poor fellows."

"And Kenny Bayst is in hospital, badly hurt."

"Oh dear." His distress was genuine. He really cared.

'I know that Kenny Bayst was insured with you. At least, he told me he was going to be. And after this I should think you would be flooded with more applications."

"I expect you're right. You seem to understand things, just like Charles does."

"Did Charles have any plans for giving the scheme a quick boost to begin with?"

"I don't follow you, my dear chap."

"What happened to the Accident Fund," I asked casually, "after that bomb exploded in the airplane which had been carrying Colin Ross?"

He looked enthusiastic. "Do you know, a lot of people told me they would join. It made them think, they said. I asked Charles if they had really done anything about it, and he said yes, quite a few inquiries had come in. I said that as no one had been hurt, the bomb seemed to have done the Fund a lot of good, and Charles was surprised and said so it had."

Charles had met the Duke through Rupert Tyderman. Rupert Tyderman had set off the bomb. If ever there was a stone-cold certainty, it was that Charles Carthy-Todd was the least surprised on earth that cash had followed combustion. He had reckoned it would. He had reckoned right.

"Charles sent out a pamphlet urging everyone to insure against bombs on the way home," I said.

The Duke smiled. "Yes, that's right. I believe it was very effective. We thought, do you see, that as no one had been hurt, there would be no harm in it."

"And as it was Colin Ross who was on board, the bomb incident was extensively covered on television and in the newspapers . . . and had a greater impact on your Fund than had it been anyone else."

The Duke's forehead wrinkled. "I'm not sure I understand."

"Never mind, sir. I was just thinking aloud."

"Very easy habit to fall into. Do it myself, you know, all the time."

Carthy-Todd and Tyderman's second sabotage, I thought, hadn't been as good. Certainly by attacking Colin they'd achieved the same impact and national coverage, but I would have thought it was too obviously slanted at one person to have had much universal effect. Could be wrong, though. . . .

"This has been the most interesting chat," said the Duke. "But, my dear fellow, the evening is passing. What was it that you wanted to see me about?''

''Er . . .'' I cleared my throat. ''Do you know, sir. I'd very much like to meet Mr. Carthy-Todd. He sounds a most go-ahead, enterprising man.''

The Duke nodded warmly.

''Do you know where I could find him?''

''Tonight, do you mean?'' He was puzzled.

''No, sir. Tomorrow will do.''

''I suppose you might find him at our office. He's sure to be there, because he knows I will be calling in myself. Warwick races, do you see?''

''The Accident Fund office . . . is in Warwick?''

''Of course.''

''Silly of me,'' I said. ''I didn't know.''

The Duke twinkled at me. ''I see you haven't joined the Fund.''

''I'll join tomorrow. I'll go to the office. I'll be at Warwick, too, for the races.''

''Great,'' he said. ''Great. The office is only a few hundred yards from the racecourse.'' He put two fingers into an inside pocket and brought out a visiting card. ''There you are, my dear chap. The address. And if you're there about an hour before the first race, I'll be there, too, and you can meet Charles. You'll like him, I'm sure of that.''

''I'll look forward to it,'' I said. I finished my whisky and stood up. ''It was kind of you to let me come . . . and I think your trains are absolutely splendid. . . .''

His face brightened. He escorted me all the way down to the front door, talking about young Matthew and the plans they had for the holidays. Would I fix Matthew's flight for Thursday, he asked. Thursday was Matthew's birthday. He would be eleven.

''Thursday it is,'' I agreed. ''I'll do it in the evening if there's a charter fixed for that day.''

''Most good of you, my dear chap.''

I looked at the kind, distinguished, uncomprehending face. I knew that if his partner Charles Carthy-Todd skipped with the accumulated premiums before paying out the Newmarket widows, as I was privately certain he would, the Honourable Duke of Wessex would meet every penny out of his own coffers. In all probability he could afford it, but that wasn't the point. He would be hurt and bewildered and impossibly distressed at having been tangled up in a fraud, and it seemed to me especially vicious that anyone should take advantage of his vulnerable simplicity and goodness.

Charles Carthy-Todd was engaged in taking candy from a child and then making it look as though the child had stolen it in the first place. One couldn't help but feel protective. One couldn't help but want to stop it.

I said impulsively, ''Take care of yourself, sir.''

''My dear chap . . . I will.''

I walked down the steps from his front door toward Honey's Mini waiting in the drive, and looked back to where he stood in the yellow oblong of light. He waved a hand gently, and slowly closed the door, and

I saw from his benign but slightly puzzled expression that he was still not quite sure why I had come.

It was after one o'clock when I got back to the caravan. Tired, hungry, miserable about Nancy, I still couldn't stay asleep. Four o'clock I was awake again, tangling the sheets as if in fever. I got up and splashed my itching eyes with cold water: lay down, got up, went for a walk across the airfield. The cool starry night came through my shirt and soothed my skin but didn't do much for the hopeless ache between my ears.

At eight in the morning, I went to fetch Honey after filling her tank with the promised petrol at the nearest garage. She had made a gallon or two on the deal, I calculated. Fair enough.

What was not fair enough, however, was the news with which she greeted me.

"Colin Ross wants you to ring him up. He rang yesterday evening about half an hour after you'd buzzed off."

"Did he say . . . what about?"

"He did ask me to give you a message, but honestly I forgot. I was up in the tower until nine, and then Uncle was impatient to get home, and I just went off with him and forgot all about coming down here with the message . . . and anyway what difference would a few hours make?"

"What was the message?"

"He said to tell you his sister didn't meet anyone called Chanter at Liverpool. Something about a strike, and this Chanter not being there. I don't know . . . there were two aircraft in the circuit and I wasn't paying all that much attention. Come to think of it, he did seem pretty anxious I should give you the message last night, but, like I said, I forgot. Sorry, and all that. Was it important?"

I took a deep breath. Thinking about the past night, I could cheerfully have strangled her. "Thanks for telling me."

She gave me a sharp glance. "You look bushed. Have you been making love all night? You don't look fit to fly."

"Seldom felt better," I said with truth. "And no, I haven't."

"Save yourself for me."

"Don't bank on it."

"Beast."

When I rang Colin's number from the telephone in the lounge, it was Midge who answered. The relief in her voice was as overwhelming as my own.

"Matt! . . ." I could hear her gulp, and knew she was fighting against tears. "Oh, Matt—I'm so glad you've rung. She didn't go after Chanter. She didn't. It's all right. Oh dear . . . just a minute. . . ." She sniffed and paused, and when she spoke again she had her voice under control. "She rang yesterday evening and we talked to her for a long time. She said she was sorry if she had upset us, she had really left because she was so angry with herself, so humiliated at having made up such silly dreams about you. . . . She said it was all her own fault, that you hadn't deceived her in any way, she had deceived herself. . . . She wanted to tell us that it wasn't because she was angry with you that she ran out, but because she felt she had made such a fool of herself. . . . Anyway, she said she had cooled off a good deal by the time her train got to Liverpool and she was simply miserable by then, and then when she found Chanter had gone away because of the strike, she said she was relieved, really. Chanter's landlady told Nancy where he had gone—somewhere in Manchester, to do a painting of industrial chimneys, she thought—but Nancy decided it wasn't Chanter she wanted. . . . And she didn't know what to do, she still felt muddled. . . . And then outside the art school she met a girl who had been a student with us in London. She was setting off for a camping holiday near Stratford and—well—Nancy decided to go with her. She said a few days' peace and some landscape painting would put her right . . . so she rang up here, and it was our cleaning woman who answered. . . . Nancy swears she told her it was Jill she was with, and not Chanter, but of course we never got that part of the message . . ." She stopped, and when I didn't answer immediately she said anxiously, "Matt, are you still there?"

"Yes."

"You were so quiet."

"I was thinking about the last four days."

Four wretched, dragging days. Four endless, grinding nights. All unnecessary. She hadn't been with Chanter at all. If she'd suffered about what she'd imagined about me, so had I from what I'd imagined about her. Which made us, I guessed, about quits.

"Colin told her she should have asked you about that court case instead of jumping to conclusions," Midge said.

"She didn't jump, she was pushed."

"Yes. She knows that now. She's pretty upset. She doesn't really want to have to face you at Warwick—after making such a mess of things. . . ."

"I shan't actually slaughter her."

She half laughed. "I'll defend her. I'm driving over with Colin. I'll see you there, too."

"That's marvelous."

"Colin's out on the gallops just now. We're setting off after he's come in and had something to eat."

"Tell him to drive carefully. Tell him to think of Ambrose."

"Yes. . . . Isn't it awful about that crash?"

"Have you heard what happened, exactly?"

"Apparently, Ambrose tried to pass a slow lorry on a bend and there was another one coming the other way. He ran into it head on, and one of the lorries overturned and crushed another car with three stable lads in it. There's quite a lot about it in today's *Sporting Life*."

"I expect I'll see it. And, Midge . . . thank Colin for his message last night."

"I will. He said he didn't want you to worry any longer. He seemed to think you were almost as worried about her as we were."

"Almost," I agreed wryly. "See you at Warwick."

14

HONEY HAD arranged for me to fly a Mr. and Mrs. Whiteknight and their two young daughters down to Lydd, where the daughters were to meet friends and leave on the car-air ferry to Le Touquet for a holiday in France. After waving the daughters off, the Whiteknights wanted to belt back to see their horse run in the first race at Warwick, which meant, since there was no racecourse strip, landing at Coventry and hailing a cab.

Accordingly, I loaded them up at Buckingham and pointed the nose of the Six toward Kent. The two daughters, about fourteen and sixteen, were world-weary and disagreeable, looking down their noses at everything with ingrained hostility. Their mother behaved to me with cool condescension, and autocratically bossed the family. Mr. Whiteknight, gruff, unconsulted, a downtrodden universal provider, out of habit brought up the rear.

At Lydd, after carrying the daughters' suitcases unthanked into the terminal, I went back to the Six to wait through the farewells. Mr. Whiteknight had obligingly left his *Sporting Life* on his seat. I picked it up and read it. There was a photograph of the Ambrose crash. The usual mangled metal, pushed to the side of the road, pathetic result of impatience.

I turned to the middle page to see how many races Colin was riding at Warwick. He was down for five, and in most of them was favorite.

Alongside the Warwick program, there was an advertisement in bold black letters.

"COLIN ROSS HAS INSURED WITH US. WHY DON'T YOU?" Underneath in smaller type, it went on, "*You* may not be lucky enough to survive two narrow escapes. Don't chance it. Cut out the proposal form printed below and send it with five pounds to the Racegoers' Accident Fund, Avon Street, Warwick. Your insurance cover starts from the moment your letter is in the post."

I put the paper down on my knee, looked into space, and sucked my teeth.

Major Tyderman had told Annie Villars that he and a partner of his had something going for them that would make them rich. She had thought he meant control of Rudiments, but of course it hadn't been that. The maneuvering with Rudiments had come about simply because Tyderman couldn't resist a small swindle on the side, even when he was engaged in a bigger one.

Tyderman had got Annie to introduce him to the Duke, so that he in his turn could produce Carthy-Todd. Goldenberg was incidental, needed only for placing bets. Carthy-Todd was central, the moving mind, the instigator. Everyone else, Tyderman, the Duke, Colin, Annie, myself—all of us were pieces on his chessboard, to be shoved around until the game was won.

Clean up and clear out, that was how he must have decided to play. He hadn't waited for the Fund to grow slowly and naturally; he'd blown up an airplane and used Colin Ross for publicity. He would only have stayed anyway until the claims began mounting, and if the crash victims at Newmarket were in fact insured he would be off within the week. He would stay just long enough to collect the crash-inspired rush of new premiums, and that would be that. A quick transfer to a Swiss bank. A one-way ticket to the next happy hunting ground.

I didn't know how to stop him. There would be no proof that he meant to defraud until after he'd done it. I could produce nothing to back up my belief. No one was going to lurch into drastic action on what was little more than a guess. I could perhaps telephone to the Board of Trade . . . but the Board of Trade and I were now hardly on speaking terms. The tall man might listen. He had, after all, once asked for my thoughts. Maybe the aircraft section had a hot line to the insurance section. And maybe not.

With a sigh, I folded up Mr. Whiteknight's newspaper and glanced again at the crash on the front page. Down in one corner in the left-hand column, beside the account of the accident, a paragraph heading caught my eye.

Tyderman, it said. I read the dry meager lines underneath with a vague and then mounting feeling of alarm.

"A man believed to be Major Rupert Tyderman was found dead early yesterday beside the main London to South Wales railway line, between Swindon and Bristol. His death, at first attributed to a fall from a train, was later established as having been the result of a stab wound. The police, who had wanted to interview Major Tyderman, are making inquiries."

The Whiteknight parents were walking back across the apron by the time I'd decided what to do. They were displeased when I met them and said I was going to make a telephone call. There wasn't time, they said.

"Check on the weather," I lied. They looked up at the hazy heat-wave sky and gave me deservedly bitter looks. All the same, I went on my way.

The Duke's polite manservant answered.

"No, Mr. Shore, I'm very sorry, His Grace left for Warwick half an hour ago."

"Was young Matthew with him?"

"Yes, sir."

"Do you know if he was planning to go to the Accident Fund office before he went to the racecourse?"

"I believe so, sir. Yes."

I put the receiver down, feeling increasingly fearful. Rupert Tyderman's death put the game into a different league. Lives had been at risk before, in the airplanes; the basic callousness was there; but on those occasions the intention had been expressly not to kill. But now, if Carthy-Todd had decided to clear up behind him . . . if Tyderman's blunder with Nancy's airplane, which had led to his uncovering, had also led directly to his death . . . if Carthy-Todd had stopped Tyderman giving evidence against him . . . then would he, could he possibly, also kill the simple, honest, truth-spilling Duke? . . .

He wouldn't, I thought coldly. He couldn't.

I didn't convince myself one little bit.

* * *

The Whiteknights had no cause for complaint about the speed at which I took them to Coventry, though they consented only with bad grace when I asked to share their taxi to the races. I parted from them at the main gate and walked back toward the town center, looking for the office of the Accident Fund. As the Duke had said, it wasn't far: less than a quarter of a mile.

It was located on the first floor of a small moderately well-kept town house which fronted straight onto the pavement. The ground floor seemed to be uninhabited, but the main door stood open and a placard on the wall just inside announced, "Racegoers' Accident Fund. Please walk up."

I walked up. On the first landing there was a washroom, a secretary's office, and, at the front of the house, a door with a Yale lock and a knocker in the shape of a horse's head. I flipped the knocker a couple of times and the door came abruptly open.

"Hello," said young Matthew, swinging it wide. "Uncle was just saying you would miss us. We're just going along to the races."

"Come along in, my dear chap," said the Duke's voice from inside the room.

I stepped into the office. At first sight a plushy one: wall-to-wall plum-colored carpet, but of penny-pinching quality, two fat-looking easy chairs with cheap foam seats, a pair of shoulder-high metal filing cabinets, and a modern formica desk. The atmosphere of a solid, sober, long-established business came exclusively from the good proportions of the bay-windowed room, the moldings round the nineteenth-century ceiling, the carved wood and marble slab of the handsome fireplace, and some dark old gilt-framed oils on the walls. The office had been chosen with genius to convince, to reassure, to charm. And as clients of insurance companies seldom if ever visited the offices, this one must have been designed to convince, to reassure, to charm only the Duke himself.

The Duke introduced me to the man who had been sitting and who now stood behind the desk.

"Charles Carthy-Todd . . . Matthew Shore."

I shook his hand. He'd seen me before, as I'd seen him. Neither of us gave the slightest sign of it. I hoped he had not distinguished in me the minute subsidence of tension which I saw in him. The tension I felt hadn't subsided in the slightest.

He was all the Duke had said: a man with good presence, good voice, a thoroughgoing public-school gent. He would have had to be, to net the Duke; and there were all those silver-framed photographs, which the Duke had mentioned, standing around to prove it.

He had dark hair with the merest sprinkling of gray, a compact little mustache, pinkish-tan slightly oily-looking skin, and heavy black-framed glasses assisting his grayish-blue eyes.

The Duke was sitting comfortably in an armchair in the bay window, his splendid head haloed by the shining day behind. His knees were crossed, his hands relaxed, and he was smoking a cigar. From his general air of pleased well-being, it was easy to see the pride he held in his beautiful benevolent Fund. I wished sincerely for his sake that he wasn't going to have to wake up.

Charles Carthy-Todd sat down and continued with what he had been going to do when I arrived, offering young Matthew a piece of chocolate-covered orange peel from a half-empty round red-and-gold tin. Matthew took it, thanked him, ate it, and watched him with anxious reserve. Like the Duke, I trusted young Matthew's instinct. All too clearly, it had switched to amber, if not to red. I hoped for all our sakes that he would have the good manners to keep quiet.

"Give Matthew a proposal form, Charles," the Duke said contentedly. "That's what he's come for, you know, to join the Fund."

Carthy-Todd obediently rose, crossed to the filing cabinet, pulled open the top drawer, and lifted out two separate sheets of paper. One, it appeared, was the proposal form; the other a lavishly curlicued certificate of insurance. I filled in the spaces on the ultra-simple proposal while Carthy-Todd inscribed my name and a number on the certificate; then I handed over a fiver, which left me with enough to live on cornflakes until payday, and the transaction was complete.

"Take care of yourself now, Matt," joked the Duke, and I smiled and said I would.

The Duke looked at his watch. "Good gracious!" He stood up. "Come along now, everybody. Time we went along to the racecourse. And no more excuses, Charles, I insist on you lunching with me." To me he explained, "Charles very rarely goes to the races. He doesn't much care for it, do you see? But as the course is so very close . . ."

Carthy-Todd's aversion to race meetings was to my mind completely understandable. He wished to remain unseen, anonymous, unrecognizable, just as he'd been all along. Charles would choose which meetings he went to very carefully indeed. He would never, I imagined, turn up without checking with the Duke whether he was going to be there, too.

We walked back to the racecourse, the Duke and Carthy-Todd in front, young Matthew and I behind. Young Matthew slowed down a little and said to me in a quiet voice, "I say, Matt, have you noticed something strange about Mr. Carthy-Todd?"

I glanced at his face. He was half anxious, half puzzled, wanting reassurance.

"What do you think is strange?"

"I've never seen anyone before with eyes like that."

Children were incredibly observant. Matthew had seen naturally what I had known to look for.

"I shouldn't mention it to him. He might not care for it."

"I suppose not." He paused. "I don't frightfully like him."

"I can see that."

"Do you?"

"No," I said.

He nodded in satisfaction. "I didn't think you would. I don't know why Uncle's so keen on him. Uncle," he added dispassionately, "doesn't understand about people. He thinks everyone is as nice as he is. Which they're not."

"How soon can you become his business manager?"

He laughed. "I know all about trustees. I've got them. Can't have this and can't do that, that's all they ever say, Mother says."

"Does your uncle have trustees?"

"No, he hasn't. Mother's always beefing on about Uncle not being fit to control all that lucre and one day he'll invest the lot in a South Sea bubble. I asked Uncle about it and he just laughed. He told me he has a stockbroker who sees to everything and Uncle just goes on getting richer and when he wants some money for something he just tells the stockbroker and he sells some shares and sends it along. Simple. Mother fusses over nothing. Uncle won't get into much trouble about money because he knows that he doesn't know about it, if you see what I mean?"

"I wouldn't like him to give too much to Mr. Carthy-Todd," I said.

He gave me a flashing look of understanding. "So that's what I felt. . . . Do you think it would do any good if I sort of tried to put Uncle off him a bit?"

"Couldn't do much harm."

"I'll have a go," he said. "But he's fantastically keen on him." He thought deeply and came up with a grin. "I must say," he said, "that he has awfully good chocolate orange peel."

Annie Villars was upset about Kenny Bayst. "I went to see him for a few moments this morning. He's broken both legs and his face was cut by flying glass. He won't be riding again before next season, he says. Luckily he's insured with the Racegoers' Fund. Sent them a tenner, he told me, so he's hoping to collect two thousand pounds at least. Marvelous thing, that Fund."

"Did you join?"

"I certainly did. After that bomb. Didn't know it was Rupert then, of course. Still, better to do things at once rather than put them off, don't you agree?"

"Were Kitch and the stable lads insured, too, do you know?"

She nodded. "They were all Kitch's own lads. He'd advised them all to join. Even offered to deduct the premium from their wages bit by bit. Everyone in Newmarket is talking about it, saying how lucky it was. All the stable lads in the town who hadn't already joined are sending their fivers along in the next few days."

I hesitated. "Did you read about Rupert Tyderman in *Sporting Life?*"

A twinge of regret twisted her face: her mouth, for the first time since I had known her, took on a soft curve that was not consciously constructed.

"Poor Rupert. . . . What an end, to be murdered."

"There isn't any doubt, then?"

She shook her head. "When I saw the report, I rang the local newspaper down at Kemble—that's where they found him. He was lying, they said, at the bottom on an embankment near a road bridge over the railway. The local theory is that he could have been brought there by car during the night, and not fallen from a train at all. . . . " She shook her head in bewilderment. "He had one stab wound below his left shoulder blade, and he had been dead for hours and hours when he was found."

* * *

It took a good deal of lying in wait to catch the Duke without Carthy-Todd at his elbow, but I got him in the end.

"I've left my wallet in the Accident Fund office," I said. "Must have left it on the desk when I paid my premium. . . . Do you think, sir, that you could let me have a key, if you have one, so that I can slip along and fetch it?"

"My dear chap, of course." He produced a small bunch from his pocket and sorted out a bright new Yale. "Here you are. That's the one."

"Very kind, sir. I won't be long." I took a step away and then turned back, grinning, making a joke.

"What happens, sir, if it's you who gets killed in a car crash? What happens to the Fund then?"

He smiled back reassuringly, in a patting-on-the-shoulder avuncular manner. "All taken care of, my dear chap. Some of the papers I signed, they dealt with it. The Fund money would be guaranteed from a special arrangement with my estate."

"Did Charles see to it?"

"Naturally. Of course. He understands these things, you know."

Between the Duke and the main gate, a voice behind me crisply shouted.

"Matt."

I stopped and turned. It was Colin, hurrying toward me, carrying the saddle from the loser he'd partnered in the first race.

"Can't stop more than a second," he said. "Got to change for the next. You weren't leaving, were you? Have you seen Nancy?"

"No. I've been looking. I thought . . . perhaps . . . "

He shook his head. "She's here. Up there, on the balcony, with Midge."

I followed where he was looking, and there they were, distant, high up, talking with their heads together, two halves of one whole.

"Do you know which is Nancy?" Colin asked.

I said without hesitation, "The one on the left."

"Most people can't tell."

He looked at my expression and said with exasperation, "If you feel like that about her, why the bloody hell don't you let her know? She thinks she made it all up. . . . She's trying to hide it, but she's pretty unhappy."

"She'd have to live on peanuts."

"For crying out loud, what does that matter? You can move in with us. We all want you. Midge wants you—and now, not some distant time when you think you can afford it. Time for us is now, this summer. There may not be much after this." He hitched the saddle up on his arm and looked back toward the weighing room. "I'll have to go. We'll have to talk later. I came after you now, though, because you looked as though you were leaving."

"I'm coming back soon." I turned and walked along with him toward the weighing room. "Colin . . . I ought to tell someone . . . you never know . . . " He gave me a puzzled glance and in three brief sentences I told him why the Accident Fund was a fraud, how he and the bomb had been used to drum up business, and in what way Carthy-Todd was a fake.

He stopped dead in his tracks. "Good God," he said. "The Fund was such a great idea. What a bloody shame."

Saturday afternoon. The Board of Trade had gone home to its lawn-mowing and the wife and kids. I put down the telephone and considered the police.

The police were there, on the racecourse, all ready and able. But willing? Hardly. They were there to direct the traffic; a crime not yet committed would not shift them an inch.

Both lots, if they believed me, might eventually arrive on Carthy-Todd's doorstep. By appointment, probably; especially the Board of Trade.

There would be no Carthy-Todd to welcome them in. No records. No Fund. Possibly no Duke . . .

I always told myself to stay out of trouble.

Never listened.

No clocks ticked in Carthy-Todd's office. The silence was absolute. But it was only in my mind that it was ominous and oppressive. Carthy-Todd was safe at the races and I should have a clear hour at least: or so my brain told me. My nerves had other ideas.

I found myself tiptoeing across to the desk. Ridiculous. I half laughed at myself and put my feet down flat on the soundless carpet.

Nothing on the desk top except a blotter without blots, a tray of pens and pencils, a green telephone, a photograph of a woman, three children, and a dog in a silver frame, a desk diary, closed, and the red-and-gold tin of chocolate orange peel.

The drawers contained stationery, paper clips, stamps, and a small pile of the "insure against bombs on the way home" brochures. Two of the four drawers were completely empty.

Two filing cabinets. One unlocked. One locked.

The top of the three drawers of the unlocked cabinet contained the packets of proposal forms and insurance certificates and a packet of claim forms; the second contained the completed and returned forms of those insured, filed in a rank of folders from A–Z; and the third, almost empty, contained three folders only, one marked "Claims settled," one "Claims pending," and one "Receipts."

"Claims settled" embraced the records of two separate outgoing payments of one thousand pounds, one to Acey Jones and one to a trainer in Kent who had been kicked in the face at evening stables. Three hundred pounds had been paid to a stable girl in Newmarket in respect of fracturing her wrist in a fall from a two-year-old at morning exercise. The claim forms, duly filled in with doctor's certificates attached, were stamped "Paid," with a date.

"Claims pending" was fatter. There were five letters of application for claim forms, annotated "forms sent," and two forms completed and returned, claiming variously for a finger bitten off by a hungry hurdler and a foot carelessly left in the path of a plow. From the dates, the claimants had been waiting only a month for their money: and few insurance companies paid out quicker than that.

The thin file "Receipts" was in many ways the most interesting. The record took the form of a diary, with the number of new insurers entered against the day they paid their premiums. From sporadic twos and threes during the first week of operation, the numbers had grown like a mushroom.

The first great spurt was labeled in the margin, in small tidy handwriting, "A. C. Jones, etc." The second, an astronomical burst, was noted "Bomb!" The third, a lesser spurt, "Pamphlet." The fourth, a noticeable upthrust, "Electric failure." After that, the daily average had gone on climbing steadily. The word, by then, had reached pretty well every ear.

The running total in two months had reached 5,472. The receipts, since some insurers had paid double premiums for double benefits, stood at £28,040.

With the next inrush of premiums after the Kitch-Ambrose accident (which Carthy-Todd certainly had not engineered, as only nonclaiming accidents were any good to him), there would have been almost enough in the kitty to settle all the claims. I sighed, frowning. It was, as Colin had said, a bloody shame. The Duke's view of the Fund was perfectly valid. Run by an honest man, and with its ratio of premiums to payoff slightly adjusted, it could have done good all round.

I slammed the bottom drawer shut with irritation and felt the adrenalin race through my veins as the noise reverberated round the empty room.

No one came. My nerves stopped registering tremble; went back to itch.

The locked second cabinet was proof only against casual eyes. I tipped it against the wall and felt underneath, and sure enough it was the type that worked on one connecting rod up the back: pushed the rod up from the bottom and all the drawers became unlocked.

I looked through all of them quickly, the noise I had made seeming to act as an accelerator. Even if I had all the time in the world, I wanted to be out of there, to be gone.

The top drawer contained more folders of papers. The middle drawer contained a large gray metal box. The bottom drawer contained two cardboard boxes and two small square tins.

Taking a deep breath, I started at the top. The folders contained the setting-up documents of the Fund and the papers which the Duke had so trustingly signed. The legal language made perfect camouflage for what Carthy-Todd had done. I had to read them twice, to take a strong grip and force myself to concentrate, before I understood the two covenants the Duke had given him.

The first, as the Duke had said, transferred one hundred thousand pounds from his estate into a guarantee trust for the Fund, in the event of his death. The second one at first sight looked identical, but it certainly wasn't. It said in essence that if the Duke died within the first year of the Fund, a further one hundred thousand pounds from his estate was to be paid into it.

In both cases, Carthy-Todd was to be sole trustee.

In both cases, he was given absolute discretion to invest or use the money in any way he thought best.

Two hundred thousand pounds. . . . I stared into space. Two hundred thousand pounds if the Duke died. A motive to make tongue-silencing look like child's play.

The twenty-eight thousand of the Fund money was only the beginning. The bait. The jackpot lay in the dead Duke.

His heirs would have to pay. Young Matthew, to be precise. The papers looked thoroughly legal, with signatures witnessed and stamped, and in fact it seemed one hundred per cent certain that Carthy-Todd wouldn't have bothered with them at all if they were not foolproof.

He wouldn't waste much more time, I thought. Not with the claims for the Ambrose accident coming in. With the Duke dead, the two hundred thousand would have to be paid almost at once, because the covenants would be a first charge on his estate, like debts. There would be no having to wait around for probate. If Carthy-Todd could stave off the claims for a while, he could skip with both the Duke's money and the whole Fund.

I put the papers back in their folder, back in the drawer. Closed it. Gently. My heart thumped.

Second drawer. Large metal box. One could open it without removing it from the cabinet. I opened it. Lots of space, but few contents. Some cotton wool, cold cream, glue, and a half-used stick of grease paint. I shut the lid, shut the drawer. Only to be expected.

Bottom drawer. Knelt on the floor. Two small square tins, one seemed empty, one full and heavy and fastened all round with adhesive tape. Looked inside two cardboard boxes first and felt the breath go out of my body as if I'd been kicked.

The cardboard boxes contained the makings of a radio bomb. Solenoids, transmitters, fuse wire, a battery, and a small container of gunpowder in the first box. Plastic explosive wrapped in tin foil in the other.

I sat on my heels looking at the small square heavy tin. Heard in my mind the tall man from the Board of Trade: the tighter you pack a bomb, the more fiercely it explodes.

Decided not to open the small square tin. Felt the sweat stand out in cold drops on my forehead.

I shut the bottom drawer with a caution which seemed silly when I remembered the casual way I'd tilted the whole cabinet over to open it. But then the bomb wouldn't go off until it got the right signal . . . and it wouldn't get the signal where it was, not with those precious documents in the cabinet just above.

I wiped my hand over my face. Stood up. Swallowed.

I'd found everything I came to find, and more. All except for one thing. I glanced round the office, looking for somewhere else. Somewhere to hide something big . . .

There was a door in the corner behind Carthy-Todd's desk which I assumed connected with the secretary's office next door. I went over to it. Tried the handle. It was locked.

I let myself out of Carthy-Todd's office and went into the secretary's room, whose door was shut but had no keyhole. Stared, in there, at an L-shaped blank wall. No connecting door to Carthy-Todd. It was a cupboard, with the door on his side.

I went back to Carthy-Todd's office and stood contemplating the door. If I broke it open, he would know. If I didn't, I could only guess at what was inside. Evidence of a fraud committed, which would spur the Board of Trade to action. Evidence that would make the Duke rescind his covenants, or at least rewrite them so that they were no longer death warrants. . . .

Carthy-Todd hadn't been expecting trouble. He had left the key to the cupbord on his desk in the tray of pens and pencils. I picked up the single key which lay there, and it fitted.

Opened the cupboard door. It squeaked on its hinges, but I was too engrossed to notice.

There he was. Mr. Acey Jones. The crutches, leaning against the wall. The white plaster cast lying on the floor.

I picked up the cast and looked at it. It had been slit neatly down the inside leg from the top to the ankle. One could put one's foot into it like a boot, with the bare toes sticking out of the end and the metal walking support under the arch. There were small grip clips like those used on bandages sticking into the plaster all down the opening. Put your foot into the cast, fasten the clips, and bingo, you had a broken ankle.

Acey Jones, loudly drumming up business for the Fund.

Acey Jones, Carthy-Todd. Confidence tricksters were the best actors in the world.

I didn't hear him come.

I put the cast back on the floor just where it had been, and straightened up and started to shut the cupboard door and saw him moving out of the corner of my eye as he came into the room. I hadn't shut the office door behind me when I'd gone back. I hadn't given myself any time at all.

His face went rigid with fury when he saw what I'd seen.

"Meddling pilot," he said. "When the Duke told me he'd given you the key—" He stopped, unable to speak for rage. His voice was different, neither the Rugby of Carthy-Todd nor the Australian of Acey Jones. Just ordinary uninflected English. I wondered fleetingly where he came from, who he really was—a thousand different people, one for every crime.

Unblinking behind the black-framed glasses, the pale blue-gray eyes all but sizzled. The incongruous white eyelashes, which Matthew had noticed, gave him now a fierce, fanatical ruthlessness. The decision he was coming to wasn't going to be for my good.

He put his hand into his trouser pocket and briefly pulled it out again. There was a sharp click. I found myself staring at the knife which had snapped out, and thought with a horrific shiver of Rupert Tyderman tumbling down dead beside the railway line. . . .

He took a step sideways and kicked shut the office door. I twisted round toward the mantelshelf to pick up whatever I could find there—a photograph, a cigarette box, anything I could use as a weapon or a shield.

I didn't even get as far as taking anything into my hand, because he didn't try to stab me with the knife.

He threw it.

15

IT HIT me in the left shoulder blade, and the jolt threw me forward on my twisting legs so that I hit my forehead solidly on the edge of the marble slab mantelshelf. Blacking out, falling, I put out a hand to stop myself, but there was nothing there, only the empty black hollow of the fireplace and I went on, right down, smashing and crashing among the brass fire irons . . . but I heard them only dimly . . . and then not at all.

I woke up slowly, stiffly, painfully, after less than a quarter of an hour. Everything was silent. No sound. No people. Nothing.

I couldn't remember where I was or what had happened. Not until I tried to get up. Then the tearing soreness behind my shoulder stung me straight back into awareness.

Had a knife sticking in my back.

Lying face down among the fire irons, I felt gingerly round with my right hand. My fingers brushed like feathers against the hilt. I cried out at my own touch. It was frightful.

Stupid the things you think of in moments of disaster. I thought: Damn it, only three weeks and one day to my medical. I'll never pass it. . . .

Never pull knives out of wounds, they say. It makes the bleeding worse. You can die from pulling knives out of wounds. Well . . . I forgot all that. I could see only that Acey-Carthy-Todd had left me for dead, and if he found me alive when he came back he would most certainly finish the job. Therefore I had to get out of his office before he came back. And it seemed incongruous, really, to walk round Warwick with a knife in one's back. So I pulled it out.

I pulled it out in two stages and more or less fainted after each. Kidded myself it was concussion from the mantelshelf, but I was crying as well. No stoic, Matt Shore.

When it was out, I lay where I was for a while, looking at it, snivelling weakly and feeling the sticky warmth slowly spread, but being basically reassured because I was pretty certain by then that the knife had not gone through into my lung. It must have hit my shoulder blade at an angle: it had been embedded to three or four inches, but slanting, not straight in deep. I wasn't going to die. Or not yet.

After a while, I got up onto my knees. I didn't have all the time in the world. I put my right hand on Carthy-Todd's desk; pulled myself to my feet.

Swayed. Thought it would be much much worse if I fell down again. Leaned my hip against the desk and looked vaguely round the office.

The bottom drawer of the second filing cabinet was open.

Shouldn't be. I'd shut it.

Open.

I shifted myself off the desk and tried a few steps. Tottered. Made it. Leaned gingerly against the wall. Looked down into the drawer.

The two cardboard boxes were still there. The empty tin was still there. The small square heavy tin wasn't.

Realized coldly that the future no longer meant simply getting myself to safety out of that office, but getting to the Duke before the bomb did.

It was only four hundred yards. . . . Only . . .

I'd have to do it, I thought, because if I hadn't searched the office Carthy-Todd wouldn't now be in a tearing hurry. When I didn't turn up to ferry home the Whiteknights—or turn up anywhere again, for that matter, except with a stab wound in a ditch—the Duke would say where I had been last . . . and Carthy-Todd would want to avoid a police investigation like a slug shrinking away from salt. He wouldn't wait for that. He would obliterate my tracks.

There was something else missing from the office. I didn't know what it was, just knew it was something. It niggled for a moment, but was gone. Didn't think it could be important. . . .

Walked with deliberation to the door. Opened it, went outside. Stopped dead at the top of the stairs, feeling dizzy and weak.

Well. Had to get down them somehow. Had to.

The handrail was on the left-hand side. I couldn't bear to lift my left arm. Turned round, hung on tightly, and went down backward.

"There you are," I said aloud. "You bloody can." Didn't convince myself. It took Carthy-Todd to convince.

I laughed weakly. I was a fully paid-up insurer with the Fund. Like to see Carthy-Todd pay my claim . . . a thousand smackers for a knife in the back. Lovely.

Rolled out into the hot sunlit street as lightheaded as a blonde.

Blond Acey Jones . . .

Acey Jones was being pushed. Hurried. Knowing I'd found him out but still believing he could retrieve the situation. Still make his two hundred thousand. If he kept his nerve. If he killed the Duke immediately, this afternoon, and somehow made it look like an accident. If he dumped me somewhere later, as he had the Major. . . .

He would think he could still do it. He didn't know I'd told Colin, didn't know that Colin knew he was Carthy-Todd. . . .

The empty street had got much longer during the afternoon. Also it wouldn't stay absolutely still. It shimmered. It undulated. The pavement was uneven. Every time I put my foot down, the paving stones reached up and stabbed me in the back.

I passed only an elderly woman on the way. She was muttering to herself. I realized that I was, too.

Half way. I squinted along at the gate of the car park. Had to make it. Had to. And that wasn't all. Had to find someone to go and fetch the Duke, so that I could explain . . . explain . . .

Felt myself falling and put a hand out toward the wall. Mustn't shut my eyes. . . . I'd be done for. . . . Spun heavily against the bricks and shuddered at the result. Rested my head against the wall, trying not to weep. Couldn't spare the time. Had to get on.

I pushed myself back into a moderately upright walking position. My feet couldn't tell properly how far it was down to the pavement: half the time I was climbing imaginary steps.

Weird.

Something warm on my left hand. I looked down. My head swam. Blood was running down my fingers, dripping onto the pavement. Looked up again, along to the course. Head swam again. Didn't know if it was concussion or heat or loss of blood. Only knew it reduced the time factor. Had to get there. Quickly.

One foot in front of the other, I told myself . . . just go on doing that: one foot in front of the other. And you'll get there.

Concentrate.

I got there. Gate to the car park. And no official guarding it. At that time in the afternoon, they'd given up expecting further customers.

I said, "Ohhh," in weak frustration. Have to go still further. Have to find someone. . . . I turned in to the car park. Through the car park there was a gate into the paddock. Lots of people there. Lots . . .

I went between the cars, staggering, holding on to them. feeling my knees bending, knowing the dizzy weakness was winning, and caring less and less about the jagged pain of every step. Had to find someone. Had to.

Someone suddenly called to me from quite close.

"Matt!"

I stopped. Looked slowly round. Midge was climbing out of Colin's parked Aston Martin down the row and running to catch me up.

"Matt," she said, "we've been looking for you. I came back to the car because I was tired. Where have you been?"

She put her hand with friendship on my left arm.

I said thickly, "Don't . . . touch me."

She took her hand away with a jerk. "Matt!"

She looked at me more closely, at first in puzzlement and then in anxiety. Then she looked at her fingers, and where she'd grasped my coat there were bright red smears.

"It's blood," she said blankly.

I nodded a fraction. My mouth was dry. I was getting very tired.

"Listen. . . . Do you know the Duke of Wessex?"

"Yes. But—" she protested.

"Midge," I interrupted. "Go and find him. Bring him here. . . . I know it sounds stupid . . . but someone is trying to kill him . . . with a bomb."

"Like Colin? But that wasn't—"

"Fetch him, Midge," I said. "Please."

"I can't leave you. Not like this."

"You must."

She looked at me doubtfully.

"Hurry."

"I'll get you some help, too," she said. She turned lightly on her heel and half walked, half ran toward the paddock. I leaned the bottom of my spine against a shiny gray Jaguar and wondered how difficult it would be to prevent Carthy-Todd from planting his bomb. That tin . . . it was small enough to fit into a binocular case . . . probably identical with the one which had destroyed the Cherokee. I would have sweated at the thought of so much confined explosive power if I hadn't been sweating clammily already.

Why didn't they come? My mouth was drier. . . . The day was airless. . . . I moved restlessly against the car. After I'd told the Duke, he'd have to go off somewhere and stay safely out of sight until the Board of Trade had dealt with Carthy-Todd. . . .

I dispassionately watched the blood drip from my fingers onto the grass. I could feel that all the back of my coat was soaked. Couldn't afford a new one, either. Have to get it cleaned, and have the slit invisibly mended. Get myself mended, too, as best I could. Harley wouldn't keep the job for me. He'd have to get someone else in my place. The Board of Trade doctors wouldn't let me fly again for weeks and weeks. If you gave a pint of blood as a donor, they grounded you for over a month. . . . I'd lost more than a pint involuntarily, by the looks of things . . . though a pint would make a pretty good mess if you spilled it. . . .

I lifted my lolling head up with a jerk. Got to stay awake until they came. Got to explain to the Duke. . . .

Things were beginning to fuzz round the edges. I licked my dry lips. Didn't do much good. Didn't have any moisture in my tongue either.

I finally saw them, and it seemed a long way off, coming through the gate from the paddock. Not just Midge and the Duke, but two others as well. Young Matthew, jigging along in front.

And Nancy.

Chanter had receded into the unimportant past. I didn't give him a thought. Everything was as it had been before, the day she flew to Haydock. Familiar, friendly, trusting. The girl I hadn't wanted to get involved with, who had melted a load of ice like an acetylene torch.

Across the sea of cars, Midge pointed in my direction and they began to come toward me, crossing through the rows. When they were only twenty or so yards away, on the far side of the row in front of me, they unaccountably stopped.

Come on, I thought. For God's sake, come on.

They didn't move.

With an effort, I pushed myself upright from the Jaguar and took the few steps past its bonnet, going toward them. On my left, six cars along, was parked what was evidently the Duke's Rolls. On the bonnet stood a bright red-and-gold tin. Matthew was pointing, wanting to cross over and fetch it, and Midge was saying urgently, "No, come on, Matt said to come quickly, and he's bleeding. . . . "

Matthew gave her a concerned look and then nodded, but at the last second temptation was too much and he ran over and picked up the tin and started back to join them.

Bright red-and-gold tin. Containing sticks of orange peel dipped in chocolate. It had been on the desk. And afterward . . . not on the desk. Something missing. Red-and-gold tin.

Missing from Carthy-Todd's desk.

My heart bumped. I shouted, and my voice came out hopelessly weak.

"Matthew, throw it to me."

He looked up doubtfully. The others began to walk through the row of cars toward him. They would reach him before I could. They would be standing all together, Nancy and Midge and the Duke and young Matthew, who knew, too, that I'd been in Carthy-Todd's office that day.

I scanned the car park desperately, but he was there. He'd put the tin on the car and simply waited for them to come out of the races. The last race was about to start . . . the horses had gone down to the post and at that moment the loudspeakers were announcing, "They're under starter's orders". . . . He knew it wouldn't be long before they came. . . . He was standing over nearer the rails of the course, with his black head showing and the sun glinting on his glasses. He had meant just to kill young Matthew and the Duke, but now there were Nancy and Midge as well . . . and he didn't know he couldn't get away with it . . . didn't know Colin knew . . . and he was too far away for me to tell him. . . . I couldn't shout . . . could barely talk.

"Matthew, throw me the tin." It was a whisper, nothing more. I began to walk toward him, holding out my right arm. Stumbled. Swayed. Frightened him.

The others were closing on him.

No more time. I took a breath. Straightened up.

"Matthew," I said loudly. "To save your life, throw me that tin. Throw it now. At once."

He was upset, uncertain, worried.

He threw the tin.

It was taking Carthy-Todd several seconds to press the transmission buttons. He wasn't as adept at it as Rupert Tyderman. He wouldn't be able to see that he had missed his opportunity with the Duke, and that now there was only me. But whatever he did, he'd lost the game.

The red-and-gold tin floated toward me like a blazing sun and seemed to take an eternity crossing the fifteen feet from Matthew. I stretched my right arm forward to meet it, and when it landed on my hand I flung it with a bowling action high into the air behind where I was standing, back as far as I could over the parked rows, because behind them, at the rear, there was empty space.

The bomb went off in the air. Three seconds out of my hand, six seconds out of Matthew's. Six seconds. As long a time as I had ever lived.

The red-and-gold tin disintegrated into a cracking fireball like the sun, and the blast of it knocked both young Matthew and me with a screeching jolt flat to the ground. The windows in most of the cars in the car park crashed into splinters, and the two Fords just below the explosion were thrown about like toys. Nancy and Midge and the Duke, still sheltered between two cars, rocked on their feet and clung to one another for support.

Along in the stands, we heard later, no one took much notice. The race had started and the commentator's voice was booming out, filling everyone's ears with the news that Colin Ross was lying handy and going nicely on the favorite half a mile from home.

Young Matthew picked himself up smartly and said in amazement, "What was that?"

Midge completed the four steps to his side and held his hand.

"It was a bomb," she said in awe. "As Matt said, it was a bomb."

I was trying to get myself up off the grass. Even though the Duke was for the present safe, the Fund money was not. Might as well try for set and match. . . .

On my knees, I said to Matthew, "Can you see Carthy-Todd anywhere? It was his tin . . . his bomb. . . . "

"Carthy-Todd?" repeated the Duke vaguely. "It can't be. Impossible. He wouldn't do a thing like that."

"He just did," I said. I was having no success in getting up any further. Had nothing much left. A strong arm slid under my right armpit, helping me. A soft calm voice said in my ear, "You look as if you'd be better staying down."

"Nancy. . . . "

"How did you get into this state?"

"Carthy-Todd . . . had a knife. . . . "

"There he is!" Matthew suddenly shouted. "Over there."

I wobbled to my feet. Looked where Matthew was pointing. Carthy-Todd, running between the rows. Nancy looked, too.

"But that's," she said incredulously, "that's the man I saw in the car with Major Tyderman. I'd swear to it."

"You may have to," I said.

"He's running to get out," Matthew shouted. "Let's head him off."

It was almost a game to him, but his enthusiasm infected several other racegoers who had come early out of the races and found their windows in splinters.

"Head him off," I heard a man shout, and another, "There, over there. Head him off."

I leaned in hopeless weakness against a car, and dimly watched. Carthy-Todd caught sight of the growing number converging on him. Hesitated. Changed course. Doubled back on his tracks. Made for the only free and open space he could see. The green grass behind him. The racecourse itself.

"Don't. . . . " I said. It came out a whisper, and even if I'd had a microphone he wouldn't have heard.

"Oh, God," Nancy said beside me. "Oh, no."

Carthy-Todd didn't see his danger until it was far too late. He ran blindly out across the course, looking over his shoulder at the bunch of men who had suddenly, aghast, stopped chasing him.

He ran straight in front of the thundering field of three-year-olds sweeping round the last bend to their final flying effort up the straight.

Close-bunched, they had no chance of avoiding him. He went down under the pounding hoofs like a rag into a threshing machine, and a second later the flowing line of horses broke up into tumbling chaos . . . crashing at thirty miles an hour . . . legs whirling . . . jockeys thudding to the ground like bright blobs of paint . . . a groaning shambles on the bright green turf. . . . And side-stepping, swaying, looking over their shoulders, the rear ones in the field swerved past and went on to a finish that no one watched.

Nancy said in anguish "Colin!" and ran toward the rails. The pink-and-white silks lay still, a crumpled bundle curled in a protective ball. I followed her, plod by plod, feeling that I couldn't go any farther, I simply couldn't. One car short of the rails, I stopped. I clung on to it, sagging. The tide was going out.

The pink-and-white ball stirred, unrolled itself, stood up. Relief made me even weaker. Crowds of people had appeared on the course, running, helping, gawping, closing in like a screen round the strewn bodies. . . . I waited for what seemed an age, and then Colin and Nancy reappeared through a thronging wall of people and came back toward the car park.

"Only stunned for a second," I heard him say to a passing inquirer. "I shouldn't go over there . . . " But the inquirer went on, looking avid.

Nancy saw me and waved briefly, and ducked under the rails with Colin.

"He's dead," she said abruptly. She looked sick. "That man—he—he was Acey Jones. . . . Colin said you knew—his hair was lying on the grass—but it was a wig—and there was this bald white head and that pale hair—and you could see the line of grease paint—and the black mustache. . . . " Her eyes were wide. Full of horror.

"Don't think about it," Colin said. He looked at me. "She shouldn't have come over. . . . "

"I had to—you were lying there," she protested. He went on looking at me. His expression changed. He said, "Nancy said you were hurt. She didn't say how badly." He turned abruptly to Nancy and said, "Fetch the doctor."

"I tried to before," she said. "But he said he was on duty and couldn't see to Matt before the race in case he was needed. . . . " She tailed off and looked over at the crowd on the course. "He'll be over there, seeing to those two jockeys. . . . " She looked back at Colin with sudden fright. "Midge said Matt had cut his arm. . . . Is it worse? . . . "

"I'll fetch him," Colin said grimly, and ran back to the battlefield. Nancy looked at me with such flooding anxiety that I grinned.

"Not as bad as all that," I said.

"But you were walking. . . . You threw that bomb with such force . . . I didn't realize. . . . You do look ill."

The Duke and young Matthew and Midge reappeared from somewhere. I hadn't seen them come. Things were getting hazier.

The Duke was upset. "My dear chap," he said over and over again. "My dear chap. . . . "

"How did you know it was a bomb?" Matthew asked.

"Just knew."

"That was a pretty good throw."

"Saved our lives," said the Duke. "My dear chap. . . . "

Colin was back.

"He's coming," he said. "Immediately."

"Saved our lives," said the Duke again. "How can we repay . . . "

Colin looked at him straight. "I'll tell you how, sir. Set him up in business . . . or take over Derrydowns . . . give him an air-taxi business, based near Newmarket. He'll make you a profit. He'll have me for a customer, and Annie, and Kenny . . . and in fact the whole town, because the Fund can go on now, can't it?" He looked at me inquiringly, and I fractionally nodded. "It may cost a bit to put it right," Colin said, "but your Fund can go on, sir, and do all the good it was meant to. . . . "

"An air-taxi business. Take over Derrydowns," the Duke repeated. "My dear Colin, what a splendid idea. Of course. Of course."

I tried to say something . . . anything . . . to begin to thank him for so casually thrusting the world into my fingers . . . but I couldn't say anything . . . couldn't speak. I could feel my legs collapsing. Could do nothing any more to stop them. Found myself kneeling on the grass, keeping myself from falling entirely by hanging on to a door handle of the car. Didn't want to fall. Hurt too much.

"Matt!" Nancy said. She was down on her knees beside me. Midge, too. And Colin.

"Don't bloody die," Nancy said.

I grinned at her. Felt lightheaded. Grinned at Colin. Grinned at Midge.

"Want a lodger?" I asked.

"Soon as you like," Colin said.

"Nancy," I said. "Will you . . . will you . . . "

"You nit," she said. "You great nit."

My hand slipped out of the door handle. Colin caught me as I fell. Everything drifted quietly away, and by the time I reached the ground I couldn't feel anything at all.

ABOUT THE AUTHOR

DICK FRANCIS, a former jockey turned newspaper columnist and, finally, best-selling mystery writer, was born in 1920 in Tenby, South Wales. He grew up around horses and learned to ride early, eventually becoming a champion steeplechase jockey who rode for Britain's Queen Elizabeth, the Queen Mother.

Francis served in the Royal Air Force in World War II (and several of his books, in addition to being set in the world of horses and racing, also incorporate his knowledge of airplanes and flying). At the age of thirty-six Francis retired from the jockey's life, began writing a weekly racing column for the London *Sunday Express*, and, finally, went all the way to full-fledged fiction.

Dick Francis is the author of some two dozen mystery novels, many of them best sellers, including *Reflex, Twice Shy* and *Banker*. He currently lives in Oxfordshire, England, with his wife, and still rides whenever he can.